New Eves

SCIENCE FICTION ABOUT THE THE EXTRAORDINARY WOMEN OF TODAY AND TOMORROW

Edited By

JANRAE FRANK
JEAN STINE
&
FORREST J ACKERMAN

LONGMEADOW PRESS

Stamford, Connecticut

Published by Longmeadow Press, 201 High Ridge Road, Stamford, Connecticut 06904. All rights reserved. No part of this book may be reproduced or utilized in any form or by any means, electronic or mechanical, including photocopying, recording or by any information storage or retrieval system, without permission in writing from the Publisher.

Longmeadow Press and the colophon are trademarks.

Interior Design by Pamela C. Pia

This Longmeadow Press edition is printed on archival quality paper. It is acid-free and conforms to the guidelines established for permanence and durability by the Council of Library Resources and the American National Standards Institute. ∞™

Library of Congress Cataloging-in-Publication Data
New Eves : science fiction about the extraordinary women of today and tomorrow / edited by Janrae Frank, Jean Stine, Forrest J Ackerman — 1st Longmeadow Press ed.
    p.   cm.
    ISBN 0-681-00525-4
    1. Science Fiction, American—Women authors.   2. Women—Fiction.
    I. Frank, Janrae.   II. Stine, Jean.   III. Ackerman, Forrest J
PS648.S3N42   1994
813'.08762089287—dc20

                                                                94-38214
                                                                CIP

Printed and bound in the United States of America.
First Longmeadow Press edition.
0 9 8 7 6 5 4 3 2 1

Dedication

TO THE PIONEERING WOMEN
WHO EDITED SCIENCE FICTION MAGAZINES
1928-1981

Miriam Bourne
Amazing Stories
1926 - 1932

Mary Gnaedinger
Famous Fantastic Mysteries, Fantastic Novels
1939 - 1953

Beatrice Mahaffey
Other Worlds, Universe, Super Science
1949 - 1955

Marge Saunders Budwig
Other Worlds, Universe, Super Science
1949 - 1955

Kay Tarrent
Astounding/Analog
1949 - 1972

Lila Shaffer
Amazing, Fantastic
1948 - 1954

Evelyn Paige
Galaxy
1951 - 1956

Frances Hamling
Imagination
1951 - 1958

Marie A. Park
Dorothy B. Seador
The Original Science Fiction Stories, Future, Science Fiction Quarterly
1953 - 1960

Eve Wulff
If, Worlds of Science Fiction
1954 - 1957

Lenore Hailparn
Infinity, Science Fiction Adventures
1955 - 1956

Lee Hoffman
Infinity, Science Fiction Adventures
1956 - 1957

Cylvia Kleinman
Satellite
1957 - 1959

Elaine Wilber
If, Worlds of Science Fiction
1958

Cele Goldsmith
Amazing Stories, Fantastic Stories
1958

Diane Sullivan
Galaxy, Worlds of If
1964 - 1966

Judy-Lynn Benjamin
Galaxy, Worlds of If
1966 - 1973

Elinor Mavor
Amazing, Fantastic
1979 - 1981

Contents

PART FOUR: THE 60s & 70s

PART FIVE: THE 80s — AND BEYOND

Introduction

NEW EVES AND NEW GENESIS:
the extraordinary women who write science fiction
and the women they write about

The Judeo-Christian tale of Eve, Adam and the apple is open to many interpretations. What is clear is that Eve had the courage to defy social precepts that prevented the human race from obtaining knowledge about the universe. Typically, this angered the powers that be, and those who blindly accepted their precepts (consider what happened to Prometheus, Pandora and others).

The first Genesis had created Eve. In eating of the tree of forbidden knowledge, Eve recreated herself in her own Genesis. Ever since women have burned with the thirst for forbidden knowledge and the desire to recreate their role in society.

Only science fiction, of all forms of literature, gives women the freedom to completely reinvent themselves. Contemporary novels can only show women as oppressed or as rebelling against oppression. Accurate historical fiction might paint an even dimmer picture. But in science fiction, women have always been at liberty to postulate any kind of society, and to imagine women fulfilling every possible kind of role within it. In short, to create new Geneses for women and extraordinary New Eves from among them.

In this book, you will find a sampling of those new Geneses — and the New Eves that accompany them — drawn from the entire seventy some year span of magazine science fiction. Although women writers have created daring, even rebellious women in mainstream fiction, they have been until quite recently the exception; and rarely does the author of mimetic fiction have a better prescription for women's ills than the obvious perception that something is wrong and needs to be changed. How things might be changed, and how those changes would in turn affect women, are not the subjects of speculation in contemporary fiction.

Women with extraordinary perceptions and imaginations, who wished to pose solutions, to present New Eves and new Geneses, had to place their stories not merely elsewhere, but elsewhen. Most found themselves projecting their stories into the future — where women's lot would certainly have to be better. Yet, because they challenged the status quo, and challenged people to imagine, these women were largely ignored by readers and critics, while their sisters, whose teary romantic opuses endorsed the status quo, found favor among both.

THE FIRST WARM WELCOME

Before *Amazing Stories*, science fiction appeared one book at a time, one story at a time, without the kind of strong genre identity necessary to make a specialized fiction form commercially and popularly viable (the way mysteries, romances and westerns had already done for themselves). As a result, neither it nor its writers made a significant impact, with the exception of Mary Shelley, Jules Verne and H. G. Wells — who were considered unique, unduplicatable prodigies. The closest to a focal point magazine science fiction achieved was in Frank A. Munsey's *All-Story*, which contained tales from every genre, but specialized in the "different" story or "scientific romance" (as science fiction was then called) and published more than fifty science fiction novels, and hundreds of stories in its brief two decades. *All-Story*, like most magazines of its era, was a "family" publication, with stories and a contents page aimed at men, women and children, so that female science fiction authors like Francis Stevens ("Friend Island") Florence Crew-Jones *The New Eve*, and Margaret Prescott ("The Great Sleep Tanks") — and their New Eves — found ready welcome between its covers.

When the first science fiction magazine came along in 1926, reaping the benefit of an anxious market left bereft by *All-Story's* demise, its founder, Hugo Gernsback, eagerly welcomed women writers and correspondents along with men. A scientific visionary, who pioneered early radio broadcasting, and an inventor with many successful patents to his name, Gernshack aimed at using science fiction to inspire scientifically-minded young people — whatever their gender — to take up science and become the researchers, technicians, engineers and inventors of succeeding generations. The pages of the early *Amazing* were frequently graced with the names of women writers like Lilith Lorraine, L. Taylor Hansen, Leslie Francis Stone, Hazel Heald, Mina Irving, and others.

Better yet, Gernsback was equally receptive to the messages of these extraordinary women. Indeed, he was receptive to any questioning of social and gender roles, from whatever source. For all his faults, Gernsback included social speculation in his view of science fiction along with the more obvious technological speculations of Verne. In just the short four year period from 1929 to 1932, *Amazing* printed a number of important stories with new Geneses in which future worlds were ruled by women, including David Keller's "The Feminine Metamorphosis," Margaret F. Rupert's "Via the Hewitt Ray," Edmond Hamilton's "The Last Man," Leslie Francis Stone's "The Conquest of Gola," Richard Vaughan's "The Woman from Space" and Lilith Lorraine's "Into the 28th Century." Nor does this list of New Eves count the typically courageous and daring heroines of stories like Rupert H. Romans *The Moon Conquerors* (in which, in a delicious reversal of teens and twenties male science fiction conventions, Dorothy Brewster finances and spearheads an expedition to the Moon to rescue a handsome young prince she has seen menaced through a super telescope), or Leslie F. Stone's "Women with Wings" or the final turning in Hazel Heald's "Man of Stone." (None of this should be surprising, considering Gernsback's pioneering scientific vision extended to championing birth control, women's rights — and the founding of pioneer *Sexology* magazine, when most public discussion of such issues was banned as pornographic.)

WHEN WOMEN WERE FROZEN OUT

Then in 1930, an event occurred which was to have a devastating impact on the women who wrote science fiction, an event from which neither they nor the field would recover for more than two full decades: Hugo Gernsback lost control of *Amazing Stories* — and the rest of his publishing empire — supposedly through the machinations of his then business rival, Bernarr Macfadden. *Amazing* passed into the hands first of TEC Publications, and then into the hands of the Ziff-Davis pulp chain, where it fell under the editorship of the notorious Ray Palmer. At the same time, Gernsback's second set of futuristic publications, *Wonder Stories*, etc. ended in the hands of the Standard Magazine group, where Mort Weisinger quickly transformed it into *Thrilling Wonder Stories*. While, over at Clayton Publications, a new science fiction pulp, *Astounding Stories of Super Science*, had risen under the editorship of Harry Bates.

Bates, Weisinger and Palmer saw that if science fiction was to sell for their publishers, it could only be marketed as a subcategory of pulp magazine men's adventure fiction. To a certain degree, considering the cultural climate of the time (particularly the way women were discouraged from scientific interests and curiosity), and that 90+% of *Amazing* and *Wonder Stories'* readership had been male, these three editors were probably right. (And, due to cultural and other factors, science fiction's audience would remain largely male until the 1970s, when the shopping mall emerged as the major point of distribution for American books — causing a seismic upheaval that resulted in an almost complete reversal of the field's readership, with women, who visit malls far more frequently than men, becoming its dominant market, and hence, inevitably, the dominant writers, of science fiction.)

The immediate consequence of the realignment of magazine science fiction away from a vehicle of scientific and social extrapolation in the tradition of Verne and Wells — and into a lineal descendent of boys' adventure fiction (from Robert Lewis Stevenson to Doc Savage) — was a radical diminution in the number of women writers, and their visions of woman's possibilities, in the field. Just as few female readers of romance novels feel a male writer could capture a woman's emotional shadings well enough to pen a credible romance — so men of the 1930s were unwilling to believe that a female writer could capture convincingly the reactions of a brawny, two-fisted masculine hero. Thus, women writers were to disappear almost overnight from the pages of science fiction magazines and remain in exile for the next twenty years. (Talents such as Lilith Lorraine and Leslie Francis Stone simply had no reason to go on writing, and no place to publish their work if they had — while the women who continued in the field were forced to channel their narratives exclusively into fantasy and horror publications like *Weird Tales*, where issues without one, or even two women gracing the contents page were rare.) The only woman writer whose work received any welcome at all during this period was Helen Weinbaum ("Honeycombed Satellite," "The Genius Bureau"), who probably had no idea the reason her fine work saw publication was that she was riding on what editors saw as the drawing power of her more famous brother's last name.

WOMEN WITHOUT NAMES

Fortunately, science fiction has its own integrity, in spite of all attempts to consign it to narrow formulas, and by the late 30s and early 40s, it had become apparent that what attracted readers to stories, and sold the greatest number of copies of a magazine over the long run, was not mindless action and meaningless shoot 'em-ups — but stories with sharp, innovative ideas and sympathetic characters. This realization was inarguably brought about by the success of the one publication which might be considered a spiritual heir of Gernsback's celebration of the 20th century miracles brought about by science, John W. Campbell, Jr.'s *Astounding* (a lurid title he inherited, never comfortable with, and with considerable foresight transformed into the more sedate *Analog* three decades later).

It was primarily in the pages of Campbell's publication, that women began to make their reappearance in the field. And just as women writers were given space to reassert themselves in the pages of Campbell's publications, so were women characters first given leave to assume positions of authority and influence over events that during the previous era would have been reserved, and considered believable, only in male characters. (The women in Heinlein's stories, for instance, were physicists, mathematicians — anything but mere housewives.) Like Gernsback, Campbell had no serious operant prejudices against race, creed or gender — as long as a writer was capable of working with scientific ideas, and developing them in a logical way. It was the quality of the mind that counted with Campbell, and he found himself intellectually drawn to any male or female he met with a brain he felt was on a plane near his own.

However, Campbell had to deal with the marketing powers that be at his own corporate headquarters. These conservative East Coast establishment gentlemen dictated that writers whose names were ethnic (especially Jewish) adopt Anglo-Saxon pseudonyms, and that women's names not appear in *Astounding*'s pages at all. The women writers who could meet Campbell's vigorous intellectual standards were forced to cloak their real gender behind ambiguous first names or initials. Catherine L. Moore became C. L. Moore, Amelia Reynolds Long became A. R. Long, Eona Mayne Hull, E. Mayne Hull, while Leigh Brackett's moniker sounded masculine enough to allow her safe passage under her full name in the science fiction pulps. (Ironically, it was the discovery that the public revelation of Brackett's gender caused no decrease in her massive popularity, or more importantly the enormous sales value of her name at the newsstand, that finally made the publishers realize such constraints were no longer necessary — and perhaps never had been. In consequence, women writers such as Margaret St. Clair, Miriam Allen DeFord and Katherine MacLean were suddenly able to launch their careers successfully without having to disguise their names (and without ever knowing they once would have had to).

WHAT CAN'T WOMEN DO?
Campbell and *Astounding* dominated science fiction throughout the 1940s, a decade during which World War II (and the period immediately following) made real what the science fiction of the 1900s and the 1930s had forecast: Women working as equals alongside and even replacing men in every aspect of the American workforce — from business to science, from factories to foundries — had proved just how extraordinary "ordinary" women could be. Women's equality was no longer a matter of theory; it was a matter of demonstrated fact. To open minded science fiction writers — and readers — of both genders, the next question was clear: If women could perform mental and physical labor every bit as well as men, then what could women not do? The New Eves they envisioned and the new Geneses that created them began to multiply.

C. L. Moore *(Judgment Night)* and A. E. Van Vogt *(The Weapon Shops of Isher)* saw them as potentially capable of anything including galactic rule. Leigh Brackett *(The Black Amazon of Mars,* "Water Pirate"*),* Arthur Barnes *(Interplanetary Huntress),* and others, saw them as daring adventuresses every bit the equal of any brawny, brawling hero of the pulps. Others like Leslie Perri ("Space Episode") and Robert A. Heinlein *(Methuselah's Children, Beyond this Horizon)* saw them as spaceship pilots, project engineers, even soldiers.

Yet, even while these writers were exploring the possibilities of the distant future, women like St. Clair (with her "Oona" series), Judith Merril ("That Only a Mother") and DeFord ("Throwback") were exploring the implications of what life might hold for somewhat more "ordinary" Eves in the near future. It is hardly surprising that by the end of the forties, more and more women writers were beginning to find a warm welcome in the pages of science fiction magazines again.

AN EXPLOSION OF WOMEN WRITERS
With this climate, the 1950s saw an explosion of women writers and New Eves. By the end of the decade, more new female authors had made their appearance between the covers of science fiction magazines than had appeared in the field's

entire forty year history. There were two major reasons for this:

The first was that, in the Western World, at least, women's view of themselves was changing, in large part as a result of the war. Women had discovered during W.W.II that they could do welding, figure the square root of a hypotenuse, dispatch trains and make executive decisions as well as any man — and had received far greater educational opportunities than women of earlier generations (who else was there to swell the ranks of war-years colleges, with men off fighting the war). As a result, there was a quantum jump in the number of women with the scientific or educated bent of mind needed to write — or read — science fiction.

The second reason so many women suddenly appeared in the field is that even if they hadn't felt a strong urge to write science fiction there were editors, male editors, particularly H. L. Gold at *Galaxy*, and the duo of McComas and Boucher at *The Magazine of Fantasy and Science Fiction*, who were willing to go out and recruit them. Though there were differences in slant, both editorial forces shared certain common fifties sensibilities: One was disillusionment with the utopian promise of technology. Their generation had seen "wonders" of science, that seemed to promise so much in the 1920s and 1930s, subverted to war and Madison Avenue-driven consumerism. Their approach to science fiction was also wider than Campbell's, more Wellsian. It still included the gadget or alien puzzle story, but now that shared their pages with social commentary, satire and character study.

The ability to write knowledgeably about buss-bars and transistors was "out." The ability to observe people and social trends and skewer both with equal deftness was "in." Such observations are best made by "outsiders" — who possess a more objective eye — and here, women had a monopoly over men. For they were the fifties' ultimate outsiders (just as blacks would be in the 60s and 70s and gays in the 80s and 90s).

H. L. Gold, whose real taste was for social commentary and satire, particularly wanted women in his pages, encouraging any woman he met whose intelligence, wit or literary ability impressed him as having what it took to write science fiction. He even made a monthly round of calls to his favorite women authors (as he did with his favorite male writers) dunning them for stories. (It is hardly a coincidence, that when the magazine changed editors, lacking Gold's constant encouragement his stable of women writers, many award-winners in other fields, vanished from *Galaxy*'s pages; Fred Pohl, who succeeded him, though perfectly willing to buy a good story by a woman if he received one, did not consider it of vital importance to number women among his stable).

But during the heyday of Gold and Boucher-McComas, it was a rare issue of *Galaxy* or *F&SF* that didn't have at least one woman author, and frequently two or more, listed on their contents pages. When women like St. Clair, DeFord, MacLean, and Merril, found their work was suddenly, not merely tolerated, but in demand (and at considerably higher rates), their productivity began to rise.

Meanwhile their appearance in both magazines' pages encouraged other women with a yen to write science fiction to submit their own efforts. Soon names like Evelyn E. Smith, Wynona McClintic, Ruth Sterling, Sonya Dorman, Helen Clarkson, Helen Urban, Mildred Clingerman, Zenna Henderson, Carol Emshwiller, Sylvia Jacobs, Phyllis Sterling Smith, Pauline Ashwell, Wilmar Shiras (Campbell's two sole fifties female discoveries), and others, joined their sisters' ranks.

With women back in the field, as colleagues, as readers and as inspiration, the fifties produced a small, but significant body of work by writers of both genders exploring the outermost limit of current thought about what women might actually be — once the sweeping tide of change which had affected every institution since the turn of the century, began to subside. What if women turned out to be neither superior nor different, no worse and no better than men? In that case, there would be no big heroics in their lives, only small ones; the same kind of every day triumphs and failures that males experienced. Rather than being empresses and space huntresses, the New Eves would be ordinary women — who revealed the extraordinary in every woman. They might be doctors as in Judith Merril's "The Lady Was a Tramp," or artists as in Betsy Curtis' "A Peculiar People," or even thieves as in Andre Norton's "All Cats Are Grey." But in the fifties, mostly they would be wives and homemakers, plain-Jane Does (the way their husbands were plain-John Doe working-stiffs), as in Helen Clarkson's "The Last Day," or Zenna Henderson's "Subcommittee," or Sonya Dorman's "The Putnam Tradition," or Evelyn E. Smith's inverted "The Captain's Mate."

THE INVASION

Women science fiction writers began to make their presence felt in a serious way in the 1950s. But it was only a small beachhead compared to the invasion that was to come. For in the 1960s and 70s, women began to enter the field with an explosive impact that would alter its shape and character forever. There would still be plenty of boy's adventure fiction (now girl's adventure fiction, with swashbuckling New Eves who grew increasingly larger than life, and appealing to both "girls" and "boys"). But there would also be far more "serious" work; so much more that by the end of the 1970s, women would have produced more serious science fiction than all the men writing before 1960 added together.

Equally importantly, for whatever reason, the quality of these extraordinary women's writings was much higher than that of the men who had been writing science fiction up to that time. This resulted in many lesser male science fiction authors dropping out or being squeezed out of the field; others in rising to the challenge and elevating the quality of their own work; and the entrance of a number of male authors who might once have spurned science fiction as crude or juvenile.

Even a partial list of the women who launched their careers during these all-important two decades (an astonishing number of award-winners among them) reveals that both the growth and quality curves had suddenly gone from mathematical to exponential: Suzette Hayden Elgin, Jane Gaskill, Phyllis Gottlieb, Anne McCaffrey, Ursula K. LeGuin, Doris Piserchia, Jane Roberts, Susan K. Putney, G. McDonald Walsh, Joanna Russ, Josephine Saxton, Marion Zimmer Bradley, Kate Wilhelm, Naomi Mitchison, Jane Gallion, Jo Clayton, Tanith Lee, C. J. Cherryh, Sydney Van Scyoc, Phyllis Eisenstein, Lisa Tuttle, James Tiptree, Jr. (Alice Racoona Sheldon), Elizabeth Lynn, Pamela Sargent, Vonda McIntyre, Suzy McKee Charnas, Joan Vinge.

The women who wrote science fiction in previous generations made an impact for themselves through writing about women's concerns or by bringing a special and distinct "feminine" sensitivity to their work. The new generation writing in the sixties would tackle and master every kind of story and sub-genre in which it had previously been thought that only men could excel. Phyllis Gotlieb (*O Master Caliban*), Sydney Van Scyoc (*Cloudcry*, "Bluewater Dreams"), and Ursula K. LeGuin (*The World for World is Forest*) invaded the harder and more rigorous realms of science based science fiction; George Rosel Brown (*The Waters of CENTAURUS*) and C. J. Cherryh (*Downbelow Station, Chandur's Pride*) proved that slam-bang rip-roaring space opera was no longer a male preserve; while Suzette Hayden Elgin (*At the Seventh Level*), and Kate Wilhelm (*The Killer Thing*, "The Last Days of the Captain") proved that a woman could write an intellectual puzzle story that was up to any previous standard.

FROM LIBERATION TO REVOLT

Throughout the sixties and seventies a single predominant current can be charted in the work of the women writing science fiction: a movement from liberation (the joyous dropping of intellectual and gender-role fetters) to feminism (defiant rebellion against and determined assault on the patriarchal system they believed had fettered them). The 50s had come in like a lamb, but — due to the advent of effective birth control — it went out in the greatest explosion of sexual activity and gender redefinition the world had ever witnessed. Science fiction writers, with their eyes ever fixed on the implications of current developments, couldn't help (as Sturgeon puts it) "asking the next question": If the freedom from the danger of childbirth had liberated women to find their own identities within their gender, how much more so might freedom from the burden of reproduction alter their lives and identities?

In a series of novels and stories in which their vigorous, assertive New Eves seemed creatures of a genesis that left them remarkably free of concern about the possibility of pregnancy, writers like Anne McCaffrey (*Dragonrider*) and Marion Zimmer Bradley (*Hawkmistress,* "Death Between the Stars"), Naomi Mitchison *(Memoirs of a Spacewoman)*, and others demonstrated that for future woman — liberated from all previous biological constraints through the new Geneses created by biology — life was just as full of sexual opportunity and breathless adventure as for any male.

The answers were plain and so was the next question about women to be grappled with and explored in science fictional terms: Freed from early death in childbirth and the constraints of involuntary conception, women had been proved man's intellectual and creative equal, and could make every bit as much of her life. So was it tolerable to project futures in which men and women were not on a fundamentally equal basis — or for historically and technologically outdated social mores to prevent women from expressing the full range of their capabilities in any aspect of contemporary society they choose?

As the possibilities of worlds of unlimited opportunity for women opened up, many of the women writing science fiction, and the women reading it —and more critically still, the women who were about to write it — were beginning to feel their entire gender had been unfairly confined by rigid sex-roles and to seethe with resentment at a patriarchal society they believed had repressed them (although the social critics of two decades before, female and male, had been decrying civilization's millennia long domination by a matriarchal society).

So while feminism was just beginning to be discussed in the popular media, and become a subject of discussion only among enclaves of women in urban centers and the more progressive universities — feminism in just three years (between 1969 and 1972) became the main subject of discourse within the world of science fiction. Even women and men who did not embrace it in their fiction were at least forced to acknowledge or excoriate its existence. No one, however, was able to ignore it and remain a commercially viable writer.

SWORDS AGAINST THE PATRIARCHY

In fact, from the late-60s through the late-70s the central focus of the women writing in the field became a continuous broadside at what they viewed as the confinement and anguish inherent in the role women had been assigned in humanity's patriarchal past; and against the negative characteristics that had to be inherent in the male of the species, to have suppressed and mistreated women as they had throughout history.

Women who had begun their careers identifying with men and writing about strong male protagonists, soon switched to heroines, portraying these New Eves ill-treatment at the hands of a male dominated society: among them, Marion Zimmer Bradley *(Hawkmistress, The Shattered Chain)*, Ursula LeGuin *(The Dispossessed)*, Anne McCaffrey *(Dragondrums, Dragonsong)*, Andre Norton *(Witchworld)*.

The new group of women writers, perhaps taking heart from their elders, seemed to arrive with their own broadsides readied. Led by authors like Joanna Russ (*We Who Are About to Die*, "Gleepsite"), Vonda McIntyre *(Dreamsnake)*, Suzy McKee Charnas *(Walk to the End of the World)*, Suzette Hayden Elgen *(Furthest)*, James Tiptree, Jr. ("Houston, Houston, Do You Read?"), "The Snows Are Melted, The Snows Are Gone"), and Jo Clayton (Diadem from the Stars). For a period every New Eve's blasters and swords seemed raised against the repressive tyranny of the patriarchy.

SOFT MEN AND HARD WOMEN

But reactions to long-perceived repression are always extreme (Paris, 1794) and tend to first perceive all those in any way associated with the cause of that repression as black — and everything associated with their own side as white. After a time, when greater liberty has been obtained and reason reasserts itself, it is realized (at the least) that there are good and bad people on both sides. So it was with science fiction and doctrinaire, anti-male science fiction.

While many major writers who emerged in the 80s, such as Jo Clayton continued to write consciously feminist works, they no longer constituted the majority even in the early years of the decade and by the end of the decade were wholly outnumbered by conscious egalitarians like Mary Caraker, Elizabeth Moon, Susan Schwartz, Alison Tellure, Shelia Finch, Nancy Kress, Melissa Michaels, Melissa Scott, Sharon Webb, Connie Willis, Mary Gentle, Barbara Hamley, Nina Kiriki Hoffman, Lisa Mason, Ardath Mayhar, Cynthia Morgan.

Long before what would be known as post-feminism entered the mainstream culture, the women who were writing science fiction, and particularly the new generation that was growing up in the freer climate their elder sisters had won, were beginning to question the precepts that all males were evil and all sisterhood good. In 1979, Charnas who had launched a lethal salvo against men with *Walk to the End of the World*, fired the opening salvo in a whole new revolution with its sequel *Motherlines*, a novel whose post-feminist sensibilities, debunking the myth of the Edenic matriarchal society, reflected what was to become the dominant attitude in the work of the women who would enter the ranks of science fiction writers during the 1980s and into the 1990s.

They not only didn't see men as evil, they didn't view them as different, either. They had grown up in a world where, increasing freedom had allowed women to successfully prove they could do every job that it had been previously thought only males could handle physically or mentally (from dock work to military combat). The obvious conclusion was that women and men were not necessarily, at base, as distinctly different from one another as had been thought.

Ironically, by the late 1970s these trends, coupled with a major move in the location of bookstores from the streets into shopping malls (where surveys showed an average of 70% to 80% of the patrons are female) combined to place women in the majority among science fiction writers and readers, bringing them to dominance in what was once an almost exclusively male province. At the same time, an explosion of new genre magazines, led by *Isaac Asimov's, Science Fiction Age, Aboriginal,* and others, created a large and eager market for science fiction by and about women. This situation, however, was not without it's own ironic consequences: For with the increased demand for science fiction works by identifiably female authors, a great number of works by lesser talents and visions found their way into print. Whereas in the 1970s women writers had clearly, for their proportions, held the lions share of the talent, their average standard of work was no longer superior to that of the male writers in the field.

BEYOND GENDER

Science fiction, stripping away one-by-one the social myths that had shrouded the nature of women and men for centuries, had finally come face to face with nothing less than the very meaning of gender: What actually constitutes being female or male — both in relationship to themselves and to each other? Which roles and characteristics, if any were inherently gender-based, and which arbitrarily evolved by society?

Together, the women who write science fiction and their male colleagues, extrapolating from the social and biological changes around them, began to find tentative answers. The men in their stories were likely to be "soft", and earn their keep by intellect or artistic talent rather than brain or brawn; their women "hard," earning their keep through wielding power or violence (Barbara Hambly's *The Silent Tower*). Or they might be complex combinations of both, as in Octavia Butler's "Speech Sounds." Or perhaps neither male nor female but a mixture of both, as in LeGuin's "Winter's King"; or able to change sexes at will as in John Varley's *Steel Beach*.

Even the question of just which gender New Eves came from and belonged to became blurred. In a society where women ruled and men were repressed, raised to be helpless and ineffectual — wouldn't males who found the strength to assert themselves be the New Eves (Marion Zimmer Bradley's *Ruins of Isis*)?

With the characteristics of the genders revealed to be so interchangeable, the final question came in sight: Considering all this, if it made no difference what gender one was, what difference did it make what gender one's partner was? Science fiction had already made it clear that love between women and men of different humanoid species (feline, avian and other) was as beautiful and worthy as love between Homo Sapiens. As the eighties and nineties progressed, it made the same thing clear about same sex love. The New Eves were women who could love anyone (and any thing). Homosexual love was treated as matter of factly and with as much sensitivity and erotic subtlety as heterosexual love as in Anne McCaffery's "Changeling," Melissa Scott's *The Kindly Ones*, Frank Robinson's *The Dark Beyond the Stars*, Pamela Sargent's "Fears," Maureen F. McHugh's "The Missionary's Child," Michael Flynn's "Werehouse" and Mary Rosenblum's "California Dreamers," Bisexuality was almost tacitly endorsed (if not practiced) as the sanest of the sexualities.

TOMORROW'S WOMEN: THE NEW EVES

As society at large began to come face-to-face with these very issues, science fiction, and the women who wrote it, were already moving on, eyes on the distant implications of this trend too. For when all was said and done, the women of the 1990s seemed to conclude that if at base men and women were essentially the same, and the choice of sexual partners of equal unimportance — then all that was left was — people. Though gender themes still appear, from the pens of women and men alike, they are a receding wave.

To the women writing science fiction at the turn of the 21st century — and perhaps beyond — stories are about themselves, not about gender or sexuality. Their characters are simply whatever they are — women or men or any of the genders in between. In the works of such cutting-edge authors as Nancy Kress

("Down Behind Cuba Lake"), Sheila Finch ("A Long Way Home"), Lee Killough, ("Symphony for a Lost Traveler"), Karen Joy Fowler ("The Lake was Full of Artificial Things"), and others, the issues simply did not exist, as they had for four generations of their sisters.

Their New Eves live in a world reborn, whose Genesis has made gender, for the most part, simply not an issue — was not even, in fact, worth worrying about. And this, perhaps, is the most extraordinary thing about these stories, their characters, and the women who write them. Now, when they reach out for knowledge, it is no longer forbidden them. It may be self-knowledge, scientific discovery, contact with the wonders offered by alien races. It may confer great benefits, or bring disaster. They can know this in advance, no more than men can. But these New Eves can reach for that knowledge confidently, knowing they have the freedom and the ability to make the best of whatever consequences it brings.

A WORD ABOUT THE MEN WHO WRITE SCIENCE FICTION AND THE WOMEN THEY WRITE ABOUT

Many people who write about the history of science fiction mistakenly believe that until women began to enter the field seriously in the late sixties, all the female characters portrayed by male authors (especially during the early pulp era of the 30s and 40s) were weak, passive, helpless victims —easily captured or endangered — whose *de rigueur* rescue by the hero provided the ersatz jeopardy and action that motivated the story. Actually, with the exception of the worst hacks, almost all the women populating the pages of science fiction were strong, intelligent and resolute.

The reason for this is simple. The men who write science fiction are hardly typical men, and hardly liked typical women — especially not the simpering, passive, empty-headed type. They were generally attracted to intelligent women of character, and generally wrote about intelligent women of character. In a pinch their heroines were more likely to grab a weapon and have at the villain, or outsmart him, than to faint or swoon at his threats.

From George Allan England *(The Flying Legion)*, Edgar Rice Burroughs *(A Princess of Mars, Tarzan the Terrible)*, and David H. Keller in the 20s, to Stanley G. Weinbaum *(The Red Peri)*, Arthur K. Barnes *(Interplanetary Hunter)*, John Taine *(The Greatest Adventure)* Edward E. Smith (the "Lens" series) and John Russell Fearn *(The Golden Amazon)* in the 30s, to Wallace West *(The Bird of Time)*, Nelson S. Bond ("The Priestess who Rebelled"), Robert A. Heinlein *(The Puppet Masters)*, Isaac Asimov *(I, Robot)*, L. Sprague de Camp *(The Queen of Zamba, The Hand of Zei)* in the 40s, to Fred Pohl *(Gravy Planet/The Space Merchants)*, James Schmitz *(The Witches of Karres)*, Stephen Barr ("The Back of Our Heads"), and on into the present with Varley, Ellison, Niven, Benford, Bear, Simmons — and just about everybody else.

The image of the science fictional heroine as victim seems to have been generated almost entirely by viewing the covers of old pulps. Designed to lure their prospective adolescent male readers, these always portrayed a woman (usually in futuristic bra, g-string and high-heels, even when the hero wore a complete spacesuit), usually being saved by a hero with a blazing raygun from the fearsome BEM (bug-eyed monster) into whose arms she has helplessly fainted — and whose use for her, either sexual or gastronomic, defies all scientific logic. Since few people can afford these magazines, and not even one percent of the stories they contain have ever been reprinted, most modern essayists have assumed the covers to be representative of the contents. But here, too, lurking behind their lurid exteriors, New Eves flowered in abundance.

Authors' Note

The stories that follow were selected because they met at least one of three criterion, either they were representative of: the author's work, the story's era, or a key theme in the evolution of science fiction's view of women and their place in the universe. They were not chosen for political correctness. We believe that to censor, denigrate or ignore the ideas and attitudes of the women who founded the field, because we now feel some of those ideas and attitudes to be antiquated, dangerous or wrong, is to imply that our own (which are sure to be viewed in much the same light by our progeny) are no more worthy of serious consideration in future times. Courage, we believe, lies in the strength to stand up and be counted in whatever way one believes right, regardless of whether we believe in it or not.

New Eves aims at showing the entire range of stories women science fiction authors have written about their extraordinary heroines. So expect to find some stories that will shock you, and some that will disturb you, and some that will make you think. Also expect to find some that will make you laugh, some that will make you cry, some that will touch your innermost hearts. Along with some that are for fun, some that are pell-mell adventure, some that are intellectual puzzles, and some that are cutting-edge science.

Those eager to read more by these extraordinary writers, and to encounter the New Eves they, and their male colleagues, created, may be disappointed to discover there is no "recommended reading" list here. The reason is simple: with the exception of a rare anthologization, the works of all the women (and men) who wrote science fiction before the mid-1960s are out of print, and considering the current structure of the publishing industry, likely to remain so. Their books can only be found by lucky browsers in used bookstores; whereas stories by women who wrote before 1950, are simply unobtainable, except to the wealthy, who can afford to pay premium prices for the moldering pulps that alone contain their work. Even the early books of many writers who began their careers in the 1970s and 80s are now out of print — while those of most current women authors can easily be found in one's local bookstore. Until such time as these conditions change, we can only offer this sampler of eight generations of stories by and about the extraordinary New Eves of science fiction.

JANRAE FRANK

JEAN STINE

FORREST J ACKERMAN

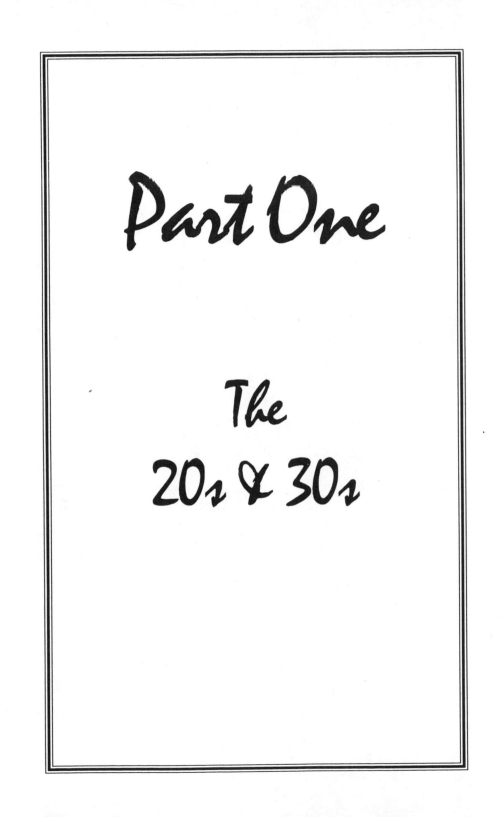

Part One

The
20s & 30s

Friend Island

FRANCIS STEVENS

ABOUT FRANCIS STEVENS
AND *FRIEND ISLAND*

Friend Island *was first published:*
All-Story Weekly, *September 7, 1918*

Science fiction historiographer Sam Moskowitz rightly calls Francis Stevens: "The greatest woman writer of science fantasy in the period between Mary Wolstonecraft Shelly and C.L. Moore." In spite of this, the work of Francis Stevens is almost unknown today. Only her books Citadel of Fear *and* Claimed *have ever been widely reprinted, her other novels* Labyrinth *and* Sunfire *and* Serapion *have sadly never been printed in book form*

Francis Stevens, whose real name was Gertrude Bennett took up writing when her husband's death on a treasure hunting expedition in 1910 left her with an 18 month old daughter to support. After selling a few short stories, Ms. Stevens secured a secretarial position with the University of Pennsylvania, supplementing her income with part-time typing for students. Her immediate financial needs taken care of, Stevens apparently lost her only motivation for writing and ceased contributing to the magazines of the time.

Her genius might have been lost to us entirely had the death of her father around 1916 not added the responsibility of caring for her invalid mother. From that date until her mother's death around 1920, Francis Stevens enjoyed her major period of productivity, penning a number of classic science fiction and fantasy novels. With her mother's death the byline Francis Stevens disappeared, never to reappear on a book or story again. Some twenty years later, she apparently died in California, for a letter written to her by her daughter in the winter of 1939 was returned as undeliverable.

Francis Stevens began writing at a time before women received the franchise to vote, during the climactic years of the suffragette movement for full equality. "Friend Island" is set in a future where that battle has been won. The story is told by a retired female sea captain (an absolute impossibility in the world of 1918). "Friend Island," then, can be considered one of the first and most important works of feminism to appear in an American pulp magazine. In spite of its feminist slant, and its satiric jibs at men's weaknesses, the story is unusually fairly balanced, containing more than a few satiric jibs at women as well. As Moskowitz points out Francis Stevens, "widowed early, with a child to support did not find men as useless as does the lead character of this story. Nor does she magnify their faults all out of proportion in the way that many modern feminist writers do."

Friend Island

by FRANCIS STEVENS

I T WAS UPON the waterfront that I first met her, in one of the shabby little tea shops frequented by able sailoresses of the poorer type. The uptown, glittering resorts of the Lady Aviators' Union were not for such as she.

Stern of feature, bronzed by wind and sun, her age could only be guessed, but I surmised at once that in her I beheld a survivor of the age of turbines and oil engines — a true sea-woman of that elder time when woman's superiority to man had not been so long recognized. When, to emphasize their victory, women in all ranks were sterner than today's need demands.

The spruce, smiling young maidens — engine-women and stokers of the great aluminum rollers, but despite their profession, very neat in gold-braided blue knickers and boleros—these looked askance at the hard-faced relic of a harsher day, as they passed in and out of the shop.

I, however, brazenly ignoring similar glances at myself, a mere male intruding on the haunts of the world's ruling sex, drew a chair up beside the veteran. I ordered a full pot of tea, two cups and a plate of macaroons, and put on my most ingratiating air. Possibly my unconcealed admiration and interest were wiles not exercised in vain. Or the macaroons and tea, both excellent, may have loosened the old sea-woman's tongue. At any rate, under cautious questioning, she had soon launched upon a series of reminiscences well beyond my hopes for color and variety.

"When I was a lass," quoth the sea-woman, after a time, "there was none of this high-flying, gilt-edged, leather-stocking luxury about the sea. We sailed by the power of our oil and gasoline. If they failed on us, like as not 'twas the rubber ring and the rolling wave for ours."

She referred to the archaic practice of placing a pneumatic affair called a life-preserver beneath the arms, in case of that dreaded disaster, now so unheard of, shipwreck.

"In them days there was still many a man bold enough to join our crews. And I've knowed cases," she added condescendingly, "where just by the muscle and brawn of such men some poor sailor lass has reached shore alive that would have fed the sharks without 'em. Oh. I ain't so down on men as you might think. It's the spoiling of them that I don't hold with. There's too much preached nowadays that man is fit for nothing but to fetch and carry and do nurse-work in big child-homes. To my mind, a man who hasn't the nerve of a woman ain't fitted to father children, let alone raise 'em. But that's not here nor there. My time's past, and I know it, or I wouldn't be setting here gossipin' to you, my lad, over an empty teapot."

I took the hint, and with our cups replenished, she bit thoughtfully into her fourteenth macaroon and continued.

"There's one voyage I'm not likely to forget, though I live to be as old as Cap'n Mary Barnacle, of the *Shouter*. 'Twas aboard the old *Shouter* that this here voyage occurred, and it was her last and likewise Cap'n Mary's. Cap'n Mary, she was then that decrepit, it seemed a mercy that she should go to her rest, and in good salt water at that."

"I remember the voyage for Cap'n Mary's sake, but most I remember it because 'twas then that I come the nighest in my life to committin' matrimony. For a man, the man had nerve; he was nearer bein' companionable than any other man I ever seed; and if it hadn't been for just one little event that showed up the — the *mannishness* of him, in a way I couldn't abide, I reckon he'd be keepin' house for me this minute."

"We cleared from Frisco with a cargo of silkateen petticoats for Brisbane. Cap'n Mary was always strong on petticoats. Leather breeches or even half-skirts would ha' paid far better, they being more in demand like, but Cap'n Mary was three-quarters owner, and says she, land women should buy petticoats, and if they didn't it wouldn't be the Lord's fault nor hers for not providing 'em."

"We cleared on a fine day, which is an all sign — or was, then when the weather and the seas o' God still counted in the trafficking of the humankind. Not two days out we met a whirling, mucking bouncer of a gale that well nigh threw the old *Shouter* a full point off her course in the first wallop. She was a stout craft, though. None of your featherweight, gas-lightened, paper-thin alloy shells, but toughened aluminum from stern to stern. Her turbine drove her through the combers at a forty-five knot clip, which named her a speedy craft for a freighter in them days."

"But this night, as we tore along through the creaming green billows, something unknown went 'way wrong down below."

"I was forward under the shelter of her long over-sloop, looking for a hairpin I'd dropped somewheres about that afternoon. It was a gold hairpin, and gold still being mighty scarce when I was a girl, a course I valued it. But suddenly I felt the old *Shouter* give a jump under my feet like a plane struck by a shell in full flight. Then she trembled all over for a full second, frightened like. Then, with the crash of doomsday ringing in my ears, I felt myself sailing through the air right into the teeth o' the shrieking gale, as near as I could judge. Down I come in the hollow of a monstrous big wave, and as my ears doused under I thought I heard a splash close by. Coming up, sure enough, there close by me was floating a new, patent, hermetic, thermo-ice chest. Being as it was empty, and being as it was shut up air-tight, that ice chest made as sweet a life-preserver as a woman could wish in such an hour. About ten foot by twelve, it floated high in the raging sea. Out on its top I scrambled, and hanging on by a handle I looked expectant for some of my poor fellow-women to come floating by. Which they never did, for the good reason that the *Shouter* had blowed up and went below, petticoats, Cap'n Mary and all."

"What caused the explosion?" I inquired

"The Lord and Cap'n Mary Barnacle can explain," she answered piously. "Besides the oil for her turbines, she carried a power of gasoline for her alternative engines, and likely 'twas the cause of her ending so sudden like. Anyways, all I ever seen of her again was the empty ice chest that Providence had well-nigh hove upon my head. On that I sat and floated, and floated and sat some more, till by-and-by the storm sort of blowed itself out, the sun come shining — this was next morning — and I could dry my hair and look about me. I was a young lass, then, and not bad to look upon. I didn't want to die, any more than you that's sitting there this minute. So I up and prays for land. Sure enough toward evening a speck heaves up low down on the horizon. At first I took it for a gas liner, but later found it was just a little island, all alone by itself in the great Pacific Ocean."

"Come, now, here's luck, thinks I, and with that I deserts the ice chest, which being empty, and me having no ice to put in it, not likely to have in them latitudes, is of no further use to me. Striking out I swum a mile or so and set foot on dry land for the first time in nigh three days."

"Pretty land it were, too, though bare of human life as an iceberg in the Arctic."

"I had landed on a shining white beach that run up to a grove of lovely, waving palm trees. Above them I could see the slopes of a hill so high and green it reminded me of my own old home, up near Couquomgomoc Lake in Maine. The whole place just seemed to smile and smile at me. The palms waved and bowed in the sweet breeze, like they wanted to say, 'Just set right down and make yourself to home. We've been waiting a long time for you to come.' I cried, I was that happy to be made welcome. I was a young lass then, and sensitive-like to how folks treated me. You're laughing now, but wait and see if or not there was sense to the way I felt."

"So I up and dries my clothes and my long, soft hair again, which was well worth drying, for I had far more of it than now. After that I walked along a piece, until there was a sweet little path meandering away into the wild woods."

"Here, thinks I, this looks like inhabitants. Be they civil or wild, I wonder? But after traveling the path a piece, lo and behold it ended sudden like in a wide circle of green grass, with a little spring of clear water. And the first thing I noticed was a slab of white board nailed to a palm tree close to the spring. Right off I took a long drink; for you better believe I was thirsty, and then I went to look at this board. It had evidently been tore off the side of a wooden packing box, and the letters was roughly printed in lead pencil."

" 'Heaven help whoever you be,' I read. 'This island ain't just right. I'm going to swim for it. You better too. Good-by. Nelson Smith.' That's what it said, but the spellin' was simply awful. It all looked quite new and recent, as if Nelson Smith hadn't more than a few hours before he wrote and nailed it there."

"Well, after reading that queer warning I begun to shake all over like in a chill. Yes, I shook like I had the ague, though the hot tropic sun was burning down right on me and that alarming board. What had scared Nelson Smith so much that he had swum to get away? I looked all around real cautious and careful, but not a single frightening thing could I behold. And the palms and the green grass and the flowers still smiled that peaceful and friendly like. 'Just make yourself to home,' was wrote all over the place in plainer letters than those sprawly lead pencil ones on the board."

"Pretty soon, what with the quiet and all, the chill left me. Then I thought, 'Well, to be sure, this Smith person was just an ordinary man, I reckon, and likely he got nervous of being so alone. I likely he just fancied things which was really not. It's a pity he drowned himself before I come, though likely I'd have found him poor company. By his record I judge him a man of but common education.' "

"So I decided to make the most of my welcome, and that I did for weeks to come. Right near the spring was a cave, dry as a biscuit box, with a nice floor of white sand. Nelson had lived there too, for there was a litter of stuff — tin cans — empty — scraps of newspapers and the like. I got to calling him Nelson in my mind, and then Nelly, and wondering if he was dark or fair, and how he come to be cast away there all alone, and what was the strange events that drove him to his end. I cleaned out the cave, though. He had devoured all his tin-canned provisions, however he come by them, but this I didn't mind. That there island was a generous body. Green milk-coconuts, sweet berries, turtle eggs and the like was my daily fare."

"For about three weeks the sun shone every day, the birds sang and the monkeys chattered. We was all one big, happy family, and the more I explored that island the better I liked the company I was keeping. The land was about ten miles from beach to beach, and never a foot of it that wasn't sweet and clean as a private park."

"From the top of the hill I could see the ocean, miles and miles of blue water, with never a sign of a gas liner, or even a little government running-boat. Them running-boats used to go most everywhere to keep the seaways clean of derelicts and the like. But I knowed that if this island was no more than a hundred miles off the regular courses of navigation, it might be many a long day before I'd be rescued. The top of the hill, as I found when first I climbed up there, was a wore-out crater. So I knowed that the island was one of them volcanic ones you run across so many of in the seas between Capricorn and Cancer."

"Here and there on the slopes and down through the jungly tree-growth, I would come on great lumps of rock, and these must have came up out of that crater long ago. If there was lava it was so old it had been covered up entire with green growing stuff. You couldn't have found it without a spade, which I didn't have nor want."

"Well, at first I was happy as the hours was long. I wandered and clambered and waded and swum, and combed my long hair on the beach, having fortunately not lost my side-combs nor the rest of my gold hairpins. But by-and-by it begun to get just a bit lonesome. Funny thing, that's a feeling that, once it starts, it gets worse and worser so quick it's perfectly surprising. And right then was when the days begun to get gloomy. We had a long, sickly hot spell, like I never seen before on an ocean island. There was dull clouds across the sun from morn to night. Even the little monkeys and parrakeets, that had seemed so gay, moped and drowsed like they was sick. All one day I cried, and let the rain soak me through and through — that was the first rain we had —and I didn't get thorough dried even during the night, though I slept in my cave. Next morning I got up mad as thunder at myself and all the world."

"When I looked out the black clouds was billowing across the sky. I could hear nothing but great breakers roaring in on the beaches, and the wild wind raving through the lashing palms."

"As I stood there a nasty little wet monkey dropped from a branch almost on my head. I grabbed a pebble and slung it at him real vicious. 'Get away, you dirty little brute!' I shricks, and with that there come a awful blinding flare of light. There was a long, crackling noise like a bunch of Chinese fireworks, and then a sound as if a whole fleet of *Shouters* had all went up together."

"When I come to I found myself 'way in the back of my cave, trying to dig further into the rock with my finger nails. Upon taking thought, it come to me that what had occurred was just a lightning-clap, and going to look, sure enough there lay a big palm tree right across the glade. It was all busted and split open by the lightning, and the little monkey was under it, for I could see his tail and his hind legs sticking out."

"Now, when I set eyes on that poor, crushed little beast I'd been so mean to. I was terrible ashamed. I sat down on the smashed tree and considered and considered. How thankful I had ought to have been. Here I had a lovely, plenteous island, with food and water to my taste, when it might have been a barren, starvation rock that was my lot. And so, thinking, a sort of gradual peaceful feeling stole over me. I got cheerfuller and cheerfuller, till I could have sang and danced for joy."

"Pretty soon I realized that the sun was shilling bright for the first time that week. The wind had stopped hollering, and the waves had died to just a singing murmur on the beach. It seemed kind o' strange, this sudden peace, like the cheer in my own heart after its rage and storm. I rose up, feeling sort of queer, and went to look if the little monkey had came alive again, though that was a fool thing, seeing he was laying all crushed up and very dead. I buried him under a tree root, and as I did it a conviction come to me."

"I didn't hardly question that conviction at all. Somehow, living there alone so long, perhaps my natural womanly intuition was stronger than ever before or since, and so I *knowed*. Then I went and pulled poor Nelson Smith's board off from the tree and tossed it away for the tide to carry off. That there board was an insult to my island!"

The sea-woman paused, and her eyes had a far-away look. It seemed as if I and perhaps even the macaroons and tea were quite forgotten.

"Why did you think that?" I asked, to bring her back. "How could an island be insulted?"

She started, passed her hand across her eyes, and hastily poured another cup of tea.

"Because," she said at last, poising a macaroon in mid-air, "because that island — that particular island that I had landed on — had a heart!"

"When I was gay, it was bright and cheerful. It was glad when I come, and it treated me right until I got that grouchy it had to mope from sympathy. It loved me like a friend. When I flung a rock at that poor little drenched monkey critter, it backed up my act with an anger like the wrath o' God, and killed its own child to please me! But it got right cheery the minute I seen the wrongness of my ways. Nelson Smith had no business to say, 'This island ain't just right,' for it was a righter place than ever I seen elsewhere. When I cast away that lying board, all the birds begun to sing like mad. The green milk-coconuts fell right and left. Only the monkeys seemed kind o' sad like still, and no wonder. You see, their own mother, the island, had rounded on one o' them for my sake!"

"After that I was right careful and considerate. I named the island Anita, not knowing her right name, or if she had any. Anita was a pretty name, and it sounded kind of South Sea like. Anita and me got along real well together from that day on. It was some strain to be always gay and singing around like a dear duck of a canary bird, but I done my best. Still, for all the love and gratitude I bore Anita, the company of an island, however sympathetic, ain't quite enough for a human being. I still got lonesome, and there was even days when I couldn't keep the clouds clear out of the sky, though I will say we had no more tornadoes."

"I think the island understood and tried to help me with all the bounty and good cheer the poor thing possessed. None the less my heart give a wonderful big leap when one day I seen a blot on the horizon. It drawed nearer and nearer, until at last I could make out its nature."

"A ship, of course," said I, "and were you rescued?"

"'Tweren't a ship, neither," denied the sea-woman somewhat impatiently. "Can't you let me spin this yarn without no more remarks and fool questions? This thing what was bearing down so fast with the incoming tide was neither more nor less than another island!"

"You may well look startled. I was startled myself. Much more so than you, likely. I didn't know then what you, with your book-learning, very likely know now — that islands sometimes float. Their underparts being a tangled-up mess of roots and old vines that new stuff's growed over they sometimes break away from the mainland in a brisk gale and go off for a voyage, calm as a old-fashioned, eight-funnel steamer. This one was uncommon large, being as much as two miles, maybe, from shore to shore. It had its palm trees and its live things, just like my own Anita, and I've sometimes wondered if this drifting piece hadn't really been a part of my island once — just its daughter like, as you might say."

"Be that, however, as it might be, no sooner did the floating piece get within hailing distance than I hears a human holler and there was a man dancing up and down on the shore like he was plumb crazy. Next minute he had plunged into the narrow strip of water between us and in a few minutes had swum to where I stood."

"Yes, of course it was none other than Nelson Smith!"

"I knowed that the minute I set eyes on him. He had the very look of not having no better sense than the man what wrote that board and then nearly committed suicide trying to get away from the best island in all the oceans. Glad enough he was to get back, though, for the coconuts was running very short on the floater what had rescued him, and the turtle eggs wasn't worth mentioning. Being short of grub is the surest way I know to cure a man's fear of the unknown."

"Well, to make a long story short, Nelson Smith told me he was a aeronauter. In them days to be an aeronauter was not the same as to be an aviatress is now. There was dangers in the air, and dangers in the sea, and he had met with both. His gas tank had leaked and he had dropped into the water close by Anita. A case or two of provisions was all he could save from the total wreck."

"Now, as you might guess, I was crazy enough to find out what had scared this Nelson Smith into trying to swim the Pacific. He told me a story that seemed to fit pretty well with mine, only when it come to the scary part he shut up like a clam, that aggravating way some men have. I give it up at last for just man-foolishness, and we begun to scheme to get away."

"Anita moped some while we talked it over. I realized how she must be feeling, so I explained to her that it was right needful for us to get with our kind again. If we stayed with her we should probably quarrel like cats, and maybe even kill each other out of pure human cussedness. She cheered up considerable after that, and even, I thought, got a little anxious to have us leave. At any rate, when we begun to provision up the little floater, which we had anchored to the big island by a cable of twisted bark, the green nuts fell all over the ground, and Nelson found more turtle nests in a day than I had in weeks."

"During them days I really got fond of Nelson Smith. He was a companionable body, and brave, or he wouldn't have been a professional aeronauter, a job that was rightly thought tough enough for a woman, let alone a man. Though he was not so well educated as me, at least he was quiet and modest about what he did know, not like some men, boasting most where there is least to brag of."

"Indeed, I misdoubt if Nelson and me would not have quit the sea and the air together and set up housekeeping in some quiet little town up in New England, maybe, after we had got away, if it had not been for what happened when we went. I never, let me say, was so deceived in any man before nor since. The thing taught me a lesson and I never was fooled again."

"We was all ready to go, and then one morning, like a parting gift from Anita, come a soft and favoring wind. Nelson and I run down the beach together, for we didn't want our floater to blow off and leave us. As we was running, our arms full of coconuts, Nelson Smith, stubbed his bare toe on a sharp rock, and down he went. I hadn't noticed, and was going on."

"But sudden the ground begun to shake under my feet, and the air was full of a queer, grinding, groaning sound, like the very earth was in pain."

"I turned around sharp. There sat Nelson, holding his bleeding toe in both fists and giving vent to such awful words as no decent sea-going lady would ever speak nor hear to!"

" 'Stop it, stop it!' I shrieked at him, but 'twas too late."

"Island or no island, Anita was a lady, too! She had a gentle heart, but she knowed how to behave when she was insulted."

"With one terrible, great roar a spout of smoke and flame belched up out o' the heart of Anita's crater hill a full mile into the air!"

"I guess Nelson stopped swearing. He couldn't have heard himself, anyways. Anita was talking now with tongues of flame and such roars as would have bespoke the raging protest of a continent."

"I grabbed that fool man by the hand and run him down to the water. We had to swim good and hard to catch up with our only hope, the floater. No bark rope could hold her against the stiff breeze that now blowing, and she had broke her cable. By the time we scrambled aboard great rocks was falling right and left. We couldn't see each other for a while for the clouds of fine gray ash."

"It seemed like Anita was that mad she was flinging stones after us, and truly I believe that such was her intention. I didn't blame her, neither!"

"Lucky for us the wind was strong and we was soon out of range."

" 'So!' says I to Nelson, after I'd got most of the ashes out of my mouth, and shook my hair clear of cinders. 'So, that was the reason you up and left sudden when you was there before! You aggravated that island till the poor thing druv you out!' "

" 'Well,' says he, and not so meek as I'd have admired to see him, 'how could I know the darn island was a lady?' "

" 'Actions speak louder than words,' says I. 'You should have knowed it by her ladylike behavior!' "

" 'Is volcanoes and slingin' hot rocks ladylike?' he says. 'Is snakes ladylike? T'other time I cut my thumb on a tin can, I cussed a little bit. Say — just a li'l bit! An' what comes at me out o' all the caves, and out o' every crack in the rocks, and out o' the very spring o' water where I'd been drinkin'? Why snakes! *Snakes,* if you please, big, little, green, red and sky-blue-scarlet! What'd I do? Jumped in the water, of course. Why wouldn't I? I'd ruther swim and drown than be stung or swallowed to death. But how was I t' know the snakes come outta the rocks because I cussed?' "

"'You, couldn't,' I agrees, sarcastic. 'Some folks never knows a lady till she up and whangs 'em over the head with a brick. A real, gentle, kind-like warning, them snakes were, which you would not heed! Take shame to yourself, Nelly,' says I, right stern, 'that a decent little island like Anita can't associate with you peaceable, but you must hurt her sacredest feelings with language no lady would stand by to hear!' "

"I never did see Anita again. She may have blew herself right out of the ocean in her just wrath at the vulgar, disgustin' language of Nelson Smith. I don't know. We was took off the floater at last, and I lost track of Nelson just as quick as I could when we was landed at Frisco."

"He had taught me a lesson. A man is just full of mannishness, and the best of 'em ain't good enough for a lady to sacrifice her sensibilities to put up with."

"Nelson Smith, he seemed to feel real bad when he learned I was not for him, and then he apologized. But apologies weren't no use to me. I could never abide him, after the way he went and talked right in the presence of me and my poor, sweet lady friend, Anita!"

Now I am well versed in the lore of the sea in all ages. Through mists of time I have enviously eyed wild voyagings of sea rovers who roved and spun their yarns before the stronger sex came into its own, and ousted man from his heroic pedestal. I have followed — across the printed page — the wanderings of Odysseus. Before Gulliver I have burned the incense of tranced attention; and with reverent awe considered the history of one Munchausen, a baron. But alas, these were only men!

In what field is not woman our subtle superior?

Meekly I bowed my head, and when my eyes dared lift again, the ancient mariness had departed, leaving me to sorrow for my surpassed and outdone idols. Also with a bill for macaroons and tea of such incredible proportions that in comparison therewith I found it easy to believe her story!

The Man
of Stone

HAZEL HEALD

ABOUT HAZEL HEALD
AND
THE MAN OF STONE

The Man of Stone was *first published:*
Wonder Stories, *October 1932*

Hazel Heald's literary output was restricted almost entirely to fantasy. And her handful of short stories (which reputedly had the final drafts glossed by no less a luminary than H.P. Lovecraft) appeared almost entirely in the pages of Weird Tales. *Her sole appearance in science fiction was restricted to "The Man of Iron" in Hugo Gernsback's* Wonder Stories.

Modern readers should be warned Ms. Heald was born in an age when women did not yet possess the vote. One in which, in the rural backwoods of the world, woman's condition was no better than that of a chattel slave, and often considerably lower than that of a good hunting dog.

That as recently as sixty years ago (and probably more recently) women in the western world could be routinely whipped and beaten by their husbands and see nothing unusual or objectionable in the experience or the man, may seem shocking to many women today. Yet the era of which Ms. Heald writes is at most our grandmothers' era (and what tales those ladies might have had to tell if only we had possessed the wit to seek them out and ask). Fortunately, in science fictional guise Heald tells us one of those tales.

The Man Of Stone

by HAZEL HEALD

Ben Hayden was always a stubborn chap, and once he had heard about those strange statues in the upper Adirondacks, nothing could keep him from going to see them. I had been his closest acquaintance for years, and our Damon and Pythias friendship made us inseparable at all times. So when Ben firmly decided to go — well, I had to trot along too, like a faithful collie.

"Jack," he said, "you know Henry Jackson, who was up in a shack beyond Lake Placid for that beastly spot in his lung? Well, he came back the other day nearly cured, but had a lot to say about some devilish queer conditions up there. He ran into the business all of a sudden and can't be sure yet that it's anything more than a case of bizarre sculpture; but just the same his uneasy impression sticks."

"It seems he was out hunting one day, and came across a cave with what looked like a dog in front of it. Just as he was expecting the dog to bark he looked again, and saw that the thing wasn't alive at all. It was a stone dog — but such a perfect image, down to the smallest whisker, that he couldn't decide whether it was a supernaturally clever statue or a petrified animal. He was almost afraid to touch it, but when he did he realized It was surely made of stone."

"After a while he nerved himself up to go in the cave — and there he got a still bigger jolt. Only a little way in there was another stone figure or what looked like it — but this time it was a man's. It lay on the floor, on its side, wore clothes, and had a peculiar smile on its face. This time Henry didn't stop to do any touching, but beat it straight for the village, Mountain Top, you know. Of course he asked questions — but they did not get him very far. He found he was on a ticklish subject, for the natives only shook their heads, crossed their fingers, and muttered something about a 'Mad Dan' — whoever he was."

"It was too much for Jackson, so he came home weeks ahead of his planned time. He told me all about it because he knows how fond I am of strange things — and oddly enough, I was able to fish up a recollection that dovetailed pretty neatly with his yarn. Do you remember Arthur Wheeler, the sculptor who was such a realist that people began calling him nothing but a solid photographer? I think you knew him slightly. Well, as a matter of fact, he ended up in that part of the Adirondacks himself. Spent a lot of time there, and then dropped out of sight. Never heard from again. Now if stone statues that look like men and dogs are turning up around there, it looks to me as if they might be his work — no matter what the rustics say, or refuse to say, about them."

Of course a fellow with Jackson's nerves might easily get flighty and disturbed over things like that: but I'd have done a lot of examining before running away.

"In fact, Jack, I'm going up there now to look things over — and you're coming along with me. It would mean a lot to find Wheeler — or any of his work. Anyhow, the mountain air will brace us both up."

So less than a week later, after a long train ride and a jolting bus trip through breathlessly exquisite scenery, we arrived at Mountain Top in the late, golden sunlight of a June evening. The village comprised only a few small houses, a hotel, and the general store at which our bus drew up; but we knew that the latter would probably prove a focus for such information. Surely enough, the usual group of idlers was gathered around the steps; and when we represented ourselves as health-seekers in search of lodgings they had many recommendations to offer.

Though we had not planned to do any investigating till the next day, Ben could not resist venturing some vague, cautious questions when he noticed the senile garrulousness of one of the ill-clad loafers. He felt, from Jackson's previous experience, that it would be useless to begin with references to the queer statues; but decided to mention Wheeler as one whom we had known, and in whose fate we consequently had a right to be interested.

The crowd seemed uneasy when Sam stopped his whittling and started talking, but they had slight occasion for alarm. Even this barefoot old mountain decadent tightened up when he heard Wheeler's name, and only with difficulty could Ben get anything coherent out of him.

"Wheeler?" he had finally wheezed, "Oh, yeh — that feller as was all the time blastin' rocks and cuttin' 'em up into statues. So yew knowed him, hey? Wal, they ain't much we kin tell ye, and mebbe that's too much. He stayed out to Mad Dan's cabin in the hills — but not so very long. Got so he wa'nt wanted no more. . . . by Dan, that is. Kinder soft-spoken and got around Dan's wife till the old devil took notice. Pretty sweet on her, I guess. But he took the trail sudden, and nobody's seen hide nor hair of him since. Dan must a told him sumthin' pretty plain — bad feller to git agin ye, Dan is! Better keep away from thar, boys, for they ain't no good in that part of the hills. Dan's ben workin' up a worse and worse mood, and ain't seen about no more. Nor his wife, neither. Guess he's penned her up so's nobody else kin make eyes at her!"

As Sam resumed his whittling after a few more observations, Ben and I exchanged glances. Here, surely, was a new lead which deserved intensive following up. Deciding to lodge at the hotel, we settled ourselves as quickly as possible; planning for a plunge into the wild hilly country on the next day.

At sunrise we made our start, each bearing a knapsack laden with provisions and such tools as we thought we might need. The day before us had an almost stimulating air of invitation — through which only a faint undercurrent of the sinister ran. Our rough mountain road quickly became steep and winding, so that before long our feet ached considerably.

After about two miles we left the road — crossing a stone wall on our right near a great elm and striking off diagonally toward a steeper slope according to the chart and directions which Jackson had prepared for us. It was rough and briery traveling, but we knew that the cave could not be far off. In the end we came upon the aperture quite suddenly — a black, bush-grown crevice where the ground shot abruptly upward, and beside it, near a shallow rock pool, a small, still figure stood rigid — as if rivaling its own uncanny petrification.

It was a grey dog — or a dog's statue — and as our simultaneous gasp died away we scarcely knew what to think. Jackson had exaggerated nothing, and we could not believe that any sculptor's hand had succeeded in producing such perfection. Every hair of the animal's magnificent coat seemed distinct, and those on the back were bristled up as if some unknown thing had taken him unaware. Ben, at last half-kindly touching the delicate stony fur, gave vent to an exclamation.

"Good God, Jack, but this can't be any statue! Look at it — all the little details, and the way the hair lies! None of Wheeler's technique here! This is a real dog — though Heaven only knows how he ever got in this state. Just like stone — feel for yourself. Do you suppose there's any strange gas that sometimes comes out of the cave and does this to animal life? We ought to have looked more into the local legends. And if this is a real dog — or was a real dog — then that man inside must be the real thing too."

It was with a good deal of genuine solemnity — almost dread — that we finally crawled on hands and knees through the cave mouth, Ben leading. The narrowness looked hardly three feet, after which the grotto expanded in every direction to form a damp, twilight chamber floored with rubble and detritus. For a time we could make out very little, but as we rose to our feet and strained our eyes we began slowly to descry a recumbent figure amidst the greater darkness ahead. Ben fumbled with his flashlight, but hesitated for a moment before turning it on the prostrate figure. We had little doubt that the stony thing was what had once been a man, and something in the thought unnerved us both.

When Ben at last sent forth the electric beam we saw that the object lay on its side, back toward us. It was clearly of the same material as the dog outside, but was dressed in the same mouldering and unpetrified remains of rough sport clothing. Braced as we were for a shock, we approached quite calmly to examine the thing; Ben going around to the other side to glimpse the averted face. Neither could possibly have been prepared for what Ben saw when he flashed the light on those stony features. His cry was wholly excusable, and I could not help echoing it as I leaped to his side and shared the sight. Yet it was nothing hideous or intrinsically terrifying. It was merely a matter of recognition for beyond the least shadow of a doubt this chilly rock figure with its half-frightened, half-bitter expression had at one time been our old acquaintance, Arthur Wheeler.

Some instinct sent us staggering and crawling out of the cave, and down the tangled slope to a point whence we could not see the ominous stone dog. We hardly knew what to think, for our brains were churning with conjections and apprehensions. Ben, who had known Wheeler well, was especially upset; and seemed to be piecing together some threads I had overlooked.

Again and again as we paused on the green slope he repeated "Poor Arthur, poor Arthur!" but not till he muttered the name "Mad Dan" did I recall the trouble into which, according to old Sam Poole, Wheeler had run just before his disappearance. Mad Dan, Ben implied, would doubtless be glad to see what had happened. For a moment it flashed over both of us that the jealous host might have been responsible for the sculptor's presence in this evil cave, but the thought went as quickly as it came.

The thing that puzzled us, most was to account for the phenomenon itself. What gaseous emanation or mineral vapor could have wrought this change in so relatively short a time was utterly beyond us. Normal petrification we know, is a slow chemical replacement process requiring vast ages for completion; yet here were two stone images which had been living things — or at least Wheeler had — only a few weeks before. Conjecture was useless. Clearly, nothing remained but to notify the authorities and let them guess what they might; and yet at the back of Ben's head that notion about Mad Dan still persisted. Anyhow, we clawed our way back to the road, but Ben did not turn toward the village, but looked along upward toward where old Sam had said Dan's cabin lay. It was the second house from the village, the ancient loafer had wheezed, and lay on the left far back from the road in a thick copse of scrub oaks. Before I knew it Ben was dragging me up the sandy highway past a dingy farmstead and into a region of increasing wildness.

It did not occur to me to protest, but I felt a certain sense of mounting menace as the familiar marks of agriculture and civilization grew fewer and fewer. At last the beginning of a narrow, neglected path opened up on our left, while the peaked roof of a squalid, unpainted building showed itself beyond a sickly growth of half-dead trees. This, I knew, must be Mad Dan's cabin; and I wondered that Wheeler had ever chosen so unprepossessing a place for his headquarters. I dreaded to walk up that weedy, uninviting path, but could not lag behind when Ben strode determinedly along and began a vigorous rapping at the rickety, musty-smelling door.

There was no response to the knock, and something in its echoes sent a series of shivers through one. Ben, however, was quite unperturbed; and at once began to circle the house in quest of unlocked windows. The third that he tried — in the rear of the dismal cabin — proved capable of opening, and after a boost and a vigorous spring he was safely inside and helping me after him.

The room in which we landed was full of limestone and granite blocks, chiselling tools and clay models, and we realized at once that it was Wheeler's erst while studio. So far we had not met with any sign of life, but over everything hovered a damnably ominous dusty odor. On our left was an open door evidently leading to a kitchen on the chimney side of the house, and through this Ben started, intent on finding anything he could concerning his friend's last habitat. He was considerably ahead of me when he crossed the threshold, so that I could not see at first what brought him up short and wrung a low cry of horror from his lips.

In another moment, though, I did see — and repeated his cry as instinctively as I had done in the cave. For here in this cabin far from any subterranean depths which could breed strange gases and work strange imitations — were two stony figures which I knew at once were no products of Arthur Wheeler's chisel. In a rude armchair before the fireplace, bound in position by the lash of a long rawhide whip, was the form of a man — unkempt, elderly, and with a look of fathomless horror on its evil, petrified face.

On the floor beside it lay a woman's figure; graceful, and with a face betokening considerable youth and beauty. Its expression seemed to be one of sardonic satisfaction, and near its outflung right hand was a large tin pail, somewhat stained on the inside, as with a darkish sediment.

CHAPTER II
The Diary of "Mad Dan"

We made no move to approach these inexplicably petrified bodies, nor did we exchange any but the simplest conjectures. That this stony couple had been Mad Dan and his wife we could not well doubt, but how to account for their present condition was another matter. As we looked horrifiedly around we saw the suddenness with which the final development must have come — for everything about is seemed, despite a heavy coating of dust, to have been left in the midst of commonplace household activities.

The only exception to this rule of casualness was on the kitchen table; in whose cleared center, as if to attract attention, lay a thin, battered, blank-book weighted down by a sizable tin funnel. Crossing to read the thing, Ben saw that it was a kind of diary or set of dated entries, written in a somewhat cramped and none too practiced hand. The very first words riveted my attention, and before ten seconds had elapsed he was breathlessly devouring the halting text — I avidly following as peered over his shoulder. As we read on — moving as we did so into the less loathsome atmosphere of the adjoining room — many obscure things became terribly clear to us, and we trembled with a mixture of complex emotions.

This is what we read — and what the coroner read later on. The public has seen a highly twisted and sensationalized version in the cheap newspapers, but not even that has more than a fraction of the genuine terror which the simple original held for us as we puzzled it out alone in that musty cabin among the wild hills, with two monstrous stone abnormalities lurking in the deathlike silence of the next room. When we had finished Ben pocketed the book with a gesture half of repulsion, and his first words were "Let's get out of here."

Silently and nervously we stumbled to the front of the house, unlocked the door, and began the long tramp back to the village. There were many statements to make and questions to answer in the days that followed, and I do not think that either Ben or I can ever shake off the effects of the whole harrowing experience. Neither can some of the local authorities and city reporters who flocked around — even though they burned a certain book and many papers found in attic boxes, and destroyed considerable apparatus in the deepest part of that sinister hillside cave. But here is the text itself:

"Nov. 5 — My name is Daniel Morris. Around here they call me 'Mad Dan' because I believe in powers that nobody else believes in nowadays. When I go up on Thunder Hill to keep the Feast of the Foxes they think I am crazy — all except the back country folks that are afraid of me. They try to stop me from sacrificing the Black Goat at Hallow Eve, and always prevent my doing the Great Rite that would open the gate. They ought to know better, for they know I am a Van Kauran on my mother's side, and anybody this side of the Hudson can tell what the Van Kaurans have handed down. We come from Nicholas Van Kauran, the wizard, who was hanged in Wijtgaart in 1587, and everybody knows he had made the bargain with the Black Man."

"The soldiers never got his Book of Eibon when they burned his house, and his grandson, William Van Kauran, brought it over when he came to Rensselacrwyck and later crossed the river to Esopus. Ask anybody in Kingston or Hurley about what the William Van Kauran line could do to people that got in their way. Also, ask them if my uncle Hendrick didn't manage to keep hold of the Book of Eibon when they ran him out of town and he went up the river to this place with his family."

"I am writing this and am going to keep on writing this — because I want people to know the truth after I am gone. Also, I am afraid I shall really go mad if I don't set things down in plain black and white. Everything is going against me, and if it keeps up I shall have to use the secrets in the Book and call in certain Powers. Three months ago that sculptor Arthur Wheeler came to Mountain Top, and they sent him up to me because I am the only man in the place who knows anything except farming, hunting, and fleecing summer boarders. The fellow seemed to be interested in what I had to say, and made a deal to stop here for $13.00 a week with meals. I gave him the back room beside the kitchen for his lumps of stone and his chiseling, and arranged with Nate Williams to tend to his rock blasting and haul his big pieces with a drag and yoke of oxen."

"That was three months ago. Now I know why that cursed son of hell took so quick to the place. It wasn't my talk at all, but the looks of my wife Rose, that is Osborn Chandler's oldest girl. She is sixteen years younger than I am, and is always casting sheep's eyes at the fellows in town. But we always managed to get along fine enough till this dirty rat showed up, even if she did balk at helping me with the Rites on Roodmas and Hallowmass. I can see now that Wheeler is working on her feelings and getting her so fond of him that she hardly looks at me, and I suppose he'll try to elope with her sooner or later."

"But he works slow like all sly, polished dogs, and I've got plenty of time to think up what to do about it. They don't either of them know I suspect anything, but before long they'll both realize it doesn't pay to break up a Van Kaursn's home. I promise them plenty of novelty in what I'll do."

"Nov. 25 — Thanksgiving Day! That's a pretty good joke! But at that I'll have something to be thankful for when I finish what I've started. No question but that Wheeler is trying to steal my wife. For the time being, though, I'll let him keep on being a star boarder. Got the Book of Eibon down from Uncle Hendrik's old trunk in the attic last week, and am looking up something good which won't require sacrifices that I can't make around here. I want something that'll finish these two sneaking traitors, and at the same time get me into no trouble. If it has a twist of drama in it, so much the better. I've thought of calling in the emanation of Yoth, but that needs a child's blood and I must be careful about the neighbors. The Green Decay looks promising, but that would be a bit unpleasant for me as well as for them. I don't like certain sights and smells."

"Dec.10 — *Eureka!* I've got the very thing, at last! Revenge is sweet — and this is the perfect climax! Wheeler, the sculptor — this is too good! Yes, indeed, that damned sneak is going to produce a statue that will sell quicker than any of the things he's been carving these past few weeks! A realist, eh? Well — the new statuary won't lack any realism! I found the formula in a manuscript insert opposite page 679 of the Book. From the handwriting I judge it was put there by my great-grandfather Bareut Picterse Van Kauran — the one who disappeared from New Paltz in 1839. *Ia! Shub-niggurath!* The Goat With a Thousand Young!"

"To be plain, I've found a way to turn those wretched rats into stone statues. It's absurdly simple, and really depends more on plain chemistry than on the Outer Powers. If I can get hold of the right stuff I can brew a drink that'll pass for homemade wine, and one swig ought to finish any ordinary being short of an elephant. What it amounts to is a kind of petrification infinitely speeded up. Shoots the whole system full of calcium and barium salts and replaces living cells with mineral matter so fast that nothing can stop it. It must have been one of those things my great-grandfather got at the Great Sabbat on Sugar-Loaf in the Catskills. Queer things used to go on there. Seems to me I heard of a man in New Paltz — Squire Hasbrouck — turned to stone or something like that in 1834. He was an enemy of the Van Kauran's. First thing I must do is order the five chemicals I need from Albany and Montreal. Plenty of time later to experiment. When everything is over I'll round up all the statues and sell them as Wheeler's work to pay for his overdue board bill! He always was a realist and an egoist — wouldn't it be natural for him to make a self-portrait in stone, and to use my wife for another model — as indeed he's really been doing for the past fortnight? Trust the dull public not to ask *what quarry* the queer stone came from!"

"Dec. 25 — Christmas. Peace on earth, and so forth! Those two swine are goggling at each other as if I didn't exist. They must think I'm deaf, dumb, and blind! Well, the barium sulphate and calcium chloride came from Albany last Thursday, and the acids, catslytics, and instruments are due from Montreal any day now. The mills of the gods — and all that! I'll do the work in Allen's Cave near the lower wood lot, and at the same time will be openly making some wine in the cellar here. There ought to be some excuse for offering a new drink — though it won't take much planning to fool those moonstruck nincompoops. The trouble will be to make Rose take wine, for she pretends not to like it. Any experiments that I make on animals will be down at the cave, and nobody ever thinks of going there in winter. I'll do some woodcutting to account for my time away. A small load or two brought in will keep him off the track."

"Jan. 20 — It's harder work than I thought. A lot depends on the exact proportions. The stuff came from Montreal, but I had to send again for some better scales and an acetylene lamp. They're getting curious down at the village. Wish the express office weren't in Steenwyck's store. Am trying various mixtures on the sparrows that drink and bathe in the pool in front of the cave — when it's melted. Sometimes it kills them, but sometimes they fly away. Clearly, I've missed some important reaction. I suppose Rose and that upstart are making the most of my absence — but I can afford to let them. There can be no doubt of my success in the end.

"Feb. 11 — Have got it at last! Put a fresh lot in the little pool — which is well melted today — and the first bird that drank toppled over as if he were shot. I picked him up a second later, and he was a perfect piece of stone, down to the smallest claws and feather. Not a muscle changed since he was poised for drinking, so he must have died the instant any of the stuff got to his stomach. I didn't expect the petrification to come so soon. But a sparrow is a fair test of the way the thing would act with a large animal. I must get something bigger to try it on, for it must be the right strength when I give it to those swine. I guess Rose's dog Rex will do. I'll take him along the next time and say a timber wolf got him. She thinks a lot of him, and I shan't be sorry to give her something to sniffle over before the big reckoning. I must be careful where I keep this book. Rose sometimes pries around in the queerest places."

"Feb. 15 — Getting warm! Tried it on Rex and it worked like a charm with only double the strength. I fixed the rock pool and got him to drink. He seemed to know something queer had hit him, for he bristled and growled, but he was a piece of stone before he could turn his head. The solution ought to have been stronger, and for a human being ought to be very much stronger. I think I'm getting the hang of it now, and am about ready for that cur Wheeler. The stuff seems to be tasteless, but to make sure I'll flavor it with the new wine I'm making up at the house. Wish I were surer about the tastelessness, so I could give it to Rose in water without trying to urge wine on her. I'll get the two separately — Wheeler out here and Rose at home. Have just fixed a strong solution and cleared away all strange objects in front of the cave. Rose whimpered like a puppy when I told her a wolf had got Rex, and Wheeler gurgled a lot of sympathy."

"March 1 — Iä R'lyeh! Praise the Lord Tsathoggua! I've got that son of hell at last! Told him I'd found a new ledge of friable limestone down this way, and he trotted after me like the yellow cur he is! I had the wine-flavored stuff in a bottle on my hip, and he was glad of a swig when we got here. Gulped it down without a wink — and dropped in his tracks before you could count three. But he knows I've had my vengeance, for I made a face at him that he couldn't miss. I saw the look of understanding come into his face as he keeled over. In two minutes he was solid stone."

"I dragged him into the cave and put Rex's figure outside again. That bristling dog shape will help to scare people off. It's getting time for the spring hunters, and besides, there a damned 'lunger' named Jackson in a cabin over the hill who does a lot of snooping around in the snow. I wouldn't want my laboratory and storeroom to be found just yet! When I got home I told Rose that Wheeler had found a telegram at the village summoning him suddenly home. I don't know whether she believed me or not but it doesn't matter. For form's sake, I packed Wheeler's things and took them down the hill, telling her I was going to ship them after him. I put them in the dry well at the abandoned Rapelye place. Now for Rose!"

"March 3 — Can't get Rose to drink any wine. I hope that stuff is tasteless enough to go unnoticed in water. I tried it in tea and coffee, but it forms a precipitate and can't be used that way. If I use it in water I'll have to cut down the dose and trust to a more gradual action. Mr. and Mrs. Hoog dropped in this noon, and I had hard work keeping the conversation away from Wheeler's departure. It mustn't get around that we say he was called back to New York when everybody at the village knows no telegram came, and that he didn't leave on the bus. Rose is acting damned queer about the whole thing. I'll have to pick a quarrel with her and keep her locked in the attic. The best way is to try to make her drink that doctored wine — and if she does give in, so much the better."

"March 7 — Have started in on Rose. She wouldn't drink the wine so I took a whip to her and drove her up in the attic. She'll never come down alive. I pass her a platter of salty bread and salt meat, and a pail of slightly doctored water, twice a day. The salt food ought to make her drink a lot, and it can't be long before the action sets in. I don't like the way she shouts about Wheeler when I'm at the door. The rest of the time she is absolutely silent."

"March 9 — It's damned peculiar how slow that stuff is in getting hold of Rose. I'll have to make it stronger — probably she'll never taste it with all the salt I've been feeding her. Well, if it doesn't get her there are plenty of other ways to fall back on. But I would like to carry this neat statue plan through! Went to the cave this morning and all is well there. I sometimes hear Rose's steps on the ceiling overhead, and I think they're getting more and more dragging. The stuff is certainly working, but it's too slow. Not strong enough. From now on I'll rapidly stiffen up the dose."

"March 11 — It is very queer. She is still alive and moving. Tuesday night I heard her piggling with a window, so went up and gave her a rawhiding. She acts more sullen than frightened, and her eyes look swollen. But she could never drop to the ground from that height and there's nowhere she could climb down. I have had dreams at night, for her slow, dragging pacing on the floor above gets on my nerves. Sometimes I think she works at the lock of the door."

"March 1 — Still alive, despite all the strengthening of the dose. There's something queer about it. She crawls now, and doesn't pace very often. But the sound of her crawling is horrible. She rattles the windows, too, and fumbles with the door. I shall have to finish her off with the rawhide if this keeps up. I'm getting very sleepy. Wonder if Rose has got on her guard somehow. But she must be drinking the stuff. This sleepiness is abnormal — I think the strain is telling on me. I'm sleepy . . ."

(Here the cramped handwriting trails out in a vague scrawl, giving place to a note in a firmer, evidently feminine handwriting, indicative of great emotional tension.)

"March 16 — 4 A. M. — This is added by Rose C. Morris, about to die. Please notify my father, Osborne E. Chandler, Route 2, Mountain Top, N. Y. I have just read what the beast has written. I felt sure he had killed Arthur Wheeler, but did not know how till I read this terrible notebook. Now I know what I escaped. I noticed the water tasted queer, so took none after the first sip. I threw it all out of the window. That one sip has half paralyzed me, but I can still get about. The thirst was terrible, but I ate as little as possible of the salty food and was able to get a little water by setting some old pans and dishes that were up here under places where the roof leaked."

"There were two great rains. I thought he was trying to poison me, though I didn't know what the poison was like. What he has written about himself and me is a lie. We were never happy together and I think I married him only under one of those spells that he was able to lay on people. I guess he hypnotized both my father and me, for he was always hated and feared and suspected of dark dealings with the devil. My father once called him The Devil's Kin, and he was right."

"No one will ever know what I went through as his wife. It was not simply common cruelty — though God knows he was cruel enough, and beat me often with a leather whip. It was more — more than anyone in this age can ever understand. He was a monstrous creature, and practised all sorts of hellish ceremonies handed down by his mother's people. He tried to make me help in the rites — and I don't dare even hint what they were. I would not, so he beat me. It would be blasphemy to tell what he tried to make me do. I can say he was a murderer even then, for I know what he sacrificed one night on Thunder Hill. He was surely the Devil's Kin. I tried four times to run away, but he always caught and beat me. Also, he had a sort of hold over my mind, and even over my father's mind."

"About Arthur Wheeler I have nothing to be ashamed of. We did come to love each other, but only in an honorable way. He gave me the first kind treatment I had ever had since leaving my father's, and meant to help me get out of the clutches of that fiend. He had several talks with my father, and was going to help me get out west. After my divorce we would have been married."

"Ever since that brute locked me in the attic I have planned to get out and finish him. I always kept the poison overnight in case I could escape and find him asleep and give it to him somehow. At first he waked easily when I worked on the lock of the door and tested the conditions at the windows, but later he began to get more tired and sleep-sounder. I could always tell by his snoring when he was asleep."

"Tonight he was so fast asleep that I forced the lock without waking him. It saw hard work getting downstairs with my partial paralysis, but I did. I found him here with the lamp burning — asleep at the table, where he had been writing in this book. In the corner was the long rawhide whip he had so often beaten me with. I used it to tie him to the chair so he could not move a muscle. I lashed his neck so that I could pour anything down his throat without his resisting."

"He waked up just as I was finishing and I guess he saw right off that he was done for. He shouted frightful things and tried to chant mystical formulas, but I choked him off with a dish towel from the sink. Then I saw this book he had been writing in, and stopped to read it. The shock was terrible, and I almost fainted four or five times. My mind was not ready for such things. After that I talked to that fiend for two or three hours steady. I told him everything I had wanted to tell him through all the years I had been his slave, and a lot of other things that had to do with what I had read in this awful book."

"He looked almost purple when I was through, and I think he was half delirious. Then I got a funnel from the cupboard and jammed it into his mouth after taking out the gag. He knew what I was going to do, but was helpless. I had brought down the pail of poisoned water, and without a qualm, I poured a good half of it into the funnel."

"It must have been a very strong dose, for almost at once I saw that brute begin to stiffen and turn a dull stony grey. In ten minutes I knew he was solid stone. I could not bear to touch him, but the tin funnel *clinked* horribly when I pulled it out of his mouth. I wish I could have given that Kin of the Devil a more painful, lingering death, but surely this was the most appropriate he could have had."

"There is not much more to say. I am half-paralyzed, and with Arthur murdered I have nothing to live for. I shall make things complete by drinking the rest of the poison after placing this book where it will be found. In a quarter of an hour I shall be a stone statue. My only wish is to be buried beside the statue that was Arthur — when it is found in that cave where the fiend left it. Poor trusting Rex ought to lie at our feet. I do not care what becomes of that stone devil tied in the chair. . . ."

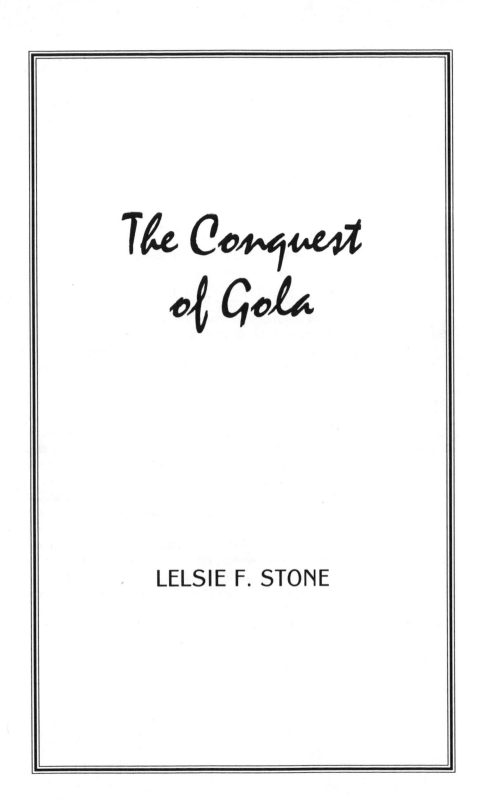

The Conquest of Gola

LELSIE F. STONE

ABOUT LESLIE F. STONE
AND
THE CONQUEST OF GOLA

The Conquest of Gola *was first published:*
Wonder, *April 1931*

Leslie F. Stone was not the first woman author her family produced; she derived her inspiration at her mother's knee. Her mother, Lillian Spellman (Stone), was a celebrated turn of the century author and poet. Not surprisingly with this background, Leslie F. Stone became the leading female light of Hugo Gernsback's inner circle. Her first story "Men With Wings" was quickly followed by a story whose title might have symbolized all that was to be written by women science fiction writers in the future, "Women With Wings."

Unfortunately with the death of the Gernsback magazines and the sudden transmutation of science fiction to a subcategory of men's and boy's adventure pulps, the market for Leslie Stone's work dried up quickly. Although she appeared frequently in the pages of Gernsback's publications fifteen times between 1929 and 1935, she appeared only four times in the genre over the next ten years. It is impossible to over estimate the significance of her loss to the field. But we believe the "Conquest of Gola" (reprinted here for the first time in more than fifty years) will go a long way toward showing the incalculable legacy and contribution to the field she might have made had she been encouraged to keep writing over the next several decades in the way that such male contemporaries as Jack Williamson, Clifford D. Simak and Murray Leinster were. The fact that Ms. Stone's story prefigures by almost four decades, and with equal depth and grace, Joanna Russ' "When It Changed," is we believe sufficient testimony to the field's loss.

The Conquest Of Gola

by LESLIE F. STONE

HOLA, my daughters (sighed the Matriarch), it is true indeed, I am the only living one upon Gola who remembers the invasion from Detaxal. I alone of all my generation survive to recall vividly the sights and scenes of that past era. And well it is that you come to me to hear by free communication of mind to mind, face to face with each other.

Ah, well I remember the surprise of that hour when through the mists that enshroud our lovely world, there swam the first of the great smooth cylinders of the Detaxalans, fifty *tas** in length, as glistening and silvery as the soil of our land, propelled by the man-things that on Detaxal are supreme even as we women are supreme on Gola.

In those bygone days, as now, Gola was enwrapped by her cloud mists that keep from us the terrific glare of the great star that glows like a malignant spirit out there in the darkness of the void. Only occasionally when a particularly great storm parts the mist of heaven do we see the wonders of the vast universe, but that does not prevent us, with our marvelous telescopes handed down to us from thousands of generations before us, from learning what lies across the dark seas of the outside.

Therefore we knew of the nine planets that encircle the great star and are subject to its rule. And so are we familiar enough with the surfaces of these planets to know why Gola should appear as a haven to their inhabitants who see in our cloud-enclosed mantle a sweet release from the blasting heat and blinding glare of the great sun.

So it was not strange at all to us to find that the people of Detaxal, the third planet of the sun, had arrived on our globe with a wish in their hearts to migrate here, and end their days out of reach of the blistering warmth that had come to be their lot on their own world.

Long ago we, too, might have gone on exploring expeditions to other worlds, other universes, but for wlnat? Are we not happy here? We who have attained the greatest of civilizations within the confines of our own silvery world. Powerfully strong with our mighty force rays, we could subjugate all the universe, but why?

Are we not content with life as it is, with our lovely cities, our homes, our daughters, our gentle consorts? Why spend physical energy in combative strife for something we do not wish, when our mental processes carry us further and beyond the conquest of mere terrestrial exploitation?

On Detaxal it is different, for there the peoples, the ignoble male creatures, breed for physical prowess, leaving the development of their sciences, their philosophies, and the contemplation of the abstract to a chosen few. The greater part of the race faces forth to conquer, to lay waste, to struggle and fight as the animals do over a morsel of worthless territory. Of course we can see why they desired Gola with all its treasures, but we can thank Providence and ourselves that they did not succeed in "commercializing" us as they have the remainder of the universe with their ignoble Federation.

Ah yes, well I recall the hour when first they came, pushing cautiously through the cloud mists, seeking that which lay beneath. We of Gola were unwarned until the two cylinders hung directly above Tola, the greatest city of that time, which still lies in its ruins since that memorable day. But they have paid for it — paid for it well in thousands and tens of thousands of their men.

We were first apprised of their coming when the alarm from Tola was sent from the great beam station there, advising all to stand in readiness for an emergency. Geble, my mother, was then Queen of all Gola, and I was by her side in Morka, that pleasant seaside resort, where I shall soon travel to partake of its rejuvenating waters.

With us were four of Geble's consorts, sweet gentle males, that gave Geble much pleasure in those free hours away from the worries of state. But when the word of the strangers' descent over our home city, Tola, came to us, all else was forgotten. With me at her side, Geble hastened to the beam station and there in the matter transmitter we dispatched our physical beings to the palace at Tola, and the next moment were staring upward at the two strange shapes etched against the clouds.

What the Detaxalan ships were waiting for we did not know then, but later we learned. Not grasping the meaning of our beam stations, the commanders of the ships considered the city below them entirely lacking in means of defense, and were conferring on the method of taking it without bloodshed on either side.

It was not long after our arrival in Tola that the first of the ships began to descend toward the great square before the palace. Geble watched without a word, her great mind already scanning the brains of those whom she found within the great machine. She transferred to my mind but a single thought as I stood there at her side and that with a sneer "Barbarians!"

Now the ship was settling in the square and after a few moments of hesitation, a circular doorway appeared at the side and four of the Detaxalans came through the opening. The square was empty but for themselves and their flyer, and we saw them looking about surveying the beautiful buildings on all sides. They seemed to recognize the palace for what it was and in one accord moved in our direction.

Then Geble left the window at which we stood and strode to the doorway opening upon the balcony that faced the square. The Detaxalans halted in their tracks when they saw her slender graceful form appear and removing the strange coverings they wore on their heads they each made a bow.

Again Geble sneered, for only the male-things of our world bow their heads, and so she recognized these visitors for what they were, nothing more than the despicable males of the species! And what creatures they were!

Imagine a short almost flat body set high upon two slender legs, the body tapering in the middle, several times as broad across as it is through the center, with two arms almost as long as the legs attached to the upper part of the torso. A small column-like neck of only a few inches divides the head of oval shape from the body, and in this head only are set the organs of sight, hearing, and scent. Their bodies were like a patchwork of a misguided nature.

Yes, strange as it is, my daughters, practically all of the creature's faculties had their base in the small ungainly head, and each organ was perforce pressed into serving for several functions. For instance, the breathing nostrils also served for scenting out odors, nor was this organ able to exclude any disagreeable odors that might come its way, but had to dispense to the brain both pleasant and unpleasant odors at the same time.

Then there was the mouth, set directly beneath the nose, and here again we had an example of one organ doing the work of two, for the creature not only used the mouth with which to take in the food for its body, but it also used the mouth to enunciate the excruciatingly ugly sounds of its language forthwith.

Never before have I seen such a poorly organized body, so unlike our own highly developed organisms. How much nicer it is to be able to call forth any organ at will, and dispense with it when its usefulness is over! Instead these poor Detaxalans had to carry theirs about in physical being all the time so that always was the surface of their bodies entirely marred.

Yet that was not the only part of their ugliness, and proof of the lowliness of their origin, for whereas our fine bodies support themselves by muscular development, these poor creatures were dependent entirely upon a strange structure to keep them in their proper shape.

Imagine if you can a bony skeleton somewhat like the foundations upon which we build our edifices, laying stone and cement over the steel framework. But this skeleton instead is inside a body which the flesh, muscle and skin overlay. Everywhere in their bodies are these cartilaginous structures — hard, heavy, bony structures developed by the chemicals of the being for its use. Even the hands, feet and head of the creatures were underlaid with these bones — ugh, it was terrible when we dissected one of the fellows for study. I shudder to think of it.

Yet again there was still another feature of the Detaxalans that was equally as horrifying as the rest, namely their outer covering. As we viewed them for the first time out there in the square we discovered that parts of the body, that is the part of the head which they called the face, and the bony hands were entirely naked without any sort of covering, neither fur nor feathers, just the raw, pinkish-brown skin looking as if it had been recently plucked.

Later we found a few specimens that had a type of fur on the lower part of the face, but these were rare. And when they doffed the head coverings which we had first taken for some sort of natural covering, we saw that the top of the head was overlaid with a very fine fuzz of fur several inches long.

We did not know in the beginning that the strange covering on the bodies of the four men, green in color, was not a natural growth, but later discovered that such was the truth, and not only the face and hands were bare of fur, but the entire body, except for a fine sprinkling of hair that was scarcely visible except on the chest, was also bare. No wonder the poor things covered themselves with their awkward clothing. We arrived at the conclusion that their lack of fur had been brought about by the fact that always they had been exposed to the bright rays of the sun so that without the dampness of our own planet the fur had dried up and fallen away from the flesh!

Now thinking it over I suppose that we of Gola presented strange forms to the people of Detaxal with our fine circular bodies, rounded at the top, our short beautiful lower limbs with the circular foot pads, and our short round arms and hand pads, flexible and muscular like rubber.

But how envious they must have been of our beautiful golden coats, our movable eyes, our power to scent, hear and touch with any part of the body, to absorb food and drink through any part of the body most convenient to us at any time. Oh yes, laugh though you may, without a doubt we were also freaks to those freakish Detaxalans. But no matter, let us return to the tale.

On recognizing our visitors for what they were, simple-minded males, Geble was chagrined at them for taking up her time, but they were strangers to our world and we Golans are always courteous. Geble began of course to try to communicate by thought transference, but strangely enough the fellows below did not catch a single thought. Instead, entirely unaware of Geble's overture to friendship, the leader commenced to speak to her in most outlandish manner, contorting the red lips of his mouth into various uncouth shapes and making sounds that fell upon our hearing so unpleasantly that we immediately closed our senses to them. And without a word Geble turned her back upon them, calling for Tanka, her personal secretary.

Tanka was instructed to welcome the Detaxalans while she herself turned to her own chambers to summon a half dozen of her council. When the council arrived she began to discuss with them the problem of extracting more of the precious tenix from the waters of the great inland lake of Notauch. Nothing whatever was said of the advent of the Detaxalans, for Geble had dismissed them from her mind as creatures not worthy of her thought.

In the meantime Tanka had gone forth to meet the four who of course could not converse with her. In accordance with the Queen's orders she led them indoors to the most informal receiving chamber and there had them served with food and drink which by the looks of the remains in the dishes they did not relish at all.

Leading them through the rooms of the lower floor of the palace she made a pretence of showing them everything which they duly surveyed. But they appeared to chafe at the manner in which they were being entertained.

The creatures even made an attempt through the primitive method of conversing by their arms to learn something of what they had seen, but I Tanka was as supercilious as her mistress. When she thought they had had enough, she led them to the square and back to the door of their flyer, giving them their dismissal.

But the men were not ready to accept it. Instead they tried to express to Tanka their desire to meet the ruling head of Gola. Although their hand motions were perfectly inane and incomprehensible, Tanka could read what passes through their brains, and understood more fully than they what lay in their minds. She shook her head and motioned that they were to embark in their flyer and be on their way back to their planet.

Again and again Detaxalans tried to explain what they wished, thinking Tanka did not understand. At last she impressed upon their savage minds that there was nothing for them but to depart, and disgruntled by her treatment they reentered their machine, closed its ponderous door and raised their ship to the leave of its sister flyer. Several minutes passed and then, with thanksgiving, we saw them pass over the city.

Told of this, Geble laughed. "To think of mere man-things daring to attempt to force themselves upon us. What is the universe coming to? What were their women back home considering when they sent them to us? Have they developed too many males and think that we can find use for them?" she wanted to know.

"It is strange indeed," observed Yabo, one of the council members. "What did you find in the minds of these ignoble creatures, O August One?"

"'Nothing of particular interest, a very low grade of intelligence, to be sure. There was no need of looking below the surface."

"It must have taken intelligence to build those ships."

"None aboard them did that. I don't question it but that their mothers built the ships for them as playthings, even as we give toys to our 'little ones,' you know. I recall that the ancients of our world perfected several types of space-flyers many ages ago!"

"Maybe those males do not have 'mothers' but instead they build the ships themselves. Maybe they are the stronger sex on their world!" This last was said by Suiki, the fifth consort of Geble, a pretty little male, rather young in years. No one had noticed his coming into the chamber, but now everyone showed surprise at his words.

"Impossible!" ejaculated Yabo.

Geble, however, laughed at the little chap's expression. "Suiki is a profound thinker," she observed, still laughing, and she drew him to her gently hugging him.

And with that the subject of the men from Detaxal was closed. It was reopened, however, several hours later when it was learned that instead of leaving Gola altogether the ships were seen one after another by the various cities of the planet as they circumnavigated it.

It was rather annoying, for everywhere the cities' routines were broken up as the people dropped their work and studies to gaze at the cylinders. Too, it was upsetting the morale of the males, for on learning that the two ships contained only creatures of their own sex they were becoming envious wishing for the same type of playthings for themselves.

Shut in, as they are, unable to grasp the profundities of our science and thought, the gentle, fun-loving males were always glad for a new diversion and this new method developed by the Detaxalans had intrigued them.

It was then that Geble decided it was high time to take matters into her own hands. Not knowing where the two ships were at the moment it was not difficult with the object-finder beam to discover their whereabouts, and then with the attractor to draw them to Tola magnetically. An *ous* later we had the pleasure of seeing the two ships rushing toward our city. When they arrived above it, power brought them down to the square again.

Again Tanka was sent out, and directed the commanders of the two ships to follow her in to the Queen. Knowing the futility of attempting to converse with them without mechanical aid, Geble caused to be brought her three of the ancient mechanical thought transformers that are only museum pieces to us but still workable. The two men were directed to place them on their heads while she donned the third. When this was done she ordered the creatures to depart immediately from Gola, telling them that she was tired of their play.

Watching the faces of the two I saw them frowning and shaking their heads. Of course I could read their thoughts as well as Geble without need of the transformers, since it was only for their benefit that these were used, so I heard the whole conversation, though I need only to give you the gist of it.

"We have no wish to leave your world as yet," the two had argued.

"You are disrupting the routine of our lives here," Geble told them, "and now that you've seen all that you can there is no need for you to stay longer. I insist that you leave immediately."

I saw one of the men smile, and thereupon he was the one who did all the talking (I say "talking," for this he was actually doing, mouthing each one of his words although we understood his thoughts as they formed in his queer brain, so different from ours).

"Listen here," he laughed, "I don't get the hang of you people at all. We came to Gola (he used some outlandish name of his own, but I use our name of course) with the express purpose of exploration and exploitation. We come as friends. Already we are in alliance with Damin (again the name for the fourth planet of our system was different, but I give the correct appellation), established commerce and trade, and now we are ready to offer you the chance to join our federation peaceably."

"What we have seen of this world is very favorable; there are good prospects for business here. There is no reason why you people as those of Damin and Detaxal can not enter into a nice business arrangement congenially. You have far more here to offer tourists, more than Damin. Why, except for your clouds this would be an ideal paradise for every man, woman and child on Detaxal and Damin to visit, and of course with our new cloud dispensers we could clear your atmosphere for you in short order and keep it that way. Why, you'll make millions in the first year of your trade.

"'Come now, allow us to discuss this with your ruler — king or whatever you call him. Women are all right in their place, but it takes the men to see the profit of a thing like this — you are a woman, aren't you?"

The first of his long speech, of course, was so much gibberish to us, with his prate of business arrangements, commerce and trade, tourists, profits, cloud dispensers and what not, but it was the last part of what he said that took my breath away, and you can imagine how it affected Geble. I could see straightway that she was intensely angered, and good reason too. By the looks of the silly fellow's face I could guess that he was getting the full purport of her thoughts. He began to shuffle his funny feet and a foolish grin pervaded his face.

"Sorry," he said, "if I insulted you — I didn't intend that, but I believed that man holds the same place here as he doe's on Detaxal and Damin, but I suppose it is just as possible for woman to be the ruling factor of a world as man is elsewhere."

That speech naturally made Geble more irate, and tearing off her thought transformer she left the room without another word. In a moment, however, Yabo appeared wearing the transformer in her place. Yabo had none of the beauty of my mother, for whereas Geble was slender and as straight as a rod, Yabo was obese, and her fat body overflowed until she looked like a large dumpy bundle of *yat* held together in her furry skin. She had very little dignity as she waddled toward the Detaxalans, but there was determination in her whole manner, and without preliminaries she began to scold the two as though they were her own consorts.

"There has been enough of this, my fine young men," she shot at them. "You've had your fun, and now it is time for you to return to your mothers and consorts. Shame on you for making up such miserable tales about yourselves. I have a good mind to take you home with me for a couple of days, and I'd put you in your places quick enough. The idea of men acting like you are!"

For a moment I thought the Detaxalans were going to cry by the faces they made, but instead they broke into laughter, such heathenish sounds as had never before been heard on Gola, and I listened in wonder instead of excluding it from my hearing, but the fellows sobered quickly enough at that, and the spokesman addressed the shocked Yabo.

"I see," said he, "it's impossible for your people and mine to arrive at an understanding peaceably. I'm sorry that you take us for children out on a spree, that you are accustomed to such a low type of men as is evidently your lot here."

"I have given you your chance to accept our terms without force, but since you refuse, under the orders of the Federation I will have to take you forcibly, for we are determined that Gola become one of us, if you like it or not. Then you will learn that we are not the children you believe us to be.

"You may go to your supercilious Queen now and advise her that we give you exactly ten hours in which to evacuate this city, for precisely on the hour we will lay this city in ruins. And if that does not suffice you, we will do the same with every other city on the planet! Remember, ten hours!"

And with that he took the mechanical thought transformer from his head and tossed it on the table. His companion did the same and the two of them strode out of the room and to their flyers which arose several thousand feet above Tola and remained there.

Hurrying in to Geble, Yabo told her what the Detaxalan had said. Geble was reclining on her couch and did not bother to raise herself.

"Childish prattle," she conceded and withdrew her red eyes on their movable stems into their pockets, paying no more heed to the threats of the men from Detaxal.

I, however, could not be as calm as my mother, and I was fearful that it was not childish prattle after all. Not knowing how long ten hours might be I did not wait, but crept up to the palace's beam station and set its dials so that the entire building and as much of the surrounding territory as it could cover were protected in the force zone.

Alas, that the same beam was not greater. But it had not been put there for defense, only for matter transference and whatever other peacetime methods we used. It was the means of proving just the same that it was also a very good defensive instrument, for just two *ous* later the hovering ships above let loose their powers of destruction, heavy explosives that entirely demolished all of Tola and its millions of people and only the palace royal of all that beauty was left standing!

Awakened from her nap by the terrific detonation, Geble came hurriedly to a window to view the ruin, and she was wild with grief at what she saw. Geble, however, saw that there was urgent need for action. She knew without my telling her what I had done to protect the palace. And though she showed no sign of appreciation, I knew that I had won a greater place in her regard than any other of her many daughters and would henceforth be her favorite as well as her successor, as the case tuned out.

Now, with me behind her, she hurried to the beam station and in a twinkling we were both in Tubia, the second greatest city of that time. Nor were we to be caught napping again, for Geble ordered all beam stations to throw out their zone forces while she herself manipulated one of Tubia's greatest power beams, attuning it to the emanations of the two Detaxalan flyers. In less than an *ous* the two ships were seen through the mists heading for Tubia. For a moment I grew fearful, but on realizing that they were after all in our grip, and the attractors held every living thing powerless against movement, I grew calm and watched them come over the city and the beam pull them to the ground.

With the beam still upon them, they lay supine on the ground without motion. Descending to the square Geble called for Ray C, and when the machine arrive she herself directed the cutting of the hole in the side of the flyer and was the first to enter it with me immediately behind, as usual.

We were both astounding by what we saw of the great array of machinery within. But a glance told Geble all she wanted to know of their principles. She interested herself only in the men standing rigidly in whatever position our beam had caught them. Only the eyes of the creatures expressed their fright, poor things, unable to move so much as a hair while we moved among them untouched by the power of the beam because of the strength of our own minds.

They could have fought against it if they had known how, but their simple minds were too week for such exercise.

Now glancing about among the stiff forms around us, of which there were one thousand, Geble picked out those of the males she desired for observation, choosing those she judged to be their finest specimens, those with much hair on their faces and having more girth than the others. These she ordered removed by several workers who followed us, and then we emerged again to the outdoors.

Using hand beam torches the picked specimens were kept immobile after they were out of reach of the greater beam and were borne into the laboratory of the building Geble had converted into her new palace. Geble and I followed, and she gave the order for the complete annihilation of the two powerless ships.

Thus ended the first foray of the people of Detaxal. And for the next two *tels* there was peace upon our globe again. In the laboratory the thirty who had been rescued from their ships were given thorough examinations both physically and mentally and we learned all there was to know about them. Hearing of the destruction of their ships, most of the creatures had become frightened and were quite docile in our hands. Those that were unruly were used in the dissecting room for the advancement of Golan knowledge.

After a complete study of them, which yielded little, we lost interest in them scientifically. Geble, however, found some pleasure in having the poor creatures around her and kept three of them in her own chambers so she could delve into their brains as she pleased. The others she doled out to her favorites as she saw fit.

One she gave to me to act as a slave or in what capacity I desired him, but my interest in him soon waned, especially since I had now come of age and was allowed to have two consorts of my own, and go about the business of bringing my daughters into the world.

My slave I called Jon and gave him complete freedom of my house. If only we had foreseen what was coming we would have annihilated every one of them immediately! It did please me later to find that Jon was learning our language and finding a place in my household, making friends with my two shut-in consorts. But as I have said I paid little attention to him.

So life went on smoothly with scarcely a change after the destruction of the ships of Detaxal. But that did not mean we were unprepared for more. Geble reasoned that there would be more ships forthcoming when the Detaxalans found that their first two did not return. So, although it was sometimes inconvenient, the zones of force were kept upon our cities.

And Geble was right, for the day came when dozens of flyers descended upon Gola from Detaxal. But this time the zones of force did not hold them since the zones were not in operation!

And we were unwarned, for when they descended upon us, our world was sleeping, confident that our zones were our protection. The first indication that I had of trouble brewing was when, awakening, I found the ugly form of Jon bending over me. Surprised, for it was not his habit to arouse me, I started up only to find his arms about me, embracing me. And how strong he was! For the moment a new emotion swept me, for the first time I knew the pleasure to be had in the arms of a strong man, but that emotion was short lived, for I saw in the blue eyes of my slave that he had recognized the look in my eyes for what it was, and for the moment he was tender.

Later I was to grow angry when I thought of that expression of his, for his eyes filled with pity, pity for me! But pity did not stay, instead he grinned and the next instant he was binding me down to my couch with strong rope. Geble, I learned later, had been treated as I, as were the members of the council and every other woman in Gola!

That was what came of allowing our men to meet on common ground with the creatures from Detaxal, for a weak mind is open to seeds of rebellion and the Detaxalans had sown it well, promising dominance to the lesser creatures of Gola.

That, however, was only part of the plot on the part of the Detaxalans. They were determined not only to revenge those we had murdered, but also to gain mastery of our planet. Unnoticed by us they had constructed a machine which transmits sound as we transmit thought and by its means had communicated with their own world, advising them of the very hour to strike when all of Gola was slumbering. It was a masterful stroke, only they did not know the power of the mind of Gola — so much more ancient then theirs.

Lying there bound on my couch I was able to see out the window and, trembling with terror, I watched a half dozen Detaxalan flyers descend into Tubia, guessing that the same was happening in our other cities. I was truly frightened, for I did not have the brain of a Geble. I was young yet, and in fear I watched the hordes march out of their machines, saw the thousands of our men join them.

Free from restraint, the shut-ins were having their holiday and how they cavorted out in the open, most of the time getting in the way of the freakish Detaxalans who were certainly takin over our city.

A half *ous* passed while I lay there watching, waiting in fear at what life we had led up to the present and trembled over what the future might be when the Detaxalans had infested us with commerce and trade, business propositions, tourists and all of their evil practices. It was then that I received the message from Geble, clear and definite, just as all the women of the globe received it, and hope returned to my heart.

There began that titanic struggle, the fight that won us victory over the simple-minded weaklings below who had presumptuously dared to conquer us. The first indication that the power of our combined mental concentration at Geble's orders was taking effect. They tried to shake us off, but we knew we could bring them back to us.

At first the Detaxalans paid them no heed. They knew not what was happening until there came the wholesale retreat of the Golan men back to the buildings, back to the chambers from which they had escaped. Then grasping something of what was happening the already defeated invaders sought to retain their hold on our little people. Our erstwhile captives sought to hold them with oratorical gestures, but of course we won. We saw our creatures return to us and unbind us.

Only the Detaxalans did not guess the significance of that, did not realize that inasmuch as we had conquered our own men, we could conquer them also. As they went about their work of making our city their own, establishing already their autocratic bureaus wherever they pleased, we began to concentrate upon them, hypnotizing them to the flyers that had disgorged them.

And soon they began to feel of our power, the weakest ones first, feeling the mental bewilderment creeping upon them. Their leaders, stronger in mind, knew nothing of this at first, but soon our terrible combined mental power was forced upon them also and they realized that their men were deserting them, crawling back to their ships! The leaders began to exhort them into new action, driving them physically. But our power gained on them and now we began to concentrate upon the leaders themselves. They were strong of will and they defied us, fought us, mind against mind, but of course it was useless. Their minds were not suited to the test they put themselves to, and after almost three ous of struggle, we of Gola were able to see victory ahead.

At last the leaders succumbed. Not a single Detaxalan was abroad in the avenues. They were within their flyers, held there by our combined wills, unable to act for themselves. It was then as easy for us to switch the zones of force upon them, subjugate them more securely and with the annihilator beam to disintegrate completely every ship and man into nothingness! Thousands upon thousands died that day and Gola was indeed revenged.

Thus, my daughters, ended the second invasion of Gola.

Oh yes, more came from their planet to discover what had happened to their ships and their men, but we of Gola no longer hesitated, and they no sooner appeared beneath the mists than they too were annihilated until at last Detaxal gave up the thought of conquering our cloud-laden world. Perhaps in the future they will attempt it again, but we are always in readiness for them now, and our men — well, they are still the same ineffectual weaklings, my daughters . . .

Honeycombed Satellite

HELEN WEINBAUM

ABOUT HELEN WEINBAUM
AND
HONEYCOMBED SATELLITE

Honeycombed Satellite *was first published:*
Thrilling Wonder, *June 1940*

After the death of her brother, Stanley Weinbaum, in 1935, his sister Helen finished one of his uncompleted works, "Tidal Moon," and then apparently bit by the writing bug went on to produce half a dozen stories under her own name. Unfortunately, like all the women writers of the early 1940s who choose to write under clearly feminine surnames, Ms. Weinbaum's work was relegated to the smaller fringe pulps that typically paid a quarter and half a cent a word "on lawsuit." Her first solo story appeared in July 1940 and the last only 18 months later in September of 1941.

In the interim however she managed to produce "Honeycombed Satellite." In this delicious outer space romp, Christine Murray, of husband and wife planeteer team, Christine and Philip Murray, outwits a villain and solves a scientific mystery (all this, plus their little dog Toto!). From the internal evidence it is clear that Ms. Weinbaum's loss to the field was equal to that of her brother.

Honeycombed Satellite

by HELEN WEINBAUM

PHILIP MURRAY nosed his space toward the north pole of Themis, last discovered of Saturn's moons. Below toward the lofty, steepled structures of the termite like inhabitants of the tiny satellite, the Cacochauns, who seemed neither to know nor care that Earth-exiled criminals searched their hive for blue amber.

Only on Themis was blue amber found — and there only in the Cacochaun hive — for the inner element was so perishable that it oxidized in air, leaving a dull, blue powder. In the honeycomb, however, live particles had been covered by exudations from the Cacochaun's pores. Thus preserved by the fossil resin, it had lain for centuries undisturbed, until a space traveler taking a few pieces to Earth had discovered that by using it as the plate in a vacuum tube, short waves far below the normal range might be received.

Now, by means of vacuum tubes containing the blue amber, Earth was able to keep in constant, secret communication with her possessions — Saturn and all her moons, Uranus and Venus. Enemy powers, through lack of the element, were unable to catch waves far below the sensitivity of their receivers.

A little thing! Yet on it now rested the fate of the tiny planet, Venus. For Mars, the little Napoleon of the Universe, had ambitions, and it was well known that her eye rested longingly on Venus — Venus with her vast platinum mines and coal fields!

Let Mars come into possession of the element, blue amber, and create a tube delicate enough to catch the short wave messages from the experimental laboratories of Earth directing the placement of Venus's new defenses, and the cause was lost!

Lately, shipments of blue amber had fallen off. The Government of Earth, fearful of leakage to the enemy power, took steps at once to investigate conditions in the penal colony of Themis. The job fell to Philip Murray.

Outside of the Cacochauns, there was no civilization on the satellite. No one knew the engineering secret of the underground combs, stretching endlessly beneath the minarets and spires which towered like a frosted wedding cake from the forty-mile diametered satellite.

The civilization within the honeycomb was a matriarchy, the whole brood offspring of the Queen, a huge, inert egg-laying machine who ruled telepathically from an inner cell. Under the Queen were four castes: the first, fertile males whose sole function was to cohabit with the Queen; the second, a food producing type on whose bodies grew strange fungus sprouts; the third, farmers who gathered the sprouts and brought food from outside as well; and the fourth, workers, the builders of the honeycomb itself.

On all Themis there was but one hive, one Queen, one civilization.

This, then, was the world to which Philip and Christine Murray came — certainly no place to spend a honeymoon. But the Government order to check on the dropping off in shipments of blue amber had come so soon after their marriage, that Christine had insisted on accompanying him.

"I married an adventurer," she said. "High time I found out how one does adventuring."

Now, stepping from the landed ship, Philip looked admiringly at her slim figure in the short, flared leather skirt and tight leggings.

"Brrr." Her teeth chattered, despite valiant efforts to control them.

"Didn't you oil your face?"

She shook her head, made tiny by the close fitting helmet, raising her green eyes sheepishly.

"No. It was such nasty stuff."

"Nasty or not," he said sternly, "it keeps out the cold. Put a thick layer on immediately! It's better than having your nose frozen! I'm afraid, Chris," he continued, "you're going to be a lot of trouble. I should have left you home."

"Don't be mean, Philip. I'm still a bride. Besides, you take Toto everywhere."

"Toto doesn't eat, at any rate. He gets his nourishment from air and rain."

He patted the queer, three-legged pup bounding excitedly at his feet, smiling at the monkey face crowned with huge rabbit ears which perched saucily atop a pyramid-shaped body.

"Totodozeneat," the pup squealed, cocking one ear and rolling large black eyes. "Totodozeneatatanyrate — Totodozen —"

"*Sh!*" Toto shut up; it was the only word he understood. Released from the confines of the space ship, the pup bounded on his three legs, bringing his circulation to where it could withstand the terrific cold of the satellite.

Christine, her face now shining with a thick coat of the cold resistant oil, looked curiously about. This was her first trip through space.

"Look at the horizon!" she exclaimed.

"It's right next to us. It's like standing on the bottom of an upsidedown bowl."

"Of course, silly. The whole circumference is only some hundred and twenty miles."

"Ofcoursillythewholehundred — of coursillythewhole — is — twenty — ofcours—"

"Oh, Toto," she laughed as she picked him up. "You're all bawled up. Now shush!"

Philip set the electro-magnetic time-lock on the space ship for two Themisian days and carefully closed the door.

"Why bother?" the girl asked. "We may be through sooner."

"It's the surest way to keep current flowing through the lock," he answered. "Don't forget, this is a criminal colony, and some of the fellows may be a little tired of Themis. They're all here for life, you know. A nice unlocked space ship might be too much of a temptation."

As they walked toward the barracks, his rugged face sobered at thought of the investigation which lay ahead. The only non-criminal here was Sime Conner, Governor of the satellite. He managed the exiles — not too hard a task, as there was little choice between working in the Cacochaun hive and eking out an existence in the wastes of Themis — but if shipment of blue amber had fallen off, Conner must be responsible.

By the dim light the room at first looked empty. But as Philip's eyes grew more accustomed to the gloom, he saw a loose, slovenly figure slouched over a table at the far end. Surely this could not be the slim, fastidious Governor whom he had met some years ago. But yes, something in the face was familiar.

Leaving Christine just inside the door, he walked toward the man, his voice booming briskly, his lean, wind-toughened features in sharp contrast to the governor's sagging jowls.

"Hello."

"Hellohellohellohel—" Toto squeaked.

Startled, the man raised bleary eyes.

"Who are you?"

"Philip Murray. I was here a few years ago. Remember?"

"No." The man tipped a filthy, half-filled bottle to his lips. "What's that?" pointing to Toto.

"Just a pup from Callisto. He's harmless."

"Ugh." The man grunted, wiping his loose lips with the back of one hand.

Removing his heavy outer garment, Philip sat down, stretching long legs before him. Sime Conner watching his every movement through narrowed, suspicious eyes.

"Well, wadda ya want?" he growled. "Not just stopping here for a visit, are you?"

"No. I've been sent by the Interplanetary Division of the Government of Earth."

"Whafor?" Conner took another drink and looked up blearily. "Wadda they wanna know? I'm doin' my job, sick as I am."

Philip glanced pointedly at the bottle.

"Doctor's perscripshun," Conner said defensively. "I gotta drink the stuff. He said so."

"Who said so?"

"My doctor — Shrimp. One a the criminals here."

"Oh. Well, Conner," Philip leaned forward, "I'm afraid you're *not* doing your job. Shipments of blue amber have fallen off to nothing."

"Thassa lie!" The man rose swaging to his feet. "I'm doin' my job as well as anyone could in this God-forsaken Hell."

"Sit down and talk, Conner!" Philip spoke sternly.

The man obeyed.

"What's the matter with production?" Philip continued more kindly. "That's all I'm here to find out. Surely the combs aren't dry of blue amber —"

"Surelythecombsaren'tdry —" Toto squeaked. "— surelythecombs —"

"Shut that thing up!" Conner screamed. "Nothing's the matter with production!"

Philip rose. They were talking in circles.

"I'll have a look around the combs myself. Maybe I can find out what's wrong."

The burly figure of Conner blocked his way.

"No visitors allowed," he growled. "*I'll* give you a report for your sainted Government."

Philip waited as Conner sank into a chair and rubbed a hand over his forehead.

"Report" — Conner paused — "I wish the Shrimp was here," he said weakly. "I can't remember what he told me about —" He stopped abruptly, looking up slyly to see if his words had caught.

"Who's in command?" Philip asked impatiently. "You or the Shrimp?"

Conner took another drink. "I am. But he's a smart fellow. Helped me a lot. Donno what I'd do without this medicine — distills it for me himself — from the shrubs of —"

"Give me the report," Philip interrupted. "Why aren't you producing blue amber?"

"Sa long story. Can't you wait for the Shrimp? He'll explain how the men won't work and —" His voice trailed off.

Philip rose angrily. "No! I certainly can't wait! Sit here and swill your — medicine!" He stared toward the door.

Conner grasped his arm and swung him around, putting his bleary face close. "Tha's treason!" He straightened swaying. "I'm Governor here. Tha's just tha same as King. Apologize for your tone of voice!"

"My apology is — this!" Philip swung. Conner fell —

"Nice work."

Philip looked up to see Christine beside him. For the moment, he had forgotten her.

"Nice to know you approve." He rose, straightening his clothes and walked with her to the door.

"I know," she said, "don't tell me. I'm a nuisance."

"Right." He tried to pinch her cheek, but his fingers slid off its oily surface. "What am I going to do with you? You certainly can't stay with *him*."

"Where are you going? I'll go with you."

"You won't like it, baby," he warned. "I'm going into the honeycomb."

"It sounds lovely, just like —" She stopped abruptly, pointing ahead.

A giant, featherless bird, its long spiked tail curled forward between its feet, blacked the sky. Quickly Philip pulled her down to the ground. An instant later, the bird whizzed over, its sharp forked tail missing their bodies by inches. For a moment more they lay quietly, then cautiously, Philip raised his head. The bird had turned! Flying low, its forked tail cutting the rubber shrubs like so much paper, it beat toward them again.

Philip fumbled for his gun and, firing almost on the draw, rolled aside, pushing Christine out of range of the crashing body. Toto let out little squeals of fear.

"Don't be a baby, Toto," Christine admonished in a trembling voice. "This is how an adventurer adventures. Look at me. I'm not scared."

"Must have been a Black Drongo," Philip said grimly, "a Themislan species of Drongo-shrike."

His skin tingled with crawling mites, picked up from contact with the ground. Hastily he pulled Christine to him, wiping first her face with his glove and then his own, fearing some among the parasites might be the lichen leech, a fungus growth, part plant, part animal, which attached itself to the second caste of Cacochauns. The cold resistant oil might keep them from taking root. He hoped so anyway. On humans, the lichen leech was fatal.

The only entrance to the Cacochaun hive was at ground level, though windowless towers stretched some five stories upward. Cacochauns, a man-sized species of termite, crawled on six legs with their bodies parallel to the ground. To enter the hive Philip and Christine had to get down on all fours. Once through the entrance, however, it was possible to stand erect. Compared to the outside temperature, the air was hot.

The cell in which they found themselves had a slanting floor triangular in shape. Its walls and ceiling were spotted with the green flares of electric malops which clung by means of suction pads on their stomachs. Their eel-like bodies formed a broken circle, the head a few inches from the tail. Across the gap sparks leaped, filing the interior of the cell with a greenish brilliance.

"Don't touch them," Philip warned, putting Toto under one arm for safety "unless you want to get electrocuted"

"Don't worry," she answered indignantly. "I think they're horrible."

In the next cell they came upon a man lying on his back, leisurely dangling one ankle in the air. The floor was wet with the not yet hardened exudation of the Cacochauns, but he seemed unconscious of the sticky mess in which he lay. At their entrance, he jumped up quickly.

"How did *you* get in?" His voice was angry.

"The usual way," Philip answered. "Any objections?"

The man's manner changed suddenly; his voice was oily smooth.

"Of course not. It's just that we have visitors so seldom." His snappy black eyes dwelt curiously on Christine and Toto. "You took me by surprise. A collector, I suppose?"

"Acollectorlsupp —" Toto began.

"Don't mind him," Christine said. "Sa-ay. You don't look like a crim —"

"I'm not a collector," Philip interrupted loudly. "I'm here on another mission." He glared at Christine from the corner of his eye.

The man smiled at his embarrassment.

"The lady is right," he said suavely. "I am not a criminal. I am a scientist — Dr. Charles Waite. That is, I *was* Dr. Charles Waite. One loses identity here. They call me Shrimp."

"Oh." Philip stared satirically. "You're the one who prescribes for Conner. He seems to depend a lot on you — on liquor too!"

"I do what I can for him," the doctor answered. "That's more than the others do. I'm surprised at myself sometimes. After fifteen years in this Hell, one *should* lose the milk of human kindness."

'Fifteen years," Christine murmured. "That's a long time."

"A long time," the doctor mused. "A long time to pay for an error."

"An error," Philip repeated incredulously. "What error?"

"I killed a woman."

Christine drew back.

"But death through error," Philip objected, "or in the interests of science — I thought men were exiled to Themis only for premeditated murder."

"It was that stupid, dull-witted jury," Dr. Waite answered. "They couldn't see it. I was going a great work of research, of inestimable value to the world." His voice was matter-of-fact. "But I needed money to continue, so I killed my wife — for her insurance. However, it was *all* in the interests of science. I even killed her scientifically — a new virus I had discovered. Quick and painless."

Christine tugged at Philip's sleeve. Obviously, her eyes said, he's a little touched. Let's get away.

Dr. Waite put a hand on Philip's arm, his voice suddenly soft, sane — that of a kindly man trying to help.

"Why are you here?"

"To inspect the honeycombs. I represent the Interplanetary Division of the Government of Earth."

"Hum," the scientist said thoughtfully. "An official visit! Well," he shrugged, "let me take you through. The honeycombs are complicated for a stranger."

Stepping carefully to keep from falling on the slimy floor, they entered the next cell. Six men knelt in a circle, picking earnestly at a cleared space in the center. Beside them lay two blue ambers, their fire-stabbed brilliance startling against the dull floor.

At their entrance the men looked up.

"Who are they, Shrimp?" one yelled. "New exiles?"

"Visitors." The doctor's voice was steely. "Get back to work!"

There was no doubt, Philip reflected, as to who was in command inside the honeycomb.

"I got the impression from Sime Conner," Philip said slowly, "that the men wouldn't work He said you'd explain more fully why Earth is receiving such meager shipments of blue amber."

The scientist shook his head. "It's a hard task he's set me. Under my discipline, the men *do* work. That isn't the cause." He paused, then shrugged. "Well, I suppose I must tell you." He turned suddenly. "Have you ever been in the honeycombs before?"

"No. I've been on Themis, but not in the honeycombs."

"Nononono," Toto squealed, gaining courage in the safety of Philip's arms.

"That," Dr. Waite said softly, "puts a different face on the matter."

"'Ugh!" Christine gasped in disgust.

A huge, wet, red Cacochaun had entered from the next cell, drawing its heavy body across the floor on six fleshless legs. Long, furry antennae waved slowly as its iron-strong jaws opened and closed with every step. Toto squealed shrilly. The Cacochaun continued unperturbed on its way, noticing neither the strangers, nor the chatterings of Toto.

"It's maddening," Dr. Waite said. "They act as if we weren't here. There are thirty-one men in the hive right now, but they pay no attention." He brushed his tousled hair excitedly. "To be ignored so completely by slimy, filthy Themis monsters — it's too much to bear. I'd like to kill them!"

"Personally," Christine put in faintly, "I'd rather not be noticed."

At the sound of her voice, the man calmed.

Unerringly he led them through a maze of cells, turning now right, now left, until his companions were entirely confused. Each cell was identical: the triangular sloping floor about ten feet on a side, slippery with Cacochaun exudation, and the walls and ceilings brilliant with light-giving malops. In some cells Earth exiles worked in the scum. Through others Caeochauns passed carrying food in their strong mandibles to the newest brood of the Queen. At an unoccupied cell, the doctor paused.

"As you already suspect," he began abruptly, "blue amber is being stolen."

Philip paled.

"But as yet none has been sold to Mars," the doctor continued softly.

"How do you know of Mars' expansion policy? You've been here fifteen years —"

"Collectors talk," Dr. Waite answered. "But as I said, the stolen blue amber is still on Themis. You see, Sime Conner has had no way of leaving — until now!"

"Sime Conner!" Philip grasped his arm excitedly. "And by 'until now' you mean in *our* space ship." He turned quickly and started back through the combs.

"Wait, my friend." The doctor's voice was oily. "Your space ship is safe for a time. Sime Conner will not leave without the blue amber — and he does not have them now. *I know where they are!*"

"Where?"

"Wherewherewhere," Toto repeated.

Dr. Waite glared at the pup. "You'll have to keep *that* quiet, however, or you'll never get past the guards. In fact, it's too great a risk for more than one to try. You'll have to go alone."

Christine stared incredulously. "Do you mean to say Sime Conner has *men* guarding the blue amber he has stolen?"

"Not men," the doctor answered, "Cacochauns. And they're not guarding the blue amber, but the cell of their Queen. Sime Conner chose his hiding place well. And don't let their chant confuse you." He turned back to Philip. "It's meaningless. In fact, I doubt that they know why they chant or what they protect. The only thing they do know is to keep anything but Cacochauns from entering the Queen's cell. That's a natural instinct to assure perpetuation of their race, for all eggs come from the Queen."

"And where's the blue amber?" Philip asked.

Stooping, Dr. Waite traced in the slime of the floor a diagram of small triangles fit together to form an inverted triangle, the bottom point resting on a small circle and an arc reaching from the right top angle to the circle.

"The blue amber," he said slowly, "is behind the stone bearing this symbol in the ceiling of the Queen's cell."

"In the Queen's cell," Christine repeated. "Won't *she* object to Philip's entering?"

"The Queen sleeps soundly," Dr. Waite answered.

As they went farther into the combs, it became harder to get a foothold in the slime of the sloping floors. Often they caught themselves just about to put a steadying hand on an uncoiled malop, for unless the malop's head was within a few inches of the tail, the green sparks of warning did not flash. Let a man touch either end, however, and instantly the other end flipped around, sending hundreds of volts of electricity through his body.

In the lower depths, Dr. Waite stopped, covering his face and hands with lengths of material he brought from his pocket.

"In the next few cells are the second caste of Cacochauns," he explained, "the ones with the lichen leech growth. Don't expose any part of your skin to the floating spores. If one touches you —" He shrugged.

Through the mesh of the material covering their eyes, they got a hard, repulsive glimpse of the fungus-covered Cacochauns. Christine clung to a fold of Philip's coat and Toto chattered in the unwonted darkness beneath it. At an empty cell they sighed with relief and started to remove their coverings.

"Don't!" Dr. Waite yelled suddenly. "Leave them on!"

With a slush of dragging feet, a lurching, fungus-covered form approached. If the Cacochauns were repulsive, this creature was far more so. Half bloody splotches, half long fungus ferns which waved feebly as he walked, beneath his loathsome exterior he was, unmistakably, a man.

Christine gasped and drew nearer to Philip.

At sight of the strangers, the man laughed wildly, tearing the long, furry growth out by the roots and throwing it madly about the cell, leaving his skin torn and bleeding beneath. Suddenly he calmed and came closer.

"Scratch me," he pleaded. "Scratch my back. It itches."

"Kill him," Dr. Waite whispered. "Kill him, if you have a gun. He's mad from the itching."

It was the humane thing to do. But until the repulsive fungus-covered arm reached to snatch the covering from Christine's face, Philip could not bring himself to move. He turned his gun outward, firing through the cloth of his garment.

"He would have died soon anyway," Dr. Waite said, "as soon as the roots reached his heart. Besides, if he hadn't escaped, we'd have done away with him before he got so bad."

A little farther on, Philip drew Christine aside.

"When you leave me," he whispered, "go straight through the honeycomb and wait at the space ship. I won't be long."

As he pressed his gun into her hand, he saw her eyes glisten with adventure.

Now a faint sound reached their ears, a sound starting high in the scale and going down note by note, each one sustained a shorter time than the one before.

"The chant of the guard," Dr. Waite said.

Fascinated, Philip listened. As he had no knowledge of the Cacochaun language, the chant was meaningless, yet strangely he found himself counting the beats. On each new note it lessened by two, until finally it reached a beat of one. Then, without pause, it started over in the shrill note of its beginning, holding it for sixty-one beats. Each beat was a long *ck* sound, coming strangely liquid from the larynxes of the Cacochauns.

As they advanced and the chant grew louder, a picture formed in Philip's mind — the diagram of the inverted triangle formed of triangular cells by which Dr. Waite had said he could identify the hiding place of the stolen blue amber.

Before he could satisfactorily find an explanation, the scientist broke his thoughts.

"We must leave now. The guard cell is very close. Keep bearing right and you can't miss it. Now, in order to pass through, you must distract their attention. Throw something alive in their midst — that pup of yours will do — and while they are occupied, walk through behind them."

"Thatpupofyours," Toto squealed gleefully, "thatpupofyourswilldo — that —"

Philip turned on Waite angrily. "If that's the best suggestion you can make —"

"He'd just as soon throw me," Christine said.

The scientist shrugged. "Well, if you want to risk it, use an uncoiled malop. But you'll have to throw it quickly."

As he turned to leave, it occurred to Philip to wonder why he was taking the trouble to expose Sime Conner's thievery. What could he, a life exile, hope to gain from helping the Government?

"There is no reprieve from a murder sentence," Philip said. "Why do you trouble yourself with the affairs of Earth?"

Again Dr. Waite shrugged, darting his small, black eyes into Philip's.

"Sime Conner is free," he said. "Every day I look at his fat loathsome face and think 'Sime Conner is free, I am not.' For that I hate him. Sime Conner can leave this filthy, Cacochaun infested satellite whenever he chooses, and he does not leave. For that I despise him. And Sime Conner has abused his freedom. For that I expose him."

He beckoned Christine to leave.

"Don't forget what I told you," Philip whispered to her. "Wait at the space ship!"

"I will, honey." She patted his arm reassuringly. "But hurry." She looked distastefully at Dr. Waite's back.

It took but a few minutes to traverse the remaining cells. As the chant grow louder, Philip again counted its beats, and again came that strange picture — the inverted triangle formed of triangular cells.

Now, on the low notes, the beats were few. Soon would come that triumphant bass growl which meant the end. Involuntarily, Philip thought of the bottom point of the triangle resting on the circle. Strange that that picture should keep recurring to his mind. Suddenly he looked up to find himself at the guard's cell.

Four Cacochauns lay on the sloping triangular floor, their jaw moving quickly with the *ck ck ck* beat of the chant.

Picking his spot carefully, Philip grasped an uncoiled malop from the wall, hurling it quickly into the cell. As one the Cacochauns ceased their chant, and before the writhing malop had a chance to bring its two ends together, all four had sunk their mandibles into the black flesh.

Hurriedly, Philip entered, stepping carefully behind them — but half-way across, Toto wriggled from his grasp. The near Cacochaun turned, snapping viciously at the small pyramid shaped body. Philip kicked the under part of its neck, sending it crashing against a wall, and quickly picked Toto from the floor unharmed. But now the three others were upon him, snapping at the leather of his shoes, tearing at the thick cloth about his legs.

It was almost hopeless, to fight four Cacochauns without a gun and with Toto wriggling and squealing in his arms. Kicking madly, Philip stunned two, but the first had come to life behind him and fastened its mandibles in the flesh of his leg. Unable to move for the pain, he stood helpless for a moment, until with a mighty effort he twisted his body free. Then, seizing an uncoiled malop he hurled it at another Cacochaun.

There was a sharp crackle as the malop made connections. The smell of burning flesh filled the cell. The Cacochaun writhed and twitched as the electric charge went through him. For the moment there was only one more to be dealt with. Philip threw another malop and, hardly waiting to see whether it hit its mark, limped into the next cell, nerves tensed to meet whatever danger it had to offer.

On a circular dais centered in the triangular floor lay the most repulsive monster he had ever see — giant orange and black striped Cacochaun. The thick, furry antennae slowly waved their four-foot lengths. The six legs, covered with coarse black hairs, were dwarfed by the fat body. Despite the movement of her antennae, the Queen was sleeping. For the moment, there was no danger.

As he set Toto down that he might better search the diagrammed stone in the ceiling, Philip's eyes were caught by a rich, fire-stabbed blue light in the filth and slime of the floor. Gently, he picked it up, almost fearing to touch its beauty and, for a moment, lost consciousness of his surroundings in contemplation of its magnificent color.

At last, drawing his eyes away, he dropped the blue amber in his pocket. Here was his first evidence, probably lost from the loot of Sime Conner. That thought brought the business at hand to mind and he raised his eyes to the ceiling to search the marked stone.

At the moment, few malops gave their greenish sparks, and he strained his eyes upward in the half gloom. Then at last he saw it — the strange, inverted triangle with one side embraced by an arc. — just as Dr. Waite had drawn it.

But, it was in the part of the ceiling directly over the Queen. *And the only way he could reach it was to stand on her dais!*

Tiptoeing over he mounted carefully. Hastily he searched his pocket for a knife. He had a feeling of distaste for what he was about to do, but he overcame his reluctance, and when the knife struck an obstruction he pushed harder until it brought down from the crack a heavy, wire handle.

From beside him he heard an angry *ck ck*. The Queen had awakened! Hurriedly he pulled on the wire, not anxious to feel her mandibles bite his flesh — the wound from his last encounter still pained him — and, as the stone did not move, used all the strength he had in him.

And then it gave! He reached for the cache of blue amber. But the space above the stone was — empty! A second later there was a sickening crack. The ceiling was giving way — quickly widening cracks spreading across it!

Helplessly he watched, hearing the patter of small rocks as they fell. From above came creaks and groans, and finally heavy, dull thuds as tons of rock came thundering down. The whole honeycomb was collapsing!

Toto ran wildly, chattering in terror as rocks crashed around him. At last, giving a frenzied leap, he landed in Philip's outstretched arms.

Then, for the first time, Philip became aware that the dais on which he stood was sinking — another proof of the engineering genius of the Cacochauns! For the stone he had removed must be the keystone of the hive, on which all the cells and towers above were dependent for support. Hopelessly he remembered Christine and wondered if she had been caught in the crumbling comb. But there was little time to think.

Even as the cell walls gave, the dais with the Queen, Toto and himself upon it was below floor level. A heavy door closed over, shutting out sight of the ruined combs.

In the dark sub chamber they could hear the crack of falling rocks; the ceiling shook with the weight upon it. But it held!

Cautiously, he stepped from the dais, feeling for solid ground before he shifted his weight. Behind him the Queen clucked angrily and Toto, frightened in the damp darkness, imitated her *ck ck ckk* in his squeaky voice.

Aside from the angry Queen, there was danger in staying too long in the sealed sub chamber with no way of getting air.

He stood helpless with anger as suddenly the thought dawned that he had been tricked! Dr. Waite had known that by removing the keystone he would

collapse the whole honeycomb. Sime Conner had no cache of blue ambers —
No, worse! He *had* one — *But it had never been hidden in the Queen's cell!*

As soon as the time lock on the space ship opened, Sime Conner and Dr.
Waite would escape to Mars and sell their blue ambers to the enemy power.

And Christine! Christine was either dead — buried in the debris of the
collapsed hive, doomed to flee with a drunkard and a murderer to a strange
planet — or — worse! — left alone, the only human thing on Themis! For all
the convicts must have died in the ruined honeycomb.

His racing thoughts drove him mad! In helpless anger he paced the cell.
Yet — yet — there was — there must be a chance.

Feverishly he covered every inch of wall surface with his bare hands,
wishing at least one electric malop had come down with the sinking dais to
give him light. He found no opening in the smooth circular walls. Still there
must be some way out! Of what value was it to protect the Queen, if she
and her potential brood must starve in this sub chamber? Despondently, he
calmed himself and tried to think.

As the constant *ck ckk ck ckk ckk* of the Queen penetrated his consciousness, the chant of the Cacochaun guards recurred to his mind and he
remembered how the diagram of the inverted triangle had haunted him at the
sound of it. Suddenly the reason dawned. He slapped his knee at its simplicity.

The guards' chant was a sound picture of the hive's construction — sound
picture of the symbol on the keystone! The chant had sixty-one beats on the
first note; the diagram had sixty-one triangular cells across the top. Each
graded down to one: the last beat of the chant; the last triangular cell — the
Queen's chamber.

Now he was getting somewhere! The circle on which the bottom point of
the triangle — the Queen's cell — rested, was, of course, this cell. His
solution was here. He had only to find it.

Again he retraced the sequence in his mind: the chant, the keystone, the
diagram. And then, simultaneously, he remembered both the unexplained
mystery of the construction of the honeycomb from the bottom up and the
arc on the diagram enclosing one angle and the bottom circle.

Now he had it! He was almost breathless with excitement! The arc
represented the curvature of Themis, and the combs, instead of going
straight down to the interior of the satellite, had been built on a chord of the
sphere, parallel to and only slightly below the surface. As the diameter of
Themis was only forty miles, a chord near her pole must be far less.
Accordingly, this cell *must* be at the surface on the opposite side of the
sphere from the towers of the honeycomb. This was the cell from which the
Cacochaun builders had started!

He started to rise to go over the wall surface once more, putting a band
on the floor to keep the weight from his wounded leg, but he stopped short
as he felt regular indentations beneath his fingers. He traced them carefully.
It was the keystone symbol, the inverted triangle embraced by an arc.

Breathless he ran his knife around the edges of the stone, hoping against hope to meet the obstruction which meant a handle. At last he found it, a heavy wire which rose with the pressure of his knife. He pulled with all the strength he had in him until, at last, the stone moved.

Beneath it a narrow passageway ran parallel to the cell floor. If his deductions were correct, it would slant upward to the surface farther on. That was his only hope!

Behind him the Queen clucked angrily, filling the cell with her rumbling sounds. There was the sound of movement as she raised her fat body and descended from the dais.

Hastily he pushed the chattering Toto into the passageway and, crawling on all fours, followed. The Queen was behind him. He could feel her heavy jaws snapping at the soles of his feet.

He pushed on desperately, and at last found himself in the freezing outside air.

The Queen emerged behind him. Still clucking in anger, she snapped at his feet. He strode a few steps away to pick up Toto, confident that she could not approach his speed with her heavy body, and started across the surface of the satellite.

He hurried in the direction of the pole, tripping sometimes in the brush, moving his feet quickly to numb his mind — to keep from wondering whether his wife, Christine, were alive or dead — and if alive, whether the space ship were still there to take her from this unlucky moon.

At last, after what seemed years of running, he saw a pile of debris on the near horizon. A pile of debris! All that remained of the minarets and towers of the honeycomb! He ran quickly, hoping against hope, that the space ship was still there.

It was! And standing before it was Christine — alive!

A shout of joy died in his throat as he saw Dr. Waite a few feet away training a gun on her. Silently he crept closer, praying Toto would have no crazy impulse to chatter now and reveal his presence. Then, suddenly, he dropped the pup and dove at the doctor's legs.

Waite went down with a thud, but turning quickly raised both legs, kicking Philip in the stomach and forcing the breath from him. With a strong effort, Philip dove again, and the two men rolled over and over in the scrubby brush. Tired from his hurried trek across the satellite, Philip felt his strength ebbing. Straining, he tried to loose the gun from Dr. Waite's grasp, but he could not. Nor could he spare an arm to knock the man senseless. So, for a moment, they lay, strength pitted against strength, and the one who gave first — the loser!

A figure approached, but Philip could not spare the energy to raise his eyes. Suddenly, Dr. Waite gave a hoarse shout and wrenched his body, the gun falling, from his hand. In a flash, Christine retrieved it and leveled it at the scientist.

"I did it." She smiled at Philip. "I did it with a little pin."

Later, soaring through space with the only two survivors of the Themisian colony — Dr. Waite tied securely and Sime Conner sleeping drunkenly beside him — Philip tried to piece together the scattered fragments of his knowledge.

There *had* been a cache of stolen blue amber, though the thief had been, not Sime Conner, but Dr. Waite, who, little by little, had taken control of the colony from the weak governor's hands, urging Conner to drink in order to dull his senses. And Conner, completely under the mad doctor's thumb, had not questioned his instructions to keep official visitors, who might see too much blue amber being found, from the honeycombs until Dr. Waite had been warned. All the while, of course, the scientist had but one aim in view: somehow to escape from Themis and sell his loot to the enemy power, Mars.

Suddenly Philip remembered the blue amber he had picked up in the moment before he had removed the keystone and destroyed the hive. He took it from his pocket, dropping it into Christine's lap.

"Oooh." She cupped her hands around it, fascinated by its fire-stabbed blue. "It's really as beautiful as a jewel. I like it better than a Xanadu stone."

"I hope it's beautiful enough," he said ruefully, "so that the Government of Earth won't remember it's the last she'll ever get." He sighed. "I sure left the Cacochaun hive a shambles —"

Christine's face sobered. "It's always seemed foolish to me," she said, "to wait for the Cacochaun exudation to fossilize in order to get blue amber."

He looked at her through narrowed eyes for a moment.

"Honey, I'll bet you're right." His hand brushed her cheek softly. "There must be a lot of the inner element buried on Themis. All they have to do is cover it with liquid glass or something before it gets a chance to oxidize. The Cacochaun exudation is only a preservative after all; it's the blue they use in tubes."

"I'm smart," she said impersonally. "I wondered when you'd realize it. Look how I stuck that pin into Dr. Waite. And look how I fooled him before."

"Sa-ay." He tipped her chin up so be could peer into her eyes. "It looks more as if he fooled you. I gave *you* the gun. How did he get it?"

She jerked her chin away petulantly.

"He took it. When he started dashing through the honeycomb I suspected something wrong. So I told him I'd shoot if he didn't stop and tell me what the hurry was. Then he just took the gun out of my hand and dragged me after him."

"Hm!" Philip tightened his lips. "I see. He just took it. Well, why didn't he just take the space ship then? The time lock opened hours ago."

She winked knowingly at her puzzled husband.

"That's where I fooled him. You see, I didn't want to leave — I thought perhaps you'd been hurt a little when the honeycomb collapsed. I knew you were too smart to get killed and I insisted on going to look for you. That's why he had the gun trained on me. He was afraid I'd escape."

"Escape? Well, he had the ship. Why did he care?"

'That's how I fooled him." Her green eyes rolled mischievously. "When be asked me if I'd ever flown a space ship I said yes. You see, neither Sime Conner nor he had the slightest idea of how to run one."

Part Two

The 40s

Space Episode

LESLIE PERRI

ABOUT LESLIE PERRI
AND
SPACE EPISODE

Space Episode *was first published:*
Future, *December 1941*

Leslie Perri penned only four science fiction stories between 1941 and 1956. A long time science fiction fan, and editor of a motion picture magazine, her marriages to Hugo winners Frederik Pohl and Richard Wilson may have provided the initial impetus to her science fiction writing. Her four stories ("In The Forest," "Under The Skin," "The Untouchables" and "Space Episode") constitute a small but wickedly barbed body of work.

In "Space Episode," Ms. Perri takes a classic situation from 1930s and 1940s pulp adventure science fiction and gives it her own wicked, feminist twist. It's a story that ought well to have found its way into a more distinguished publication, but the tale's reversal of standard plot situations, and the fact that its heroics are performed by a heroine rather than a hero, relegated "Space Episode," as it did the works of Helen Weinbaum and the latter stories of Leslie Francis Stone, to the lowest of the pulps.

Space Episode

by LESLIE PERRI

SHE STARED at her two companions for a moment and then a sickening revulsion replaced fear, the fear that held each of the three in a terrible grip of inertia. Her slim hands bit hard into the back; of one of the metal seats. The tiny rocket ship was plummeting to destruction, careening dizzily through space. Here, in the atmosphereless void, their motion was negligible to them, but instruments told a grim story; unless they could blast the forward rockets very soon they would be caught in the Earth's titanic grip and drawn with intensifying acceleration to its surface. They would come screaming down like some colossal shell and the planet's surface would become a molten sore where they struck. And now, while precious seconds fled, the three of them stood transfixed, immobile.

What had happened? A simple thing, an unimportant thing in space. They had encountered a meteor swarm, one utterly infinitesimal in the sight of the looming worlds about them. But it had left one of its members jammed in their forward rocket nozzles, the tubes which determined whether they would land safely or crash in a blaze of incandescence. They had turned off their operating power rather than wreck the ship completely; with no escape for the rocket-blasts, their motors would be smashed to pieces.

The first they knew of disaster, striking unheralded from space, was the ear-shattering impact of the meteor. No sound; just concussion that was worse than any deafening crash. Then the power generator dial shot to the danger line; the ship began to plunge, teleplate showing the universe seemingly turning fast somersaults as their ship careened end over end. The truth was evident at once; that impediment must be removed from the forward tubes. One of them must volunteer to clear away the obstruction, or all were doomed.

A time for heroics, this, but none of them felt like heroes. Erik and Michael stood side by side, a sort of bewildered terror on their faces — a "this can't happen to us" look. Neither had moved or spoken a word since the first investigation. Erik, upon discovering that the outer door was gone, had flung his space suit to the floor with an impotent curse. For that shorn-off door meant that whoever left the ship now could never return; it was a one-way passage. The taller of the two men played with the instruments, spinning them this way and that, then stood waiting. Waiting for heaven alone knew what miracle to happen.

Lida found her confidence in them, that fine confidence she had known up to now, dissolving away, leaving her with an empty feeling which was greater than any fear could have been. She could not square them, as they were now, with the men she had known before — through innumerable Terrestrial dangers on land, sea, and in the clouds. The three had had a planet-wide reputation as reckless and danger-despising. And now. . . .

"Erik!" she cried suddenly. "Damn it, this is not a tea party! We have to do something now. Toss coins or draw lots. Either one of us goes out there now, or we all crack up."

Michael glanced at her dully as she spoke, his tongue moving over dry lips. Erik closed his eyes, brushing his hair with a limp gesture. Lida's hands tightened on the back seat; what was wrong with them? She bent forward slightly, her heart beating like a dull and distant drum. The dials on the control board frightened her; she whispered now. "You see what little time we have left? Nothing's going to happen unless we make it happen. We're falling, falling fast."

Michael slumped in his seat, dropped his head to his knees groaning. Erik looked at her vaguely for a long second, then turned his eyes to the teleplate. Cold perspiration stood on his forehead. This was the dashing Erik Vane, one-time secret dream hero, close companion since that day, years back, when he and Mike had fished her out of the wreck of her plane somewhere in the Pacific. Suddenly, it all seemed amusing to her; the question of sacrifice lay between Michael and Erik — this was strictly men's work. But they were finding life a sweet thing — a sudden burst of laughter overcame her. There was such an amusing impotency to Erik's strength and the dash of his clothes; the knuckles stood white on his hands, cold damp fear glittering on his forehead.

And what of Michael, the gallant? He slumped in his seat, holding his face in shaking hands. Could this be the same man who had saved them all by scaling what was virtually a sheer cliff by night and obtaining help from neighboring aborigines? All the dangers they had faced together and overcome together now crowded in her memory, one piling upon another. Scores of times one of them had unhesitatingly faced unpleasant death for the sake of all; she had been no exception.

And there was another picture that made her laugh, too, but it wasn't a gay laugh. The picture of Michael opening the outer door of the rocket on the night they left bowing gallantly speaking extravagantly dear words of welcome to her on their first space flight. Lida clung to a chair, eyes blurring, as she gazed at the control panel, now a welter of glittering metal, polished and useless.

Michael's head shot up suddenly. "Stop laughing! Stop it!" He covered his face with his hands and Lida felt sick; he was crying.

She paused, her eyes filled with bitterness and contempt. Then she smiled wearily, feeling strangely akin to the vacuum outside them. There was only a sudden decision and she made it. This was her exit and to hell with heroes!

She bowed to them scornfully, waving aside their fears with a flippant sweep of her hand. Only one regret remained now. They could have chosen fairly, made a pretense of flipping a coin. She looked cocky and defiant now, gathering tools for her job. A grin twisted her mouth into a quivering scarlet line. Would she make a television headline? Would they name a ramp after her, or, perhaps, some day, a rocket division? There were several photos of her in newspaper files; she hoped they would pick a good one when they ran the story. Oh, hers would be a heroic end.

She put aside the word "end" mentally and turned her attention to what had to be done. Her decision made, she would have to act swiftly or the sacrifice would be useless. The cabin's interior was becoming unreal and horrible with apathy. She ignored the others; they were like figures in a nightmare.

The outer door had been destroyed, no doubt about that. Erik was almost blown from the cabin when he opened the inner door. She would need magnetic clamps from the outset; the neutralizing effect of the airlock between the two doors was gone; that spelled doom for the one who ventured beyond the cabin. Once out, there was no returning. The force of escaping air would not permit it.

On the black, glistening floor of the cabin lay Erik's glittering, iridium-woven spacesuit. He had ventured that much at least, pulled it from a locker and tossed it to the floor. Fortunately the gyroscopes were working. She stepped into the suit, smiling grimly. It was much too long and wide all over. Her fingers were swift and sure, adjusting the steel clamps.

Michael was still in a semi-coma. Erik was watching her reflection. He knew what she was doing. His shoulders were rigid now, but he made no move to stop her. And now memory played the final ironic trick. She recalled Michael saying, with his arm around her shoulders, "When we get to Mars, you'll be the glamor girl of the planet. It'll be wonderful, Lida — just the two of us." His eyes had hinted at things he did not put into words and even though she knew that nothing of the kind would happen so long as there were three of them, she had been glad for him then.

She jerked up the front zipper, trying to close her memories with the same motion. There weren't many seconds to spare now. She fastened the tools to her belt, checked them and with them her signal sending button with the receiving set on the instrument board. Then, with shaking hands she could not help, she picked up the helmet.

Michael looked up suddenly, incredulity filling his eyes. Erik wheeled around from the teleplate.

"Lida!" he said, his voice hoarse.

Gone was the bitterness and contempt now. "So long, Erik," she replied softly. "I'll do the best I can. Watch for the signal on the control board. I'll send it through when the rocket nozzles are clear — that is, if I'm not blown from the ship."

He swayed for an instant, lurched over to where she stood. "I can't let you do it. Give me the suit, Lida. I'll go." She looked at him, cynical and proud, her eyes glittering like steel and her small chin thrust forward determinedly. These words he had said — what were they but words he flung from him, reaching out to pull together the tatters of his self-respect? She pitied him.

"There's no time for that now," she replied crisply. "Good luck."

On a sudden impulse she darted over to Michael and struck him sharply across the face. He looked up suddenly, his eyes widening in amazement. "Aren't you going to say — goodbye?"

"Lida," he muttered, "don't go. Don't leave us now; it won't do any good, Lida. Take off the suit and we'll all go together."

She shook her head defiantly. "No! There's still time. Goodbye, Michael." She fastened on the helmet, her hands cold.

Steeling herself against the sudden chill of terror that was seeping through her, she forced herself to the inner door. She pressed the electric release, her hands, heavily swathed, clinging to the steel ring. The panel slid open slowly; a buzzing sound would be filling the cabin now, but she could not hear it. She could feel their eyes on her. With a magnetic clamp in readiness, she waited for the moment when the aperture would be wide enough. Then suddenly, pressing the button in reverse, she plunged through and was hurtled against the wall of the air lock. The magnetic clamp held!

Breathing a deep sigh of relief, Lida glanced around her. The inner door was shut already; this, then, was her final goodbye. There could be no returning to the cabin. She was conscious of a dull, throbbing pain in her arm. It was numb from the impact. Frantically, trying to save time, she worked it up and down until gradually life returned to it. Then she made her way to the ragged-edged gash in the hull. Nothing remained of the outer door. Clinging to a large metal splinter, she made a hurried survey.

The path of the meteor and the damage it had done was clearly visible. It had ploughed a deep welt-like furrow in the side of the ship and piled melted metal and large chunks from the side over the nozzle ends. There were probably meteor fragments as well. But her job would be easy even so. Judicious blasting with the torch would take care of everything. Placing a heavily padded foot in the still glowing furrow, she detached a magnetic clamp from her belt.

Space lay around her and, as she worked, she felt a nameless dread seep into her being. The face of the planet was directly *above*. Desperately, she tried not to look at it. Despite her efforts, she could not help but glance upward at its looming immensity, cringing as she did so. It was so horribly large — falling on her. It seemed to be drawing her *up*, the way an electromagnet catches a piece of scrap-iron. And around her was space, space filled with pinpoints, billiard balls, and footballs of light. She knew she must not stop to look at them. They would charm away her senses and burn out her eyes. She knew this without ever having been told. There was a horror in space, not anything alive, but a dread that chilled and stole away one's life.

Slowly, carefully, she made her way up the side of the ship, using her torch, when necessary, to clear obstructions. Finally she reached the nose, rested against the boldly painted nameplate. *Ares.* A sense of the horrible irony of the situation struck her. If they had immediately fired the forward rockets when the meteor struck, the tremendous blast furnace would have melted the obstruction, for, she saw now, it was very slight. Given a chance to harden, however, it was a different story; to blast now, with it there, would blow out the tubes.

She understood, now, why men who had faced all manner of Terrestrial dangers had become weak and helpless here. They had been fools, all of them, to come on this flight without conditioning — space was no place for humans unless they had been conditioned to it gradually. And they had thought themselves so clever in the way they had evaded the requirements for a license.

She pressed the signal button at her waist as the last trace of the obstruction was eaten away. An instant later, there was an answering flash in the small metal tube next to it; they had been watching the control button. A single tear ran down her nose as she thought: "I hope they go to hell, damn them."

Pulling her hand from the magnetic clamp, she straightened up stiffly, and, with a hard, quick push jumped clear of the ship. It swerved suddenly and with dizzying violence knocked her clear of their rockets. She had not considered the imminence of them before. The thought of being charred....

Earth loomed above her. She had not the acceleration of the ship. Soon it would leave her behind. She would float out here in an orbit of her own, a second moon. Perhaps a meteor would strike her some day; perhaps in the future space-voyagers would find her and bring her home. Soon, within an hour at the most, there would be no more air. But why wait hours? With a sudden movement, she threw open the helmet of her suit.

The ship was gone now. Michael and Erik were safe. And something tenuous had clamped itself over her nose and mouth so that she could no longer breathe. For an instant she struggled, lungs bursting, as in the throes of a nightmare. Her thoughts cried out, "Michael! Michael!"

The darkness gathered her in.

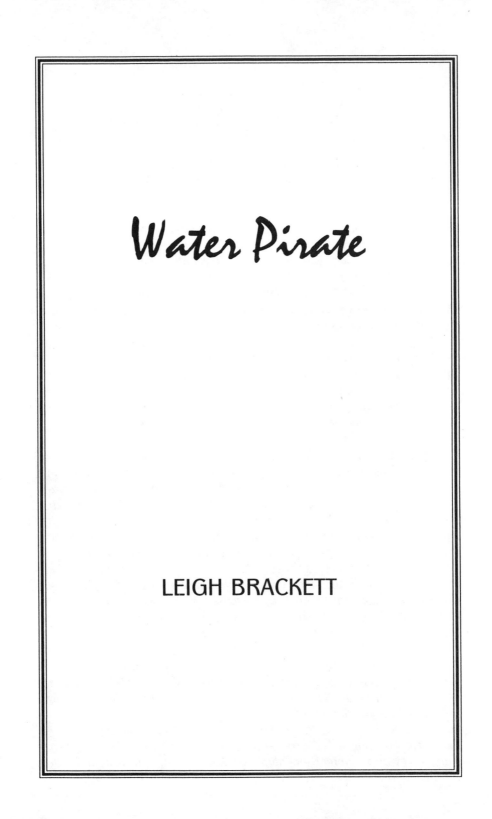

Water Pirate

LEIGH BRACKETT

ABOUT LEIGH BRACKETT
AND *WATER PIRATE*

Water Pirate *was first published:*
Super Science Stories, *January 1941*

Leigh Brackett was the first woman science fiction writer to become a bowl-em-over fan favorite. (C. L. Moore had come close, but then disappeared behind a flurry of pseudonyms, including her husband's by-line.) Not so coincidentally, Brackett was also the first top-notch woman science fiction writer. The secret of her success was simple, like her heirs (Norton, Bradley, McCaffrey), she wrote vigorous, well-realized action stories, setting deeply felt characters against colorful, exotic alien worlds. Exactly, in fact, the kind of story male fan favorites wrote.

Though the protagonist in Brackett's stories is usually male, presumably because she (like many women writers) strongly identified with the kind of role only men were allowed to play in her society, the second hero is usually a heroine. In the dynamic little space opera that follows, her second hero(ine) recapitulates all the standard reactions of a Brackett hero: takes a courageous stand, has sense enough to know when not to fight, and personally intervenes to assure the villain's destruction.

Leigh Brackett's tales of masculine adventure are so unremittingly vigorous that no one suspected her gender for many years (a situation paralleled in a somewhat different form in the symbolically autobiographical Black Amazon of Mars*) possessed a unique poetic voice that colored her fiction with a brooding, lyric quality that lifted them far beyond the literary quality of her fellow pulp writers of the time. She wrote, from the very first, with the fine, precisely controlled, sense of normal outrage that fueled the work of all great writers (visible in stories as various "All the Colors of the Rainbow," where green-skinned honeymooners, visiting dignitaries from another planet, are subjected to brutality and outrage by the narrow minded racists they encounter deep in the American heartland and her award nominee suspense tale,* An Eye for An Eye, *which take the theme of brutal assault and its aftermath several steps further).*

Leigh Brackett successfully, almost casually comes to terms with and acknowledges the male libido, she appears to have embraced it's existence with as much gusto as she has embraced the rest of her natural surroundings; she displays a genuine liking for men and maleness, particularly as it was conceived during her era, in a way that is ahead of its time even today. Leigh Brackett's work suggests a stronger identification with the male gender than with her own; a common phenomenon among author's of both genders throughout recorded history.

Water Pirate

by LEIGH BRACKETT

T WAS early in 2418 that the Solar System realized that there was a Water Pirate. The great tanker ships, carrying water to the rich dry-world mines and colonies, began to vanish from the space-lanes, with their convoys. The Trans-Galactic Convoy Fleet, which for two hundred years had kept the spaceways safe, was suddenly helpless. Ships and men vanished without a trace or an explanation, and there was no clue to be found.

For four solid weeks not a drop of water got through. The storage tanks dropped lower and lower; a panic fear of thirst swept the dry worlds. The Interplanetary Trade Marts shook in the wind of that fear, and the economic system trembled with it.

Old Johan Gray, Chief of Special Duty of the Convoy Fleet, played his last card. His son Jaffa went through the worst hellspots of the System, searching for something that might show them some way to fight.

And on a moon-washed Martian night, Jaffa Gray stood in the shadow of the Valkis slave-market and cursed, bitterly and softly; a stocky, strong-boned man, his square face hard with the failure that he had at last to admit.

For the first time in the two days he had been in Valkis, he took off his peaked spaceman's cap, wanting the desert wind on his head and not giving a damn who saw his trademark — the broad streak where his hair had come in white over a scar. He raked his fingers through it, swearing out the last of his vocabulary; and a voice said out of the darkness: "Jaffa Gray!"

He whirled, his heat-gun blurring into his hand. A boy stepped into the moonlight. His arrow-straight body was clad like Jaffa's in dark spaceman's leather, but where Jaffa's dark hair was cropped short, the boy's rose in a shining crown, bound with the thin metal chains that marked him already a warrior in Kesh, a barbarian state in the Martian drylands.

Jaffa's face hardened. He had seen that gleaming pile of hair almost everywhere in Valkis. "All right, Keshi, you've caught up with me. Talk, and talk fast!"

The boy came closer, fearless of the gun, and his words were a breathless whisper. *"I can take you to the Water Pirate!"*

Jaffa stood like a graven image. He had risked his neck on an invisible trail. The last possible covert had drawn blank. He had been going home defeated; and now Fate dropped the whole thing neatly in his lap! His lips curled in a silent laugh. His left hand shot out to clamp the Keshi's tunic in a throttling grip; his right jammed the gun-muzzle in the boy's ribs. "Now," he said easily, "what's your game?"

The Keshi didn't flinch. "You are Jaffa Gray; I was sure when I saw your hair. You are hunting the Water Pirate. I can take you to him. There is no game."

Jaffa's eyes blazed. "If you were telling the truth. . . ."

The boy grinned in his face, a fighting grin. "Feel my chin, Jaffa Gray, if you want proof!"

Puzzled, the Earthman slid the fist of his gun-hand along the upthrust jaw. His breath hissed in sharply. Intently he retraced the jawline, ran downward along the smooth curve of the throat. Then he let go of the tunic abruptly, as though it had burned him.

"By the Nine Red Hells of Jupiter!" he whispered. "A woman!"

"Now do you believe?" mocked the low voice. "Would I have risked Valkis to tell you a lie? What would those wolves do to me, if they found out? I need you, Jaffa Gray, and you need me!"

The white lock gleamed as Jaffa's blunt fingers rumpled it. Then he nodded shortly and shrugged his heavy shoulders.

"I'll take a chance," he grunted. "Let's go. We can talk aboard my ship."

The Kallman two-seater was ready to fly. Behind the bolted space-port they were safe from spying, and the warrior-girl of Kesh told her story in rapid sentences.

"My name is Lhara. My brother Lhar was pilot on one of the tanker ships that disappeared. The Water Pirate holds him prisoner, along with the men from the other ships, but one man escaped. My brother sent me a message by him; told me to find you, because you were the one man in the System who could bring the Water Pirate in.

"The pilot, who escaped in one of the Pirate's own ships, was to have helped us. But something went wrong; we crashed, and he was killed. You've got to fix the ship."

"Why not just use my own?" asked Jaffa.

"How close do you think you'd get to the Pirate's hideout?" returned Lhara impatiently. "Besides, it has much better weapons than any of our ships."

Jaffa's ears pricked. "Who exactly is the Water Pirate?"

"I don t know. None of the men has ever seen him."

Jaffa nodded. "Where did you crash?"

"Near the Teka range, about three hundred miles from here."

"Just a minute," demanded Jaffa suspiciously. "How'd you get across the desert to Valkis?"

The girl's grey eyes were contemptuous. "I am a Keshi." She touched the chains in her tawny hair. "I have earned these honestly. It was not hard to steal a *thak* from a village across the first range. I rode to Valkis."

Jaffa shook his head. "You win. But warrior or no warrior, if you're lying to me I'll wring your pretty neck. What's your position?"

He was admiring the pretty neck as he slid the strato-wings out of the hull and set the air-rotors going.

"By the Nine Red Hells of Jupiter!" Jaffa shoved back his cap and whistled. "Where did this crate come from?"

He was standing in the open port of a wrecked space ship, lying at a slight angle in the red sand of the Teka desert. It was the weirdest ship he had ever seen, and he had seen plenty. A flattened oval, rather than the familiar cylinder of the System, the alloy of its metal and the use of various gadgets projecting from the hull were both a mystery. Inside, the control cabin was furnished with queer low couches and upholstered all over with a peculiar silky stuff that flowed in quavering patterns of green and blue and brown.

A small ship, carrying four at the outside on a long voyage.

To Jaffa's right as he stood was the control panel, and beyond it, the buckled bow-plates that had sustained the brunt of the crash. Ahead was a wall pierced with thick quartzite visiports. To his left was a bulkhead; the heavy door into the rear cabins was closed. And at his feet. . . .

At his feet was the maddest thing of the whole crazy ship. Covering most of the floor space was an oval pit some six feet deep, tiled in a pattern of outlandish marine growths. It was bone dry; whatever moisture had been there had long ago gone out into the dry Martian air. But it was undoubtedly a pool of some sort, and Jaffa wondered profanely what lunatic would cart a swimming pool through space.

He whirled as bolts shot to behind him. Whirled; and dropped in a jointless heap on the narrow floor. Lhara looked grimly down at him, the paralysis-gun that Jaffa had not taken from her steady in her hand. Mutely, Jaffa raged. He had not disarmed her, for there was no way beyond actual imprisonment to keep her from the Kallman's gun-rack; and Jaffa had been reluctant to risk alienating her help. Also, he had had no real reason to believe she lied. Now he could have kicked himself.

From a locker she produced manacles and chained him securely, wrist and ankle, taking his gun. "I'm sorry, Jaffa Gray," she said steadily, as she stood at last over him. "That was an unworthy trick. But I have told you no lie. My brother is a prisoner, I need your help, and I can take you to the Water Pirate!"

Then she was gone, out into the desert.

Jaffa glared bitterly after her. The paralyzing charge had not been strong, and the life came back into him quickly. He struggled against his chains, knowing it was useless. Then he lay still, too bitter against himself and

Lhara even to curse.

After a bit there came a thundering shock that rocked the desert under the ship. Sand pelted against the ports, and the sagging bow-plates shook in the surge of ruptured air. Jaffa swore. Only one thing could have made that explosion; Lhara had bombed his Kallman. His only hope of escape now lay in this queer ship that he must make fly.

The girl came back, carrying a bundle of Jaffa's things, her hair shaken in a tawny veil across her shoulders and full of sand. Subconsciously Jaffa saluted the courage it had taken to heaven a sub-atomic bomb into the ship and then lie in the sand with that explosion roaring over her.

Lhara freed his hands, lengthened the chain between his ankles so that he could walk after a fashion, the paralysis-gun ready to topple him if he made a false move.

"Go look at the damage, Jaffa. You'll find everything you need here. And I advise you to hurry."

He went, grappling the problem of why, if Lhara had been telling the truth as she said, she was acting this way. She must have gone to a good deal of trouble to track him to Valkis, for he was not in the habit of leaving guide-posts behind him; and she hadn't done it simply because she needed a man to repair the ship, or even to fly it. Almost anyone else would have answered that purpose as well as he. There was something more behind it, something damned queer.

He tried to solve the mystery by the simple method of asking questions. But Lhara, along with the chains in her hair, had learned a warrior's trick of keeping her jaw shut.

He learned nothing.

The damage to the ship was not great. The bow-plates had been broken so that the cabin was not space-worthy, but the instrument panel had not suffered much. The pilot had died of a broken neck, according to the girl. Jaffa studied the controls. Unfamiliar in pattern, they yet bore a resemblance to those he knew, and the ship ran on the same vibratory atom-smashing principle. He nodded in grim admiration as he saw what had made the disappearances of the tanker ships and their convoys possible. A powerful vibratory field was created by means of exterior electrodes, neutralizing the vibrations in the atom-smashing units of the System ships, rendering the engines useless. The vibrations also blanketed the radios, preventing communication. After that, the huge electro-magnets simply clamped on and towed the helpless ships like fish on a line.

A queer, wonderful ship. But he knew he could fly it; and given the proper materials, he could fix the damage in two days.

"Of course," he added, when he made his surly report to the girl, "if the mechanism of the ship has been sprung or damaged. . . ."

"It hasn't," she assured him, and he wondered how she knew.

That night the two of them bunked in the control cabin. Jaffa never thought of being alone with a woman. They brought up their girls to be men in Kesh. Lhara simply chained her prisoner securely, lay down and went to sleep. The door in the bulkhead remained closed. Jaffa tried more questions, but finally gave up and went to sleep too.

Sometime much later he came awake, not starting up, but simply ceasing to be asleep. Both moons were up, shooting crazy shadows across the narrow floor and the dry pool. Lhara's couch was empty.

Jaffa realized suddenly what had waked him. There was a sense almost of fog in his nostrils, a warm moisture faintly tinged with an unfamiliar smell. The dry, cold air sucked it up before he could analyze it. But it had been there; and Lhara was gone.

He sat up. His ankle-chain passed around a stanchion, but from where he was he could see that the bolts of the space-lock were shot from the inside, and the hatch into the engine rooms below was locked.

His eyes fastened on the bulkhead door. Lhara was there, behind it; there was no place else for her to be. Something else was there, too, something that made warm moisture in a climate drier than the Earthly Sahara. What?

Jaffa lay awake, waiting, trying till his head ached to answer his own question. He lay so that he could see the door and still seem to be asleep; when at last the heavy door swung cautiously open, he held his breathing to an even rhythm, though he strained every sense to see what was beyond.

Nothing. Just darkness, against which Lhara's unbound hair shone like a silver cape in the moonlight. But there came again that gush of moist warmth that had wakened him, and the strange odor was a thought stronger. Then the door swung to again, and the thirsty air swallowed all trace.

Lhara stood over him a moment, listening to his breathing. Then she went back to her couch; and in spite of his rage against her, Jaffa dreamed of her, and pleasantly.

Two days of hard work saw the bow-plates once more tight. That evening Jaffa faced the Keshi girl.

"All right," he grunted. "Your crate will fly. Now what?"

"Now you try it. " Lhara shot the space-bolts home. "Take her up. If she's all right, go on. If not, come back and finish the repairs."

"Had you thought we might not be able to get back?" asked Jaffa dryly.

Lhara's jaw set. "Those are the orders, Jaffa Gray."

"Yours — or someone else's?"

"That doesn't concern you." The ever-present paralysis-gun motioned him to the pilot's seat. Jaffa shrugged and obeyed.

He switched on the air pumps and the purifying system, watching the gauges intently. The needles held steady for a moment, then wavered back to the danger point.

"What is it?" asked Lhara sharply. "Cut in your rockets!"

Jaffa pointed to the gauges: The girl's eyes hardened abruptly with suspicion. "The pumps were all right when we tested for tightness an hour ago."

"You can see them now," retorted Jaffa indifferently. "If you go up with them this way, you'll not live two hours."

She wavered a moment, for the first time uncertain. She suspected a trap, but she knew nothing of machinery. In the end, she gave in; there was nothing else to do.

"All right. You'll have to go below and fix them, and you well know there's only room for one down there. But hear me, Earthman!" Her grey gaze was steel-hard, her jaw stern. "You can't escape from there. And if you make a single false move, I'll drop you in your tracks!"

Jaffa shrugged and slid his manacled feet down the hatch.

A single narrow runway ran between the great bulkheaded power units, back to the fuel feed and the vibration chamber, where the special heavy atoms were smashed to power the rocket tubes. He found the air unit without any trouble, stood staring speculatively at the gleaming mass of machinery. There was nothing wrong with it; he himself had caused the reaction on the gauges. But there was an idea at the back of his mind, an unformed thing made of closed doors and cryptic actions and warm moisture in cold, dry air. With the queer inventiveness of a man on the brink of a mysterious fate, something had occurred to him; a fantastic thing, that might, just possibly come in handy. Anyway, it was all he could do, and anything was better than nothing.

He set to work with quick, sure hands. For nearly an hour he was at it, answering Lhara's shouted questions with surly plausibilities. When at last he climbed the ladder back to the control chamber, there was something in the air-unit that had not been there before.

He took the strange ship up, testing her in every way and finding her sound. Lhara gave him his course; he stared at it, raking the white streak in his hair with blunt fingers.

"The Asteroid Belt, eh? Trust the Water Pirate to do something no crook has done since the Fleet got its long-range detectors thirty years ago! I'll be interested to see how he does it!"

"By the Nine Red Hells of Jupiter!" Jaffa said it, very slow and soft. Impossibility was manifest before his eyes.

Mars was back of them, across the curve of space. All around them the Asteroids hurtled on their far-flung way. Ahead, where Jaffa, under Lhara's pistol-enforced order, was steering, was a tiny world-pebble a mile or so in diameter. It seemed a long way to come to commit suicide, but Jaffa held the ship steady, straight for the barren surface.

Then the impossible happened. Emptiness yawned behind a back-slid portion of the asteroid itself; Jaffa, goggling, took the ship in. The strange space door closed behind them.

"We must wait until the air is replenished," said Lhara, as though she were reciting a lesson, and Jaffa waited, staring.

A vast space had been hollowed in the rock of the asteroid, probably with powerful disintegrators, and fitted out for a hangar. Ranged neatly in ranks were the convoy ships that had vanished with the tankers; of the clumsy tankers themselves, there was no sign. There was no other ship like the one he flew, and Jaffa smiled. That fitted his embryonic theory. The floor was sheeted in metal, and he guessed at magnetic gravity plates.

A green light flashed against the wall. The Keshi girl got up and shot the space-bolts back. "Come," she said, and Jaffa, shuffling in his ankle chains, followed obediently.

Lhara guided him, muttering directions under her breath as though she had memorized them. There was a barrack room where men of the Convoy Fleet sat in strange, quiescent alertness, like robots of flesh and blood. Lhara's eyes went in anxious pain to a tall Keshi in the uniform of the tanker company; but there was no recognition in his face, and she did not pause. Then there was a little terminal room where a car waited on a curved trough. Lhara motioned her prisoner in. Then she pressed a button, and the car shot down a green-lit tube straight for the heart of the asteroid.

With a dizzying, vertiginous suddenness, the car shot out of the metal tube into one of glass. Space opened around them — space filled with water, swarming with queer sea-creatures, suffused by a curious pale radiance. Jaffa realized, with a suffocating sensation, that the water filled the whole hollowed-out center of the asteroid.

Lhara's face was set and pale; he could not read her expression. But her knuckles were white on the grip of the ray-gun, and her breast rose to deep-drawn fighter's breathing.

There were glassite buildings ahead in the water's blur. The tube went straight into one, closing transparent walls around them. They went down a ramp and into a small room, furnished as the spaceship had been, and at Jaffa's feet there was a sunken pool, broad each way as two tall men.

Jaffa followed the Keshi girl through swinging doors into a room that stretched vastly under curving crystal walls. Intricate mechanisms, control panels, coils and vacuum tubes and gigantic things of cryptic identity filled every foot of available space; there were ray lamps and heating apparatus and rack upon rack of cultures in gleaming tubes.

And there was water, in a deep sunken pool tiled green and brown in a pattern of water-weeds.

Lhara led her captive to the brink of the pool and stopped. They stood waiting, and there was a silence like a holding of breath in the laboratory.

The water in the pool stirred suddenly, lapping against the tiles. Far down, cloaked in the rippling refractions, a solid something moved, sending a stream of crystal bubbles up along the surge of the disturbed water.

Something that was swift and sure and graceful; something that gleamed with a golden sheen as the light struck it; something that was panther-lithe and supple, and had areas of shimmering iridescence at its extremeties. Jaffa's blunt fingers raked his white-streaked hair and did not feel it.

The head broke water.

A strange, unearthly face. Fine golden fur-covered features that were strong and clear and as streamlined as a space-cruiser. Eye and nostril were fitted with protective membranes, and there were no outward ears; but Jaffa, looking into fire-shot dark eyes, knew that this was a man, with no taint of the hybrid in his blood.

In one light surge the stranger gained the tiles beside the pool. The close golden fur that covered him shed the water in glistening streams down a smooth-muscled body, as human in shape as Jaffa's own, save that at wrist and ankle there were fanlike membranes. There was a strange, triumphant fire burning in the swimmer as he stood looking at Jaffa; and the Earthman realized abruptly that Lhara was trembling.

"You have done well, girl," murmured the golden Being, and Lhara's voice burst out of a tight throat.

"Give me my brother and let me go!"

The water-man might not have heard her. His dark gaze was fastened on Jaffa. "The gods are with me!" he said softly. "I shall succeed."

Jaffa's face was hard as carven stone. "I seem to be the sacrifice," he observed. "Is it permitted that I know for what?"

The golden swimmer swung about, reaching for a switch, "I'll show you, Earthman!" The light went out, leaving a suffocating blackness. After a moment a pale square of light gleamed; the strange voice, that had a liquid music in it, called them closer. "Look here, into this ultravisor. It will explain better than any words."

Jaffa looked, hearing the taut breathing of the Keshi girl beside him. Something, a spinning blur, took shape in the screen, resolved itself into a planet, revolving about a triple sun. The focus drew in, blotting out the suns; the curve of the globe flattened, became a concave bowl of water, stretching to the limits of the screen. Here and there tiny islands raised swampy heads, barely above the face of the warm, teeming sea; in the shallows around them were domes of gleaming glassite, housing cities.

Closer still; into the streets of the under-water cities, where there were great buildings fallen to ruin and disuse, all save the temples. No children played, and the homes were desolate. Only the temples had life — and the taverns. There were as many taverns as they were temples, and here the sunken pools were filled with stuff that was not water; those who wallowed in them were mere sodden, licentious hulks.

The cities faded to show writhing undersea forests, growing on oozy mud. Amongst the towering fronds of weeds and the amorphous bulks of giant sponges swam monstrous shadows, things with gills and dorsal fins that were yet not fish. They were to the beings in the cities as the apes are to man, and their faces were bestial beyond anything Jaffa had ever seen. They swam around the glassite domes, nuzzling the transparent surfaces, glaring hungrily at the men within; and here and there a shining dome was cracked before the strength of their numbers. The sea-things rode the spurting water through the rifts, and the men who had time to drown were the lucky ones.

Lhara gasped, and Jaffa sensed her averted head. Then, as the screen flickered out and the light came up again, the voice of the golden swimmer spoke, low and sombre.

"I, Rha, was the last child to be born on Vhila."

They stood waiting, the man and the woman. The alien one faced them, his muscles drawn taut.

"Vhila is a dying world. Once, as you saw, she was great. But we are an old people, and we have seen our doom approaching for centuries. The sea-dwellers out-breed us a thousand to one. One by one our cities fall, and my people have fallen too, under the load. You saw them; some wait for death in the temples, some in the *kulha*-tanks. But learning and work and hope are dead on Vhila.

"Can you understand that, Earthman? A world of living dead! No future, no life, just a dumb acceptance and an endless waiting. I revolted. I lived alone in the empty colleges, the laboratories, the museums; I learned all the ancient knowledge of my race. And I turned my eyes to your solar system, where I dreamed of a new life for what remains of my people. When I was ready, I took a spaceship from the museum, stocked it with the tools I would need, but no weapons, for we are a peaceful race."

"I landed first on the Venus. You call guess why, Earthman; we are amphibious, taking water through the skin. We cannot live in a dry world. But instead of the peaceful welcome I had expected, I was attacked and driven off. The people feared me. They would have killed me if they could. I knew then that my people could not come in peace. We are alien."

"I found this asteroid, and changed it to suit me. Then I studied your system more thoroughly, by means of the ultravisor, that I might find means to conquer it. I have no wish to kill, only to force recognition of my wishes and to gain the power to carry them out. I found that your civilization rests basically on the water trade that permits your far-flung colonies to live. Fitting, was it not? I could prey on this water trade, bring you to the brink of destruction, and then make my demands. Under the circumstances, there could be no refusal."

Again the fire-shot eyes rested on Jaffa. "The gods have been kind. So far I have succeeded."

Jaffa raised his head. "Where do I fit in?"

Rha smiled. "I need a hostage, to insure that my demands are believed, understood, and carried out promptly. You are the son of Johan Gray. The Chief of Special, I have learned, is really the most powerful man in the

System, for he sits at the secret head of all the activities of the planets. To him, through you, I shall make my demands."

Jaffa nodded, his eyes hooded behind dropped lids. "And if he refuses?"

Rha sighed and spread his hands.

For the first time Lhara spoke. Both men started. Her voice was sharp and fearless as a sword, and the paralysis-gun was steady in her hand.

"I've been a fool, Rha! I knew none of this; only that if I brought you this man, you would cure my brother and let him go. I thought you were only a clever bandit, and I was willing to barter with you for my brother's life. If I had known, I would have killed Lhar with my own hands before I would have obeyed you!"

She flung quick words over her shoulder at Jaffa. "I am sorry, Earthman, for what I did. Stand by me now!"

Rha did not flinch. "You cannot escape. The doors are closed, and my pilots, who are my slaves since I injected them with a special hormone, guard the hangar. Only I can take you out of here."

Wills met and locked. Then Lhara bowed before the truth. Rha took the gun from her unresisting hand.

"Now," he said. "We will go out again in my spaceship, away from here so that my position cannot be traced by the radio carrier-waves, and contact Johan Gray. You will not be stubborn, Jaffa, I am sure."

Jaffa's eyes were still hidden, and there was a ghost of a smile on his lips. He asked: "Why did you come back here at all? You were aboard the ship back on Mars."

"You guessed it, did you?" Rha nodded as he led the way out of the laboratory. "The Martian air is so dry I couldn't leave my cabin, and I was afraid if you knew, you'd try something. An unfortunate thing, that smash-up, especially the pilot's death. But I had to have you, Jaffa, and I had to have Lhara to get you.

"I came back here for two reasons. The water, air, and food were nearly exhausted; but particularly I wanted you to see my stronghold and my laboratory, so that you would know I made no idle boasts. Vhila has scientific secrets your people won't guess at for several centuries yet."

They made a silent trio on the trip back to the hangar. Rha picked up three armed pilots from the barrack room. He smiled at Lhara as he motioned her into his ship, saying: "I feel safer with you where I can watch you." Then the ship roared out through the space door. The bulkhead door was closed, and the pool in the control cabin was newly filled.

At a safe distance Rha brought the ship to a standstill. And as the throb of the motors died, Jaffa came to his feet. His chains clashed as he hurled himself in a desperate dive for the control panel. Before anyone could stop him, he had landed all his weight on a knife-switch set beside the controls, smashed it down to the end of its slot.

Down in the bowels of the ship there was a grating clash. The water in the pool began to bubble and hiss, and a whitish gas rolled sluggishly over the brink to spread across the floor. In the time it took Jaffa to regain his feet, it had covered the floor-plates and was lapping the ankles of the thunderstruck people who watched it.

"That gas," said Jaffa steadily, "is highly explosive. I should advise the men not to fire their heat-guns."

Rha snapped his orders. "Take him — but don't fire!"

The three pilots moved forward like plastic robots. Jaffa faced them; without shifting his eyes he called to Lhara, "Keep your head above the mist!" Rha stood quietly, waiting, but his eyes were on a switch above the one Jaffa had thrown, and he said "Hurry!" very quietly.

The white gas billowed sluggishly at their wrists.

The rest, afterwards, was a blur to Jaffa's memory. One man missed his footing on the narrow floor and vanished into the pool. The other two came on, holding their heat-guns clubbed. The Earthman caught a glimpse of Lhara, stalking like a panther behind Rha. Then he had grappled the two pilots and gone lurching down into the sea of mist.

The swirling opacity blinded him; he held his breath while he struggled, praying that his chest wouldn't burst until he had what he wanted. The pilots fought doggedly to hold him while they regained their feet. But Jaffa had the desperation of a man clutching his last chance; and he knew that above the rising flood of gas, Rha was reaching for the switch that would mean defeat.

His hand closed on a flailing heat-gun. His head was ringing, his lungs burned with the agony of suffocation. Dimly he knew that one man had fallen limply to the floor, unconscious. He wrenched desperately at the gun, knowing he couldn't last much longer. The distorted face close to his loosed a burst of breath that set the white gas swirling. Then the empty lungs sucked in; the hand went limp.

With the last of his strength Jaffa surged upward. The gas had risen; how high? Above his head, perhaps. Perhaps it had choked all air from the cabin, pouring up faster than the air conditioners could work. Perhaps Rha and Lhara were lying under it, dying of anoxia. And suddenly, through his pain and desperation, Jaffa knew something. The hard-held air in his lungs broke from him in a cry.

"Lhara!"

Like a swimmer, his head broke the surface. The gas lapped his chin, but there was air still. He gulped it in. Rha's head was rigid above the rising tide, and behind it, Lhara's, her hair fallen in a bright cloak that gleamed through the mist.

Jaffa raised his gun and fired.

In a crackling fury of sparks the flying controls fused to a blackened ruin. Jaffa lurched forward, dragged at the switch above the one he had pressed before. The handle scorched his palm, so near had the destructive blast come to it. A gurgling rush came from the pool, and the gas sucked downward in a sullen whirlpool. Jaffa leaned weakly against the bulkhead, and knew that he was laughing at the two thunderstruck faces.

"Dry ice!" he gasped. "I diverted carbon dioxide from the air purifiers and improvised a compression unit with one of the pressure tanks. Then I connected the compression tank release with a cut-in on the feed-pipe for this pool, the only one that can be emptied from the control panel. When I pulled that switch I dumped about ten pounds of dry ice into the water. That gas was the released carbon dioxide, perfectly harmless, except that it can suffocate."

Lhara released the arm she had been holding in a vise-grip behind Rha's back; the grip that had kept him from getting to that all-important switch and wrecking Jaffa's plans. Together they got the men up above the last of the gas that hovered above the empty pool. When they were breathing properly again, Jaffa turned to Rha.

"You realize your position. Very soon after I radio, Fleet ships will come to take us in tow. In the ordinary course of events, you will be destroyed as a danger to the welfare of the Solar System."

"But I don't think you are a menace, Rha. I think you're a very courageous man, and a great scientist; and on those grounds, I'll make a bargain with you. My father, as you said, has influence. I think, after I explain, that I can persuade him to arrange a colony for you, provided you give your word to live in peace. And that's what you really want, isn't it, Rha?"

"I ask only a useful life for my people." For a long, long moment Rha looked into the Earthman's eyes. Then he bowed his head, and his voice was deep as he answered:

"I accept your offer, Jaffa Gray."

Jaffa sighed relievedly and turned to the radio. Lhara sat on a couch beside it.

"You'll go back to Kesh now?" he asked abruptly.

"As soon as my brother is free." She faced him frankly. "I'm sorry for what I did, Jaffa. But since it's turned out this way. . . ."

"I think," said Jaffa, " If I were to come to Kesh, and you were to try very hard, I might forgive you."

Aleph Sub One

MARGARET ST. CLAIR

ABOUT MARGARET ST. CLAIR
AND
ALEPH SUB ONE

Aleph Sub One *was first published:*
Startling, *January 1948*

From the beginning, Margaret St. Clair was a purveyor of highly-polished, satirically barbed prose. Beginning her career at the height of the pulp era, she was, naturally, virtually without a market at first — finding welcome only in the pages of Startling. *Only with the advent of* F&SF *and* Galaxy, *which actively welcomed sophistication, wit and women, did St. Clair truly come into her own. Even then, as her work reached its highest levels of polish and literary attainment, she was constantly pushing the limits by appealing only to the most sophisticated readership. (Perhaps not so coincidentally, she achieved her greatest fame, and all her literary awards, in the mystery field.)*

Who was the first series heroine written by a woman to appear in a science fiction magazine? Answer: Oona, the delightful 1940s heroine St. Clair employed to poke fun at urban young sophisticates. Like many women writers, St. Clair evenhandedly exposes the foibles of both genders. Though "Aleph Sub One" is hardly characteristic of her later work, we felt she was best represented here by a story featuring this nearly forgotten, breakthrough character.

Aleph Sub One

by MARGARET ST. CLAIR

"YES, but I don't understand what you mean by 'to ten as a base,' " Oona said doubtfully.

Jick sighed.

"It's perfectly simple, honey," he said. "Ordinarily logarithms are made to the base ten. Of course, it's not the only base possible. Napierian logs are done to the base E, which is a transcendental. But you don't need to worry your little head about *that*. The thing for you to try to remember is that the log of ten is one."

"One?" Oona replied.

She didn't know — sometimes she almost wished Jick would stop trying to teach her about mathematics. It was sweet of him to share his interests with her — gee, lots of husbands never spoke to their wives except to complain about the cooking — and he never made fun of her or got impatient when she couldn't understand.

In junior college he'd taken a lot of math, and though he'd never done anything with it after he got out, she knew it meant a lot to him. He had a whole shelf of books about it.

Only — well, Jick was as sweet as sugar, but was he really such a good teacher? He'd spent the quieter moments of their honeymoon (they had taken an inexpensive skatosphere trip around the world) trying to teach her about calculus.

Oona didn't know much about math, but wasn't that sort of advanced — especially as she'd only had half a term each of algebra and geometry in high school. And he explained everything, he explained all about everything right from the start clear through to the end. He explained so much she got mixed up listening to him.

"Well, if the log of ten is one, what number is it that has a log of two?" Jick asked, leaning forward and looking at her questioningly.

"A — a hundred?" Oona answered uncertainly.

Jick beamed. "I knew you'd get it," he said. "You're a smart girl. It was just a question of explaining it enough. Well, if the log of one hundred is two, what number is it whose log is three?"

"I — unh — two hundred?"

Jick sighed. The disappointed expression she so much disliked seeing on his face appeared again.

"No, honey, a thousand," he said gently.

There was a pause. "You know, Oona," Jick said thoughtfully, pinching his lower lip, "Austin was telling me about something that might help you."

Oona stiffened. She didn't much care for Austin. He was a teaching fellow in the math department at City College, perfectly respectable and polite and well-mannered and all that, but she didn't like his influence on Jick.

Not that he led Jick into gambling or things like that — Oona might have been able to understand it better if he had. But every time Austin came to see them he arrived with a wild gleam in his eye and some sort of mathematical puzzle (Austin called them mathematical recreations) for Jick to work.

The last time he'd called he had kept Jick up two hours after midnight arguing with him over the solution, and Jick had had to go to work the next day with only four hours' sleep. She wished Austin would find some nice girl and get married and settle down.

"It's something the heads of the math and physics departments have been working on for the last seven years," Jick said. "Austin says it has the finest robot brain ever yet devised. At first it filled up the whole laboratory; now they've got it down to table size. It's called the Vizi-math."

"What does it do?" Oona asked. Usually she didn't talk much when Jick was explaining mathematics to her for fear she'd say something silly, but she could hardly go wrong with a question like that.

"As I understand it, they were trying to get a sort of super calculating machine, one that you could do cube root and the higher mathematical operations on easily. But what they finally came out with, Austin says, is the answer to the dumb student's prayer.

"You write any mathematical expression on a piece of paper, feed it into the machine — it has a scanner, of course and watch the vizi-plate. What you get is a translation into visual terms of the mathematical expression you were interested in. Austin says he'd always been a little shaky about vector analysis, and the Vizi-math cleared the subject up for him in a way he wouldn't have thought possible."

"I don't see how it works," Oona said. What was it Jick had just said — that the Vizi-math translated mathematics into visual terms? So you could see it? Well, how could you see something that didn't exist, like that square root — minus one, it was — Jick had told her about once?

Jick laughed. "Neither does anyone else, honey," he said. "Austin says that some of the stuff you get on the vizi-plate in higher math almost frightens him. Uncanny, sort of.

"Last week he tried an expression with a transcendental and he got a big black spot on the vizi-plate and a lot of stars. But you don't need to worry about that. What we want is something to clear up the few simple things that bother you."

"Well. . . ." Oona said.

Austin brought the Vizi-math over the next day at noon.

"I had a lot of trouble getting Dr. Preeble to let me have it," he said as he carried his burden pantingly into the kitchen. "You'll be careful with it, won't you, Mrs. Ritterbush?"

"Oh, sure."

Austin cleared a place for the Vizi-math by sweeping his arm — along the counter where the chronnox stood. A bottle of feijoa extract and two cans of spilal paste toppled and fell to the floor. Oona stooped to pick them up.

"I brought the Vizi-math in here," Austin explained, pulling the plugs of the chronnox out of the socket and inserting that of the Vizi-math, "because it has to go on an appliance circuit. It needs a lot of power. There. What do you think of it?"

Oona stepped back and looked at the thing. The machine was about three feet long, the shape of a rather plump cigar, and plated all over with some bright metal which had a faintly bluish cast. Oona didn't know why, but for some reason it reminded her of a coffin, a coffin for an abnormally small adult or a child.

She tried to think of something nice to say about it. "It certainly is scientific-looking," she brought out at last.

Austin nodded thoughtfully and rubbed his upper lip. "A great deal of research went into it," he observed. "Dr. Preeble was telling me this morning that he thinks it may mean the beginning of a new era in mathematics. Well. Would you like me to demonstrate it for you?"

"Um-hum."

"Mr. Ritterbush said you'd had trouble with the binomial expansion, eh?"

Oona nodded. She didn't remember it especially, but it was probably true. She had trouble with so many things.

On a piece of paper he got out of his pocket (Oona thought it looked like a laundry bill) Austin wrote:

$$(a+b)^2=a^2+2ab+b^2$$

He put the bit of paper into a small orifice on the front of the Vizi-math, pressed an inconspicuous button on the side, and said, "Now, watch."

A large section of the plating along the top of the Vizi-math became faintly luminous. The metal grew translucent, then transparent.

"The Vizi-plate's warming up," Austin said.

On the lighted surface two horizontal lines of unequal length appeared, one of them labeled *a*, the other *b*. They moved toward each other, joined. Three new lines, all labeled *a+b*, joined themselves at right angles to the original *a+b* to make a square, corresponding *a* and *b* portions opposite on opposite sides.

From the points *ab* on each of the sides new lines moved at right angles toward the center. The original $a+b$ square was now divided into a small square, labeled b^2, a large one denominated a^2, and two rectangles bearing the legend ab.

While Oona watched, the Vizi-math went on with the visualization. It printed a^2 across the surface of the vizi-plate (the a-square became outlined in bright blue light) $+^2ab$ (the two rectangles were vividly outlined in red) $+b^2$ (the small b-square stood out in yellow light.)

The four members of the $a+b$ square moved away from each other and came back together several times. The vizi-plate read $(a+b)^2=a^2+2ab+b^2$. The Vizi-math seemed to be determined that Oona got the idea.

She was watching almost open-mouthed. So *that* was what they meant when they talked about squaring a number. Not just multiplying it by itself, or whatever Jick had said, but turning it into an honest-togoodness square, something a person could look at and understand.

Mathematics, then, wasn't just a lot of numbers and letters and foolishness. It meant something, and a mathematical expression was like a sentence with something to say.

"What do you think of it, Mrs. Ritterbush?" Austin asked.

Oona looked at him. She had to draw a deep breath before she could speak.

"It's *elegant!*" she said warmly. "It's simply the most zestful thing I ever saw! I'm glad you brought it. Gee, I had no idea it would be like that!"

Austin looked pleased. "Of course, that was a very simple example," he said modestly. "Let's try it with the cube."

He got another dog-eared bit of paper out of his pocket, scribbled on it for a moment, and passed it in to the machine. There was a pause, and then the lines a and b appeared once more. This time the square grew into a highly three-dimensional cube, very solid and real-looking. It wasn't, Oona thought like the picture of a cube — there seemed to be a cube inside the machine.

The demonstration went on smoothly. When the Vizi-math had gone through its paces and the vizi-plate was opaque again, Oona, for the first time in her life, was clear about what $a^3+3a^2b+3ab^2+b^3$ meant.

"You get the general idea," Austin said at last. "When Mr. Ritterbush comes home tonight you can try anything else that bothers you."

Oona nodded radiantly. Her inability to follow Jick's patient explanations must have weighed on her mind more than she had realized. At any rate, now that she knew she *could* understand mathematical things after all, there was a sort of bubbling elation in her veins.

No more seeing Jick look so disappointed and hurt, no more listening to him talk, talk, talk, while she wondered what in the System he was talking about. From now on she'd take her troubles to the Vizi-math. For a moment she thought of giving Austin (though he had a face like a Venusian quohaug) a grateful, sisterly kiss, but decided against it. He wouldn't understand.

"Thanks a myriad," she said, "thanks ever so much."

After Austin had gone, she got a piece of paper, wrote on it, "What's a sine?" and turned it over to the Vizi-math.

She was a little doubtful whether the machine would work with that, because it wasn't really a mathematical expression at all, and it did seem that the Vizi-math sort of hesitated before it made-up its mind.

But the visualization, when it came, was up to the quality of the other two, and the idea, once she got it, was so simple that Oona wondered why it had eluded her for so long.

She looked at the chronologue on her wrist. Oh, gee! According to the dial, today was the fifth, and she had an appointment at the beauty shop at 14:20. She'd have to hurry in order to make it.

Being a verdette was an awful nuisance, Oona thought as she quickly sprayed and dried her face. Of course, the color was becoming to her, and it did look lovely when it was sprinkled lightly with dust of pearl. And all the fashion experts insisted that the "mermaid influence" was better than ever this season. But she was always having to have her hair bleached and regreened.

Sometimes she wished that women would go back to natural colored hair. But probably by now it would seem as old-fashioned and queer as it would if they stopped putting lacquer on their faces. No doubt by next year she'd be wearing her hair magenta or kingfisher blue.

She halted at the front door and looked at her chronologue again. Maybe it wouldn't matter if she was a little late for her appointment — she was a steady customer. And she did hate to go away without trying any more math on the machine in the kitchen. It was the most wonderful thing she'd ever seen in her life. She'd put one more expression in it, something with a lot of a's and n's and e's, and see what she got.

She fetched a notepad from the desk and began to write. Make it complicated, that was the idea. Jick had written so many equations for her when he was trying to teach her that she knew all kinds of things to put in the one she was making up, though she didn't know what most of them meant.

She wrote steadily for nearly five minutes, sprinkling her work liberally with dx's, nth powers and a good many e's, and then paused. It was all right so far, but she wanted a real clincher, something to make the Vizi-math hump itself. What would it be?

Oona went over to the shelf where Jick kept his math books and pulled one out. Yes, she had some of those wiggly things and one of those double o's that looked like eyes. There must be something else.

She turned the page. Up at the top there was a peculiar looking sign, sort of like an x, with a zero under it. Jick had told her once that it was the first letter of the Hebrew alphabet, and added that a man named Cantor had invented it. Its name was *zarf* or *alpha* or something. She'd put that in her question, only with a one instead of a zero under it.

Oona added the *aleph* with its subscript to her work, followed it with an equals sign, and paused for inspiration. Equals what? Well, n^2 ought to be about right.

It looked pretty good, she thought, reading it over. But wasn't n^2 for the answer a little too vague? *N* ought to be something more definite. Under her equation, in her round, childish penmanship, *N=five*.

She hurried into the kitchen — moondust! she was late and fed her slip of paper into the Vizi-math. Gradually the vizi-plate warmed up. It turned a light tan. Short lines appeared momentarily on the surface and then vanished. In the upper corner a whirl of reddish colors spun and disappeared.

Very briefly, so briefly that Oona couldn't be sure whether she had really seen it or not, a thing like a cube, like a bunch of cubes, a thing that made her eyes smart, appeared. Perhaps she'd imagined it. Then the vizi-plate lost its tan coloring and became its ordinary self. The visualization seemed to be at an end.

Oona clicked her tongue in vexation. Was that going to be all? Here she'd made herself late for her appointment and everything — she'd have to fly the family 'copter instead of taking the bus, she was so late — just so she could see a few lines and a thing a little like a cube that probably hadn't been there at all. A few more times like this, and she was going to lose her confidence in the Vizi-math.

It occurred to her as she set the 'copter down inexpertly on the roof of the beauty shop that what had happened wasn't entirely the mathematical machine's fault. She'd tried to make up an equation that would make it hump itself; she had simply succeeded too well. Her equation had stumped the Vizi-math. She'd made up something that couldn't be visualized.

Oona got through dreadfully late. The girl at the beauty shop had given her appointment to a Mrs. Nicker when Oona got there and Oona had had to wait until Mrs. Nicker was under the aridifier before she could get her own hair regreened. It was too bad. Jick would be home before her, and though she could get dinner in ten minutes, she knew how Jick disliked coming home to an empty house.

Oona piloted the 'copter to just over the hangarage, pressed the button that, by remote control, made the roof of the building below her open up, and looked into the periscope. O.K., but what was that blurry business off to the side of the house? Funny. She'd take a look when she got out.

Oona shut off the power receiver and stepped out of the 'copter. She opened the door in the side of the hangarage that led through into the house. The house wasn't there.

For a moment Oona couldn't take it in. She held on to the doorknob — her eyes wide open and her lips apart — and looked.

The house — their house, the house she and Jick had worked on so hard, the house they had just barely finished paying for — was gone. An unnatural reddish blur, a thing that rotated slowly and was shaped like the whirlpool you get when water runs out of the sink, seemed to have taken its place.

What had happened? Oona hadn't felt like this since the time they had called from the hospital to say that Jick had been hurt in an accident and when she'd asked how badly hurt the nurse had hesitated before she replied. What had happened, anyhow?

" 'Lo, baby," a voice behind her said.

Oona whirled around. It was Jick; everything ought to be all right, now that he was here. Gee, she was glad to see him. She threw her arms around his neck.

"I'm scared," she said, her emerald tresses against his cheek. "What is it, Jick? What do you s'pose it is?"

He shook his head.

"Honey, I'm a little scared myself." He was silent for an instant, while Oona tipped back her head and looked at him. He seemed to be struggling with an idea. ". . . Did Austin bring over the Vizi-math, kid?"

The Vizi-math! Could it be was it —? Oh, my gosh!

"Yes, he did," Oona replied.

"Hum. Unh — listen, Oona — unh — you didn't do anything to it, did you? Fool with the machinery or anything?"

Even through her makeup, Oona could feel herself turn red. It was unbecoming, but she didn't care. What kind of an idiot did he think she was? Fool with the machinery, for Pete's sake!

"I did not!" she said indignantly. "Austin brought it over and worked a couple of equations on it and then I asked it what a sine was. Then I put an equation in, but nothing much happened. Do you think it could be out of order, Jick? You said nobody knew how it worked."

"I don't think so — you say you put an equation in and nothing happened? You mean nothing at all?"

"Well, the vizi-plate got sort of tan and there were some lines on it and a sort of fancy thing like a cube that hurt my eyes. It just wasn't there at all, no time at all. It was an awfully looking thing."

"And that's all that happened. Um." Jick I rubbed his forehead. "What was the equation, dear?"

"Oh, it had all sorts of things in it. *X*'s and *d*'s and *e*'s and squiggly things. Oh, and I put a *zarf* in it with a number underneath."

"*Zarf?*"

"One of those signs you showed me once, like an *x*. Why ? Do you think my equation had something to do with it?"

Jick ignored her question.

"We'd better get the 'copter out of here," he said, "that red stuff seems to be expanding. And I'm going to call Austin. This looks like something in his line."

Austin arrived as Jick was gulping down the last of the sandwich Oona had persuaded him to eat. He brought a whole bunch of people from the university with him, and they started an immediate conference in front of the reddish thing which had engulfed Oona's house. They walked about and shook their heads and wrote things in notebooks while Oona, standing first on one foot and then the other, watched them miserably.

Finally Mrs. McClure, who lived on down the street (a wonderful housekeeper — there wasn't a place in her house where you could relax), had taken pity on her and asked her to come in and try to rest. Oona had gone dutifully to bed, as Mrs. McClure suggested but she couldn't get to sleep. She looked at her chronologue. It was nearly twenty-four.

Jick and Austin and the people from the university were carrying on their conference in Mrs. McClure's living room. A representative from the fire department and another from the city police were with them.

Through the closed louvers of Mrs. McClure's guest couchchamber Oona could see the reddish glow of the Vortex (that was what the people from the university were calling it).

The end of the street where Oona's house was — *had* been — was full of policemen, reporters, stereo-casters, and spectators. No wonder she couldn't get to sleep.

Dr. Preeble and Dr. Garth (the heads of the math and physics departments) had asked her over and over what had been in the equation she had put in the Vizi-math. She'd told them as well as she could remember, and they'd sighed and gone back to their eternal conference.

Oona put her arms under her head and stared up into the dark, trying to think. Was it her fault? She didn't honestly think it was. Jick and Austin — especially Austin — should have known better than to let her have the Vizi-math.

As she understood it, from what the scientists were saying, it was by the merest fluke that she'd made up an equation which had driven the Vizi-math, in its frantic attempt to visualize it, to creating a sort of superdimensional whorl. Dr. Preeble had said that that odd-looking cube affair she'd seen had been an instaneous tesseract. If that meant anything.

Yes, Austin was to blame. Still, Oona couldn't help feeling responsible. If only she hadn't put that aleph with the one under it in! She felt sure that it was the cause of all the trouble. And what was going to happen? Would the Vortex grow and grow until — well, until it swallowed up the world?

A little after two Jick came softly in the room. "Sorry to disturb you, sweetheart," he said, "but Preeble thinks we'd better evacuate this house. The Vortex has already expanded twice, and though they can't work out a formula for its expansion, it looks as if it might be logarithmic. Based on e."

Soggily, Oona began to put on her clothes.

"Have they found out any way to stop it yet?" she asked as she stepped into her brogans.

"Well, not just yet, but they're bound to, pretty soon. Any time now, Oona, any time."

Any time now, Oona thought sardonically late the next afternoon as she sat against the wall of the living room of the house (it belonged to a couple named Roux) Jick and the others were currently using as headquarters. Sure, any time now. Whenever they got around to it. Meantime, the Vortex had swallowed up an area six city blocks square and was expanding at unpredictable but frequent intervals.

Oh, they were doing all they could. They'd sprayed the Vortex with firehoses, sent volunteers (who hadn't been seen afterwards) into it, and tried to blow it up with dynamite. They had even got permission from the Security Council and dropped a small, carefully-shielded, atomic bomb. The Vortex had paid no attention of any kind to these attacks. It rotated slowly and kept on looking like the water running out of a sink.

The state police were there and so was an infantry company from the Fort. Jick had told her as he rushed by that the U.N. was sending a task force. It didn't make any difference: Oona hadn't a gram of confidence in any of them. If it was left up to them, the Vortex would swallow up the whole darned universe. They were dopes.

She walked over to the window and looked out. The glow from the Vortex had tinged the whole sky a sickly pink. She'd heard Dr. Grath say that by tomorrow the entire city would have been taken over by it. Meantime there they sat, talking their fool heads off.

Well. What was it her Aunt Nellie used to say? "For every evil under the sun, there is a remedy —" (the rhyme went on, "or there is none," but Oona wasn't going to think about that part of it.). What was the remedy for this evil.

Her equation, particularly that *aleph* with the one under it was the cause of everything, Oona felt sure. If there was only some way of canceling it out, of neutralizing it, of making it opposite to itself!

Oona halted in her thoughts, struck by a sudden idea. Here she'd been concentrating all the time on the *e*'s and *dx*'s, the *aleph* and infinity signs and so on in the *front* part of her equation, when after all the n^2 on the other side of the *equals* sign was every bit as important, maybe more so. What was it she had told the Vizi-math? — that *n* equalled *five*? Um. Well, what was the opposite of five?

This part was easy: Oona was sure what the answer was. Zero is the opposite of any number. Zero, then, is the opposite of five.

She opened her handcase and fished a notepad and stylo out of it. Using the handcase for a desk, she wrote:

I made a mistake. I'm sorry. *N* doesn't equal five. Zero (o) is what *n* is equal to.

Oona.

She looked over her production with a critical frown. She'd taken great pains to write clearly, so the Vizi-math couldn't possibly go wrong. But wasn't the signature a little informal for a note like this one?

She wrote "Ritterbush" after the "Oona" and, frowning still more, followed her last name with "Mrs." in parentheses.

There. Now all she had to do was to get the note into the Vortex.

It might not be so, easy. She was well within the evacuated area, and the bulk of the soldiers and policemen were stationed outside, to keep people from busting in to see what was going on.

Inside that area guards had been posted all around the Vortex about fifty feet apart. And if any of them suspected what she was trying to do, they'd stop her, of course.

She walked down the steps of the Roux house and sauntered toward the Vortex and the guards. One of them was rather nice, and he'd probably let her get up close.

How was she going to get her note in though? She thought for a moment of rolling it up around one of her earrings and tossing it in, but that wouldn't do; the Vizi-math might not be able to read it.

There was the same objection to folding the note into a dart, the way they had done it in school, and sailing it at the Vortex. What she needed was a long thin stick.

Wait a minute. Wasn't there a folding meterstick in her handcase? She'd bought it on Tuesday so she could get the hem straight on that frock she was making, and had forgotten to take it out of the case. What luck! Of course, it might ruin the meterstick, but this was no time to be economical.

"Howdy, Mrs. Ritterbush," the guard greeted her. "Come to look at our phenomenon? It's worth looking at."

"It certainly is," Oona agreed. Privately, she didn't think it was. She'd heard a stereo-caster referring to the Vortex as, "The red doom that rides across the western sky," but to her it just looked like a big red thing the shape of the water running out of the kitchen sink.

"Don't get too close. Say, do you know anything new from headquarters?"

Oona had managed to open the meterstick behind her back. Now, in a series of contortions she hoped the guard wasn't noticing, she attached the note with a paper clip.

"They say the U.N. is sending specialists who are sure to stop it," she replied. "Look! Isn't that them coming now?" She pointed.

As the guard turned to see what she was pointing at, Oona hurled the meterstick, javelin-style, straight at the Vortex's edge.

As it met the line of red, there was an enormous, soundless flash. Oona later described it by saying that it was like seeing a noise or hearing a light. For a moment the universe seemed to wobble on the edge of an abyss. Then it appeared to shrug its shoulders and decide to settle down.

Later, after the commotion and the fuss had pretty much died away, after the photographers had taken dozens of pictures and the stereo-casters had interviewed everybody, Oona went out in the kitchen to have another look at the Vizi-math.

She'd already been through the house and seen that everything was all right. Everything in the area the Vortex had covered *was* all right. The volunteers who had vanished in it turned up with no recollection whatever of the passage of time since they had walked into it, and Oona had found her meterstick.

But she wanted to take another look at the thing that had caused so much trouble before Austin came to take it away.

For a long moment Oona stared at the Vizi-math. Really, it was a sort of disappointing looking thing. Wait, though. Wasn't there something on the floor in front of it?

Oona stooped over and scooped up the object on a piece of paper. She didn't much want to touch it, since it probably had come out of the Vizi-math.

What was it? She prodded it gingerly with the edge of one fingernail. It seemed like a lattice-work of cubes set at right angles to each other, and it was still faintly warm. Oona thought it looked like an attempt to make an ordinary model, in ordinary space, of that very extraordinary thing she had seen for an instant in the vizi-plate. A tesseract — wasn't that what Dr. Preeble had said?

It was perfectly plain what had happened. After she had thrown her note into the Vizi-math, it had gone to work visualizing the amended equation and had ended up with a model of a tesseract.

What should she do with it? After a moment Oona carried the tesseract, still on the piece of paper, to the bedroom. She got up on a chair in her closet and dropped the tesseract, paper and all, in a hatbox.

For the first week or ten days after she put it away, Oona thought about the tesseract all the time. It worried her; she supposed it was all right, but it *had* come out of the Vizi-math. But after a month or so had gone by, she thought about it less and less frequently. Jick had given up teaching her math and was trying to acquaint her with the rules of three-board chess.

Six months later she'd nearly forgotten it, and when she had a grand cleaning-out of the closet two years or so afterwards, she had to sit down and look at the tesseract before she could remember what it was.

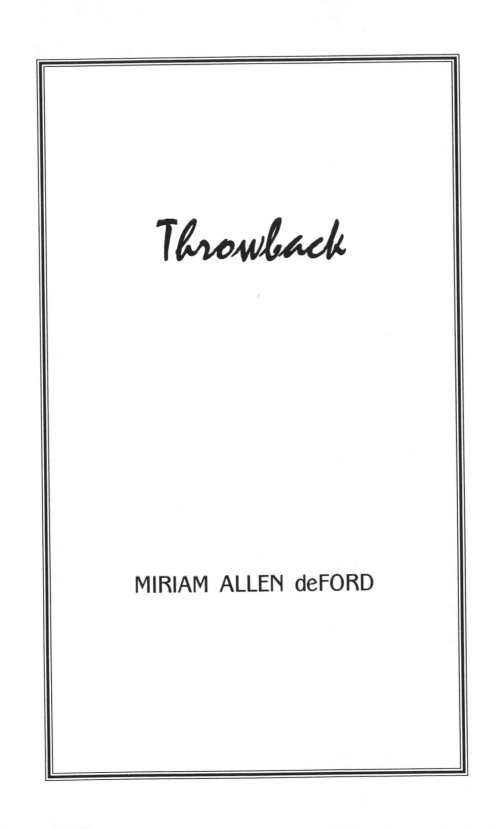

Throwback

MIRIAM ALLEN deFORD

ABOUT MIRIAM ALLEN deFORD
AND
THROWBACK

Throwback *was first published:*
Startling Stories, *October 1952*

Although undeservedly obscure today, Miriam Allen deFord was one of the leading women stylists of science fiction in the 1940s and 1950s. Unfortunately literary polish and incisive characterization were rarely high priorities with the science fiction readers of her era and Ms. deFord's work, although highly acclaimed by her fellow writers, was generally ignored by the genre's fans.

As a result Ms. deFord received a much more enthusiastic welcome in the mystery field, which honored her with no less than two Edgars, causing her to focus most of her efforts on that field during the last several decades of her life. A former feature writer for the Boston Post, *the best of her science fiction has been collected in* Exneogenesis and Elsewhere, Elsewhen, and Elsehow. *The* Science Fiction Encyclopedia *writes: "Her examination of themes such as nuclear devastation and sexual roles is conducted in a crisp, clear cut style."*

Of herself Ms. deFord has written "I am active as a feminist and a secularist. My work is included in at least one hundred anthologies and countless magazines (Harper's, F&SF, Ellery Queen's etc.)." She attributed her involvement with science fiction to the fact that "My husband was a writer and lecturer in science, and I have always read much in the field especially in biology and psychology." These last two undoubtedly account for her long involvement with Galaxy *and the* Magazine of Fantasy and Science Fiction *with their strong emphasis on these elements of science fiction.*

"Throwback" is an archtypal example of a theme tackled frequently by women science fiction writers of her era. deFord's revolution is equally typical and echoes statements made by Marion Zimmer Bradley and others in the letter columns and stories of the era (a position which now undoubtedly causes Bradley and many others to blush — and which shows that what (people) consider an eternal variety in one era they may see as an absurdity in another).

Throwback

by MIRIAM ALLEN deFORD

"STOP being so jittery," Kathrin admonished herself sternly. "The only way you're going to see this thing through is by keeping your head."

Nevertheless, her hands shook a little as she parked by one of the rows of meters on the roof, and her knees trembled as she stepped out of the copter.

If she had only let Jon into this first it wouldn't have been so bad. Together, somehow, they might have worked it out. She hadn't been sure enough of him: that was the inescapable fact. And now she had involved and imperiled him as well as herself. It was up to her. It had been so overwhelming an impulse that it had swept her away. She didn't see the glimmering of a solution, but one would have to be found, and quickly; and she was the one who was going to have to find it.

As she dropped down the shaft Kathrin tried to remember if she had ever known an unregistered child. There was Bill North — people used to say he must have been unregistered; but that was probably just slander, because he was so odd. Come to think of it, his forehead was unmarked, and once she had seen him vote, so it was just libel and he must have been a full citizen. The colonies, of course had plenty of them — they didn't need an optimum population law yet, and everybody there was as good as everybody else. They said the mayor of Venusberg was an unregistered.

Kathrin shivered. She didn't want to leave the earth forever, to be a permanent exile — though she would, if she had to. All her friends, her associations, were here on earth; in all her twenty-six years she had made only two vacation tours to the Moon and one to Mars, and she hadn't the least desire to become a permanent resident of either of them. Where, in the provincial life of the colonies, would there be a market for Kathrin Clayborn's sophisticated plasto-ceramics, which were earning banked credits and a solid reputation for her here?

And Jon. The colonies wanted hydroponic farmers and sub-atomic engineers and prefabrication builders; they had no need for a specialist in fourteen-tone music. But if Jon wouldn't go, there was no reason to live at all.

The carrier stopped at the 141st floor and Kathrin opened the door to the lobby of the suite of offices. Baby-faced Lane sat facing her at the visiboard.

She smiled good morning. Lane was one of the fancier touches of Amalgamated Art Enterprises; an ordinary business office would have had a robot visicom operator.

"CCD's been calling you, Clayborn," Lane said brightly.

"Put them on for me."

This was it: she would have to think fast. She entered the studio that was more like a laboratory — fitted in light blue and silver, she always noted amusedly, because Amalgamated Art Enterprises never missed a bet and Kathrin Clayborn was a silver blonde — and almost immediately the visiscreen flashed.

"This is Central Contraception Department, Clayborn," said the robot voice. "Our records show that you missed your contraceptone injection which was due on February 28th."

Good old government procrastination! It was now April 28th by the new thirteen-month-plus-Year-Day calendar. Kathrin had been banking on that.

Alternative excuses flashed through her mind with the speed of neutrons. "I should have notified you," she apologized smoothly. "I'm applying to the Selection Board."

"You are not supposed to do that without giving us six months' notice," said the robot voice severely. "The matter will be investigated and we shall report back."

Now she *really* had to work fast. "Get me the Selection Board," she told Lane.

As she asked to have the application forms sent to her, she was calculating swiftly. They would have to be returned before CCD got around to verifying. But the Board would take at least three months, she was sure, before making its examination. Then she would be in trouble for fair. But at least she would have a breathing-space in which to plan what to do next.

Kathrin started work on the day's orders, but it was hard to keep her thoughts away from her problem. It was futile now to wish that she could have been telling the truth to CCD. Never in her life had she thought of applying to the Selection Board in all sincerity. She didn't want motherhood as a career, to spend all her fertile years incubating and bearing children at ordered, stated intervals. And she didn't want babies by artificial insemination, either, carefully chosen in somebody's laboratory and to guaranteed to be the best eugenic combination. She wanted Jon's baby.

That was how it had started. Like everybody else, Kathrin had had plenty of temporary affairs. But this was permanent, the real thing, what they used to call marriage, a thousand years ago; Jon and she both felt that. The yearning, the excitement, perhaps even the vast tenderness, they could get and had got, both of them, from others; but not this feeling of belonging, of being necessary to each other, of being safe together against the world.

But now they weren't safe, and it was she herself who had jeopardized their safety. Musing, as her hands deftly shaped a plastic abstract, Kathrin reflected that she must be feeling as it had been normal for a woman to feel in — oh, say, the twentieth century. She wanted the old primitive unit, man and woman and child. And not a child to be taken away as soon as the pediatricians and psychologists ruled it ready for mass rearing, but a child to be reared with its parents, knowing them, loving them and being loved by them. In other words, what they used to call a family.

Kathrin blushed as if she had said an obscene word aloud, but she might as well be honest with herself. By some quirk of heredity, she was a throwback, an atavistic reversion, a freak.

And yet, In spite of everything — in the face of loss of citizenship, imprisonment, death itself — she had obeyed that atavistic impulse. And now she faced the probability of losing the child even if she alone contrived to bear it. Even worse, she might lose Jon as well.

As if she had called to him, the door opened and Jon stood there.

"Jon! What in the galaxy are you doing here?" Instinctively she darted a glance at the door, at the visiscreen.

He laughed and stretched out his arms.

"My shy girl! I have permission to you, my love. I'm running over to Capetown this afternoon, and I find I'll have to stay and look over Bloemer's stuff, so I can't get back till tomorrow."

As always, Kathrin felt a brief twinge of envy of Jon's mobility. In a sense he was a World Government employee, commissioned to find and evaluate the latest compositions in fourteen-tone scale music, and was meant to hop to Australia or Greenland. Kathrin, tied all her working life to office hours, and knowing few persons except Jon who weren't, often wondered what it would be like to be free to go here and there at will. Instead, she might find out soon what it would be like to be confined in a rehabilitation camp!

"Why didn't you just visicom to tell me you'd be gone for the night?"

"Because I couldn't kiss you good-by by visicom. Like this." He demonstrated thoroughly. "Great Sun, Kathrin, don't be such a roboty little mouse! Anybody'd think you'd broken a law, the way you tremble at every tiny breach of government regulations."

"Jon —" she said suddenly. If he only knew. No, this wasn't the time or the place. She would have a night alone now, to think how she could tell him.

"What?"

"Nothing, darling. Did you check to see if your overnight things were in the plane?"

"I did. Good-by, dearest. I'll be there when you get home tomorrow."

"Good-by, Jon. I hope you find Bloemer's wonderful."

He wave and was gone. Kathrin was with her problem again.

What did one do when one had a problem too hard for one's own solution? Go to the Counselor, of course.

But would the Counselor help when a question of — almost of treason was involved? What was even more important, was the Counselor really safe? There was supposed to be only one copy made of the microfilm record, which the consultant took away with him. But suppose, unknown to ordinary citizens, a secret duplicate was made which went to the consultant's dossier in World Government files?

Kathrin had been to the Counselor twice before, once to have her talent evaluated, to see if it was worth while for her to take the intensive art training, once at the time she had first met Jon, when she had had a tempting offer of a position in Turkey to balance against the growing realization that Jon, whose work was based in America, was going to be one of the most important factors of her existence. Both times she had received sound advice and was glad to have followed it, and neither time had she heard any echo from the consultation. But this would be different.

Back in the suburban apartment, a hundred miles from the city, Kathrin set herself to serious meditation. For the first time in her life she really thought about unregistered children.

They were something people didn't talk about; something the poor creatures themselves couldn't hide, and that decent people pretended to ignore. How did they happen? Contraceptone never failed; either the mother must have let her injection date go by through pure stupid carelessness, or she had deliberately skipped it as Kathrin had done herself. But that meant that other women must be throwbacks too. She had a sudden vision of a vast, secret society of women whose atavistic emotions had impelled them into this dangerous adventure.

What about the fathers of the unregistered, she wondered. Men, of course, did not have to undergo contraceptone injections; any man might be chosen at any time by the Selection Board, and she had never heard of one who had refused his common civic duty. But had some of the fathers of unregistered children known and approved beforehand, hoping too for the impossible were there male throwbacks as well as female? Or if they hadn't known, what a shock and grief when they learned about it, if they loved the women concerned. For inevitably as soon as the fact became unhidable, the woman was taken into custody, and as soon as the baby was old enough to be taken away from her and reared in a Pediatricum — with that dreadful red circle tattooed on its forehead, to make it recognizable for life — the mother was either sent to a rehabilitation camp or euthanized. The government could take no chances on upsetting the balance of nature by an epidemic of unregistered births.

Suddenly Kathrin remembered a tragedy of several years before — a couple she had known slightly, who were found dead in their apartment. The man had ray-gunned the woman and then himself, and nobody ever discovered why. Was that the reason? Had the woman confessed, and had this been his heartbroken way out? Kathrin thought of Jon, and shivered. What a fool she had been; what an impulsive fool. But she realized why she had not tried first to secure Jon's co-operation. The impulse had been too overwhelming. She could not risk his probable recoil and refusal.

Now it was too late.

No sleep-inducer vibrations did any good to Kathrin that night. But desperation brings its own calm.

Her voice was quite steady the next morning as she asked the Counseling Office for a special appointment. Fifty credit-units extra for not waiting her turn, but what did that matter?

The robot clerk in the waiting room checked her number, then let her into the little room where the towering Counselor took up all of one wall. She shut the inward-locking door, peered through the one-way glass to watch the robot go back to its desk, and lay down on the long couch.

The Counselor lighted up immediately. The mechanical voice repeated her number, indicating that her dossier was before it for reference, and recited the opening formula: "This is a confidential consultation lasting one hour. What is our problem?" The microfilm began to pour out from the slot into the plastic container in which she would carry it away afterwards.

It was hard to begin. For a moment Kathrin had the embarrassing feeling that the Counselor was a human being, like the human psychoanalysts in ancient times she had read about. The voice had to reiterate: "What is your problem, please?"

Again, she felt with a sinking heart, she had been too precipitate. Most certainly she should have waited for Jon to come home; she should have told him everything, have made sure of his co-operation, before she made an appointment with the Counselor. But last night it had seemed such a wonderful inspiration. Now she must go on with it.

"As my dossier shows, Counselor," she began hesitantly, "I am by profession a maker of plasto-ceramics. Most of these have been designed for use as interior decoration or as house furnishings. But I have also made some advances in the use of plasto-ceramics as pure sculpture. I have twice won the World Prize for rhythmic three-dimensional art."

"All this is on record," said the Counselor, in what would have been an impatient tone if a machine could display emotion.

"Just so. My dossier also shows that for two years now I have been in unit-relation with Jon Grover, who is conceded to be the foremost authority on fourteen-tone scale music. Naturally we have talked much together about our separate arts."

"And now —" Kathrin took a deep breath and prepared for the plunge — "we are on the verge of something altogether new in cultural history — a synthesis of the two aspects of rhythmic force."

"The Counselor is not competent to give technical advice."

"That is not my — not our problem. It is that such a project requires much time and complete attention. It has become apparent that we shall not be able to bring it to fruition while both of us are actively engaged in our usual work."

"How much time would be required?"

"That is difficult to say. No one could even promise success in such an experiment; we might find in the end that it could not be accomplished at all. All I can say is that we feel we are on the right track, and that if we could have — oh, say a year, under suitable conditions and with the opportunity to devote ourselves exclusively to the task, without demands or interruptions of any sort, we should at least be able to demonstrate whether or not such a synthesis could be brought about."

"One can see the magnitude of such a discovery. It would be as important as was the color-touch synthesis of Stjern and Harasuki. You would both be willing to undergo a year of unmitigated isolation and distasteful privacy to conduct your experiment?"

Kathrin's heart beat fast. She stifled the joyful relief that rose in her. Throwback she might be, but she had been reared in this era; she knew very well its compulsive gregariousness, its horror of being alone even in couples.

"If that were the only condition," she said carefully, "our devotion to the progress of civilization is great enough to make us willing to endure even that."

"It might be possible," the Counselor said, "for you both to secure a year's leave of absence and for arrangements to be made for you to spend it in Patagonia."

"We would have to live in reasonable comfort, with facilities for our work," Kathrin interposed quickly.

"Your knowledge of geography is deficient," retorted the Counselor. "Patagonia, it is true, has been for some four hundred years preserved as an example of natural uninhabited terrain. But its climate has been adjusted to human requirements, and buildings have been erected for the use of visiting scientists from earth and the other planets. There is even a resident curator, who is a Martian, naturally, since Martians do not mind loneliness as human beings do. You could have one of those buildings, fully equipped for human habitation; your food and the materials and supplies you might need could be teleported to you on order; and of course you would be in visicom communication with all World Government areas."

"If you and Grover are willing to undertake this onerous task, and believe you could bear such isolation without physical or mental breakdown, application to the World Arts Department would probably be granted. The Counselor would add its own recommendation."

"But be very sure, before you apply, first that there is at least a good chance of your succeeding in this project, and secondly that you feel confident of your ability to endure the strain. Remember, not even the Martian curator nor the occasional visitors would be permitted to associate with you, and your visicom would be strictly censored so that you could use it only for utilitarian purposes, not for social communication."

"I understand."

"Make your application, then. The reputation you both possess in your respective fields of art will eliminate the need of any extensive inquiry or examination."

"There is one difficulty —"

"Oh, yes," replied the Counselor smoothly. "You mean your recent application to the Selection Board. It is the latest item in your dossier. Why did you do that?"

"It is hard to explain, I know. It was the outcome of discouragement. Discouragement with the prospects of being able to devote myself to this synthesis experiment, I mean," she added hastily. "Naturally I realize that to be chosen by the Selection Board is the highest social honor that could be given any citizen. So I thought, if I couldn't serve the World Government by advancing cultural progress, perhaps it would let me serve it by producing worthy offspring."

"And then you changed your mind? That does not augur very well for your psychological stability."

"I did not change my mind. Actually, as you will notice, I have not even really applied to the Board. All I have done is to ask them to send me the blanks. That does not commit me unless I send them in. What I wanted was to be provided with an alternative, if you could give me no hope of an opportunity to accomplish this other project."

"Citizen, you are a little too free with your individualistic schemes and actions. The government is willing to make allowances for the aberrancies of people with artistic talents, but you are in danger of carrying it too far. However, in view of the real importance of the project you have in mind, the government will probably let this too be adjusted. Your application to the Selection Board might be withdrawn without prejudice."

"But in your dossier there appears another serious discrepancy. You are two months overdue for your contraceptone injection."

"Yes, I — I let it go when I first thought of applying to the Board."

"Now that, citizen, is what is meant by carrying your individualistic tendencies too far. You must know the danger you have run by failing to keep your injections up to date. Suppose in consequence you had become pregnant? Then, no matter what your potential value to the community, it would have been necessary to treat you like any other lawbreaking woman who conceives an unregistered child.

"In fact, irrespective of this other matter of the synthesis experiment, it is imperative that some penalty be inflicted on you for this criminal carelessness.

"The Counselor will strongly recommend that you and Grover be given a year's leave in Patagonia, with full pay and maintenance, to make your experiment. But it will also recommend that, as a penalty for your disobedience to a fundamental law, you be debarred from the protection of contraceptone until after your return to civilization. You need a lesson in self-control, citizen. You will either exercise it during your leave, or you will take your chances on having an unregistered child, with all that that implies. And since, if that should happen, it would also obviously implicate your companion, he would incur the same consequences."

"Do you still wish to go ahead?"

"I still wish to go ahead," Kathrin said quietly.

She glanced at the ceiling, on which, as on every ceiling on earth, moving hands on a lighted dial told the time. Her hour was up.

"Your consultation with the Counselor is at an end," the voice intoned as the lights flicked off. Kathrin rose from the couch, picked up the microfilm container, and opened the door. The robot clerk checked her number as she passed its desk.

Katherin Clayborn and Jon Grover sat hand in had at the view window of their twentieth-story suburban apartment, watching the peaceful countryside, with the moon making silver lace of the shadows of leaves on the river bank below them. Behind them, in the rosy glow to which they had switched the wall-tubes, music like a muted echo played a soft uninterrupting accompaniment to their voices. Kathrin had set the stage with infinite care. This was the final, crucial moment.

"Jon."

"Yes, darling?"

"You love me very much, don't you?"

"More than I have ever loved anyone in my life."

"I have something to tell you. I have done something — perhaps you'll think it was dreadful. You may never forgive me."

He kissed her and laughed.

Then she told him.

There was a long silence. Kathrin sat stiffly, trying to master the trembling that had seized her whole body.

Through the long day many versions of Jon's possible response had passed before her mind. Sometimes, in moments of optimism, he cried: "You too? I never dared to hope! Now we'll fight it out together, we two — we three —!"

But in the version that came most often, a voice she did not recognize said bitterly: "You must be out of your mind. Had you no concern for your own work, or for mine? You have ruined them both, and us with them. This is 2952, not 1952. I fell in love with a thirtieth-century woman, not with a freakish reversion to the days of our primitive barbarian ancestors!"

Never, in her most fantastic guesses, had she been prepared for what he really did say.

"I know already, dearest. I know about it. I've just been waiting for you to tell me yourself."

"You know? How could you?"

But of course. How had she been stupid enough to trust them, to believe that anything touching even the fringes of government could be really secret or confidential? Everything that had happened, everything she had said and done, had been taken down and put on file; and after her interview with the Counselor they had communicated with Jon immediately before she could see him, wherever he had been, in South Africa or on his way home.

She turned to him uncertainly.

"Then what —"

He took her in his arms.

"It's all right, darling," he soothed her, his voice tender. "It was touch and go for awhile; they gave me a real scare. They insisted you must be insane. You know what that would have meant." He shuddered. "But I used every bit of influence I have. I got some pretty important psychologists on the job right away, and we convinced the authorities it was only a temporary collapse from overwork and overstrain, such as might affect any highstrung artist. It helped a bit that this plasto-music synthesis you dreamed up really is quite logical — though at present it is also quite impossible."

"You're going to be perfectly safe; I have their absolute guarantee. Just a short stay in a mental hospital, and it will all be as if nothing had ever happened."

"But Jon —" Kathrin could scarcely find her voice. "You don't understand. I'm pregnant now — I told you that! They couldn't have known that."

"They guessed it, my dear," he said dryly. "But don't worry. That can be taken care of very easily; we're in plenty of time."

She looked at him, incredulous horror in her eyes.

"Jon — Jon — no! Our child!"

"Don't you understand, darling? You needn't *have* the child. You *never* need have one."

She tried once more desperately.

"But I want it, Jon. That was my whole idea in getting the Counselor to back my plan — so that we could go to Patagonia together and then maybe escape on a space ship somehow and be together always — all three of us."

"Now, now, Katherin! Don't you realize, dear, that this is all part of your mental upset? Just stop worrying and leave things to me. I've taken care of everything. It will be all right."

He held her to him, gently and firmly, and signaled with his head. His face twisted with loving concern, he handed her over — dazed, no longer protesting — to the two men in white uniforms who had been waiting in concealment.

Part Three

The 50s

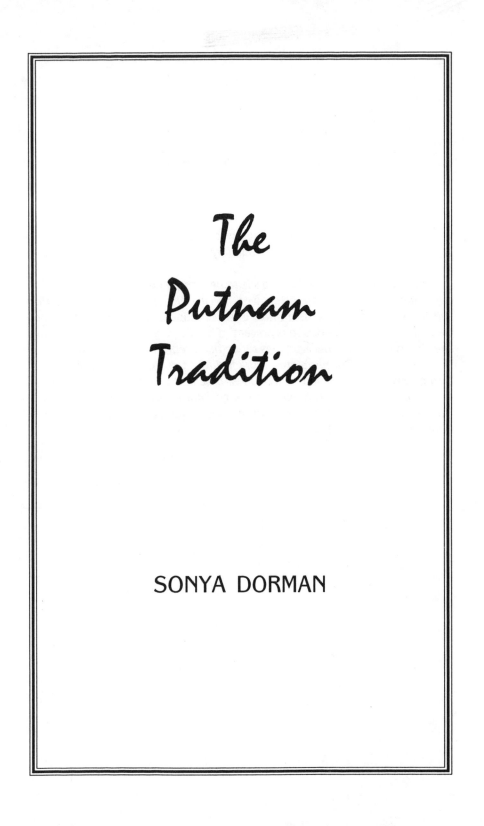

The
Putnam
Tradition

SONYA DORMAN

ABOUT SONYA DORMAN
AND
THE PUTNAM TRADITION

The Putnam Tradition *was first published:*
Amazing, *January 1963*

Sonya Dorman is one of America's leading women poets. She is also one of our leading women science fiction writers. Only the small number of stories she has published in the field (most of which appeared in a brief flourish of creativity in the late 1960s) has prevented her from achieving the reputation she deserves. In fact, her work has rarely been reprinted or anthologized.

The best of Ms. Dorman's other work includes the stories "Blind Bird, Blind Bird go away from me" and "The Deepest Blue in the World." John Clute calls her work "Intensely written sometimes highly metaphorical." This is especially true of "The Putnam Tradition," her first published story, which tells of the unusual women of a staid New England family.

The Putnam Tradition

by S. DORMAN

IT WAS an old house not far from the coast, and had descended generation by generation to the women of the Putnam family. Progress literally went by it: a new four-lane highway had been built two hundred yards from the ancient lilacs at the doorstep. Long before that, in the time of Cecily Putnam's husband, power lines had been run in, and now on cold nights the telephone wires sounded like a concert of cellos, while inside with a sound like the breaking of beetles, the grandmother Cecily moved through the walls in the grooves of tradition.

Simone Putnam, her granddaughter; Nina Putnam, her great-granddaughter; the unbroken succession of matriarchs continued, but times the old woman thought that in Simone it was weakened, and she looked at the four year old Nina askance, waiting, waiting, for some good sign.

Sometimes one of the Putnam women had given birth to a son, who grew sickly and died, or less often, grew healthy and fled. The husbands were usually strangers to the land, the house, and the women, and spent a lifetime with the long-lived Putnam wives, and died, leaving their strange signs: telephone wires, electric lights, water pumps, brass plumbing.

Sam Harris came and married Simone, bringing with him an invasion of washer, drier, toaster, mixer, coffeemaster, until the current poured through the walls of the house with more vigor than the blood in the old woman's veins.

"You don't approve of him," Simone said to her grandmother.

"It's his trade," Cecily Putnam answered. "Our men have been carpenters, or farmers, or even schoolmasters. But an engineer. Phui!"

Simone was washing the dishes, gazing out across the windowsill where two pink and white Murex shells stood, to the tidy garden beyond where Nina was engaged in her private games.

She dried the dishes by passing her hand once above each plate or glass, bringing it to a dry sparkle. It saved wear on the dishtowels, and it amused her.

"Sam's not home very much," she said in a placating voice. She herself had grown terrified, since her marriage, that she wouldn't be able to bear the weight of her past. She felt its power on her and couldn't carry it. Cecily had brought her up, after her father had disappeared and her mother had died in an unexplained accident. Daily she saw the reflection of her failure in the face of her grandmother, who seemed built of the same seasoned and secure wood as the old Putnam house. Simone looked at her grandmother, whom she loved, and became a mere vapor."

"He's not home so much," Simone said.

Her face was small, with a pointed chin, and she had golden-red hair which she wore loose on her shoulders. Nina, too, had a small face, but it was neither so pale nor so delicate as her mother's, as if Sam's tougher substance had filled her out and strengthened her bone structure. If it was true that she, Simone, was a weak link, then Sam's strength might have poured into the child, and there would be no more Putnam family and tradition.

"People don't change that easily," the old woman said.

"But things —" Simone began. The china which had a history of five generations slipped out of her hands and smashed; Sam's toaster wouldn't toast or pop up; Simone couldn't even use the telephone for fear of getting a wrong number, or no number at all.

"Things, things!" her grandmother cried. "It's blood that counts. If the blood is strong enough, things dissolve. They're just garbage, all those things, floating on the surface of our history. It's our history that's deep. That's what counts."

"You're afraid of Sam," the young woman accused.

"Not afraid of any man!" Cecily said, straightening her back. "But I'm afraid for the child. Sam has no family tradition, no depth, no talent handed down and perfected. A man with his head full of wheels and wires."

Simone loved him. She leaned on him and grew about him, and he supported her tenderly. She wasn't going to give him up for the sake of some abstract tradition —

"— it's not abstract," her grandmother said with spirit. "It's in your blood. Or why don't you sweep the floors the way other women do? The way Sam's mother must?"

Simone had begun to clean the house while she was thinking, moving her hand horizontally across the floor, at the height of her hip, and the dust was following the motion of her hand and moving in a small, sun-brightened river toward the trash basket in the kitchen corner. Now Simone raised her hand to her face to look at it, and the river of dust rose like a serpent and hung a foot below her hand.

"Yes," she agreed, "at least I can clean the house. If I don't touch the good china, and look where I'm going."

"Phui," the old woman said again, angrily. "Don't feel so sorry for yourself."

"Not for myself," Simone mumbled, and looked again toward the garden where her daughter was doing something with three stones and a pie plate full of spring water.

"I do despair of Nina," Cecily said, as she had said before. "She's four, and has no appearance. Not even balance. She fell out of the applerose tree, and couldn't even help herself." Suddenly the old woman thrust her face close to her granddaughter. It was smooth, round, and sweet as a young kernel of corn. The eyes, sunk down under the bushy grey brows, were cold and clear grey.

"Simone," the old woman said. "You didn't lie to me? You did know she was falling, and couldn't get back in time to catch her?"

A shudder passed through Simone's body. There was no blood in her veins, only water; no marrow in her bones, they were empty, and porous as a bird's. Even the roots of her hair were weak, and now the sweat was starting out on her scalp as she faced her grandmother and saw the bristling shapes of seven generations of Putnam women behind her.

"You lied," the old woman said. "You didn't know she was falling."

Simone was a vapor, a mere froth blowing away on the first breeze.

"My poor dear," the old woman said in a gentle voice. "But how could you marry someone like Sam? Don't you know what will happen? He'll dissolve us, our history, our talents, our pride. Nina is nothing but an ordinary little child."

"She's a good child," Simone said, trying not to be angry. She wanted her child to be loved, to be strong. "Nina isn't a common child," she said, with her head bent. "She's very bright."

"A man with his head full of wheels, who's at home with electricity and wires," the old woman went on. "We've had them before, but never allowed them to dominate us. My own husband was such a man, but he was only allowed to make token gestures, such as having the power lines put in. He never understood how they worked." She lowered her voice to a whisper, "Your Sam understands. I've heard him talk to the water pump."

"That's why you're afraid of him," Simone said. "Not because I'm weak, and he might take something away from me, but because he's strong, and he might give us something. Then everything would change, and you're afraid of that. Nina might be our change." She pointed toward the garden.

Following white line of her granddaughter's finger, Cecily looked out into the garden and saw Nina turn toward them as though she knew they were angry. The child pointed with one finger directly at them in the house. There was a sharp crackle, and something of a brilliant and vibrating blue leaped between the out-stretched fingers of mother and daughter, and flew up like a bird to the power lines above.

"Mommy," Nina called.

Simone's heart nearly broke with wonder and fright. Her grandmother contemptuously passed through the kitchen door and emerged on the step outside, but Simone opened the door and left it open behind her. "What was that?" she asked Nina. "Was it a bluebird?"

"Don't be silly," Nina said. She picked up the pie plate and brought it toward them. Cecily's face was white and translucent, one hand went to her throat as the child approached.

Brimful of crackling blue fire with a fluctuating heart of yellow, the pie plate came toward them, held between Nina's small, dusty hands. Nina grinned at them. "I stole it out of the wires," she said.

Simone thought she would faint with a mixture of joy and fear. "Put it back," she whispered. "Please put it back."

"Oh Mommy," Nina said, beginning to whine. "Not now. Not right away. I just got it. I've done it lots of times." The pie plate crackled and hissed in the steady, small hands.

Simone could feel the old woman's shocked silence behind her. "You mustn't carry it in a pie plate, it's dangerous," Simone said to her child, but she could see Nina was in no danger. "How often have you done this?" She could feel her skirt and her hair billow with electricity.

"Lots of times. You don't like it, do you?" She became teasing and roguish, when she looked most like Sam. Suddenly she threw back her head and opened her mouth, and tilting up the pie plate she drank it empty. Her reddish gold hair sprang out in crackling rays around her face, her eyes flashed and sparks flew out between her teeth before she closed her mouth.

"Nina!" the old woman cried, and began to crumple, falling slowly against Simone in a complete faint. Simone caught her in trembling hands and lowered her gently. She said to her daughter, "You mustn't do that in front of Grandy. You're a bad girl, you knew it would scare her," and to herself she said: I must stop babbling, the child knows I'm being silly. O isn't it wonderful, isn't it awful, O Sam, how I love you.

"Daddy said it would scare you," Nina admitted. "That's why I never showed you before." Her hair was softly falling into place again, and she was gazing curiously at her great-grandmother lying on the doorstep.

"It did scare me," Simone said. "I'm not used to it, darling. But don't keep it secret any more."

"Is Grandy asleep?"

Simone said hastily, "Oh yes, she's taking a nap. She is old, you know, and likes to take naps."

"That's not a nap," Nina said, leaning over and patting the old woman's cheek. "I think she's having a bad dream."

Simone carried her grandmother into the house. If that old, tired heart had jumped and floundered like her own, there must be some damage done to it. If anything happened to her grandmother, the world would end, Simone thought, and was furious with Nina, and at the same time, full of joy for her.

Cecily Putnam opened her eyes widely, and Simone said, "It does change, you see. But it's in the family, after all."

The old woman sat upright quickly. "That wicked child!" she exclaimed. "To come and frighten us like that. She ought to be spanked." She got up with great strength and rushed out to the garden.

"Nina!" she called imperiously. The child picked up one of the small stones from the pie plate now full of spring water, and came to her great-grandmother.

"I'll make something for you, Grandy," she said seriously. She put the stone in the palm of her hand, and breathed on it, and then held out her hand and offered the diamond.

"It's lovely. Thank you," the old woman said with dignity, and put her hand on the child's head. "Let's go for a walk and I'll show you how to grow rose-apples. That's more becoming to a young lady."

"You slept on the step."

"Ah! I'm old and I like to take little naps," Cecily answered.

Simone saw them disappear among the applerose trees side by side. She was still trembling, but gradually, as she passed her hand back and forth, and the dust followed, moving in a sparkling river toward the trash basket, Simone stopped trembling and began to smile with the natural pride of a Putnam woman.

All Cats Are Gray

ANDRE NORTON

ABOUT ANDRE NORTON
AND
ALL CATS ARE GRAY

All Cats are Gray *was first published:*
Fantastic Universe, September 1953

To say that Andre Norton is the most famous and influential science fiction writer of the 1950s and the 1960s might be to seriously understate the case. Ms. Norton is the only woman science fiction writer of her era to achieve the popularity and sales of her most successful male contemporaries. This may at first been due in part to the androgyny of her chosen pseudonym and the fact that the protagonists of her first twenty or so books were all males. But it was also due in some part, to their extraordinary quality which garnered them rave reviews in major newspapers that rarely even deigned to review a Heinlein or a Asimov.

Thankfully Andre Norton is one woman writer whose work readers can easily find in today's bookstores. "All Cats are Gray" is the almost ideal Andre Norton short story, recapitulating in a few thousand words all of the major themes of her most popular novels: outcasts rejected as different because they possess some unusual talent, symbiotic human–animal linkages, high adventure, and unprecedentedly for a Norton work of the 1950s a hint of romance and sex.

All Cats Are Gray

by ANDRE NORTON

STENNA of the spaceways — that sounds just like a corny title for one of the Stellar-Vedo spreads. I ought to know, I've tried my hand at writing enough of them. Only this Steena was no glamorous babe. She was as colorless as a lunar planet — even the hair netted down to her skull had a sort of grayish cast, and I never saw her but once draped in anything but a shapeless and baggy gray spaceall.

Steena was strictly background stuff, and that is where she mostly spent her free hours — in the smelly, smoky, background corners of any stellar-port dive frequented by free spacers. If you really looked for her you could spot her — just sitting there listening to the talk — listening and remembering. She didn't open her own mouth often. But when she did, spacers had learned to listen. And the lucky few who heard her rare spoken words — these will never forget Steena.

She drifted from port to port. Being an expert operator on the big calculators, she found jobs wherever she cared to stay for a time. And she came to be something like the masterminded machines she tended — smooth, gray, without much personality of their own.

But it was Steena who told Bub Nelson about the Jovan moon rites — and her warning saved Bub's life six months later. It was Steena who identified the piece of stone Keene Clark was passing around a table one night, rightly calling it unworked Slitite. That started a rush which made ten fortunes overnight for men who were down to their last jets. And, last of all, she cracked the case of the *Empress of Mars*.

All the boys who had profited by her queer store of knowledge and her photographic memory tried at one time or another to balance the scales. But she wouldn't take so much as a cup of canal water at their expense, let alone the credits they tried to push on her. Bub Nelson was the only one who got around her refusal. It was he who brought her Bat.

About a year after the Jovan affair, he walked into the Free Fall one night and dumped Bat down on her table. Bat looked at Steena and growled. She looked calmly back at him and nodded once. From then on they traveled together — the thin gray woman and the big gray tomcat. Bat learned to know the inside of more stellar bars than even most spacers visit in their lifetimes. He developed a liking for Vernal juice, drank it neat and quick, right out of the glass. And he was always at home on any table where Stenna elected to drop him.

This is really the story of Steena, Bat, Cliff Moran, and the *Empress of Mars*, a story which is already a legend of the spaceways. And it's a damn good story, too. I ought to know, having framed the first version of it myself.

For I was there, right in the Rigel Royal, when it all began on the night that Cliff Moran blew in, looking lower than an antman's belly and twice as nasty. He'd had a spell of luck foul enough to twist a man into a slug snake, and we all knew that there was an attachment out for his ship. Cliff had fought his way up from the back courts of Venaport. Lose his ship and he'd slip back there — to rot. He was at the snarling stage that night when he picked out a table for himself and set out to drink away his troubles.

However, just as the first bottle arrived, so did a visitor. Steena came out of her corner, Bat curled around her shoulders stolewise, his favorite mode of travel. She crossed over and dropped down, without invitation, at Cliff's side. That shook him out of his sulks. Because Steena never chose company when she could be alone. If one of the man-stones on Ganymede had come stumping in, it wouldn't have made more of us look out of the corners of our eyes.

She stretched out one long-fingered hand, set aside the bottle he had ordered, and said only one thing. "It's about time for the *Empress of Mars* to appear."

Cliff scowled and bit his lip. He was tough, tough as jet lining — you have to be granite inside and out to struggle up from Venaport to a ship command. But we could guess what was running through his mind at that moment. The *Empress of Mars* was just about the biggest prize a spacer could aim for. But in the fifty years she had been following her queer derelict orbit through space, many men had tried to bring her in — and none had succeeded.

A pleasure ship carrying untold wealth, she had been mysteriously abandoned in space by passengers and crew, none of whom had ever been seen or heard of again. At intervals thereafter she had been sighted, even boarded. Those who ventured into her either vanished or returned swiftly without any believable explanation of what they had seen — wanting only to get away from her as quickly as possible. But the man who could bring her in — or even strip her clean in space — that man would win the jackpot.

"All right!" Cliff slammed his fist on the table. "I'll try even that!"

Steena looked at him, much as she must have looked at Bat that day Bub Nelson brought him to her, and nodded. That was all I saw. The rest of the story came to me in pieces, months later and in another port half the system away.

Cliff took off that night. He was afraid to risk waiting — with a writ out that could pull the ship from under him. And it wasn't until he was in space that he discovered his passengers — Steena and Bat. We'll never know what happened then. I'm betting Steena made no explanation at all. She wouldn't.

It was the first time she had decided to cash in on her own tip and she was there — that was all. Maybe that point weighed with Cliff, maybe he just didn't care. Anyway, the three were together when they sighted the *Empress* riding, her deadlights gleaming, a ghost ship in night space.

She must have been an eerie sight because her other lights were on too, in addition to the red warnings at her nose. She seemed alive, a Flying Dutchman of space. Cliff worked his ship skillfully alongside and had no trouble in snapping magnetic lines to her lock. Some minutes later the three of them passed into her. There was still air in her cabins and corridors, air that bore a faint corrupt taint which set Bat to sniffing greedily and could be picked up even by the less sensitive human nostrils.

Cliff headed straight for the control cabin, but Steena and Bat went prowling. Closed doors were a challenge to both of them and Steena opened each as she passed, taking a quick look at what lay within. The fifth door opened on a room which no woman could leave without further investigation.

I don't know what had been housed there when the *Empress* left port on her last lengthy cruise. Anyone really curious can check back on the old photo-reg cards. But there was a lavish display of silk trailing out of two travel kits on the floor, a dressing table crowded with crystal and jeweled containers, along with other lures for the female which drew Steena in. She was standing in front of the dressing table when she glanced into the mirror — glanced into it and froze.

Over her right shoulder she could see the spider-silk cover on the bed. Right in the middle of that sheer, gossamer expanse was a sparkling heap of gems, the dumped contents of some jewel case. Bat had jumped to the foot of the bed and flattened out as cats will, watching those gems, watching them and — something else!

Steena put out her hand blindly and caught up the nearest bottle. As she unstoppered it, she watched the mirrored bed. A gemmed bracelet rose from the pile, rose in the air and tinkled its siren song. It was as if an idle hand played. . . . Bat spat almost noiselessly. But he did not retreat. Bat had not yet decided his course.

She put down the bottle. Then she did something which perhaps few of the men she had listened to through the years could have done. She moved without hurry or sign of disturbance on a tour about the room. And, although she approached the bed, she did not touch the jewels. She could not force herself to do that. It took her five minutes to play out her innocence and unconcern. Then it was Bat who decided the issue.

He leaped from the bed and escorted something to the door, remaining a careful distance behind. Then he mewed loudly twice. Steena followed him and opened the door wider.

Bat went straight on down the corridor, as intent as a hound on the warmest of scents. Steena strolled behind him, holding her pace to the unhurried gait of an explorer. What sped before them was invisible to her, but Bat was never baffled by it.

They must have gone into the control cabin almost on the heels of the unseen — if the unseen had heels, which there was good reason to doubt — for Bat crouched just within the doorway and refused to move on. Steena looked down the length of the instrument panels and officers' station seats to where Cliff Moran worked. Her boots made no sound on the heavy carpet, and he did not glance up but sat humming through set teeth, as he tested the tardy and reluctant responses to buttons which had not been pushed in years.

To human eyes they were alone in the cabin. But Bat still followed a moving something, which he had at last made up his mind to distrust and dislike. For now he took a step or two forward and spat — his loathing made plain by every raised hair along his spine. And in that same moment Steena saw a flicker — a flicker of vague outline against Cliff's hunched shoulders, as if the invisible one had crossed the space between them.

But why had it been revealed against Cliff and not against the back of one of the seats or against the panels, the walls of the corridor or the cover of the bed where it had reclined and played with its loot? What could Bat see?

The storehouse memory that had served Steena so well through the years clicked open a half-forgotten door. With one swift motion, she tore loose her spaceall and flung the baggy garment across the back of the nearest seat.

Bat was snarling now, emitting the throaty rising cry that was his hunting song. But he was edging back, back toward Steena's feet, shrinking from something he could not fight but which he faced defiantly. If he could draw it after him, past that dangling spaceall. . . . He had to — it was their only chance!

"What the . . ." Cliff had come out of his seat and was staring at them.

What he saw must have been weird enough: Steena, barearmed and bareshouldered, her usually stiffly netted hair falling wildly down her back; Steena watching empty space with narrowed eyes and set mouth, calculating a single wild chance. Bat, crouched on his belly, was retreating from thin air step by step and wailing like a demon.

"Toss me your blaster." Steena gave the order calmly — as if they were still at their table in the Rigel Royal.

And as quietly, Cliff obeyed. She caught the small weapon out of the air with a steady hand — caught and leveled it.

"Stay where you are!" she warned. "Back, Bat, bring it back."

With a last throat-spitting screech of rage and hate, Bat twisted to safety between her boots. She pressed with thumb and forefinger, firing at the spaceall. The material turned to powdery flakes of ash — except for certain bits which still flapped from the scorched seat — as if something had protected them from the force of the blast. Bat sprang straight up in the air with a screech that tore their ears.

"What . . .?" began Cliff again.

Steena made a warning motion with her left hand. *"Wait!"*

She was still tense, still watching Bat. The cat dashed madly around the cabin twice, running crazily with white-ringed eyes and flecks of foam on his muzzle. Then he stopped abruptly in the doorway, stopped and looked back over his shoulder for a long, silent moment. He sniffed delicately.

Steena and Cliff could smell it too now, a thick oily stench which was not the usual odor left by an exploding blaster shell.

Bat came back, treading daintily across the carpet, almost on the tips of his paws. He raised his head as he passed Steena, and then he went confidently beyond to sniff, to sniff and spit twice at the unburned strips of the spaceall. Having thus paid his respects to the late enemy, he sat down calmly and set to washing his fur with deliberation. Steena sighed once and dropped into the navigator's seat.

"Maybe now you'll tell me what in the hell's happened?" Cliff exploded as he took the blaster out of her hand.

"Gray," she said dazedly, "it must have been gray — or I couldn't have seen it like that. I'm color-blind, you see. I can see only shades of gray — my whole world is gray. Like Bat's — his world is gray, too — all gray. But he's been compensated, for he can see above and below our range of color vibrations, and apparently so can I!"

Her voice quavered, and she raised her chin with a new air Cliff had never seen before — a sort of proud acceptance. She pushed back her wandering hair, but she made no move to imprison it under the heavy net again.

"That is why I saw the thing when it crossed between us. Against your spaceall it was another shade of gray — an outline. So I put out mine and waited for it to show against that — it was our only chance, Cliff.

"It was curious at first, I think, and it knew we couldn't see it — which is why it waited to attack. But when Bat's actions gave it away, it moved. So I waited to see that flicker against the spaceall, and then I let him have it. It's really very simple. . . ."

Cliff laughed a bit shakily. "But what *was* this gray thing. I don't get it."

"I think it was what made the *Empress* a derelict. Something out of space, maybe, or from another world somewhere. She waved her hands. "It's invisible because it's a color beyond our range of sight. It must have stayed in here all these years. And it kills — it must — when its curiosity is satisfied. Swiftly she described the scene, the scene in the cabin, and the strange behavior of the gem pile which had betrayed the creature to her.

Cliff did not return his blaster to its holder. "Any more of them aboard, d'you think?" He didn't look pleased at the prospect.

Steena turned to Bat. He was paying particular attention to the space between two front toes in the process of a complete bath. "I don't think so. But Bat will tell us if there are. He can see them clearly, I believe."

But there weren't any more and two weeks later, Cliff Steena and Bat brought the *Empress* into the lunar quarantine station. And that is the end of Steena's story because, as we have been told, happy marriages need no chronicles. Steena had found someone who knew of her gray world and did not find it too hard to share with her — someone besides Bat. It turned out to be a real love match.

The last time I saw her, she was wrapped in a flame-red cloak from the looms of Rigel and wore a fortune in Jovan rubies blazing on her wrists. Cliff was flipping a three-figured credit bill to a waiter. And Bat had a row of Vernal juice glasses set up before him. Just a little family party out on the town.

Subcommittee

ZENNA HENDERSON

ABOUT ZENNA HENDERSON
AND
SUBCOMMITTEE

Subcommittee *was first published:*
The Magazine of Fantasy & Science Fiction, *July 1962*

Until her death Zenna Henderson would have needed no introduction. In the years before Ursula LeGuin she was simply and uncontestedly the leading woman writer in the field — and one of its leading lights, period. A school teacher who wrote primarily about teachers and students, Ms. Henderson is most famous for her critically acclaimed People series, collected as Pilgrimage: the Book of the People *and* The People: No Different Flesh. *The best of her other work though by no means all of it, is collected in two further books* Holding Wonder *and* The Anything Box. *Readers who can find any of these elusive volumes can consider themselves quite fortunate.*

It can be no insult to say that one of Zenna Henderson's greatest virtues as a writer is that she brought an unmistakable and unabashed women's sensibility to the writing of science fiction — resulting in an extraordinary surge in quality. It's therefore not surprising that the protagonist or narrator of the majority of her stories is female. This is particularly true of "Subcommittee" in which (as with Sydney J. Van Scyoc's story later in this anthology) two women, because they are women possess the sensibility necessary to bridge the gap between conflicting cultures, when men are only able to deepen the divisions.

Subcommittee

by ZENNA HENDERSON

first came the sleek black ships, falling out of the sky in patterned disorder, sowing fear as they settled like seeds on the broad landing field. After them, like bright butterflies, came the vivid-colored slow ships that hovered and hesitated and came to rest scattered among the deadly dark ones.

"Beautiful!" sighed Serena, turning from the conference room window. "There should have been music to go with it."

"A funeral dirge," said Thorn, "Or a requiem. Or flutes before failure. Frankly, I'm frightened, Rena. If these conferences fail, all hell will break loose again. Imagine living another year like this past one."

"But the conference won't fail!" Serena protested. "If they're willing to consent to the conference, surely they'll be willing to work with us for peace."

"Their peace or ours?" asked Thorn, staring morosely out the window. "I'm afraid we're being entirely too naïve about this whole affair. It's been a long time since we finally were able to say, 'Ain't gonna study war no more,' and made it stick. We've lost a lot of the cunning that used to be necessary in dealing with other people. We can't, even now, be sure this isn't a trick to get all our high command together in one place for a grand massacre."

"Oh, no!" Serena pressed close to him and his arm went around her. "They couldn't possibly violate —"

"Couldn't they?" Thorn pressed his cheek to the top of her head. "We don't know, Rena. We just don't know. We have so little information about them. We know practically nothing about their customs even less about their values or from what frame of reference they look upon our suggestion of suspending hostilities."

"But surely they must be sincere. They brought their families along with them. You did say those bright ships are family craft, didn't you?"

"Yes, they suggested we bring our families and they brought their families along with them, but it's nothing to give us comfort. They take them everywhere — even into battle."

"Into battle!"

"Yes. They mass the home craft off out of range during battles, but every time we disable or blast one of their fighters, one or more of the home craft spin away out of control or flare into nothingness. Apparently they're just glorified trailers, dependent on the fighters for motive power and everything else." The unhappy lines deepened in Thorn's face. "They don't know it, but even apart from their superior weapons, they practically forced us into this truce. How could we go on wiping out their war fleet when, with every black ship, those confounded posy-colored home craft fell too, like pulling petals off a flower. And each petal heavy with the lives of women and children."

Serena shivered and pressed closer to Thorn. "The conference must work. We just can't have war any more. You've got to get through to them. Surely, if we want peace and so do they —"

"We don't know what they want," said Thorn heavily. Invaders, aggressors, strangers from hostile worlds — so completely alien to us — How can we ever hope to get together?"

They left the conference room in silence, snapping the button on the door knob before they closed it.

"Hey, lookit, Mommie! Here's a wall!" Splinter's five-year-old hands flattened themselves like grubby starfish against the greenish ripple of the ten-foot vitricrete fence that wound through the trees and slid down the gentle curve of the hill. "Where did it come from? What's it for? How come we can't go play in the go'fish pond any more?"

Serena leaned her hand against the wall. "The people who came in the pretty ships wanted a place to walk and play, too. So the Construction Corps put the fence up for them."

"Why won't they let me play in the go'fish pond?" Splinter's brows bent ominously.

"They don't know you want to," said Serena.

"I'll tell them, then," said Splinter. He threw his head back. "Hey! Over there!" He yelled, his fists doubling and his whole body stiffening with the intensity of the shout. "Hey! I wanta play in the go'fish pond!"

Serena laughed. "Hush, Splinter. Even if they could hear you, they wouldn't understand. They're from far, far away. They don't talk the way we do."

"But maybe we could play," said Splinter wistfully.

"Yes," sighed Serena. "Maybe you could play. If the fence weren't there. But you see, Splinter, we don't know what kind of — people — they are. Whether they would want to play. Whether they would be — nice."

"Well, how can we find out with that old wall there?"

"We can't, Splinter," said Serena. "Not with the fence there."

They walked on down the hill, Splinter's hand trailing along the wall.

"Maybe they're mean," he said finally. "Maybe they're so bad that the 'struction Corps had to build a cage for them — a big, big cage!" He stretched his arm as high as he could reach, up the wall. "Do you suppose they got tails?"

"Tails?" laughed Serena. "Whatever gave you that idea?"

"I dunno. They came from a long ways away. I'd like a tail — a long, curly one with fur on!" He swished his miniature behind energetically.

"Whatever for?" asked Serena.

"It'd come in handy," said Splinter solemnly. "For climbing and — and keeping my neck warm!

"Why aren't there any other kids here?" he asked as they reached the bottom of the slope. "I'd like *somebody* to play with."

"Well, Splinter, it's kind of hard to explain," Serena, sinking down on the narrow ledge shelving tiny dry water course at her feet.

"Don't esplain then," said Splinter. "Just tell me.

"Well, some Linjeni generals came in the big black ships to talk with General Worsham and some more of our generals. They brought their families with them in the fat, pretty ships. So our generals brought their families, too, but your daddy is the only one of our generals who has a little child. All the others are grown up. That's why there's no one for you to play with." I wish it were as simple as it sounds, thought Serena, suddenly weary again with the weeks of negotiation and waiting that had passed.

"Oh," said Splinter, thoughtfully. "Then there *are* kids on the other side of the wall, aren't there?"

"Yes, there must be young Linjeni," said Serena. "I guess you could call them children."

Splinter slid down to the bottom of the little water course and flopped down on his stomach. He pressed his cheek to the sand and peered through a tiny gap left under the fence where it crossed the stream bed. "I can't see anybody," he said, disappointed.

They started back up the hill toward their quarters, walking silently, Splinter's hand whispering along the wall.

"Mommie?" Splinter said as they neared the patio.

"Yes, Splinter?"

"That fence is to keep them in, isn't it?"

"Yes," said Serena.

"It doesn't feel like that to me," said Splinter. "It feels like it's to shut me out."

Serena suffered through the next days with Thorn. She lay wide-eyed beside him in the darkness of their bedroom, praying as he slept restlessly, struggling even in his sleep — groping for a way.

Tight-lipped, she cleared away untouched meals and brewed more coffee. Her thoughts went hopefully with him every time he started out with new hope and resolution, and her spirits flagged and fell as he brought back dead-end, stalemate and growing despair. And in between times, she tried to keep Splinter on as even a keel as possible, giving him the freedom of the Quarters Area during the long, sunlit days and playing with him as much as possible in the evenings.

One evening Serena was pinning up her hair and keeping half an eye on Splinter as he splashed in his bath. He was gathering up handfuls of foaming soap bubbles and pressing them to his chin and cheeks. "Now I hafta shave like Daddy," he hummed to himself. "Shave, shave, shave!" He flicked the suds off with his forefinger. Then he scooped up a big double handful of bubbles and pressed them all over his face. "Now I'm Doovie. I'm all over fuzzy like Doovie. Lookit, Mommie, I'm all over —" He opened his eyes and peered through the suds to see if she was watching. Consequently, Serena spent a busy next few minutes helping him get the soap out of his eyes. When the tears had finally washed away the trouble, Serena sat toweling Splinter's relaxed little body.

"I bet Doovie'd cry too, if he got soap in his eyes," he said with a sniff. "Wouldn't he, Mommie?"

"Doovie?" said Serena. "Probably. Almost anyone would. Who's Doovie?"

She felt Splinter stiffen on her lap. His eyes wandered away from hers. "Mommie, do you think Daddy will play with me a-morrow?"

"Perhaps." She captured one of his wet feet. "Who's Doovie?

"Can we have pink cake for dessert tonight? I think I like —"

"Who's Doovie?" Serena voice was firm. Splinter examined his thumbnail critically, then peered up at Serena out of the corner of his eye.

"Doovie," he began. "Doovie's a little boy."

"Oh?" said Serena. "A playlike little boy?"

"No," Splinter whispered, hanging his head. "A real little boy. A Linjeni little boy." Serena drew an astonished breath and Splinter hurried on, his eyes intent on hers. "He's nice people, Mommie, honest! He doesn't say bad words or tell lies or talk sassy to his mother. He can run as fast as I can — faster, if I stumble. He — he —" His eyes dropped again. "I like him —" His mouth quivered.

"Where did — how could — I mean, the fence —" Serena was horrified and completely at a loss for words.

"I dug a hole," confessed Splinter. "Under the fence where the sand is. You didn't say not to! Doovie came to play. His Mommie came, too. She's pretty. Her fur is pink, but Doovie's is nice and green. All over!" Splinter got excited. "All over, even where his clothes are! All but his nose and eyes and ears and the front of his hands!"

"But Splinter, how could you! You might have got hurt! They might have —" Serena hugged him tight to hide her face from him.

Splinter squirmed out of her arms. "Doovie wouldn't hurt anyone. You know what, Mommie! He can shut his nose! Yes, he can! He can shut his nose and fold up his ears! I wish I could. It'd come in handy. But I'm bigger'n he is and I can sing and he can't. But he can whistle with his nose and when I try, I just blow mine. Doovie's nice!"

Serena's mind was churning as she helped Splinter get into his night clothes. She felt the chill of fear along her forearms and the back of her neck. What to do now? Forbid Splinter's crawling under the fence? Keep him from possible danger that might just be biding its time? What would Thorn say? Should she tell him? This might precipitate an incident that —

"Splinter, how many times have you played with Doovie?"

"How many?" Splinter's chest swelled under his clean pajamas. "Let me count," he said importantly and murmured and mumbled over his fingers for a minute. "Four times!" he proclaimed triumphantly. "One, two, three, four whole times!"

"Weren't you scared?"

"Naw!" he said, adding hastily, "Well, maybe a little bit the first time. I thought maybe they might have tails that liked to curl around people's necks. But they haven't." Disappointed. "Only clothes on like us with fur on under."

"Did you say you saw Doovie's mother, too?"

"Sure," said Splinter. "She was there the first day. She was the one that sent all the others away when they all crowded around me. All grownups. Not any kids excepting Doovie. They kinda pushed and wanted to touch me, but she told them to go away, and they all did 'cepting her and Doovie."

"Oh, Splinter!" cried Serena, overcome by the vision of his small self surrounded by pushing, crowding Linjeni grownups who wanted to 'touch him.'

"What's the matter, Mornmie?" asked Splinter.

"Nothing, dear." She wet her lips. "May I go along with you the next time you go to see Doovie? I'd like to meet his mother."

"Sure, sure!" cried Splinter. "Let's go now. Let's go now!"

"Not now," said Serena, feeling the reaction of her fear in her knees and ankles. "It's too late. Tomorrow we'll go see them. And Splinter, let's not tell Daddy yet. Let's keep it a surprise for a while."

"Okay, Mommie," said Splinter. "It's a good surprise, isn't it? You were awful surprised, weren't you?"

"Yes, I was," said Serena. "Awful surprised."

Next day Splinter squatted down and inspected the hole under the fence. "It's kinda little," he said. "Maybe you'll get stuck."

Serena, her heart pounding in her throat, laughed. "That wouldn't be very dignified, would it?" she asked. "To go calling and get stuck in the door."

Splinter laughed. "I'd be funny," he said. "Maybe we better go find a really door for you."

"Oh, no," said Serena hastily. "We can make this one bigger."

"Sure," said Splinter. "I'll go get Doovie and he can help dig."

"Fine," said Serena, her throat tightening. *Afraid of a child,* she mocked herself. *Afraid of a Linjeni* — aggressor — invader, she defended.

Splinter flattened on the sand and slid under the fence. "You start digging," he called. "I'll be back!"

Serena knelt to the job, the loose sand coming away readily to her scooping hands, so readily that she circled her arms and dredged with them.

Then she heard Splinter scream

For a brief second, she was paralyzed. Then he screamed again, closer, and Serena dragged the sand away in a frantic frenzy. She felt the sand scoop down the neck of her blouse and the skin scrape off her spine as she forced herself under the fence.

Then there was Splinter, catapulting out of the shrubbery, sobbing and screaming, "Doovie! Doovie's drownding! He's in the go'fish pond! All under the water! I can't get him out! Mommie, Mommie!"

Serena grabbed his hand as she shot past and towed him along, stumbling and dragging, as she ran for the goldfish pond. She leaned across the low wall and caught a glimpse, under the churning thrash of the water, of green mossy fur and staring eyes. With hardly a pause except to shove Splinter backward and start a deep breath, she plunged over into the pond. She felt the burning bite of water up her nostrils and grappled in the murky darkness for Doovie — — feeling again and again the thrash of small limbs that slipped away before she could grasp them.

Then she was choking and sputtering on the edge of the pond, pushing the still struggling Doovie up and over. Splinter grabbed him and pulled as Serena heaved herself over the edge of the pond and fell sprawling across Doovie.

Then she heard another higher, shriller scream and was shoved off Doovie viciously and Doovie was snatched up into rose-pink arms. Serena pushed her lank, dripping hair out of her eyes and met the hostile glare of the rose-pink eyes of Doovie's mother.

Serena edged over to Splinter and held him close, her eyes intent on the Linjeni. The pink mother felt the green child all over anxiously and Serena noticed with an odd detachment that Splinter hadn't mentioned that Doovie's eyes matched his fur and that he had webbed feet.

Webbed feet! She began to laugh, almost hysterically. Oh, Lordy! No wonder Doovie's mother was so alarmed.

"Can you talk to Doovie?" asked Serena of the sobbing Splinter.

"No!" wailed Splinter. "You don't have to talk to play."

"Stop crying, Splinter," said Serena. "Help me think. Doovie's mother thinks we were trying to hurt Doovie. He wouldn't drown in the water. Remember, he can close his nose and fold up his ears. How are we going to tell his mother we weren't trying to hurt him?"

"Well," Splinter scrubbed his cheeks with the back of his hand. "We could hug him —"

"That wouldn't do, Splinter," said Serena, noticing with near panic that other brightly colored figures were moving among the shrubs, drawing closer — "I'm afraid she won't let us touch him."

Briefly she toyed with the idea of turning and trying to get back to the fence, then she took a deep breath and tried to calm down.

"Let's play-like, Splinter," she said. "Let's show Doovie's mother that we thought he was drowning. You go fall in the pond and I'll pull you out. You play-like drowned and I'll — I'll cry."

"Gee, Mommie, you're crying already!" said Splinter, face puckering.

"I'm just practicing," she said, steadying her voice. "Go on."

Splinter hesitated on the edge of the pond, shrinking away from away from the water that had fascinated him so many times before. Serena screamed suddenly, and Splinter, startled, lost his balance and fell in. Serena had hold of him almost before he went under water and pulled him out, cramming as much fear and apprehension into her voice and actions as she could. "Be dead," she whispered fiercely. "Be dead all over!" And Splinter melted so completely in her arms that her moans and cries of sorrow were only partly make-believe. She bent over his still form and rocked to and fro in her grief.

A hand touched her arm and she looked bright eyes of the Linjeni. The look held for a long moment and then the Linjeni smiled, showing even white teeth, and a pink, furry hand patted Splinter shoulder. His eyes flew open and he sat up. Doovie peered around from behind his mother and then he and Splinter were rolling and tumbling together, wrestling happily between the two hesitant mothers. Serena found a shaky laugh somewhere in among her alarms and Doovie's mother whistled softly with her nose.

That night, Thorn cried out in his sleep and woke Serena. She lay in the darkness, her constant prayer moving like a candle flame in her mind. She crept out of bed and checked Splinter in his shadowy room. Then she knelt and opened the bottom drawer of Splinter's chest-robe. She ran her hand over the gleaming folds of the length of Linjeni material that lay there — the material the Linjeni had found to wrap her in while her clothes dried. She had given them her lacy slip in exchange. Her fingers read the raised pattern in the dark, remembering how beautiful it was in the afternoon sun. Then the sun was gone and she saw a black ship destroyed, a home craft plunging to incandescent death and the pink and green and yellow and all the other bright furs charring and crisping and the patterned materials curling before the last flare of flame. She leaned her head on her hand and shuddered.

But then she saw the glitter of a silver ship, blackening and fusing, dripping monstrously against the emptiness of space. And heard the wail of a fatherless Splinter so vividly that she shoved the drawer in hastily and went back to look at his quiet sleeping face and unnecessarily to tuck him in.

When she came back to bed, Thorn was awake, lying on his back, his elbows winging out.

"Awake?" she asked as she sat down on the edge of the bed.

"Yes." His voice was tense as the twang of a wire. "We're getting nowhere," he said. "Both sides keep holding up neat little hoops of ideas, but no one is jumping through, either way. We want peace, but we can't seem to convey anything to them. They want something, but they haven't said what, as though to tell us would betray them irrevocably into our hands, but they won't make peace unless they can get it. Where do we go from here?"

"If they'd just go away —" Rena swung her feet up onto the bed and clasped her slender ankles with both hands.

"That's one thing we've established." Thorn was bitter. "They *won't* go. They're here to stay — like it or not."

"Thorn —" Rena spoke impulsively into the shadowy silence, "Why don't we just make them welcome? Why can't we just say, 'Come on in!' They're travelers from afar. Can't we be hospitable —"

"You talk as though the afar was just the next county — or state!" Thorn tossed impatiently on the pillow.

"Don't tell me we're back to that old equation — Stranger equals Enemy," said Rena, her voice sharp with strain. "Can't we assume they're friendly? Go visit with them — talk with them casually —"

"Friendly!" Thorn shot upright from the tangled bed-clothes. "Go visit! Talk!" His voice choked off. Then dangerously calmly he went on. "Would you care to visit with the widows of our men who went to visit the friendly Linjeni? Whose ships dropped out of the sky without warning —"

"Theirs did, too." Rena's voice was small but stubborn. "With no more warning than we had. Who shot first? You must admit no one knows for sure."

There was a tense silence, then Thorn lay down slowly, turned his back to Serena and spoke no more.

"Now I can't ever tell," mourned Serena into her crumpled pillow. "He'd die if he knew about the hole under the fence."

In the days that followed, Serena went every afternoon with Splinter, and the hole under the fence got larger and larger.

Doovie's mother, whom Splinter called Mrs. Pink, was teaching Serena to embroider the rich materials like the length they had given her. In exchange, Serena was teaching Mrs. Pink how to knit. At least, she started to teach her. She got as far as purl and knit, decrease and increase, when Mrs. Pink took the work from her, and Serena sat wide-mouthed at the incredible speed and accuracy of Mrs. Pink's furry fingers. She felt a little silly for having assumed that the Linjeni didn't know about knitting. And yet, the other Linjeni crowded around and felt of the knitting and exclaimed over it in their soft, fluty voices as though they'd never seen any before. The little ball of wool Serena had brought was soon used up, but Mrs. Pink brought out hanks of heavy thread such as were split and used in their embroidery, and, after a glance through Serena's pattern book, settled down to knitting the shining brilliance of Linjeni thread.

Before long, smiles and gestures, laughter and whistling, were not enough. Serena sought out the available tapes — a scant handful — on Linjeni speech and learned them. They didn't help much since the vocabulary wasn't easily applied to the matters she wanted to discuss with Mrs. Pink and the others. But the day she voiced and whistled her first Linjeni sentence to Mrs. Pink, Mrs. Pink stumbled through her first English sentence. They laughed and whistled together and settled down to pointing and naming and guessing across areas of incommunication.

Serena felt guilty by the end of the week. She and Splinter were having so much fun and Thorn was wearier and wearier at each session's end.

"They're impossible," he said bitterly, one night, crouched forward tensely on the front edge of his easy chair. "We can't pin them down to anything."

"What do they want?" asked Serena. "Haven't they said yet?"

"I shouldn't talk —" Thorn sank back in his chair. "Oh what does it matter?" he asked wearily. "It'll all come to nothing anyway!"

"Oh, no, Thorn!" cried Serena. "They're reasonable human —" she broke off at Thorn's surprised look. "Aren't they?" she stammered. "Aren't they?"

"Human? They're uncommunicative, hostile aliens," he said. "We talk ourselves blue in the face and they whistle at one another and say yes or no. Just that, flatly."

"Do they understand —" began Serena.

"We have interpreters, such as they are. None too good, but all we have."

"Well, what are they asking?" asked Serena.

Thorn laughed shortly. "So far as we've been able to ascertain, they just want all our oceans and the land contiguous thereto."

"Oh, Thorn, they couldn't be that unreasonable!"

"Well I'll admit we aren't even sure that's what they mean, but they keep coming back to the subject of the oceans, except they whistle rejection when we ask them point-blank if it's the oceans they want. There's just no communication." Thorn sighed heavily. "You don't know them like we do, Rena."

"No," said Serena miserably. "Not like you do."

She took her disquiet, Splinter, and a picnic basket down the hill to the hole next day. Mrs. Pink had shared her lunch with them the day before, and now it was Serena's turn. They sat on the grass together, Serena crowding back her unhappiness to laugh at Mrs. Pink and her first olive with the same friendly amusement Mrs. Pink had shown when Serena had bit down on her first *pirwit* and had been afraid to swallow it and ashamed to spit it out.

Splinter and Doovie were agreeing over a thick meringued lemon pie that was supposed to be dessert.

"Leave the pie alone, Splinter," said Serena. "It's top-off on."

"We're only testing the fluffy stuff," said Splinter, a blob of meringue on his upper lip bobbing as he spoke.

"Well, save your testing for later. Why don't you get out the eggs. I'll bet Doovie isn't familiar with them either."

Splinter rummaged in the basket and Serena took out the huge camp salt shaker.

"Here they are, Mommie!" cried Splinter. "Lookit, Doovie, first you have to crack the shell —"

Serena began initiating Mrs. Pink into the mysteries of hard-boiled eggs and it was all very casual and matter of fact until she sprinkled the peeled egg with salt. Mrs. Pink held out her cupped hand and Serena sprinkled a little salt into it. Mrs. Pink tasted it.

She gave a low whistle of astonishment and tasted again. Then she reached tentatively for the shaker. Serena gave it to her, amused. Mrs. Pink shook more into her hand and peered through the holes in the cap of the shaker. Serena unscrewed the top and showed Mrs. Pink the salt inside it.

For a long minute Mrs. Pink stared at the and then she whistled urgently, piercingly. Serena shrank back, bewildered, as every bush seemed to erupt Linjeni. They crowded around Mrs. Pink, staring into the shaker, jostling one another, whistling softly. One scurried away and brought back a tall jug of water. Mrs. Pink slowly and carefully emptied the salt from her hand into the water and then up-ended the shaker. She stirred the water with a branch someone snatched from a bush. After the salt was dissolved, all the Linjeni around them lined up with cupped hands. Each received — as though it were a sacrament — a handful of salt water. And they all, quickly, not to lose a drop, lifted the handful of water to their faces and inhaled, breathing deeply, deeply of the salty solution.

Mrs. Pink was last, and, she raised her wet face from her cupped hands, the gratitude in her eyes almost made Serena cry. And the dozens of Linjeni crowded around, each eager to press a soft forefinger to Serena' cheek, a thank-you gesture Splinter was picking up already.

When the crowd melted into the shadows again, Mrs. Pink sat down, fondling the salt shaker.

"Salt," said Serena, indicating the shaker.

"*Shreeprill,*" said Mrs. Pink.

"*Shreeprill?*" said Serena, her stumbling tongue robbing the word of its liquidness. Mrs. Pink nodded.

"*Shreeprill* good?" asked Serena, groping for an explanation for the just finished scene.

"*Shreeprill* good," said Mrs. Pink. "No *shreeprill*, no Linjeni baby. Doovie — Doovie —" she hesitated, groping. "One Doovie — no baby." She shook her head, unable to bridge the gap.

Serena groped after an idea she had almost caught from Mrs. Pink. She pulled up a handful of grass. "Grass," she said. She pulled another handful. "More grass. More. More." She added to the pile.

Mrs. Pink looked from the grass to Serena.

"No *more* Linjeni baby. Doovie — " She separated the grass into piles. "Baby, baby, baby —" she counted down to the last one, lingering tenderly over it. "Doovie."

"Oh," said Serena, "Doovie is the last Linjeni baby? No more?"

Mrs. Pink studied the words and then she nodded. "Yes, yes! No more. No *shreeprill*, no baby."

Serena felt a flutter of wonder. Maybe — maybe this is what the war was over. Maybe they just wanted salt. A world to them. Maybe —

"Salt, *shreeprill*," she said. "More, more, more *shreeprill*, Linjeni go home?"

"More, more, more *shreeprill*, yes," said Mrs. Pink. "Go home, no. No home. Home no good. No water, no *shreeprill*."

"Oh," said Serena. Then thoughtfully, "More Linjeni? More, more, more?"

Mrs. Pink looked at Serena and in the sudden silence the realization that they were, after all, members of enemy camps flared between them. Serena tried to smile. Mrs. Pink looked over at Splinter and Doovie who were happily sampling everything in the picnic basket. Mrs. Pink relaxed, and then she said.

"No more Linjeni." She gestured toward the crowded landing field. "Linjeni." She pressed her hands, palm to palm, her shoulders sagging. "No more Linjeni."

Serena sat dazed, thinking what this would mean Earth's High Command. No more Linjeni of the terrible, devastating weapons. No more than those that had landed — no waiting alien world ready to send reinforcements when these ships were gone. When these were gone — no more Linjeni. All that Earth had to do now was wipe out these ships, taking the heavy losses that would be inevitable, and they would win the war — and wipe out a race.

The Linjeni must have come seeking asylum — or demanding it. Neighbors who were afraid to ask — or hadn't been given time to ask. How had the war started? Who fired upon whom? Did anyone know?

Serena took uncertainty home with empty picnic basket. *Tell, tell, tell,* whispered her feet through the grass up the hill. *Tell and the war will end.* But how? she cried out to herself. By wiping them out or giving them a home? Which? Which?

Kill, kill, kill grated her feet across the graveled patio edge. *Kill the aliens — no common ground — not human — all our hallowed dead.*

But what about *their* hallowed dead? All falling, the flaming ships — the home-seekers — the dispossessed — the childless?

Serena settled Splinter with a new puzzle and a picture book and went into the bedroom. She sat on the bed and stared at herself in the mirror.

But give them salt water and they'll increase — all oceans, even if they said they were no good. Increase and increase and take the world — push us out — trespass — oppress —

But their men — our men. They've been meeting for over a week and can't agree. Of course they can't! They're afraid of betraying themselves to each other. Neither knows anything about the other, really. They aren't trying to find out anything really important. I'll bet not one of our men knows the Linjeni can close their noses and fold their ears. And not one of the Linjeni knows we sprinkle their life on our food.

Serena had no idea how long she sat there, but Splinter finally found her and insisted on supper and then Serena insisted on bed for him.

She was nearly mad with indecision when Thorn finally got home.

"Well," he said, dropping wearily into his chair. "It's almost over."

"Over!" cried Serena, hope flaring, "Then you've reached —"

"Stalemate, impasse," said Thorn heavily. "Our meeting tomorrow is the last. One final 'no' from each side and it's over. Back to blood-letting."

"Oh, Thorn, no!" Serena pressed her clenched fist to her mouth. "We can't kill any more of them! It's inhuman — it's —"

"It's self-defense," Thorn's voice was sharp with exasperated displeasure. "Please, not tonight, Rena. Spare me your idealistic ideas. Heaven knows we're inexperienced enough in warlike negotiations without having to cope with suggestions that we make cute pets out of our enemies. We're in a war and we've got it to win. Let the Linjeni get a wedge in and they'll swarm the Earth like flies!"

"No, no!" whispered Serena, her own secret fears sending the tears flooding down her face. "They wouldn't! They wouldn't! Would they?"

Long after Thorn's sleeping breath whispered in the darkness beside her, she lay awake, staring at the invisible ceiling. Carefully she put the words up before her on the slate of the darkness.

Tell — the war will end.

Either we will help the Linjeni — or wipe them out.

Don't tell. The conference will break up. The war will go on.

We will have heavy losses — and wipe the Linjeni out.

Mrs. Pink trusted me.

Splinter loves Doovie. Doovie loves him.

Then the little candle-flame of prayer that had so nearly burned out in her torment, flared brightly again and she slept.

Next morning she sent Splinter to play with Doovie. "Play by the goldfish pond," she said. "I'll be along soon.

Okay, Mommie," said Splinter. "Will you bring some cake?" he asked slyly. "Doovie isn't a-miliar with cake."

Serena laughed. "A certain little Splinter is a-miliar with cake, though! You run along, greedy!" And she boosted him out of the door with a slap on the rear.

"Bye, Mommie," he called back.

"Bye, dear. Be good."

"I will."

Serena watched until he disappeared down the slope of the hill, then she smoothed her hair and ran her tongue over her lips. She started for the bedroom, but turned suddenly and went to the front door. If she had to face even her own eyes, her resolution would waver and dissolve. She stood, hand on knob, watching the clock inch around until an interminable fifteen minutes had passed — Splinter safely gone — then she snatched the door open and left.

Her smile took her out of the Quarters Area to the Administration Building. Her brisk assumption of authority and destination took her to the conference wing and there her courage failed her. She lurked out of sight of the guards, almost wringing her hands in indecision. Then she straightened the set of her skirt, smoothed her hair, dredged a smile up from some hidden source of strength and tiptoed out into the hall.

She felt like a butterfly pinned to the wall by the instant unwinking attention of the guards. She gestured silence with a finger to her lips and tiptoed up to them.

"Hello, Turner. Hi, Franiveri," she whispered.

The two exchanged looks and Turner said "You aren't supposed to be here, Ma'am. Better go."

"I know I'm not," she said, looking guilty — with no effort at all. "But, Turner, I — I just want to see a Linjeni. She hurried on before Turner's open mouth could form a word. "Oh, I've seen pictures of them, but I'd like awfully to see a real one. Can't I have even one little peek?" She slipped closer to the door.

"Look!" she cried softly. "It's even ajar a little already!"

"Supposed to be," rasped Turner. "Orders. But Ma'am, we can't —

"Just one peek?" she pleaded, putting her thumb in the crack of the door. "I won't make a sound."

She coaxed the door open a little farther, her hand creeping inside, fumbling for the knob, the little button.

"But, Ma'am, you couldn't see 'em from here anyway."

Quicker than thought, Serena jerked the door open and darted in, pushing the little button and slamming the door to with what seemed to her a thunder that vibrated through the whole building. Breathlessly, afraid to think, she sped through the anteroom and into the conference room. She came to a scared skidding stop, her hands tight on the back of a chair, every eye in the room on her. Thorn, almost unrecognizable in his armor of authority and severity, stood up abruptly.

"Serena!" he said, his voice cracking with incredulity. Then he sat down again, hastily.

Serena circled the table, refusing to meet the eyes that bored into her — blue eyes, brown eyes, black eyes, yellow eyes, green eyes, lavender eyes. She turned at the foot of the table and looked fearfully up at the shining expanse.

"Gentlemen," her voice was almost inaudible. She cleared her throat. "Gentlemen." She saw General Worsham getting ready to speak — his face harshly unfamiliar with the weight of his position. She pressed her hands to the polished table and leaned forward hastily.

"You're going to quit, aren't you? You're giving up!" the translators bent to their mikes and their lips moved to hers. "What have you been talking about all this time? Guns? Battles? Casualty lists? We'll-do-this-to-you-if-you-do-that-to-us? I don't know!" she cried, shaking her head tightly, almost shuddering. "I don't know what goes on at high level conference tables. All I know is that I've been teaching Mrs. Pink to knit, and how to cut a lemon pie —" She could see the bewildered interpreters thumbing their manuals. "And already I know why they're here and what they want!" Pursing her lips, she half whistled, half trilled in her halting Linjeni, "Doovie baby. No more Linjeni babies!"

One of the Linjeni started at Doovie's name and stood up slowly, his lavender bulk towering over the table. Serena saw the interpreters thumbing frantically again. She knew they were looking for a translation of the Linjeni "baby." Babies had no place in a military conference.

The Linjeni spoke slowly, but Serena shook her head. "I don't know enough Linjeni."

There was a whisper at her shoulder. "What do you know of Doovie?" And a pair of earphones were pushed into her hands. She adjusted them with trembling fingers. Why were they letting her talk? Why was General Worsham sitting there letting her break into the conference like this?

I know Doovie," she said breathlessly. "I know Doovie's mother, too. Doovie plays with Splinter, my son — my little son. She twisted her fingers, dropping her head at the murmur that arose around the table. The Linjeni spoke again and the earphones murmured metallically. "What is the color of Doovie's mother?"

"Pink," said Serena.

Again the scurry for a word — pink — pink. Finally Serena tuned up the hem of her skirt and displayed the hem of her slip — rose-pink. The Linjeni sat down again, nodding.

Serena, General Worsham spoke as quietly as though it were just another lounging evening in the patio. "What do you want?"

Serena's eyes wavered and then her chin lifted.

"Thorn said today would be the last day. That it was to be 'no' on both sides. That we and the Linjeni have no common meeting ground, no basis for agreement on anything."

"And you think we have?" General Worsham's voice cut gently through the stir at the naked statement of thoughts and attitudes so carefully concealed.

"I know we do. Our similarities so far outweigh our differences that it's just foolish to sit here all this time, shaking our differences at each other and not finding out a thing about our similarities. We are fundamentally the same — the same —" she faltered. "Under God we are all the same." And she knew with certainty that the translators wouldn't find God's name in their books. "I think we ought to let them eat our salt and bread and make them welcome!' She half smiled and said, "The word for salt is *shreeprill.*"

There was a smothered rush of whistling from the Linjeni, and the lavender Linjeni half rose from his chair and subsided.

General Worsham glanced at the Linjeni speculatively and pursed his lips. "But there are ramifications —" he began.

"Ramifications!" spat Serena. "There are no ramifications that can't resolve themselves if two peoples really know each other!"

She glanced around the table, noting with sharp relief that Thorn's face had softened.

"Come with me!" she urged. "Come and see Doovie and Splinter together — Linjeni young and ours, who haven't learned suspicion and fear and hate and prejudice yet. Declare a — a — recess or a truce or whatever is necessary and come with me. After you see the children and see Mrs. Pink knitting and we talk this matter over like members of a family — Well, if you still think you have to fight after that, then —" she spread her hands.

Her knees shook so as they started downhill that Thorn had to help her walk.

"Oh, Thorn," she whispered, almost sobbing. "I didn't think they would. I thought they'd shoot me or lock me up or —"

"We don't want war. I told you that," he murmured.

"We're ready to grab at straws, even in the guise of snippy females who barge in on solemn councils and display their slips!" Then his lips tightened. "How long has this been going on?"

"For Splinter, a couple of than a weeks. For me, a little more than a week."

"Why didn't you tell me?"

"I tried — twice. You wouldn't listen. I was too scared to insist. Besides, you know what your reaction would have been."

Thorn had no words until they neared the foot of the hill, then he said, "How come you know so much? What makes you think you can solve —"

Serena choked back a hysterical laugh. "I took eggs to a picnic!"

And then they were standing, looking down at the hole under the fence.

"Splinter found the way," Serena defended. I made it bigger, but you'll have to get down flat."

She dropped to the sand and wiggled under. She crouched on the other side, her knees against her chest, her clasped hands pressed against her mouth, and waited. There was a long minute of silence and then a creak and a grunt and Serena bit her lips as General Worsham inched under the fence, flat on the sand, catching and jerking free halfway through. But her amusement changed to admiration as she realized that even covered with dust, scrambling awkwardly to his feet and beating his rumpled clothing, he possessed dignity and strength that made her deeply thankful that he was the voice of Earth in this time of crisis.

One by one the others crawled under, the Linjeni sandwiched between the other men and Thorn bringing up the rear. Motioning silence, she led them to the thicket of bushes that screened one side of the goldfish pond.

Doovie and Splinter were leaning over the edge of the pond.

"There it is!" cried Splinter, leaning perilously and pointing. "Way down there on the bottom and it's my best marble. Would your Mommie care if you got it for me?"

Doovie peered down. "Marble go in water."

"That's what I said," cried Splinter impatiently. "And you can shut your nose—" he put his finger to the black, glistening button, "and fold your ears." He flicked them with his forefinger and watched them fold. "Gee!" he said admiringly, I wish I could do that."

"Doovie go in water?" asked Doovie.

"Yeah," nodded Splinter. "It's my good taw and you won't even have to put on swimming trunks — you got fur."

Doovie shucked out of his brief clothing and slid down into the pond. He bobbed back up, his hand clenched.

"Gee, thanks." Splinter held out his hand and Doovie carefully turned his hand over and Splinter closed his. Then he shrieked and flung his hand out. "You mean old thing!" yelled Splinter. "Give me my marble! That was a slippy old fish!" He leaned over, scuffing, trying to reach Doovie's other hand. There was a slither and a splash and Splinter and Doovie disappeared under the water.

Serena caught her breath and had started forward when Doovie's anxious face bobbed to the surface again. He yanked and tugged at the sputtering, coughing Splinter and tumbled him out onto the grass. Doovie squatted by Splinter, patting his back and alternately whistling dolefully through his nose and talking apologetic sounding Linjeni.

Splinter coughed and dug his fists into his eyes.

"Golly, golly!" he said, spatting his hands against his wet jersey. "Mommie'll sure be mad. My clean clothes all wet. Where's my marble, Doovie?"

Doovie scrambled to his feet and went back to the pond. Splinter started to follow, then he cried. "Oh, Doovie, where did that poor little fish go? It'll die if it's out of the water. My guppy did."

"Fish?" asked Doovie.

"Yes," said Splinter, holding out his hand as he searched the grass with intent eyes. "The slippery little fish that wasn't my marble."

The two youngsters scrambled around in the grass until Doovie whistled and cried out triumphantly, "Fish!" and scooped it up in his hands and rushed it back to the pond. "There," said Splinter, "now it won't die. Looky, swimming away!"

Doovie slid into the pond again and retrieved the lost marble.

"Now," said Splinter, "watch me and I'll show you how to shoot."

The bushes beyond the two absorbed boys parted and Mrs. Pink stepped out. She smiled at the children and then she saw the silent group on the other side of the clearing. Her eyes widened and she gave an astonished whistle. The two boys looked up and followed the direction of her eyes.

"Daddy!" yelled Splinter. "Did you come to play?" And he sped, arms outstretched, to Thorn, arriving only a couple of steps ahead of Doovie who was whistling excitedly and rushing to greet the tall lavender Linjeni.

Serena felt a sudden choke of laughter at how alike Thorn and the Linjeni looked, trying to greet their offspring adequately and still retain their dignity.

Mrs. Pink came hesitantly to the group to stand in the circle of Serena's arm. Splinter had swarmed up Thorn, hugged him with thoroughness and slid down again. "Hi, General Worsham!" he said, extending a muddy hand in a belated remembrance of his manners. "Hey, Daddy, I'm showing Doovie how to play marbles, but you can shoot better'n I can. You come show him how."

"Well —" said Thorn, glancing uncomfortably at General Worsham.

General Worsham was watching the Linjeni as Doovie whistled and fluted over a handful of bright colored marbles. He quirked an eyebrow at Thorn and then at the rest of the group.

"I suggest a recess," he said. "In order that we may examine new matters that have been brought to our attention."

Serena felt herself getting all hollow inside, and she turned her face away so Mrs. Pink wouldn't see her cry. But Mrs. Pink was too interested in the colorful marbles to see Serena's gathering, hopeful tears.

Idol's Eye

CAROL EMSHWILLER

ABOUT CAROL EMSHWILLER
AND
IDOL'S EYE

Idol's Eye *was first published:*
Future, *February 1958*

Carol Emshwiller is certainly one of the few drop-dead beautiful photogra-phers models to have become a major woman of letters. Although her initial work appeared in science fiction magazines like F&SF, Future, Science Fiction Digest, *and* Super Science Stories, *the dozen or so quiet urbane, and extraordinary literate stories she wrote during the five year span between 1956 and 1961 immediately established her reputation as one of the field's few genuine literary talents.*

No one who read that early work could be surprised that twenty-five years later her work would grace the pages of the nation's finest literary publications, from the New Yorker *to the* Atlantic Review. *The irony may be that when the* Village Voice *devoted an entire page to her most recent collection of short stories, they never mentioned (and seemed to have no idea of) her roots in science fiction. Yet Carol Emshwiller has long been famous for disturbingly realistic works in the Shirley Jackson tradition like "Baby" and "Pelt," two stories, as toughly unsentimental as anything ever written by a male, and yet which could only have been written by a woman of enormous discernment and sensitivity. "Idol's Eye," her story here, is a brilliant economy on the nature of courage that offers profound and unexpected insight into the psychology "of the ugly duckling."*

Idol's Eye

by CAROL EMSHWILLER

PHILIPPA was on the back steps shelling peas when she heard the sound of footsteps. They didn't make much noise on the dry earth, but Philippa heard them; and because of the heaviness of them, and the time of day, and the way they came around to the back of the house, she knew who it was.

Her fine black hair already hung down, hiding each cheek, but she shook her head to bring it farther over her eyes in a protective screen. She peered out through the thick lenses of her ill-fitting glasses, but the only thing in focus, as usual, was the comfortable, familiar, black hair before her eyes.

There was the blurred shape of the grey barn, and the hazy, rolling line where the hills stopped and the sky began, and a new, dark shape under the green umbrella of the elm tree looking like every other blurred shape of a man or a woman. About the most Philippa saw of any of them. She knew who it was, though, and her hands tensed and she shelled peas more rapidly than before.

The shape neared and stood before her. "Hello," he said. "You're looking pretty."

She was used to being the way she was, and she didn't mind any more, not really. It was only the mockery she always felt in him that hurt her, not the words he said. When she answered, she spoke slowly and almost in a whisper. She wanted to say that if he loved her, and really wanted to marry her, he should say that she was what she was; but she didn't think there was really any love for her in him. He would rather see her something different. "I may not see very well," she said, "but I know I'm not pretty."

"You are to me." But she knew these were just words, the kind of words people always said without thinking if they meant anything.

He sat down beside her and leaned over her. He was so close she could see his uneven teeth and the bristled mustache above them almost as clearly as she saw her own hair.

"How about a kiss?"

"No," she said, "not now."

She knew he was only saying it to tease her, but still the thought made her turn her head away.

"You've got to sometime, you know."

"Maybe after we're married."

"Maybe! I guess you'd better. Anyway, I'll be the boss then." He laughed a laugh that made her shrink inside and then he got up and went on into the kitchen. She heard him call out to her mother, laugh again and say, "Philippa."

She heard the tail end of her mother's answer . . . "doesn't know when she's well off," and ". . . a strange one, Philippa."

During the conversation with him, Philippa had not stopped shelling peas, but now she did.

She looked off to where the green went the highest into the blue of the sky, to Old Hump Back Mountain — no mountain at all, but the biggest hill around — and she thought about being up there on the top, and the breeze there, and the smell of pine and the rustling animal sounds. She thought about it so she would forget about her mother and him inside.

Then she was it, clearer than she had ever seen anything before. It was almost as if she saw it with the mind's eye as well as with her real eyes. A cloud, but a clear cloud with the billowing shapes within it concisely outlined. It was purple, with a reddish tinge around the edges; it billowed upwards in a funnel shape for almost a full minute before it shrank and faded.

I saw it, she thought. I saw it as clearly as I see my own hair before my eyes. She shook the hair back, for once impatient with it, and stared at Hump Back Mountain. It was as blurry as ever.

That was seeing, she thought. That was the way everybody sees, and it's wonderful. Or perhaps it's a special way of seeing — my way.

And she thought that this was a nice thing to remember and think about; she shelled the peas again and felt happy.

They had come. This was the place and there must be one somewhere, a special one that was just right. The crystal would tell them.

They came out of the folded loop, Par and Til and Gib.

"We're doing it for the idol," said Par. The others didn't answer, but Par knew.

They set the crystal down on the pine needles, and Gib curled around it to give it what it needed. "This is a nice place in it's way," Gib said before he went "out."

"Were we seen?" Til asked.

"They can't," Par said. "It takes more than eyes sometimes."

"So, it is a nice place, in its way, to be calm and sure in," said Til. They sat and felt the breeze, smelled the pine smell, listened to the rustle of small animals, and waited.

When night came Gib uncurled from the crustal and came "to" again. "One is found," he said, "with what it needed. Shall I call?"

The others didn't answer, because there was no reason, but Gib looked into himself and knew the answer then; he called a slow call that would wait for the right time.

"This is a nice place in its way," Par said. It has been said, but not by Par. And then they all waited again.

He and Philippa and her father and mother all sat down to supper at the round table. Philippa said nothing, because she was thinking about how it was to see clearly all the way to the top of Hump Back Mountain. She shook her head till her hair was a curtain from the light above the table and the shining white dishes and the glitter from the knives and forks. All the others talked, but Philippa was lost into herself.

"You were rude tonight," her mother said afterwards, as they washed the dishes together. "You're always rude to him, and he's the only one you'll ever have a chance with. He needs a wife and he's not particular, Lord knows, but maybe he won't even have you if you're this way all the time, and then what will you do?"

"I didn't mean to be rude," Philippa said.

"Well I'm warning you, he may not be much but he's your only chance. I don't understand you, Philippa, that you can throw away your only chance. Try to be better when we go out to the front room again. Wake up and don't be so dreamy-like. Men like a girl who notices."

"I'll try."

And she did try, later in the front room, but there was something about him that shut her like a box inside, something about him that made her want to make him fuzzy not only to her eyes, but to her inner eye.

She tried though. She was noticing and kind and because of it he grew bold.

They were on the porch and her mother and father had gone to bed. I'm going to have that kiss," he said I've waited as long as an engaged man can."

"Please not now."

"Look, Philippa, I need a woman, like you can't even think how I need one. Look," he leaned close and held her arm in a bruising grip, "they brought Lucky Lady over to the Prince today. Did you hear him bellow down to the pasture?"

Philippa tried to lean away, but he held her arm tightly just below the shoulder. "I'm like the Prince," he said, "just like the Prince, I could bellow."

His hand pulled at her other shoulder in a kind of clumsy caress, coaxing her to turn to him. "We're going to be married, you know. It doesn't matter now. We can do anything." Then he pulled her hard against him. "For God's sake push back that hair," he said.

A few minutes later, Philippa managed to twist from his grip. She ran rapidly through the dark front room to the hall and the stairs. She had no need of sight, here in her home, and the dark was comfortable. He stumbled after, bumping into the small table by the door and cursing the noise he made. He dared go no farther than the stairs and by that time Philippa was in her room. She heard his heavy steps on the porch as he left, and she waited by her window until the crunching sounds on the stony earth of the driveway were gone.

She lay on her bed, and she could neither think nor sleep; but she knew that she could not marry him, in spite of her mother and father. Now she had decided that.

The hours went by rapidly for her because she had so much confusion in her mind, but finally she dozed.

She was in an orchard in a valley and the fruits on the trees were pink and ripe, because it was a holy time. There were creatures around her, unclear creatures that she saw more clearly even than she had seen the purple cloud that evening over Hump Back. The creatures came to the orchard because they loved. They loved to eat the pink fruit and they loved, in this holy season, to worship the idol here where he lived.

Then she saw him and she loved him, too, because she could see more than him.

One shoulder was higher than the other and arm was shriveled. He had lost both feet at the ankles, and a scar lumped across his forehead. Philippa saw all this, but mostly she saw his strange, blind eyes and what lay behind them. She saw him, inner eye to inner eye.

Then one of the creatures handed her a pink fruit. It had a Strange taste, neither sweet nor bitter. The sweetness was more sweet because of this, and she ate it.

She woke and remembered the grasping hands and the brutal kiss of the night before, but it was like a memory of a long time ago that didn't matter any more. A lot of things didn't matter now, for something new was inside her.

She came down to the kitchen. No one else was yet up. She made the coffee and drank some and ate an orange. She savored the sweetness of the orange and the bitterness of the coffee. *These are the tastes of my home,* she thought, *my home and my land,* and she loved the tasting. But she had a strange new taste in her mind that had a new meaning.

Her father came down and they went out to the morning milking, not speaking. Father and daughter, a disappointing, ugly, half-blind daughter; but still, in the early morning going to milk the cows, they were father and daughter.

Later in the morning, she took the garden claw and weeded the vegetable patch; then she squatted down to pick green beans for lunch. The hot sun made sweat bead along her upper lip and dampen the back of her blouse. *This is the hot sun of my land,* she thought, and loved her sweating.

After lunch she asked her mother, "Can I go for a while" for now was the time.

"There's a lot to be done," her mother said, and then she thought that this was her daughter, who had so little. "But go on, there's nothing that won't wait."

"Goodby," Philippa said.

She went out and a half an hour later she stood just where Hump Back Mountain started from the valley floor. She took off her glasses and laid them on the ground. She pushed her hair back, showing her large, staring eyes and broad nose and then she started walking through the pines towards the top of the hill.

Once the generals and the politicians and the scientific experts had searched the Earth and found six strong, healthy men — trained and intelligent men — and one of them was also a truly kind and good man with some said, a way of seeing into people. And they had sent him with the others, out in one of the six new ships built to leave the solar system. "Most of you won't come back," they said.

Some of the ships crashed, and some never got to any place that was a place, and they never heard of the men again, nor of him.

And because of what he was inside, the creatures of a strange world had planted an orchard and built a holy gate; they had seen the answer to the question he never asked, and had come where they would never venture before to find him a worthy wife.

The Last Day

HELEN CLARKSON

ABOUT HELEN CLARKSON
AND
THE LAST DAY

The Last Day *was first published:*
Satellite, *April 1958*

We have been unable to discover a single fact about Helen Clarkson. She is apparently the author only of the following science fiction story, which appeared in an obscure science fiction digest in the late 1950s. Who Ms. Clarkson was, why she wrote this story, why she never graced the pages of a science fiction magazine again — are all questions that may never be answered.

But we feel safe in saying that the following short story is one of the most brilliant and moving science fiction works ever penned by a woman, and that Ms. Clarkson's failure to author more is one of the field's greatest losses. To our knowledge this is the first appearance of Ms. Clarkson's undeservedly neglected solo effort since its original publication.

The Last Day

by HELEN CLARKSON

NO ONE SEEMED to know why there was no wind in the hollow. It was a deep cup, walled on every side by dunes. Nothing grew at the sandy bottom but a few weeds and bayberry bushes.

Ted and I found the place one brisk, August day, when we were walking along the top of the sand cliffs, looking at the wide, blue floor of ocean a hundred feet below. Up there, in wet bathing suits, we were chilled by a nagging, little sea breeze. But when we slid down the sloping side of the hollow, there was no wind at all — only peace and sunny stillness.

The dunes rose all around us like ramparts, blocking out the sea and the roofs of the fishing village that were just visible from the cliff top. It was secret as the bottom of a well. We could see nothing beyond but the sky, where white clouds drifted against soft blue. We vowed at once that we would never tell any other summer people about this discovery.

We lay on our backs, watching the beach grass at the top, waving in the wind like long, green hair. Where we were, there was no wind at all. "Even the curls at the back of your neck are frozen," said Ted. "I wonder why?"

"Configuration," I said. "Like an echo. Chance has formed this hollow so the wind can't get into it."

"Watch that bird," said Ted.

He was a small, brown bird, his wings spread wide and motionless, planing down an air current like a tiny glider, but, when he came to the air above the hollow, he lost momentum suddenly and his wings began to flutter in flight. Once beyond the hollow, he glided again.

"See?" said Ted. "Even above the hollow, there's no wind. He couldn't glide over it. He had to fly."

"I never did like the wind," I said. "It's an enemy. In a monsoon mood, it can kill you. In its milder moments, as a mistral or a foehn, it can drive you mad by its sheer monotony."

"Women never like the wind because he's a rude lover," said Ted. "He musses their hair, lifts their skirts and plasters their dresses to their bodies."

We got back to the village at sunset. Ted stopped at the wharf to buy fish from old Captain Baldwin. "I know that hollow," said the Captain. "Never has been any wind there, even in my grandfather's day. He used to call it the Hurricane's Eye.

Said it had the queer, sudden hush you notice when the heart of a hurricane is right overhead. Said he didn't believe there was any other spot quite like it anywhere else in the world. He ought to have known, for he'd been all over the world. He was in the China trade."

After supper in our rented cottage, we turned on the radio. Things had been sounding bad for a long, long time, but tonight they sounded worse than usual.

Some chief of civilian defense wound up the broadcast. He said the important thing was to keep calm, no matter what happened. And to stay in the cellar, if you had a cellar. We didn't.

"Be sure not to look back at any sudden, big flashes of light on the horizon," he warned. "And don't come out of your cellar until you hear the all-clear. No scientist knows exactly what will happen when bombs of this type are dropped in quantity, but remember — radio-active dust will be carried anywhere that the wind can go."

Ted turned off the radio. "Remember Lot's wife?"

"Not in detail."

"Sodom was punished for its sins by fire from Heaven. Lot received divine warning and left the city beforehand with his wife and daughters. They were warned not to look back. *Escape for thy life; look not behind thee . . . lest thou be consumed . . .* The very words have a strangely prophetic ring today. Of course Lot's wife did look back and she was turned into a pillar of salt."

"I've been hearing about these bombs for a long time," I said. "But they will never be dropped. For the same reason that they never used poison gas in the second war: no one can tell beforehand just which way the wind will blow."

We were both wakeful that night. About two in the morning we saw the vast, insane flash, bright as sunlight, on the horizon. There was no time to look away. I shut my eyes, but I heard Ted jump up and pull down the shades. Later we felt a shock and heard a rumbling, like an earthquake. It was far away. The house trembled, but stood. And that was all, except that when we turned on the radio we couldn't get anything.

The village had never looked more peaceful than it morning sunshine, but quite a high wind that blue surface of the bay into sparkling, wavelets and filled the sails of the fishing fleet, as it rounded the point, coming in with a dawn catch.

"Got plenty of food here way," said Captain Baldwin.

Nobody said anything just then about radioactivity.

There were no newspapers that morning and no truck deliveries from the outside world. No weekend tourists came cruising up the road in cars choked with children and dogs and daddy's best suit swinging on a coat hanger. Nobody could get anything on radio or TV. Half the village had cars, but no one seemed to feel like driving down to the nearest town.

We all felt it was up to them to get news and supplies to us. But after two whole days had passed and still there was no word, Captain Baldwin got out his battered Ford and chugged down the highway. People who had families elsewhere gave him messages to take to the telegraph office. *Say we're all right. Say everything is fine here.*

He was back in an hour. There was no telegraph office. There was no town. Only rubble. No one volunteered to go farther afield.

"We were self-contained in pioneering days," said the Captain. "We can be self-contained again. We have farms and fishing boats. What more does anybody want?"

Villagers and summer people were drawn together now, like refugees on a raft, with a sort of false cheerfulness that masked panic. Only the doctor was grave. He was watching the flag on village green as it rattled in the high wind.

"They've got too much to out there to worry about us," said the clergyman. "We'll just take care of ourselves and hope for the best until they're able to get things organized and get in touch with us again. You've plenty of medicines, haven't you, doctor?"

"Plenty of aspirin and penicillin," he answered, but I knew he was thinking of things that aspirin and penicillin couldn't cure.

There never was a more lovely summer. Just enough rain to keep things green. One golden day after another, as if earth was trying to say to us: *See how lovely I can be? Won't you be sorry to leave me?*

But we had no time to think. There was so much to be done if we were to have food for the winter.

In September the lease on our cottage was up, but no one cared. The owner had been in New York in August, when we last heard from him. Now we had no idea what had become of him.

One morning the little rosebush in our garden put out a single, improbable rose, quite out of season. It was an old-fashioned rose, deliciously fragrant and white, with the faintest blush of pink around its golden heart. Ted touched the silken petals with his fingertips and said gently: "The last rose of . . . the last summer." That night the rose bush died though it was too early for frost.

The sea gulls were the next to go. We woke one morning to a stench of dead birds. They were heaped along the wharves, some floating in the water. Next it was the songbirds and little woods animals. I hadn't realized how many songbirds there were, but now I noticed the silence in the garden, especially at dawn and dusk. Finches and robins, hares and squirrels had ranged farther afield and nibbled less discriminately than we.

A great many of us were living largely on canned food now. After the gulls died, no one dared to eat fish and the fleet stayed in port.

People were beginning to be afraid of eggs and milk, so no one minded very much when the cows and chickens died.

Finally the slow, secret rot spread to human beings. First, the children, one by one, until mothers moved through the village numb or mad with shock. Then the rest of us.

Ted and Captain Baldwin were the last of the survivors to be stricken. The old Captain went quickly, but Ted lingered, going blind before he died. Why, we didn't know. There was no one to ask. The doctor had died long ago.

There came a cold, bright day in early winter when I was the only living thing in the village and its surrounding farms. Not a cricket chirped. Not even an ant crawled after the sugar I had spilled on the kitchen floor. There was only the earth itself and the sunlight and the wind that had never really ceased blowing since the bombs fell.

I wondered about the life I couldn't see — the viruses and germs. Had cholera and influenza died with the race they preyed upon? Was the whole earth now clinically sterile?

I remembered then the hollow Ted and I had found in August. It was too small to hold even one person with the food he would need for the winter, so we had not considered it as a possible refuge. But now I wanted to see it once again, so I walked out of the village, alone, as I would be now until the day of my own death.

From the top of the sand cliff I saw again the wide, blue floor of ocean, rippled like watered silk by the skimming wings of the wind. An ocean where there were no longer fish or clams or algae or anything alive. A dead sea on a dead planet.

I came to the hollow and slid down its sandy side to the bottom. Once again I lay on my back and watched white clouds drift across a soft blue sky, but there were no gulls now diving and gliding down air currents. I closed my eyes and tried to pretend that the last few months had never happened, that this was August, that Ted would soon come to the rim of the hollow with a lunchbasket full of fried chicken and an ice bucket of Chablis and we would feast in the sun and then walk back to the village for a supper of fresh fish and turn on the radio to get some music and hear the news of the world . . .

But I couldn't make myself believe it. The world was dead. There would never be any news again. I was alone here, perhaps alone in the whole world, and I wouldn't be alive much longer.

The world had died as Sodom died for its sins. Not sins of sensuality, but sins of pride and intolerance and cruelty. *Thou shalt not kill. Thou shalt love thy neighbor as thyself.* The command had been clear and simple for nearly two thousand years, but it had not been obeyed.

I was startled out of my wits by a rustling of leaves. Had the wind reached the hollow at last and stirred the bayberry bushes? Or was there one other of God's creatures alive in this vacuum? I opened my eyes. I saw nothing, but I heard a clear, sweet trill of song and then I saw him — the small, brown bird, perched, swaying, on a twig of bayberry.

The hollow that was too small to shield and feed a human being had shielded and fed one small bird. He must have found it by chance, or instinct, before it was too late and he had stayed long enough to survive until now, living on the seeds and berries that grew here uncontaminated by the wicked wind.

One bird alone, without a mate or a nest of eggs — the last bird of all singing to the last human being.

I sat and listened while he poured forth the most joyous song I have ever heard, as if he, too, had been lonely, as if he, too, were glad to see me. I could almost hear words: *Isn't it lovely? The sun, the sea, the sky, the sand? Hasn't God been good to give us all this?*

As I listened to his innocent joy, slowly, for the first time since the bombs fell, tears began to slip down my cheeks. For I was not innocent. I shared the guilt of all my species.

After a while I lay down to sleep in the only place in the whole world that was clean and windless.

The Lady
Was a Tramp

JUDITH MERRIL

ABOUT JUDITH MERRIL
AND
THE LADY WAS A TRAMP

The Lady Was A Tramp *was first published:*
Venture, *July 1957*

Although for personal reasons she now prefers to keep as much distance between her and the world of science fiction as possible, Judith Merril was a seminal figure in the 1950s and 1960s. An editor, author, reviewer, and essayist she is one of the few women science fiction has produced so far who functioned as a genuine prodigy in much the same way as Harlan Ellison does. To each of these endeavors she brought a cutting-edge sensibility that often kept her light-years ahead of her male contemporaries. So that when the "New Wave" literary revolution broke in the late 1960s and early 70s, she was almost alone among those of her generation to embrace its arrival and principles.

Ms. Merril's own fiction was immediately recognized as being of exemplary quality; and while her work by no means focused exclusively on women, it has frequently done so, beginning with the publication of her groundbreaking first story "That Only A Mother." Her first novel Shadow on the Hearth *dropped a bombshell of equal impact with its first ever depiction of a suburban housewife's view of a post-holocaust world. As with most of Ms. Merril's work it has been lauded for "a remarkable sensitivity to emotional psychology," so much so that the science fiction encyclopedia calls her "before her time."*

Although her work has been collected in Out of Bounds, Survival Ship and other Stories, The Best of Judith Merril *it is not widely available now. "The Lady Was A Tramp" offers Merril's own pithy take on the contrasts between male and female sexuality — arriving at a far more tolerant view than many more doctrinaire feminists.*

The Lady Was A Tramp

by JUDITH MERRIL

She had been lovely once, sleek-lined and proud, with shining flanks; and men had come to her with hungry hearts and star-filled eyes, and high pulse of adventure in their blood.

Now she was old. Her hide was scarred with use, her luster dulled; though there was beauty in her still it was hidden deep. A man had to know where to look — and he had to care.

The young man left the conditioned coolness of the Administration Building and paused outside the door to orient. Then he strode briskly forward, ignoring the heat that wilted his uniform collar and damply curled the edges of the freshly stamped papers in his breast pocket. He passed the inner tier of docks, refusing to look to left or right at the twin proud heights of gleaming Navy vessels.

Beyond them, alone in the outmost ring, the *Lady Jane* sat on her base in the concrete hole, waiting. In the white-light glare of the shadowless Dome, each smallest pit and pockmark of twenty years' usage stood out in cruel relief against the weathered darkness of her hull. Potbellied, dumpy, unbeautiful, she squatted without impatience inside the steel framework of supports, while her tanks were flushed and her tubes reamed clean. When the dock gang was done, and the ravages of the last voyage repaired insofar as could be, she would set forth once more on her rounds of the ports in space. Meantime, she rested.

The young man paused. It was *Lady Jane*. He half-turned back; but it was too late now. Fury, or training, or despair, or some of all of them, moved him on.

"That's him all right," Anita smiled, and turned on the *Lady Jane's* viewpoint screen; the figure toward them with focussed clarity, and showed up on the IBMan insignia showed up on the jacket sleeve.

"Mad dogs and eye-bee-men," Chan quoted softly, and leaned forward to study the young man with mock amazement. On the tenth "day" of Lunar sunlight it was still possible to keep moderately cool inside an unsealed ship, and the central Administration Building was kept at a steady seventy, day or night. But out in the atmosphere dome, it was hot. Yet the young man walking briskly toward the ship wore formal greens, and his shirt was bound at his

neck with a knotted tie. Chandra leaned back, picked up a tall cold glass and shook his head.

"Look at him, Chan! He's a *kid*. . . ."

Chan shrugged. "You knew that before. You got the papers. . . ."

Impatiently, she shook her head. "I know. But *look* at him. . . ."

"I wasn't any older —" Chandra began.

"Yes you were! I don't know what your papers said, but — *look* at him. And you weren't an IBMan. And we were all younger then. And — darling, you were a *man!*"

He laughed and stood up, rumpling her hair as he passed. "Well, if that's all that's eating on you, babe — hell, four of us kept you happy half-way home."

He ducked through the bunk-room door as she started to rise. "Don't shoot," he called back.

"It ain't so funny, honey." She stood watching the screen. "What's bothering me is, who's going to keep *him* happy?"

Terence Hugh Carnahan, Lieutenant, U.N.N. Reserves was twenty-four years old and newly commissioned. He was stuffed to the gills with eight full years of Academy training, precision, and knowledge. The shiny new stripes on his sleeve and the dampening papers inside his breast pocket were the prices he'd worked for and dreamed of as long as it mattered. The fruits were sour now, and the dream was curdled. A man might approach the *Lady* incited by lust to a venture of greed; but the sight of her was enough to wipe out the last visions of glory.

The Lieutenant moved on, more slowly. He stopped as a three-wheeled-red-and-white-striped baggage truck swung out in a wide crazy curve from behind the Navy ship to the left and careened to a stop at the *Lady's* side.

A tall thin man in rumpled full-dress whites leaped out of the bucket, swinging a canvas suitcase in his hand. He climbed aboard the ship's waiting elevator and it started up.

Terry walked on and waited beside the truck for the cage to come down. When it did, he produced his ID card, got inside, and rode up in silence.

In the open lock, the man in the dirty whites was waiting for him. He held out his hand, and for the first time Terry saw the pilot's jets on his lapels; and the boards on his shoulders spelled Commander.

"You the new IBMan?" the pilot asked. "Where's your gear?"

"I sent it on this morning." They shook, and the pilot's slim fingers were unexpectedly cool and dry.

"Welcome to our happy home," he said. "Glad to have you aboard. And all that sort of thing. Manuel Ramon Decardez, at your service. They call me Deke."

"I'm Terry Carnahan."

"Come on in. I guess they're all waiting." Deke led the way through the open inner valve.

In the suit room, the pilot turned back. "Just take it easy, kid," he said. "It ain't like the Navy in here."

It wasn't.

The Lieutenant had been on merchant ships before. It was part of his training to know the layout and standard equipment of every jump-ship ever made. He had been on inspection tours; and a *Lady* class ship was still in Academy use for cadet instruction trips. But that one was Navy-maintained and Navy-staffed.

This *Lady* had left the service thirteen years back. The crew quarters had been torn out to make an extra hold, and the rule book had gone by the wayside along with the hammocks.

"Up here," Deke said, and Terry followed him up the ladder to Officers' Country. Then he stood in the wardroom doorway and stared at the crazy carnival scene.

To start with, the overheads were off. The only light was diffused U-V out of the algy tanks that cut two-foot swaths along opposite bulkheads. In the yellow-green dimness, the scattered lounging chairs and coffee cups and a tray with a bottle and glasses on the table, gave a ridiculous cocktail-bar effect to the whole place. And the first thing he saw was a hippy blonde, in tight black slacks and a loosely tied white shirt, who detached herself from the arm of a chair — and from the encircling arm of what looked like a naked brown-skinned man inside the chair. She ran across the room to fling herself on Deke, who picked her up bodily, kissed her with gusto.

"Where did you sneak in from?" she demanded. "We were waiting for —"

"Whoa, babe," Deke started. "If you mean —" He started to turn, began to move forward, to let Terry in, but from a shadowy corner a wiry little man in coveralls, with grease-stains on his hands and his hair and his face, broke in.

"What the hell! These two give me a pile of pitch about haulin' myself up here to give the new kid a big hello, and all I find is *this* old s.o.b instead!" *These two* appeared to be the blonde and the naked man. Deke was the s.o.b.

"You bitchin' again, Mike?" The voice was a bull-roar; it came from the only member of the *Lady's* crew Terry had met before. The Captain came down the ladder from Control, sneakers and rolled-cuff workpants first, and then the tremendous bulk of chest and arms, bristled with wiry curling red-gold hair. The room had looked crowded before. With Karl Hillstrom's two-hundred-twenty pounds added, it was jammed. "Relax," he said. "Have a drink and relax. Nita said she saw the kid comin' . . ."

Dete had given up trying to interrupt. He turned back to Terry and shrugged. "I told you —" he started, and just then the blonde saw him.

"Oh, my God!" she said, and broke into helpless laughter; so did Deke. She took a step forward toward Terry, trying to talk. He ignored it.

"Captain Hillstrom?" he said formally, as loud as possible. He felt like a school-kid in a lousy play, doing a bad job of acting the part of the butler at a masquerade.

The big man turned. "Oh, there you are!" He held out a burly hand. "You met Deke already? Anita, this is our new IBMan, Terry Carnahan. Anita Filmord, our Medic. And Mike Gorevitch, our Chief —" that was the grease-stained one —

"and Chan — Chandra Lal, our Biotech."

Terry fished in his pocket for the orders the Captain had failed to request, and noted with relief meantime that the Biotech, Chan, now unfolding himself from his chair, wasn't entirely naked after all.

It wasn't till then that he fully realized the hippy blonde was nobody's visiting daughter or friend, but a member of the crew and an officer in the Naval Reserve.

The blonde officer put a drink in his hand, and his last clear thought that night was that Deke was quite right: it wasn't like the Navy. Not at all.

When they gave him his commission, at the Examiner's Board, they had also delivered elaborate and resounding exhortations about the Great Trust being placed this day in his hands: how the work of an IBMan on a merchant ship was both more difficult and more important by far than anything done by an officer of equivalent rank on a Navy ship.

He knew all that. The ranking IBMan officer, on any ship, was fully responsible for the operation and maintenance of all material connected in any way with either solar navigation or space-warp jumps. On a tramp, there was likely to be just one IBMan to do it all, Navy Transports carried a full complement of four officers and five enlisted men. Fresh Academy graduates came on board with j.g. status only, and worked in charge of an enlisted maintenance crew on the "jump-along" — that abstract mechanical brain whose function it was to set up the obscure mathematic-symbolic relationships which made it possible for matter to be transmitted through the "holes" in spacetime, enabling a ship to travel an infinite distance in an infinitesimal time.

On a Navy transport, a full Lieutenant IBMan would be in charge of SolNav only, with two petty officers under him, both qualified to handle maintenance, and one at least with a Navy rating, capable of relieving him on duty at the control board during the five or twelve or twenty hours it might take to navigate a jump-ship in or out of the obstacle course of clutter and junk and planets and orbits of any given System.

Even the senior officer, on a Navy Transport, would never have to jump "blind," except in the rare and nearly unheard-of instance of an analog failure; only tramps and Navy Scouts ever jumped willingly on anything but a 'log-computed course. The stellar analog computers were the Navy's Topmost Secret; when you used one, nothing was required except to make sure the jump-along itself was in perfect condition, and then to pull the switch. The 'log did the rest.

Merchant ships carried 'logs for their chartered ports of call — the Lady had two — but the charter ports were the smallest part of a merchant trip. The number of destinations for which Navy analogs were available was hardly a hatfull out of the galaxies. Without a 'log to point the way for him, it was up to the IBMan to plot coordinates for where a hole ought to be. With luck and skill he could bring the ship out into normal space again somewhere within SolNav reach of the destination. With the tiniest error in computation, a ship might be lost forever in some distant universe with no stars to steer her home.

Terry Carnahan had been hoping desperately for a Navy transport job — but only because it was the route to the Scouts: the Navy's glory-boys, the two-bunk blind-jump ships that went out alone to map the edge of man's universe. It was the Scout job he'd worked for those long eight years — and dreamed about five years before, while he sweated for credits to get into Academy.

He didn't argue with his tramp assignment; nobody argued with the Board. He knew that most of the men who drew Navy assignments would envy him; the money was in the Reserves. And most of the rest, the ones who drew Transport and liked it, were there because they *couldn't* jump blind, and they knew it.

He knew all that. But when his orders came, and they told him he drew a tramp because he was tenth in his class — that's what they said: tramp work was the toughest — he also knew how close he had come to the dream, because he also knew that the top five men had been sent to Scout training.

Eight years of the most he could give it just wasn't enough. The answer was *NO!* For good.

But you didn't throw out eight years of training for a good job either. Terry went for his psychs and medics, and met Captain (U.N.N. Reserve) Karl Hillstrom; he took his two weeks' leave and reported for duty.

That first night, he fell asleep with the bunkroom spinning around him, and an obvious simple solution to the whole mess spinning with it, just out of his reach, no matter how fast he turned. When he stopped whirling, the dreams began, the dreams about naked crewmen, one of whom might have been *him*, and a terrible wonderful blonde in a sea of stars, winkin' and blinkin' and nod in a herring tramp to the smiling moon-faced girl who asked him in. . . .

In the morning, Captain Karl Hillstrom showed him around Control. It was shipshape and shiny up here, and the IBMan plunged gratefully into routine, checking and testing his board, and running off sample comps. He allowed himself only the briefest inspection of the jump-along and the keyboard and calckers attached. His first job would be solar navigation. Once they were clear of the System, there'd be three weeks on solar drive before they jumped — plenty of time to double-check the other equipment. Right now, the standard computers and solar 'log were what counted.

He worked steadily till he became aware of the Captain at his side.

"How does it look?"

"Fine so far, sir." Terry leaned back.

"Anything messed up there you can blame it on me. I worked that board coming in."

Terry remembered now — they had lost their IBMan on Betelgeuse IV, last trip, and come back short-handed, and with half the trade load still in the holds. Since no one but an IBMan could jump blind, they'd had pick up a new man — Terry.

"I haven't found anything wrong, sir," Terry said.

"You can drop the 'sir.' We go mostly by first names here." There was an edge of irritation in the Captain's voice. "It's chow time now. You want to knock off?"

Terry hesitated. This wasn't the Navy; it was a lousy tramp. If the pilot was drunk half the time, and the Chief had a dirty neck, and the Captain looked like a pirate or stevedore (the first of which he was, and the second had been), the IBMan was certainly free to work or eat when he chose.

"I'd just as lief stick with if for a while," Terry said cautiously.

"Sure. Suit yourself. Galley's open. Take what you want when you want it. . . ."

He disappeared. For a blessed two hours, alone with machines he knew and trusted, Terry ran off the standard tests and comps, noting with trained precision each tiniest deviation from perfect performance. The computer had never been built that could navigate without error. Maybe only in the tenth decimal, but that was enough for disaster. You had to know your 'log and your board and machines and make your adjustments as automatically as a man makes allowance for the sights on a rifle he's known and shot for years.

It took Terry four hours to learn this board, and he had started his first dry-run when the sandwich appeared on his arm-rest. A tall plastic glass with a straw in the top and a tempting froth came next.

"Well, thanks," he said, "but you didn't have to —"

"It's chocolate," she told him. "I ordered strawberry when your papers came in, but they haven't sent it yet."

"Chocolate is fine," he said weakly, and let himself look.

The loose-tied shirt and tight-fitting slacks of the evening had been replaced by standard-issue summer-weight fatigues. The blouse was zipped up, and she seemed to be wearing a bra underneath. Her shorts displayed no more than a reasonable length of shapely leg. She wore no makeup, and her face looked scrubbed and clean. You could hardly get mad at a woman for being good-looking. The sandwich looked toasted and crisp, and he found he was very hungry.

"Well, thanks," he said again, and took a bite, and picked up the pencil with his other hand.

"Karl had to go down to Ad," she said. He took his eyes off his paper, and figured that out. Administration office, she'd mean.

"They called him to bring down the Beetle 'log papers," she said. "He asked me to let you know — it'll be back in the morning."

He nodded, trying to match her casual air. The Betelgeuse analog was coming back from the shop tomorrow. And IBMan Carnahan would be due for his first installation — the first on his own command.

". . . we could finish your med-check in time for dinner," she was talking still. "You want to knock off up here pretty soon?"

He nodded again, and glanced over his board. The run he'd started would take most of an hour. Then some time for adjustments. . . . "Sixteen hours all right?" he asked.

"Fine. Dinner's at nineteen."

He sat there and stared at his sandwich and thought it all over, including the staggering fact of the Commander's silver leaves on the woman's faded green shirt collar.

The milk shake turned out to be good; the sandwich delicious. The run on the board got fouled up, and after a half an hour of grief, he had to admit his mind wasn't on it. There was a Manual on the wardroom shelf below, that would tell him the things he wanted to know. He switched off the board, and went down.

Page, 532, Section six, was explicit. The Medical Officer for a six-man crew had to have junior psych, as well as a senior pharmacist's or nurse's rating — *besides* being qualified sub for the Biotech. With Commander's rank, it meant she likely had more actual years of training than he did. And: "The Medical Officer shall be supplied with dossiers . . . psych ratings and personality profiles . . . responsible for well-being of personnel. . . ."

It explained some things: the milk shake and strawberry order, for instance; and why she should bother with either one. It did nothing to change the first impression of last night; or to make him forget his dreams; or — certainly — to make him feel any more at ease with Commander Anita Filmord. There were some things a woman shouldn't know about a man . . . or at least some women. . . .

There was very little Anita Filmord didn't know about Terry Carnahan three hours later. For the first half-hour she took smears and samples and scrapings with deft impersonal proficiency. Each labeled slide or tube went into its own slot or niche or clamp; then she threw a switch, and sat down to confront him with a questionnaire. To the familiar humming background of the diagnostics, she asked him all the questions he had answered twice a year for the past eight years.

"They put me through all this when I got my orders," he said at the end. "How come . . ."

"We do it every time you come on board. I'll have to run samples on Karl this evening too." The machine had run itself down. She pulled out the tape, tossed it onto her desk for reading later. "*I* don't know what you've been doing the past weeks," she pointed out, and he felt himself flush at the certainty of what she meant. "And we've got a good long time to be shut up on this ship together." She stood there looking at him. Her smile faded. "The prospect isn't too appealing, is it?"

"*You* are!" he might have said. This wasn't the Navy. The way she was dressed last night, the way she acted . . .

Last night — was it one of those dreams? He couldn't be sure, but the memory came clearly. . . . He had heard a door close, and the murmur of voices, one high and one low. Before he fell asleep again — or in his dream? — a tall figure had entered the bunkroom and flopped in the last empty sack.

Five men and one woman . . .

"*You're goddam right it's not!*" he wanted to say, but he shifted his gaze four inches, and the leaves on the collar of her short-sleeved shirt were still a Commander's.

He threw out all putative answers, and retreated to subordination.

"Yes, ma'am," he said blank-faced. "It surely is, ma'am." *Five men and one woman . . . and Deke had it all tied up!* . . .

"I'm glad to hear you say so, Lieutenant," she answered deadpan. "But if anything should turn up — any problems or questions or troubles of any kind — remember, that's why I'm here." Her smile was just a bit mechanical this time. *Good!*

"Just come if you need me," she said. "*Any time . . .*"

Five men and one woman . . . and *come*, she said, *any time* . . . maybe it wasn't just Deke. Maybe . . .

He went to the spray room and stripped and turned on the shower full blast to shut out Chandra Lal's cheerful talk. When he was finished, Chan was still in a cloud of steam, the effects of a day cleaning algy tanks now removed. While Terry rubbed himself harshly dry, Chan resumed conversation.

"How do you like the old bitch?" he asked idly.

"I'm not an expert," Carnahan said, and rubbed faster.

"Who is?" I've been here six years now, and I still get surprises. She may not look like much, but she's a hell of a mess of boat for five men to run. . . .

Five men and one woman . . . What the hell! Come off that track, boy. Chan was talking about the ship — not the Medic.

"You're right about that," Terry said, and escaped to his locker.

He wore his clean uniform like armor into the wardroom, accepted a cocktail, and sipped at it slowly. Deke, the pilot, and Captain Hillstrom were both drunk already, loudly replaying the ball game they'd just seen on the vid.

Hillstrom had shed his uniform as soon as he got back in the ship; he was bare-chested and rolled-cuffed again.

Deke at least dressed for dinner. So did Anita. Tonight, the tight-ass slacks were red, and she *did* wear a bra — also bright red — under her clear plastic shirt.

Mike wasn't dressed and he wasn't drunk. He came up just in time to sit down and eat with the rest, his face and coveralls both, if possible, one layer greasier than the day before. Chandra did not dress either: he emerged from the spray room, glowing, immaculate in the virtually non-existent trunks he'd worn the night before. Anita poured him a drink.

Obviously, she wouldn't care how — or if — Chan was dressed.

And if *she* didn't, who should?

Not Karl Hillstrom, that was clear; or perhaps he was too drunk to notice. . . .

Sleep didn't come easy that night. When all the crew's bunks but Deke's were filled, Terry gave up, and went out to the wardroom. He found Deke there, alone, watching a film. He tried to watch, too, but next to the screen, a red light on the Medic's door flashed, DON'T DISTURB! and his eyes kept seeing, instead of the picture, the curve of a thigh limned in the fiery red of her slacks, or perhaps of the bulb. . . .

He got up and prowled the room.

DON'T DISTURB. *". . . any time . . ."*

The door opened. Karl Hillstrom came out. It closed behind, and the light flicked off. She was alone now. She could be disturbed.

"Hi . . . late-late show?" Karl poured himself a drink and held up the bottle. "How about you?"

"I had it," Deke said.

"Terry?"

"Thanks. I will . . . later." He poured his own, a big one, and took it back to his bunk.

. . . any time . . . Deke didn't have it tied up, not at all . . .

At two in the morning, he remembered vaguely some provision in the Manual for refusal to serve in ships with a crew of less than ten, on grounds of personality stress. That meant a psych Board of course — and it had to go through the Medic . . . well, she might have reasons to make it easy for him. This wasn't the Navy, but it was still under Navy charter. *Lousy tramp!* He grinned, and promised himself to look it up, and went to sleep.

At three, he woke briefly, remembering she had said the Captain would have to have a new set of samples run that evening for his med records. Well, that *could* explain the DON'T DISTURB . . . At eight, they woke him to tell him the Beetle 'log was coming on board.

Mike Gorevitch drifted up from his engines to lend a hand, and the hand was a steady one, Terry found. By noon they were finished with a job that would have taken Terry more than a day by himself. His first installation was finished. Over a shared plate of cold meat in the galley, the IBMan found himself inexplicably pleased at the Chief's terse invitation to have a look below.

"Nothin' you didn't see before better on a Navy boat," Mike said, "But some of the stuff is rigged up my own way. You ever get stuck with a duty shift down there, you'll want to know . . ."

Like every jump-ship, the *Lady* was Navy built, equipped, and staffed. Even Hillstrom, who had made his stake in the Solar Fleet, had to get his Reserve Commission before they'd sell him his ship and lease him a stellar analog to hook onto the jump-along.

By now he had traded in that first cheap Sirius 'log for a prized Aldebaran, and had acquired a Betelgeuse besides. It was on Betelgeuse IV that Bailey, the IBMan who'd been with the *Lady* for nine or her thirteen years tramping, had lost his nerve. It was something that happened. The best jump-man reached the point where he'd figured he'd had it — the one more blind trip wouldn't work. Bailey quite cold, and declined even passage back.

This trip, the *Lady* carried a consignment of precision instruments for the new colony on Aldebaran III. But nobody ever got rich on consignment freight. It paid for the trip; that was all. The profit-shares came out of the other hold: the seeds and whisky and iron pigs and glassware and quick-freeze livestock embryos; the anything-and-whatsit barter goods that someone at some unchartered planet off the analog routes would pay for in some way. That was the lure that kept the crews on merchant ships: you never knew when you'd come back with the barter-hold full of uranium, or cast-gold native artifacts, or robin-egg diamonds.

And if you never knew for sure *when* you'd come back, or *where from,* or whether . . . well, that was the reason why IBMen went upstairs fast. For a man who could handle the job, there was pay and promotion, and almost anything else he might want.

What Carnahan wanted, the *Lady* didn't have.

For Mike Gorevitch, that was not the case.

The *Lady* was a tramp. She was scratched and dented and tarnished with age. She'd lost her polish, and her shape was out of date. She'd been around, and it showed.

But she had beauty in her still, if you knew where to look, and you *cared*.

"There's a dance in the old girl yet," Mike said approvingly, when he saw the IBMan's hand linger with pleasure on the smooth perfect surface of the shaft he'd ground the night before. "You read *Archy?*" he asked.

Terry shook his head. "What's that?"

"You might not like it," Mike said doubtfully. He opened a locker and pulled out a battered grease stained book. "Here. You can take it up with you if you want."

That night, Terry slept. He took the Manual and Mike's book both to the bunk with him right after dinner, and found what he wanted in one, then returned to the other. Both of them helped and so did exhaustion.

But somewhere in the night he woke long enough to note that it was Deke who came in last again, and to identify the pattern of repeated sounds from two nights back. It had *not* been a dream.

Five men and one woman . . . He wondered why Bailey had quit. Nine years, and then . . . If you took it that long . . . Well, he had the same way out if he wanted it . . . *any time* . . .

Next day, again, he worked at his board through the morning. This time it was Chandra who happened to be in the galley when Terry went down for his lunch. The pattern began to come clear: informal, haphazard, and unsystematic, but they were taking him over the ship, little by little.

The two of them sat on a white-painted bench in the Bio lab, and discoursed of algae and alien life-forms and also Anita. "Listen," Chan said abruptly, "has the blonde bombshell got you mixed up?"

"No," Terry said bitterly. "I wouldn't say that."

"It ain't like the Navy, is it kid?" Chan smiled, and it didn't matter if you knew the man had been trained for years to create just this feeling of empathy and understanding; he created it all the same. If he couldn't, they'd be in a hell of a spot on an alien planet. . . .

"Don't get me wrong," Terry said cautiously. "I like girls. If you think everyone sleeps in his own bed on a Navy ship . . ."

"I came out of Academy too," Chan reminded him.

"All right, then, you know what I mean. But this kind of deal — one dame, and the five of us, and — I just can't see it. If I go to a whore, I don't want her around me all day. And if I have a girl, I damn sure don't want every guy she sees to get into . . . you know what I mean!"

"Yeah." He was silent a moment. "I know what you mean, but I don't know if I can explain . . . Look, it's a small ship, and the payload counts. A girl friend for every guy would be nice, but . . . well, hell, kid, you'll see for yourself once we get going. All I wanted to say to begin with was if you got the idea it was all for one guy, you were wrong. Deke's always kind of hopped up before we go, and he's the guy we have to count on to get us out safe. She just naturally . . . naturally . . . anyhow, don't let him monopolize anything — not if you *want* it, that is."

"I don't," Terry said, and they went back to algae and aliens. And at least one thing emerged: Mike wasn't the only man on board who *cared.* Just what it was that mattered so much to him or to Chan, Terry wasn't quite sure: their work, or the *Lady* herself, or the dead dream she stood for. Whatever exactly it was, the *feeling* was something that Terry could understand — and that Deke and Hillstrom never could . . .

Hillstrom didn't have to. He owned the *Lady.* He wasn't obliged to understand her: only to pay the bills, and let the hired hands do their work for him. For her . . . ?

The hired help worked, all right. At least, Mike and Chan did, and Terry Carnahan. Even Deke put in a full morning up in Control, checking his board, and testing a dry run with Terry.

Even Deke? What the hell? Deke had been holding down, the driver's seat on the *Lady* for four years now. He *had* to be good. And he was; the half-hour's test was enough to show his class.

In his bunk that night, Terry improved his acquaintance with Archy the poet-cockroach, and Mehitabel the cat. Archy's opinions amused him; but in the determined dignity of the lady-cat's earthy enthusiasms, he found a philosophy sadly appropriate for the life of a *Lady* ship: and it was difficult to continue to feel entirely sad about the fit of the shoe while Mehitabel danced her wild free whirling dance, defiant and *toujoursgai* . . . *wotthehell* . . . *wotthehell* . . .

Mehitabel, Mike, and Chandra all helped. But backing them all up was the Manual.

P. 549, at the bottom: "An IBMan specialist may exercise his privilege of declaring the psychological conditions on board a ship of the specified classes unfit for blind jump at any time before plotting navigation data to the jump-off point in question. In such cases, the ship will return by analog to Lunar Base; or if unequipped to do so, will remain in its current port, pending a hearing by the Commandant."

They wouldn't jump till after the Aldebaran hop. Six weeks out, two weeks in port: there was time to wait and find out whether one lousy tramp could ruin the work and the dreams of thirteen years.

As he fell asleep, the IBMan thought with surprise that grease and nudity were perhaps as fitting uniforms in their ways for engine maintenance and bio work as knife-edge trouser creases were for precision computing. . . .

The thirty-foot-wide metal collar that encircled the lower third of the *Lady Jane*, in drydock, rose slowly out of the concrete pit. When the *Lady* had been lifted some twenty feet, the trucks moved in and extended supporting yard-wide jacks up into smaller collars, set in the underside of the wide, upper flange.

The outer lock, 'midships, swung open, and the elevator cage started down. Five figures in full-gear pressure suits emerged and took their places on the flange. They fastened the chains and winches securing the jacks in their sockets and belted themselves in position to keep a watch on the winches during the overland voyage.

One by one their voices cleared over the suit-to-suit. "All secure here . . . Okay . . . Check . . . Secure . . . That's it!" Hillstrom's was the last.

"All clear?" He waited five seconds, then waved the red flag at his side. The enormous pit jack sank downward; and the trucks started lifting alone. At fifty feet, the jet tubes were clear of the ramp. The trucks swivelled into alignment, and sixty-five earth-tons of wheelchair began to move the *Lady* away from drydock in lumbering state.

From his seat on the flange, Terence Hugh Carnahan surveyed man's moon, and found it good. Six hours away, the black knife-edge of lunar night sliced off the horizon. Ten minutes ahead, the mile-long launching tube yawned empty and waiting.

The suit-to-suit crackled with small talk and still-smaller humor. Terry almost gave in to the urge to turn it off. He'd been through the launching routine a hundred times, in mockups and dry runs, but this was his first time to ride a live ship over the face of the moon from the dock to the tube. If the schoolboy dreams of glory were dead forever . . . if the battered old hulk of the *Lady* was all he could have . . . even she had her dubious virtues, and among them the brightest was this . . . this moment, *now*, the fulfillment of, not a child's dream, but the Big Dream of a man, of mankind, for the stars.

It was sacrilege, nothing less, to be approaching the launch-site with a series of schoolboy *double entendres* supplying the background music.

He had actually reached for the switch, when a new voice floated in. "Still with us, Lieutenant?"

"Yes, *ma'am!*" He let his hand drop. The regulations made sense. Secured as they were in their seats, and spread round the bulge of the *Lady,* the audio was all the proof they had that each of them was still on post, alive and conscious. Even the Medic inside the sealed ship, watching the screen, couldn't be sure from what she could actually see, whether a man immobile inside a suit was effectively, operative.

They came up to the tube, and the great cranes reached out steel fingers, stripping and lifting the *Lady* out of her wheelchair wrappings, pushing and nudging and sliding her into place on the runway. Six moon-suited figures slid down the jacks into the trucks, and were toted back up to the airlock by the tube elevator.

There was no time for small talk now. Five hours to see for the last time that the ship was secure; once the word, *ready*, went down, it was too late to look any more.

Terry covered his section with swift methodical care. Satisfied, he went to his chair, and strapped himself in; he did a last double check on his board; then he fastened his helmet back on, and began the slow conscious relaxing of muscles and breathing that ended the ritual.

When the count-down began, he was off in a floating dream of sunshine and sparkling water. Zero *minus nine,* and he sat up erect. *Minus eight,* and he forced himself back into limpness before they hit *seven.* Breathe in . . . out . . . hold . . . in . . . six . . . *out* . . . hold . . in . . . hold . . . *five* . . . out . . . *four* . . . in . . . *three* . . out . . . *two.* . . innnnn*one*-nnnnou — *out!*

Off and out . . . down and out . . . blackness and whirlpools and terror and *kick* back, up, *out!*

His finger punched the wake-up button before he was fully aware of consciousness again. The light ahead of him flashed green, and there was an instant's prideful notice that his was the second green on. Then he forgot to be proud, and forgot to be Terry Carnahan. Green lights flashed and steadied, then yellow and blue and red. The board was a Christmas tree crossword constellation, each light a word or a number or place, their shifting patterns spelling out death and life.

Pressure eased; and the voices began — voices of engines and scanners and stresses and temps. Some he heard in the helmet and some the board told him with signals and lights. A voice in the helmet allowed him to take it off: the voice of the Bio board. A key on the pilot's board, at the chair up ahead, was depressed by a finger; the *think*-board, in this chair, flashed questioning lights. The *think*-board replied, and new figures lit up ahead, for the hands to use — the hands and direction and eyes of the *Lady,* up there at the pilot's board, steering *her* free of the multitude of menacing mites and pieces and bits of matter and mass in the populous planet-plied system.

The dance of escape begat rhythm to suit itself, and the old girl whirled on her axis, and pushed *her* way out to the stars, with a dance in her yet, wotthehell and the *think*-board was metal-and-plastic and flesh-and-blood too; part of *her,* of the steaming single mote which alone in this mote-filled single cell-of-Sol was bound to break out of bounds and escape to the endless entropic emptiness of Universe.

"Take a break, kid. We got a clear stretch here. Karl can take over."

He looked at the chrono, and didn't believe what he saw, and looked again. Five hours, and seventeen minutes past zero. Now aching muscles returned to sensation, and ego to Terry Carnahan.

Anita was standing beside him, one hand on a chair strap, the other held out to help.

"Whore!" he said. "Get away, bitch!"

She went away; Terry stayed where he was. What Deke could take, he could take too.

He took it for six hours more, through the last of the dust and debris of the System. He drank from the flask when it nuzzled his lips, and swallowed the pills she put in his mouth, and gave back what *she* needed: the readings and scannings and comps and corrections that went to the driver's seat, to the pilot's board, to Deke with the strength of ten and a in his heart.

He stayed there and took it until there was no more to do. Then he reached for the straps, and her hands were already there, unfastening him.

Bitch! he thought. *Tramp!* You don't want *me!*

He let her lead him out of the room, down the ladder, through dim yellow-green, to the door where the light would be flashing red outside.

And there he stopped. There was something important to ask her, when he found out what it was, he started to smile. *Which one do you want?*

Which *one?* How could she possibly tell?

As well ask, *Which one needs her?*

He laughed and stepped forward . . . and the tramp was his.

A Peculiar People

BETSY CURTIS

ABOUT BETSY CURTIS
AND
A PECULIAR PEOPLE

A Peculiar People *was first published:*
The Magazine of Fantasy and Science Fiction, *August 1951*

Readers of the May 1953 lead novel in Planet Stories, *"The Temptress of Planet Delight" ("It was forty years since the last G. C. Spacer . . . plenty can happen on an off galaxy world in that length of time") by "B. Curtis," may have been surprised to discover in subsequent issues of* Galaxy *and* F&SF *that the "B" stood for Betsy. Although she does not rate a mention in any of the many science fiction encyclopedias and readers guides, Betsy Curtis' work appeared frequently in* Fantasy and Science Fiction *and* Galaxy *the leading literary magazines of the 50s.*

Ms. Curtis is another one of those women the quality of whose work entitled her to larger recognition but whose output was too small to gain her the attention she deserved. Although the majority of Betsy Curtis' work appeared in the early 1950s, she was still contributing an occasional story to the field as recently as the 80s. Altogether she appears to have had around a dozen stories published in the course of a three decade career. "Peculiar People" was so highly thought of at the time of its original publication, that it was selected as one of the "best science fiction stories of the year" by Bleiler and Dikty, and reprinted among very distinguished company in their series of pioneering "best of" anthologies.

Ms. Curtis' droll tale of two unique mothers has undeservedly remained out of print ever since. Hopefully its appearance here will inspire other anthologists to seek out and reprint this excellent writer's far too neglected work.

A Peculiar People

by BETSY CURTIS

I N THE momentary privacy of the gentlemen's room, Fedrik Spens loosened the neck cord of his heavy white toga and reached for the threadlike platinum chain of his tiny adjuster key. Pulling back the pale plastissue skin from the almost invisible slit at the center of his chest, he inserted the key in the orifice of the olfactory intensificator and gave it two full turns. Three full turns for the food receptacle grinder. These official banquets could be murder. Removing the key, he retied the cord and approached the mirror, as the ambassador had insisted in last minute instructions to the several robots on the embassy staff.

"Normal respiration, human body temperature —" Fedrik could still hear the stentorian tones of the ambassador — "as there may be dancing after dinner. Check appearance carefully with a mirror. Martian security demands Terran ignorance of your mechanical nature!" (As if all of them hadn't lived like humans all their lives. It might be true, as some of the boys said, that the ambassador was subconsciously prejudiced.)

Coming out of the gentlemen's room, Spens found the ceremonial dinner procession already forming. His searching eyes found the little knot of attachés and he hurried to join his dinner partner, a statuesque blonde swathed in an ice-blue tissue tunic, and offered her his arm with appropriate compliments.

The great dinner was well under way when Fedrik, a little weary of small talk about Earth politics and fashions, let his gaze wander down and up the long resplendent table and saw the girl. Her head, demurely inclined to listen attentively to the man on her left, showed hair black and smooth as a Martian dove's wing, drawn softly back to a great Spanish knot. He stared at the gently rounded cheek and chin, proud neck and exquisitely modeled shoulders rising from folds of shiny deep green stuff — shoulders, neck, and face of the color and texture of the brown yornith blossom.

Trying to seem casual, he asked the blonde who she was, and received the noncommittal reply that she was probably the wife of one of the undersecretaries, who, she stated flatly before returning to the succulent *ambaut roatel,* were seldom invited to State Department functions.

Attaché Spens turned from his uninformative dinner partner to the imposing lady on his left and wondered at the towering mass of white hair piled on her head before he looked at her eyes and asked his question again.

"Who?" she replied. "The girl in bottle-green sataffa? Sitting this side of your Martian Emissary of Finance? Why she's Gordon Lowrie's daughter — the Minister of Terran Agriculture, you know. He's sitting down there between Alice Fanwell and Teresita Morgan." The white tower nodded almost imperceptibly down and across the table to Fedrik's left.

Fedrik looked covertly down the table where she gestured and noticed for the first time Gordon Lowrie's ageless face, the keen dark eyes, the smooth skin so dark a brown that the white, close-cropped hair seemed assumed for dramatic contrast. But not so dramatic as the daughter, Spens thought, as he stole a glance at the other end of the table.

He smoothed the magenta ribbon that crossed the glistening white folds on his chest, the ribbon that marked him as an attaché of the Martian Embassy, and smiled at the grande dame of the white hair-do. "The men in our department were jealous as anything when they found out I was coming to Earth. You earthwomen certainly outdo any of the rumors that reach us on Mars."

The lady inclined her white tower graciously, pleased. "We do have some pretty girls. But I'm sure," she added deprecatingly, "that half the effect is just seeing them in a different setting."

"No, I hate to say it, but our girls are mostly homely, like me. Attractive as anything, but homely." He grinned as she looked appraisingly at his straight red hair, craggy red brows, hawk nose and wide mouth. "You women all have a delicacy of feature that is a great pleasure to see."

White-tower's nose was tiny, straight, patrician. Spens looked down at his plate. "And the cooking. Is it always this good? I'm beginning to be sorry that I'm slated for only a year here."

"Randole is the treasure of the State Department," she informed him. "Good cooks are probably just as hard to come by here as on Mars. I hope some day you'll have a chance to eat with us at the Transport Hall. My husband, as you know, is Undersecretary Breton of Transport. We think our Ashil Blake as good as Randole, although Randole's *ambaut . . .*"

Fedrik stopped listening and began scheming.

Finding his quarry in the throng milling about the great silver ballroom was much easier than he had expected. His dinner partner had been claimed by her mustachioed husband as soon as they left the banquet hall; and as Spens circled the ballroom, he caught sight of Gordon Lowrie's white hair just beyond the shoulder of Bartok Borrl, the Martian finance chief. He joined the group casually, remarking deferentially to Borrl that the Terrans certainly put on a mighty splendid party and that "we'll have to work extra hard to give them a taste of Martian hospitality soon, won't we, sir?"

Borrl's eye searched the crowd for an instant, and it seemed to Fedrik that he performed the introductions with more than his usual enthusiasm. In fact, Fedrik had hardly begun to explain to Gordon Lowrie that he had wanted to meet him than his superior was excusing himself to the smiling girl and disappearing in the melee.

"My father," Fedrik continued, "was a tweedle and bradge farmer south of Jayfield and I grew up on the farm. He took his agricultural training here on Earth while the irrigation projects in his area were under construction; and I've always had a consuming curiosity about the Earth farms. Dad used to tell me and my brothers stories about cowboys and cattle ranching and miles of tall corn and plains of wheat rippling in the wind till we dreamt of it nights. We even used to have 'roundups' with bands of hoppy little tweedles and then throw them handfuls of bradoe and tell 'em to eat their corn and get fat now."

Anna Lowrie's laugh was a gay arpeggio.

"This part of the country is going to be a disappointment to you. Dad," she turned to Gordon, "has a few acres of choice tobacco and a prize dairy, but no prairies and no cowboys. When he's on the warpath, he insists he's part Indian, but he never gets very wild."

"We have garden corn, too, but it's Dwarf Pearl and we wouldn't think of casting it before swine," added Lowrie's rich baritone.

"Well anyhow, maybe you'll give me the address of a cow so I can tell my brothers, Donnel and Rone, that I've really seen one when I get back," Fedrik requested.

"Anna," said Gordon, "I wonder if this poor, ignorant, earnest, young man . . ."

"This seeker for wider experience, Father?"

"Exactly! Isn't it our duty to broaden his knowledge as well as to behave toward the stranger in our midst with diplomatic hospitality?"

"Mr. Spens," Anna's smile was infectious, "Daddy would like to invite you to become personally acquainted with one or several of our cows. Klover Korzybski Kreamline Garth would be charmed to know you, though you may prefer Altamont Daybird Fennerhaven, she being the petite Jersey type."

Gordon Lowrie frowned thoughtfully. "Of course, you'll have to meet them at their hours. Early morning, that is. What time do you have to be at the office?"

Fedrik was suddenly aware of his internal food chopper grinding away at speed three. "Oh, not much before eleven," he said as nonchalantly as he could.

"Then you could come right home with us now and visit with their highnesses at crack of day tomorrow and still have plenty of time to get back to stern realities by eleven." Anna was persuasive.

Fedrik could feel something, his little plans jumping up and down in his head. "Oh but . . ." he gestured toward the great shining floor where couples were turning in the slow ellipses of the xerxia, "I couldn't think of taking you away from here so early. Wouldn't you really like to dance?" He could even sacrifice the pleasure of looking at her for the pleasure of hearing more of her delicate contralto voice.

"Not tonight," she responded at once. "And everybody's used to my leaving early. I'm a government sculptress and *my* studio opens at eight, not eleven."

"You mean you do busts for halls of fame and bas-reliefs for post-offices and things like that?"

"Well . . . that's close enough. Anyhow, do come. We practically promised Mother to bring home something or someone from the party, didn't we, Dad?"

"Solemn promise, Annie. You're trapped, Mr. Spens. Trapped by two fiendishly exacting women. We'll meet you up at the copter stage as soon as we can find our robes," and Lowrie took his daughter's hand to leave the room as if there were no more to be said.

Fedrik hurried to the gentleman's room where he had left his downy black fur robe. Fortunately the room was again empty, and he turned off the empty grinder with considerable relief. Then out and up the ramp to the copter stage.

The thirty-minute copter trip seemed like ten to the young Martian as Anna and Gordon drew out the story of his winters at Jayfield Union School and Donnel's phoenix fair and Rone and Betha's trip to deep space.

At the house, Anna and her father left him to find her mother. Fedrik had only a few moments to look about at the deep, walnut-paneled room and notice the many stringed instruments lying about on tables and the top of the great black piano, the books, looking in the glow of many lamps like jewels, ruby, ultramarine, garnet, in their cases set into the paneling, the sedate smile of an old portrait, and the high, many-arched window. Anna entered almost at once, followed by a wheel chair pushed by Gordon Lowrie, which contained, feather-wool afghan across her knees, a lady in a rose sataffa wrap. Gordon eased the chair down the two broad steps to the lower level and Fedrik approached the chair.

"Mother," Lowrie bent over the chair, "this is Fedrik Spens from the Martian Embassy." He straightened. "Fedrik, this is my wife, Janet Lowrie."

Spens looked down into the sweet dark face. "So very glad, Mrs. Lowrie . . ."

"My name is Janet." The fine lines of a smile spread to her thin dark cheeks from the corners of clear brown eyes as she held out her hand. Fedrik took it and found the gentle pressure drawing him down to a chair beside her. "I won't ask you for your first impressions of Earth or what you think of Terran Woman." Fedrik grinned. "Gordon tells me that your father was a farmer; and presently we should like to hear about the Martian farm, but first let's have some real Brazilian coffee. Gordon?"

"At once, dear." He went back up the steps and out through the wide doorway.

Anna came to the other side of the chair and took her mother's other hand. "Mother's a sculptress, too, Fedrik, not a chronic invalid. She had a little accident at the studio a few weeks ago, but she's almost through with the wheel chair."

"A dangerous profession?" he asked, grave-faced, looking at the perfect modeling of Anna's head and shoulders.

"Oh no," she answered quickly. "A beaker of . . . of . . . solution fell and broke on her foot and an infection set in. By the way," her free hand waved about the room, "do you like music, and do you play a viol by any strange chance?"

"I could probably wring a tune out of this one." He rose and crossed to lift a viola d'aubade from the top of the piano. "I was the star," he bowed to the ladies, "of our grade school orchestra. Though I'm afraid I haven't played a note since."

"Daddy wrote a lovely xerxia for three viols the other day," Anna was setting up stands and handed Janet a tiny violette whose pale patina shone from use. "Let's surprise him with it."

The sweet sonority of the trio greeted Gordon's return. When the piece was finished, he set the tray before Anna and said, "Bravo, Fed. I like that even if I did write it myself. Do you know any of those rousing Martian frontier songs? *Out Along the Rim, In Ellberg Town,* or *Her Six-Ton Boots?*"

"Sure, but it's been so long since I held a viol that I don't think I could sing them and accompany at the same time."

Janet laughed. "Well, drink your coffee now and afterwards Anna can fake the harmony on the piano while you roar out those wonderful words."

Despite the cows and Anna's studio, it was one-thirty when Gordon showed Fedrik his room. An evening to remember for its fullness.

Skillfully as usual, Fedrik maneuvered the copter he had rented by the month, for the express purpose of bringing Anna home from the studio, down to the stage on the roof of the George Willis Public School to pick up Bud and Sukie, Anna's young brother and sister.

Bud waved from the crowd of children at the top of the ramp and bounded over to the copter yelling, "Hi Fed, hi Annie," at the top of his seven-year-old lungs. Sukie, six, as tall as Bud, followed more demurely and had to be boosted in, clutching a coloring book in one hand and holding a bright splashy painting on newsprint in the other.

"Hi kids. Home James, huh?" greeted Fedrik.

"Give her fifty gees and slam for the ranch!" hooted Bud from the back seat, while Sukie cuddled down on Anna's lap in the front and began a long "D'ya know what . . ." description of her school day to her older sister, who sat smiling and listening carefully.

Fed was glad he did not have to make talk as the copter carried them swiftly toward the Lowries'. This was probably the last trip, though the kids didn't know it. Neither did Anna. Nobody but himself had heard his going-over from the ambassador only an hour before.

"The Lowrie girl, Mr. Spens," the ambassador always came straight to the point with his subordinates in spite of his reputation as an interplanetary diplomat, "you're seeing a great deal of her these days."

"Yes, indeed, sir."

"That's hardly fair, Spens. Not fair to her if she's a tenth as sweet and affectionate as I imagine she is; not fair to us because there's an ever present danger that anyone who knows you too well will find that we have robots on our staff and draw the obvious conclusion that there are many of your kind on Mars. It's only human nature, you know, to be afraid of machines, and what men fear they fight."

"Yes, sir, but . . ."

"Interplanetary suspicion isn't likely to be aroused by a girl's being jilted by a young man; but I don't want it to go even that far. Lowrie's an important man to us, you know. We're still importing more than a fifth of our food, thanks to the fact that Earth farmers feel they can trust him. He's got to trust us."

"But sir, Miss Lowrie's not in love with me. It's true of course that I've been going out there to see her, but I want to be with her family, too. It's a family, sir, and they do things together — sing and talk and plan things like . . . like a garden . . . or a new cow barn . . . it's so . . . well . . . unlonely. It's more like having a new father and mother. I'm sure thy don't suspect anything." He hoped wildly that the ambassador couldn't suspect how much he needed Anna's incredibly friendly self.

The ambassador's face softened for a moment, his eyes looked far out the window. "Fathers and mothers have very sharp eyes, son. You love your Mars family too well to threaten their existence by a war, don't you? If I can't convince you that nobody on earth can hold your secret safely and that you must give up the Lowries, I'll have to ship you back home on the next flight. You'll have to get your music at concerts and your talk at receptions or not at all around here. That's all."

"Yes, sir. But may I take Miss Lowrie home this afternoon? She's expecting me."

"Of course. But make it brief. You can tell them that you've got a new assignment that's going to take a lot of time. Thank them nicely. Remember, we need Lowrie's good will."

Fedrik landed the copter gently in the plot by the house. The children dashed off into the interior and he followed Anna slowly into the paneled music room as usual. Anna slipped into her favorite chair and he brought her a frosty green glass of minth from the kulpour on a side table.

Before he could get words in order, Sukie popped into the room around the corner of the door, barefooted in a tattered old red plaid dress. "Look at me quick," she giggled and danced and bobbed about, then back to the door. "Just wait a minute now. You don't have to shut your eyes." She popped out.

In a moment she was back, resplendent in a ballet frock of spangled net, a star in her ebony curls, shining silveglas slippers on her twinkling feet. Bud followed her in reluctantly, swathed in a long mauve cape which did not entirely hide mauve knee-breeches. Sukie laughed at him gently, trillingly. "Daddy says I'm his queen of the starlings — and Bud and I are playing Cinderella. Do you like me?"

"I couldn't help myself, your majesty," Fedrik dropped gallantly to one knee and held out his hand as the little girl twirled about him.

Anna ran to the piano and added a few bars of the *Butterfly Étude* to the fun. Bud grinned condescendingly down at the kneeling Fedrik. Sukie stopped her whirling and laughed at Bud.

"You look so silly for a prince with all those teeth out," she said.

Fedrik got awkwardly to his feet. "Why Sukie, you'll look just as silly in a year or so when yours begin to drop," he observed.

"Oh no I shan't. Mine aren't going to drop," she stated saucily.

Anna got up. Her voice seemed cold. "Susan Lowrie, you know better than to say such things. Tell Bud you're sorry you teased him and then run along and play Cinderella in the nursery."

"I'm sorry, Bud," Sukie was half penitent. She followed him to the door, then turned back to Fedrik defiantly. "Just the same, I'm never going to look silly and my teeth aren't ever going to drop," and she was gone.

"Kids," Fedrik smiled, returning to the sofa, "always so jealous of their dignity."

Anna went back to her chair, stood behind it grasping the back. "Sukie mustn't learn to enjoy teasing Bud," she said quietly. "Everybody has some dignity. Bud's a right guy, but he can get perfectly miserable when he thinks he's not living up to what that little minx expects of him. Sue's got to learn to be fair."

That word *fair* again. Fed looked about the room and seemed to feel a wrench somewhere in the vicinity of his grinder. He searched his synapses for the thing to say and heard his voice, wistful, "You love children, don't you, Anna?"

Her face went blank. Her eyes stared at him. Her voice was empty. "Yes, Fedrik, I suppose I do." She walked around the tapestried chair and continued toward the steps and the door. "Please excuse me." Her voice seemed faint, confused. When she reached the door she was moving rapidly; and Fed imagined that she was running after she turned into the hall.

He had not had a chance to rise before she was gone; and he leaned forward to put his head in his hands, an unconscious imitation of Gerel Spens, who had sat like this when he was baffled.

His fingers had barely met at his temples when Janet Lowrie came through the door and down the steps, steadying herself on her husband's arm. Fedrik pulled himself off the sofa and stood up.

Gordon Lowrie assisted Janet to a tall carved chair and sat down on the arm of it. "Sit down, please, Fedrik."

Fedrik sat down.

"What was the matter with Anna, Fed? She came running out of here as if something were after her." Janet's voice was full of deep concern.

"Really, Janet, I don't know. We were talking about Bud and Sukie and suddenly she just said 'excuse me' and went out."

"Can you remember exactly what you said before she went?" asked Lowrie. "I have a particular reason for wanting to know."

"I . . . I . . . well, I guess I said she loved children, didn't she."

"Oh." Janet's dark face was full of pain and she reached for Gordon's hand where it lay on his knee.

Gordon took hers, clasped it. He looked at Fedrik. "I don't want to sound like the stern medieval father, Fedrik Spens, but I want to know if you are in love with Anna."

Here it was. There was no escape from finding words this time. Fed wondered what the ambassador would have said in his place. He tried to sit straight and matter of fact on the sofa, but it was too soft and he seemed to be wriggling deeper into the cushions.

"I'll tell you, Gordon, but it'll have to be in a sort of round-about way."

Gordon Lowrie's white head nodded, but otherwise he sat motionless.

"My father wanted to be an artist — a painter — but Mars needed farmers and his . . . his responsibilities combined with what amounted to orders from the government made him come here for training and then move out and start a family in the thick bradge country. When I used to go around with him he was always . . . exulting over colors and shadings and forms. He even used to bring home twigs of dry bradge and put them in bowls and sketch them; and when the brown and mauve yornith blossomed in the spring we used to have expeditions to the little valleys to bring home a few for a special celebration. Well, Gordon, Anna is lovely like all the things Dad showed me, and I wanted to make a special celebration for her."

Gordon glanced proudly down at Janet, who smiled up, then both turned back to Fed.

"And when I got to know her she was such a friendly encouraging sort of person and . . . and she had you. I don't know how to put it, but there's something about this house full of things you like to use and the children who don't look at you twice except as a welcome audience and ally . . . and . . . well . . . Anna is my friend. I guess that's not exactly love but there it is." He wondered how anybody could make such a lame speech as that.

Gordon's face was still serious, but he seemed somehow relieved. "It's hard, son, but that's how we hoped it was. Not love yet. Because we're going to have to ask you to see very little of us for a while."

("For the love of . . ." thought Fed, "they're going to do the breaking off and it's out of my hands." His relief was followed by the thought of the utter absence of Anna.) "Of course, if you say so, but I don't understand . . ."

"We want you to understand," Gordon said kindly, "and we want you to know because you're like one of the family and we don't want you to feel that we've cast you out. But the story of the reason is what all our government offices call a security risk; and once you know it, we could hardly let you go back to Mars." He looked hopefully at the young Martian.

"I'm afraid you better not tell me, Gordon," Fedrik replied regretfully, firmly. "The ambassador told me today that I was slated for a special mission back any day. I only came this afternoon to break the news and say good-bye."

"Would you like to stay, Fed?" Janet asked sympathetically. "Even if it meant not coming here for a while . . . that is, until Anna's married or living somewhere else?"

A soft, low voice broke in. "What about Anna, Mother? Are you planning to get rid of me?" No one had noticed her come so slowly through the door and down the two shallow carpeted steps.

Fedrik jumped and turned his head. Janet raised a beckoning hand and Anna went to sit on the other arm of her mother's chair. "What about Anna?"

"Wait a bit, dear," said Janet.

Gordon addressed Fedrik again. "I have papers in my study, Fed, that need only my signature to declare you a security risk for Earth and require that you stay here. And we really need men like you. There are a dozen excellent jobs. You can have your pick. And when you understand about us you'll probably find you want to stay and help anyway."

Fedrik sat motionless for a moment, flooded with a thought of gruesome humor . . . a security risk to both sides would be . . . well . . . too great a risk. He could imagine the interminable delicate argument between the ambassador and the President of Earth as to who was to conduct the disassembly, which side have the doubtful privilege of short-circuiting his synapses.

Gordon seemed to interpret Fedrik's silence as indecision. "There's Earth security, Fedrik, and Mars security: and then there's human security. I guess that really comes first; and that's why we need to tell you and have you understand."

Fed's memory cells flushed him a sudden picture of his father and of Betha, his father's only human child; and a feeling of affection and pity for their weakness, their kindness and their vast lovely dreams seemed mixed with the very metal of his bones. "Human security. Yes."

"So as one human being to another, I must tell you of your duties as a man as well as your privileges."

(His father had explained duty to him and Donnel and Rone so they'd understand about Betha.)

"You see, Susan and Anna here are — are our daughters, but they're not human like Bud. They're what you and Martians would think of as robots. Please don't interrupt me yet," as he saw Fed's mouth open.

"Because of the emigrations to other planets and an inexplicably declining birth rate, we came to depend more and more on intelligent machines in almost all kinds of work. And as we began to depend on them we began to be afraid — afraid of their alienness — afraid that they wouldn't always see things our way — afraid that some day we should have to choose between giving them up entirely, destroying them, or having them give us up entirely as poor, weak, selfish things who didn't deserve to clutter up their earth. We found out that we'd have to make friends of them, sons and daughters as well as bridge partners and copter mechanics . . . personalities that had to develop slowly like us, who understood and sympathized with us, no matter how much easier and more interesting and productive physical existence might be for them than for us. They had to love humanness. That's one reason why they look like humans. Both Janet and Anna," he smiled down, "are body sculptors." Janet made Anna almost as truly as if she were her real flesh-and-blood offspring.

"You're probably wondering now where the human security comes into the picture, what you and I are bound to do. Well . . . humans are a peculiar people with peculiarly human capabilities. We're bound to be fathers if we can — fathers of human children and mechanical, to grow up together under the most intelligent and loving care we can give them. Robots may be parents of robots here, but it's not the same. That's why you have a great duty that is not to Anna."

Anna added earnestly, "That's why I scolded Sukie, you see, Fed. She mustn't ever make Bud feel inferior — a feeling he might take out on his mechanical children some day. Of course Sukie's teeth won't ever drop out, although she will change her body every year for the next ten or eleven. We have our responsibilities too, in understanding you and in doing well the things we are made so well to do."

Fed traced the pattern in the wine carpet to the wall and back with his eyes as Gordon finished his revelation.

"And last of all comes interplanetary security," Gordon concluded firmly, sadly. "Your young cultures are still expanding and you rely on men still, not machines. As you can all too easily see, Mars would fear, and, when her economy is more self-sustaining, she would fight what she would think of as the alien invasion of Earth. She might try to rescue a few Janets, a few Gordons, from what she would consider the domination of unhuman interests; but most Earth humans as well as our dear foster children would be doomed. Because we humans have learned not to be type-gregarious. There are no associations here whose membership is more than about a quarter human. Janet and I have had two earlier families: this makes four children of our bodies, fifteen children given to us by the government. You must stay with us, Fedrik Spens, because you understand from knowing Anna what we can do here and why it must not be destroyed."

Martian stood up to face Earthman. He spoke deliberately but without feeling. "Settling the interplanetary angle will be even harder than you think . . . although I'm glad you told me. I imagine with care we can keep it between a few men at the top and me."

Gordon's dark face took on a shade of gray, not brown. "You don't mean that you're going to tell your ambassador?"

"It may be the best thing to do," was the reply, as Fedrik opened the neck of his conservative dark green toga and exposed the pale skin of his chest. He fumbled for the slit and pulled the edges back to show the adjustor orifices, the silver plate bearing his name and serial number. "I represent more than one security risk."

He retied the neck cord and smiled a little at last. "If I'm not officially disassembled, I might even marry Anna. That is, if she'll have me."

Anna rose and held out her hand, which he grasped as if never to let go.

Gordon began to laugh, convulsively, until he saw that Janet was weeping. He tightened his arm around her shoulders.

"I wouldn't worry about disassembly," he said. "I think your ambassador and I can make plans to write you into the charter at last without having anything to hide. And do you really want to get married?"

Two human-type mechanical faces looked only at each other.

"Then Annie, you bring me home a parentage application form from the studio tomorrow. I'll qualify you as parents first class."

"Anna," Fedrik asked, "will you make all our kids just like you?"

"Personally, I rather fancy craggy red-haired people."

" 'People' . . ." Gordon Lowrie murmured to his wife. There were tenderness and wonder and amusement in the quotation marks with which he enclosed the word.

Janet smiled up at him. "Well?" she asked.

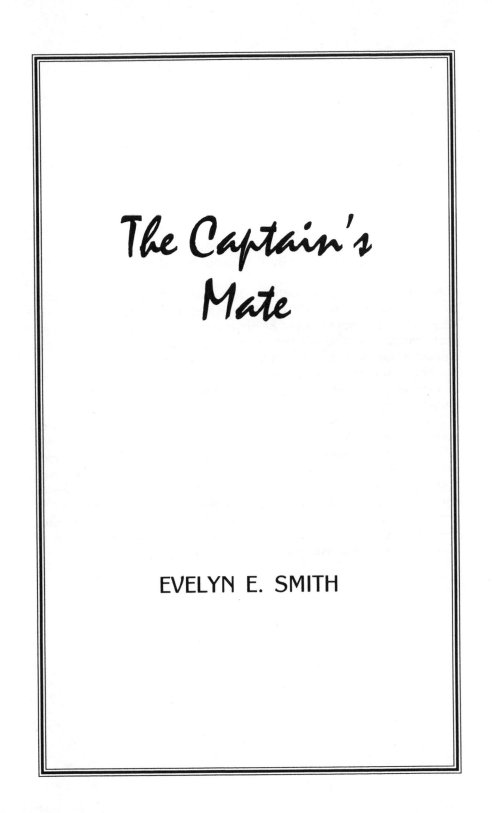

The Captain's Mate

EVELYN E. SMITH

ABOUT EVELYN E. SMITH
AND
THE CAPTAIN'S MATE

The Captain's Mate *was first published:*
The Magazine of Fantasy and Science Fiction, *March 1956*

No one who was familiar with the razor sharp satire of Evelyn E. Smith's stories for Galaxy *in the 1950s (and her subsequent if rarer appearances in* F&SF *since the 1960s) would be surprised to learn that in the last few years she has become the author of a highly successful series about a woman assassin. Evelyn E. Smith has been eagerly assassinating the Shibboleths and foibles of American culture, not to mention the absurdities of the war between the genders, for almost forty years. Thankfully she shows no sign of stopping now.*

Unfortunately almost none of her fine science fiction short stories or novels (which include The Perfect Planet *and* Unpopular Planet*) are available today. Thus readers are deprived of the pleasure of reading such delicious works as "Tea Tray in the Sky," "The Ignoble Savages," "Not Fit For Children," and "Sentry of the Sky." Until a wider republication, readers will have to content themselves with "The Captain's Mate," a mind-bending jape at gender roles that rings one more change on a hoary old theme than many readers may be expecting. Its inclusion on this anthology may make it one of our most controversial selections.*

The Captain's Mate

by EVELYN E. SMITH

"SOMETIMES, Captain," Deacon snarled, "I don't think you're even human." I looked at him. "Whoever said I was?" I replied, allowing myself to show an amusement I did not particularly feel. "Do I look human?"

At this, even the other men laughed. Deacon's face intensified in color. "You know what I mean," he retorted sullenly. "You have no feelings."

Feelings, indeed! What did this insignificant biped know of feelings! "My feelings are no concern of yours," I told him brusquely. "Similarly, yours are no concern of mine. You're paid to do a job, and I want that job done. . . . And take your greasy tentacles off my trunk!"

I pulled the chest out of his reach. It was my private property and I was damned if I'd let one of these monsters touch it.

"They're hands, do you hear me!" he yelled. "Hands, not tentacles, and I'll thank you to remember that!"

"I'll try to," I said, "if you will try to remember that I must be absolutely alone in the control room while I navigate. You know that's the shrlangi rule of space."

"I never heard it before," Spanier — the first and oldest of my three of officers — remarked. "And I've been kicking around space a good many years."

So what if I was young — if I had got my wings only a couple of days before takeoff — he didn't have to rub it in. Age and experience weren't everything, although I was beginning to realize that they might have a certain utilitarian value. "Well, you're hearing it now!" I snapped. "You've never sailed on a shrlangi ship before, have you?"

"No," he said softly. "None of us ever has. Funny coincidence, isn't it?"

"Yeah;" added little Muscat, "there's not one other shrlang aboard, even among the passengers. Just people, except for the captain. And most of the machinery wasn't made for human hands to work either." His voice was questioning.

"I'm sure you must have heard that, of all the intelligent and semi-intelligent species, only humans can breathe the same atmosphere as the shrlangi," I condescended to explain, "and I had no intention of spending over a month with my head in a tank."

"That doesn't explain why you didn't hire any shrlangi as crewmen," Deacon pointed out. He was beginning to annoy me. "It's usual to have mixed crews. Are you . . . afraid of your own kind? And why won't you at least come down to the engine room and see what's wrong? You know it's your duty."

I looked at him level-eyed, though inside my chitin I was shaking. "Telling me what my duty is, Deacon? That smacks of insubordination. Let me remind you that the irons in the brig also were designed for tentacles; human limbs might find them a bit painful."

He bit the fleshy protuberances on the lower part of his face.

"Don't blame him, sir," Spanier put in. "After all, you can't deny that things do seem a bit — well — fishy. It is rather odd for the captain never to leave his control room, even in an emergency."

I banged an anterior tentacle on the instrument panel. "When you address me, Mister Spanier," I thundered, "you'll call me *ma'am,* not *sir!*"

"Yes, ma'am," he said softly. "I always forget I'm addressing a . . . lady."

I couldn't really blame him, for no doubt to them I was as hideous a monster as they appeared to me, and the idea of femininity in my species as ludicrous as the thought that these uncouth creatures could possibly be males. However, I had picked my crew and passengers precisely because they had had little, if any, previous contact with the shrlangi. It had never occurred to me that the alien life-forms I hired would have sufficient intelligence to notice any peculiarity in the arrangements, and I was frightened, feeling that perhaps I had bitten off more than I could masticate.

The easiest way to mask fright is with anger. "Get out of the control room!" I stormed, breathing heavily through my spiracles. "All of you!"

They left without quite closing the door. "Bugs," I could hear Deacon mutter. "Just bugs. There's something about this setup that stinks to high heaven; I'll swear that leak in the auxiliary fuel tank wasn't an accident. Somebody wants to slow us down . . . and the captain's been doing everything she can to louse us up since she boarded *The Space Queen.* I'd give a week's salary to know what her little game is!"

"Yeah," agreed Muscat. "And another funny thing — what happened to her husband? His name is on the passenger list but he never came aboard. If you ask me, she doesn't want to reach Methfessel III — she's afraid the law'll be waiting for her there."

"But what good would all this stalling do her?" Spanier asked. "Eventually we'd have to make planetfall somewhere, and, wherever that was, the Intergalactics would be waiting for her. Give the gi — her a chance, maybe you're misjudging her."

"Sure," Muscat said. "Sure we're misjudging her. She's a wonderful — er — thing and a credit to space. So why won't she at least take a little trip down to the engine room and see what's wrong with the drive?"

"After all," the first officer told him, "this *is* a shrlangi ship and we aren't familiar with a lot of the equipment, or with the kind of alien mentality that constructed it. Maybe there's some good reason for all this."

"If you ask me," Deacon remarked harshly, "she doesn't know any more about running *The Space Queen* than we do. 'Two points off course already . . .'"

At that point I got up and angrily slammed the door. Then I fished my copy of the shrlangi edition of the *Intergalactic Space Manual* out of my carapace and checked it against the bewildering banks of colored lights and dials that surrounded me in all directions. Deacon was right; the ship was two points off course. I corrected it — at least I hoped that was what I did. However, the possibility existed that she was now four points off course.

I set her on automatic. Then I got up and drew the chlorophylgreen silk curtains that obscured the observation port. Only a clear plastic bubble stood between me and the vast blackness of interstellar space through which I, virtually alone, was guiding the destinies of fifty-two reasoning creatures — I, who had never even seen a spaceship before in all of my sheltered life. Everything was incredibly empty and silent except for the continuous, maddening whine of the engines in the background. I wondered, not for the first time in those two horrible weeks, whether I had not been a trifle impetuous in doing what I had done, too confident in assuming that I would be able to do it.

But what else could I have done to avoid disgrace for myself and everything I held dear? The answer was . . . *nothing.*

I closed the curtains and returned to my seat at the controls. I stroked the intricate chasings of the metal chest by my side, the chest that had been designed to hold my trousseau . . . for this voyage was to have been my honeymoon — the moment for which I had hoped and planned during all of my adolescent years. If only JrisXcha were by me to tell me what to do . . . but that was impossible now. Whatever happened, I would have to face the future alone.

There was a vast sense of unfulfillment inside of me that was more poignant than sorrow, more personal than infinity. Finally I realized it for what it was — I was hungry. The thought of food revolted me, but I must eat if I were to survive, and there were fifty-one life-forms depending upon me. From the stores in my locker, for I had known when first I set tentacle on *The Space Queen* that I would have to spend the whole month of the voyage virtually confined to the control room, I took a cake of compressed cpalKn and a container of vriClu . . . but when I tried to drink the liquor I gagged on it, remembering that, had it not been for JrisXcha's fatal predilection for that beverage, all this might not have happened. So I drank water instead and felt the better for it.

I tried to forget myself in music, so I played on my bnaloo and sang a very beautiful song about the vast emptinesses of deep space . . . but my hearts were not in it. What good is a song with no one to sing it to? At last I laid the instrument away and sat tormented by self-doubting and loneliness. Would I be able to prolong the trip until the time was right — or would we run out of fuel and drift in space until all perished? Was I right to have risked the lives of so many others — mere humans though they might be — on the slender chance of saving face and reputation?

As if in answer to my question, suddenly a tremendous explosion flung me out of my seat and across the cabin. The ship shuddered violently, as if some giant tentacle had reached out from space to rock it. For a few minutes it twisted and turned in corkscrew fashion, while I clung to a stanchion. There was another mighty thump, and then the body of the ship relapsed into a continual shivering. Meanwhile, the whine of the engines had risen to an alternate roar and rasp, diversified by the occasional crash of machinery. Far, far away I could hear the thin screams of the passengers. It looked to me as if something certainly had gone wrong.

As I picked myself and the navigation charts up from the deck, the door was flung open and the three officers burst in. From the paleness of their faces and the fixed gaze of their eyes, I deduced that they were in a disturbed state of mind.

Spanier saluted. "Ma'am," he said tersely, "we just fell out of hyperspace."

"Dear me!" I replied. "I do hope we haven't fallen on anything breakable."

"We haven't fallen *on* anything, ma'am," Spanier said. "We have fallen *into* normal space."

"Oh, we have?" I wished I could consult my *Manual*. "That is bad, isn't it? Well—uh—can't we just continue on through normal space?"

He exhaled a long breath through his facial aperture. "We can," he said, "but it would delay the voyage a hell of a lot."

I exhaled a long breath through my spiracles. This was exactly what I had hoped to accomplish, and here it had happened all by itself! "We're not in any hurry," I pointed out. "The cargo isn't perishable."

"No, but we are. Via hyperspace we would reach Methfessel III in twelve days from now, give or take a day. The same trip through normal space will take us two hundred and eighty-three years, give or take a decade."

"Oh," I murmured "that does sound rather long." I wasn't being authoritative enough. I cleared my throat. "How did it happen that we fell out of hyperspace anyhow? If someone was careless enough to drop us, it will bode ill for him."

"It was your fault!" Muscat burst out. "We tried to tell you all morning that one of the engines was on the blink, but you wouldn't listen. It finally blew up, and the detonation hurled us back into normal space."

"But we have three more," I protested. "Surely we can make do."

"The ship was built to operate on four, ma'am," Spanier said, "and it's much too heavy to get back into hyperspace on only three — especially since we lost so much reserve fuel before I could seal up the tank."

"Oh, yes," I said knowledgeably.

Maybe sneaking down that evening while everybody was at the ship's dance and boring a hole in her side hadn't been such a good idea, but it had been all I could think of at that moment.

There was a snort from Deacon. "See, what did I tell you? Doesn't know a damn thing about operating a spaceship. Probably an escaped criminal taking a desperate chance."

"That doesn't really matter now," the older man said. "At the moment all we're interested in is making planetfall."

"Ma'am," he turned to me, "our only chance of survival is to jettison the cargo and the passengers' and crew's gear. Everything that can possibly go must be dropped of. If we lighten the *Queen* enough, we might be able to get her back into hyperspace on only three engines. It's our only hope for making port. None of us can even try to fix the fourth engine now, because the shielding on the pile broke down and radiation is insidiously escaping."

I allected to ponder the question. "Well, if it must be done, I suppose it must."

"Thank you for your permission, captain," Spanier replied quietly "although I'm afraid I wouldn't have waited for it if you'd refused. . . . All right, men, pick up that chest and heave it out of the airlock."

"Wait a minute!" I cried, flying across the room and clutching my trunk frantically with all six of my appendages. "Don't you dare touch this box, you — you *man!*"

Spanier looked at me. Both his eyes were steady. "In an emergency, ma'am, I'm afraid we can play no favorites. If necessary, we'll even use force. The captain's trunk must go over the side with everybody else's gear."

The others nodded emphatically. "It's about time we saw some justice done on this ship," Deacon said darkly.

"But you don't understand!" I almost shrieked. "It's not just a chest; it has — it is — it's *vital* — necessary for running the ship!"

Muscat thrust me aside rudely and laid a tentacle on the trunk. "By God!" he declared, stepping backward on Deacon's pedal extremity. "Something moved. There's something alive inside!"

"Ouch!" the big man yelped. "Ve-ry sinister," he went on. "Let's have it open and take a look before we heave it out."

This was a real emergency! I turned around and expertly stung the three of them in rapid succession. They staggered back, groaning. Taking advantage of their temporary disablement, I pushed them out of the control room and bolted the door. It would be a matter of minutes before they blasted their way back in, but by then I hoped my problems would be solved — or, at least, taken out of my hands. If only Muscat were right . . .

Hastily I unlocked the chest. But, if Muscat had been wrong, I was lost . . . we were all lost.

And, as I threw back the lid, it looked as if he had been wrong after all. The pupa inside appeared as brown and lifeless as it had been when I had tenderly placed it there. If it didn't open now it would never have a chance to open. "JrisXcha!" I cried, wildly wringing all of my appendages that I wasn't using to stand on. "JrisXcha! Can you hear me?"

There was a faint stir and a rustle. I held my breath. A crack appeared in the cocoon; slowly it grew wider and wider. I almost fainted with relief as the chrysalis split open entirely, and JrisXcha — my wife — soared out into the control room in a flash of iridescent glory. She had got her wings at last!

"What happened, FkorKo?" she demanded, lighting on the instrument panel and staring bewilderedly around. "Where am I? All I remember is that last jug of vriClu at our mating ceremony, and then — *wham!*"

"You're in the control room of *The Space Queen,*" I told her. And for a moment I forgot the respect I had promised her at that same mating ceremony. "You fool, you knew perfectly well you weren't supposed to take alcohol of any kind for a week before pupation; your cocoon formed nineteen days too late!"

"But in that case I wouldn't have been an imago by takeoff time," she said, too bewildered to take exception to my pertness. "*The Space Queen* would have sailed under another captain, and I would have been droned out of the service — ruined. How did I get on it? And what are you doing in my carapace, FkorKo?" She began to laugh. "I must say, you look pretty damn silly in it."

"*I* matured in time," I explained, "because I was a clean-living larva, so I took your place. I could get away with pretending to be you, because the crew are all human — people, you know; I picked them specially — and the poor fools can't tell a male shrlang from a female."

My voice broke as the enormity of what I had done suddenly dawned on me. "B-but, in spite of everything I did, I'm afraid we'll never reach Methfessel III. I du-did everything I could think of to su-slow the ship du-du-down, and I'm a-a-fu-fraid I su-slowed her down pup-pup-pup-permanently!"

Now that I no longer had to pretend femininity, I could break down and indulge in the luxury of prolonged ululation.

JrisXcha came over and put three appendages around my — rather, her — chitin. "Brave little fellow," she said in a voice choked with emotion. "I don't know what I ever did to deserve a husband like you. All I can say is, I certainly was a very lucky larva." She twined her antenna with mine. "Don't worry, egg; I'll get the ship in shape again — I didn't graduate *summa cum laude* from the Hexapod Space Academy for nothing. . . . What's that noise at the door?"

"Ih—it's the officers," I sobbed. "I thu-think they're probably coming to throw me — us in the brig."

She brushed me briefly with her feelers. "Don't worry, honey, I'll take care of this. Give me the uniform." I slid out of the carapace. She donned it quickly, while I draped myself in a sari out of the silk from her cocoon. Brown wasn't really my color, but I couldn't afford to be choosy.

JrisXcIla slipped the bolts on the door and flung it open so suddenly that Deacon and Muscat fell flat on their faces, while Spanier only just managed to keep his balance. "Why the blowtorch, gentlemen?" my wife asked easily. "Surely a simple knock would have sufficed. I am not so inaccessible as all that."

Deacon's skin darkened. "Why, you . . ." he began, pointing his blaster at JrisXcha, as he rose from the door in a half-crouch. I rushed forward, ready to throw myself between them and take the charge full in my thorax.

"Wait a minute," Spanier restrained the big man. "There are two of them now!"

They stared in bewilderment, first at JrisXcha, then at me, then at the chest, standing open and empty. "So that was why she wouldn't let us jettison the trunk," Muscat said slowly. "The other one was in it all the time. I'm sorry, ma'am; I wouldn't have been so — so rude to you if I'd known you were a mother."

"I'm not, actually," JrisXcha admitted, "but I hope to be, in the very near future." She was a quick thinker. "Gentlemen, allow me to introduce you to my husband, FkorKo." She pulled me to her side with two appendages. I lowered my eyes modestly, as a dutiful husband should.

"I'm sorry there had to be all this mystery, but the whole thing was a little embarrassing you know. And against regulations. A shrlang space officer isn't allowed to bring any member of her family along while he is in—excuse the expression — the pupal state. Spouses are supposed to mature at the same time. Only FkorKo was taken suddenly ill," she said, trying not to catch my eyes, "and didn't go into the pupal state when he was supposed to."

"Oh," said Deacon, "he was in a cocoon, huh?"

"But why couldn't you have waited until he matured before you started the trip?" Muscat asked.

"Nothing is supposed to stop an officer from carrying out his duties. If I'd waited until he became an imago, I'd have lost my ship — and I'd never have got another. I'd have been cashiered and both of us would have become creditless outcasts. I do hope that I can trust you not to say anything about this . . . ?"

"I'll see that the men keep it to themselves, ma'am," Spanier said. "If we live to have any tale to tell. The ship's in a pretty sad state."

"Oh, I'm sure I'll have whatever's wrong fixed in a trice now that I can put my whole mind on it," JrisXcha assured him. "You know how it is — I was so worried about my husband I just couldn't think straight."

"Of course," Deacon said contritely.

"Gee, I can imagine," Muscat echoed. "If we had only known . . ."

I liked them even if they were human. They had feelings.

"And we won't hold it against you for stinging us," Deacon added magnanimously.

"Did I — er — I was so distraught I just didn't know what I was doing." JrisXcha pulled me close and brushed my antenna lightly with hers, although ordinarily she is not demonstrative in public. "I have a wonderful little husband," she said.

"But why didn't you tell us?" Spanier wanted to know. "No matter how we felt about you, we'd hardly throw out your husband's cocoon."

JrisXcha concealed a smile with an anterior tentacle. "Well, it was so hard to put delicately," she said. "You know, each life-form has its own taboos. . . ."

The other men looked reproachfully at Spanier. His skin reddened. "Sorry, ma'am; I didn't understand."

"Quite all right," she told him cordially. "You couldn't have been expected to know."

I repressed a nervous titter with difficulty.

"Now," she went on, "I'll just step down to the engine room with you chaps and have everything right in a jiffy. We shrlangi are unaffected by radiation, you know. . . . You just wait up here, egg, and, remember, don't put your pretty little tentacles on any of the machinery."

"No, honey," I vowed, "I'll never touch another piece of machinery again as long as I live."

My wife confidently led the way out of the control room. The three humans followed her dazedly. The situation was well in hand.

Spanler was the last out. Before he left, he turned and looked at me. "Mighty proud to know you, sir," he said. "Mighty proud." Stretching out a tentacle — a hand, rather — he grasped one of my middle appendages in his and vibrated it with, I instantly perceived, amicable intent. "You know, sir," he said, "if you're not familiar with another species, sometimes it is hard to tell one sex, let alone one individual, from another. I suppose you have the same difficulty too. But, when you've worked closely with somebody, you get to know them, whether they're human or alien — and somebody you really know and like is never an alien."

He coughed and I could see that it was in embarrassment, because he was no longer an alien either. "What I'm trying to say is this," he concluded huskily, "bug or no bug, you're a great little guy . . . captain."

Part Four

The
60s & 70s

Sense of Duty

PHYLLIS EISENSTEIN

ABOUT PHYLLIS EISENSTEIN
AND
SENSE OF DUTY

Sense Of Duty *was first published:*
Isaac Asimov's, *June 1985*

The believable cultures against which Phyllis Eisenstein sets her science fiction and fantasy are no accident. Ms. Eisenstein took her degree in anthropology . To this basic gift for understanding how social systems work and why they originate, she adds an ability to create engaging characters and a native talent for storytelling.

Her science fiction has been nominated for both the Hugo and Nebula awards. Shadow of Earth *describes in convincing detail the inner and outer trials of a contemporary woman thrust into a medieval world. Her fantasy novel,* Born to Exile, *was a recipient of the Balrog Award for the Years Best Fantasy Novel.*

In the hands of a less skilled writer, "Sense of Duty" might have been nothing more than just another misunderstood, brilliant child as "changeling" (mutant, alien, Slan) story. But under Phyllis Eisenstein's sure touch, it becomes a haunting parable about the way life imposes unchosen duties on us all. Family, job, self-fulfillment, community — each exerts its own pull. What we choose, and in what combinations, defines who we are and determines the shape of our lives. It also depends, Ms. Eisenstein says, on just where your sense of duty lies.

Sense Of Duty

by PHYLLIS EISENSTEIN

How shall I start this story, my sweet Mariana, knowing that you won't read it for such a very long time? You were sitting on my lap only an hour ago, playing pattycake, your chubby hands so small against my own, and it was hard for me to imagine you as an adult looking at your mother's words on a yellowing sheet of paper. Will you even remember me by then — my face, my voice, the way I rocked you to sleep? Will you have dreamt of me sometimes, and wondered how it would have been to grow up under my care? Or will you just hate me for what I did to you, as I once hated my own mother? Oh, I hope that won't be so, Mariana. I hope that by the time you read these words you will already have come to understand that there are no good choices in our lives, dear child, only bad ones and less bad.

My own life, I'm sure, would seem very strange to you. It was strange even to my parents, though I never suspected that while I was growing up. I myself had nothing else to compare it with, and so I thought that the place I lived was quite ordinary and that I and my parents were very much like the people around us. I thought that, even after looking through my father's glasses.

I was very young at the time, curious about everything, and the glasses were a temptation too strong to resist. The hearing aids were out of reach — my parents wore them constantly, and so there was no way I could try one in my own ear. But my father hardly ever wore his glasses, though he always kept them near him, in his breast pocket by day, on his bedside table at night. More than once, I had been told not to touch them, especially when he lifted me into his arms for a hug and they were so close to my hand that I couldn't resist the smooth, almost silky texture of their soft leather case. I had been told they were too fragile for my child's touch, and I understood that, having broken a fair number of my mother's porcelain miniatures. Still, I had no glasses of my own, and I couldn't help wondering how they would look on my face.

My chance came the morning after a heavy rainstorm. My parents' bedroom window had been left open during the night, and a small rug had been soaked and required immediate removal to the basement. As they rushed the dripping, unwieldy bundle downstairs, I noticed that, in his hurry, my father had left the glasses behind. I slipped into the room and carefully took them from their case. They were heavier than I had expected, and the hinges stiffer, but I managed to unfold them and set them on my nose. They were, of course, much too large for me, their stems projecting well behind my ears, and I had to hold them on with both hands.

I was young enough not to know that some eyes were less perfect than my own, and so I did not think it odd that the lenses let me see without any distortion. I turned to the mirror to look at myself, and I couldn't help smiling because the sight was so silly, like a caricature of an adult. And then I happened to notice the reflection of the bedroom window. I had looked out my own window some moments earlier, at the backyard, the grass all sparkling with water droplets, and at the sky, swept clean of every cloud. But the square of sky reflected in the mirror was different — still blue, but overlaid with brilliant bands of yellow, orange and magenta, like strokes from some enormous paintbrush. I turned to look at the window itself, and it was the same. But oh, when I reached the sill and saw more than that tiny square . . . to my child eyes the sight was gorgeous, curving stripes spanning from horizon to horizon, converging in clusters here and there, broad wedges of blue between them. I stared and stared until I heard my parents' voices, and then I barely had enough time to slip the glasses back into their case on the bedside table.

The lines in the sky vanished, of course, when I took them off.

I didn't tell my parents what I had done, what I had seen. I was afraid of punishment. And I was also afraid that, for some reason I could not fathom, I was not supposed to see the sky that way, and if I told them I had, something would be spoiled for me. What that something might be, I couldn't guess. But the fact that I had no glasses of my own showed clearly enough that the patterns in the sky were not for me. Still, I thought of them sometimes when I was in bed at night, saw them in my mind, and wondered why so many people I saw on the street were allowed to wear glasses while I was not.

At this point, you'll probably shake your head at my naivete. I doubt that you can imagine someone who doesn't know about those markings in the sky; they'll have been part of your life for a very long time. But remember, I said my life would be strange to you. Now I must tell you something about that strangeness.

I grew up in a very large city named Chicago. By very large, I mean a population of several million, in a country where such cities were not uncommon. My parents chose to educate me in the local government-supported school system, even though it was not of the highest available quality, because they thought interaction on a broad variety of social and intellectual levels would be good for me. In this, they were mistaken. From the beginning, most of my schoolmates disliked me, and — socially isolated by their dislike — I did very little interacting on any level at all.

At the time, I did not understand why this should be so, and I had a great deal of trouble communicating about the matter to my parents, who seemed to think that, somehow, I simply wasn't trying hard enough to be friendly. Now

I realize that my problems were due partly to the other children's resentment of my too-obviously superior intelligence, and partly to their perception, on some deep level, that I was *different*. Children, I think, have a particular sensitivity to differentness, and neither tolerance nor courtesy for those who manifest it. There were a few good moments, a few brief flashes of friendliness from individuals who themselves danced on the social peripheries at school, but on balance my childhood and early adolescence were miserable.

However, though a social failure, I was an intellectual success, completing the standard courses of primary and secondary education so effectively that I was admitted to a university of great prestige. And my life there was refreshingly different; the place was full of people who had nurtured their intellects at the expense of social integration, and who — faced for the first time in their lives with their intellectual equals — were finally beginning to form real friendships. I counted myself one of them. It was a glorious experience to sit through the afternoon talking and laughing and knowing that we were embarking together and willingly on the great journey into the accumulated knowledge of an entire species. That was heady wine for me, that great journey with stalwart friends.

And even headier was the experience of falling in love.

He was my age, a classmate and, by the standards of the time and place, physically attractive. I had never been in love before, and though the entertainment media had displayed the phenomenon to me, they had not prepared me to be so completely overwhelmed by it. If he entered a room, I could not tear my eyes from him; if he smiled, I found myself smiling, too; and if he laughed, I felt a sun burst inside me. We shared two classes, adjoining seats in both, and he appeared to be well pleased by that circumstance. In time, we began to share meals and to take long walks about the campus together. He was a charming companion, and I found myself trying hard to be charming myself, so that he would continue to enjoy my presence.

His name was Edward.

The university was located in Chicago, and therefore I continued to live with my parents during my period of instruction there. I told them, of course, about my feelings for Edward, and I even brought him home for dinner now and again. They seemed to like him personally, but I could sense that they were less than happy about the intensity of my interest in him. At the time, I believed this was because his socio-economic background did not please them. His father was a dockworker in a large city some distance away, his mother a clerk in a clothing shop, and he himself worked in the university bookstore in order to supplement the scholarship that defrayed most of his expenses. In sharp contrast, my expenses were paid by my parents, whose substantial income was derived from a flourishing air-freight company.

I thought it was social prejudice that caused my parents to introduce me to the son of one of their business associates.

He was a pleasant enough person, a few years older than I, and a partner in his parents' air-freight business. He escorted me to the theater a few times, and bought me several expensive meals. From the first, I had the impression that he was entertaining me as a favor to his parents. I tried to be friendly, as a favor to my own parents, but our meetings tended to be somewhat strained. We were two people with no real attraction to each other, like two ticket-holders waiting in line at an athletic event, passing the time cordially till the gates should open.

I only felt truly alive with Edward.

We had intellectual closeness. Physical closeness seemed inevitable. I saw all the couples roaming the university campus, holding hands, sometimes even with their arms about each others' waists. I watched them smile into each others' eyes, whisper in each others' ears, kiss. I had never been kissed, except by my parents. I had never touched Edward except by accident, a brushing of shoulders in adjoining chairs, the brief contact of hands in passing a book. Truthfully, I was a little afraid to touch him, as if some kind of electricity would leap between us at the contact, wonderful and terrible all at once.

But the time came. A time I shall never forget.

It was spring, a long twilit evening in spring, and the air itself was as new and fresh as the grass we walked on. Edward and I had both done well on an important series of examinations, and we were feeling exultant. Or, as we phrased it at the time, drunk with happiness.

Drunk with happiness, I caught his hand in mine as we walked. He smiled and closed his fingers firmly about my own. His were warm, I remember. Very warm.

We fell silent then. I was supremely conscious of the pressure of his hand, and my heart was pounding so hard that it seemed to shake me with every beat. At last we stopped under an old, gnarled tree, a tree as old as the university, its bark scarred by the brief messages of lovers who had paused there before us and thought to tell the world about themselves. We stopped, and I leaned my head on Edward's shoulder, on his warm, warm shoulder, and then he put his arms around me and kissed me, and his lips were warm, too, as if the sun had been heating them all day in preparation for this moment.

He drew back, then, and I couldn't see his face in the darkness, but his arm was still around me, and it stayed there as we walked back to the dormitory that was his campus home and the dinner that waited there. Edward's arm around me. I had never been so happy. I was too happy even to notice my parents' frowns later that evening. They wanted me to see their business associate's son again, but I just laughed and shook my head. I had no use for him.

The next day, Edward was absent from both of the classes we shared. I thought perhaps he was sick — he had been so very warm the evening before — and I called the dormitory, but he wasn't there. A little later, when I had a free hour, I slipped into the back of one of his other classes and saw him in his usual seat in the front row. My heart started to pound again, only partly with relief. It was so wonderful to see him. How empty my life had been before; Edward made up for all those unhappy years. Edward. Edward.

I waited for him just outside the classroom door. He smiled when he saw me, but slowly; a tired smile, I thought. There were dark circles under his eyes. I asked him if he was all right, but he just shrugged and said he'd promised to work an early hour at the bookstore, so he had to hurry. I said I'd see him later, but he was already loping away, and I didn't know if he had heard me.

I was at the store when his shift was over, and we walked out together. He was very quiet, and he moved slowly; I thought he looked even more tired than before. I suggested he needed some rest, but he didn't answer; he was walking toward the dormitory, though. Slowly.

It was when I tried to take his hand that he stopped.

He tried not to look at me. He tried to look past me, as if he were afraid of my face, my eyes. And when he spoke, he stammered and hesitated, and it wasn't his way of speaking at all, it was some stranger standing there in the bright sunlight, some terribly uncomfortable stranger. He apologized for the previous night, for kissing me, for holding me in his arms. He apologized for giving me the impression that he wanted some kind of physical relationship with me. He had thought about it all night, he had tossed and turned and paced his room, thinking about how to tell me that he shouldn't monopolize me any more, that I should see other people and find someone right for me.

I didn't understand at first. I didn't want to understand. I told him I didn't want to spend my time with anyone else. I told him I cared for him more than I had ever cared for anyone in my life.

And he said he was sorry but he just couldn't return that feeling.

Abruptly, he started walking again, but not slowly now, not slowly at all. I had to run to catch up, to stay beside him, talking rapidly all the while, asking him to reconsider, not to make such a hasty decision, to give himself more time, to give me more time, and he didn't answer me, he just kept going. Tears were blurring my vision by the time we reached the dormitory steps, and I stumbled and barked my shin on the concrete. He stopped then, his hand on the door, and he was breathing almost as hard as I was. He didn't help me up. He just looked down at me and said it would be better if we made a clean break. It would be better. And he went inside.

The next few days were a bitter ordeal for me. Edward attended the classes we shared, but he sat across the room instead of beside me, and not once did he glance in my direction. I knew, because I never looked away from him. I heard the instructor only dimly, and I took no notes at all. The material suddenly seemed unimportant, only Edward's face was important. Not once did that face smile at me. Not once.

I tried to say hello at first, after class, but he always hurried away. Sometimes I followed him, if I had free time, or even if I didn't, just followed him to wherever he was going, class or the bookstore or the dormitory, followed at a distance. I think I was willing him to turn around and see me, to wave, to say something, but he never did. Clean break, he had said. Oh, so very clean.

At night, I closed my bedroom door and cried into my pillow. Quietly, so that my parents wouldn't hear.

But they did hear, of course. And they saw my puffy, red-rimmed eyes at the dinner table. And one evening, as I lay on my bed, aching at the emptiness of the universe, I heard them murmuring to each other in the next room, and I knew they were talking about me.

I don't think they ever really understood how I felt about Edward. I don't think they ever dreamed that I could fall in love with one of his kind. That was their mistake, you see. They had chosen to make me what I was without at all comprehending the logical consequences of that choice. And I was the one who had to pay for their misjudgment.

They knocked softly at my bedroom door. I blotted my tears on the pillow and turned it over so the wet part wouldn't show; then I called for them to come in.

They wanted to know what was wrong, of course. I didn't want to tell them at first, but they guessed that it had to do with Edward, and at last the whole story came out, and I was crying again, into my hands this time, my eyes shut tight. I didn't want to see their faces. I didn't want to see the relief I knew must be there. They had disapproved, and now the target of their disapproval had neatly removed himself from their daughter's life. I hated them, at that moment, for perceiving anything positive in my misery.

I felt the bed give as they both sat down on it. Then I felt their hands on my arms. You mustn't feel so sad, they said. There never could have been a future for you and Edward, no more than for you and a dog or a cat. And then they told me the truth, for the very first time, the truth that a child could not have been trusted with, that I had to grow up to hear, and now I was grown up enough. That this place where I had lived all my life was not mine, not my city, not my country, not my planet. That these people I had thought were so very much like me were not even my own species. We might look similar on the outside, but inside, our structures and our chemistries were different. My pheromones were wrong, they said; and Edward could not respond to them. No member of his species could.

At first I thought they were making some sort of bizarre joke. I was a human being, *homo sapiens sapiens*. I knew that. And yet, when I looked up at them, I saw that their faces were serious, even as their mouths formed one preposterous word after another.

And then I thought, my parents are insane.

We talked through the night, the three of us. I had read about structured delusions in a psychology text, and what they told me in that long, long conversation seemed to fit a diagnosis of schizophrenia perfectly. They were officers in the military establishment of an interstellar civilization, part of a team that had come to this planet to maintain the frontier garrison and refueling station that had been established here generations ago. Their identities were false, carefully prepared by their predecessors, and complete with all the appropriate documents. Though it did produce income, the air freight company was just part of their camouflage, as other commercial transport concerns had been in earlier times. Their real job, the job of their entire thinly-spread species, was to render assistance to travelers from a vast galactic empire totally unknown to *homo sapiens sapiens*. They — and I — actually looked less human than I thought, but sophisticated cosmetic techniques had enhanced a superficial similarity, and so we passed.

They had intended to tell me all of this, they said, when they were sure that I could be trusted to keep the secret. When my local education was done. When it was time for me to join the family business, to receive my own commission and my own assignment.

I listened, thinking to humor them with my attention. How trivial my own problems must have seemed to them, I thought, in the face of this grand delusion. Yet I had to ask, how could they believe it all? If we only seemed human on the outside, how had I passed the physical examinations required for entry into school, how had I been able to undergo blood tests, vaccinations, X-rays? Surely my identity would have been exposed at some time. No, they said, for they had doctors of their own to deal with these situations. This was an old garrison, a civilization intensively studied by their own, and they had evolved many ways of evading its threats to their secrecy. Every officer intended for service here was throughly briefed before beginning a tour of duty, and so far, in all the time their species had been on this planet, there had never been any insurmountable problems.

But I had not been briefed, I said. I had no way of knowing that my body could give their secret away. What would have happened if I had been hit by a vehicle and carried off, unknown to my parents, to some hospital, to be examined by some human doctor? Where would their secret have been then? And they looked at each other — nervously, I thought, each of them trying to think of some clever rationalization — and my mother said we were a tough species, hard to damage, very hard, but if the damage were great enough to incapacitate, there was an implant beneath my heart that would instantly burn my body to a loose gray ash. It would be a bizarre and inexplicable event, but it would not give the secret away. This planet was not ready to join the galactic empire, said my mother, would not be ready for a very long time, but the garrison was here, and so the secret must be kept.

And when she said that, I thought I had the question that would shatter the delusion, if any question could. Why, I asked, was the garrison here, rather than on Mars or one of the moons of Jupiter or Saturn? Surely a spacefaring civilization knew how to recycle food and water, knew how to refine fuel from the raw materials available on an uninhabited world. Why, if there really were a secret galactic empire, did it choose as a base the one body in this whole solar system where the secret might be in jeopardy? I didn't think she could answer that; I couldn't think of a good answer for it myself. But she just laughed, a soft, rueful laugh, and said that I was quite right about the food and water and fuel, but there were fifteen officers scattered across the surface of this planet, and if they were forced to live in a sealed station on some bleak, airless rock, with no one but each other for company, they would all go mad.

It seemed very neat — I had to admit that. But I thought, of course, they've had years to develop their delusion, years to reinforce each other in it. I no longer felt like crying over my own problem. Theirs was too terrible. And I had lived my whole life with them and never suspected it. They had kept their secret supremely well.

By dawn I think they both realized that, no matter how many times I nodded at their words, I didn't really believe anything they said.

My father was the one to halt our conversation. He stood up. He seemed very tall, standing beside the bed — as tall as he had seemed when I was a small child. I had always accepted his word on the truths of the universe, and now I felt guilty that I could no longer do so. He must have read that feeling on my face, because he said it was right that I should doubt, that I should require proof for any claim, even his. The three of us would go to his office at the airport, he said, and he and my mother would show me that proof.

I looked from one of them to the other, pity and protectiveness overwhelming me, as if I were the parent and they the ailing children. I saw that they needed me desperately. They were reaching out to me by including me in their delusion, and I would be betraying them if I didn't make my best effort to shepherd them to professional help. But if I was to attempt that, they must trust me, and there was obviously only one way to prove myself worthy of their trust.

The trip to the airport was not a long one. I had been to the air freight office a number of times and was familiar with it and with the warehouse and hangars next door. Even so early in the morning, workers were already busy there, checking inventory, receiving cargo from ground vehicles, and loading it into airplanes. One of the planes was almost ready to leave, only waiting for clearance from the airport control center for the first departure of the day. My parents conducted me to that plane; the pilot, who apparently expected us, indicated three seats behind his own. We boarded and strapped ourselves in.

After we were airborne, my father took out his glasses and handed them to me.

I hadn't thought about the pattern in the sky for years, but it was still there, bright and clear, the stripes shining strongly even through scattered clouds. They looked broader from a height, each band crisper than any rainbow, forming a vast latticework, like a dome over the world. We flew level beneath them for a time, the city gradually dropping behind us till even its suburbs had given way to cornfields, and then the plane angled upward once more, almost — I thought to myself — as if heading for one particular nexus in that huge, interlocking design, a place where yellow, orange and magenta came together in a blur of color. And then, as the sky darkened from the blue of atmosphere to the black of space, the nexus loomed before us, and we passed through it as through a wall of steam. The stars came out, more stars than I had ever seen before.

They took me to the base beneath the lava plain on the far side of this planet's satellite, and I saw the installation there and met the two officers on duty. They all took turns, my father said; none of them cared to stay for long, but it was the place that travelers came to, with all the repair facilities that a spacefaring civilization required, and so someone had to be there.

The planet, of course, was the beacon, its latticework pattern, invisible without those special lenses, and undetectable to any human sense or instrument, were the message and the pointer for anyone passing near this system.

You probably won't comprehend what a shock this revelation was to me. I felt as though I were walking through a dream, even though everything about the experience was crisp and clear and tangible. After we returned to our house in Chicago, I could almost have believed I was waking up, that none of it had ever happened, except that my parents gave me my own glasses and my own hearing aid to remind me of reality. The hearing aids were, of course, our contacts with the satellite base. At the moment I first slipped mine into my ear, I became a cadet officer under my parents' tutelage. I had joined the family business.

I took some time, and several trips back to the satellite, to make my adjustment to this new identity. I had to drop out of the university — my life just wasn't large enough for two simultaneous educations. And with that, I left Edward behind, and all the yearnings he had evoked in me. No longer would I see him, even from a distance, no longer would I try to talk to him. And I told myself it was better this way. He had no place in my new life. No place at all.

But I couldn't help thinking about him sometimes, about his smile, about his arm around me, about his lips that were only warm, I knew now, because my own were cool. In that kiss, he had sensed everything that was different about me, everything that had been meaningless as long as our relationship was merely intellectual. His body had told him I was unacceptable, and he was confused, ashamed, even angry. It was only logical that he should run away from those feelings, and from me. In my rational moments, I could consider these things with cool detachment and rueful understanding.

In my less rational moments, however, I hated my parents for keeping their secret so long, for keeping their camouflage so complete, for letting me grow up under the delusion that I was a human being among my own kind. They had never thought it could hurt me. And they had never thought I could fall in love with a member of another species. They hadn't considered that love has two components, the physical and the psychological, and that I could succumb to one long before I was tested by the other. I hated them deeply, for giving me a life full of falseness, and for making me vulnerable to Edward.

So there I was, grown, a cadet in another planet's military corps, and I hadn't the faintest idea of who or what I was. I was learning about my parents' past, and it was as alien to me as this narrative will be to you. Which species was really mine, the one that formed my mind or the one that made my body? Neither, I thought. I was floating somewhere in between. I felt bewildered.

I won't say that my bewilderment faded with time. But I did become accustomed to the job my parents had given me. I did learn the history and customs of their — my — species, as a foreigner learns the history and customs of another land. I won't say that I ever internalized them. But I became a functioning member of the garrison, and eventually my commission was relayed to me; not surprisingly, I was assigned to the planet I already knew so well. And of course, I also joined that other business, air freight, which actually occupied most of my time. Not long after I received my first promotion, my parents were rotated back to the home planet, their tour of duty finished, administrative posts awaiting them, rewards for effective service. Their departure was camouflaged by an airplane crash, after which I arranged a false double funeral. I don't yet know whether or not I was sorry to see them go.

Shortly after that, I married the man who had been intended to take my mind off Edward. He was, of course, one of us, newly arrived here when I first met him. I didn't love him, but he was pleasant, unattached, and biologically compatible.

And, not very long ago, we decided to have you, Mariana. It seemed like a good decision at the time. We felt that a child would complete our lives and give us focus. I think we both wanted to love something. It was only after you were born and we did love you very, very much that I realized how bad a decision it had been. Now I know that we should have adopted a native child, one who could grow up here, stay here, and be secure in a human identity. Or we should have waited till we were rotated back to the home planet; we wouldn't have been too old to start a family then. Instead, we had chosen to perpetuate my own parents' mistake.

I blame myself for this entirely. Your father couldn't have known how it was for me. Like my own parents, he never thought about the life his child would experience outside the walls of our home, never thought how that life would mark you, shape you, claim you.

By the time you read this, you will probably already be imbued with the sense of duty that made my parents and my husband and all the other members of this garrison come to this planet. The sense of duty that has spread our species among the stars. They go, knowing they'll be far from home and loved ones for a long, long time, knowing that the lives they face will be strange and difficult to adjust to. Still, they go, as they have gone for generations, because someone must go. I don't profess to understand this. It's something I grew up without, something my parents accepted so completely that they couldn't conceive I might not share it. And yet I do have my own sense of duty. Toward you, my dear Mariana.

You will go home tomorrow, to grow up among your own kind, where the secret is common knowledge and everyone has seen the stripes in the sky. And the pheromones are appropriate. You will have your chance for happiness.

I don't know if we shall ever meet again. I don't know if, when my tour here is over, I will have the courage to return to the planet where my parents were born, to the place where, in spite of the physical traits I share with the rest of the population, I would always be a stranger. Even to you, my child, my flesh and blood, my dear, sweet Mariana. Even to you, the only person in the universe that I love. Even to you. I have made sure of that.

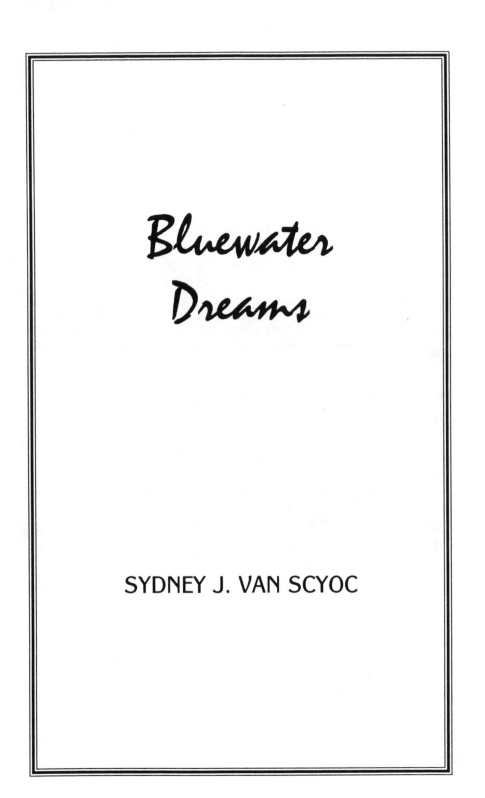

Bluewater Dreams

SYDNEY J. VAN SCYOC

ABOUT SYDNEY J. VAN SCYOC
AND
BLUEWATER DREAMS

Bluewater Dreams *was first published:*
Isaac Asimov's, *March 1986*

Sydney J. Van Scyoc has been one of the top women science fiction writers since her debut in the early 1960s. Although it is doubtful that, considering her androgynous first name, most readers of her era were aware of her gender. Indeed much of her early work featured male protagonists and tended toward the kind of vigorous action adventure generally associated with male writers. Fortunately both her work and identity have become increasingly visible in the 1980s and 1990s, particularly in several story sequences she has had running in Isaac Asimov's.

"Blue Water Dreams" is the kind of alien cultural puzzle story that used to populate the pages of Astounding/Analog *under John W. Campbell Jr. But in Ms. Van Scyoc's hands it becomes far more: a touching, insightful tale in which two women manage to bridge the gap between races on an alien world. It's a story that has much to say about the gulfs between people in what is soon to be our 21st century world.*

Bluewater Dreams

by SYDNEY J. VAN SCYOC

NAMIR WAS sleeping, the breeze on her face, when Mega slipped through the window and touched her with cold fingers. Namir woke immediately, briefly confused. "Mega?" Then, by the light of the nightlamp, she saw the swelling that disfigured her friend's face, distinguished the mottled patches that underlay Mega's fine body hair, and her heart sank. She sat with an involuntary sob. "No, Mega."

"It's come to me." Mega's voice was seldom more than a whisper. That, combined with the softness of the fine dark hair that covered her and the half-hidden glint of her eyes, made her a creature of shadow and subtlety. Tonight her voice was wispy, regretful. "It's taking me, Namir."

"No." Useless word. These things happened each time new settlers came from Zabath, Shandoar, and Perdin. Diseases that scarcely touched humans savaged Mega's kind, those who insisted upon living in the human settlement. This was a new pathology, one no one had yet named. Some tiny organism from some far world had come to Zabath and silently taken up life with its new human host, causing neither discomfort nor death. But when it rode its host to Rahndarr and met the Birleles, it was a killer.

Now the killer had found Mega — Mega, who was always so insouciant, skipping up and down the redrock steps of Rahndatown after Namir even when Namir tried to send her away. Quickly Namir embraced her friend, trying to warm her slight body. She could feel the bones through the thin flesh. In the sunlight, running, leaping, Mega was swift and dauntless. In Namir's arms, cold and afflicted, she was fragile. "If you had gone back to the mountains —" Namir said hopelessly.

She herself had lured Mega down. Music was the thing that drew Birleles to Rahndatown — singing, the ring of cymbals, the call of horns. They were fascinated by the bright sounds but could not make music themselves, just as they could not duplicate the bright colors of the cloth the human settlers wore. The Birleles lived high in the greyrock mountains with only the music of the wind in the crags and the bright color of an occasional shatterflower. Namir had sat at the foot of the greyrock mountain one day, lonely, singing songs from Shandoar and crying, and had seen bright eyes peering at her from the rocks. Sense told her to quit singing then, to chase the Birlele back up the mountain to her own kind. But sense had not been with her that day, only loneliness, and she had tempted Mega all the way back to Rahndatown with her, just to have her company. "If you had not come with me—"

Mega quivered in Namir's arms. "I would have come to Rahndatown one day anyway. I'm one of the ones who has to come here and know the human things."

Yes, just as there were many Birleles in the mountains who would never come to Rahndatown, who resisted the call of music and color and new experience. Namir had often thought about them and wondered if they were the strong ones, or if the strong ones were the ones like Mega, who risked themselves for the new experience.

"I would have come," Mega repeated, "and one day I would have gone back to my mountain. Now I must go tonight."

Namir's arms stiffened. She released her friend, keenly aware of the chill of her room, of the weight of her blankets. "You can't — you can't go back there. You've heard —"

"Namir, I have to go to the dreaming ponds," Mega whispered with shivering intensity. "I need my dreams now. They're calling me." Through puffy lids, her eyes were earnest, pleading.

Namir shivered. The dreaming ponds lay high on the mountain where Mega's people lived. The Birleles bathed in them at important times and had dreams then to guide them. "Namir —"

Mega's eyes glinted faintly. "Namir, I've had my child-dreams my naming-dreams, my hunting-dreams. Now it is time for my dying-dreams." One slight hand closed on Namir's arm. "You have dreams too, Namir. You know the call of them."

Yes, she dreamed often enough, but always in her bed and always of Shandoar. "Mega — you can't go. Your people — they won't let you go up the mountain with disease." At least that was what the separatists said when they went before the Council of Governors to request laws to send the Birleles who lived in Rahndatown back to the mountains. The Birleles took disease too easily, they said, and when they tried to go back to their mountains to die, their mountain kin caught them on the lower slopes and bled them, rather than letting them carry disease to the high Birlele habitats.

"They will stop me, perhaps," Mega said. "But when I tell them I go for my dying-dreams, they will let me pass."

"No, Mega. The separatists —"

"Namir, do you believe the separatists? Over me? They say they want to send us back for our own good, but they have other reasons — other reasons for not wanting us here."

Namir frowned. Yes, there was more than altruism behind the separatists' vehemence. There was a fear of the non-human intelligence of the Birleles, even a fear of their strange shadowed beauty. Not everyone was attracted by the alien. Many were frightened and repelled by it. "But the dead Birleles that have been found on the lower paths —" She had heard of the way they died, their blood drained from their bodies.

"Namir, you know there are predators on the mountain. Many of them."

"I — I don't know what to believe, Mega." Even if the Birleles would let Mega pass, Namir was reluctant to let her go tonight. The Birleles exhibited a wide range of body temperatures and changed in many ways with the warm and cold of day and night. By night they were slow-moving and sometimes confused. If their body temperatures fell below a certain level, compensatory mechanisms came into play and warmed them, and then their minds cleared. But by day, with sunlight warming them, they moved swiftly and their thoughts were quicksilver. "At least wait for morning, when it's warm. You'll walk faster then."

"I'll go farther if I start now, before I become weaker. Namir —"

"Mega — wait and I'll sing for you. You have to let me sing for you a last time." She said it as an inducement but immediately recognized it for a plea. She needed to sing for Mega again. They had begun their friendship with singing. If it must end, then it must end that way.

And perhaps after she had sung, Mega would realize she couldn't risk the walk to the mountain. Perhaps —

She didn't wait for consent. Holding the fragile body, she began to rock, singing a wordless melody from her creche days on Shandoar. She felt Mega first resist, then fall to the spell of the song. Her lids hooded her eyes and her breath grew deep and sighing. Once she said, querulously, "Namir —" But Namir knew Mega's weakness and she continued singing, softly, wordlessly, trying to warm Mega with her own body heat.

"Namir — please. I have to go."

Namir did not release her. She sang until her song finally lulled them both to sleep. Even then she seemed to feel the catch of her voice in her throat, until sometime much later when she woke and realized that she was sobbing rather than singing. She sat with a start. First dawn was in the sky and she was alone.

There was unreality in her room. Surely she had imagined Mega's visit. Other Birleles fell victim to infection; never Mega. Mega had been her special friend for three years and would be until Namir took her first year-mate.

But she knew she had not dreamed the visit, the disease or the plea. Certainly she had not dreamed Mega's disappearance. Mega had gone to the dreaming ponds.

Alone, and there were predators on the mountain. Whether they were Mega's own kind or other species, there was danger and Mega would be too weak to resist it. The chill of dawn entered Namir's bones. She had brought Mega to the valley — never mind that she had tried many times to send her away — and now Mega was dying of human-borne Infection.

Quickly Namir left her bed and dressed, her fingers trembling. This was the coldest time, the hour before sunrise, and Mega would travel slowly. If Namir could find her before she reached the mountain and bring her back —

She had hoped to leave the dwelling unnoticed. But her father was awake. She encountered him in the passageway, the anger of a new day already on his face. He was not happy in Rahndatown, where new settlers pressed in on all sides. His chronic dissatisfaction found ready focus in Namir's behavior. "Early today," he said, a hard undertone in his voice.

"I couldn't sleep." For once she was anxious not to rankle him.

"People seldom sleep when they are singing. And I saw your friend as she left."

"She came this way?" Usually Mega came and went through Namir's bedroom window.

"Would I have seen her otherwise? And I saw her disease." He turned, and for a moment his eyes gleamed fiercely. "She won't be back, you know. She is gone for good now."

Namir sucked a painful breath. "Father —"

"Don't dispute me. I told you never to sing to a Birlele and you did. I told you to send her back when you first brought her here and you did not. I told you to close your window and your door to her and you said you would do what you pleased. Now you have done it."

Yes, and Mega would die. Namir released her breath in an angry sob. It was useless to argue with him, to remind him that she had tried many times to send Mega back. And if she had closed her window and door to her, Mega would simply have become another wistful Rahndatown Birlele, taking food and shelter where she could find it. "And I'd do it again!" she said angrily, suddenly full of her own grievance. "She's the only thing I've had here! I left everything else behind on Shandoar — my school-sisters, my friends —"

She had touched a nerve. "You left them to make a new life here! And so you will! Do you expect to have everything you had on Shandoar — at once? I've waited all my life to have what you will have here in a few years more."

"The mines?" she demanded sharply, forgetting that she did not want to rankle him. "Is that what you're giving me?"

Even in the dim light of the passageway, she saw his face congest. He wrenched at her arm. "Have I ever asked you to use pick and lantern? Have I ever sent anyone but myself down those tunnels to dig?"

"No but you'd be happier if you could!" she shot back — unfairly. Why she always deflected his own bitterness back at him twofold, why she always fought, she didn't know. "With two of us digging, we could move to the farlands that much sooner."

"We'll be there in good enough time." Namir's mother had appeared in the doorway of her bedroom, frowning, her hands clenched.

Namir's father turned, releasing Namir's arms. He seemed caught between them, a big man, angry. "No time in Rahndatown is good time."

"Yet we can't go to the farlands until we can go," Namir's mother reminded him. "And you make it worse by going to the tunnels without your mask and tank. You make yourself mindsick." Her voice was low, contained, but with a sharp edge. "You know there are gasses in the tunnels. Ask anyone who watches the miners come up at the end of the day. We can tell from the faces which ones have used their masks. Those are the ones who look tired. The others, the ones who are angry, the way you are always angry —"

"You wouldn't be angry when you came here to grow wintergrasses in the farlands and then had to mine the mountain to buy emigration permits?"

"You knew about the permits when we came. And you know about the gasses in the mine too."

It was a familiar argument, his bitter impatience pitted against her gritty persistence. It would go on until he left for the tunnels. Silently Namir slipped down the passageway and out the door. Neither of them noticed.

Rahndatown was little more than a series of cavities cut into the redrock mountainside: windows, doors, ventholes, hollowed-out rooms. Its look was bleak by dawn, as if the mountain were beset with parasites. And its paths and stairs were shaggy with weeds and litter. Rahndatown was no proud place, and every fresh shipload of immigrants added a new tawdriness.

Yet there was music and color too, during the bright hours of day. The settlers from Shandoar had a tradition of music and those from Perdin dyed and wove their own cloth so they could wear the brilliant colors they chose in designs that pleased them. The Zabathi cheerfully adopted both traditions and added a few of their own. As Namir slipped down the steps that led to the lower levels, she was aware of an occasional Birlele peering at her from rocky shelter wondering if she would sing, wondering if when it grew warm and she removed her jacket, there would be colorsilks beneath.

Namir averted her eyes and hurried. Most of these Birlele had no particular friend. They lived as they could, seldom well by human standards. Yet friendship had not saved Mega.

Once beyond the burrowed settlement, she ran through the slagpiled regions at the foot of the mountain, past the timbered mouth of the mine, down streets of quikpanel warehouses that held export and import materials. There were already people and machinery at work among the warehouses and in the sorting and assembling sheds. And in the distance, the smelters offered fiery sparks to the grey morning sky.

Once or twice she recognized a face among the workers and wanted to stop and ask if Mega had come this way. But what other way was there through the valley toward the greyrock mountains?

None. Namir ran.

Soon she left Rahndatown behind. And soon the morning sun climbed over the crags of the distant mountains and banished grey from the sky. Namir turned once and peered back toward Rahndatown, trying to find something there to warm her. But she could see nothing there to stand comparison with her memory of Shandoar's muraled buildings and green parks.

Her eyes stung. *I never minded that people pressed us on all sides. I never minded that everything on Shandoar had already been built and there was nothing more to build. I never minded any of that.*

But I do mind the roughness and emptiness here. We have to lock the flute and horn in cases to keep grit front scarring them. We hardly take them out anymore. And my voice — how long will my voice be sweet here?

The morning began to warm and she sang, testing her voice against the air. If Mega had not run too far ahead, if she heard Namir singing —

But there was no sign that Mega heard. Namir watched the brush that choked the valley for sign of her friend, or for fresh footprints. Several times she saw crushed vegetation and once she found a place where someone had uprooted sweetroot and chewed the starchy tuber. That could have been anyone, Birlele or human.

Pausing, discouraged, she pulled sweetroot and chewed it herself. Then she continued to the lowermost slopes of the mountain where she had first met Mega.

She found her there on the path, her slight body sprawled gracelessly, her breath harsh. For a moment, Namir only wanted to turn back and forget seeing her like this. If she could remember her running in the sun instead, limbs flashing, dark hair gleaming —

Mega stirred and pulled herself to a sitting position. Her swollen face was grotesque and mottled patches glared angrily through her dark hair. " 'Mir — you've come to carry me."

Namir forced herself forward. "I — I've come to take you back. Yes."

Mega struggled to her feet, her limbs thrashing almost angrily. "No — no. You've come to carry me to the ponds. You have to carry me, 'Mir. I thought I could walk, but I can't. It's taking me — this disease."

Namir felt a quick twist of fear. "Mega — no. I can't take you there."

Despite her infirmity, Mega's eyes glinted. "You believe them then — the people who want to keep us in the mountains. You believe that my own people will catch us on the paths and kill us. You're afraid of them."

Was she? Afraid of Mega's kind? Namir could not deny it. The Birleles who lived in Rahndatown were eager and whispering, caught up in the excitement of human activity and color. That made them somehow childish. Those who lived in the seclusion of the mountains were surely different. They were not susceptible to human ways. They were an intelligent species with rituals and traditions and — Mega said — legends. Intelligent enough, certainly, to know that if they permitted humans to penetrate the upper reaches of the mountains where they lived, they would take disease and die. Namir wet her lips with her tongue. "Mega, maybe there is something the doctors can give you. If you let me take you back —"

Mega peered up at her unwinkingly. "You know there is nothing, 'Mir. What I need are my dreams. The dreamwaters call me."

Namir hesitated, torn. If the separatists were right, if it was the mountain Birleles who had killed those returning Birleles found dead on the lower slopes — She peered up the mountainside. The greyrock was stark and harsh-shadowed, a stern environment. But somewhere were the dreams Mega remembered — dreams much like Namir's memories of Shandoar, precious, tantalizing, evanescent.

Certainly she had never heard of any Birlele harming any human. Perhaps that was simply because no human had climbed the greyrock mountains.

Perhaps not. Deciding, she took her friend in her arms. "I'll take you to the ponds." To the dreams. Perhaps someone would take her back to Shandoar one day, to the silken park grasses and muraled walls she remembered. She could hope.

Although Mega stood half as tall as Namir, carrying her up the mountain path was like carrying nothing. According to Birlele legend, the Birlele were descended from avians. The webbed membrane that connected Mega's upper arms to her slight torso seemed testimony to the authenticity of the legend. And she was light, her bones insubstantial. Occasionally, imagining watchful Birlele soaring on mountain air currents, Namir glanced up the mountain apprehensively.

But the Birleles had not flown for hundreds of centuries, and they did not fly today. Instead, at midafternoon, they suddenly perched in numbers upon the rocks that overlooked the path, their breath a menacing hiss. Namir halted, peering up at them, her nerves frozen. They had appeared silently, without warning. Mega sighed and opened her eyes.

Namir fought a suddenly-thick tongue. "Mega — will they understand me? If I talk to them?" The hissing grew louder. The Birlele were two dozen, and they hunched as if ready to spring. Their body hair was denser than Mega's, darker, glossier. Their bodies were more muscular. And their faces were twisted in warning.

Mega summoned a weak whisper. "They will understand if you sing."

Namir shivered. Sing to two dozen mountain trail with her friend dying them, Mega —"

"I don't have to talk to them. They know I'm going to the dreamwaters. Every Birlele goes there to die, and I am dying."

Namir caught her breath involuntarily. "Mega — you told me you wanted to dream in the ponds."

"I do. But that's where we die too, Namir — in the warm water." She looked up into Namir's face. "Don't be afraid — I will talk to them." Summoning strength, she spoke a few sibilant words to the Birlele at the side of the path.

The exchange was brief, hissing. Three of the Birlele spoke with Mega in turn and then drew back, folding their arms over their chests.

"They are glad I've come," Mega told Namir. "Only a few others have come this far who were sick. But they ask that you not let me touch ground. That way I will not soil the paths. And — they ask that you sing. They won't come to the valley for songs, but they would like them here, to know what they are like."

Namir's mouth was suddenly dry. The Birleles at the side of the path regarded her stonily. She could not believe they wanted to hear her. She could only believe they wanted to savage her. "We won't soil the paths," she said, and hoped the hissing Birleles understood.

Certainly they seemed to understand her songs. As she continued up the trail, holding Mega's chill body close, stroking her dark hair, she sang every song she knew of Shandoar. She sang its clipped grasses and its white buildings, its black beaches and the foamed water that washed them. She sang the bright clothes the people wore, and the happy voices of schools of children running to recitation. She sang all her memories of there and then she sang the memories she wished she might have had, of growing to adulthood there, of walking the parks and city-trails as a woman, of laughing under trimmed trees with her own children and the children of her school-sisters.

At first the Birleles followed warily, shoulders hunched, faintly hissing. But when Namir paused and carefully removed her jacket, never letting Mega touch ground, when she pulled her brightly patterned blouse free from its confining sash and let the colors ripple in sunlight, the Birleles quieted.

Finally they were silent, and only Namir's voice rang in the grey-rock mountains.

Despite Mega's assurances, she dared not sit to rest. She dared not let her song trail away. On their mountain, the Birleles were more alien than she had ever imagined and her voice was the only thing she had familiar. It reassured her, quenching the worst of her fear. When dark came, she pulled her jacket back over her blouse and continued up the trail, Mega directing her.

Did she only imagine during the final hour of their climb that she tasted something in the air she had never tasted before on Rahndarr? And that something — Welcome? Joy?

Then the scent in the air changed and became heavy. They reached the dreaming ponds soon after the moon rose and Namir paused, sampling the sulphur taint in the air. The ponds, three of them, were yellow-crusted yet vividly blue. The moon floated upon each smooth-glass surface, three times sister to itself. Namir paused and thought she had never seen it so full, so silver. Nor had she ever seen the stars of Rahndarr so vivid in the black sky.

There are many things I haven't seen here. Things I haven't wanted to see, she realized, *because I've only wanted to see Shandoar.*

Certainly she had never seen the geyser that plumed from the rocks and rose moon-silver against the night while she stood at the edge of the nearest pond. She watched its magical play with drawn breath until it sank back into the rocks. Then her breath sighed away.

I could sing about that.

. . . if Mega were not dying. Mega seemed to have shrunk in her arms. Her skin was chill, her eyes vacant. "You will have to carry me into the pond," she whispered. "Don't put me down until you can put me into the water."

"I could put you into the water now," Namir said. She stepped forward, breaking the yellow crust that ringed the pond. Warm water seeped into her boots.

"No, take me to the center of the pond. And don't be afraid of the stings, Namir."

"Stings?" Involuntarily Namir stiffened, peering down into the moonlit depths of the pool.

"Yes, they make the dreams. Sometimes I wonder about that, you know — I wonder if the stings would make you dream too. I dream like a human sometimes, at night when I sleep."

Namir hesitated at the edge of the pond. She could see nothing in the pond that might sting her. There were no insects and the bottom of the pond was of greyrock pebbles. She stroked Mega's hair. The night was cold and Mega was confused.

The Birleles who crouched behind them were not confused. They peered at Namir silently, their eyes bright and unreadable. There were several dozen of them now, some of them very old, others very young. As she hesitated, they edged forward and those nearer her raised their arms, fanning out their vestigial flight-membranes. Their shadows became grotesque on the pebbled ground.

Were they threatening her? Were they observing some ritual? Or were they simply urging her forward?

How could she know? Namir stepped forward quickly, pond water lapping up her pants legs to her thighs, her hips, her waist. It was hotter than she had guessed, almost scalding. Gasping, she stumbled toward the center of the pond.

And then she felt the stings. Something rippled up from the bottom of the pond, something irregular and grey — it might have been a pebble — and brushed against her leg. And stung, sharply. She jerked in surprise. "Mega —" A second object broke from the pond bottom and struck at her. This time there was numbness. It spread quickly up and down her leg. She attempted to step back, to escape the pond. Her leg buckled and instead she fell forward into the water.

Mega seemed not to notice her distress. She squirmed free of Namir's grasp and arched fluidly into the depths of the pond. As she swept underwater to the bottom of the pond, Namir saw a look of ecstatic anticipation on her swollen face. Then pebble-like objects bobbed from the bottom of the pond and swirled around her, striking at her in a quick frenzy.

Namir struggled to her feet. "No!" Without thinking, she flung herself into the water after Mega, grappling for her. Sulphur water stung her eyes and was sucked into her half-open mouth. *"Mega!"*

Mega did not reach for rescue. Instead she swam swiftly away across the pond, her dark hair washing in the water, the expression on her face intent now, expectant.

As Namir slipped and stumbled after her, she was stung again and again. With an anguished cry, she fell forward into the water, suddenly too weak to swim. Still the pebble-like objects darted at her and stung her and Mega swam just beyond reach.

Namir was aware of overwhelming weakness and terrible dizziness. Gasping, coughing, she fought to mobilize her lifeless legs, her numbing arms. She had lost voluntary control of both. Finally she sank into the pond, hot mineral water burning in her respiratory passages.

At some point consciousness faded.

At some other point it returned, in fragments. Namir gathered the fragments and realized that she lay on the verge of the pond, that it was daylight, and that she was alone. Whatever Birlele had pulled her from the water had gone with all the others. She stared up into the noonday sun. Her throat burned and her head ached. And she had the strange sense that she had dreamed.

She lay for a moment, trying to capture the substance of her dreams. The images were alien and came in incomprehensible juxtapositions — as if the dreams had not been her own but someone else's, created not from her reality of Shandoar-lost but from some other reality of Rahndarr-gained. The welcome, the joy she had felt the night before — somehow they had become part of her dreams.

"The meadows —" she said, hardly aware that she spoke. She had always thought shatterflowers coarse, those that grew in Rahndatown. Now she knew that in the meadows that lay far beyond the town, their gaudy colors would be vibrant. "The fields —" Her father had described them to her often enough, the fields of wintergrass they would grow in the farlands: lush, green, sweeping in the sun. She had imagined them as a terrible emptiness. Now she saw them as he must see them: vividly, hungrily. She wanted them as badly as he did.

But there was something else she wanted and that she could not have. "Mega," she said with a sob, and sat.

Mega hung in the blue water of the dreaming pond, her limbs lax, only her face breaking the water's surface. Her arms were spread, and her flight-membranes seemed to flutter despite the stillness of the pond.

Had the Birleles simply left her here like this? Left her to bloat in the water? Almost angrily Namir took her feet. If she could reach Mega's body before she was stung to unconsciousness again, pull it back to the pond's edge —

Before she could enter the water, Mega rolled to her stomach in the water and kicked herself across the pond to Namir.

Namir found herself holding her friend, holding the body that should have been stiff and cold — the body that was water-hot and living. "Mega — your face —" she stammered. The swelling was gone. So were the vivid discolorations that marked the course of the disease.

"Did you dream?" Mega demanded, her eyes lively. "Did the stings make you dream?"

"I — I think I did dream. A little. But —"

Mega nodded eagerly, shaking herself, making water fly. "I dreamed everything I wanted to dream. I spoke with the wind, I tumbled with the rocks, I rode the clouds over the mountains. Do you see them, Namir? I rode those clouds." She pointed, radiant. "We are that much alike at least. The stings made you dream too. A little."

"Yes." Perhaps. And perhaps she had dreamed simply because she often did, dreamed strangely because the last day had changed her in some way. "But Mega —" Namir peered down into the clear pond. Why was Mega alive? Why was she well? None of the Birleles in Rahndatown had recovered from this disease.

None of the Birleles in Rahndatown had come to the dreaming ponds. They had been too weak to come so far alone, and few of them had special friends to help them. None had special friends foolish enough to climb to the Birlele habitat. Namir stroked Mega's shoulder. It was fever hot, as if —

As if — "Mega," she realized, "you needed fever."

Mega was preening herself, deftly grooming her wet hair, sweeping it into dark whorls. "Fever?"

"You needed fever to kill the disease. And your body — your body doesn't make fever. When you got sick, you became cold instead. You had to come here to make yourself warm enough to kill the infection." Could it be that simple? Could the Birleles who lived among the humans survive human diseases simply by submersion?

"I had to come here to die," Mega corrected her. "But I had healing dreams instead of dying dreams. It happens sometimes. We dream of being well and live again."

Namir nodded. Perhaps the solution was not so simple. Perhaps there had been some subtle interaction between the heat of the dreaming pond and the venom of whatever it was that stung. Perhaps even that interaction would not suffice against all human-borne infections. Perhaps only this one.

Still Namir did not feel any sinking discouragement. Mega had stepped from the pond well. Namir had had her dreams of Rahndarr, whatever their origin. And she would tell the Council of Governors what had happened. The Council had declared for the right of the Birleles to live where they pleased on their native world, whatever the dangers. Perhaps they could do something now to alleviate the worst of those dangers. She brushed at her clothes. They were stiff in places, damp in others. "Mega, will you come back to Rahndatown with me?" Did she hope for a yes or a no?

Mega had completed her grooming and she peered up at Namir with momentary sadness. "No, Namir, I have been in Rahndatown three years and I have seen and heard what I wanted. Now there are places I dreamed and I want to visit them. The caves where my sisters live, the crags dark at night, the deep crevices where we hunt shadowleaf —"

Namir nodded, understanding. There were meadows and grasslands she wanted to see, urgently. "The others — you're sure they won't hurt you?"

Mega's eyes glinted. "Namir, they came into the pond and dreamed with me while I was healing. They were glad I returned, and they asked why others have not."

The separatists were wrong then. The Birleles had let her walk up their mountain paths; they had saved her from drowning in the dreampond; and they had welcomed Mega back, even sick.

They gazed at each other. It was awkward parting. There were things Namir wanted to say. Yet all she could think was, "Mega when I dreamed, you were there." Was it a lie? Hadn't there been a quick shape moving through her half-recalled dreams? Hadn't she glimpsed it in the meadows and in the farlands?

"Then I will see you again." Noon restlessness was on Mega and her limbs moved eagerly. But before she darted away, she touched the bright sash that held Namir's blouse. "Will you leave me this?"

"Of course." Namir stripped it off, eager to prolong their parting. "And I'll sing for you."

At that Mega laughed, hoarsely, coughing, as Birleles laughed. "No, Namir. Don't sing until you get back to the valley. Then if there is someone there sick, sing when you carry her up the trail and we will all dream with her. Will you?"

Come up the mountain again past hissing Birleles? For a moment fear returned, unreasoning. Namir dismissed it. "Of course." She would make herself friend of those Birleles in Rahndatown who had no special friend. If they needed her, she would be there, either to speak to the Council of Governors for them or to carry them to the dreaming ponds when they were stricken.

"Then that is when I will see you," Mega said, and she leapt away as swift and dauntless as Namir remembered.

When she was gone, Namir started down the trail. Occasionally she saw Birleles watching her from the rocks. When she paused they hissed. She longed for something familiar to reassure herself by — some song to guard against strangeness. But she looked closely and found a little bit of Mega in each watching Birlele, and she did not sing again until she reached the valley.

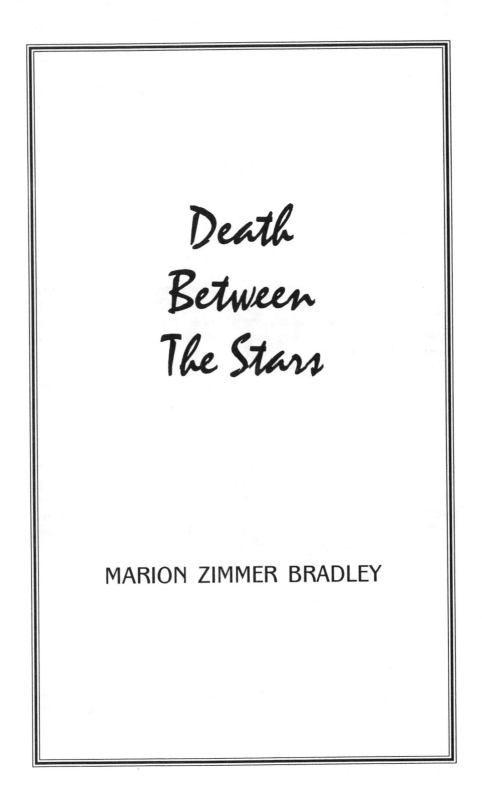

Death
Between
The Stars

MARION ZIMMER BRADLEY

ABOUT MARION ZIMMER BRADLEY
AND
DEATH BETWEEN THE STARS

Death Between The Stars *was first published:*
Fantastic Universe, *March 1956*

The three bestselling women science fiction writers in history have been Andre Norton, Marion Zimmer Bradley and Anne McCaffrey. It can be no coincidence that the work of all three shares many common elements. Each writes vigorous action adventure with a strong moral undercurrent and a deep sensitivity to the experiences of the "outsider."

Nor is it any coincidence that Norton was a deep influence on Bradley and Bradley an important influence on McCaffrey. But the three most profound influences on Ms. Bradley's work appear to be Abraham Merritt, Henry Kuttner and Leigh Brackett (the last two themselves who deeply influenced by Merritt). Merritt's influence can be seen in the moodiness of Bradley's early picturesque novels, while Kuttner's and Brackett's can be seen in Bradley's commitment to the full intellectual and emotional characterization of her protagonists. The irony of her success as a science fiction writer may be that the Darkover novels are really fantasies with a slight SF rationale, in which magic crystals become matrix jewels, etc. But when Ms. Bradley began her career there was no market for fantasy and those who hoped to sell it were forced to add at least a patina of scientific underpinning to their work.

Although like many of the women in this anthology Bradley's earliest work portrayed the adventures of swashbuckling masculine heroes, women came to play an increasingly dominant role in her writings until they took full stage in her work beginning in the late 1970s and early 1980s. "Death Between the Stars," one of Ms. Bradley's least known tales, was more than a decade ahead of its time in presenting the kind of no compromises heroine that would one day become the staple of science fiction. The story mixes many of her traditional themes in an atypical space opera that tackles cultural prejudice, gender discrimination, and the sometimes unexpected consequences of doing what's right even when it's the last thing in the world one feels like doing.

Death Between The Stars

by MARION ZIMMER BRADLEY

THEY ASKED ME about it, of course, before I boarded the starship. All through the Western sector of the Galaxy, few rules are stricter than the one dividing human from nonhuman, and the little Captain of the *Vesta* — he was Terran, too, and proud in the black leather of the Empire's merchantman forces — hemmed and hawed about it, as much as was consistent with a spaceman's dignity.

"You see, Miss Vargas," he explained, not once but as often as I would listen to him, "this is not, strictly speaking, a passenger ship at all. Our charter is only to carry cargo. But, under the terms of our franchise, we are required to transport an occasional passenger, from the more isolated planets where there is no regular passenger service. Our rules simply don't permit us to discriminate, and the Theradin reserved a place on this ship for our last voyage."

He paused, and re-emphasized, "We have only the one passenger cabin, you see. We're a cargo ship and we are not allowed to make any discrimination between our passengers."

He looked angry about it. Unfortunately, I'd run up against that attitude before. Some Terrans won't travel on the same ship with nonhumans even when they're isolated in separate ends of the ship.

I understood his predicament, better than he thought. The Theradin seldom travel in space. No one could have foreseen that Haalvordhen, the Theradin from Samarra, who had lived on the forsaken planet of Deneb for eighteen of its cycles, would have chosen this particular flight to go back to its own world.

At the same time, I had no choice. I had to get back to an Empire planet — *any* planet — where I could take a starship for Terra. With war about to explode in the Procyon sector, I had to get home before communications were knocked out altogether. Otherwise — well, a Galactic war can last up to eight hundred years. By the time regular transport service was re-established, I wouldn't be worrying about getting home.

The *Vesta* could take me well out of the dangerous sector, and all the way to Samarra — Sirius Seven — which was, figuratively speaking, just across the street from the Solar System and Terra. Still, it was a questionable solution. The rules about segregation are strict, the anti-discriminatory laws are stricter, and the Theradin had made a prior reservation.

The captain of the *Vesta* couldn't have refused him transportation, even if fifty human, Terran women had been left stranded on Deneb IV. And sharing a cabin with the Theradin was ethically, morally and socially out of the question. Haalvordhen was a nonhuman telepath; and no human in his right senses will get any closer than necessary even to a human telepath. As for a nonhuman one —

And yet, what other way was there?

The captain said tentatively, "We *might* be able to squeeze you into the crewmen's quarters—" he paused uneasily, and glanced up at me.

I bit my lip, frowning. That was worse yet. "I understand," I said slowly, "that this Theradin — Haalvordhen — has offered to allow me to share *its* quarters."

"That's right. But, Miss Vargas —"

I made up my mind in a rush. "I'll do it," I said. "It's the best way, all around."

At the sight of his scandalized face, I almost regretted my decision. It was going to cause an interplanetary scandal, I thought wryly. A human woman — and a Terran citizen — spending forty days in space and sharing a cabin with a nonhuman!

The Theradin, although male in form, had no single attribute which one could remotely refer to as sex. But of course that wasn't the problem. The nonhuman were specifically prohibited from mingling with the human races. Terran custom and taboo were binding, and I faced, resolutely, the knowledge that by the time I got to Terra, the planet might be made too hot to hold me.

Still, I told myself defiantly, it was a big Galaxy. And conditions weren't normal just now and that made a big difference. I signed a substantial check for my transportation, and made arrangements for the shipping and stowing of what few possessions I could safely transship across space.

But I still felt uneasy when I went aboard the next day — so uneasy that I tried to bolster up my flagging spirits with all sorts of minor comforts. Fortunately the Theradin were oxygen-breathers, so I knew there would be no trouble about atmosphere-mixtures, or the air pressure to be maintained in the cabin. And the Theradin were Type Two nonhumans, which meant that the acceleration of a hyperspeed ship would knock my shipmate into complete prostration without special drugs. In fact, he would probably stay drugged in his skyhook during most of the trip.

The single cabin was far up toward the nose of the starship. It was a queer little spherical cubbyhole, a nest. The walls were foam-padded all around the sphere, for passengers never develop a spaceman's skill at maneuvering their bodies in free-fall, and cabins had to be designed so that an occupant, moving unguardedly, would not dash out his or her brains against an unpadded surface. Spaced at random on the inside of the sphere were three skyhooks — nested cradles in swinging pivots — into which the passenger was snugged during blastoff in shock-absorbing foam and a complicated Garensen pressure-apparatus and was thus enabled to sleep secure without floating away.

A few screw-down doors were marked LUGGAGE. I immediately unscrewed one door and stowed my personal belongings in the bin. Then I screwed the top down securely and carefully fastened the padding over it. Finally, I climbed around the small cubbyhole, seeking to familiarize myself with it before my unusual roommate arrived.

It was about fourteen feet in diameter. A sphincter lock opened from the narrow corridor to cargo bays and crewmen's quarters, while a second led into the cabin's functional equivalent of a bathroom. Planetbound men and women are always surprised and a little shocked when they see the military arrangements on a spaceship. But once they've tried to perform normal bodily functions in free-fall, they understand the peculiar equipment very well.

I've made six trips across the Galaxy in as many cycles. I'm practically an old hand, and can even wash my face in free-fall without drowning. The trick is to use a sponge and suction. But, by and large, I understand perfectly why spacemen, between planets, usually look a bit unkempt.

I stretched out on the padding of the main cabin, and waited with growing uneasiness for the nonhuman to show up. Fortunately, it wasn't long before the diaphragm on the outer sphincter-lock expanded, and a curious, peaked face peered through.

"Vargas Miss Hel-len?" said the Theradin in a sibilant whisper.

"That's my name," I replied instantly. I pulled myself upward, and added, quite unnecessarily, "You are Haalvordhen, of course."

"Such is my identification," confirmed the alien, and the long, lean, oddly-muscled body squirmed through after the peaked head. "It is kind, Vargas Miss, to share accommodation under this necessity."

"It's kind of you," I said vigorously. "We've all got to get home before this war breaks out!"

"That war may be prevented, I have all hope," the nonhuman said. He spoke comprehensibly in Galactic Standard, but expressionlessly, for the vocal chords of the Theradins are located in an auxiliary pair of inner lips, and their voices seem reedy and lacking in resonance to human ears.

"Yet know you, Vargas Miss, they would have hurled me from this ship to make room for an Empire citizen, had you not been heart-kind to share."

"Good heavens!" I exclaimed, shocked, "I didn't know that!"

I stared at him, disbelieving. The captain couldn't have legally done such a thing — or even seriously have entertained the thought. Had he been trying to intimidate the Theradin into giving up his reserved place?

"I—I was meaning to thank *you*," I said, to cover my confusion.

"Let us thank we-other, then, and be in accord," the reedy voice mouthed.

I looked the nonhuman over, unable to hide completely my curiosity. In form the Theradin was vaguely humanoid — but only vaguely — for, the squat arms terminated in mittened "hands" and the long sharp face was elfin, and perpetually grimacing.

The Theradin have no facial muscles to speak of, and no change of expression or of vocal inflection is possible to them. Of course, being telepathic, such subtleties of visible or auditory expression would be superfluous on the face of it.

I felt — as yet — none of the revulsion which the mere presence of the Theradin was *supposed* to inspire. It was not much different from being in the presence of a large humanoid animal. There was nothing inherently fearful about the alien. Yet he was a telepath — and of a nonhuman breed my species had feared for a thousand years.

Could he read my mind?

"Yes," said the Theradin from across the cabin. "You must forgive me. I try to put up barrier, but it is hard. You broadcast your thought so strong it is impossible to shut it out." The alien paused. "Try not to be embar-rass. It bother me too.

Before I could think of anything to say to that a crew member in black leather thrust his head, unannounced, through the sphincter, and said with an air of authority, "In skyhooks, please." He moved confidently into the cabin. "Miss Vargas, can I help you strap down?" he asked.

"Thanks, but I can manage," I told him.

Hastily I clambered into the skyhook, buckling the inner straps, and fastening the suction tubes of the complicated Garensen apparatus across my chest and stomach. The nonhuman was awkwardly drawing his hands from their protective mittens and struggling with the Garensens.

Unhappily the Theradin have a double thumb, and handling the small-size Terran equipment is an almost impossibly delicate task. It is made more difficult by the fact that the flesh of their "hands" is mostly thin mucus membrane which tears easily on contact with leather and raw metal.

"Give Haalvordhen a hand," I urged the crewman. "I've done this dozens of times!"

I might as well have saved my breath. The crewman came and assured himself that *my* straps and tubes and cushions were meticulously tightened. He took what seemed to me a long time, and used his hands somewhat excessively. I lay under the heavy Garensen equipment, too inwardly furious to even give him the satisfaction of protest.

It was far too long before he finally straightened and moved toward Haalvordhen's skyhook. He gave the alien's outer straps only a perfunctory tug or two, and head to grin at me with a totally uncalled-for familiarity.

"Blastoff in ninety seconds," he said, and wriggled himself rapidly out through the lock.

Haalvordhen exploded in a flood of Samarran could not follow. The vehemence of his voice, however, was better than a dictionary. For some strange reason I found myself sharing his fury. The unfairness of the whole procedure was shameful. The Theradin had paid passage money, and deserved in any case the prescribed minimum of decent attention.

I said forthrightly, "Never mind the fool, Haalvordhen. Are you strapped down all right?"

"I don't know," he replied despairfully. "The equipment is unfamiliar —"

"Look —" I hesitated, but in common decency I had to make the gesture. "If I examine carefully my own Garensens, can you read my mind and see how they should be adjusted?"

He mouthed, "I'll try," and immediately I fixed my gaze steadily on the apparatus.

After a moment, I felt a curious sensation. It was something faint, sickening feeling of being touched and pushed about, against my will, by a distasteful stranger.

I tried to control the surge of almost physical revulsion. No wonder that humans kept as far as possible from the telepathic races . . .

And then I saw — did I see, I wondered, or was it a direct telepathic interference with my perceptions? — a second image superimpose itself on the Garensens into which I was strapped. And the realization was so disturbing that I forgot the discomfort of the mental rapport completely.

"You aren't nearly fastened in," I warned. "You haven't begun to fasten the suction tubes — oh, *damn* the man. He must have seen in common humanity —" I broke off abruptly, and fumbled in grim desperation with my own straps. "I think there's just time —"

But there wasn't. With appalling suddenness a violent clamor — the final warning — hit my ears. I clenched my teeth and urged frantically: "Hang on! Here we go!"

And then the blast hit us! Under the sudden sickening pressure I felt my lungs collapse, and struggled to remain upright, choking for breath. I heard a queer, gagging grunt from the alien, and it was far more disturbing than a human scream would have been. Then the second shockwave struck with such violence that I screamed aloud in completely human terror. Screamed — and blacked out.

I wasn't unconscious very long. I'd never collapsed during takeoff before, and my first fuzzy emotion when I felt the touch of familiar things around me again was one of embarrassment. What had happened? Then, almost simultaneously, I became reassuringly aware that we were in free fall and that the crewman who had warned us to alert ourselves was stretched out on the empty air near my skyhook. He looked worried.

"Are you all right, Miss Vargas?" he asked, solicitously. "The blastoff wasn't any rougher than usual —"

"I'm all right," I assured him woozily. My shoulders jerked and the Garensens shrieked as I pressed upward, undoing the apparatus with tremulous fingers. "What about the Theradin?" I asked urgently. "His Garensens weren't fastened. You barely glanced at them."

The crewman spoke slowly and steadily, with a deliberation I could not mistake. "Just a minute, Miss Vargas," he said. "Have you forgotten? I spent *every moment* of the time I was in here fastening the Theradin's belts and pressure equipment."

He gave me a hand to assist me up, but I shook it off so fiercely that I flung myself against the padding on the opposite side of the cabin. I caught apprehensively at a handhold, and looked down at the Theradin.

Haalvordhen lay flattened beneath the complex apparatus. His peaked pixie face was shrunken and ghastly, and his mouth looked badly bruised. I bent closer, then jerked upright with a violence that sent me cascading back across the cabin, almost into the arms of the crewman.

"You must have fixed those belts *just now*," I said accusingly. "They *were not* fastened before blastoff! It's malicious criminal negligence, and if Haalvord-hen dies —"

The crewman gave me a slow, contemptuous smile. "It's my word against yours, sister," he reminded me.

"In common decency, in common humanity —" I found that my voice was hoarse and shaking, and could not go on.

The crewman said humorlessly, "I should think you'd be glad if the geek died in blastoff. You're awfully concerned about the geek — and you know how *that* sounds?"

I caught the frame of the skyhook and anchored myself against it. I was almost too faint to speak. "What were you trying to do?" I brought out at last. "*Murder* the Theradin?"

The crewman's baleful gaze did not shift from my face. "Suppose you close your mouth," he said, without malice, but with an even inflection that was far more frightening. "If you don't, we may have to close it for you. I don't think much of humans who fraternize with geeks."

I opened and shut my mouth several times before I could force myself to reply. All I finally said was, "You know, of course, that I intend to speak to the captain?"

"Suit yourself." He turned and strode contemptuously toward the door. "We'd have been doing you a favor if the geek had died in blastoff. But, as I say, suit yourself. I think your geek's alive, anyhow. They're hard to kill."

I clutched the skyhook, unable to move, while he dragged his body through the sphincter lock and it contracted behind him.

Well, I thought bleakly, I had known what I would be letting myself in for when I'd made the arrangement. And since I was already committed, I might as well see if Haalvordhen were alive or dead. Resolutely I bent over his skyhook, angling sharply to brace myself in free-fall.

He wasn't dead. While I looked I saw the bruised and bleeding "hands" flutter spasmodically. Then, abruptly, the alien made a queer, rasping noise. I felt helpless and for some reason I was stirred to compassion.

I bent and laid a hesitant hand on the Garensen apparatus which was now neatly and expertly fastened. I was bitter about the fact that for the first time in my life I had lost consciousness! Had I not done so the crewman could not have so adroitly covered his negligence. But it was important to remember that the circumstance would not have helped Haalvordhen much either.

"Your feelings do you nothing but credit!" The reedy flat voice was almost a whisper. "If I may trespass once more on your kindness — can you unfasten these instruments again?"

I bent to comply, asking helplessly as I did so, "Are you sure you're all right?"

"Very far from all right," the alien mouthed, slowly and without expression.

I had the feeling that he resented being compelled to speak aloud, but I didn't think I could stand that telepath touch again. The alien's flat, slitted eyes watched me while I carefully unfastened the suction tubes and cushioning devices.

At this distance I could see that the eyes had lost their color, and that the raw "hands" were flaccid and limp. There were also heavily discolored patches about the alien's throat and head. He pronounced, with a terribly thick effort.

"I should have been drugged. Now it's too late. *Argha maci* " the words trailed off into blurred Samarran but the discolored patch in his neck still throbbed sharply, and the hands twitched in the agony which, being dumb, seemed the more fearful.

I clung to the skyhook, dismayed at the intensity of my own emotion. I thought that Haalvordhen had spoken again when the sharp jolt of command sounded, clear and imperative, in my brain.

"Procalamine!" For an instant the shock was all I could feel — the shock, and the overwhelming revulsion at the telepathic touch. There was no hesitation or apology for it now, for the Theradin was fighting for his life. Again the sharp, furious command came: *"Give me procalamine!"*

And with a start of dismay, I realized that most nonhumans needed to drug, which was kept on all spaceships to enable them to live in free-fall.

Few nonhuman races have the stubbornly persistent heart of the Terrans, which beats by muscular contraction alone. The circulation of the Theradin, and similar races, is dependent on gravity to keep the vital fluid pulsing. Procalamine gives their main blood organ just enough artificial muscular spasm to keep the blood moving and working.

Hastily I propelled myself into the "bathroom" — wiggled hastily through the diaphragm, and unscrewed the top of the bin marked FIRST AID. Neatly pigeonholed beneath transparent plastic were sterile bandages, antiseptics clearly marked HUMAN and — separately, for the three main types of nonhuman races, in one deep bin — the small plastic globules of vital stimulants.

I sorted out two purple fluorescent ones — little globes marked *procalamine* — and looked at the warning, in raised characters on the globule. It read: FOR ADMINISTRATION BY QUALIFIED SPACE PERSONNEL ONLY. A touch of panic made my diaphragm catch. Should I call the *Vesta*'s captain, or one of the crew?

Then a cold certainty grew in me. If I did, Haalvordhen wouldn't get the stimulant he needed. I sorted out a fluorescent needle for nonhuman integument, pricked the globule and sucked the dose into the needle. Then, with its tip still enclosed in the plastic globe, I wriggled myself back to where the alien still lay loosely confined by one of the inner straps.

Panic touched me again, with the almost humorous knowledge that I didn't know where to inject the stimulant, and that a hypodermic injection, in space presents problems which only space-trained men are able to cope with. But I reached out notwithstanding and gingerly picked up one of the unmittened "hands." I didn't stop to think how I knew that this was the proper site for the injection. I was too overcome with strong physical loathing.

Instinct from man's remote past on Earth told me to drop the nonhuman flesh and cower, gibbering and howling as my simian antecedents would have done. The raw membrane was feverishly hot and unpleasantly slimy to touch. I fought rising queasiness as I tried to think how to steady him for the injection.

In free-fall there is no steadiness, no direction. The hypodermic needle, of course, worked by suction, but piercing the skin would be the big problem. Also, I was myself succumbing to the dizziness of no-gravity flight, and realized coldly that if I couldn't make the injection in the next few minutes I wouldn't be able to accomplish it at all.

For a minute I didn't care, a primitive part of myself reminding me that if the alien died I'd be rid of a detestable cabinmate, and have a decent trip between planets.

Then, stubbornly, I threw off the temptation. I steadied the needle in my hand which convinced me that I was looking both up and down at the Theradin.

My own center of gravity seemed to be located in the pit of my stomach, and I fought the familiar space voyaging instinct to curl up in the foetal position and float. I moved slightly closer to the Theradin. I knew that if I could get close enough, our two masses would establish a common center of gravity, and I would have orientation while I made the injection.

The maneuver was unpleasant, for the alien seemed unconscious, flaccid and still, and mere physical closeness to the creature was repellent. The feel of the thick wettish "hand" pulsing feebly in my own was almost sickeningly intimate. But at last I managed to maneuver myself close enough to establish a common center of gravity between us — an axis on which I seemed to hover briefly suspended.

I pulled Haalvordhen's "hand;' into this weight-center in the bare inches of space between us, braced the needle, and resolutely stabbed with it.

The movement disturbed the brief artificial gravity, and Haalvordhen floated and bounced a little weightlessly in his skyhook. The "hand" went sailing back, the needle recoiling harmlessly. I swore out loud, now quite foolishly angry, and my own jerky movement of annoyance flung me partially across the cabin.

Inching slowly back, I tried to grit me teeth, but only succeeded with a snap that jarred my skull. In terse anger, I seized Haalvordhen's "hand," which had almost stopped its feverish pulsing, and with a painfully slow effort — any quick or sudden movement would throw me, in recoil, across the cabin again — I wedged Haalvordhen's "hand" under the strap and anchored it there.

It twitched faintly — the Theradin was apparently still sensible to pain — and my stomach rose at that sick pulsing. But I hooked my feet under the skyhook's frame, and flung my free arm down and across the alien, holding tight to the straps that confined him.

Still holding him thus wedged down securely, I jabbed again with the needle. It touched, pricked — and then, in despair, I realized it could not penetrate the Theradin integument without weight and pressure behind it.

I was too absorbed now in what had to be done to care just how I did it. So I wrenched forward with a convulsive movement that threw me, full-length across the alien's body. Although I still had no weight, the momentum of the movement drove the hypodermic needle deeply into the flesh of the "hand."

I pressed the catch, then picked myself up slowly, and looked around to see the crewman who had jeered at me with his head thrust through the lock again, regarding me with the distaste he had displayed toward the Theradin from the first. To him I was lower than the Theradin, having degraded myself by close contact with a nonhuman.

Under that frigid, contemptuous stare, I was unable to speak. I could only silently withdraw the needle and hold it up. The rigid look of condemnation altered just a little, but not much. He remained silent, looking at me with something halfway between horror and accusation.

It seemed years, centuries, eternities that he clung there, just looking at me, his face an elongated ellipse above the tight collar of his black leathers. Then, without even speaking, he slowly withdrew his head and the lock contracted behind him, leaving me alone with my sickening feel of contamination and an almost hysterical guilt.

I hung the needle up on the air, curled myself into a ball, and, entirely unstrung, started sobbing like a fool.

It must have been a long time before I managed to pull myself together, because before I even looked to see whether Haalvordhen was still alive, I heard the slight buzzing noise which meant it was a meal-period and that food had been sent through the chute to our cabin. I pushed the padding listlessly aside, and withdrew the heat-sealed containers — one set colorless, the other nonhuman fluorescent.

Tardily conscious of what a fool I'd been making of myself, I hauled my rations over to the skyhook, and tucked them into a special slot, so that they wouldn't float away. Then, with a glance at the figure stretched out motionless beneath the safety-strap of the other skyhook, I shrugged, pushed myself across the cabin again, and brought the fluorescent containers to Haalvordhen.

He made a weary, courteous noise which I took for acknowledgment. By now heartily sick of the whole business, I set them before him with a bare minimum of politeness and withdrew to my own skyhook, occupying myself with always-ticklish problem of eating in free-fall.

At last I drew myself up to return the containers to chute, knowing we wouldn't leave the cabin during the entire trip. Space, on a starship, is held to a rigid minimum. There is simply no room for untrained outsiders moving around in the cramped ship, perhaps getting dangerously close to critically delicate equipment, and the crew is far too busy to stop and keep an eye on rubbernecking tourists.

In an emergency, passengers can summon a crewman by pressing a call-button. Otherwise, as far as the crew was concerned, we were in another world.

I paused in midair to Haalvordhell's skyhook. His containers were untouched and I felt moved to say, "Shouldn't you try to eat something?"

The flat voice had become even weaker and more rasping now, and the nonhuman's careful enunciation was slurred. Words of his native Samarran intermingled with queer turns of phrase which I expected were literally rendered from mental concepts.

"Heart-kind of you, *thakkava* Vargas Miss, but late. Haalvordhen-I deep in grateful wishing —" A long spate of Samarran, thickly blurred followed, then as if to himself, "Theradin-we, die nowhere only on Samarra, and only a little time ago Haalvordhen-I knowing must die, and must returning; to home planet. *Saata*. Knowing to return and die there where Theradin-we around dying —" The jumble of words blurred again, and the limp "hands" clutched spasmodically, in and out.

Then, in a queer, careful tone, the nonhuman said, "But I am not living to return where I can stop-die. Not so long Haalvordhen-I be lasting, although Vargas-you Miss be helping most like *real* instead of alien. Sorry your people be most you unhelping —" he stopped again, and with a queer little grunting noise, continued, "Now Haalvordhen-I be giving Vargas-you stop-gift of heritage, be needful it is."

The flaccid form of the nonhuman suddenly stiffened, went rigid. The drooping lids over the Theradin's eyes seemed to unhood themselves, and in a spasm of fright I tried to fling myself backward. But I did not succeed. I remained motionless, held in a dumb fascination.

I felt a sudden, icy cold, and the sharp physical nausea crawled over me again at the harsh and sickening touch of the alien on my mind, not in words this time, but in a rapport even closer — a hateful touch so intimate that I felt my body go limp in helpless fits and spasms of convulsive shuddering under the deep, hypnotic contact.

Then a wave of darkness almost palpable surged up in my brain. I tried to scream, *"Stop it, stop it!"* And a panicky terror flitted in my last conscious thought through my head. *This is why, this is the reason humans and telepaths don't mix —*

And then a great dark door opened under my senses and I plunged again into unconsciousness.

It was not more than a few seconds, I suppose, before the blackness swayed and lifted and I found myself floating, curled helplessly in mid-air, and seeing with a curious detachment, the Theradin's skyhook below me. Something in the horrid limpness of that form stirred me wide awake.

With a tight band constricting my breathing, I arrowed downward. I had never seen a dead Theradin before, but I needed no one to tell me that I saw one now. The constricting band still squeezed my throat in dry gasps, and in a frenzy of hysteria I threw myself wildly across the cabin, beating and battering on the emergency button, shrieking and sobbing and screaming . . .

They kept me drugged all the rest of the trip. Twice I remember waking and shrieking out things I did not understand myself, before the stab of needles in my arm sent me down into comforting dreams again. Near the end of the flight, while my brain was still fuzzy, they made me sign a paper, something to do with witnessing that the crew held no responsibility for the Theradin's death.

It didn't matter. There was something clear and cold and shrewd in my mind, behind the surface fuzziness, which told me I must do exactly what they wanted, or I would find myself in serious trouble with the Terran authorities. At the time I didn't even care about that, and supposed it was the drugs. Now, of course, I know the truth.

When the ship made planetfall at Samarra, I had to leave the *Vesta* and trans-ship for Terra. The *Vesta*'s little captain shook me by the hand and carefully avoided my eyes, without mentioning the dead Theradin. I had the feeling — strange, how clear it was to my perceptions — that he regarded me in the same way he would regard a loaded timebomb that might explode at any moment.

I knew he was anxious to hurry me aboard a ship for Terra. He offered me special reservations on a linocruiser at a nominal price, with the obvious lie that he owned a part interest in it. Detachedly I listened to his foundering lies, ignored the hand he offered again, and told a lie or two of my own. He was angry. I knew he didn't want me to linger on Samarra.

Even so, he was glad to be rid of me.

Descending at last from the eternal formalities of the Terran landing zone, I struck out quickly across the port city and hailed a Theradin ground-car. The Theradin driving it looked at me curiously, and in a buzzing voice informed me that I could find a human conveyance at the opposite corner. Surprised at myself, I stopped to wonder what I was doing. And then —

And then I identified myself in a way the Theradin could not mistake. He was nearly as surprised as I was. I clambered into the car, and he drove me to the queer, block-shaped building which my eyes had never seen before, but which I now knew as intimately as the blue sky of Terra.

Twice, as I crossed the twisting ramp, I was challenged. Twice, with the same shock of internal surprise, I answered the challenge correctly.

At last I came before a Theradin whose challenge crossed mine like a sure, sharp lance, and the result was startling. The Theradin Haalvamphrenan leaned backward twice in acknowledgment, and said — not in words — "Haalvordhen!"

I answered in the same fashion. "Yes. Due to certain blunders, I could not return to our home planet, and was forced to use the body of this alien. Having made the transfer unwillingly, under necessity, I now see certain advantages. Once within this body, it does not seem at all repulsive, and the host is highly intelligent and sympathetic.

"I regret the feeling that I am distasteful to you, dear friend. But, consider. I can now contribute my services as messenger and courier, without discrimination by these blind Terrans. The law which prevents Theradin from dying on any other planet should now be changed."

"Yes, yes," the other acquiesced, quickly grasping my meaning. "But now to personal matters, my dear Haalvordhen. Of course your possessions are held intact for you."

I became aware that I possessed five fine residences upon the planet, a private lake, a grove of Theirry-trees, and four hattel-boats. Inheritance among the Theradin, of course, is dependent upon continuity of the mental personality, regardless of the source of the young. When any Theradin died, transferring his mind into a new and younger host, the new host at once possessed all of those things which had belonged to the former personality. Two Theradin, unsatisfied with their individual wealth, sometimes pooled their personalities into a single host-body, thus accumulating modest fortunes.

Continuity of memory, of course, was perfect. As Helen Vargas, I had certain rights and privileges as a Terran citizen, certain possessions, certain family rights, certain Empire privileges. And as Haalvordhen, I was made free of Samarra as well.

In a sense of strict justice, I "told" Haalvamphrenan how the original host had died. I gave him the captain's name. I didn't envy him, when the *Vesta* docked again at Samarra.

"On second thought," Haalvamphrenan said reflectively, "I shall merely commit suicide in his presence."

Evidently Helen-Haalvordhen-I had a very long and interesting life ahead of me.

So did all the other Theradin.

The Snows Are Melted, The Snows Are Gone

JAMES TIPTREE, JR.

ABOUT JAMES TIPTREE, JR.
(ALICE RACOONA SHELDON)
AND
THE SNOWS ARE MELTED, THE SNOWS ARE GONE

The Snows are Melted, The Snows are Gone *was first published:*
Venture, *November 1969*

James Tiptree Jr. , the only male name to apparently grace these pages, was as most people know a pseudonym for the indisputably female Alice Racoona Sheldon. The amazing thing is that Tiptree was able to carry off the masquerade so successfully considering that the protagonists of so many of her stories were women written from a distinctively female point of view. While even the stories featuring men were, to say the least, unusually sympathetic to women.

The author's success in part may have been due to her years spent working for the OSS and the CIA (and perhaps to her own Ph.D. in psychology). But accustomed as she was to spies and spy games, Ms. Tiptree was apparently unprepared for the assiduousness with which science fiction fans seek out and collate information about their favorite authors. Where foreign spies failed, science fiction fans succeeded, revealing her real identity to the world. Thus while this anthology contains a number of gender-bending stories, Ms. Tiptree may have been our most gender-bending writer.

Had she started writing earlier and lived longer, Ms. Tiptree might well have become the field's leading woman writer in terms of both quality and sales. Although her work is now only fitfully available in print, the best of her short stories were collected in Ten Thousand Light Years From Home, Starsongs of an Old Primate, *and* Warm World and Otherwise. *Her novels, all tour de forces include* Up The Walls of the World *and* Brightness Falls From The Sky. *As John Clute has pointed out her work interpenetrates "complexity with considerable narrative impact . . . from densely conceived psychological narrative to the broadest of sense of wonder revelations." And John Clute is equally discerning when he notes that her limited production "should not disguise the weight of her contribution to SF." Her story here, "The Snows are Melted, the Snows are Gone," is a story only James Tiptree Jr. could have written, combining life experiences from Africa, the Pentagon and her own quirky brand of feminism, into a subtle and unforgettable narrative.*

The Snows Are Melted, The Snows Are Gone

by JAMES TIPTREE, JR.

T HE COLD, silent land was lightening as the human figure walked up to the ridge. Against pale rock the figure was a dark fork, too thin. Serpent-shouldered. It sank into shadowy bushes below the crest, turned a small face up to the sky, crouched again.

Something moved in silhouette, circling the ridge. A large dog; no, a very large wolf. The animal drifted onto the rocks above the human, froze. His brush was held stiffly, showing a broken crook. The dawn was coming fast now, but the valley on the west was still dark. From the valley a howling rose and ceased.

The dog-wolf faded off the ridge, reappeared by the scrub where the human crouched. The figure bowed its head. Dawnlight slid on wolf canines as he snapped sidewise carrying away a dark cap.

A flood of light hair spilled loose, flew as the human tossed it back. The wolf dropped the cap, sat down and began to worry at something on its chest.

Light welled into the niche below the rocks. The figure was now clearly visible, a young girl in jacket and breeches shaking out her hair. The shoulders of her jacket ended in pads. It had no arms. Nor had she, none at all: A phocomorph. She settled herself beside the beast, who showed now as bulge-headed, with oddly curling fur.

The wolf had drawn out a small object which he laid on the rock between them. They were face to face, dawn glinting yellow from his eyes, blue in the girl's. His pan went to the object, clicked.

"Patrol to base," the girl said softly.

Tiny squeak of reply.

"We're at the ridge. The river's about five km west. There's a trail below us, it hasn't been used since the rains. We heard the dogs. We'll wait here til dark. After this we'll be in radio shadow. We'll signal when we're out, maybe night after next."

Squeaking louder; a woman's voice. Wolf jaws widened, girl lips grinned.

"We always take care. Out."

The wolf clicked off, and then bent and delicately gripped her boottip in his jaws. The armless girl pulled her foot free, flexed her slim prehensile toes in the cold light. When the other boot was off, the girl used her toes to unhitch the pack harness from his dense fur. He stretched hugely, flung himself down and rolled, revealing a rich cream underbelly.

The girl toed out a foodpack and a canteen. He got up and carried it to a spring beneath the outcrop, pawing it under to fill. They ate and drank, the girl lying on her back and clangling the canteen over her face by its strap. Once she let out a gurgle of laughter. His paw struck her head, pushing her face into her knees. They finished eating, went to relieve themselves. It was broad day now, the sun moving straight up from the eastern hills as if pulled on a string. A wind rose with it, howling over the rocky rim.

The wolf belly-crawled to the crest, watched awhile, returned to the girl. They pulled brush around themselves, curled together on the laterite shelf.

The sun mounted, struck through the wind's chill. No bird flew, no furred animal appeared. In the brush tangle, silence. Once a mantislike thing rattled near the brush. A yellow eye opened at ground level. The thing whirred away; the eye closed.

During the afternoon the wind carried a faint cawing sound to the outcrop. In the brush, yellow eyes were joined by blue. The murmur faded, the eyes disappeared again. Nothing more happened. The equatorial sun dropped straight down the west into the valley, quieting the wind.

As shadow flowed over the outcrop, the brush was pulled aside. Girl and wolf came out together to the stream and lapped, she bending like a snake. They ate again, and the girl toed the pack together, fastened the wolf's harness. He nosed the transmitter into its pouch in his chest-fur, and picked up a boot for her to thrust her foot inside. When she was shod he hooked a fang into the edge of her cap; she let her pale hair coil into it and he pulled it over her head, adjusting it delicately away from her eyes. It was dark now, a quarter-moon behind them in the east. She twisted to her feet like a spring, and they set off down the escarpment into the valley.

It was arid scrubland, eroded by old floods, with forest further down. The two moved carefully in single file, following a faint trail. When the moon had passed zenith, they halted to carry out laborious rearrangements of brush and stone. They went on into the trees, halted again to labor. Trails branched here; they moved on with greater care.

The moon was setting before them when they reached the ruined canyon walls. Beyond them a broad sheet of river muttered in the night. They crossed at a silver riffle, circled quietly down stream. The scent was a reek now; smoke fish, sweat and excrement, coming from a bend around the canyon crags. A dog howled, was joined by another, cut off with yelps.

Girl and wolf came out on the crags. Below them eight ragged thatches huddled in a cove. Smoke rose from a single ash-pile. The huts were in shadow. A last moonray silvered a pile of offal by the shore.

The two on the crag watched quietly. It was warm here, but no insects flew. In the huts below a dog whimpered, was silenced. The moon set, the river turned dark. A fish splashed.

The wolf rose, drifted away. The girl listened to the river. He returned, and she followed him upriver to a cranny in the canyon wall, around a bend from the huts. In the river below, the water gurgled around a line of crazy stakes. The two ate and drank in silence. When the world lightened they were curled together in sleep.

Sunlight struck the canyon wall, shadow fled east. From the cove came a thin clamour of children's voices, deeper voices, a thud, a cry. On the cranny above, sunlight reflected yellow glints behind dry weeds. The wind was rising, blowing toward the sun across the river. Between the gusts came snarls, chirrupings, undecipherable shouts, the crackle of fire. The eyes waited.

In mid-morning, two naked women came into view below, dragging something along the shore. Seven more came after, paused to gesture and gabble. Their skin was angry red, pale at crotch and armpits. White scars stood out, symmetrical chevrons on the bulging bellies. All had thick, conelike nipples; two of them appeared close to term. Their hair was rusty, grease-streaked mats.

Above on the crag, blue eyes had joined yellow. The women were wading into the river now, their burden revealed as a crude net, which they proceeded to string between the stakes. They shrieked at each other, "Gah! Gah! "A small flock of children was straggling around the bend, several of the larger carrying babies. "Gah! Gah!" they echoed, high-voiced. A stake collapsed, was retrieved with shrieks, would not stand, was abandoned.

Presently larger figures appeared on the shore path: the men. Seven of them, ruddy and naked like the women, but much more scarred. None was beyond first youth. The smallest was dark; all the rest had carroty hair and beards. Behind them trailed three dogs, tails tucked, ready to run.

The men shouted imperiously and walked on upriver. The women came out of the water and trotted after them. At the next bend, the whole party waded in and began to splash and flail, driving fish down to the nets. A baby screamed. The pair on the rocks watched intent.

One of the men noticed the dogs skulking by the net and hurled a stone. They fled, hovered. This man was larger than the others, active and well-formed. As the splashing people neared the nets, the big man looked ahead, saw the gap in the nets and raced around on shore to pull it taut. On the cliff above, wolf eyes met human eyes. Wolf teeth made a tiny click.

The fish were foaming in the nets now. The humans closed upon them, hauling at the nets while fish sluiced and leaped through, dogs splashed in to snap. Shouting, screams, floundering splashes. They dragged the squirming mass ashore, dropped it to grab at the escaping fish. The young giant stood grinning, biting alternately at a fish in each hand. At his feet the children scrambled in the thrashing mess. He gave a loud, wordless shout, threw the fish high.

Finally the women dragged the catch along the shore path out of sight, and the river was empty again. Girl and wolf stretched, lay down unrelaxed. Smoke blew from the cove around the bend. It was hot in the rocks, out of the wind.

Below on the sand the fish-parts glittered, but no flies appeared. From the cove, silence, interrupted briefly by a child's wail. The sun was dropping behind them; shadow ran down their cliff.

Presently shadow filled the canyon, and the sky turned lilac with a waxing moon in the east, to which a column of smoke was rising from the cove. In the stillness, vague voices rose and joined in a rhythmic chorus, underlaid with pounding. This continued for a time, interspersed with shouts, bursts of shrieking. The smoke column wavered, gouted sparks. More shrieks, general shouting. The uproar died to grumbles, then to silence. The rocks clicked in the night chill.

The wolf left the cranny. The girl sighed, remained. Around the bend a dog began to howl, squealed and was silent. The girl toed intricate patterns in a sandy basin. The wolf returned, wetlegged, and they ate and drank. While the moon set they napped.

Before dawn they left that place and circled back across the river to the side on which they had entered the valley. The canyon wall was eroded to a tumble here. The two went slowly several times between shore and rocks as the sky paled. Finally they sat down to wait at the water's edge, behind a screen of alders. Across the river were the huts.

When light struck into the canyon the girl rose and faced the wolf. Her jacket wrapped around her waist, ending in a large loop. He caught a fang in this loop, flicked it free, and had the jacket open. Beneath the jacket she was bare. She stood patiently while he worried the jacket back across her shoulders like a cape. Her shoulders were smooth, scarless knobs above her small breasts. The cold air puckered their pink tips, stirred the patches of gold silk in what should have been her armpits.

Deftly, he had laid the folds of the jacket so they mimicked arms. He jerked his big head, satisfied, and then began to tug at the elastic waistband of her breeches, drawing them down delicately to expose her body and upper thighs. As he worked she began to smile, moved. He growled faintly. The wind blew on her bareness. She leaned against his warm fur. They waited.

Sounds were coming from the huts across the river. People appeared, ambling down to the river brink to stand or squat. Girl and wolf watched an alder-grove, across the river farther from the huts. Presently leaves began to shiver; a man was coming through. Wolf-head nodded; it was the big young one. The man appeared, moving familiarly along a sandpit, and stood to relieve himself.

Carefully the wolf drew back a low branch. The girl took an awkward pace forward, putting her naked body full in sunlight. The man's head swung, fixed on her. His body tensed. She gave a low call, swaying herself.

A surging ran up his legs, his foot spurned sand. Instantly the branch thrashed back around her. The wolf was yanking up her breeches, tugging her jacket around. Then they were running, pelting through the alders, racing out of the river-bottom on the line toward their trail.

Behind them, splashing. It turned upstream. The wolf had chosen well, there was a deep cut which the man must get around to gain their shore. They leaped up the bluffs, the girl agile as a goat. When they were out of the canyon the wolf turned aside and vanished in the trees.

The man came over the bluff to see the girl running alone through the tunnel-like path, far ahead. He plunged after, strong legs eating space. But she was at the electric age for running, childlight and trained hard; when he slowed from his first burst into a pound she was well ahead and going tirelessly, a peculiar weaving motion of her torso making up the balance for lost arms. As she ran her eyes roamed in search of the slashes they had left upon the trees beside the trail.

Suddenly there were new voices behind her: The dogs had joined the chase. The girl frowned, speeded up. A big grey shadow swerved alongside, stopped with lifted leg beside one tree and another. The girl smiled, let her pace slow.

Shortly she heard the dogs' voices change when they came to the wolf-sign. Shouts from the man, a yelp. No more sound of dogs.

She ran on. It was trot and trot now, uphill, with the sun towering to noon. She was panting hard when she came to the first of the places they had arranged. She leaped aside, catching the shadow of grey among the trees, and jogged on up the rising ground.

Behind her came a sharp yell and then the grunts and flounder of the bogged man. She leaned against a dead termitary. The trees were thinning here, the wind came through to carry her tiredness away.

Presently the wolf appeared, jerking his head irritably. The man was free. She turned and trotted on, the wind at her back. Over the valley trees the rim-rocks were a blue line far ahead. Trot and trot; the man held her in view now, and he was gaining.

Finally she heard behind her the crack of breaking branches and the angry shout. When she paused, the wolf stood by her, and they listened together to the sound of the man's struggles. She resumed of her own accord, knowing now that she could not outrun him on the rising ground. The wolf stayed, watching from cover.

The sun was yellowing into the high dust-haze when she topped the final ridge and turned to look. This was the limit of the wild men's trails; would he follow on beyond? The dying wind told her nothing. The wolf appeared, motioning her to a sunlit ledge, butting her into position with his nose. Then he pulled her jacket apart, and she gave a clear girl trill, ending in laughter.

As the echo died he sent her running down the rocks, past their old resting-place. In a moment he joined her, grinning toothily, and then leaped behind a rock to let her trot on alone across the unrolling shadows. She glanced behind; a ruddy figure was bobbing down the rocks. No dogs followed.

Shadows pooled, became quick twilight around her. As the twilight turned to moonlight and ink, the wolf ranged ahead with his crooked tail held high, and she followed its flag across the plain. This was old goat land, knobbed with clumps of thorn trees whose young were springing everywhere now that the goats were gone. They had slowed to walking, pausing now and again to listen for the footfalls behind; no other sound was here.

Finally he halted her and drifted back, silent as fog. He came back satisfied, and led her to a thorn clump. She freed her toes and drank, and ate greedily and drank again, and rested while he inspected and licked her feet. But he would not let her unharness him, nor release her hair, and he made her put her boots back on before he got out the transmitter.

"We've got one. He's very strong. Is Bonz all right?"

Questions rattled out at them. The wolf cut off, and pushed the girl's body earthward. Then he removed himself from her warm odors, and leaped up an ant-castle to lie facing the way they had come, head on crossed paws and one eye open under his heavy brow.

The dawn showed them to be on an amba, a high tableland backed by a line of cliffs. These turrets were their goal, but there was the empty plain to cross. The girl was well out upon it, trotting alone, when the ruddy figure appeared behind. The man wavered, ready to turn back until the sight of his prey gripped him and he was racing hard on her trail.

She speeded up and held the space between them almost steady for a kilometer before he began to gain. She forced her legs; it was wind against wind here across the bare plain. The plain was sliced with deep dry gullies; as her endurance failed her she was able to take advantage of the known terrain, doubling to lure him into delusive short-cuts. At two of the deepest arroyos she found the wolf waiting for her. She crossed by springing onto his back, where her pursuer would have to clamber up and down.

But for all she could do the man gained steadily. She was winded to gasping when she reached the tumbled hummocks at the foot of the cliffs. He was close, now. She began to toil upwards, remembering the stone that had been flung at the dog. How far could that powerful strange limb propel a rock? She did not know, and dodged upward with searing lungs, all her hope focussed on the tunnel.

This was the crucial part: If he should know these rocks.

But he was coming straight up behind her, not stopping to throw. Gravel sprayed, she could hear him grunt above her own grasping. He was only paces behind.

Suddenly shadow closed over her; she was in the old culvert. Hanging ropes touched her. She flung her weight into a harness, spun dizzily. Then everything gave and she struck the ground in a shower of darkness. At her heels, cascading thunder of rockslide pouring into the culvert mouth, cutting him off.

She panted for awhile in the ringing dust, and then made her way up through darkness. After a time there was grey light. She scrabbled, pushing herself on her shoulder pads, on up. This was an old skill; as an infant she had rubbed her shoulders raw.

Finally she emerged onto the old road bed where the wolf was waiting, and they went together to look over the brink of the cliff. It was blowing hard here; she leaned against him to peer down.

Far below a red figure scrabbled at the rocks before the tunnel. The cliff between them hung sheer; he could not get up that way. The girl sighed, still panting. She nuzzled the wolf's back, found the canteen mouth and sucked deep.

When she was breathing easily, they went again through the ritual of exposing her body. As he dragged her breeches down she giggled. He growled and nipped at her belly. Then he reared up and pulled off her cap to let the blonde silk blow.

She advanced to the cliff edge, called into the wind. A red face turned up to her. Its mouth opened and worked. She motioned with her head, took a few steps to the left. To that side the roadway was chasmed with a rockfall, where he could climb.

Finally he left off staring and mouthing, and began to circle toward the rockfall, stopping often to look up. She paced along as if to meet him until rocks came between.

Then the wolf dressed her peremptorily, and sent her staggering down the road in the other direction, away from the man. She took up a steady jog, going northwest now with the wind and the sun in her face. In less than a kilometer the old highway left the brow and cut inward through the turrents. There were higher blue crests beyond them to her right; they had once been called Harar. The road began to run straight across another mesa top. There were ruins here; adobe shells, ditches, littered yards under isolated big eucalyptus trees. There were metal fragments by the roadside. A rusting pump stood like a man as she jogged by. It was dusty and she was beginning to limp.

Now and then the wolf ranged up alongside and settled to watch her pursuer pass. The man was in sight on the straight road now. He came on doggedly, veering away from the strange shapes by the road. They were both walking as the light began to change. The distance between them was shrinking fast.

The girl was hobbling when she reached a ravine where the bridge had lay in wreckage. A little time could be saved here, but not much; she was spent. Beyond the chasm the road curved around walls, ran along an old square. The girl turned aside here and fell to her knees by the wall. The man was already leaping through the fallen bridge.

Beside her the wolf grunted urgently. She shook her head, panting. He grunted again and began to yank at her clothing, shouldering her up.

When the man strode around the bend she was standing alone, her body brilliant in the level light. He stopped, eyes rolling white at the walls. Then he took a step toward her and was suddenly in charging onrush. She stood quiet. He leaped, arms grappling her head, and she went down under him onto the hard dirt.

As they fell together a jet of gas came from between her lips into his face. He convulsed, crushingly. The wolf was on them, dragging at his arm. Still flailing, the giant was rolled aside while the girl coughed and gagged. When the man had flopped to inertness, the wolf pounced over her and nosed to raise her head.

Her gagging changed timbre; she wrapped both legs around the wolf and tried to roll him. He roughed her face with his tongue, planted his paw in her navel and pulled free. When she quieted he was holding the transmitter in front of her face. A snoring noise was coming from the man on the ground.

They looked together at his big body. He was half again the wolf's weight.

"If we tie him to you and drag him he'll get all torn," the girl said. "Do you think you can drive him?"

The wolf laid the transmitter down and grunted noncommittally, frowning at the man.

"We're only at that place west of Goba," the girl told the transmitter. "I'm sorry. He's much stronger than we thought. You — wait!"

The wolf was out on the road, standing tense. She listened too, heard nothing. Then a shiver in the ground, a tiny rumble. The transmitter began to squawk.

"It's all right!" the girl told it. "Bonz is here!"

"What do you mean, Bonz is there?"

"We can hear him coming, he must have got through the break."

"Damned idiots," said the voice. "You're all wasting energy. Base out."

Girl and wolf squatted together in the dusk beside the snoring man. Once she prodded at him curiously with her booted foot. Her teeth had begun to chatter.

The throbbing turned to a clashing roar, and a fan of light swung around the far end of the square. Behind the light was the dark nub of a small tractor cab. It was towing a wagon.

The girl stood up, swung her hair.

"Bonz! Bonz, we've got one!"

The tractor rattled up beside them and a pale head leaned out. The dashlight showed a boy's face, a bony, knife-edged version of the girl's.

"Where is he?"

"Here! Look, how big he is!"

The tractor's light swung, flooded the prone man.

"You'll have to get him on the wagon," the boy said. His eyes were smudged with fatigue. He made no move to leave the cab.

The wolf was at the sidewall of the wagon, pulling at a latch. The wall clanged down, forming a ramp to the low cart bed. Girl and wolf began to roll the red body sideways, toward the ramp.

"Wait," said the boy suddenly. "Don't hurt him. What have you done to him?"

"He's all right," said the girl. The man's shoulders were lolling against her knees, his upper arm slashed red where the wolf had gripped him.

"Wait, let me look," said the boy. He made no move to get out, but sat staring, licking his thin lips.

"Our saviour," he said. "There's your damned y-chromosome. He's filthy."

He pulled his head back, and they tumbled the unconscious man up onto the cart. There were hasps and straps in the floor. The girl got her boots off and fastened him down, her bruised toes clumsy. As they got him secure he began to groan. The girl pulled back her lips to reveal the syringe fastened between teeth and cheek and carefully jetted more vapor on his face.

The boy watched them through the back window, twisted in his seat. He was drinking from a canteen. On the wagon the girl unhitched her companion's pack and they ate and drank too. They grinned at the boy. He did not grin back; his eyes were on the great red-gold man.

The girl toed him idly, jostled him.

"Don't do that!" the boy called sharply. It was quite cold now.

"Do you think he needs a blanket?" asked the girl.

"No! Yes." The boy's voice sounded crumpled.

When the wolf reared up beside the cab door the boy was bent over, hauling blankets from behind his seat. The cab's interior was cluttered with tubing and levers. On the floor, where the boy's feet should have been, was an apparatus from which tubes led upwards. When he straightened up it could be seen that he had no legs; his torso was strapped to the seat and ended in a cocoon of canvas into which tubing led. His face was wet-streaked.

"We can all go die, now," he said in a hard voice. He pushed the blankets out the cab window, ramming with sinewy arms. Wetness ran down his thin jaw, fell on the blanket. The girl peered around the side, said nothing. The wolf grabbed a double corner of blanket and slung the rest back over his withers as he dropped to all fours. The boy hung his arms around the steering-wheel, let his head go down.

Girl and wolf covered the man on the cart and fastened up its side. He draped a blanket around her, leaped to the ground. The boy's head came up. He started the tractor and they lurched out into the road. Above them, no bat flew, no nightbird hunted, here or anywhere in the empty world. Only the tractor moved across the moonlit plain, a grey beast trotting behind. No insects came to its yellow lights. Before them the road stretched away neutrally to the crests above the Rift, in the land that had been Ethiopia.

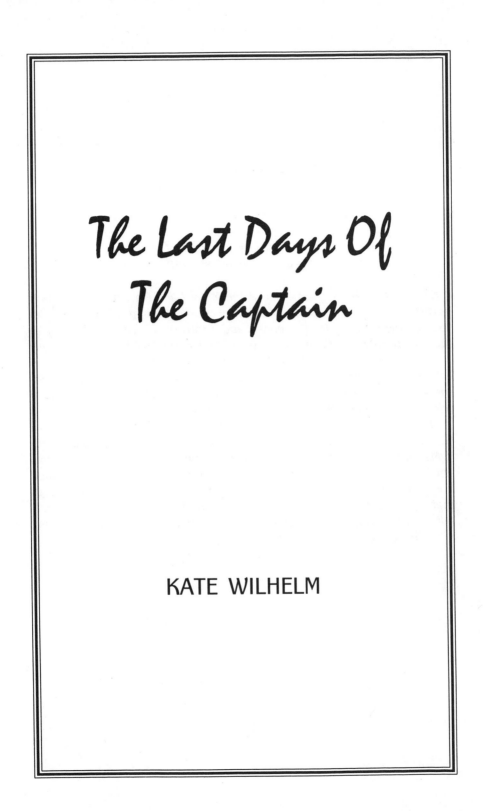

The Last Days Of
The Captain

KATE WILHELM

ABOUT KATE WILHELM
AND
THE LAST DAYS OF THE CAPTAIN

The Last Days Of The Captain *was first published:*
Amazing, *November 1962*

Kate Wilhelm is the godmother of the Milford and Clarion science fiction workshops. From here earliest appearances in the mid 1950s, Wilhelm distinguished herself for the power and depth of her characterization. It was not however until the late 1960s and early 1970s that she really came into her own as a writer. Beginning with The Downstairs Room, Let The Fire Fall, Where Late The Sweet Bird Sang, through the Clewston Test, she produced a body of work that, while it satisfied all the requirements of science fiction fans, also verged closer and closer on the mainstream.

"The Last Days of the Captain" was a ground-breaking story when it was first written and would probably be received as a major contemporary work if Ms. Wilhelm had penned it last week. Subtle and moving, it tackles among other subjects, issues like fidelity through infidelity, the unfulfilled hungers in the human heart, and the times when "a woman knows things that aren't said and mustn't be said." Powerfully characterized and deeply felt "The Last Days of the Captain" is a story that lingers in the mind long after the last pages are turned.

The Last Days Of The Captain

by KATE WILHELM

KEITH looked up scowling as the mayor entered his temporary office. "Well?" he snapped.

"Captain Winters, there are problems. Some of the people don't wish to leave . . . Their crops, their homes . . ." Mayor Stebbins edged into the room hesitantly. "If you'd talk to them . . ."

"Mayor Stebbins, don't you have any power over these people? Won't they follow you?" Keith asked sharply.

"How can they adjust so fast, Captain? Only this morning they arose with everything normal, and now they are told they have to leave what they've worked for all their lives. How can I explain it to them?"

Keith's eyes filmed over as he stared at the little man. Slowly he said, "I'll talk to them. In an hour. And, Mayor, three loads of your people will leave tonight as Taros sets. You decide which ones. I'll want the information as soon as possible."

The meeting was held in the church. Keith studied the uneasy, pale faced congregation with an emotionless expression. They had silenced their buzzing whispers at his approach with the mayor and now waited. As Stebbins stepped forward to introduce him, he took his elbow and put him to one side, standing solidly behind the dais himself.

"Ladies and gentlemen," he started, his voice authoritative and hard, "you know who the Amories are and that they have literally burned up three inhabited worlds. The Space Exploration Control has learned that they plan to attack Kulane in sixteen days, and for that reason the entire population is being evacuated. Following the evacuation there will be a surprise counter attack. You will be put aboard a stellar ship at Lanning and transferred to safety." He paused and regarded them stonily, seeing not individuals but articles to be moved out. Here and there audible sobs were heard, but for the most part they were stunned and still.

Briskly he concluded, "Your mayor will sit in on a briefing shortly and he will be able to answer your questions later. I cannot stress too strongly how important it is to give the appearance of normalcy. We have located alien scanners on Taros and there's another one in orbit to coincide with the sun's motions. There may be others that we have not found. They must not report any undue activity!"

He strode through the empty street with the sound of the congregation's mass voice raised in hymns ringing in his ears. By the time he reached his makeshift office in the mayor's house, a cynical grin had replaced his earlier frown. Sheep!

Seven days later he climbed a hill overlooking the village. He sat watching until darkness came and one after another of the house lights flicked on. Very faintly he could make out the figures that appeared now and again in the streets, and he nodded his satisfaction. He glanced once toward the glowing disk of a moon that hovered just above the tops of the mammoth conifers that made up the terrain of the planet Kulane. Very tiredly he pushed himself up from the ground and prepared to return to the village. This last night, and then he'd leave with the last truck load of settlers, mission accomplished. He stiffened and pivoted to face the shadowy tree trunks.

"Who's there?" He had heard of the giant cats of Kulane and his tight lips curled as his fingers became part of his smooth sonic gun.

"Oh, I didn't know you were up here. I'm sorry." It was a woman, her face a pale blank in the faint light of the moon. She stopped at the sight of the gun.

"What are you doing in the woods?" He didn't put the gun back in his tunic.

"Captain, please . . ." She advanced toward him, her hands held out so that he could see they were empty. "I'm Marilyn Roget. I came up here to wait for my husband and son. They'll come this way. Every night I come."

Stephan Roget, he remembered, was hunting the cats with his twelve year old son. He stared at the woman for a moment and then sheathed his gun. "You'd better be getting back," he said starting down the hill.

"Captain! I've tried to see you, but they said you were busy. Please listen to me!"

"Waiting for your husband?" he said, but he stopped.

"Captain, I don't care what you think. You can't just go off and leave them. Stevie is only twelve. What will happen to them?"

"There's nothing I can do. We have to have this village emptied by tomorrow morning and if they aren't back by then, we'll have to leave them." His tone was remote and again he turned to start back.

She ran to his side and caught his arm. "But . . ." She let her hand fall and raised her head very high. "Of course, you have to obey orders, don't you. But I don't. I'll stay and wait. We can get out in one of the flyers." At the look on his face she rushed on, "Not flying it. We'll use it as a ground car. We do it when there's a high storm."

"And what if they don't get back in time to make Lanning?"

"I'll hide in the forest until the battle's over. Until the time comes to hide, I could stay right down there and give it a real look of authenticity. What if something goes wrong with the robots. What if the generators fail? Someone should stay and make sure everything looks real right up to the end. I'll do it, and then hide in the woods later."

Savagely Keith swung around to blaze at her, "You fool! There will be no battle! No fight! The Amories will bombard Kulane from out in space and leave it a seething mass of radioactivity down to the deepest root of the tallest tree! We don't intend to let them suspect that the Control knows anything of it!"

Marilyn stared at him, incomprehension giving away to horror and fear. "I don't believe you," she whispered. "I don't believe you! I DON'T BELIEVE YOU! She flung herself at him and beat at his face with hard, tight fists.

Keith jerked away and slapped her angrily. "Come on," he said roughly grasping her arm and forcing her ahead of him. Taros dipped behind a swaying branch of needles and left them dark shadows that stumbled down the hill.

He held her arm tightly as they walked among the robots dressed in the villagers' clothes. She was weeping quietly now, making no sound, not even shaking, just steady tears flowing down her cheeks. Keith muttered a curse and shouted for Sorenson who was giving last minute instructions to the few remaining villagers waiting for the setting of the moon. The atom powered ground car stood loaded with supplies for the journey.

"Sorenson, take care of her. Put her to bed in the mayor's house. Change in plans. You take this group and I'll come out tomorrow with her."

Sorenson looked from the woman back to Keith. "But how will you make it out?" he blurted.

"We'll use a flyer on the ground. If her husband and son get back, they'll come with us. Otherwise, I'll bring her alone."

When Taros vanished Sorenson and the last of the villagers sped out of sight toward the towering trees. Despite the cheerful lighting of the houses, the village had an air of abandonment which deepened as one by one the house lights blinked out. In the rear of the mayor's house Marilyn slept fitfully under sedation, and finally Keith stretched out on the lounge in his office and also slept.

He cooked their breakfast when he heard her moving about, and by the time she appeared, he was ready to pour the coffee. She sat down opposite him, her eyes fastened on the plate before her.

"Better eat," he said. "We have lots to do today. You'll have to help get the flyer ready."

"Yes," she answered. When he finished his eggs, she rose and cleared the table. Her food was untouched.

Keith stripped down the craft as Marilyn made up a list of supplies for the trip. He noticed without comment that she prepared enough food for four. Toward noon the flyer was packed and ready. There was nothing more to be done until Taros set that night.

He studied his charts and calculated quickly the times for traveling during the next eight nights. It would take every minute of time they had. He frowned as he arrived at the figure one hundred ten miles per hour for the sixty four and two-thirds hours when it would be dark and Taros and its companion scanner would not be keeping watch.

The afternoon wore on and Keith put away his charts to prowl restlessly about the mayor's house. Contemptuously he fingered the stuff that covered the old fashioned lounge and glanced over the outdated books and ornaments that cluttered the room. He had been in the Space Exploration Control since his eighteenth birthday, seventeen years earlier. This assignment had come as a blow to him, baby sitting a bunch of colonists. Like most of the Control officers he had nothing but scorn for the earthbound dirt grubbers and their petty, smug lives. By God, he thought, if someone had come to him and told him he had to leave his ship, he'd tell him to go to hell, and put him there if necessary. But these people had crossed their hands and had sung a few hymns and had moved without an argument. He shook his head angrily; their psychology was as alien to him almost as that of the Amories. It hadn't been worth the risk of discovery. He wheeled about as Marilyn entered the room hesitantly. Like her, he thought, scared to death of him. Ready to run like a rabbit.

"Captain, you should rest now if you're going to drive all night. Lieutenant Sorenson gave me these capsules . . . If you'd like one . . ."

Keith's mouth curled in an unpleasant smile and he said coolly, "Keep them. Just call me at 1030." She turned to leave and he added icily, "And, Mrs. Roget, don't leave. I've made all the flyers inoperative and I set the lock for the one we're to use."

The woman turned sharply. "I'm not going with you, Captain!" she cried fiercely. "I demand one of the flyers to use to look for them! What harm can that do? We use the flyers all the time, and I'd be going away from Lanning, not toward it."

"Those scanners aren't to pick up a single flyer, nothing to make them look twice."

"I'll walk then," she cried. "Don't you understand? I can't just leave them here to die! I can't !"

Keith shrugged and turned from her taking a paper from the desk and handing it to her. "Read it, Mrs. Roget. It gives specific directions for your husband to follow if he returns before takeoff time. If he does get back and does follow those instructions, he'll beat us to Lanning. But flying is strictly forbidden until on the very last day; he'll wait until then for the time lock to be released. Now stop being a child." He pulled off his boots as he spoke and sat on the side of the lounge.

"You're not lying?" Marilyn asked, wanting to believe.

"Read the instructions," he said brusquely and lay down. He listened to her footsteps as she replaced the paper on the desk and left.

The roads through the forest were merely wide, cleared thoroughfares between the giant trees, held as nearly as possible to straight lines. Since the ground cars and trucks actually never touched the ground except when at rest, the trailing vines that covered the forest floor were allowed to grow undisturbed. Skimming eighteen inches above it, it took on the appearance of smooth, oiled concrete, and would feel just as hard if they should hit an obstruction at the speed Keith held. Marilyn sat motionless beside him oblivious to the streak of trees and vines they passed at speeds that often hit one hundred thirty. Keith's face set in lines of intense concentration as he gazed steadily into the opening among the trees and with part of his mind listened to the roar of the jet streams of air. After three hours without slowing once, he brought the flyer to a dead stop, braking in quickly and smoothly.

"What's wrong?" Marilyn asked almost disinterestedly.

"Trees are having a hypnotic effect," he said shortly. They were thinner here and he adjusted the light downward. Marilyn handed him coffee and he drank it quickly. Five minutes later they were racing along the forest road again.

They traveled for nine hours and sixteen minutes that first night, and when dawn brought the second scanner into play, Keith slumped over the wheel of the flyer letting his muscles jerk and twitch as they found relaxation. They ate wordlessly and slept encased in air mattresses.

When he awakened, he thought she had gone. He was alone by the flyer and the forest was noisy with birds. The plastic mattress cover was now too warm as the sun advanced across the sky. He got up and repacked his bed and cover in the flyer and munched on a biscuit. He didn't hear her return until she was nearly up to the flyer and then he stared. She was dressed in a green, two-piece knit suit that covered her entirely from her wrists to her ankles. She was delicately slender and well formed. He realized he was staring at her only when she flushed slightly and turned away. With a disturbing sensation that he had made a mistake in not letting her wait for her husband he jerked his chart from the flyer and walked to the trees to sit down and mark off one night. Later in the afternoon he strapped on his sonic gun and hoped one of the cats would make an appearance that day.

The third night they came upon the first of a series of boulders that jutted out into the clearing. By day, or even by night, at a reasonable speed, it would have been simple to avoid them. As it was he had to cut his speed in half, and then some more, to keep the flyer above them, and out of the trees. Left to itself it would try to maintain the eighteen inches he had set, but in doing so, it would veer upward and meet disaster against the branches of the trees. Four hours after starting he called a halt for coffee.

"How did they find out an attack was coming?" Marilyn asked, holding her cup in both hands to warm them.

Keith leaned back, grudgingly grateful to her, and forced his mind off the boulders he knew lay ahead of them. He demanded obedience from his muscles and nerves, compelling himself to untense. "One of your teachers from Lanning had a group of boys on Taros for a holiday and geology trip and he came across the scanner. He had enough sense not to disturb it and reported it immediately to the Control. From his description they decided it was probably a heat-sensing device and this plan fit. There were several alternative plans already drawn up, if the opportunity ever came to use them. The fleet was dispatched to maneuver in this sector for cover and then ostensibly withdraw again. When they leave, every person on Kulane is to be aboard the ships ready to take off. That will give us two days or more to finish setting the trap; it'll take them at least that long to gather in the sector, but this time it will be different."

"But you said there'd be no battle," she said quickly, a note of hope making her voice husky.

"There won't be. They'll think they've done it again. Hit and run. But we'll have a fix on them and follow them to home base."

"I see." Her voice went flat again. "Kulane will be destroyed as the other worlds were. Why didn't you tell them the truth?"

"This was the only way," Keith said coldly. "As it is, this mass evacuation is a calculated risk, and if there had been four thousand more inhabitants, it wouldn't have been attempted." He started the motor again, remembering the look on her face when he set the lock on the two seater flyer that was fast enough to get from the village to Lanning in a single night.

In eight and a half hours they made only five hundred fifty miles. Keith drank his coffee quickly and stalked away. He walked several miles scouting the road that lay ahead of them and returned in a vicious mood. Marilyn avoided his eyes as she handed him the rest of his breakfast.

"Do you think the others are having trouble?" she asked after a long silence.

"It'll be easier for them. Those trucks, cars, or whatever you call them, are made for skimming. The flyer isn't." He didn't add that there were also enough men to drive in shifts.

She nodded gravely and prepared her bed.

He wondered if she slept and knew she must sometime despite the growing hollows beneath her eyes and the darkness of the hollows.

That afternoon he unloaded some of the food and replaced it with boulders. Marilyn helped, rearranging the remaining food, straining to help lift the heavy stones into the flyer. "Might do some good," Keith grunted wiping his face with the back of his hand.

"Do you think we'll make it to Lanning in time?" she asked quietly.

"Not if we have many nights like last night. Afraid?" He could feel the sweat trickling down his back where his tunic didn't touch and he hunched his shoulders letting the material soak it up.

"There's a stream about a quarter of a mile down there," Marilyn said pointing. She was perspiring and moist and her hail had begun to curl about her face where little stray ends worked loose from the roll high on her head.

"Are you afraid?" he repeated.

"I don't know," she answered simply as if she hadn't considered it. "I keep praying Stephan and Stevie have got the message and will be there waiting for us. Perhaps I am afraid." Her eyes met his and she added, "But not of dying."

Keith turned sharply snatching his clean uniform from the flyer. "I'll go wash first and get dried. We'll freeze when the sun goes down," he said in the same voice he used with his sergeant.

That night they drove for eight hours and fifteen minutes and covered five-hundred twenty miles.

"I can't believe one lone flyer in the sky would be disastrous," Marilyn exclaimed, breaking into his monotonous swearing. "You can't stand many more nights like that and you know it."

"We can't take that risk!" he shot back at her. "One object in the sky might draw attention that would make this whole trek stand out. We don't even know for sure what kind of scanners they are using."

"Then be sensible and stop cursing those rocks. That isn't going to move them!" She slapped the can she was holding to the ground angrily, "What's happened to that perfect Control training, Captain? Are you afraid you'll be stuck here in the forest when the Amories attack?"

"Goddam it! Shut up! I've got a squadron to lead on a battleship! That's where I belong, not out here in a wilderness leading a bunch of moon faced settlers home to safety. This shouldn't have been tried in the first place! We'll give it all away and the Amories will bypass Kulane and hit somewhere else while we're playing nursemaid. Our first chance at them and some big brass has to louse it up with a stunt like this!"

"You would have voted against us, wouldn't you?" she asked softly a look of repugnance crossing her face. "Captain Winters, just what are you fighting for?"

Keith felt his hands become fists and involuntarily he took a step toward her. Abruptly he turned and stalked off, conscious of her following stare until he passed from her sight.

He walked unthinking until his legs throbbed and only then did he turn back. She was standing before the flyer and without raising her voice she said urgently, "There's a cat to my left! It's ready to spring."

Keith faded back several steps to get a view of the rear of the flyer, but he didn't dare risk hitting the ship. He could see the great beast moving, agonizingly slow, between the ten foot tree trunks. It was cat-like only in its tawny color and its crouching, ready-to-spring stalking. Its hairless head was long with a mouth that could open a foot wide; the rest of it, covered with stubby yellowish hair, seemed to be mostly long powerful legs built for leaping.

"I'll attract it over here," Keith called and stepped in front of the flyer.

"It won't change its prey," Marilyn answered. "Walk around behind me. As soon as I start to move it will jump. It will make two leaps; one to snatch me up and the next back to the trees. You'll have to be fast. If it misses me it will keep going and try again before you know it. I'll count three, take two steps away from the flyer and dive back under at three."

"Marilyn, stand still!" Keith shouted and was furious with himself. "I'll circle it."

"They're never alone," she said. She glanced at him then and said steadily, "one." She took a step away from the ship. "Two." Another step. "Three." She whirled and dived and the beast was in the air higher than Keith's head. It landed without stopping its forward momentum, its claws raking the spot where she had been the second before. Keith's gun fired and the creature crashed to the ground and moved no more. He ran to Marilyn and they climbed into the flyer before the cat's mate appeared at the edge of the woods. It sniffed their presence, hesitated momentarily, then seized its partner and dragged it off through the trees.

"It won't be back," Marilyn said calmly as it disappeared.

"Is that what your . . . your people hunt?" Keith asked. He knew he wouldn't choose hunting the beasts for sport.

The boulders were left behind them that night and when they stopped they had crossed off another eight hundred fifty-one miles.

The weather was growing steadily colder and they slept in the flyer. He was acutely aware of her breathing as his legs jerked and muscles untied. The strain of following that one bright, low light among the tree trunks, of being alert to changes in the terrain and anticipating curves and turns was telling on his nervous system.

He listened to her sigh in her sleep and he wondered vaguely what it would be like to live with her, go hunting with her, see her in his bed, feel her at his side, share the breakfast table with her day by day. He wondered if she dimpled when she laughed, what it took to make her laugh. He let the fantasies loose and drifted of into sleep.

He wakened hearing her scream. Just the one scream of terror. He slipped from his seat and groped for her.

She fell against him shaking unable to speak and he stroked her hair until she was still. He hadn't known she took her hair down when she slept. It was long nearly to her waist, and incredibly soft. He held her and stroked her hair and remembered the thoughts he'd had while falling asleep. He pushed her from him and asked self-consciously, "Are you all right?"

"I'm sorry," she said weakly fighting for control again. "I must have dreamed."

He knew she was weeping although her voice didn't break. "Try to rest some more," he said. "I'll see about coffee."

Nine hundred miles and they both took the sleeping medicine and huddled under their covers. He was groggy and heavy when he woke up, his appetite dulled and a bitter taste in his mouth. Marilyn was walking back and forth beside the flyer, a heavy tunic pulled over her green suit. There was no sign of the sun high over the trees.

Let it rain, he thought viciously. That was all he needed, to drive through a rain storm. It didn't however. They talked in a desultory manner, and regularly they got out and stamped up and down along the clearing. Neither of them mentioned the dream.

Night after night their traveling time had grown shorter as Taros set later. Kulane had thirty-two hour days and by the sixth night they were using only seven and three quarters hours of it for their journey. The day dragged interminably, and after sunset they still had eight hours to wait for Taros to go down. Keith sat stoically trying to ignore the cold that numbed his fingers. "You should have gone with the others," he said. "They'll be warmer inside the trucks."

Her voice floated back from the rear seat of the ship. "I'm all right. Why did you wait?"

"It was the least I could do."

"You were glad," she said with a note of finality. "You didn't want to be confined with them for so long."

"Why don't you try to sleep. It's going to be rough when we do get started."

"Why don't you answer me? I could sense it every time I saw you, how you hated us all. You came so cold and hard, despising us, seeing us as things that stood in your way." Her voice was low and meditative, as if she were thinking aloud. "They all knew exactly how the Amories left the other worlds they found. What good could they have done on the ground? You'll never know how much strength it took for them to leave."

Keith turned on his side and pretended to sleep. She was a stupid, ignorant peasant, he thought. All she knew was farming and hunting in the deep forests and how to keep her son and husband fed and content. Like animals all they had was acceptance for whatever came along. Strength! Were sheep strong? He dozed fitfully and the vision of her standing beside a slightly smaller version of her, a boy version of her, smiling, kept intruding in his dreams.

That night he got the speed up to a hundred quickly. One ten, fifteen, twenty, thirty. The trees were a blur as they raced by them and only the opening before him was real and straight. The small craft edged past one thirty and the gauge needle reached for the one forty mark and held there. His arms ached after the first hour, and his eyes burned as if he had a fever as he stared ahead watching for a sudden curve or dip that could send them hurtling up into the trees. The way was ruler straight and the inclines long and rolling. The needle crept past the forty mark and held the fifty indicator. The trees were a solid wall, dark and impenetrable, gleaming back at him the reflection from the stabbing light.

Suddenly a boulder loomed ahead, and before he could react to it, the flyer arced up. It missed the first branch of the tree and climbed higher as he struggled to regain control. He headed the craft upward through the branches, reducing speed, hearing the snapping of branches as the nose of the flyer cut through them. Then they were above the trees and in the sky.

Without a moment's hesitation Keith turned the light downward and hovered above the branches looking for a way back in. Finally, very cautiously, he began to lower it, maneuvering it carefully among the tree limbs, feeling pain every time he heard the inevitable scraping. At last they were back on the ground and he turned for the first time to look at Marilyn.

"Are you all right?"

A long shudder passed over her and she nodded. She pressed both hands into her face and shook but made no sound. Keith frowned helplessly, feeling the same need for release from tension. He started to reach for the coffee, but instead found himself gathering her into his arms.

"It's all right, Marilyn. It's all right now. I'm sorry." He held her murmuring quietly, his eyes closed, until she pushed back, calmed again. He tightened his arm about her shoulders.

"Please," she whispered tightly, "leave me alone."

Abruptly he pulled away and got the coffee out. He avoided looking at her, staring into the blackness outside instead. After swallowing the hot coffee he fingered the starter again. "I'm going to see if it will go," he said. "Ready?"

"Yes," she said steadily.

There were no more of the boulders and he held the speed on one forty almost hoping they would crash into one of the trees. It would be quick and painless, but the tunnel was smooth and he followed the wide curves without slackening speed until the sky was starting to lighten in streaks barely visible through the covering of the needles above. When he brought the flyer to a halt and felt the faint bump as it met the ground, he let his head fall forward cradled in his arms over the control panel. Wearily he noted that they had made one thousand miles. He slept.

Something awakened him. He shifted his cramped position slightly without opening his eyes and a nearly inaudible gasp brought him to complete alertness. He didn't move, but tried to hear, and there was nothing else. Very deliberately he inched his hand across the seat to his gun, and he could have cursed. It wasn't there. Then he did open his eyes, just enough to see in the edge of his field of vision that Marilyn had the gun and she was watching him. The gun was pointed at his head.

He let his eyes close and waited. Do it now, kid, he thought. Do it! Do it! Take the flyer and go look for them. You have that much coming to you. Do it!

He couldn't hold the position after several more minutes; his legs were sending cramping pains up through his hips, and his hand was asleep on the seat where his gun had been. Keeping his eyes closed he shifted again. Damn her! She was a coward after all! She couldn't do it. Gradually he untensed and fatigue dulled his thoughts. Coward, the word kept parading through his mind, and it was not clear whether he meant her for not shooting, or himself for wanting her to shoot.

Marilyn's voice roused him and he had no awareness of passage of time. "Keith," she said again, "you should eat and lie down. You'll be so cramped."

He pulled himself away from the seat reluctantly. He was aching all over, from both cold and cramped muscles. The gun was once more by him. Had he dreamed it then? Quickly he looked out at her. "Did I sleep long?" he asked.

"Several hours. She had her cover draped about her and her face was pinched and very cold looking.

He ate before he went out to inspect the damage the tree had done. It was surprisingly little. The sharp nosed, wingless craft was Sturdy with no protuberances to catch and break. Apparently it had slid between the woody limbs with little more than scratching to show it.

From behind him she said, "It would have been so easy once you were up there to open up and cover five or six hundred miles during that lost hour. Didn't it occur to you?"

"I thought of it," he admitted tiredly arranging his cover on the front seat.

"But you wouldn't do it, would you? Not even for yourself."

He turned to look at her and her eyes were very bright and remote, almost glassy. "Not even for you," he said distinctly.

She turned her curiously bright eyes to his and took a step toward him. "I'm so cold," she said faintly.

Her face was ashen, but her eyes burned into him. He went to her, taking her in his arms gently. She was stiff and cold in his arms. He felt nearly unendurable pain as her soft fingers that were so strong clutched at his back.

When she slept he carefully covered her and crawled into the other seat where he lay watching her for a long time until he too slept.

The moon was shining when they awoke and it lighted them as they ate. Afterward they sat inside the flyer, she in the rear seat and he up front. The trees shadowed the flyer and the dark grew deeper until he could see nothing and their voices when they spoke came from a void and sounded briefly and left nothingness behind.

"The ships will be uncomfortable," he said. "It would have been too risky sending regular passenger cruisers, so they stripped down cargo ships. Nothing left inside but the engine rooms and floors. You'll be crowded and uncomfortable."

"That doesn't matter," she replied after a pause. "Just so they all get out."

They were silent a very long time and finally Keith said, "I'll get coffee. We should be eating, I suppose."

They ate little, however, but sipped the hot drink slowly savoring the warmth and strength of it.

"Marilyn, I want you to take one of those pills Sorenson gave you."

In the dim light he could see her wide, luminous eyes still burning with an unnatural light. "I'm all right," she said. "I can take it as long as you can drive."

"I know you can. I don't want you to have to."

"Keith," Marilyn said in a low voice, "I understand. Sometimes a woman knows things that aren't said and mustn't be said. I'm not afraid."

"And sometime, a long time from now, can I see you?"

She ducked her head not answering and he reached for the controls.

It was a nightmare in which there was no let-up of speed, no curve to break the monotony of the abyss that drew them along. As the miles were left behind with totals changing at dizzying speeds he kept thinking of Stevie, almost as big as she. Her son. Her husband. How could she see him again? He didn't stop for a break although his arms ached and dragged leadenly at his commands and a numbness crept upward through his legs. They were entering Lanning when dawn was still several hours away.

Lt. Sorenson met them jubilantly. "I knew you'd make it, sir. Mrs. Roget, you're to go to room A-3 in the administration building. They'll direct you."

Keith ignored the man and helped Marilyn from the flyer. She started to walk toward the building, but turned and said, "Make it a very long time, Captain." The fierce brightness of her eyes was gone and there was only a deep, dull hurt there.

"What's that mean?" Sorenson asked and not waiting for a reply added, "You sure can't figure these colonists, can you? Wouldn't you have thought she'd at least ask about her husband and son?"

"Sorenson, shut your mouth!" Keith's voice was ominous. "These people are the only reason we have for even existing." He wheeled about and strode away remembering to hold himself as erect and proud as she had done. The pain in his own eyes, deep where it wasn't easily discernible, very nearly matched hers.

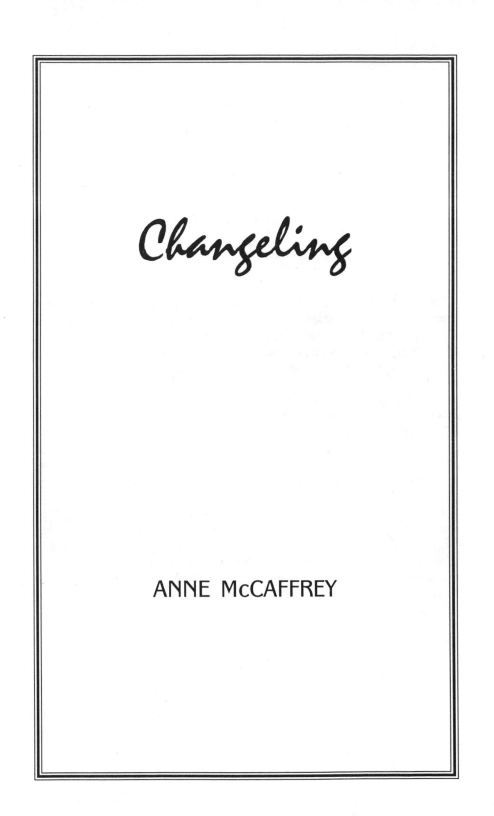

Changeling

ANNE McCAFFREY

ABOUT ANNE McCAFFREY
AND
CHANGELING

Changeling *was first published:*
God of the Unicorn, *1977*

   Anne McCaffrey is one of the world's bestselling science fiction writers, and unquestionably it's bestselling woman writer. Not bad for someone who, a little more than two decades ago, could not give her stories away. According to McCaffrey she had so much trouble selling her work that she had almost given up when a despairing letter she wrote provoked a reply from the late, great John W. Campbell Jr. that changed the course of her career.

   Campbell who could be credited with encouraging almost any author, regardless of gender, capable of writing the kind of story which interested him, suggested the hoary old wisdom of writing about what McCaffrey knew the most about. That turned out to be horses. A slight transposition of horses to dragons led first to "Weyrsearch," and when the public turned out to be as interested in dragons as Ms. McCaffrey was in horses, to her bestselling "Dragons of Pern" series.

   In its treatment of surrogacy at least ten years before the fact, "Changeling" is one of the author's rare pieces of genuine science fiction prophecy. Originally written for Harlan Ellison's Dangerous Visions anthology, it was rejected in favor of the story "Bones Do Lie." But the author has always considered "Changeling" — which is part of an unfinished story cycle and has a great deal to say about gender roles, parenthood, and the definition of "family" — the far more dangerous story.

Changeling

by ANNE McCAFFREY

CLAIR GLANCED QUICKLY at Roy again, her mind churning with astonishment, fury, and confusion. She simply had to persuade him to bring her back to City. Prenatal instructions blithely stated that the first birth was apt to take longer, but never how long. Claire knew that she had a wide pelvis, and she'd done all the strengthening exer — She concentrated on deep-breathing as the uterine muscles contracted strongly.

Good God, was this why Roy had been so faithful in attending the prenatal courses? She and Chess had thought that it was only because this baby was Roy's and, because of his sexuality, likely to be his only issue. Had Roy planned *this* all along?

She swallowed, for the nausea was acute.

"Roy, I'm going to be sick," she said, amazed that she could speak so calmly.

"Don't!"

The order was frightening, almost as frightening as the speed with which he skipped the uneven terrain, barely skimming the low ridges as the helicar climbed higher and higher into the Alleghenies.

He must be taking me somewhere, but where? Claire thought desperately. And why? Why?

A short, strong contraction pulled at her and she gasped inadvertently. Roy looked at her then, his almond-shaped eyes narrowing slightly.

"That's too soon. Are they increasing?"

"Yes, yes."

"No."

A flat-out, inarguable negative.

"For your baby's sake, Roy . . ." The soft entreaty, intense despite her quiet voice, caused the perfect curve of his wide mouth to flatten in anger.

Claire felt bereft of all courage. Roy was not going to be dissuaded from whatever insane course he had inaugurated. And that was very like Roy . . . and terribly unlike him. Why? *Why?* Where had she miscalculated with this brilliant, beautiful, complicated personality. What had she, after all, done wrong? Artificial insemination had solved his basic problem in the matter of becoming a father. Had he so little confidence in her after the years they'd lived so equably together? What maggot had got into his mind over this baby? He couldn't be jealous of Chess . . . or Ellyot? That was the prime reason for her having Roy's child first.

Claire had to stop thinking to concentrate on breathing as the contractions renewed. As she checked the sweep second hand on the heli's panel, she realized that Roy, too, was timing the spasms.

Oh, God, what is the matter with him? Why is he acting this way? We thought we'd covered every possible reaction. But to kidnap me? At the onset of labor? Roy, Roy, what did I do wrong?

Claire fought back tears, which would infuriate Roy. She wanted to scream but such a distressingly female reaction would not serve. It was the calm, rational quality of their relationship, the experts had told her, that was so essential to Roy's stability. The fact that Claire was always serene, so much the antithesis of the flamboyant feminine emotionalism which was repugnant to Roy Beach, had sustained this unusual experiment in human relationships. Now, every instinct in her rebelled noisily against his actions. But every last shred of disciplined rationality she had cried caution, patience, containment.

What had possessed him that he was compelled to act in this fashion? Things could go wrong, even at the last minute, and if they were so far from the City's obstetrical help, what could she do? Then Claire remembered again that Roy had attended every prenatal lesson and had read more books than she had. She bit her lips to contain an hysterical sob. Now she knew that it had not been complacent acceptance that Roy had exhibited, but twisted planning.

No, not twisted planning, she hurriedly corrected her thoughts. Roy wasn't twisted: he just saw things from a different angle. A very different angle, since he regarded women as a different species, useless in his environment. Up to the present moment, she'd been the sole exception. And how could she have been so dense as to imagine that he would react in any normally predictable fashion at the moment of parturition of the one child he was likely to sire?

The groan that issued from Claire's despair, part pain.

Roy glanced at her again, his eyes sliding around, through, beyond her, without seeming to pause long enough to admit her existence. He did note the contractions that rippled across her swollen belly. He frowned slightly as he looked back across the hills. Judging, Claire realized, whether he had enough time to make his destination before the birth occurred.

Where could he be taking her? Did Ellyot know? Or Chess? Ellyot surely, of the four of them, should have caught an inkling of Roy's plans. Roy barely noticed her these last few months, but he was constantly with Ellyot and Chess. The grotesqueness of her once slender, perfect figure would be repugnant to him: she'd expected that. Her physical perfection had first attached Roy to her. So it was reasonable for him to be revolted by her gravid condition even though it was his child that warped her body. She had dressed as concealingly and fashionably as possible and then kept out of his way — to the point of ducking into closets whenever she heard his quick light step in the house.

Unable to look at him or at the blurring green of the forest over which the heli passed, Claire closed her eyes and shuddered again. She forced herself to relax into the contractions. They were unquestionably stronger — and longer. She could tell that without recourse to the chronometer. And Roy was timing them, too. Let Roy take over. He had. Let him do his worst. He would be the biggest loser. By God and all the growing insight of modern psychiatry, she had done her best. Between pains, she cast back into memory and tried to reason out this extraordinary abduction.

Roy Beach, Praxiteles, Adonis, Apollo, call him Male Beauty in the classic mode, and adore him . . . at a distance. Always at a distance, please. He is not to be touched, he is untouchable. The crisp golden curls that fall in stylish sweeps across the high forehead; the wide-set, slightly slanting almond-shaped, green-green eyes over broad cheekbones, eyes that looked with such ruthless intensity at the wonders of the world, assessing its hidden beauties, disclosing its accepted horrors; the fine straight nose with sensitive flaring nostrils; the sensuous lips, neither too full nor too thin, graceful in the double curve of an Apollonian bow; the firm wide jaw. An incredibly beautiful face — and a beautiful body, tall, straight, deep-chested, muscular with graceful strength, hairlessly smooth. Then Nature compounded her gifts and gave him an intelligence that ranked him one of the most brilliant geopoliticians of the past three centuries. Nature, not always kind, added one final quirk to the psyche of Roy Beach, prince among men, to ensure that no princess would rouse tender, heterosexual feelings in his superb breast. And yet . . .

Claire Simonsen met Roy Beach in City University Complex. If they had not chanced to attend the same seminar, they would doubtless have been introduced by some meddler or other. As Roy Beach was a sleeping prince of godly perfection, Claire Simonsen was Snow White. Hair black as coal, skin white as snow, lips red as drops of blood on a queen mother's linen, she was gracious and gentle, and the fairest in the land — at least, in Penn City and its environs. She was also an extremely intelligent young woman: not equal to Beach as a theoretician — for her talent was in personal relationships which translated into human terms the geopolitical equations — but she was both able to follow and interpret his theories up to the point where he made the final ascent of intuitive genius.

At the time they met, Roy had not yet admitted his sexual preference and was intensely aggravated by the importunities of both sexes. Claire, for the same reason, saw in him the answer to her insistent suitors.

"I don't like females," Roy had told her that first evening in his quarters. "But I also haven't found a man with whom I can form an attachment." Roy never equivocated. "I may never find someone congenial. If you do, you have my blessings. Until that time —" and one of his rare and beatific smiles touched the perfect lips "— be my guest?"

"With you, candor has become an art," Claire had replied.

"If we are to continue to deal pleasantly together candor is essential."

Claire distinctly remembered that she had been strolling around his study room (even as a student, he rated status quarters), admiring the simplicity and elegance of its furnishings, the knowing placement of the few paintings, the Britton bronze, the Flock marble statuette. Unquestionably, Roy had been the model.

"You feel compelled to preserve the image of masculinity?" she had asked.

He had shrugged, his almond, green-green eyes expressionless.

"I am the image of masculinity."

"But not its substance."

He had frowned slightly, then he again awarded her that incredible smile. This time, it lit his eyes with humor.

"Sexuality in this day and age is, thank God, a personal, not a social choice. However, there is subtle pressure to pair off, and until this has been done, one is subjected to constant entreaties." He paused, nodding understandingly as Claire shuddered. Until Roy had blatantly annexed her that evening, she had been pestered by three quarrelsome and competitive fellow freshmen. "You are the most beautiful woman I have met. It is a pleasure to listen to your voice, to watch you move across a room." Roy smiled wryly. "Artistically, we complement each other."

"We do," Claire could not help grinning back at their reflections in the mirror surface of the darkened terrace doors. "God and witch. White and black."

"Are you always so tactful, Claire?"

She was a trifle startled at the laughter in his voice, at the definite twinkle in the intensely green eyes. Whatever reservations she had faded. Without humor, Roy Beach would have been insufferable.

"Let us see how we deal together, then," she replied. "It'll be a relief, even if we split up next Saturday, to have those hot-handed louts off my . . . my back."

Smoothly, Claire had adapted herself to Roy's ways. It was never mentioned but it was obvious to a girl with Claire's perceptions that the weight of compromise in the arrangement would always be hers. However, it was a small price to pay for being left alone once the word got abroad that Roy Beach and Claire Simonsen were quartering together. There might have been intense private speculation, but custom forbade probing. They were welcomed everywhere and were soon the acknowledged leaders of their University class.

The key, Claire had discovered, to Roy's intricate personality was to accept him at his own evaluation, a fluid standard which she understood intuitively at first, then intellectually as she penetrated deeper into Human Behavioral Sciences, until she could not have said why she knew how to suit him but invariably did. Theirs could never be a physical relationship, but Claire occasionally thought she was his mental alter ego. However, in his own way, he was devoted to her and as aware of her emotional needs as she was of his; once to the point of being demonstrably tender with her when one of her brief love affairs dissolved painfully.

It had been a tempestuous affair and ended in a bitter quarrel. Claire had run blindly back to Roy's quarters to find him waiting for her, and patient with her distress.

"You appeared to enjoy him," Roy had remarked when she paused at one point in her harangue. "He's got a reputation for proficiency, at any rate. Or didn't he make a good lover, after all?"

Claire had pulled the remnants of her pride together and looked at Roy.

"He is certainly physically attractive," Roy had said thoughtfully, taking her by the arm and leading her toward her old room. "But not your intellectual equal. You'd've fought sooner or later. Here's a trank: it'll ease the worst of the withdrawal."

He had pushed her onto her bed, tugged off her boots, gave her water to down the medication, and, to her immense surprise, had kissed her cheek lightly after he arranged covers over her.

With amazement, she detected a faint shadow of worry in his eyes.

"*We* understand each other, Claire. We complement each other. Do not settle for less than the best your own excellence can command."

As she drifted off to sleep, Claire was oddly comforted that Roy regarded her as a personality in her own right, and not as an adjunct or supplement to his own consequence.

There had been further brief associations for her, but always the standard that Roy had set for her governed the flare of sexual desire. On those occasions she had terminated the relationship — until Ellyot Harding was introduced to Roy at the Eastern Conference of Cities.

When Roy brought the slender dark man back to the flat — Roy and Claire had moved, of course, to civilian quarters after obtaining their advanced degrees — Claire was instantly aware of the bond between the two men, and of her own attraction for Ellyot. She was also aware of the surprise that rocked Ellyot Harding at her presence in Roy's quarters. She could all but hear his startled thought, What's a *woman* doing with him?

But Ellyot was quick to perceive subtleties and, on the heels of the first shock, came comprehension. He had instantly stepped forward, to grip her hand, to place a cool kiss on her cheek.

"You *must* be Claire Simonsen," for Roy had not yet had a chance to introduce her. "I followed your programmed analysis of the Deprivation Advantage with intense interest. In fact, I have allowed for that factor in the renewal project currently planned in my City. Oh, I apologize . . . Roy is rescuing me from the sterility of Transient Accommodations, and the inevitability of having to talk shop with other victims trapped there."

Ellyot's good-natured smile never touched just his lips, his whole face was involved in it.

"Go right ahead," Roy urged, turning to dial drinks at the console. "I rather thought you two would have overlapping interests. Explore them while I order a dinner suitable for this momentous occasion."

The look on Ellyot's face was mirrored in Claire's for both caught the nuance, the unspoken assumption in Roy's bland directive. Ellyot smiled, raised his eyebrows in a question.

"Yes, it is indeed an occasion," Claire said. "You might like our northern scallops, Ellyot — tender, sweet, delicious."

"The North has much to recommend it," Ellyot replied, leading Claire to the deep wall lounger. His manner was both triumphant and entreating.

Ellyot did not return to the Transient Accommodations or to the southern City which had sent him to the Conference. Claire's supervisor hired him immediately he made known his willingness to transfer. By the time City Management reviewed accreditation in the fall, the three had enough status to move to a larger single dwelling on the outskirts of the City. In fact, Claire was surprised at the outsized dwelling Roy chose for them.

"It's marvelous to have such space to spread out in, Roy, but it'll take every accommodation credit we own to manage this place," she had said.

"Not for long," was all Roy said, imperturbably.

He looked insufferably pleased with himself during the few weeks it took them to arrange and settle into the new house. Claire noticed that Ellyot was unusually irritable and put that down to Roy's insistence on each of them having a separate sleeping room. In fact, relations, up until then extremely harmonious, became strained.

"What is he up to?" Ellyot demanded of Claire one evening when Roy was at a meeting. "I know he's being coy about something."

"So do I, but I thought you'd know."

"Well, I don't. You've known him longer, Claire, can't you hazard what's on his mind?"

"Did you think I've some magic talisman to see into Roy's mind? I don't even sleep with him."

"That's the first catty thing I've heard you say."

"It wasn't catty, Ellyot, truly," she said in gentle apology even as he blurted out a request for pardon.

"You're a remarkable woman, Claire. Why have you never cut out? Why aren't you — well, jealous or . . ." He hesitated and, to her surprise, blushed. "I mean, you're so obviously hetero, and yet . . ." He gestured vaguely around the high-ceilinged living room.

"It's as much Roy for me as for you, Ellyot," she heard herself say, and then stopped, having finally voiced that admission. "Yes, it is Roy. We have never been lovers — never — but there's nothing of misplaced maternity in my relationship with Roy, or sisterly affection for that matter. It's a relationship . . . of the spirit. No platonic nonsense, either. I honestly, truly, deeply admire, respect, and . . . and love Roy. I cannot live fully without him and I cannot —"

"I know exactly what you mean," Ellyot said softly, with a ghost of a smile on his lips, but none in his eyes. He leaned back against the couch. "You remember the day we met? I'd a hetero marriage contract set up in my old City, you know, but half an hour in Roy's company and that was all over." He grinned. "I wanted children, you see, but Roy was too much."

Now Ellyot turned his head toward her, his eyes reflecting her image. She felt his hand touch hers, spread her fingers against his palm.

"She was no match for Roy . . . or you." He dropped her hand and abruptly stood up, almost glaring at her. 'And this is not fair to you, either. You've enough status to have a child of your own from a lover. Get out of here, have a child, marry, don't waste your life on us . . . on Roy. He doesn't mean to be exclusive. He just is."

His outburst surprised him as much as did her, for he dropped down on the sofa, one arm behind her, and scowled earnestly as he covered both her hands in a tight grasp.

"Yes, he just is," Claire said softly. "I cannot leave him, Ellyot, any more than I can leave you. There's no other company I'd rather keep, you know." She gently returned the pressure of his hand.

"But I *know* you want children. I've seen you pausing by the playyards. I've seen the longing in your face.

"I'm in no hurry. I'll find someone . . ."

Ellyot snorted his opinion of that naïveté. "You haven't even had a lover in the past year. All you've done is work . . . work."

"You've been keeping tabs on me?" Claire was touched by his sudden protectiveness. That was more Roy's role than Ellyot's.

"Neither of us wants you wasting your womanhood on just anybody . . . or no one."

Claire shook her head slowly, conscious of a deep and tender affection for Ellyot. "Did neither of you think to ask my opinion?"

Ellyot glanced sharply down at her. His eyes darkened and he pulled in a deep startled breath just as he bent to kiss her fully and passionately on the mouth.

When she and Ellyot emerged from her room the next morning, Roy merely nodded pleasantly and invited them to join him at the table. Breakfast for three had already been dialed.

Nor was there any embarrassment. Almost, Claire once mused, as if Roy had expected something of this sort and was relieved that it had finally taken place. After the first occasion, Claire had to be the aggressor with Ellyot, though he was never reluctant.

However, in the course of the next few months, Claire realized that the lovemaking she shared with Ellyot could become invidious. It was impossible to make love with Ellyot and not sense Roy, not make love with Roy through Ellyot, not hunger for Roy's magnificent body when Ellyot's covered hers.

Roy had brought Ellyot into their circle for his own ease and solace. Triangularity could deteriorate the relationship. Claire must find a fourth member.

She wasn't getting any younger, and Ellyot was correct about how much she longed for a child.

Claire was convinced that Roy had perceived her turn of thought. Of course, they had been talking about building a real kitchen into the house the next time City Management raised their total income. Roy was intensely interested in raw food preparation and increasingly annoyed with the mass-produced combinations available from the public kitchens, despite the interesting variations he achieved with what came out of the dispensers. But it was Claire, restless, increasingly dissatisfied, who undertook to find an architect who would design a kitchen room for them.

The first firm she consulted laughed at the notion of an entire room devoted to the preparation of food for consumption. The second thought she wanted a rough arrangement such as could be installed in a retreat too far from a City or Center for regular facilities. They recommended another firm that did reconstruction work for museums. That was how she met Chess Baurio.

"He's very busy, you know," she was told over the telephone by the receptionist. "But the notion is bizarre enough that he might just like to try it." An appointment was made and she went directly to his office, not far from their home.

It could never be called love at first sight, for he was extremely antagonistic from the moment she introduced herself. Only because he'd never attempted to solve such a design problem did he reluctantly agree. And then, under the stipulation that it was done his way. He knocked down one after another of her plans, sarcastically deriding her painstaking research. In fact, when she had finally got him to agree to come to the house and examine the proposed site, Claire wondered why she had put up with his manner and attitude for one session, much less contemplate a further association.

Still, when he arrived the next morning, he was unexpectedly pleasant, even charming — until Roy walked in. If Roy Beach was the personification of the classic concept of the male manner, Chess Baurio was the twenty-first century's. Compact, lean, healthily attractive, alert, he was the antithesis of Roy's studied indolence. Roy was the aloof, detached, arrogant observer; Chess was the involved, enthusiastic, vital participator.

As Roy strode up to the terrace where she and Chess were discussing the location of the kitchen room, the air became charged with electric hostility.

Claire looked at Chess, saw that his eyes were snapping with anger, that the smile on his face was set, that his movements as he leaned forward slightly to shake Roy's hand were jerky. His manner became stilted, false. She glanced at Roy, who was his usual urbane self.

"Chess Baurio? You designed the new theater complex at Northwest 4," Roy said by way of greeting. "Now, why did you use polyfoam instead of Mutual's acoustical shielding?"

"Ever heard the wows in the Fine Arts Theater at Washington South?"

"Can't say that I've been in that theater, but wasn't it John Bracker, Claire, who was so vehement in his objections to playing in that hall?"

"He did mention he'd rather play under Niagara Falls," she said lightly, hoping to ease the tension.

"And polyfoam corrects wow?" Roy demanded of Chess.

"In that size building, or in amphitheater form." Baurio's voice had a bitten quality.

"I've been advised to use it in our music room," Roy went on, blandly, dialing out three coffees and passing them round as if Chess would naturally take his black as they did. "What's your opinion on its use in a small room?"

"As a consultant?"

The rudeness in Chess' tone surprised Claire. People were rarely rude to Roy. He simply didn't elicit that kind of response. She held her breath. Roy did not appear to notice.

"The kitchen room comes before the music room, but we always combine efforts. I believe that Ellyot . . . Ellyot Harding," and that was the first time Claire ever heard Roy qualify any acquaintance so pointedly, "is the third member of the house . . . has a preference for natural woods as acoustical materials, rather than manmade products."

Hostility fairly bristled from Baurio now.

"We have not really discussed the music room. I imagine, however, Designer Baurio, that if the kitchen room is successful, we'll get busy on the other," Claire said, trying to sound relaxed and gracious. Why was anything Roy said so offensive to this Baurio?

"I'm not at all sure," Baurio said icily, putting down his untouched cup of coffee, "if anything I designed would be successful in this . . . this kind of ménage."

Not even Roy could ignore that, and he slowly turned toward Baurio, his eyes glittering.

"You object to polyandry?"

"I object . . . I object to such a monopoly, to the sheer waste of . . ." He broke off, glaring savagely from Claire to Roy before he spun around and strode out of the house.

"What on earth possessed you to come out with statements like that, Roy?" Claire asked. "He was . . . to design a kitchen room . . . What happened?"

Roy smiled down at her. "He'll be back. And you must make him stay."

After the most tempestuous three months in her entire life, she did, but only when their marriage contract had been registered in the City. And that came about only because Roy and Ellyot cornered Chess privately at the end of a particularly bitter quarrel.

The end of the mad abduction and the cessation of a particularly painful contraction — her muscles were beginning to hurt despite training and control — were simultaneous. Claire opened her eyes to a leafy vista, the tops of trees below the heli's landing gear. Startled, she peered down. The heli was perched on the edge of a sudden, sharp drop, the bottom of which was hidden by foliage. Wildly she turned to Roy. His eyes wouldn't focus on her, his breath was uneven.

"Can you move?" he asked.

"Where?" She couldn't control the quaver in her voice.

He threw up the hatch and jumped out, ignoring the gasp she made as she had a flash of him disappearing over the precipice, leaving her alone and at the mercy of her body's birth-drive in the cramped nose of the heli.

"Put your hands on my shoulders," he ordered, and she found herself obeying.

She moved as quickly as she could, knowing that a spasm was seconds away. It seized her as she reached out to him and sent her reeling into his arms. He had seen the look of pain on her face, and deftly caught her to him, holding her firmly despite the awkward position for them both.

It seemed an age until the contraction passed. She submitted weakly as he swung her up and strode off. She buried her face against his shoulder.

Does he intend for me to have the child in the woods, like an animal? she wondered.

"You'll have to open the door," he said in her ear.

She looked down and fumbled for the crude latch, surprised that there should be a door, for she had only the fleeting impression of the façade of the retreat, its rustic logs, the heli's floatons apparently resting on the surface which camouflaged the retreat. Vaguely, she hoped the roof was firmly supported against the heli's weight.

As Roy angled her through the doorway, she caught a glimpse of the superb view of the valley below them, the mountains beyond. When had he acquired such a retreat? Or who had lent it to him? Stupefied, Claire wondered if Ellyot had suspected this and kept silent.

A contraction. She couldn't suppress the groan, which deafened her to a statement Roy muttered under his breath. But, seemingly a century later, he laid her on a bed and was arranging her body in the best position to ease the strain.

"A hard one, huh?" he said as she lay, panting. She didn't resist as his hands turned her gently and stripped off her maternity sack, or as they felt her writhing abdomen.

How can he bear to touch me? He has scarcely looked at me for five months.

The next moment she became aware of other preparations for the coming birth and she began to struggle fastidiously.

"Don't resist. This has to be done. For the child's sake."

Hearing the anger and distaste in his voice for what he had to do, she forced herself to relax and endure his ministrations.

Her waters broke while she was on the toilet and she began to whimper, more from embarrassment and tension than pain.

"What is it?" His voice was clinical.

"The waters broke."

He got her back to the bed, on her back, and examined her with the deftness of her obstetrician.

"The head is in the birth canal," he said just as she experienced the first of the second-stage contractions. "That's right. Push down!"

She fought the hand that pressed down on the upper part of her belly.

"No, no Roy. Leave me alone. Get a doctor. Please, Roy!"

His face loomed suddenly above her so that she was forced to open her eyes wide and look at him.

"I know what to do, Claire. The child is *mine!*"

"But you could have assisted at the hospital, Roy," she cried, slowly perceiving through her pain and anxiety what motivated him.

"With Chess listed as your legal spouse? We haven't that right yet. No, Claire, this is my child."

"It's mine, too," she screamed.

"Is the pain unbearable? I'll fix the mask for you."

"Mask?"

"I have assembled everything that might be needed," he told her in that odd flat voice. "Do you need the mask now?"

"No, no. No!" She couldn't succumb to the desire for relief from the pain, though it was fierce now, fierce and inexorable, convulsing her body, seizing her with a steadily increasing rhythm, permitting her not so much as a moment to relax straining muscles.

"Good. Press harder. Press downward." She heard his voice through a mist of sweat and tears and pain.

She grabbed at the bed, flailed wildly around for something to hang onto and was rewarded with a strong wrist to grasp. But for that hand, she was lost in a nightmare of stretch, strain, pant and gasp, of a body that was not hers, that responded to primal urgings. The comforting hand, the reassuring voice were part of it and apart from it. The rhythm increased, unbearable, constant, exhausting, and then, wrenched by a terrible spasm, her body arched. She was sure she had been torn apart.

The pain was gone. Sweat dripped into her eyes. She felt almost lifeless, certainly weightless but . . . serene, strangely enough. Her legs were spread wide, the thigh muscles ached, her vagina throbbed, and all pain was replaced by the languor of exhaustion. She became conscious of movement within the room, of a harsh breathing, a wet splat, and then the tiny gasp as infant lungs sucked in air and complained mewlingly.

She raised herself on her elbow, one hand reaching for the sound.

"Roy?" She dashed sweat and damp hair from her eyes.

Roy's back was to her. When he turned, she was startled to see a surgical mask across his face, the translucence of plastic gloves high up his muscled forearms. And, dangling from his left hand, a tiny, armwaving inverted form, the cord still attaching it to her.

"Oh, God, Roy, give him to me."

Roy's eyes were full of tears as he laid the child on her belly.

"I have delivered my son," Roy said in the gentlest voice. "Don't touch him," he added, knicking her hand away with the bare part of his forearm. "You're not sterile."

"He's mine, too," she protested, but did not reach out.

She watched as Roy deftly tied off the umbilical cord, swabbed the child's mouth, painted his eyes. As he tenderly oiled the reddish skin, Claire craned her neck to glimpse with greedy eyes at the perfection of the tiny form.

And the baby was perfect, from the delicate kicking feet to the twitching fists. His head bones were still pointed, but there was a fineness about the angrily screwed features. Despite the unconventionality of his birth, he was alive and obviously healthy. She did not protest when Roy swathed the child in a receiving blanket and laid him in the portable crib that he pushed gently to one side of the bed.

"Now, you." Again all emotion was leached from his voice.

With the heel of his hand, he pressed into her flattened belly. She screamed for the pain of it and was seized, to her horror, with another contraction that brought a flood of tears to her eyes.

"You leave me alone!" she cried, feebly batting at his arms.

"The afterbirth!"

And it was delivered.

Utterly exhausted, she lay back. She felt but did not move as he sewed the torn skin of her, only vaguely wondering that he knew how. She was too weary to help as he cleaned her, changed the soiled sheets. She was only grateful that the pain and the shame were over as he covered her tightly bound body with a light blanket. She could hear the baby snuffling somewhere in the room and his continuing vigor was more reassuring than anything else. She felt herself drifting off into sleep and tried to fight it. She must stay awake. She couldn't afford to sleep. He might try to leave her now he had the child he had wanted so desperately.

And that thought stuck in her mind. The child Roy wanted so desperately was born. That was why he had acted so rashly. His child. His child! She had, after all, and however deviously, become the mother of his child.

A tiny voice, insistent and undeniable for all its lack of volume, roused her. She felt hands turn back the covers that lay so comfortingly around her. She felt her upper body lifted, supported with pillows. Drowsily, she evaded full consciousness until she felt her arm crooked, felt the scrape of linen against her skin, the warmth of a small rounded form, hands against her right nipple, the coolness of a wet sponge, then the fumbling of small wet lips and the incredible pleasurable pain caused by a suckling child.

She opened her eyes to the dim light. Roy was sitting on the edge of her bed, his hand securing her lax hold on the child. She was fully aware in that instant, aware and awake. She glanced down at the tiny face, eyes tight, lips working instinctively for the nourishment she could feel it drawing from her breast.

Roy did not remove his hand, yet it was not as if he did not trust Claire.

And suddenly she understood all that must have been driving him since she had blithely announced her desire to have his child first. She had taken him, of them all, by surprise. She had astounded and startled him. She had given him a hope, a promise that Roy Beach had never even considered, given the circumstances of his sexuality. She had given him the child of his own flesh, yet she had not soiled him with her femininity.

She understood now why he had been unwilling to trust anyone but himself with the responsibility of delivering his child.

The pressure in her other breast was painful. She disengaged the nipple from the searching, protesting mouth and quickly shifted the babe, taking a sensuous delight in the tug and pull of the eager lips as they fastened on the new food source.

Then she looked up at Roy. She smiled at him as their eyes met. She felt that she saw directly into his heart and soul for the first time in their long association. With her free hand, she reached for his and placed it on their son.

"I called Chess, and told him where you are. He said Ellyot made him understand."

Claire tried to tell him with her eyes that she did, too, but all she could say was. "Does he plan to come here?"

There was a quick start in Roy's body and his eyes plowed deep into hers as if he, too had to know her heart, at least this once.

"It would be more peaceful," she added, holding onto his gaze, "to have the first few days alone, if you can stand it."

"If *I* can stand it . . ."

Claire had to close her eyes against the look of intense joy, of almost painful jubilation in Roy's face. She felt him lean toward her, across the child, so that the baby kicked against the constriction. She felt his lips on hers, her body responding unreasonably to his benediction.

When she opened her eyes again, he was smiling down at the babe with untroubled pride and affection.

And that was how it must be forever, Claire reflected and deliberately put aside that brief, tantalizing glimpse of the forbidden paradise.

Fears

PAMELA SARGENT

ABOUT PAMELA SARGENT
AND
FEARS

Fears *was first published:*
Fantasy and Science Fiction, *February 1972*

Pamela Sargent is one of the leading lights of contemporary science fiction as literature. The editor of the pioneering Women of Wonder *collections, she is also the author of such critically celebrated science fiction novels as* Cloned Lives, Shore of Women, Watchstar, *and* Venus of Dreams. *A multiple award winner including the Nebula and Hugo awards, Ms. Sargent is currently editing two new Women of Wonder Anthologies.*

Her work has been described as "marked by qualities of plausibility rooted in realism and an unusual focus on characterization." "Fear," her story here, plays with notions of sex and gender, slyly subverting our expectations and revealing just how flexible these "givens" really are. In terms of traditional points of view, "Fears" may be the most radical story in this collection.

Fears

by PAMELA SARGENT

I WAS ON my way back to Sam's when a couple of boys tried to run me off the road, banging my fender a little before they sped on, looking for another target. My throat tightened and my chest heaved as I wiped my face with a handkerchief. The boys had clearly stripped their car to the minimum, ditching all their safety equipment, knowing that the highway patrol was unlikely to stop them; the police had other things to worry about.

The car's harness held me; its dashboard lights flickered. As I waited for it to steer me back onto the road, the engine hummed,. choked, and died. I switched over to manual; the engine was silent.

I felt numb. I had prepared myself for my rare journeys into the world outside my refuge, working to perfect my disguise. My angular, coarse-featured face stared back at me from the mirror overhead as I wondered if I could still pass. I had cut my hair recently, my chest was still as flat as a boy's, and the slightly padded shoulders of my suit imparted a bit of extra bulk. I had always been taken for a man before, but I had never done more than visit a few out-of-the-way, dimly lighted stores where the proprietors looked closely only at cards or cash.

I couldn't wait there risking a meeting with the highway patrol. The police might look a bit too carefully at my papers and administer a body search on general principles. Stray women had been picked up before, and the rewards for such a discovery were great; I imagined uniformed men groping at my groin, and shuddered. My disguise would get a real test. I took a deep breath, released the harness, then got out of the car.

The garage was half a mile away. I made it there without enduring more than a few honks from passing cars.

The mechanic listened to my husky voice as I described my problem, glanced at my card, took my keys, then left in his tow truck, accompanied by a younger mechanic. I sat in his office, out of sight of the other men, trying not to let my fear push me into panic. The car might have to remain here for some time; I would have to find a place to stay. The mechanic might even offer me a lift home, and I didn't want to risk that. Sam might be a bit too talkative in the man's presence; the mechanic might wonder about someone who lived in such an inaccessible spot. My hands were shaking; I thrust them into my pockets.

I started when the mechanic returned to his office, then smiled nervously as he assured me that the car would be ready in a few hours; a component had failed, he had another like it in the shop, no problem. He named a price that seemed excessive; I was about to object, worried that argument might only provoke him, then worried still more that I would look odd if I didn't dicker with him. I settled for frowning as he slipped my card into his terminal, then handed it back to me.

"No sense hanging around here." He waved one beefy hand at the door. "You can pick up a shuttle to town out there, comes by every fifteen minutes or so."

I thanked him and went outside, trying to decide what to do. I had been successful so far; the other mechanics didn't even look at me as I walked toward the road. An entrance to the town's underground garage was just across the highway; a small, glassy building with a sign saying "Marcello's" stood next to the entrance. I knew what service Marcello sold; I had driven by the place before. I would be safer with one of his employees, and less conspicuous if I kept moving; curiosity overcame my fear for a moment. I had made my decision.

I walked into Marcello's. One man was at a desk; three big men sat on a sofa near one of the windows, staring at the small holo screen in front of them. I went to the desk and said, "I want to hire a bodyguard."

The man behind the desk looked up; his mustache twitched. "An escort. You want an escort."

"Call it whatever you like."

"For how long?"

"About three or four hours."

"For what purpose?"

"Just a walk through town, maybe a stop for a drink. I haven't been to town for a while, thought I might need some company."

His brown eyes narrowed. I had said too much; I didn't have to explain myself to him. "Card."

I got out my card. He slipped it into his outlet and peered at the screen while I tried to keep from fidgeting, expecting the machine to spit out the card even after all this time. He returned the card. "You'll get your receipt when you come back." He waved a hand at the men on the sofa. "I got three available. Take your pick."

The man on my right had a lean, mean face; the one on the left was sleepy-eyed. "The middle guy."

"Ellis."

The middle man stood up and walked over to us. He was a tall black man dressed in a brown suit; he looked me over, and I forced myself to gaze directly at him while the man at the desk rummaged in a drawer and took out a weapon and holster, handing them to my escort.

"Ellis Gerard," the black man said, thrusting out a hand.

"Joe Segor." I took his hand; he gripped mine just long enough to show his strength, then let go. The two men on the sofa watched us as we left, as if resenting my choice, then turned back to the screen.

We caught a shuttle into town. A few old men sat near the front of the bus under the watchful eyes of the guard; five boys got on behind us, laughing, but a look from the guard quieted them. I told myself again that I would be safe with Ellis.

"Where to?" Ellis said as we sat down. "A visit to a pretty boy? Guys sometimes want escorts for that."

"No, just around. It's a nice day — we could sit in the park for a while."

"I don't know if that is such a good idea, Mr. Segor."

"Joe. "

"Those crossdressers hang out a lot there now. I don't like it. They go there with their friends and it just causes trouble — it's a bad element. You look at them wrong, and then you've got a fight. It ought to be against the law."

"What?"

"Dressing like a woman. Looking like what you're not." He glanced at me. I looked away, my jaw tightening.

We were in town now, moving toward the shuttle's first stop. "Hey!" one of the boys behind us shouted. "Look!" Feet shuffled along the aisle; the boys had rushed to the right side of the bus and were kneeling on the seats, hands pressed against the window; even the guard had turned. Ellis and I got up and changed seats, looking out at what had drawn the boys' attention.

A car was pulling into a spot in front of a store. Our driver put down his magazine and slowed the bus manually; he obviously knew his passengers wanted a look. Cars were not allowed in town unless a woman was riding in one; even I knew that. We waited. The bus stopped; a group of young men standing outside the store watched the car.

"Come on, get out," a boy behind me said. "Get out of the car."

Two men got out first. One of them yelled at the loiterers, who moved down the street before gathering under a lamppost. Another man opened the back door, then held out his hand.

She seemed to float out of the car; her long pink robe swirled around her ankles as she stood. Her hair was covered by a long, white scarf. My face grew warm with embarrassment and shame. I caught a glimpse of black eyebrows and white skin before her bodyguards surrounded her and led her into the store.

The driver pushed a button and picked up his magazine again; the bus moved on. "Think she was real?" one of the boys asked.

"I don't know," another replied.

"Bet she wasn't. Nobody would let a real woman go into a store like that. If I had a girl, I'd never let her go anywhere."

"If I had a trans, I'd never let her go anywhere."

"Those trans guys — they got it made." The boys scrambled toward the back of the bus.

"Definitely a trans," Ellis said to me. "I can tell. She's got a mannish kind of face."

I said, "You could hardly see her face."

"I saw enough. And she was too tall." He sighed. "That's the life. A little bit of cutting and trimming and some implants, and there you are — you don't have to lift a finger You're legally female."

"It isn't just a little bit of cutting — it's major surgery."

"Yeah. Well, I couldn't have been a transsexual anyway, not with my body." Ellis glanced at me. "You could have been, though."

"Never wanted it."

"It's not a bad life in some ways."

"I like my freedom." My voice caught on the words.

"That's why I don't like crossdressers. They'll dress like a woman, but they won't turn into one. It just causes trouble — you get the wrong cues."

The conversation was making me uneasy; sitting so close to Ellis, hemmed in by his body and the bus's window, made me feel trapped. The man was too observant. I gritted my teeth and turned toward the window. More stores had been boarded up; we passed a brick school building with shattered windows and an empty playground. The town was declining.

We got off in the business district, where there was still a semblance of normal life. Men in suits came and went from their offices, hopped on buses, strolled toward bars for an early drink.

"It's pretty safe around here," Ellis said as we sat on a bench. The bench had been welded to the ground; it was covered with graffiti and one leg had been warped. Old newspapers lay on the sidewalk and in the gutter with other refuse. One bore a headline about the African war; another, more recent, the latest news about Bethesda's artificial womb program. The news was good; two more healthy children had been born to the project, a boy and a girl. I thought of endangered species and extinction.

A police car drove by, followed by another car with opaque windows. Ellis gazed after the car and sighed longingly, as if imagining the woman inside. "Wish I was gay," he said sadly, "but I'm not. I've tried the pretty boys, but that's not for me. I should have been a Catholic, and then I could have been a priest. I live like one anyway."

"Too many priests already. The Church can't afford any more. Anyway, you'd really be frustrated then. They can't even hear a woman's confession unless her husband or a bodyguard is with her. It's just like being a doctor. You could go nuts that way."

"I'll never make enough to afford a woman, even a trans."

"There might be more women someday," I said. "That project at Bethesda's working out."

"Maybe I should have gone on one of those expeditions. There's one they let into the Philippines, and another one's in Alaska now."

I thought of a team of searchers coming for me. If they were not dead before they reached my door, I would be; I had made sure of that. "That's a shady business, Ellis."

"That group in the Amazon actually found a tribe — killed all the men. No one'll let them keep the women for themselves, but at least they have enough money to try for home." Ellis frowned. "I don't know. Trouble is, a lot of a guys don't miss women. They say they do, but they really don't. Ever talk to a real old-timer, one that can remember what it was like?"

"Can't say I have."

Ellis leaned back. "A lot of those guys didn't really like girls all that much. They had places they'd go to get away from them, things they'd do together. Women didn't think the same way, didn't act the same — they never did as much as men did." He shaded his eyes for a moment. "I don't know — sometimes one of those old men'll tell you the world was gentler then, or prettier, but I don't know if that's true. Anyway, a lot of those women must have agreed with the men. Look what happened — as soon as you had that pill that could make you sure you had a boy if you wanted, or a girl, most of them started having boys, so they must have thought, deep down, that boys were better."

Another police car drove past; one of the officers inside looked us over before driving on. "Take a trans," Ellis said. "Oh, you might envy her a little, but no one really has any respect for her. And the only real reason for having any women around now is for insurance — somebody's got to have the kids, and we can't. But once that Bethesda project really gets going and spreads, we won't need them anymore."

"I suppose you're right."

Four young men, dressed in work shirts and pants, approached us and stared down at us silently. I thought of the boys I had once played with before what I was had made a difference, before I had been locked away. One young man glanced quickly down the street; another took a step forward. I stared back and made a fist, trying to keep my hand from shaking; Ellis sat up slowly and let his right hand fall to his waist, near his holster. We kept staring until the group turned from us and walked away.

"Anyway, you've got to analyze it." Ellis crossed his legs. "There's practical reasons for not having a lot of women around. We need more soldiers — everybody does now, with all the trouble in the world. And police, too, with crime the way it is. And women can't handle those jobs."

"Once people thought they could." My shoulder muscles were tight; I had almost said we.

"But they can't. Put a woman up against a man, and the man'll always win." Ellis draped an arm over the back of the bench. "And there's other reasons, too. Those guys in Washington like keeping women scarce, having their pick of the choice ones for themselves — it makes their women more valuable. And a lot of the kids'll be theirs, too, from now on. Oh, they might loan a woman out to a friend once in a while, and I suppose the womb project'll change things some, but it'll be their world eventually."

"And their genes," I said. I knew that I should change the subject, but Ellis had clearly accepted my pose. In his conversation, the ordinary talk of one man to another, the longest conversation I had had with a man for many years, I was looking for a sign, something to keep me from despairing. "How long can it go on?" I continued. "The population keeps shrinking every year — there won't be enough people soon."

"You're wrong, Joe. Machines do a lot of the work now anyway, and there used to be too many people. The only way we'll ever have more women is if someone finds out the Russians are having more, and that won't happen — they need soldiers, too. Besides, look at it this way — maybe we're doing women a favor if there aren't as many of them. Would you want to be a woman, having to be married by sixteen, not being able to go anywhere, no job until she's at least sixty-five?"

And no divorce without a husband's permission, no contraception, no higher education — all the special privileges and protections could not make up for that. "No," I said to Ellis. "I wouldn't want to be one." Yet I knew that many women had made their peace with the world as it was, extorting gifts and tokens from their men, glorying in their beauty and their pregnancies, lavishing their attention on their children and their homes, tormenting and manipulating their men with the sure knowledge that any woman could find another man — for if a woman could not get a divorce by herself, a man more powerful than her husband could force him to give her up if he wanted her himself.

I had dreamed of guerrillas, of fighting women too proud to give in, breeding strong daughters by a captive male to carry on the battle. But if there were such women, they, like me, had gone to ground. The world had been more merciful when it had drowned or strangled us at birth.

Once, when I was younger, someone had said it had been a conspiracy — develop a foolproof way to give a couple a child of the sex they wanted, and most of them would naturally choose boys. The population problem would be solved in time without having to resort to harsher methods, and a blow would be leveled at those old feminists who had demanded too much, trying to emasculate men in the process. But I didn't think it had been a conspiracy. It had simply happened, as it was bound to eventually, and the values of society had controlled behavior. After all, why shouldn't a species decide to become one sex, especially if reproduction could be severed from sexuality? People had believed men were better, and had acted on that belief. Perhaps women, given the power, would have done the same.

We retreated to a bar when the sunny weather grew cooler. Ellis steered me away from two taverns with "bad elements," and we found ourselves in the doorway of a darkened bar in which several old and middle-aged men had gathered and two pretty boys dressed in leather and silk were plying their trade.

I glanced at the newscreen as I entered; the pale letters flickered, telling me that Bob Arnoldi's last appeal had failed and that he would be executed at the end of the month. This was no surprise; Arnoldi had, after all, killed a woman, and was always under heavy guard. The letters danced on; the President's wife had given birth to her thirteenth child, a boy. The President's best friend, a California millionaire, had been at his side when the announcement was made; the millionaire's power could be gauged by the fact that he had been married three times, and that the prolific First Lady had been one of the former wives.

Ellis and I got drinks at the bar. I kept my distance from one of the pretty boys, who scowled at my short, wavy hair and nestled closer to his patron. We retreated to the shadows and sat down at one of the side tables. The table top was sticky; old cigar butts had been planted on a gray mound in the ashtray. I sipped my bourbon; Ellis, while on the job, was only allowed beer.

The men at the bar were watching the remaining minutes of a football game. Sports of some kind were always on holo screens in bars, according to Sam; he preferred the old pornographic films that were sometimes shown amid war coverage and an occasional boys' choir performance for the pederasts and the more culturally inclined. Ellis looked at the screen and noted that his team was losing; I commented on the team's weaknesses, as I knew I was expected to do.

Ellis rested his elbows on the table. "This all you came for? Just to walk around and then have a drink?"

"That's it. I'm just waiting for my car." I tried to sound nonchalant. "It should be fixed soon."

"Doesn't seem like enough reason to hire an escort."

"Come on, Ellis. Guys like me would have trouble without escorts, especially if we don't know the territory that well."

"True. You don't look that strong." He peered at me a little too intently. "Still, unless you were looking for action, or going to places with a bad element, or waiting for the gangs to come out at night, you could get along. It's in your attitude — you have to look like you can take care of yourself. I've seen guys smaller than you I wouldn't want to fight."

"I like to be safe."

He watched me, as if expecting me to say more.

"Actually, I don't need an escort as much as I like to have a companion — somebody to talk to. I don't see that many people."

"It's your money."

The game had ended and was being subjected to loud analysis by the men at the bar; their voices suddenly died. A man behind me sucked in his breath as the clear voice of a woman filled the room.

I looked at the holo. Rena Swanson was reciting the news, leading with the Arnoldi story, following that with the announcement of the President's new son. Her aged, wrinkled face hovered over us; her kind brown eyes promised us comfort. Her motherly presence had made her program one of the most popular on the holo. The men around me sat silently, faces upturned, worshipping her — the Woman, the Other, someone for whom part of them still yearned.

We got back to Marcello's just before dark. As we approached the door, Ellis suddenly clutched my shoulder. "Wait a minute, Joe."

I didn't move at first; then I reached out and carefully pushed his arm away. My shoulders hurt and a tension headache, building all day, had finally taken hold, its claws gripping my temples. "Don't touch me." I had been about to plead, but caught myself in time; attitude, as Ellis had told me himself, was important.

"There's something about you. I can't figure you out."

"Don't try." I kept my voice steady. "You wouldn't want me to complain to your boss, would you? He might not hire you again. Escorts have to be trusted."

He was very quiet. I couldn't see his dark face clearly in the fading light, but I could sense that he was weighing the worth of a confrontation with me against the chance of losing his job. My face was hot, my mouth dry. I had spent too much time with him, given him too many chances to notice subtly wrong gestures. I continued to stare directly at him, wondering if his greed would win out over practicality.

"Okay," he said at last, and opened the door.

I was charged more than I had expected to pay, but did not argue about the fee. I pressed a few coins on Ellis; he took them while refusing to look at me. He knows, I thought then; he knows and he's letting me go. But I might have imagined that, seeing kindness where there was none.

I took a roundabout route back to Sam's, checking to make sure no one had followed me, then pulled off the road to change the car's license plate, concealing my own under my shirt.

Sam's store stood at the end of the road, near the foot of my mountain. Near the store, a small log cabin had been built. I had staked my claim to most of the mountain, buying up the land to make sure it remained undeveloped, but the outside world was already moving closer.

Sam was sitting behind the counter, drumming his fingers as music blared. I cleared my throat and said hello.

"Joe?" His watery blue eyes squinted. "You're late, boy."

"Had to get your car fixed. Don't worry — I paid for it already. Thanks for letting me rent it again." I counted out my coins and pressed them into his dry, leathery hand.

"Any time, son." The old man held up the coins, peering at each one with his weak eyes. "Don't look like you'll get home tonight. You can use the sofa there — I'll get you a nightshirt. "

"I'll sleep in my clothes." I gave him an extra coin.

He locked up, hobbled toward his bedroom door, then turned. "Get into town at all?"

"No." I paused. "Tell me something, Sam. You're old enough to remember. What was it really like before?" I had never asked him in all the years I had known him, avoiding intimacy of any kind, but suddenly I wanted to know.

"I'll tell you, Joe." He leaned against the doorway. "It wasn't all that different. A little softer around the edges, maybe, quieter, not as mean, but it wasn't all that different. Men always ran everything. Some say they didn't, but they had all the real power — sometimes they'd dole a little of it out to the girls, that's all. Now we don't have to anymore."

I had been climbing up the mountain for most of the morning, and had left the trail, arriving at my decoy house before noon. Even Sam believed that the cabin in the clearing was my dwelling. I tried the door, saw that it was still locked, then continued on my way.

My home was farther up the slope, just out of sight of the cabin. I approached my front door, which was almost invisible near the ground; the rest of the house was concealed under slabs of rock and piles of deadwood. I stood still, letting a hidden camera lens get a good look at me. The door swung open.

"Thank God you're back," Julia said as she pulled me inside and closed the door. "I was so worried. I thought you'd been caught and they were coming for me."

"It's all right. I had some trouble with Sam's car, that's all."

She looked up at me; the lines around her mouth deepened. "I wish you wouldn't go." I took off the pack loaded with the tools and supplies unavailable at Sam's store. Julia glanced at the pack resentfully. "It isn't worth it."

"You're probably right." I was about to tell her of my own trip into town, but decided to wait until later.

We went into the kitchen. Her hips were wide under her pants; her large breasts bounced as she walked. Her face was still pretty, even after all the years of hiding, her lashes thick and curly, her mouth delicate. Julia could not travel in the world as it was; no clothing, no disguise, could hide her.

I took off my jacket and sat down, taking out my card, and my papers. My father had given them to me — the false name, the misleading address, the identification of a male — after I had pleaded for my own life. He had built my hideaway; he had risked everything for me. Give the world a choice, he had said, and women will be the minority, maybe even die out completely; perhaps we can only love those like ourselves. He had looked hard as he said it, and then he had patted me on the head, sighing as though he regretted the choice. Maybe he had. He had chosen to have a daughter, after all.

I remembered his words. "Who knows?" he had asked. "What is it that made us two kinds who have to work together to get the next batch going? Oh, I know about evolution, but it didn't have to be that way, or any way. It's curious."

"It can't last," Julia said, and I did not know if she meant the world, or our escape from the world.

There would be no Eves in their Eden, I thought. The visit to town had brought it an home to me. We all die, but we go with a conviction about the future; my extinction would not be merely personal. Only traces of the feminine would linger — an occasional expression, a posture, a feeling in the flat-breasted male form. Love would express itself in fruitless unions, divorced from reproduction; human affections are flexible.

I sat in my home, in my prison, treasuring the small freedom I had, the gift of a man, as it seemed such freedom had always been for those like me, and wondered again if it could have been otherwise.

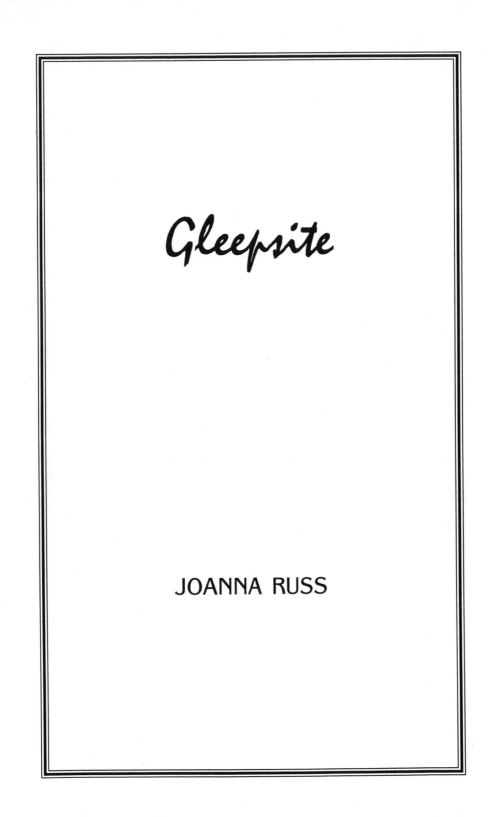

Gleepsite

JOANNA RUSS

ABOUT JOANNA RUSS
AND
GLEEPSITE

Gleepsite *was first published:*
Orbit 9, *1971*

Joanna Russ ranks with Ursula Le Guin as one of the leading lights among the women who began writing science fiction in the 1970s. Her work started out determinedly feminist and became increasingly so as it progressed. From the polemical Female Man *to* We Who Are About To . . . *and* The Two of Them, *her motifs increasingly became dominated with themes of women "achieving identity through the murder of a man," according to feminist critic Diane Parkin-Speer. Ms. Russ' best stories have been collected in the* Zanzibar Cat *and* Extraordinary People. *While her all too infrequent appearances continue to garner her award nominations with great consistency.*

"Gleepsite" will be no disappointment to Ms. Russ' diehard fans. It opens in a world where men have been reduced to less than three percent of the population and women are in control. Though science fiction, it may involve an element generally associated only with fantasy (we'll let the readers make up their own mind at the end). As Don Wollheim and Art Saha noted: "After you have read this story read it over again and perhaps read it a third time and then, you may find that you will see things you did not notice before."

Gleepsite

by JOANNA RUSS

I TRY TO MAKE my sales at night during the night shift in office buildings; it works better that way. Resistance is gone at night. The lobbies are deserted, the air filters on half power; here and there a woman stays up late amid piles of paper; things blow down the halls just out of the range of vision of the watch-ladies who turn their keys in the doors of unused rooms, who insert the keys hanging from chains around their necks in the apertures of empty clocks, or polish with their polishing rags the surfaces of desks, the bare tops of tables. You make some astonishing sales that way.

I came up my thirty floors and found on the thirty-first Kira and Lira, the only night staff: two fiftyish identical twins in the same gray cardigan sweaters, the same pink dresses, the same blue rinse on their gray sausage-curls. But Kira wore on her blouse (over the name tag) the emblem of the senior secretary, the Tree of Life pin with the cultured pearl, while Lira went without, so I addressed myself to the (minutes-) younger sister.

"We're closed," they said.

Nevertheless, knowing that they worked at night, knowing that they worked for a travel agency whose hints of imaginary faraway places (Honolulu, Hawaii — they don't exist) must eventually exacerbate the longings of even the most passive sister, I addressed myself to them again, standing in front of the semicircular partition over which they peered (alarmed but bland), keeping my gaze on the sans-serif script over the desk — or is it roses! — and avoiding very carefully any glance at the polarized vitryl panels beyond which rages hell's own stew of hot winds and sulfuric acid, it gets worse and worse. I don't like false marble floors, so I changed it.

Ladies.

"We're closed!" cried Miss Lira.

Here I usually make some little illusion so they will know who I am; I stopped Miss Kira from pressing the safety button, which always hangs on the wall, and made appear beyond the nearest vitryl panel a bat's face as big as a man's: protruding muzzle, pointed fangs, cocked ears, and rats' shiny eyes, here and gone. I snapped my fingers and the wind tore it off.

No, no, no, no! cried the sisters.

May I call you Flora and Dora? I said. *Flora and Dora in memory of that glorious time centuries past when ladies like yourselves danced on tables to the applause of admiring gentlemen, when ladies wore, like yourselves, scarlet petticoats, ruby stomachers, chokers and bibs of red velvet, pearls and maroon high-heeled boots, though they did not always keep their petticoats decorously about their ankles.*

What you have just seen, ladies, is a small demonstration of the power of electrical brain stimulation — mine, in this case — and the field which transmitted it to you was generated by the booster I wear about my neck, metallic in this case, though they come in other colors, and tuned to the frequency of the apparatus which I wear in this ring. You will notice that it is inconspicuous and well designed. I am allowed to wear the booster only at work. In the year blank-blank, when the great neurosurgical genius, Blank, working with Blank and Blank, discovered in the human forebrain what has been so poetically termed the Circle of Illusion, it occurred to another great innovator, Blank, whom you know, to combine these two great discoveries, resulting in a Device that has proved to be of inestimable benefit to the human race. (We just call it the Device.) Why not, thought Blank, employ the common, everyday power of electricity for the stimulation, the energization, the concretization of the Center of Illusion or (to put it bluntly) an aide-mémoire, crutch, companion, and record-keeping book for that universal human talent, daydreaming? Do you daydream, ladies? Then you know that daydreaming is harmless. Daydreaming is voluntary. Day dreaming is not night dreaming. Daydreaming is normal. It is not hallucination or delusion or deception but creation. It is an accepted form of mild escape. No more than in a daydream or reverie is it possible to confuse the real and the ideal; try it and see. The Device simply supplements the power of your own human brain. If Miss Kira —

"No, no!" cried Miss Lira, but Miss Kira had already taken my sample ring, the setting scrambled to erase the last customer's residual charge.

You have the choice of ten scenes. No two persons will see the same thing, of course, but the parameters remain fairly constant. Further choices on request. Sound, smell, taste, touch, and kinesthesia optional. We are strictly prohibited from employing illegal settings or the use of variable condensers with fluctuating parameters. Tampering with the machinery is punishable by law.

"But it's so hard!" said Miss Kira in surprise. "And it's not real at all!" That always reassures them. At first.

It takes considerable effort to operate the Circle of Illusion even with mechanical aid. Voltage beyond that required for threshold stimulation is banned by law; even when employed, it does not diminish the necessity for effort, but in fact increases it proportionately. No more than in life, ladies, can you get something for nothing.

Practice makes perfect.

Miss Kira, as I knew she would, had chosen a flowery meadow with a suggestion of honeymoon; Miss Lira chose a waterfall in a glade. Neither had put in a Man, although an idealized figure of a Man is standard equipment for our pastoral choices (misty, idealized, in the distance, some even see him with wings) and I don't imagine either sister would ever get much closer.

Miss Lira said they actually had a niece who was actually married to a man.

Miss Kira said a half-niece.

Miss Lira said they had a cousin who worked in the children's nursery with real children and they had holidays coming *and if I use a variable condenser, what's it to you?*

Behind me, though I cannot imagine why, is a full-length mirror, and in this piece of inconstancy I see myself as I was when I left home tonight, or perhaps not, I don't remember: beautiful, chocolate-colored, naked, gold braided into my white hair. Behind me, bats' wings.

A mirror, ladies, produces a virtual image, and so does the Device.

Bats' faces.

Hermaphroditic.

It is no more addicting than thought.

Little snakes waving up from the counter, a forest of them. Unable to stand the sisters' eyes swimming behind their glasses, myopic Flora and Dora, I changed the office for them, gave them a rug, hung behind them on the wall original Rembrandts, made them younger, erased them, let the whole room slide, and provided for Dora a bedroom beyond the travel office, a bordello in white and gold baroque, embroidered canopy, goldfish pool, chihuahuas on the marble and bats in the belfry.

I have two heads.

Flora's quite a whore.

The younger sister, not quite willing to touch the ring again, said they'd think about it, and Kira, in a quarrel that must have gone back years, began in a low whisper —

Why, they're not bats at all, I said, over at the nearest vitryl panel; *I was mistaken,* and Lira, Don't open that! We'll suffocate!

No one who is sane, of course, opens anything any more into that hell outside, but this old, old, old place had real locks on the vitryl and real seams between, and a narrow balcony where someone had gone out perhaps fifty years ago (in a diving suit) to admire the updrafts between the dead canyons where papers danced on the driving murk and shapes fluttered between the raw lights; one could see several streets over to other spires, other shafts, the hurricane tearing through the poisoned air. Nighttime makes a kind of inferno out of this and every once in a while someone decides on a gaudy exit: the lungs eaten away, the room reeking of hydrosulfurous acid, torn paper settling on the discolored rug.

When you have traveled in the tubes as much as I have, when you have seen the playground in Antarctica time after time, when your features have melted enough between black and brown and white, man and woman, as plastic as the lazy twist of a thought, you get notions. You get ideas. I saw once in a much more elegant office building a piece of polished wood, so large, so lovely, a curve fully six feet long and so beautiful that if you could have made out of that wood an idea and out of that idea a bed, you could have slept on that bed. When you put your hand on the vitryl panels at night, the heat makes your hand sweat onto the surface; my hand's melted through many times, like oil on water. I stood before the window, twisting shapes for fun, seeing myself stand on the narrow balcony, bored with Kira and Lira, poor Kira, poor Lira, poor as-I-once-was, discussing whether they can afford it.

". . . an outlet for creativity . . ."

". . . she *said* it's only . . ."

What effort it takes, and what an athlete of illusion you become! able to descend to the bottom of the sea (where we might as well be, come to think of it), to the manless moon, to the Southern Hemisphere where the men stay, dreaming about us; but no, they did away with themselves years ago, they were inefficient, the famous Blank and Blank (both men) saw that men were inefficient and did themselves in (I mean all the men except themselves) in blank-blank. Only three percent of the population male, my word!

". . . legal . . ."

". . . never. . ."

"Don't!" cried Miss Kira.

They know what I'm going to do. Ever since I found out those weren't bats' faces. As Miss Kira and Miss Lira sign the contract (thumbsy-up, thumbsy-down) I wrench the lock off the vitryl and squeeze through, what a foul, screaming wind! shoving desperately at the panels, and stumble off the narrow, railless balcony, feeling as I go my legs contract, my fingers grow, my sternum arch like the prow of a boat, little bat-man-woman with sketchy turned-out legs and grasping toes, and hollow bones and fingers down to my ankles, a thumb-and-forefinger grasper at the end of each wing, and that massive wraparound of the huge, hollow chest, all covered with blond fur; in the middle of it all, sunk between the shoulders, is the human face; Miss Kira would faint. I would come up to Miss Lira's waist. Falling down the nasty night air until I shrug up hard, hard, hard, into a steep upward glide and ride down the currents of hell past the man-made cliff where Kira and Lira, weeping with pain, push the vitryl panel back into place. The walls inside are blackening, the fake marble floor is singed. It is comfy-cold, it is comfy-nice, I'm going to mate in midair, I'm going to give shuddering birth on the ledge of a cliff, I'm going to scream at the windows when I like. They found no corpse, no body.

Kira and Lira, mouths like O's, stare out as I climb past. They do a little dance.

> She was a Floradora baby
> With a chance to meet the best,
> But she had to go and marry Abie,
> The drummer with the fancy vest!

Tampering with the machinery is punishable by law, says Kira.

Oh my dear, we'll tinker a bit, says Lira.

And so they will.

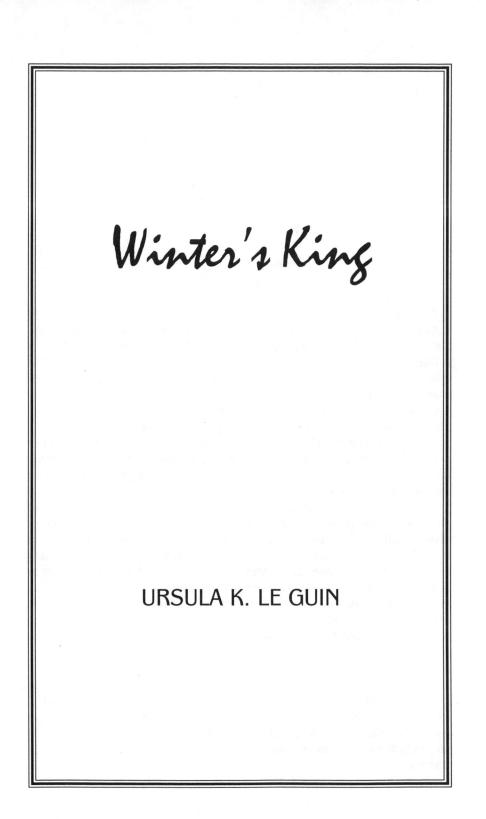

Winter's King

URSULA K. LE GUIN

ABOUT URSULA K. LE GUIN
AND
WINTER'S KING

Winter's King *was first published:*
Orbit 5, *1969*

For a time Ursula Le Guin was the only woman science fiction writer to achieve a literary reputation equal to or surpassing that of Ray Bradbury. Since then writers like Nancy Kress have begun to equal her in skill, craft and brilliance, though none have as yet equaled her reputation. Oddly Le Guin made no impact on the field until the appearance of her fourth novel Left Hand of Darkness. *With the book's appearance, it became evident that her first few books had been warm-up exercises and that now Ms. Le Guin was about to proceed with a serious career. Only a few books later she had become a darling of the* New York Times *and other literary circles who attempted to overlook the unfortunate fact that her work was published as science fiction (an error her publishers were quick to rectify by removing the label from Le Guin's subsequent books).*

Her enormous gift for weaving credible alien cultures may be a gift of her parents Dr. Alfred Krober, the celebrated anthropologist, and Theodora Krober, author of the bestselling Ishi: the Story of the Last Wild Indian in North America. *Ms. Le Guin's master's thesis was on "Ideas of Death in Ronsard Poetry" suggesting a deep affinity for poetry which was proven when a small publisher issued a collection of her poems, "Wild Angels." These various influences may explain why* The Science Fiction Encyclopedia *claims the hallmark of her work is "an intelligent and feeling use of image structures, in the manner of a poet, and not least, an example that shows how the interest of the traditional novelist, in questions of character and moral growth, need not be alien to SF."*

"Winter's King" is set on the same planet as Left Hand of Darkness, *but some years earlier. Like that book and Evelyn E. Smith's "The Captain's Mate," this story involves major gender-bending. Though its inclusion is more than justified by Ms. Le Guin's use of the pronouns "she" and "her." In fact, the story might also have been entitled "Winter's Queen" as readers will shortly discover.*

Winter's King

by URSULA K. LE GUIN

WHEN WHIRLPOOLS appear in the onward run of time and history seems to swirl around a snag, as in the curious matter of the Succession of Karhide, then pictures come in handy: snapshots, which maybe taken up and matched to compare the parent to the child, the young king to the old, and which may also be rearranged and shuffled till the years run straight. For despite the tricks played by instantaneous interstellar communication and just-sub-lightspeed interstellar travel, time (as the Plenipotentiary Axt remarked) does not reverse itself; nor is death mocked.

Thus, although the best-known picture is that dark image of a young king standing above an old king who lies dead in a corridor lit only by mirror-reflections of a burning city, set it aside a while. Look first at the young king, a nation's pride, as bright and fortunate a soul as ever lived to the age of twenty-two; but when this picture was taken the young king had her back against a wall. She was filthy, she was trembling, and her face was blank and mad, for she had lost that minimal confidence in the world which is called sanity. Inside her head she repeated, as she had been repeating for hours or years, over and over, "I will abdicate. I will abdicate. I will abdicate." Inside her eyes she saw the red-walled rooms of the Palace, the towers and streets of Erhenrang in falling SNOW, the lovely plains of the West Fall, the white summits of the Kargav, and she renounced them all, her kingdom. "I will abdicate," she said not aloud and then, aloud, screamed as once again the person dressed in red and white approached her saying, "Majesty! A plot against your life has been discovered in the Artisan School," and the humming noise began, softly. She hid her head in her arms and whispered, "Stop it, please stop it," but the humming whine grew higher and louder and nearer, relentless, until it was so high and loud that it entered her flesh, tore the nerves from their channels and made her bones dance and jangle, hopping to its tune. She hopped and twitched, bare bones strung on thin white threads, and wept dry tears, and shouted, "Have them—Have them—They must—Executed—Stopped—Stop!"

It stopped.

She fell in a clattering, chattering heap to the floor. What floor? Not red tiles, not parquetry, not urine-stained cement, but the wood floor of the room in the tower, the little tower bedroom where she was safe, safe from her ogre parent, the cold, mad, uncaring king, safe to play cat's cradle with Piry and to sit by the fireside on Borhub's warm lap, as warm and deep as sleep. But there was no hiding, no safety, no sleep. The person dressed in black had come even here and had hold of her head, lifted it up, lifted on thin white strings the eyelids she tried to close.

"Who am I?"

The blank, black mask stared down. The young king struggled, sobbing, because now the suffocation would begin: she would not be able to breathe until she said the name, the right name—"Gerer!"— She could breathe. She was allowed to breathe. She had recognized the black one in time.

"Who am I?" said a different voice, gently, and the young king groped for that strong presence that always brought her sleep, truce, solace. "Rebade," she whispered, "tell me what to do. . . ."

"Sleep."

She obeyed. A deep sleep, and dreamless, for it was real. Dreams came at waking, now. Unreal, the horrible dry red light of sunset burned her eyes open and she stood, once more, on the Palace balcony looking down at fifty thousand black pits opening and shutting. From the pits came a paroxysmic gush of sound, a shrill, rhythmic eructation: her name. Her name was roared in her ears as a taunt, a jeer. She beat her hands on the narrow brass railing and shouted at them, "I will silence you!" She could not hear her voice, only their voice, the pestilent mouths of the mob that hated her, screaming her name. "Come away, my king," said the one gentle voice, and Rebade drew her away from the balcony into the vast, red-walled quiet of the Hall of Audience. The screaming ceased with a click. Rebade's expression was as always composed, compassionate. "What will you do now?" she said in her gentle voice.

"I will — I will abdicate —"

"No," Rebade said calmly. "That is not right. What will you do now?"

The young king stood silent, shaking. Rebade helped her sit down on the iron cot, for the walls had darkened as they often did and drawn in all about her to a little cell. "You will call . . ."

"Call up the Erhenrang Guard. Have them shoot into the crowd. Shoot to kill. They must be taught a lesson." The young king spoke rapidly and distinctly in a loud, high voice. Rebade said, "Very good, my lord, a wise decision! Right. We shall come out all right. You are doing right. Trust me."

"I do. I trust you. Get me out of here," the young king whispered, seizing Rebade's arm: but her friend frowned. That was not right. She had driven Rebade and hope away again. Rebade was leaving now, calm and regretful, though the young king begged her to stop, to come back, for the noise was softly beginning again, the whining hum that tore the mind to pieces, and already the person in red and white was approaching across a red, interminable floor. "Majesty! A plot against your life has been discovered in the Artisan School —"

Down Old Harbor Street to the water's edge the street lamps burned cavernously bright. Guard Pepenerer on her rounds glanced down that slanting vault of light expecting nothing, and saw something staggering up it towards her. Pepenerer did not believe in porngropes, but she saw a porngrope, sea-beslimed, staggering on thin webbed feet, gasping dry air, whimpering. . . . Old sailors' tales slid out of Pepenerer's mind and she saw a drunk or a maniac or a victim staggering between the dank grey warehouse walls. "Now then! Hold on there!" she bellowed, on the run. The drunk, half naked and wild-eyed, let out a yell of terror and tried to dodge away, slipped on the frost-slick stones of the street and pitched down sprawling. Pepenerer got out her gun and delivered a half-second of stun, just to keep the drunk quiet; then squatted down by her wound up her radio and called the West Ward for a car.

Both the arms, sprawled out limp and meek on the cold cobbles, were blotched with injection marks. Not drunk; drugged. Pepenerer sniffed, but got no resinous scent of orgrevy. She had been drugged, then; thieves, or a ritual clan-revenge. Thieves would not have left the gold ring on the forefinger, a massive thing, carved, almost as wide as the fingerjoint. Pepenerer crouched forward to look at it. Then she turned her head and looked at the beaten, blank face in profile against the paving-stones, hard lit by the glare of the street lamps. She took a new quarter-crown piece out of her pouch and looked at the left profile stamped on the bright tin, then back at the right profile stamped in light and shadow and cold stone. Then, hearing the purr of the electric car turning down from the Longway into Old Harbor Street, she stuck the coin back in her pouch, muttering to herself, "Damn fool."

King Argaven was off hunting in the mountains, anyhow, and had been for a couple of weeks; it had been in all the bulletins.

"You see," said Hoge the physician, "we can assume that she was mindformed; but that gives us almost nothing to go on. There are too many expert mindformers in Karhide, and in Orgoreyn for that matter. Not criminals whom the police might have a lead on, but respectable mentalists or physicians. To whom the drugs are legally available. As for getting anything from her, if they had any skill at all they will have blocked everything they did to rational access. All clues will be buried, the trigger-suggestions hidden, and we simply cannot guess what questions to ask. There is no way, short of brain-destruction, of going through everything in her mind; and even under hypnosis and deep drugging there would be no way now to distinguish implanted ideas or emotions from her own autonomous ones. Perhaps the Aliens could do something, though I doubt their mindscience is all they boast of; at any rate it's out of reach. We have only one real hope."

"Which is?" Lord Gerer asked, stolidly.

"The king is quick and resolute. At the beginning, before they broke her, she may have known what they were doing to her, and so set up some block or resistance, left herself some escape route. . . ."

Hoge's low voice lost confidence as she spoke, and trailed off in the silence of the high, red, dusky room. She drew no response from old Gerer who stood, black-clad, before the fire.

The temperature of that room in the King's Palace of Erhenrang was 12° C where Lord Gerer stood, and 5° midway between the two big fireplaces; outside it was snowing lightly, a mild day only a few degrees below freezing. Spring had come to Winter. The fires at either end of the room roared red and gold, devouring thigh-thick logs. Magnificence, a harsh luxury, a quick splendor; fireplaces, fireworks, lightning, meteors, volcanoes; such things satisfied the people of Karhide on the world called Winter. But, except in Arctic colonies above the 35th parallel, they had never installed central heating in any building in the many centuries of their Age of Technology. Comfort was allowed to come to them rare, welcome, unsought: a gift, like joy.

The king's personal servant, sitting by the bed, turned towards the physician and the Lord Councillor, though she did not speak. Both at once crossed the room. The broad, hard bed, high on gilt pillars, heavy with a finery of red cloaks and coverlets, bore up the king's body almost level with their eyes. To Gerer it appeared a ship breasting, motionless, a swift vast flood of darkness, carrying the young king into shadows, terrors, years. Then with a terror of her own the old councillor saw that Argaven's eyes were open, staring out a half-curtained window at the stars.

Gerer feared lunacy; idiocy; she did not know what she feared. Hoge had warned her: "The king will not behave 'normally,' Lord Gerer. She has suffered thirteen days of torment, intimidation, exhaustion, and mindhandling. There may be brain damage, there will certainly be side- and after-effects of drugs." Neither fear nor warning parried the shock. Argaven's bright, weary eyes turned to Gerer and paused on her blankly a moment; then saw her. And Gerer, though she could not see the black mask reflected, saw the hate, the horror, saw her young king, infinitely beloved, gasping in imbecile terror and struggling with the servant, with Hoge, with her own weakness in the effort to get away, to get away from Gerer.

Standing in the cold midst of the room where the prowlike head of the bedstead hid her from the king, Gerer heard them pacify Argaven and settle her down again. Argaven's voice sounded reedy, childishly plaintive. So the Old King, Emran, had spoken in her last madness with a child's voice. Then silence, and the burning of the two great fires.

Korgry, the king's bodyservant, yawned and rubbed her eyes. Hoge measured something from a vial into a hypodermic. Gerer stood in despair. My child, my king, what have they done to you? So great a trust, so fair a promise, lost, lost. . . . So the one who looked like a lump of half-carved black rock, a heavy, prudent, rude old courtier, grieved and was passion-racked, her love and service of the young king being the world's one worth to her.

Argaven spoke aloud: "My child —"

Gerer winced, feeling the words torn out of her own mind; but Hoge, untroubled by love, comprehended and said softly to Argaven, "Prince Emran is well, my liege. She is with her attendants at Warrever Castle. We are in constant communication. All is well there."

Gerer heard the king's harsh breathing, and came somewhat closer to the bed, though out of sight still behind the high headboard.

"Have I been sick?"

"You are not well yet," the physician said, bland.

"Where—"

"Your own room, in the Palace, in Erhenrang."

But Gerer, coming a step closer, though not in view of the king, said, "We do not know where you have been."

Hoge's smooth face creased with a frown, though, physician as she was and so in her way ruler of them all, she dared not direct the frown at the Lord Councillor. Gerer's voice did not seem to trouble the king, who asked another question or two, sane and brief, and then lay quiet. Presently the servant Korgry, who had sat with her ever since she had been brought into the Palace (last night, in secret, by side doors, like a shameful suicide of the last reign, but all in reverse), Korgry committed lèse-majesté: huddled forward on her high stool, she let her head droop on the side of the bed, and slept. The guard at the door yielded place to a new guard, in whispers. Officials came and received a fresh bulletin for public release on the state of the king's health, in whispers. Stricken by symptoms of fever while vacationing in the High Kargav, the king had been rushed to Erhenrang, and was now responding satisfactorily to treatment, etc. Physician Hoge rem ir Hogeremme at the Palace has released the following statement, etc., etc. "May the Wheel turn for our king," people in village houses said solemnly as they lit the fire on the altarhearth, to which elders sitting near the fire remarked, "It comes of her roving around the city at night and climbing mountains, fool tricks like that," but they kept the radio on to catch the next bulletin. A very great number of people had come and gone and loitered and chatted this day in the square before the Palace, watching those who went in and out, watching the vacant balcony; there were still several hundred down there, standing around patiently in the snow. Argaven XVII was loved in her domain. After the dull brutality of King Emran's reign that had ended in the shadow of madness and the country's bankruptcy, she had come: sudden, gallant, young, changing everything; sane and shrewd, yet magnanimous. She had the fire, the splendor that suited her people. She was the force and center of a new age: one born, for once, king of the right kingdom.

"Gerer."

It was the king's voice, and Gerer hastened stiffly through the hot and cold of the great room, the firelight and dark.

Argaven was sitting up. Her arms shook and the breath caught in her throat; her eyes burned across the dark air at Gerer. By her left hand, which bore the Sign-Ring of the Harge dynasty, lay the sleeping face of the servant, derelict, serene. "Gerer," the king said with effort and clarity, "summon the Council. Tell them, I will abdicate."

So crude, so simple? All the drugs, the terrorizing, the hypnosis, parahypnosis, neurone-stimulation, synapse-pairing, spotshock that Hoge had described, for this blunt result? But reasoning must wait. They must temporize. "My liege, when your strength returns—"

"Now. Call the Council, Gerer!"

Then she broke, like a bowstring breaking, and stammered in a fury of fear that found no sense or strength to flesh itself in; and still her faithful servant slept beside her, deaf.

In the next picture things are going better, it appears. Here is King Argaven, XVII in good health and good clothes, finishing a large breakfast. She talks with the nearer dozen of the forty or fifty people sharing or serving the meal (singularity is a king's prerogative, but seldom privacy), and includes the rest in the largesse of her courtesy. She looks, as everyone has said, quite herself again. Perhaps she is not quite herself again, however; something is missing, a youthful serenity, a confidence, replaced by a similar but less reassuring quality, a kind of heedlessness. Out of it she rises in wit and warmth, but always subsides to it again, that darkness which absorbs her and makes her heedless: fear, pain, resolution?

Mr. Mobile Axt, Ambassador Plenipotentiary to Winter from the Ekumen of the Known Worlds, who had spent the last six days on the road trying to drive an electric car faster than 50 kph from Mishnory in Orgoreyn to Erhenrang in Karhide, overslept breakfast, and so arrived in the Audience Hall prompt, but hungry. The old Chief of the Council, the king's cousin Gerer rem ir Verhen, met the Alien at the door of the great hall and greeted him with the polysyllabic politeness of Karhide. The Plenipotentiary responded as best he could, discerning beneath the eloquence Gerer's desire to tell him something.

"I am told the king is perfectly recovered," he said, "and I heartily hope this is true."

"It is not," the old Councillor said, her voice suddenly blunt and toneless. "Mr. Axt, I tell you this trusting your confidence; there are not ten others in Karhide who know the truth. She is not recovered. She was not sick."

Axt nodded. There had of course been rumors.

"She will go alone in the city sometimes, at night, in common clothes, walking, talking with strangers. The pressures of kingship . . . She is very young." Gerer paused a moment, struggling with some suppressed emotion. "One night six weeks ago, she did not come back. A message was delivered to me and the Second Lord, at dawn. If we announced her disappearance, she would be killed; if we waited a half-month in silence she would be restored unhurt. We kept silent, lied to the Council, sent out false news. On the thirteenth night she was found wandering in the city. She had been drugged and mindformed. By which enemy or faction we do not yet know. We must work in utter secrecy; we cannot wreck the people's confidence in her, her own confidence in herself. It is hard: she remembers nothing. But what they did is plain. They broke her will and bent her mind all to one thing. She believes she must abdicate the throne."

The voice remained low and flat; the eyes betrayed anguish. And the Plenipotentiary turning suddenly saw the reflection of that anguish in the eyes of the young king.

"Holding my audience, cousin?"

Argaven smiled but there was a knife in it. The old Councillor excused herself stolidly, bowed, left, a patient ungainly figure diminishing down a long corridor.

Argaven stretched out both hands to the Plenipotentiary in the greeting of equals, for in Karhide the Ekumen was recognized as a sister kingdom, though not a living soul had seen it. But her words were not the polite discourse that Axt expected. All she said, and fiercely, was, "At last!"

"I left as soon as I received your message. The roads are still icy in East Orgoreyn and the West Fall, I couldn't make very good time. But I was very glad to come. Glad to leave, too." Axt smiled saying this, for he and the young king enjoyed each other's candor. What Argaven's welcome implied, he waited to see, watching, with some exhilaration, the mobile, beautiful, adrogynous face.

"Orgoreyn breeds bigots as a corpse breeds worms, as one of my ancestors remarked. I'm glad you find the air fresher here in Karhide. Come this way. Gerer told you that I was kidnapped, and so forth? Yes. It was all according to the old rules. Kidnapping is a quite formal art. If it had been one of the anti-Alien groups who think your Ekumen intends to enslave the earth, they might have ignored the rules; I think it was one of the old clan-factions hoping to regain power through me, the power they had in the last reign. But we don't know, yet. It's strange, to know that one has seen them face to face and yet can't recognize them; who knows but that I see those faces daily? Well, no profit in such notions. They wiped out all their tracks. I am sure only of one thing. *They* did not tell me that I must abdicate."

She and the Plenipotentiary were walking side by side up the long, immensely high room toward the dais and chairs at the far end. The windows were little more than slits, as usual on this cold world; fulvous strips of sunlight fell from them diagonally to the red-paved floor, dusk and dazzle in Axt's eyes. He looked up at the young king's face in that somber, shifting radiance. "Who then?"

"I did."

"When, my lord, and why?"

"When they had me, when they were remaking me to fit their mold and play their game. Why? So that I can't fit their mold and play their game! Listen, Lord Axt, if they wanted me dead they'd have killed me. They want me alive, to govern, to be king. As such I am to follow the orders imprinted in my brain, gain their ends for them. I am their tool, their machine, waiting for the switch to be thrown. The only way to prevent that, is to . . . discard the machine."

Axt was quick of understanding, that being a minimal qualification of a Mobile of the Ekumen; besides, the manners and affairs of Karhide, the stresses and seditions of that lively kingdom, were well known to him. Remote though Winter was, both in space and in the physiology of its inhabitants, from the rest of the human race, yet its dominant nation, Karhide, had proved a loyal member of the Ekumen. Axt's reports were discussed in the central councils of the Ekumen eighty lightyears away; the equilibrium of the Whole rests in all its parts. Axt said, as they sat down in the great stiff chairs on the dais before the fire, "But they need not even throw switches, if you abdicate."

"Leaving my child as heir, and a Regent of my own choice?"

"Perhaps," Axt said with caution, "they chose your Regent for you."

The king frowned. "I think not," she said.

"Whom had you thought of naming?"

There was a long pause. Axt saw the muscles of Argaven's throat working as she struggled to get a word, a name, up past a block, a harsh constriction; at last she said, in a forced, strangled whisper, "Gerer."

Axt nodded, startled. Gerer had served as Regent for a year after Emran's death and before Argaven's accession; he knew her honesty and her utter devotion to the young king. "Gerer serves no faction!" he said.

Argaven shook her head. She looked exhausted. After a while she said, "Could the science of your people undo what was done to me, Lord Axt?"

"Possibly. In the Institute on Ollul. But if I sent for a specialist tonight, he'd get here twenty-four years from now. . . . You're sure, then, that your decision to abdicate was —" But a servant, coming in a side door behind them, set a small table by the Plenipotentiary's chair and loaded it with fruit, sliced bread-apple, a silver tankard of ale. Argaven had noticed that her guest had missed his breakfast. Though the fare on Winter, mostly vegetable and that mostly uncooked, was dull stuff to Axt's taste, he set to gratefully; and as serious talk was unseemly over food, Argaven shifted to generalities. "Once you said, Lord Axt, that different as I am from you, and different as my people are from yours, yet we are blood kin. Was that a moral fact, or a material one?"

Axt smiled at the very Karhidish distinction. "Both, my lord. As far as we know, which is a tiny corner of dusty space under the rafters of the Universe, all the people we've run into are in fact human. But the kinship goes back a million years and more, to the Fore-Eras of Hain. The ancient Hainish settled a hundred worlds."

"We call the time before my dynasty ruled Karhide 'ancient.' Seven hundred years ago!"

"So we call the Age of the Enemy 'ancient,' and that was less than Six hundred years ago. Time stretches and shrinks; changes with the eye, with the age, with the star; does all except reverse itself — or repeat"

"The dream of the Ekumen, then, is to restore that truly ancient commonalty; to regather all the peoples of all the worlds at one hearth?"

Axt nodded, chewing bread-apple. "To weave some harmony among them, at least. Life loves to know itself, out to its furthest limits; to embrace complexity is its delight. Our difference is our beauty. All these worlds and the various forms and ways of the minds and lives and bodies on them — together they would make a splendid harmony."

"No harmony endures," said the young king.

"None has ever been achieved," said the Plenipotentiary. "The pleasure is in trying." He drained his tankard, wiped his fingers on the woven-grass napkin

"That was my pleasure as king," said Argaven. "It is over."

"Should —"

"It is finished. Believe me. I will keep you here, Lord Axt, until you believe me. I need your help. You are the piece the game-players forgot about! You must help me. I cannot abdicate against the will of the Council. They will refuse my abdication, force me to rule, and if I rule, I serve my enemies If you will not help me, I will have to kill myself." She spoke quite evenly and reasonably; but Axt knew what even the mention of suicide, the ultimately contemptible act, cost a Karhider.

"One way or the other," said the young king.

The Plenipotentiary pulled his heavy cloak closer round him; he was cold. He had been cold for seven years, here. "My lord," he said, "I am an alien on your world, with a handful of aides, and a little device with which I can converse with other aliens on distant worlds. I represent power, of course, but I have none. How can I help you?"

"You have a ship on Horden Island."

"Ah. I was afraid of that," said the Plenipotentiary, sighing. "Lord Argaven, that ship is set for Ollul, twenty-four lightyears away. Do you know what that means?"

"My escape from my time, in which I have become an instrument of evil."

"There is no escape," said Axt, with sudden intensity. "No, my lord. Forgive me. It is impossible. I could not consent —"

Icy rain of spring rattled on the stones of the tower, wind whined at the angles and finials of the roof. The room was quiet, shadowy. One small shielded light burned by the door. The nurse lay snoring mildly in the bed, the baby was head down, rump up in the crib. Argaven stood beside the crib. She looked around the room, or rather saw it, knew it wholly, without looking. She too had slept here as a little child. It had been her first kingdom. It was here that she had come to suckle her child, her first-born, had sat by the fireplace while the little mouth tugged at her breast, had hummed to the baby the songs Borhub had hummed to her. This was the center, the center of everything.

Very cautiously and gently she slipped her hand under the baby's warm, damp, downy head, and put over it a chain on which hung a massive ring carved with the token of the Lords of Harge. The chain was far too long, and Argaven knotted it shorter, thinking that it might twist and choke the child. So allaying that small anxiety, she tried to allay the great fear and wretchedness that filled her. She stooped down till her cheek touched the baby's cheek, whispering inaudibly, "Emran, Emran, I have to leave you, I can't take you, you have to rule for me. Be good, Emran, live long, rule well, be good, Emran. . . ."

She straightened up, turned, ran from the tower room, the lost kingdom.

She knew several ways of getting out of the Palace unperceived. She took the surest, and then made for the New Harbor through the bright-lit, sleet-lashed streets of Erhenrang, alone.

Now there is no picture: no seeing her. With what eye will you watch a process that is one hundred millionth percent slower than the speed of light? She is not now a king, nor a human being; she is translated. You can scarcely call fellow-mortal one whose time passes seventy thousand times slower than yours. She is more than alone. It seems that she is not, any more than an uncommunicated thought is; that she goes nowhere, any more than a thought goes. And yet, at very nearly but never quite the speed of light, she voyages. She is the voyage. Quick as thought. She has doubled her age when she arrives, less than a day older, in the portion of space curved about a dustmote named Ollul, the fourth planet of a yellowish sun. And all this has passed in utter silence.

With noise now, and fire and meteoric dazzle enough to satisfy a Karhider's lust for splendor, the clever ship makes earthfall, settling down in flame in the precise spot it left from some fifty-five years ago. Presently, visible, unmassive, uncertain, the young king emerges from it and stands a moment in the exitway, shielding her eyes from the light of a strange, hot sun.

Axt had of course sent notice of her coming, by instantaneous transmitter, twenty-four years ago, or seventeen hours ago, depending on how you look at it; and aides and agents of the Ekumen were on hand to greet her. Even pawns did not go unnoticed by those players of the great game, and this Gethenian was, after all, a king. One of the agents had spent a year of the twenty-four in learning Karhidish, so that Argaven could speak to someone. She spoke at once: "What news from my country?"

"Mr. Mobile Axt and his successor have sent regular summaries of events, and various private messages for you; you'll find all the material in your quarters, Mr. Harge. Very briefly, the regency of Lord Gerer was uneventful and benign; there was a depression in the first two years, during which your Arctic settlements were abandoned, but at present the economy is quite stable. Your heir was enthroned at eighteen, and has ruled now for seven years."

"Yes. I see," said the person who had kissed that year-old heir last night.

"Whenever you see fit, Mr. Harge, the specialists at our Institute over in Belxit —"

"As you wish," said Mr. Harge.

They went into her mind very gently, very subtly, opening doors. For locked doors they had delicate instruments that always found the combination; and then they stood aside, and let her enter. They found the person in black, who was not Gerer, and compassionate Rebade, who was not compassionate; they stood with her on the Palace balcony, and climbed the crevasses of nightmare with her up to the room in the tower; and at last the one who was to have been first, the person in red and white, approached her saying, "Majesty! A plot against your life —" And Mr. Harge screamed in abject terror, and woke up.

"Well! That was the trigger. The signal to begin tripping off the other instructions and determine the course of your phobia. An induced paranoia. Really beautifully induced, I must say. Here, drink this, Mr. Harge. No, it's just water! You might well have become a remarkably vicious ruler, increasingly obsessed by fear of plots and subversions, increasingly disaffected from your people. Not overnight, of course. That's the beauty of it. It would have taken several years for you to become a real tyrant; though they no doubt planned some boosts along the way, once Rebade wormed his way—her way— a way into your confidence. . . . Well, well, I see why Karhide is well spoken of, over at the Clearinghouse. If you'll pardon my objectivity, this kind of skill and patience is quite rare. . . ." So the doctor, the mindmender, the hairy, greyish, one-sexed person from somewhere called the Cetians, went rambling on while the patient recovered herself.

"Then I did right," said Mr. Harge at last.

"You did. Abdication, suicide, or escape were the only acts of consequence which you could have committed of your own volition, freely. They counted on your moral veto on suicide, and your Council's vote on abdication. But being possessed by ambition themselves, they forgot the possibility of abnegation, and left one door open for you. A door which only a strong-minded person, if you'll pardon my literalness, could choose to go through. I really must read up on this other mindscience of yours, what do you call it, Foretelling? Thought it was some occultist trash, but quite evidently . . . Well, well, I expect they'll be wanting you to look in at the Clearinghouse soon, to discuss your future, now that we've put your past where it belongs, eh?"

"As you wish," said Mr. Harge.

She talked with various people there in the Clearinghouse of the Ekumen for the West Worlds, and when they suggested that she go to school, she assented readily. For among those mild persons, whose chief quality seemed a cool, profound sadness indistinguishable from a warm, profound hilarity — among them, the ex-king of Karhide knew herself a barbarian, unlearned and unwise.

She attended Ekumenical School. She lived in barracks near the Clearinghouse in Vaxtsit City, with a couple of hundred other aliens, none of whom was either androgynous or an ex-king. Never having owned much that was hers alone, and never having had much privacy, she did not mind barracks life; nor was it so bad as she had expected to live among single-sexed people, although she found their condition of perpetual kemmer tiresome. She did not mind anything much, getting through the works and days with vigor and competence but always a certain heedlessness as of one whose center is somewhere else. The only discomfort was the heat, the awful heat of Ollul that rose sometimes to 35° C in the blazing interminable season when no snow fell for two hundred days on end. Even when winter came at last she sweated, for it seldom got more than ten degrees below freezing outside, and the barracks were kept sweltering — she thought — though the other aliens wore heavy sweaters all the time. She slept on top of her bed, naked and thrashing, and dreamed of the snows of the Kargav, the ice in Old Harbor, the ice scumming one's ale on cool mornings in the Palace, the cold, the dear and bitter cold of Winter.

She learned a good deal. She had already learned that the Earth was, here, called Winter, and that Ollul was, here, called the Earth: one of those facts which turn the universe inside out like a sock. She learned that a meat diet causes diarrhea in the unaccustomed gut. She learned that single-sexed people, whom she tried hard not to think of as perverts, tried hard not to think of her as a pervert. She learned that when she pronounced Ollul as Orrur some people laughed. She attempted also to unlearn that she was a king. Once the School took her in hand she learned and unlearned much more. She was led, by all the machines and devices and experiences and (simplest and most demanding) words that the Ekumen had at its disposal, into an intimation of what it might be to understand the nature and history of a kingdom that was over a million years old and trillions of miles wide. When she had begun to guess the immensity of this kingdom of humanity and the durable pain and monotonous waste of its history, she began also to see what lay beyond its borders in space and time, and among naked rocks and fumacesuns and the shining desolation that goes on and on she glimpsed the sources of hilarity and serenity, the inexhaustible springs. She learned a great many facts, numbers, myths, epics, proportions, relationships, and so forth, and saw, beyond the borders of what she had learned, the unknown again, a splendid immensity. In this augmentation of her mind and being there was great satisfaction; yet she was unsatisfied. They did not always let her go on as far as she wanted into certain fields, mathematics, Cetian physics. "You started late, Mr. Harge," they said, "we have to build on the existing foundations. Besides, we want you in subjects which you can put to use."

"What use?"

They—the ethnographer Mr. Mobile Gist represented Them at the moment, across a library table—looked at her sardonically. "Do you consider yourself to be of no further use, Mr. Harge?"

Mr. Harge, who was generally reserved, spoke with sudden fury: "I do."

"A king without a country," said Gist in his flat Terran accent, "self-exiled, believed to be dead, might feel a trifle superfluous. But then, why do you think we're bothering with you?"

"Out of kindness."

"Oh, kindness . . . However kind we are, we can give you nothing that would make you happy, you know. Except . . . Well. Waste is a pity. You were indubitably the right king for Winter, for Karhide, for the purposes of the Ekumen. You have a sense of balance. You might even have unified the planet. You certainly wouldn't have terrorized and fragmented the country, as the present king seems to be doing. What a waste! Only consider our hopes and needs, Mr. Harge, and your own qualifications, before you despair of being useful in your life. Forty or fifty more years of it you have to live, after all . . ."

The last snapshot taken by alien sunlight: erect, in a Hainish-style cloak of grey, a handsome person of indeterminate sex stands, sweating profusely, on a green lawn beside the chief Agent of the Ekumen in the West Worlds, the Stabile, Mr. Hoalans of Alb, who can meddle (if he likes) with the destinies of forty worlds.

"I can't order you to go there, Argaven," says the Stabile. "Your own conscience —"

"I gave up my kingdom to my conscience, twelve years ago. It's had its due. Enough's enough," says Argaven Harge. Then she laughs suddenly, so that the Stabile also laughs; and they part in such harmony as the Powers of the Ekumen desire between human souls.

Horden Island, off the south coast of Karhide, was given as a freehold to the Ekumen by the Kingdom of Karhide during the reign of Argaven XV. No one lived there. Yearly generations of seawalkies crawled up on the barren rocks, and laid and hatched their eggs, and raised their young, and finally led them back in long single file to the sea. But once every ten or twenty years fire ran over the rocks and the sea boiled on the shores, and if any seawalkies were on the island then they died.

When the sea had ceased to boil, the Plenipotentiary's little electric launch approached. The starship ran out a gossamer-steel gangplank to the deck of the launch, and one person started to walk up it as another one started to walk down it, so that they met in the middle, in midair, between sea and land, an ambiguous meeting.

"Ambassador Horrsed? I'm Harge," said the one from the starship, but the one from the launch was already kneeling, saying aloud, in Karhidish, "Welcome, Argaven of Karhide!"

As he straightened up the Ambassador added in a quick whisper, "You come as yourself — Explain when I can —" Behind and below him on the deck of the launch stood a sizable group of people, staring up intently at the newcomer. All were Karhiders by their looks; several were very old.

Argaven Harge stood for a minute, two minutes, three minutes, erect and perfectly motionless, though her grey cloak tugged and riffled in the cold sea wind. She looked then once at the dull sun in the west, once at the grey land north across the water, back again at the silent people grouped below her on the deck. She strode forward so suddenly that Ambassador Horrsed had to squeeze out of the way in a hurry. She went straight to one of the old people on the deck of the launch. "Are you Ker rem ir Kerheder?"

"I am."

"I knew you by the lame arm, Ker." She spoke clearly; there was no guessing what emotions she felt. "I could not know your face. After sixty years. Are there others of you I knew? I am Argaven."

They were all silent. They gazed at her.

All at once one of them, one scored and scarred with age like wood that has been through fire, stepped forward one step. "My liege, I am Bannith of the Palace Guard. You served with me when I was Drillmaster and you a child, a young child." And the grey head bowed down suddenly, in homage, or to hide tears. Then another stepped forward, and another. The heads that bowed were grey, white, bald; the voices that hailed the king quavered. One, Ker of the crippled arm, whom Argaven had known as a shy page of thirteen, spoke fiercely to those who still stood unmoving: "This is the king. I have eyes that have seen, and that see now. This *is* the king!"

Argaven looked at them, face after face, the bowed heads and the unbowed.

"I am Argaven," she said. "I was king. Who reigns now in Karhide?"

"Emran," one answered.

"My child Emran?"

"Yes, my liege," old Bannith said; most of the faces were blank; but Ker said in her fierce shaking voice, "Argaven, reigns in Karhide! I have lived to see the bright days return. Long live the king!"

One of the younger ones looked at the others, and said resolutely, "So be it. Long live the king!" And all the heads bowed low.

Argaven took their homage unperturbed, but as soon as a moment came when she could address Horrsed the Plenipotentiary alone she demanded, "What is this? What has happened? Why was I misled? I was told I was to come here to assist you, as an aide, from the Ekumen —"

"That was twenty-four years ago," said the Ambassador, apologetically. "I've only lived here five years, my lord. Things are going very ill in Karhide. King Emran broke off relations with the Ekumen last year. I don't really know what the Stabile's purpose in sending you here was at the time he sent you; but at present, we're losing Winter. So the Agents on Hain suggested to me that we might move out our king."

"But I am *dead*," Argaven said wrathfully. "I have been dead for sixty years!"

"The king is dead," said Horrsed. "Long live the king."

As some of the Karhiders approached, Argaven turned from the Ambassador and went over to the rail. Grey water bubbled and slid by the ship's side. The shore of the continent lay now to their left, grey patched with white. It was cold: a day of early winter in the Ice Age. The ship's engine purred softly. Argaven had not heard that purr of an electric engine for a dozen years now, the only kind of engine Karhide's slow and stable Age of Technology had chosen to employ. The sound of it was very pleasant to her.

She spoke abruptly without turning, as one who has known since infancy that there is always someone there to answer; "Why are we going east?"

"We're making for Kerm Land."

"Why Kerm Land?"

It was one of the younger ones who had come forward to answer. "Because that part of the country is in rebellion against the — against King Emran. I am a Kermlander: Perreth ner Sode."

"Is Emran in Erhenrang?"

"Erhenrang was taken by Orgoreyn, six years ago. The king is in the new capital, east of the mountains — the Old Capital, actually, Rer."

"Emran lost the West Fall?" Argaven said, and then turning full on the stout young noble, "Lost the West Fall? Lost Erhenrang?"

Perreth drew back a step, but answered promptly, "We've been in hiding behind the mountains for six years."

"The Orgota are in Erhenrang?"

"King Emran signed a treaty with Orgoreyn five years ago, ceding them the Western Provinces."

"A shameful treaty, your majesty," old Ker broke in, fiercer and shakier than ever. "A fool's treaty! Emran dances to the drums of Orgoreyn. All of us here are rebels, exiles. The Ambassador there is an exile, in hiding!"

"The West Fall," Argaven said. "Argaven I took the West Fall for Karhide seven hundred years ago—" She looked round on the others again with her strange, keen, unheeding gaze. "Emran—" she began, but halted. "How strong are you in Kerm Land? Is the Coast with you?"

"Most Hearths of the South and East are with us."

Argaven was silent a while. "Did Emran ever bear an heir?"

"No heir of the flesh, my liege," Bannith said. "She sired six."

"She has named Girvry Harge rem ir Orek as her heir," said Perreth.

"Girvry? What kind of name is that? The kings of Karhide are named Emran," Argaven said, "and Argaven."

Now at last comes the dark picture, the snapshot taken by firelight — firelight, because the power plants of Rer are wrecked, the trunk lines cut, and half the city is on fire. Snow flurries heavily down above the flames and gleams red for a moment before it melts in mid air, hissing faintly.

Snow and ice and guerrilla troops keep Orgoreyn at bay on the west side of the Kargav Mountains. No help came to the Old King, Emran, when her country rose against her. Her guards fled, her city burns, and now at the end she is face to face with the usurper. But she has, at the end, something of her family's heedless pride. She pays no attention to the rebels. She stares at them and does not see them, lying in the dark hallway, lit only by mirrors that reflect distant fires, the gun with which she killed herself near her hand.

Stooping over the body Argaven lifts up that cold hand, and starts to take from the age-knotted forefinger the massive, carved, gold ring. But she does not do it. "Keep it," she whispers, "keep it." For a moment she bends yet lower, as if she whispered in the dead ear, or laid her cheek against that cold and wrinkled face. Then she straightens up, and stands a while, and presently goes out through dark corridors, by windows bright with distant ruin, to set her house in order: Argaven, Winter's king.

Part Five

The
80s & Beyond

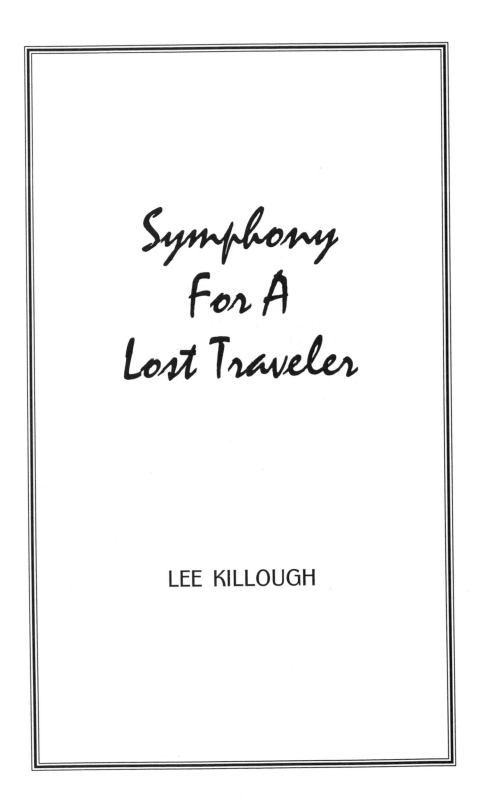

Symphony For A Lost Traveler

LEE KILLOUGH

ABOUT LEE KILLOUGH
AND
SYMPHONY FOR A LOST TRAVELER

Symphony For A Lost Traveler *was first published:*
Analog, *March 1984*

Lee Killough's glittering action adventure novels are so effortlessly written that the depth of her characterization often goes unnoted. The more successful her ongoing series about policewoman Janna Brill and her male sidekick "Mama" Maxwell (Doppleganger Gambit, Spider, and Dragon's Teeth) becomes, the more likely Ms. Killough's exceptional gifts for characterization are to remain unheralded.

Although her short stories generally deal with "men and women who strive for better lives, frequently without understanding that is wrong with their present ones," there is often a distinctly feminist undertone to her work. This is true of such novels as Liberty's World, The Monitor, The Miners and the Shree, Deadly Silence, and the justly famous A Voice Out of Rama in which a male disguises himself as a woman in order to thwart an evil priesthood and learns a great deal about gender discrimination in the process.

"Symphony For A Lost Traveler" (which appears here for the first time complete, with the final paragraphs that were dropped by the magazine's editors) captures what James Gunn calls Killough's "fine ability to portray . . . minds that are psychologically complex and emotionally vulnerable." Returning to an age-old theme of science fiction (how to motivate our reluctant citizenry into supporting those who wish to see humankind liberated from its confinement to the planet Earth) Killough posits a unique solution and offers wry commentary on the nature of carrots and sticks. Readers who are aware only of Ms. Killough's near future detective stories are in for a delightful surprise.

Symphony For A Lost Traveler

by LEE KILLOUGH

THEY WALKED in a moving band of light, into and out of darkness. The floor and ceiling panels of the corridor brightened as Cimela and the butler — in formal black-and-silver jumpsuit — entered each new section; glowing milky white, then dimming out behind them. The passage bored straight through the moon's rock. A glassy sheen of fused stone reflected back at Cimela between the succession of contemporary and classic paintings decorating the walls: abstracts by Tanguy, a Bosch, Seth Koerner's bleak planetscapes, and starships and aliens signed *Herring* and *Whelan*.

Cimela frowned. Kerel Mattias Ashendene's artistic taste ran to the fantastic. Why, then, had he sent expensive shuttle and Moon rocket tickets along with the enigmatic invitation to his lunar retreat — *I would like lo discuss the creation of a truly unique symphony* — to a composer whose work celebrated nature?

She wished she had been able to learn more about the man than public facts: that his Interstellar Mining and Drilling, Inc. issued franchises to more than half the independent miners in the asteroids and Jupiter and Saturn's moons, that he owned controlling interests in numerous other corporations, including those manufacturing pharmaceuticals and computers and contragrav units. Journalist friends could supply only two pieces of tape on him, both eleven years old. One recorded his removal from the twisted wreckage of his sailcar and the other his departure from the hospital months later in a floatchair.

The butler clapped his hands. A section of wall opened to reveal an elevator. "Ask for level four, madam. Mr.Ashendene is waiting."

He was sending her alone into the lion's den? Cimela reflected wryly.

Near-normal gravity returned briefly, but faded again when the car stopped rising. The doors opened.

Cimela gasped in horror. Before her lay the open surface of the Moon, the side and bottom of a crater dropping away in a sharp pattern of light and shadow!

For a moment she did not see distorted smear of her reflection on the inside of a transparent surface . . . the bittersweet of her jumpsuit a flame beneath her mahogany face and the ebony velvet of her close-cropped hair. Then breath returned in a gasp of relief. A dome! Even so, stepping out of the elevator, she felt for the polyplastic to reassure herself.

"You're quite safe," a deep resonant voice said.

She turned toward the sound and found herself in a large, circular room. An assortment of tables and chairs floated above the glowing floor along with a bed, a computer station, and a desk piled with papers and minidisk files. Cimela barely noticed the furnishings. Above the waist-high cabinets and bookcases around the edge—filled with genuine printed and bound volumes—the dome and wire lattice generating its meteor screen rose invisibly, creating the illusion that nothing separated the room from the lunar crater. Earth hung overhead, a brilliant sapphire suspended against midnight velvet studded with diamonds. With difficulty, she dragged her eyes from the view to the man gliding toward her in a floatchair.

He extended a hand. "I've been looking forward to meeting you."

"And I you." His hand crushed hers. Eyes the color of moondust slid over her, assessing, dissecting. Where in them, and in the assured voice, craggy features, gray-touched hair, and iridescent jumpsuit was the person who bought those paintings? "Tell me about your proposal."

"Will you join me for tea?" He used the controls on one sweeping armrest to back his chair toward a table floating above the glowing floor.

Cimela accepted the cup he handed her and folded into a freeform chair. Suddenly, from somewhere, music flooded the dome. She instantly recognized her *Requiem For a Vanishing World*, even without the holo track. It flowed around her, stately bass notes representing whales booming along under the high music of birds and the sinuous rhythms of predators, all intermixed with the sounds of the animals' own voices: twittering, whale songs, howls, snarls.

Ashendene's moondust eyes continued to search her. "I never would have thought one could make music using DNA as the score. Four notes sounds so limiting."

She quirked a brow. "Nature manages well enough with them." She expected some reply, but he only continued to stare at her. The scrutiny brought a rush of irritation. "Am I not what you expected?"

The moondust eyes flickered. "Oh, yes . . . black and all."

She started. Could the man read minds?

"I researched you, of course. Cimela Bediako, thirty-one years old, single, born in Ghana, bioengineer father, music training in Sidney, lead singer and song writer for the Neo-Renaissance band the Rococo Roos until you switched to symphonic music and presented *World Primeval* at the San Francisco Opera House five years ago. If I'm staring, it's in admiration of one not only supremely talented and beautiful, but a veritable Pied Piper as well."

Cimela blinked. "Pied Piper?"

Whale songs cried in counterpoint to the howl of wolves.

Ashendene said, "*World Primeval* generated a renewed interest in dinosaurs,

I understand, and your wildlife symphonies have inspired a growing conservation movement."

"I hope so!" She glanced up at the luminous sapphire above them, so un-flawed at this distance. "We're spreading out across the galaxy, but we're not leaving anything to come home to."

"Not quite across the galaxy. We haven't left the solar system yet."

Cimela shrugged. "Well, there's no practical star drive. Star ships would also take metals away, and we don't even know there's anywhere to go."

The moondust eyes flicked over her. "Those are just the excuses we've concocted for abandoning the stars . . . all invalid. We do have an efficient drive, and there's not only somewhere to go, but someone to meet."

Her breath stuck in her chest. "Someone . . . "

Ashendene leaned toward her. "Three years ago a miner I franchised found a derelict ship in the asteroids. It's three thousand years old."

Her throat went dry. "We've been in the asteroids for only a century."

"Yes." He sat back. "My scientists have taken the ship apart and learned the principles behind the drive. I want to put that drive in human ships now. That's why I asked you here. I plan to announce my plans at a dinner for potential investors and I want music to celebrate the occasion. In addition to keeping all rights to the music and being my guest while you work, you will, of course, receive monetary remuneration."

He named a figure that any other time would have left Cimela dazzled, but now she could feel only the bitter stab of disappointment. Background music! *This* was his idea of a unique musical work? She stood. "No, thank you. I don't do commercials or waiting room music."

The moondust eyes went chill as the crater outside. "Perhaps you would be polite enough to hear me out. The credit I spent bringing you here entitles me to at least that much of your time."

She sat down again, stiffly, on the edge of the chair.

Ashendene frowned. "I want very special music, a long piece to be per-formed after dinner by an orchestra, something arranged as only you can do it, on DNA. That ship wasn't empty, Ms. Bediako."

Searing hot and cold shot through Cimela like an electric charge. Every hair on her body raised. "You found . . . people?" she whispered.

"What remained of them. Now are you interested.?"

His sarcasm went unnoticed over the crescendo of her heart. People. Aliens! Life different from any that had ever walked this world ! How were they built? Did all life share the same nucleotides, or would their genetic matter sing a different song? And Ashendene offered her the chance to see first. Breathlessly, she asked, "When may I see a printout of the nucleotide sequence?"

A thin smile crossed his mouth. "Today. I'll have it brought to your room. There's a computer station and synthesizer already there for you, but if you need anything else, just ask for it. Albert will show you the way."

Her "room" consisted of a large suite, one entire wall of which had been built of the same polyplastic as the dome and looked out into the crater. Neither Earth nor Ashendene's study were visible from it; just moonscape, starkly lifeless in patterns of black and silver, with the crater ringwall rising jaggedly into the velvet-and-diamond canopy of sky.

Staring out, she caught a reflection of the room: the butler entering with an overall-clad young woman pushing a contra-gee cart piled with computer printout. Cimela lost all interest in the crater. Pulse leaping, she spun on the cart and fingered the printout in anticipation. "Did you bring holos of the aliens, too?"

The young woman shook her head. "They didn't give me any."

Cimela frowned. She needed them to pick appropriate instruments and tempi, and to build the holo track. She would have to ask Ashendene for them.

The butler and technician set the printout on the floor while Cimela unpacked her electronic keyboard. After the door slid closed behind them, she arranged the paper in a circle on the carpet, creating her own ringwall. Then she sat cross-legged in the center, keyboard in her lap, and began reading through the nearest stack of printout.

Some corner of her mind remembered a servant serving supper, and that she flung herself on the bed for a while; but most of her awareness focused on the nucleotide sequences. She saw nothing else and heard only the music they made in her head and on the keyboard.

The computer had not printed out the chemical structure, either as formulas or zig-zag diagrams, but the terminology told her the aliens' "DNA" differed from humans': A', G', C', and T' where A, G, C, and T usually stood for the nucleotides, plus two more named PU-3 and PY-3, indicating an addition purine and pyrimidine. Six nucleotides! Their genetics must be very complex . . . but more than that, this time she had six notes to work with.

Except that a seventh, out of key, kept intruding. She tried to ignore it.

"Ms. Bediako!"

Cimela started with enough force to lift her off the carpet. Turning, she met the keen gaze of moondust eyes regarding her from the doorway.

Ashendene floated his chair into the room. "I came to check on you. Alfred said you didn't touch breakfast or lunch and wouldn't answer the door chime."

Meals? Door chime? Oh . . . the seventh note. She grimaced. "I should have warned you how engrossed I become when I work."

A brow quirked. "Indeed. However, I didn't bring you here to expire from anorexia. To reassure me of your nutrition, will you have dinner with me this evening?"

Dinner? That would mean losing two or three hours of working time. Still, it might also give her the chance to learn where the steely businessman became the lover of fantasy. "Thank you. What time and where?"

"I take my meals in my room normally. Alfred will be pouring the wine at nineteen hundred hours. It's a house vintage, from grapes in our hydroponics farm. I think you'll like it."

Spinning his chair, Ashendene sailed it out of the room. Only after the door had closed behind him did Cimela remember that she had forgotten to ask him for holos of the aliens. Shrugging, she returned to work.

By eighteen hundred hours she had decided on the length of the symphony, chosen the key, and decided that the notes from *Mi* up to *Do* would comprise her scale. She stood stiffly, stretching, ready for a break before looking for the strand sequences to harmonize with and make a counterpoint to the main sequence .

Ashendene greeted her with a nod of approval . "Lovely."

Cimela smiled. Though this was just a break in work, she had dressed carefully, choosing a gauzy gold jumpsuit with the voluminous sleeves and legs, snuggly cuffed at wrists and ankles, that the Moon's low gravity inspired in this year's fashions. Sitting down at the round library-type table where dinner had been set, she looked out at the crater and up to the luminous globe of Earth overhead. "Do you like this room best for its view of Earth or the moon?"

"The stars." Ashendene said.

The butler poured wine and served dinner, gliding over the glowing floor silent and efficient as a robot. Her *Kings of the Air* played softly around them, a chorus of strings singing the nucleotide sequences of the great raptors.

Ashendene asked, "How did you happen to begin using DNA as a score?"

Cimela sipped her wine. It was delicious, pale and lightly sweet as moonlight. "My father once gave my mother a birthday card that was a sheet of music with notes assigned to nucleotide sequences that resulted in the pigmentation of her hair, skin, and eyes. 'The song is you,' I remember him telling her. That fascinated me. I started playing with DNA tunes. Even the music I wrote for the Rococo Roos had DNA sequence themes, and later, when I began writing about life that had vanished or seemed about to, what better than to let the very substance of those animals plead for them'? *World Primeval* sounds like any symphony, but even its themes are expanded from nucleotide sequences of the shark, lizard, echidna, and platypus."

Ashendene laughed. "I'm astonished how well it all sounds with such a restricted form, but even more amazed at the profound emotional effect your music has on people."

That always surprised her, too. "A friend once came up with a theory in an enebriated moment. He said the response results from resonance, a recognition on a deeply subconscious level of its similarity to the pattern of our own genetic structure. It's as good as any other explanation I've heard. I'll be interested in seeing how people react to an alien coding."

The moondust eyes flickered. "I would think they'd feel the same, given that the music uses human instrumentation."

She frowned. Human instrumentation. Could that be wrong? Perhaps aliens deserved new and more exotic sounds. She would play with the synthesizer. Which reminded her — knowing what they looked like would help her select appropriate sounds. "Mr. Ashendene, I need tapes or holos of the aliens."

He sipped his wine and grimaced. "There aren't any worth seeing."

She shrugged. "I don 't care how poor they are; I need something for a basis of the visual track."

"The bodies were too badly damaged to tell much about their appearance. The 'DNA' has been read from a few cells that froze quickly enough to be thawed without destroying the internal structure."

"Even damaged bodies are worth something," she protested. "Are they large or small? How many limbs do they have? What's their clothing like? What about the ship?"

The moondust eyes stared into her, then went thoughtful. "I see what you mean. We have holos of the ship and you'll have them by morning. We're working on a computer reconstruction of the aliens based on a composite and skeletal structure and you'll have that too, as soon as it's finished. From what I saw, the aliens are a bit smaller than we are, covered with . . . bronze or gold feathers."

Golden bird people? She grinned in delight. Perhaps flutes and strings, or chimes, should carry the musical theme. She played with the idea in her head the rest of dinner, and afterward programmed the synthesizer in her room for airy instrumental sounds.

Cimela kept working with the synthesizer, at the same time deciding on secondary and tertiary musical lines. During rests she studied the holos of the ship. It appeared strictly utilitarian, without decoration or color. Ceilings pressed low overhead, barely centimeters above the squatly arched doorways. The crew apparently never used furniture except tables and something like low blanket racks with padded bars. Water-filled mats on the floor served as beds. Beyond that the holos told her nothing about the aliens. She set them aside .

Every evening she ate with Ashendene in the domed study. The floor glowed beneath them; Earth shone overhead; moonwine filled their glasses like luminous silver. Ashendene entertained her with stories about his early days mining the asteroids.

"IMDI was just me, five buddies, and a patched junk ship in those days."

Cimela smiled at him over her wine glass. "You sound like you enjoyed it. Why did you give it up for a desk?"

He shrugged, looking past her at the sky. "The asteroids are just a way station."

After dinner they took tea in the study, or he showed her through another portion of the house. It had the facilities of a small colony: laboratories, work-shops, staff apartments, and a hydroponics farm. Working on the ship here, no wonder he had been able to keep his find a secret. At some point they passed to a first-name basis, and one evening during her second week there she had the chance to learn about his love of fantastic art.

"I respect people who dream," he said, "even if it's nightmares, like Bosch. So few people dream these days. And speaking of dreaming, how is your work coming?"

The question had been inevitable. She sighed. "Slowly, as always. I'm still undecided about the lead instruments. Perhaps I'll use a recorder and samisen."

He blinked. "A what?"

"The samisen is a three-stringed Japanese guitar with a long neck. The recorder is a very old flute that's played like a clarinet. It went out of common use about the time of Bach, at least until the Neo-Renaissance movement revived interest in it. It has a lovely mellow sound."

A crease appeared between the moondust eyes. "Don't forget you're writing this for modern ears."

As though modern sound could not come out of old instruments. But that was what came of discussing instruments with a non-musician. "Of course. When do I need to be finished?"

"The dinner will wait for the music. Oh, I almost forgot. Albert." He beckoned to the butler. "Will you bring Cimela the envelope from my desk?"

Her heart went into fortissimo at the sight of the small, square gray envelope. "The alien construct program?"

Ashendene finished his wine. "Now you can start on the holo track, too, and stop being underworked."

She laughed at his teasing, but could hardly wait to finish eating. Ashendene appeared to read her mind. He said little the remainder of the meal and did not ask her to stay for tea afterward.

Back in her rooms, Cimela slipped the minidisc into her computer and waited curled cross-legged in her chair. The image appeared one line at a time, as though being sketched inside the screen. It pivoted at the same time, the far side of the three-dimensional shape remaining visible through the forming lines of the near side. With every turn, however, more details appeared — feathers, the facets of compound eyes, fingernails — followed by textures and finally by color, until the screen held a construction that did not look like a computer drawing but a holophoto of an actual being.

The alien stood on two muscular legs that bent strangely but carried him like coiled springs. He had no wings after all: small arms, also oddly jointed, folded across the golden chest, ending in hands with a thumb and two long, many-jointed fingers. Feather-fringed ears belled out from the sides of the broad head. Faceted opal eyes dreamed placidly above nasal slits and a smiling bow of mouth.

Cimela sighed in satisfaction. He was alien, yes, completely inhuman — she could not even identify the tools hanging on his belt — but utterly fascinating.

She plunged happily into her doubled task and over the next several weeks used the computer to create and store the thousands of images that would be projected as the visual track, while at the same time experimenting with countless nucleotide sequences played against each other in the voices of several dozen musical instruments . . . culling, choosing, refining choices. She lived, breathed, and dreamed the symphony, aware of little else. Even at dinner with Ashendene they spoke only of the work.

He did not appear to mind. He listened intently, and once Cimela looked up from the computer to find his chair in the doorway, his expression hungry. How long he had sat there Cimela could not begin to guess, and she eyed him, suddenly aware how isolated the house was, and that leaving would entail more effort than just hailing a cab, if she needed to escape unwanted attentions.

"Is that part of the final thing?" he asked.

She did not know whether to be relieved or disappointed. His passion was for the symphony, not her. "Do you like it?"

The hunger flared brighter in the moondust eyes. "It's even better than I dreamed. Have you titled it yet?"

"How about *The Lost Traveler*?"

"Perfect. Will you think I'm impatient if I ask how close you are to being finished?"

"Yes." But she smiled. "I'll answer, though. I'm almost finished. So plan your dinner and give me an orchestra for rehearsals. Do you really plan to bring an entire orchestra all the way from Earth?"

He smiled back. "No, just around the Moon. The Chinese have a very nice orchestra at the Celestial Village complex." His smile broadened. "Maybe the samisen is appropriate after all."

Now work really began: printing out the score for each instrument, working with the butler to assign rooms to the several dozen musicians who flooded the house. Her days filled with hours of rehearsals, all held where the dinner and performance would be given: the ballroom, a dome like the study but many times larger. How she had missed seeing it before Cimela did not know, for it appeared to sit almost in the center of the crater, the rugged ringwall rising on all sides.

She had little time to admire the view, however. Though she spoke little Chinese and the conductor knew even less English, the two of them argued endlessly over tempi and other details.

Ashendene, attending one of the rounds, murmured, "Maybe we should have settled for a synthesizer."

Cimela shook her head. "I've been through this before. Wu Chien and I will work out our differences or I'll turn him into Peking duck."

Ashendene raised a skeptical brow, but by the day of the dinner she and the conductor were indeed bowing and smiling at one another. He shook his head. "Remarkable talent indeed."

The house filled to bursting. Each of the men and women Ashendene had invited moved in with companions and personal staff. They arrived a shuttle-load at a time from the Americans' Port Heinlein for two days before the dinner, and though one or two did not arrive until the last moment, by seventeen hundred hours on the appointed day all were gathering in the ballroom for cocktails.

Ashendene hovered outside the elevator like a king on a throne, greeting his guests and introducing them to Cimela, who stood beside him in gold velvet.

The group had the glitter of an international opening night, the women wrapped in jewels and expensive fabrics, the men dressed in elegant formal versions of jumpsuits, kimonos, and dashikis . . . but it was neither that nor their names, most of which Cimela failed to recognize, that kept her heart in allegro tempo. The aura of power curled around them visibly. Without being told, Cimela knew that she shook hands with the men and women who really ran the world, and whose web of influence extended even out to the edge of the solar system.

The scene had the surrealism of one of Ashendene's paintings: the tables, impeccably set with the finest china, crystal, and sterling, arranged in a circle on the milky glow of the floor; and outside the circle the guests, milling together wearing their power as easily and elegantly as their formal clothing, chatting, seemingly unaware or uncaring that they did so in the center of a lunar crater. Light from hidden spotlights flooded the crater. No Earth or Sun shone in the sky, however. The jagged teeth of the ringwall framed a breathtaking vista of stars alone, infinitely vast and far, yet so brilliant that each distant sun — which one warmed the world of the golden-feathered people? — looked close enough for Cimela to reach up and pluck .

She sat at the head table beside Ashendene, completely unable to distinguish what she ate. Instead Cimela stared up at the glorious blaze overhead and wondered how the guests could ignore it for shop talk and gossip. "Don't they ever look up?" she whispered to Ashendene .

"Perhaps after tonight they will." Grasping the edge of the table, he pulled himself upright. "Ladies and gentlemen!" He waited while the roar of conversation died away. When only the occasional clink of a dessert spoon against glass remained, he went on. "I want to thank you all for coming."

As he spoke, Cimela noticed that a square in the center of the floor dropped and slid aside.

"I hope you've enjoyed the food and wine. In a few minutes the Celestial Village Symphony Orchestra will present the new work by Cimela Bediako that I promised you."

"Before that, however, let me relieve your curiosity about the business proposal I used to entice you here. In a word, I am offering you the stars."

Cimela saw several people start to frown, but before they could complete the expression the air swirled above the circle of tables. It solidified into a holo projection of the aliens' battered ship, a blunt cigar shape wrapped in a scaffold-like spiral. Brows arched around the tables, then dipped again speculatively as the guests recognized the strange craft's aged appearance. The eyes widened when Ashendene explained what the ship was and how and where it had been found. Then the ship dissolved and in its place a holo of the alien appeared, just as Cimela had first seen it: a pivoting outline, rapidly filling with detail, texture, and color. A sigh of indrawn breath swept the circle.

"We have learned to duplicate the drive," Ashendene said. "Star travel is now possible in flights of weeks and months instead of enduring for generations. All we need is a company to build the ships."

The physics behind the drive and the talk about bent space did not interest Cimela. The expressions around the tables did, and she bit her lip. She had seen closed faces like those before . . . on critics who decided even before the conductor raised his baton that her work could not possibly contain real artistic merit, only novelty, gimmickry. These people had no interest in investing money to build star ships.

". . . opportunity to establish trade," Ashendene was saying now. "If we'll use this drive, the universe and whatever profit may lie out there are ours. And now, refill your wine glasses and prepare for pleasure." The alien holo dissolved. "I present the Celestial Village Symphony Orchestra playing the most beautiful and talented Cimela Bediako's *The Lost Traveler*." He dropped back into his chair.

Sometime during his speech the orchestra had slipped into its place at the end of the room. Cimela laced her fingers tightly in her lap, her heart thundering like kettledrums, and nodded at Wu Chien.

After the first few bars, however, she forgot her nervousness, and even Ashendene and his guests. Nothing existed but the music. It soared, the main melody carried by a descant recorder, samisen, and harp. Other strings, the brass, and woodwinds sang behind them, playing complementary nucleotide sequences. And in the center of the tables the computer projected the visual track: golden-feathered aliens with faceted opal eyes, stretching upward or striding along on their powerful legs, circling and embracing in a minuet-like dance, all against the backdrop of moonscape and starfields.

Cimela closed her eyes and let the sound possess her, reverberate through her bones and blood, hypnotic. How foolish people were to think that they created music, she mused. Nature did it first, and better, in the voices of wind and water and animals, and even in the very substance of what made all life what it was. The aliens might come from a different sun and a different sea, but in the very center of them their cells sang a song not that different from those of the trees, insects, and men of Earth.

When the music stopped, such absolute silence filled the dome that Cimela heard the sigh of breathing and the beat of her own heart. She opened her eyes hesitantly to find every guest sitting blinking at the empty air in the circle. She swung around to meet Wu Chien's eyes, stomach plunging. Oh, no! They hated it. She tried to look an apology at the orchestra.

But then the applause began . . . a single pair of hands, joined by another, then another, the sound swelling until the thunder of it shook the dome. Ashendene grinned and urged her onto her feet. And one by one the guests stood, too. The most powerful men and women in the solar system rose to their feet, their hands still pounding together in approval .

Cimela remembered bowing to the guests and orchestra, remembered the orchestra bowing; then everything blurred into a crowd of people surrounding her with congratulations. She floated on a cloud of euphoria that did not dissipate even when the ballroom emptied and she stood alone with Ashendene and a few servants.

She hugged him in sheer joy, throwing herself into his lap. "Kerel, thank you for giving me the chance to write this symphony."

"I thank *you* for *creating* it. Every one of them has asked to invest in the starship corporation." Then his arms tightened around her.

Somehow, without much surprise, she found herself in his private dome, in his bed; and the lovemaking made a celebration indeed, sweet and deeply satisfying as moonwine and her music together. Ashendene might be crippled, but not disabled, she discovered.

Some long time later she woke beneath the glorious blaze of stars and sat up in the bed, dreamily watching them. What happened next? Her contract with Ashendene gave her all rights to *Lost Traveler*, so she supposed she should take it back to Earth. After news of the alien ship spread, interest ought to run high .

She sat up more, smiling at the room, a place as surreal as the paintings: bookcases and the overburdened desk beneath stars and the lunar ringwall. She would miss the room, and probably Ashendene.

Cimela slid out of bed to pad naked along the bookcases, touching the antique objects and peering at their titles: fairy tales, science fiction, astrophysics, planetology, psychology. One book lay on the desk: another collection of fairy tales with a square of stiff paper marking "The Pied Piper of Hamlyn." Amused, she started to read the story, then noticed that the other side of the marker held a holophoto. But what *of*? She tilted it to the light of the floor, frowning. The thing looked like a misshapen porpoise. No . . . more like a giant slug, except that grey-green feathery-looking scales covered it and one end sprouted three tentacle limbs, two tipped in triple talons, the third ending in a cluster of smaller tentacles, and all situated around a great fang-filled maw. Eyes scattered back along the great body, faceted opals peering through the fronds .

Faceted opals? The hair raised on Cimela's back.

The book of fairy tales dropped forgotten to the desk as she pawed through the rest of the papers piled there. What she wanted lay under where the book had lain: more holos and a lengthy report. Cimela studied every holo and read the report, anger boiling up in her. That lying bastard!

"What are you doing, Cimela?"

She slapped the report down on the desk and whirled. "You lying son of a bitch! Golden-feathered aliens? The only similarity between the fraud and these holos is the eyes!"

He sat up. "Yes."

Her hands clenched to keep from spreading into claws. "You let me make *Lost Traveler* a fraud!"

Ashendene frowned. "Only the visuals are . . . inaccurate."

"Only!" He destroyed her artistic integrity and said *only?* "You —" No pejorative seemed vile enough to describe him. "Why did you do it!"

The moondust eyes regarded her solemnly. "Because I want man to go to the stars, and they won't if they think that the stars are inhabited by fanged slugs."

Angrily Cimela paced, flinging her head. "That's ridiculous. You lied about the age of the ship, too. That report says it's three *million* years old — and the aliens were chlorine breathers. They could be extinct by now, and even if they aren't, we don't have much chance of contacting or trading with them. It doesn't make any difference if they're out there."

He piled pillows up and leaned back against them. "Most people won't believe that. All they'll pay attention to is what they see — and you and I, of all people, know how much appearance influences what people think of something or someone."

Anger drained out of Cimela. She bit her lip. Oh yes, she knew. She sighed. "Why tell anyone about the aliens at all? Say *you* invented the drive."

His mouth twisted wryly. "Do you really think just having a drive will rekindle the star dream? No, they'll still talk about wilderness and lack of cost effectiveness. Some explorers go into wilderness just because they want to know what's there, but most people need a reason: population pressure, military advantages, trade. Greed is most effective, I think. Promise of profit will goad people into going places they'd never dream of otherwise."

Cimela sat down on the foot of the bed and hugged her knees. "So you invented attractive aliens and used me to dangle a trade carrot in front of your guests," she said bitterly.

"I had no other choice."

"You might have told me what you were trying to do. You could have asked me to help."

"After you parroted the words of every stay-at-home who's scoffed at my dream of the stars?"

That stung, but she saw his point. "What happens when they learn the truth?"

To her surprise he grinned, shrugging. "It may not be. That's a big galaxy; no one will expect to find our feathered visitors right away. Even if the truth does eventually leak, we'll be out there; and once people go into wilderness they usually stay."

The man was incorrigible, totally without conscience. In disbelief, she said, "You'd really base a star culture on a lie?"

He looked up at the blaze above them. "If that's what it takes. Babies don't remain in the womb forever. We're crippling mankind's growth by clinging to Earth and the Sun." His gaze dropped to meet hers. "Think of the possibilities. The trip doesn't have to be one-way. *I* can even go, and not have to be content with going by proxy. Think of what we can find. Wouldn't you like to visit a new world and play the music in the cells of the life there?"

Her breath caught at the flood of possibilities.

He leaned toward her. "Let me take you there. All I ask is that you help me bring the rest of Mankind, too."

He never stopped manipulating, did he? She almost regretted admiring his motives.

Cimela eyed the fiery blaze overhead. She ought to redo the holo track and make *Traveler* an honest symphony. And yet . . . a universe of life to make music on . . . Longing throbbed in her. Damn the man!

"Cimela? What do you say?" His hand touched her wrist. The heat of it spread up her arm. "Come on. Help me."

Sighing, she yielded to siren call above and within her. "All right. You win. You've bought yourself a Pied Piper."

Speech Sounds

OCTAVIA E. BUTLER

ABOUT OCTAVIA BUTLER
AND
SPEECH SOUNDS

Speech Sounds *was first published:*
Isaac Asimov's, *December 1983*

Recipient of two consecutive Hugo Awards, Octavia Butler brings a unique ethnic background to science fiction which adds unusual depth and texture to her work. This is particularly true of her award-winning story here. "Speech Sounds," pits a woman possessed of an ordinary talent against a period when that talent has become extraordinary. It paints a portrait, in which hope and darkness are equally mixed, of a possible future in which many details are certain to come to pass.

Ms. Butler's most celebrated work is the "Patternmaster" series, which consists of a double-decker set of trilogies showing the conflicts between two groups over the span of nearly four thousand years. Themes of prejudice, discrimination, slavery, and the search for self-fulfillment, not surprisingly fill this series as well as many of her other works. As in "Speech Sounds," a woman often figures at the center of these novels.

Speech Sounds

by OCTAVIA E. BUTLER

THERE WAS TROUBLE aboard the Washington Boulevard bus. Rye had expected trouble sooner or later in her journey. She had put off going until loneliness and hopelessness drove her out. She believed she might have one group of relatives left alive a brother and his two children twenty miles away in Pasadena. That was a day's journey one-way, if she were lucky. The unexpected arrival of the bus as she left her Virginia Road home had seemed to be a piece of luck–until the trouble began.

Two young men were involved in a disagreement of some kind, or, more likely, a misunderstanding. They stood in the aisle, grunting and gesturing at each other, each in his own uncertain "T" stance as the bus lurched over the potholes. The driver seemed to be putting some effort into keeping them off balance. Still, their gestures stopped just short of contact — mock punches, hand-games of intimidation to replace lost curses.

People watched the pair, then looked at each other and made small anxious sounds. Two children whimpered.

Rye sat a few feet behind the disputants and across from the back door. She watched the two carefully, knowing the fight would begin when someone's nerve broke or someone's hand slipped or someone came to the end of his limited ability to communicate. These things could happen any time.

One of them happened as the bus hit an especially large pothole and one man, tall, thin, and sneering, was thrown into his shorter opponent.

Instantly, the shorter man drove his left fist into the disintegrating sneer. He hammered his larger opponent as though he neither had nor needed any weapon other than his left fist. He hit quickly enough, hard enough to batter his opponent down before the taller man could regain his balance or hit back even once.

People screamed or squawked in fear. Those nearby scrambled to get out of the way. Three more young men roared in excitement and gestured wildly. Then, somehow, a second dispute broke out between two of these three probably because one inadvertently touched or hit the other.

As the second fight scattered frightened passengers, a woman shook the driver's shoulder and grunted as she gestured toward the fighting.

The driver grunted back through bared teeth. Frightened, the woman drew away.

Rye, knowing the methods of bus drivers, braced herself and held on to the crossbar of the seat in front of her. When the driver hit the brakes, she was ready and the combatants were not. They fell over seats and onto screaming passengers, creating even more confusion. At least one more fight started.

The instant the bus came to a full stop, Rye was on her feet, pushing the back door. At the second push, it opened and she jumped out, holding her pack in one arm. Several other passengers followed, but some stayed on the bus. Buses were so rare and irregular now, people rode when they could, no matter what. There might not be another bus today—or tomorrow. People started walking, and if they saw a bus they flagged it down. People making intercity trips like Rye's from Los Angeles to Pasadena made plans to camp out, or risked seeking shelter with locals who might rob or murder them.

The bus did not move, but Rye moved away from it. She intended to wait until the trouble was over and get on again, but if there was shooting, she wanted the protection of a tree. Thus, she was near the curb when a battered, blue Ford on the other side of the street made a U-turn and pulled up in front of the bus. Cars were rare these day — as rare as a severe shortage of fuel and of relatively unimpaired mechanics could make them. Cars that still ran were as likely to be used as weapons as they were to serve as transportation. Thus, when the driver of the Ford beckoned to Rye, she moved away warily. The driver got out—a big man, young, neatly bearded with dark, thick hair. He wore a long overcoat and a look of wariness that matched Rye's. She stood several feet from him, waiting to see what he would do. He looked at the bus, now rocking with the combat inside, then at the small cluster of passengers who had gotten off. Finally he looked at Rye again.

She returned his gaze, very much aware of the old forty-five automatic her jacket concealed. She watched his hands.

He pointed with his left hand toward the bus. The dark-tinted windows prevented him from seeing what was happening inside.

His use of the left hand interested Rye more than his obvious question. Left-handed people tended to be less impaired, more reasonable and comprehending, less driven by frustration, confusion, and anger.

She imitated his gesture, pointing toward the bus with her own left hand, then punching the air with both fists.

The man took off his coat revealing a Los Angeles Police Department uniform complete with baton and service revolver.

Rye took another step back from him. There was no more LAPD, no more any large organization, governmental or private. There were neighborhood patrols and armed individuals. That was all.

The man took something from his coat pocket, then threw the coat into the car. Then he gestured Rye back, back toward the rear of the bus. He had something made of plastic in his hand. Rye did not understand what he wanted until he went to the rear door of the bus and beckoned her to stand there. She obeyed mainly out of curiosity. Cop or not, maybe he could do something to stop the stupid fighting.

He walked around the front of the bus, to the street side where the driver's window was open. There, she thought she saw him throw something into the bus. She was still trying to peer through the tinted glass when people began stumbling out the rear door, choking and weeping. Gas.

Rye caught an old woman who would have fallen, lifted two little children down when they were in danger of being knocked down and trampled. She could see the bearded man helping people at the front door. She caught a thin old man shoved out by one of the combatants. Staggered by the old man's weight, she was barely able to get out of the way as the last of the young men pushed his way out. This one, bleeding from nose and mouth, stumbled into another and they grappled blindly, still sobbing from the gas.

The bearded man helped the bus driver out through the front door, though the driver did not seem to appreciate his help. For a moment, Rye thought there would be another fight. The bearded man stepped back and watched the driver gesture threateningly, watched him shout in wordless anger.

The bearded man stood still, made no sound, refused to respond to clearly obscene gestures. The least impaired people tended to do this — stand back unless they were physically threatened and let those with less control scream and jump around. It was as though they felt it beneath them to be as touchy as the less comprehending. This was an attitude of superiority and that was the way people like the bus driver perceived it. Such "superiority" was frequently punished by beatings, even by death. Rye had had close calls of her own. As a result, she never went unarmed. And in this world where the only likely common language was body language, being armed was often enough. She had rarely had to draw her gun or even display it.

The bearded man's revolver was on constant display. Apparently that was enough for the bus driver. The driver spat in disgust, glared at the bearded man for a moment longer, then strode back to his gas-filled bus. He stared at it for a moment, clearly wanting to get in, but the gas was still too strong. Of the windows, only his tiny driver's window actually opened. The front door was open, but the rear door would not stay open unless someone held it. Of course, the air conditioning had failed long ago. The bus would take some time to clear. It was the driver's property, his livelihood. He had pasted old magazine pictures of items he would accept as fare on its sides. Then he would use what he collected to feed his family or to trade. If his bus did not run, he did not eat. On the other hand, if the inside of his bus were torn apart by senseless fighting, he would not eat very well either. He was apparently unable to perceive this. All he could see was that it would be some time before he could use his bus again. He shook his fist at the bearded man and shouted. There seemed to be words in his shout, but Rye could not understand them. She did not know whether this was his fault or hers. She had heard so little coherent human speech for the past three years, she was no longer certain how well she recognized it, no longer certain of the degree of her own impairment.

The bearded man sighed. He glanced toward his car, then beckoned to Rye. He was ready to leave, but he wanted something from her first. No. No, he wanted her to leave with him. Risk getting into his car when, in spite of his uniform, law and order were nothing — not even words any longer.

She shook her head in a universally understood negative, but the man continued to beckon.

She waved him away. He was doing what the less-impaired rarely did — drawing potentially negative attention to another of his kind. People from the bus had begun to look at her.

One of the men who had been fighting tapped another on the arm, then pointed from the bearded man to Rye, and finally held up the first two fingers of his right hand as though giving two-thirds of a Boy Scout salute. The gesture was very quick, its meaning obvious even at a distance. She had been grouped with the bearded man. Now what?

The man who had made the gesture started toward her.

She had no idea what she intended, but she stood her ground. The man was half-a-foot taller than she was and perhaps ten years younger. She did not imagine she could outrun him. Nor did she expect anyone to help her if she needed help. The people around her were all strangers.

She gestured once a clear indication to the man to stop. She did not intend to repeat the gesture. Fortunately, the man obeyed. He gestured obscenely and several other men laughed. Loss of verbal language had spawned a whole new set of obscene gestures. The man, with stark simplicity, had accused her of sex with the bearded man and had suggested she accommodate the other men present — beginning with him.

Rye watched him wearily. People might very well stand by and watch if he tried to rape her. They would also stand and watch her shoot him. Would he push things that far?

He did not. After a series of obscene gestures that brought him no closer to her, he turned contemptuously and walked away.

And the bearded man still waited. He had removed his service revolver, holster and all. He beckoned again, both hands empty. No doubt his gun was in the car and within easy reach, but his taking it off impressed her. Maybe he was all right. Maybe he was just alone. She had been alone herself for three years. The illness had stripped her, killing her children one by one, killing her husband, her sister, her parents. . . .

The illness, if it was an illness, had cut even the living off from one another. As it swept over the country, people hardly had time to lay blame on the Soviets (though they were falling silent along with the rest of the world), on a new virus, a new pollutant, radiation, divine retribution. . . . The illness was stroke-swift in the way it cut people down and strokelike in some of its effects. But it was highly specific. Language was always lost or severely impaired. It was never regained. Often there was also paralysis, intellectual impairment, death.

Rye walked toward the bearded man, ignoring the whistling and applauding of two of the young men and their thumbs-up signs to the bearded man. If he had smiled at them or acknowledged them in any way, she would almost certainly have changed her mind. If she had let herself think of the possible deadly consequences of getting into a stranger's car, she would have changed her mind. Instead, she thought of the man who lived across the street from her. He rarely washed since his bout with the illness. And he had gotten into the habit of urinating wherever he happened to be. He had two women already — one tending each of his large gardens. They put up with him in exchange for his protection. He had made it clear that he wanted Rye to become his third woman.

She got into the car and the bearded man shut the door. She watched as he walked around to the driver's door — watched for his sake because his gun was on the seat beside her. And the bus driver and a pair of young men had come a few steps closer. They did nothing, though, until the bearded man was in the car. Then one of them threw a rock. Others followed his example, and as the car drove away, several rocks bounced off it harmlessly.

When the bus was some distance behind them, Rye wiped sweat from her forehead and longed to relax. The bus would have taken her more than halfway to Pasadena. She would have had only ten miles to walk. She wondered how far she would have to walk now—and wondered if walking a long distance would be her only problem.

At Figuroa and Washington where the bus normally made a left turn, the bearded man stopped, looked at her, and indicated that she should choose a direction. When she directed him left and he actually turned left, she began to relax. If he was willing to go where she directed, perhaps he was safe.

As they passed, blocks of burned, abandoned buildings, empty lots, and wrecked or stripped cars, he slipped a gold chain over his head and handed it to her. The pendant attached to it was a smooth, glassy, black rock. Obsidian. His name might be Rock or Peter or Black, but she decided to think of him as Obsidian. Even her sometimes useless memory would retain a name like Obsidian.

She handed him her own name symbol—a pin in the shape of a large golden stalk of wheat. She had bought it long before the illness and the silence began. Now she wore it, thinking it was as close as he was likely to come to Rye. People like Obsidian who had not known her before probably thought of her as Wheat. Not that it mattered. She would never hear her name spoken again.

Obsidian handed her pin back to her. He caught her hand as she reached for it and rubbed his thumb over her calluses.

He stopped at First Street and asked which way again. Then, after turning right as she had indicated, he parked near the Music Center. There, he took a folded paper from the dashboard and unfolded it. Rye recognized it as a street map, though the writing on it meant nothing to her. He flattened the map, took her hand again, and put her index finger on one spot. He touched her, touched himself, pointed toward the floor. In effect, "We are here." She knew he wanted to know where she was going. She wanted to tell him, but she shook her head sadly. She had lost reading and writing. That was her most serious impairment and her most painful. She had taught history at UCLA. She had done freelance writing. Now she could not even read her own manuscripts. She had a house full of books that she could neither read nor bring herself to use as fuel. And she had a memory that would not bring back to her much of what she had read before.

She stared at the map, trying to calculate. She had been born in Pasadena, had lived for fifteen years in Los Angeles. Now she was near L.A. Civic Center. She knew the relative positions of the two cities, knew streets, directions, even knew to stay away from freeways which might be blocked by wrecked cars and destroyed overpasses. She ought to know how to point out Pasadena even though she could not recognize the word.

Hesitantly, she placed her hand over a pale orange patch in the upper right corner of the map. That should be right. Pasadena.

Obsidian lifted her hand and looked under it, then folded the map and put it back on the dashboard. He could read, she realized belatedly. He could probably write, too. Abruptly, she hated him — deep, bitter hatred. What did literacy mean to him — a grown man who played cops and robbers? But he was literate and she was not. She never would be. She felt sick to her stomach with hatred, frustration, and jealousy. And only a few inches from her hand was a loaded gun.

She held herself still, staring at him, almost seeing his blood. But her rage crested and ebbed and she did nothing.

Obsidian reached for her hand with hesitant familiarity. She looked at him. Her face had already revealed too much. No person still living in what was left of human society could fail to recognize that expression, that jealousy.

. She closed her eyes wearily, drew a deep breath. She had experienced longing for the past, hatred of the present, growing hopelessness, purposelessness, but she had never experienced such a powerful urge to kill another person. She had left her home, finally, because she had come near to killing herself. She had found no reason to stay alive. Perhaps that was why she had gotten into Obsidian's car. She had never before done such a thing.

He touched her mouth and made chatter motions with thumb and fingers. Could she speak?

She nodded and watched his milder envy come and go. Now both had admitted what it was not safe to admit, and there had been no violence. He tapped his mouth and forehead and shook his head. He did not speak or comprehend spoken language. The illness had played with them, taking away, she suspected, what each valued most.

She plucked at his sleeve, wondering why he had decided on his own to keep the LAPD alive with what he had left. He was sane enough otherwise.

Why wasn't he at home raising corn, rabbits, and children? But she did not know how to ask. Then he put his hand on her thigh and she had another question to deal with.

She shook her head. Disease, pregnancy, helpless, solitary agony . . . no. He massaged her thigh gently and smiled in obvious disbelief.

No one had touched her for three years. She had not wanted anyone to touch her. What kind of world was this to chance bringing a child into even if the father were willing to stay and help raise it? It was too bad, though. Obsidian could not know how attractive he was to her—young, probably younger than she was, clean, asking for what he wanted rather than demanding it. But none of that mattered. What were a few moments of pleasure measured against a lifetime of consequences?

He pulled her closer to him and for a moment she let herself enjoy the closeness. He smelled good — male and good. She pulled away reluctantly.

He sighed, reached toward the glove compartment. She stiffened, not knowing what to expect, but all he took out was a small box. The writing on it meant nothing to her. She did not understand until he broke the seal, opened the box, and took out a condom. He looked at her and she first looked away in surprise. Then she giggled. She could not remember when she had last giggled.

He grinned, gestured toward the back seat, and she laughed aloud. Even in her teens, she had disliked back seats of cars. But she looked around at the empty streets and ruined buildings, then she got out and into the back seat. He let her put the condom on him, then seemed surprised at her eagerness.

Sometime later, they sat together, covered by his coat, unwilling to become clothed near-strangers again just yet. He made rock-the-baby gestures and looked questioningly at her.

She swallowed, shook her head. She did not know how to tell him her children were dead.

He took her hand and drew a cross in it with his index finger, then made his baby-rocking gesture again.

She nodded, held up three fingers, then turned away, trying to shut out a sudden flood of memories. She had told herself that the children growing up now were to be pitied. They would run through the downtown canyons with no real memory of what the buildings had been or even how they had come to be. Today's children gathered books as well as wood to be burned as fuel. They ran through the streets chasing each other and hooting like chimpanzees. They had no future. They were now all they would ever be.

He put his hand on her shoulder and she turned suddenly, fumbling for his small box, then urging him to make love to her again. He could give her forgetfulness and pleasure. Until now, nothing had been able to do that. Until now, every day had brought her closer to the time when she would do what she had left home to avoid doing: putting her gun in her mouth and pulling the trigger.

She asked Obsidian if he would come home with her, stay with her.

He looked surprised and pleased once he understood. But he did not answer at once. Finally he shook his head as she had feared he might. He was probably having too much fun playing cops and robbers and picking up women.

She dressed in silent disappointment, unable to feel any anger toward him. Perhaps he already had a wife and a home. That was likely. The illness had been harder on men than on women—had killed more men, had left male survivors more severely impaired. Men like Obsidian were rare. Women either settled for less or stayed alone. If they found an Obsidian, they did what they could to keep him. Rye suspected he had someone younger, prettier keeping him.

He touched her while she was strapping her gun on and asked with a complicated series of gestures whether it was loaded.

She nodded grimly.

He patted her arm.

She asked once more if he would come home with her, this time using a different series of gestures. He had seemed hesitant. Perhaps he could be courted.

He got out and into the front seat without responding.

She took her place in front again, watching him. Now he plucked at his uniform and looked at her. She thought she was being asked something, but did not know what it was.

He took off his badge, tapped it with one finger, then tapped his chest. Of course.

She took the badge from his hand and pinned her wheat stalk to it. If playing cops and robbers was his only insanity, let him play. She would take him, uniform and all. It occurred to her that she might eventually lose him to someone he would meet as he had met her. But she would have him for a while.

He took the street map down again, tapped it, pointed vaguely northeast toward Pasadena, then looked at her.

She shrugged, tapped his shoulder then her own, and held up her index and second fingers tight together, just to be sure.

He grasped the two fingers and nodded. He was with her.

She took the map from him and threw it onto the dashboard. She pointed back southwest—back toward home. Now she did not have to go to Pasadena. Now she could go on having a brother there and two nephews—three right-handed males. Now she did not have to find out for certain whether she was as alone as she feared. Now she was not alone.

Obsidian took Hill Street south, then Washington west, and she leaned back, wondering what it would be like to have someone again. With what she had scavenged, what she had preserved, and what she grew, there was easily enough food for him. There was certainly room enough in a four-bedroom house. He could move his possessions in. Best of all, the animal across the street would pull back and possibly not force her to kill him.

Obsidian had drawn her closer to him and she had put her head on his shoulder when suddenly he braked hard, almost throwing her off the seat. Out of the corner of her eye, she saw that someone had run across the street in front of the car. One car on the street and someone had to run in front of it.

Straightening up, Rye saw that the runner was a woman, fleeing from an old frame house to a boarded-up storefront. She ran silently, but the man who followed her a moment later shouted what sounded like garbled words as he ran. He had something in his hand. Not a gun. A knife, perhaps.

The woman tried a door, found it locked, looked around desperately, finally snatched up a fragment of glass broken from the storefront window. With this she turned to face her pursuer. Rye thought she would be more likely to cut her own hand than to hurt anyone else with the glass.

Obsidian jumped from the car, shouting. It was the first time Rye had heard his voice—deep and hoarse from disuse. He made the same sound over and over the way some speechless people did, "Da, da, da!"

Rye got out of the car as Obsidian ran toward the couple. He had drawn his gun. Fearful, she drew her own and released the safety. She looked around to see who else might be attracted to the scene. She saw the man glance at Obsidian, then suddenly lunge at the woman. The woman jabbed his face with her glass, but he caught her arm and managed to stab her twice before Obsidian shot him.

The man doubled, then toppled, clutching his abdomen. Obsidian shouted, then gestured Rye over to help the woman.

Rye moved to the woman's side, remembering that she had little more than bandages and antiseptic in her pack. But the woman was beyond help. She had been stabbed with a long, slender, boning knife.

She touched Obsidian to let him know the woman was dead. He had bent to check the wounded man who lay still and also seemed dead. But as Obsidian looked around to see what Rye wanted, the man opened his eyes. Face contorted, he seized Obsidian's just-holstered revolver and fired. The bullet caught Obsidian in the temple and he collapsed.

It happened just that simply, just that fast. An instant later, Rye shot the wounded man as he was turning the gun on her.

And Rye was alone with three corpses.

She knelt beside Obsidian, dry-eyed, frowning, trying to understand why everything had suddenly changed. Obsidian was gone. He had died and left her—like everyone else.

Two very small children came out of the house from which the man and woman had run—a boy and girl perhaps three years old. Holding hands, they crossed the street toward Rye. They stared at her, then edged past her and went to the dead woman. The girl shook the woman's arm as though trying to wake her.

This was too much. Rye got up, feeling sick to her stomach with grief and anger. If the children began to cry, she thought she would vomit.

They were on their own, those two kids. They were old enough to scavenge. She did not need any more grief. She did not need a stranger's children who would grow up to be hairless chimps.

She went back to the car. She could drive home, at least. She remembered how to drive.

The thought that Obsidian should be buried occurred to her before she reached the car, and she did vomit.

She had found and lost the man so quickly. It was as though she had been snatched from comfort and security and given a sudden, inexplicable beating. Her head would not clear. She could not think.

Somehow, she made herself go back to him, look at him. She found herself on her knees beside him with no memory of having knelt. She stroked his face, his beard. One of the children made a noise and she looked at them, at the woman who was probably their mother. The children looked back at her, obviously frightened. Perhaps it was their fear that reached her finally.

She had been about to drive away and leave them. She had almost done it, almost left two toddlers to die. Surely there had been enough dying. She would have to take the children home with her. She would not be able to live with any other decision. She looked around for a place to bury three bodies. Or two. She wondered if the murderer were the children's father. Before the silence, the police had always said some of the most dangerous calls they went out on were domestic disturbance calls. Obsidian should have known that — not that the knowledge would have kept him in the car. It would not have held her back either. She could not have watched the woman murdered and done nothing.

She dragged Obsidian toward the car. She had nothing to dig with here, and no one to guard for her while she dug. Better to take the bodies with her and bury them next to her husband and her children. Obsidian would come home with her after all.

When she had gotten him onto the floor in the back, she returned for the woman. The little girl, thin, dirty, solemn, stood up and unknowingly gave Rye a gift. As Rye began to drag the woman by her arms, the little girl screamed, "No!"

Rye dropped the woman and stared at the girl.

"No!" the girl repeated. She came to stand beside the woman. "Go away!" she told Rye.

"Don't talk," the little boy said to her. There was no blurring or confusing of sounds. Both children had spoken and Rye had understood. The boy looked at the dead murderer and moved farther from him. He took the girl's hand. "Be quiet," he whispered.

Fluent speech! Had the woman died because she could talk and had taught her children to talk? Had she been killed by a husband's festering anger or by a stranger's jealous rage? And the children . . . they must have been born after the silence. Had the disease run its course, then? Or were these children simply immune? Certainly they had had time to fall sick and silent. Rye's mind leaped ahead. What if children of three or fewer years were safe and able to learn language? What if all they needed were teachers? Teachers and protectors.

Rye glanced at the dead murderer. To her shame, she thought she could understand some of the passions that must have driven him, whoever he was. Anger, frustration, hopelessness, insane jealousy . . . how many more of him were there -- people willing to destroy what they could not have?

Obsidian had been the protector, had chosen that role for who knew what reason. Perhaps putting on an obsolete uniform and patrolling the empty streets had been what he did instead of putting a gun into his mouth. And now that there was something worth protecting, he was gone.

She had been a teacher. A good one. She had been a protector, too, though only of herself. She had kept herself alive when she had no reason to live. If the illness let these children alone, she could keep them alive.

Somehow she lifted the dead woman into her arms and placed her on the back seat of the car. The children began to cry, but she knelt on the broken pavement and whispered to them, fearful of frightening them with the harshness of her long unused voice.

"It's all right," she told them. "You're going with us, too. Come on." She lifted them both, one in each arm. They were so light. Had they been getting enough to eat?

The boy covered her mouth with his hand, but she moved her face away. "It's all right for me to talk," she told him. "As long as no one's around, it's all right." She put the boy down on the front seat of the car and he moved over without being told to, to make room for the girl. When they were both in the car Rye leaned against the window, looking at them, seeing that they were less afraid now, that they watched her with at least as much curiosity as fear.

"I'm Valerie Rye," she said, savoring the words. "It's all right for you to talk to me."

The
Missionary's
Child

MAUREEN F. MCHUGH

ABOUT MAUREEN F. MCHUGH
AND
THE MISSIONARY'S CHILD

The Missionary's Child *was first published:*
Isaac Asimov's Science Fiction Magazine, *October 1962*

Although she had been writing only a few short years as of the publication of this anthology, Maureen F. McHugh has already discovered that her most serious competition is going to be herself. In 1993 China Mountain Zhang was up for the Hugo Award for best novel, while her story "Protection" was up for best novella. Other novels and stories will no doubt follow and a collection of her short stories is bound to make an appearance soon.

"Missionary's Child" is space opera with a distinctive 1990s sensibility. Though it delivers as much exotic action and locale as any story of the 1930s, Ms. McHugh's story is also deeply characterized, moves to a strong and memorable conclusion, and, like her novel, plays seriously with gender-bending.

The Missionary's Child

by MAUREEN F. MCHUGH

"**A**RE YOU BLIND?**"** the woman asks.

I'm looking right at her. "No," I say, "I'm foreign."

Affronted, the woman straightens up in a swirl of rose-colored robe and chouli scent, clutching her veil. Here in the islands, they don't see very many blond-haired, blue-eyed barbarians; people have asked me if I can see normally, if all northerners are blue-eyed. But this is the first time someone has ever asked me that. Maybe she thinks that my eyes are filmed, like the milky-white of old people.

She thought I was begging — I must look pretty tattered. I should have said yes, then I could go get something to drink, get out of the sun. I'm sitting down by the water. I'm broke, and I've been hungry for awhile, and I'm listless and a little stupid from the heat and lack of food. I feel fifty instead of thirty-one.

I should go back to the hiring area, wait around with a couple of other thugs for some sort of nasty work. I should oil my sword. It's a waste of time; no one needs a mercenary here, the Celestial Prince doesn't hire foreigners in his army.

But I don't want to go back. Up in the market, some yammerhead had been rattling on about our Cousins from the stars. The Cousins haven't come to the islands in any numbers yet, and I'll wager he's never met any. Listening to this stonker gave me a headache. Wouldn't he be surprised if he knew that the Cousins think of us all about the way the woman who asked me if I was blind thinks of me. They think that we're barbarians. They think that we're stupid because we call what they do magic instead of science. Or they feel sorry for us.

I know better than thinking bitter; time to head back to the market, see if anybody will hire a tokking foreigner to dig ditches or something.

But I sit, my head aching with hunger and heat, too stupid to do anything about it. And I'm still sitting there a dine later, the sun is still high in the sky baked the color of celedon. Not awake, not asleep.

I'm going to have to start selling my gear, the slow road to starvation.

I open my eyes and watch a ship come in on the deep green sea. It has red eyes rimmed in violet and violet sails; from far away, I can see a person wearing dark clothes that are all of one piece. A Cousin, standing at the prow. On the boathouse there is a light, star-magic, like a third eye, blind and white. Here in the islands, when you see Cousins, they are with the rich and the powerful.

What would the Cousin think if I spoke a little of his/her language? I only remember a few phrases. "Hello," "My name is," and a phrase from my lessons, "Husband and wife Larkin have three children, a boy and two girls." Would the Cousin be curious enough to take me aboard? Recognize the debt for what the Cousins did to my kin, help me get back to the mainland?

The ship docks, three guildmen and a Cousin disembark, and come down the quay. Southerners will stare at any foreigner, but they stare double at a Cousin, and who can blame them? The Cousin is a woman, with her hair uncovered, dressed like a man, but not looking like a man, no. That amuses me. Southern women pull their veils around their mouths and stop to watch.

She comes down the quay with studied indifference. I can understand that; what does one do when people stare day after day? Pretend not to notice.

She is tall, taller than me, but Cousins are usually tall, and I'm shorter than many men. She looks up directly at me while I am smiling by chance. The length of a man between us. I can see that she has light eyes.

"Hello," I say in the trade language of the Cousins. The word just pops out.

It stops her, though, like a roped stabros calf. "Hello," she says, in the same tongue. Consternation among the guildmen; two in dark red and one in green, all with shaven heads dull with the graphite sheen of stubble. "You speak lingua?" she says.

"A little," I say.

Then she rattles on, asking me something, "where da-da da-da da."

I shrug. Search my memory. My lessons in lingua were a lifetime ago; I remember almost nothing. Something comes to me that I often said in class: "I don't understand," I say, "I speak little."

"Where did you learn?" she says in Suhkhra, the language of the southerners. "Starport?"

"Up north." No real answer. Already I'm sorry I spoke. Bad *enough* to be a tokking foreigner; worse to be a spectacle. And my head aches, and I am tired from three days' lack of food

"Did you work at the port?" she asks, probing

"No," I say. Flat.

She frowns. Then, like a boat before bad winds, another direction. She speaks in my own language, the language of home. "What is your name?" She is careful and stilted in that one phrase.

"Jahn," I say, probably the commonest name among northern men. "What is yours?" I ask, without regard for courtesy.

"Sulia," she says. "Jahn, what kin-kind?"

"My kin are all dead," I say, "Jahn no-kin-kind."

But she shakes her head. "I'm sorry," she says in Suhkhra, "I don't understand. I speak very little Krerjian. What did you say your name was?"

"Jahn Sckarline," I say. And then, in my own tongue, "Go away." Because I am tired of her, tired of everything, tired of starving.

She isn't listening, and probably doesn't understand anyway. "Sckarline,' she says. "I thought everyone from Sckarline —"

"Is dead," I say. "Thank you, Cousin. I am pleased you keep my kinname." It's awkward to say in Suhkra. The Suhkra aren't good at irony anyway.

"Sulia Cousin," one of the guildmen says deferentially, "they are waiting for us."

She shakes him off. "I know about the settlement at Sckarline," she says to me. "You're a mission boy. You have an education. Why don't you work at a port?"

"And live in a *ghetto?*" The word comes back to me in her trade lingua. "With the other *natives?*"

"Isn't it better to get a tech job than to live like this?" she asks.

Better than a shantytown, I think, huddled together while the starships come screaming overhead, making one's teeth ache and one's goods rattle?

I look at her, she looks at me. I search my memory for the words in lingua, but my mind isn't sharp and it was too long ago. "Go away," I finally say in Suhkhra, "people are waiting."

She stands there hesitant, but the guildman does not. He strides forward and smacks me hard in the side of my head for my disrespect. I know better than to defend myself. Oh, Heth, my poor head! Southerners are a bad lot, they have no concept of a freeman.

So, having been knocked over, I stay still, with my nose near the stones, waiting to see if he'll hit me again, smelling dust, and sea, and the smell of myself, which is probably very distasteful to everyone else.

He crouches down, and I wait to be smacked again, empty-headed. But it isn't him, it's her. "What are you doing here?" she asks. She probably means how did you come here, but I find myself wondering, what am I doing here? Looking for work. Trying to get passage home. But home is gone, should never have existed in the first place.

What does any person do in a lifetime? I give her an answer out of the Proverbs. "Putting off death," I say. "Go away, before you complicate my task—you people have done enough to me."

She looks unhappy. Cousins are like that, a sentimental people. "If I could help you, I would," she says.

"I know," I say, "but your help would make me need you. And then I would be just one more local on one more backward world." Everywhere the Cousins go across the sky, it's the same. Wanji used to tell us about her people, about the Cousins. About other worlds like ours. Where two cultures meet, she said, one of them usually gives way.

The Cousin searches through her pockets, puts a coin, a rectangular silver piece, in the dust. I wait, not moving, until they go on.

I pick up the coin. A proud person would throw it after her. I'm not proud, I'm hungry. I take it.

In the market, it's rabbit and duck day—kids herding ducks with long switches, cages of rabbits for sale, hanging next to that cheap old staple, thekla lizard drying in strips. I dodge past tallgrass poles with craken-dyed cloth hanging startling yellow, and cut through between two vegetable stands. Next to the hiring area, they're grilling stabos jerky on sticks, and selling pineapple slices dipped in saltwater to make them sweeter.

I use the Cousin's silver to buy noodles and red peanut paste, spicy with proyakapiti, and I eat slowly. I'm three days empty of food, and if I eat too fast, I'll be sick. I learned about going without food during a campaign, when I first started soldiering. On the long walk to Bashtoy. I know all about the different kinds of hunger; the first sharp stabs of appetite, then the strong hunger, how your stomach hurts after awhile and then how you forget, and then how hunger comes back, like swollen joints in an old woman. And how it wears you down, how you become tired and stupid, and how then finally it leaves you altogether, and your jaw bone softens until your teeth rock in their sockets, and you have been hungry so long you don't know what it means anymore.

The yammerhead is on the other side of the hiring area, still going on about how the guilds monopolize the Cousins. How the guilds were nothing until ten years ago, when the Cousins came and brought magic, and then no one could trade without permission of the guild. I close my eyes feeling sleepy after food, and I can see the place where I grew up. I was born in Sckarline, a magic town. I remember the white houses, the power station where Ayuedesh taught boys to cook stabos manure and get swamp air from it, then turned that into power that sang through copper and made light. At night, we had light for three or four dine after sunset. Phrases in the lingua the Cousins speak, Appropriate Technology.

I am lost in Sckarline, looking for my mother, for kin. I see Trevin, and I follow him. He's way ahead, in leggings, in dark blue with fur on his shoulders. But the way he leads me is wrong, the buildings are burned, just blackened crossbeams jutting up, he is leading me toward —

"I'm looking for a musician." I jerk awake.

A flat-faced southerner waiting for hire says, "Musicians are over there." People who wait here are like me, looking for anything.

A portly man with a wine-colored robe says, "I'm looking for a musician who knows a little about swords."

"What kind of musician?" I ask. I always talk quietly, it's a failing, and the portly man doesn't hear me. He cocks his head.

"What kind of musician?" the flat-faced southerner repeats.

"Doesn't matter." The portly man shrugs, hawks so loudly it sounds as if he's clearing his tokking head, and spits.

Tokking southerners. They spit all the time, it drives me crazy. I hear them clear their throat, and I cringe and start looking to step out of the way. Heth knows I'm not squeamish, but they all do it, men, women, children.

"Sikha," the portly man offers. A sikha is a kind of southern lute, only they pick the strings on the neck as well as the ones on the body.

"How about flute?" I offer.

"Flute?" the portly man says. His robe is of good quality, but stained, and he has a negligent air. The robe gapes open to the belted waist, showing his smooth chest and the soft flab like breasts. "You play the flute, northerner?"

No, I want to say, I just wanted to help us think of some instruments. Patience. "Yes," I say, "I play the flute."

"Let's hear you."

So I dig out my wooden flute and make pretty sounds. He waves his hands and says, "How good are you with a sword?"

I dig into my pack and pull my cloak out of the bottom. It's crushed and wrinkled, people don't wear cloaks much in the south, but I spread it out so that he can see the badge on the breast: a white mountain against a red background. The survivors of the March to Bashtoy got them — that, and sixty gold coins. The sixty gold coins have been gone for a couple of years, but the badge is still on the cloak.

People murmur. The portly man doesn't know badges, he's not a fighter, but the flat-faced southerner does, and it shows in the sudden respect in his face, and that ends any question of my swordplay — which is fine because, badge or no badge, I'm only mediocre at swordplay. I'm just not tall enough or big enough.

Surviving a campaign is as much a matter of luck and cleverness as skill with a sword, anyway.

But that's why Barok hires me to play flute at his party.

He offers me twenty In silver, which is too much money. He pays me five right away. He must want me to be a bodyguard, and that means that he thinks that he'll *need* one. I like guard duty, or, better than that, something like being a sailor. But I didn't realize until I jumped ship that, here in the Islands, not just *anybody* can be a sailor. I shouldn't take this job, it sounds like trouble, but I've got to do something.

All boat trade except local fishing is controlled by the four Navigation Orders, all the Cousins's magic by the two Metaphysical Orders. I don't pay much attention to Magic; I'm just a whistler, a mercenary. I have three spells myself (but simple ones), that Ayuedesh Engineer, the old Cousin, wired into my skull when we knew that Scathalos High-on was going to attack Sckarline. A lot of good spells did us in the end, with all of two twenties of us and four Cousins, everybody in Sckarline who could fight at all, against the Scathalos High-on, Kin-leader's army.

I am supposed to report my spells to the Metaphysical Orders, but I'm not *that* stupid. Just stupid enough to come *here*.

A man who hires a sword to play music must have unusual parties and I wait to hear what he wants of me.

"You'll need better clothes," he says. "And bathe, would you?"

I promise to meet him in the market in three dine or so. And then I finger the coppers left from the Cousin's silver and the five silver coins he's given me. First I go to the bath house, and I pay for a private bath. I hate bath houses. It is not, as the southerners all think, that northerners hate to bathe; I just find bath houses . . . uncomfortable. Even in a private room, I strip furtively, keeping my back to the door. But Heth, it is good to be clean, to not itch! I even wash my clothes, wring them out as best I can. The water runs black, and I have to put on wet clothes, but I imagine they'll dry fast enough.

Back at the market, I find a stall that sells used clothes. I go through piles until I find a black jacket with a high neck, fairly clean. And I have my hair trimmed.

I use much of my three dine and about half of the Cousin's silver, but when the time comes, I am back at the hiring area, cleaner, neater, with Barok's five silver still in my pocket, and ready to earn the other fifteen silver. And I don't wait long for my employer, who looks me over and spits, by which he means I have passed inspection.

I assume from his lavish way with silver and his manner that we will head to one of the better parts of town. After all, a lot of silver went into the feeding of that smooth belly and flacid chest. But we head down toward where the river meets the ocean. It's a wide, tame river, enclosed by stone walls and arched — so they claim — by fourteen stone bridges. But this far down, all poor. The closer we get, the more rank it smells. We go down a stone stairs to the water, past women washing clothes, and out onto a small city of permanently moored boats.

The sunbleached boats have eyes painted on the prows, even though they never go anywhere. They're homes to families, each living the length of my arm from the next, all piled up together with brown dusty chickens, laundry flapping, brown children running from boat to boat, wearing nothing but a yellow gourd on a rope tied around their waist (if they fall overboard, the gourd floats, holding them up until some adult can fish them out of the water).

I've never been out here before; it's a maze, and it would be worth my life to step on these boats alone. Even walking with Barok, I feel the men's eyes follow me with hard gazes. We cross from boat to boat, they rise and fall under our feet. The boats bob, the green river stinks of garbage and rotting fish, and my poor head swirls a bit. I've been here two and half years, I speak the language, but only southerners can live piled up on top of each other this way.

Out near where the middle is kept clear for river traffic, we climb a ramp up onto a larger boat, maybe the length of five men head to foot, the home of Barok. A tiny brown woman wrapped in blue is shoving charcoal into a tampis jar, a jar with a place in the bottom to put fuel to heat the stuff cooking in the top. It's a big tampis jar. I smell meat; there's smooth creamy yogurt in a blue and white bowl next to her. I'm hungry again. She glances up, and looks back down. Barok ignores her and steps over a neat pyramid of pale lavender boxfruit, one split to show the purple meat. As I step over them, I reach down and hook one.

"Hie!" she snaps, "that is not for you!"

Barok doesn't even look back, so I wink at her and keep walking.

"Yellow-haired dog-devil!" she shrieks. I follow Barok down into the hold, now a good sized apartment, if rather warm, and get my first surprise. There's a young girl, bare-armed and bare-haired, sitting at the table, drawing with brush and paper.

"Shell-sea," Barok growls.

So intent she is that she ignores him for a moment, and I get a chance to see what she's drawing — a long squiggling line that she's tracing as if every twist and curve has meaning. Which it clearly doesn't, since it meanders all over the page.

"Shell-sea! Take it in the back!"

She says sullenly, "It's too hot back there," and then looks up. I'm blond and sunburned, quite a sight for a southern girl who has probably never seen someone who didn't have dark hair in her life. She stares at me as she gathers her papers, and then walks to the back, her eyebrows knit into a dark line, clumping her feet heavily, like someone whose wits aren't right.

Barok watches her go as if he doesn't like the taste of something. "My guests will be here later. Wait on deck."

"What am I supposed to do?" I ask.

"Play music and watch the guests," he says.

"That's all?" I ask. "You're paying me twenty in silver to watch?" He starts to answer sharply, and I say, "If you tell me what to watch for, I might do a better job."

"You watch for trouble," he says. "That's enough."

This is bad, my stomach knows. An employer who doesn't trust his guests or his employees is like a dog with thrum — *everyone* gets bitten. I could quit, hand him back the five silvers, take the boxfruit, and go. I still have a little less than half of the Cousin's silver; I can do fine on that for a week, if I sleep down on the docks.

"There's food on the stern deck; help yourself, and ignore the woman if she complains."

So I keep the job. Stomach-thinking. Heth says in the Proverbs that our life hinges on little things. That's certainly true for me.

I eat slowly and carefully; I know that if I eat too much, I'll be sleepy. But I fill my pack with boxfruit, pigeon's egg dumplings, and red peanuts. Especially red peanuts — a person can live a long time on red peanuts. While I'm eating, Shell-sea comes up and sits on the stern to watch me. As I said, I'm not tall, most men have a bit of reach on me, and she's nearly my height. She's wearing a school uniform, the dark red of one of the orders, and her thick hair is tied back with a red cord. The uniform would be fine on a young girl, but only emphasizes that she's not a child. She's too old for bare arms, for uncovered hair, too old for the cord that belts the robe high under her small breasts. She is probably just past menses.

After I eat, I use a bucket to rinse my hands and face. After awhile she says "Why don't you take off your shirt when you wash?"

"You are a forward child," I say.

She has the grace to blush, but she still looks expectant. She wants to see how much hair I have on my chest. Southerners don't have much body hair.

"I've already bathed today," I say. Southerners waiting to see if I look like a hairy termit make me very uncomfortable. "Why do you have such an unusual name?" I ask.

"It's not a name, it's a nickname." She stares at her bare toes and they curl in embarrassment. I thought she was a bit of a half-wit, but away from Barok she's quick enough, and light on her feet.

I wonder if she's his fancy girl. Most southerners don't take a pretty girl until they already have a first wife.

"Shell-sea? Why do they call you that?"

"Not 'Shell-sea'," she says, exasperated, "*Chalcey*. What kind of name is 'Shell-sea'? My name is Chalcedony. I bet you don't know what that is."

"It's a precious stone," I say.

"How did you know?"

"Because I've been to the temple of Heth in Thelahckre," I say, "and the Shesket-lion's eyes are two chunks of chalcedony." I rinse my bowl in the bucket, then dump the water over the side; the soap scums the green water like oil. I'd been to a lot of places, trying to find the right place. The islands hadn't proven to be any better than the city of Lada on the coast. And Lada no better than Gibbun, which was supposed to be full of work, but the work was all for the new star port that the Cousins were building. My people forgetting their kin, living in slums. And Gibbun no better than Thelahckre.

"Why don't you have a beard?" she asks. Southerners can't grow beards until they're old, and then only long, bedraggled, wispy white things. They believe that all northerner men have them down to their belts.

"Because I don't," I say, irritated. "Why do you live with Barok?"

"He's my uncle."

We both stop then to watch a ship come down the river to the bay. Like the one the Cousin came in on, it has red eyes rimmed in violet, and violet sails. "'Temperance,'" I read from the side.

Chalcey glances at me out of the corner of her eye.

I smile, "Yes, some northerners can even read."

"It's a ship of the Brothers of Succor," she says. "I go to the school of the Sisters of Clarity."

"And who are the Sisters of Clarity?" I ask.

"I thought you knew everything," she says archly. When I don't rise to this, she says, "The Sisters of Clarity are the sister order to the Order of Celestial Harmony."

"I see," I say, watching the ship glide down the river.

Testily, she adds. "Celestial Harmony is the first Navigation Order."

"Do they sail to the mainland?"

"Of course," she says, patronizing.

"What does it cost to be a passenger? Do they ever hire cargo-handlers or bookkeepers or anything like that?" I know the answer, but I can't help myself from asking.

She shrugs, "I don't know, I'm a student." Then, sly again, "I study drawing."

"That's wonderful," I mutter.

Passage out of here is my major concern. No one can work on a ship who isn't a member of a Navigational Order, and no order is likely to take a blond-haired northerner with a sudden vocation. Passage is expensive .

Even food doesn't keep me from being depressed.

The guests begin to arrive just after sunset, while the sky is still indigo in the west. I'm in the hold with two food servers. I'm sweltering in my jacket, they're (both women) serene in their blue robes. I play simple songs. Barok comes by and says to me, "Sing some northern thing."

"I don't sing," I say.

He glares at me, but I'm not about to sing, and he can't replace me now, so that's that. But I feel guilty, so I try to be flashy, playing lots of trills, and some songs that I think might sound strange to their ears.

It's a small party, only seven men. Important men, because five boats clunk against ours. Or rich men. It's hard for me to make decisions about southerners, they act differently and I don't know what it means. For instance, southerners never say "no." So at first, I decided that they were all shifty bastards, but eventually I learned how to tell a "yes" that meant *no* from a "yes" that meant *yes*. It's not so hard — if you ask a shopkeeper if he can get you ground proyakapiti, and he says, "yes," then he *can*. If he giggles nervously and then says "yes," he's embarrassed, which means that he doesn't want you to know that he *isn't* able to get it, so you smile and say that you will be back for it later. He knows you are lying, you know he knows; you are both vastly relieved.

But these men smile and shimmer like oil, and Barok smiles and shimmers like oil, and I don't know what's cast, only that if tension were food, I could cut thick slices out of the air and dine on it.

There are no women except servers. I don't know if there are ever women at southern parties, because this is my first one. If a southern man toasts another, he cannot decline the toast without looking like a gelded stabos, so they drink a great deal of wine. After awhile, it seems to me that a man in green, ferret-thin, and a man in yellow are working together to get Barok drunk. If one of them toasts Barok, a bit later the other one does too. Barok would be drinking twice as much as they are, except that Barok himself toasts his guests, especially the ferret, a number of times, so it's hard to say. Besides, Barok is portly and can drink a great deal of wine.

But the servers are finished and cleaning up on deck, and Barok is near purple himself when he finally raps on the table for silence. I stop playing, and tap the bare sword under the serving table behind me with my foot, just to know where it is.

Barok clears a space on the long thin banquet table and claps his hands. Chalcey comes in, dressed in a robe the color of her school uniform but with her arms and hair decently covered. The effect is nice, or would be if she didn't have that sullen, half-wit face she wears around her uncle.

She puts two rolled papers on the table, and then draws her veil close around her chin and crouches down like a proper girl. Barok opens one of the rolls, and I crane my head before the men close around it. All I get is a glimpse of is one of Chalcey's squiggly-line drawings, with some writing on it. The men murmur. The man in yellow says, "What is this?"

"Galgor coast," Barok points, "Lesian and Cauldor Islands, the Liliana Strait."

Charts? Navigation charts of the Islands? How could Barok have gotten . . . or rather, how could Chalcey have drawn . . She is studying drawing with an Order though, isn't she? *Chalcey* drew the charts? But the Cousins have sold magic to the Navigational Orders to make sure students *can't* take out so much as a piece of paper. How does she get them out of the school?

The ferret spits on the wooden floor and I wince. "What else have you got?" the ferret asks, brusque, rude.

"Only the Liliana Straits and the Hekkhare Cove," Barok says.

"Hekkhare!" the man in blue says, "I can buy *that* off any fisherman."

"Ah, but you can compare this chart with your own charts of Hekkhare to see how my source is. And there are more coming, I can assure you." Barok fairly oozes.

"These look as if they were drawn by an amateur," ferret says. Chalcey sticks out her lower lip and beetles her eyebrows. She needs a mother around to tell her not to do that.

"If you want pretty, go to the market and buy a painting," Barok says.

"I'm not interested in artistry, I'm interested in competence," ferret snaps. "What's to say you didn't copy Hekkhare from some fisherman?" A black market in navigation charts! Maybe Barok would be able to steer me to someone who smuggled, or whatever they did with them. I might be able to work my passage out of here. "I'd like to know a little more about this source," ferret says, tapping his teeth.

"It's within one of the Orders," Barok says, "that's all I can tell you."

Yellow robe says, "You're telling me that a member of the order would sell charts? That they can counter the spellbind?"

"I didn't say a 'member of the order,' " Barok says, "I said someone *within* the order."

"This stinks," ferret says, and silently I agree.

Barok shrugs. "If you don't want them, don't take them." But the dome of his forehead is slick and shining in the lamplight.

Ferret looks at Barok. The ferret is the power in this room; the others wait on him, Barok talks to him, yellow is his flunky. These men came in boats, boats that *go* somewhere in these islands mean money, and maybe some influence with the Navigational Order. And Barok — Barok lives in a slum. A two-bit nothing trying to sell to the big lizards. Oh, Heth, I am in trouble!

Ferret contemplates, and the others wait. "All right, I'll take these to verify their validity. If these prove accurate, we'll see about the next set."

"No," Barok says, "I'm giving you Hekkhare; you pay me the 200 for Liliana."

"What if I just take the charts?" ferret asks.

"You don't know my source," Barok says, desperate.

"So? Who *else* would you sell them to? The Orders?" the ferret says, bored.

"Two hundred for Liliana," Barok says stubbornly.

Ferret rolls the charts up. "I don't think so," he says blandly.

My knees turn to water. I've fought in battle, scared off a thief in a warehouse once, but never done anything like this. Still, I start to crouch for my sword.

"Tell your barbarian to be still," ferret snaps. Yellow has a knife, so do the others. I don't need to be told again.

"These aren't free!" Barok says, "I have expenses, I —, I owe people money, Sterler. I don't pay people, you'll never get another chart! They're good, I swear they're good!"

"We'll negotiate the next ones," the ferret says, and nods at the rest. They rise and start to go.

I know that Barok is going to lunge, although it is a tokking stupid thing to do. But he does it, his hands hooked to claw at ferret. I think he only wants the charts, that he can't bear to see them go, but yellow reacts instantly. I see the flash of metal from under his robe, but I don't think Barok does. It isn't a good blow, they are all drunk, and Barok is a fleshy man. The knife handle stands out of his belly at about his liver, and Barok staggers back against the table. For a moment, he doesn't know about the knife — sometimes a knife-wound feels just like a punch.

"You can't have it," he says, "I'll tell them about you!" Then he sees the knife, and the wine-colored stain on his dark robe, and his mouth opens, pink and wet and helpless.

"Find out his source," the ferret says.

Chalcey is staring, blank-faced. I do not want her to see. I remember what it is like to see.

Yellow robe takes the knife handle and holds on to it, his face only a foot or so from Barok's. I smell shit. Barok looks at him, his face slack with disbelief, and starts to blubber. Some men's minds snap when they die.

"Who gets them for you?" yellow robe asks.

Arterial blood, dark and mixed with stomach blood, pumps out around the knife. Barok is silent. Maybe Barok is refusing to betray his niece, but I think the truth is that he has lost his wits. He has certainly voided his bowels. When yellow robe twists the knife, he screams, and then blubbers some more, his saliva not yet bloodied. He wants to go to his knees, but yellow robe has the knife handle, and Barok's hung on that blade like meat on a hook.

Chalcey is crouched, wrapped in her veil. She edges backward away from the men, her hands behind her, scooting backward like a crab until she bumps into my legs and stifles a little scream.

Ferret turns to us. "What do you know?"

I shrug casually, or as casually as I can. "I was hired today; he wouldn't tell me what he hired me for."

He looks down at Chalcey. I say, "He hired her right after he hired me."

Barok begins to say, over and over again, "Stop it, stop it, please stop it," monotonously, his hands making little clutching motions at his belly, but afraid of the knife.

"Tell me your source," yellow robe says.

Barok doesn't seem to understand. "Stop it, please stop it," he whimpers. *Die,* I think. Die before you say anything, you fat old man!

"Tok it," ferret says, "You've ruined it."

I whisper to Chalcey, "Scream and try to run up the stairs."

She rolls her eyes at me, but doesn't move.

Yellow robe shouts in Barok's face, "Barok! Listen to me!" He slaps the dying man. "Who is your source? You want it to stop? Tell me your source!"

"Help me," Barok whispers. There is blood in his mouth, now. The shadows from the lamps are hard, the big red-robed belly is in the light, and he is starting to spill flesh and bowels. The smell is overwhelming; one of the men turns and vomits, and adds that to the stench.

"Tell me where you get the charts, we'll get you a healer," yellow robe says. A lie, it's too late for a healer. But a dying man has nothing to lose by believing a lie. His eyes flicker toward Chalcey. Does he even know what is happening, understand what they are demanding? He licks his lips as if about to speak. I can't let him speak. So I whistle, five clear discordant notes, to waken one of the spells in my skull, the one that eats power, light and heat, and all the lights go out.

Black. Star-magic is easy to do, hard to engineer.

"TOK!" someone shouts in the dark, and Barok screams, a high, white noise. Things fall, I push Chalcey toward the stairs and grab my sword. I'm almost too frightened to move myself; maybe if it wasn't for Chalcey, I wouldn't, but sometimes responsibility lifts me above my true nature.

I collide with someone in the dark, slap at their face with my sword, and feel something hook in my jacket, tear at my shirt and the bindings I wear under it, then burn in my side. Then the person is gone. Ferret is screaming, "The stairs! Block the stairs!" when I fall over the bottom step.

The darkness only lasts a handful of heartbeats. It's a whistler spell, better against real power like the Cousins's lights then against natural things like a lamp, and it always makes me tired later. I turn at the stairs just as the lights come back. Blinded for a moment, I slap with my sword for the flame and knock it flying. Burning oil sprays across the room, I see blue robe cover his face, and, gods help him, poor Barok squirming on the floor.

The boat is tinder dry, and instantly the pools of oil from the lamp are full of licking blue flames. I run up the stairs. Chalcey is standing — not by the gangplank but next to the rail. My pack is there, and in the pack the cloak with the badge, and my chain vest and bracers — all I own in the world. I go for the girl and the pack, my shield arm clenched against my burning side. Ferret and the others will come boiling out of the hold like digger bees at any moment. I look down over the railing and see one of the sailboats, a soft Cousins's light clipped to the mast, and, In the glow, a green-robed adolescent with a cleric's shaven head, looking up at me. I grab Chalcey's arm and shout, "Jump!" and we land on top of the poor bastard, Chalcey's shrieking and my oomph! drowning the boy's bleat of surprise. Chalcey tumbles, but I have aimed truer, breaking his arm and probably his collar bone, so that he lies stunned and wide-eyed. I pitch him out of the boat. He is struggling in the water as I shove us off. I hope to Heth he can swim; I can't.

Our boat has a simple, single sail; it's a pleasure boat rather than a real fisherman's boat, but it will have to do. I run the sail up awkwardly. The wind will drive us downriver, toward the harbor. I don't see the boats of the others.

There is no pursuit. I think that ferret and the others have cut across the gangplank rather than make for the sailboats. I crouch next to the tiller and gingerly explore my injury with my fingers, a long flat scrape that crossed the ribs before the shirt and bindings and jacket hung it up. It bleeds freely, but it's not deep.

Chalcey curls in the prow of the boat, looking back toward her uncle's boat. The fire must have eaten the wood in huge bites. When we reach the bridge, I look back and see that the boat has been cut away and floats free in the river, burning bright and pouring out black, oily smoke. Two sailboats skitter away like dragonflies, silhouettes against the flames. Then we are enveloped in black smoke and ash which hides the boat from us, and hides us from everyone else.

Coughing and hacking, and, Heth forgive me, spitting, I keep us in the smoke as lone as I can.

When we are almost out of the harbor, Chalcey asks, "Where are we going?"

"I don't know," I say. "I wish we had one of your charts."

It's a clear night, we have a brisk breeze and no moon yet. A good night to escape. I follow the coast, away from the city. On the shore, dogs bark at us, and to each other, distant and lonely. The sound chains along the coast as we sail.

"Was that magic?" Chalcey says.

"Was what magic," I say absently. I'm tired and not feeling well; it is painful to cough and spit ash and soot when your side is cut open.

"When it got dark. When you whistled."

I nod in the darkness, then realize she can't see it. "Yes, that was a little magic."

"Are you a mage?"

Do I *look* like a mage? Would I be living this way if I could smelt metal, and make starstuff in bright colors, and machines and lights? "No, littleheart," I say, talking sweet because my thoughts are not nearly so patient, "I'm just a whistler. A fighter with no money and only a little skill."

"Do you think they'll get a healer for my uncle?"

No answer to give but the truth. "Chalcey, your uncle is dead."

She doesn't say anything for a long time, and then she starts to cry. It's chilly, and she's tired and frightened. It doesn't hurt her to cry. Maybe I cry a little, too; it wouldn't be the first time.

We bob along, the waves going *chop, chop, chop* against the prow of the little boat. Dogs bark, to us and to each other. Along our left, the lights from the city are fewer and fewer, the houses darker and smaller. It smells like broom trees out here, not city. In the wake of our little sailboat, craken phosphoresce. I wonder, since their light is blue, why is craken dye yellow?

Chalcey speaks out of the dark, "Could we go to my grandmother?"

"I don't know, sweet, where is your grandmother?"

"Across the Liliana Strait. On Lesian."

"If I knew where it was, I could try, even without a chart, but I'm a foreigner, littleheart."

"I can draw a chart. I drew those charts."

She sounds like a little girl. I smile tiredly into the darkness. "But I don't have anything for you to copy."

"I don't need to copy," she says. "They're in my head. If I have drawn a chart, even once, I never forget it. That's why my Uncle Barok brought me to the Order to go to school. But we've only practiced with Hekkhare and now Liliana Strait."

"So you drew those charts from your head?" I ask.

"Of course," she tosses her hair, her veil around her shoulders, and I can see her against the sky, just for the moment the imperious and sly girl who tried to impress the northern barbarian. "Everybody thinks that the charts are safe, all the paper and everything is spellbound. But I don't carry any papers or anything; it's all in my head."

"Chalcey," I breathe. "Can you draw one?"

"We don't have any paper, and it's dark."

"We'll land in a few hours and get some sleep. Then you can use my knife and draw it on the bottom of the boat."

"On the bottom of the boat?" She is diffident.

But I'm elated. Two people hiding from the rest of the island, in a small sailboat not meant for the open sea, going on a young girl's memory of a chart. But it's better than *Barok's* choices.

We have a fair breeze, the little sailboat is quiet except for the slap of the sail. The water is close, right at my hand. Chalcey says she's cold. I tell her to dig my cloak out of my pack and see if she can get some sleep.

I think she sleeps awhile. I keep pushing us on, thinking to go a little farther before we rest, passing places to pull the boat up, until I see the line of gray that means dawn and take us into a stream that cuts down to the ocean.

"Chalcey," I say, "when the boat stops, jump out and pull."

We come aground, and I try to stand up, and nearly fall over. My legs are numb from crouching, and my side has stiffened in the night.

"What's wrong?" Chalcey says, holding the prow to get out.

"Nothing," I say, "be careful when you get out of the boat."

The cold water is up to my waist and makes me gasp, but at the prow Chalcey is in water only to her shins. I grit my teeth and push, sliding against the uneven bottom, and she pulls, and together we get the boat well aground. I lash it to a tree, the tide is still coming in and I don't want to lose it, and then I grab my pack and stumble up the bank.

I should check the area, but I ache and I'm exhausted, so tired. I'm a little dizzy, so I promise myself I'll only rest for a minute. I prop my head against the pack and close my eyes. The world swirls. . . .

Some tokking hero, I think, and then laugh. That's one quality to which I have never aspired.

We're in heavy trees, tall pale yellow fronds of broom trees, heavily tasseled at this time of year. I'm covered with chukka bites, and the cut in my side is hot; I can feel my pulse beating in it.

There's no sign of Chalcey.

I lever myself painfully up on my elbow and listen. Nothing. Could she have wandered off and gotten lost?

"Chalcey," I hiss.

No answer.

"Chalcey!" I say, louder.

"Here!" comes a voice from over the bank, and then her head pops up floating above the soft lemon brush as if it had been plopped on a bush. Maybe I'm feverish.

"Are you in the water?" I ask.

"No," she says, "I'm in the boat. What's your name, anyway?"

"Jahn," I say.

"I took your knife, but you didn't wake up. Are you —" she hesitates, wide-eyed, and my heart lurches, "I mean, is your hurt bad?"

"No," I say, attempting to sit up naturally and failing.

"I drew a chart in the bottom of the boat, and then I used mud to make the lines darker." She shakes her head, "Drawing with a knife isn't the same as drawing with a pen."

She comes up on the bank, and we breakfast on boxfruit and red peanuts out of my pack. Breakfast and water improve my spirits immensely. I check Chalcey's drawing. She clenches her hands nervously while I look at it. As soon as a wave puts a little water in the bottom of the boat, the mud will wash out of the lines, and I have no way of judging how accurate it might be anyway, but I tell her it looks wonderful.

To hide her pleasure, she turns her head and spits matter-of-factly into the stream. I wince, but don't say anything.

We have nothing to store water in.

"How far is it to Lesian?" I ask.

She thinks it's about two days. "Jahn," she says, self-conscious about my name, "where did you learn your magic?"

"One of the Cousins put copper and glass in the bones of my head," I say. Not exactly true, but close enough.

That silences questions for awhile.

We get some good drinks of water and relieve ourselves, and maybe she prays to her deities, I don't know. Then we raise our pineapple-green sail, and we are off.

She chatters awhile about school. I like listening to her chatter. When it gets hot at midday, I have her spread my cloak across the prow and crawl into the shade underneath it. I stay with the tiller and wish for a hat. I've been browned by the sun, but the light off the green water is blinding and bright, and my nose suffers.

She sleeps during the heat of the day, and I nod. We are headed for a promontory which marks where we cut across the strait. In the afternoon, we have some bruised boxfruit out of my pack, which helps our thirst a bit. The way west is suddenly blocked by a spit of land; if Chalcey's drawing can be trusted, that's our promontory. Chalcey's chart indicates that it's not good to go ashore here, otherwise I'd stop for fresh water. We head for open sea, and I pray that the breeze holds up. I'm stiff, and tacking accurately all the way across is probably beyond my navigational skills.

I'm thirsty; Chalcey must be, too. She doesn't complain, but she gets quiet. The farther we go into the strait, the smaller the land behind us gets; the smaller the land, the quieter she gets. Once I ask her what the crossing was like when she came to live with her uncle. "It was a big boat," is all she'll say.

I'm lightheaded from the sun and thirst and fever by the time evening comes, and the cool is a relief. The sun goes down with the sudden swiftness of the south. I dig the pigeon's egg dumplings out of my pack, but they're too salty and just make me thirstier. Chalcey is hungry, though, and eats hers and half of mine.

"Jahn?" she says.

"Yes?"

"The Cousins — why do they call them that?"

"Because we are all kin," I say. "It is like in my home, when a place gets too big, and there isn't enough land to let all the stabos graze, part of the kin go somewhere else, and start a new home. Our many times elders were the Cousins. The stars are like islands for them. Some came here to live, but there was a war and the ships no longer came, and our elders' ships grew too old, and we forgot about the Cousins except for stories. Now they have found us again."

"And they help us?" she asks.

"Not really," I say. "They help the high-ons, mostly."

"What are 'high-ons'?" she asks. Southern doesn't have a word for high-ons, so I always just use the two southern words.

"High-ons, the old men who run things and have silver. Or the guilds, they are like high-ons."

"Were you a high-on?" she asks.

I laugh, which hurts my side. "No, littleheart," I say. "I am the unlucky child of unlucky parents. They believed that some of the Cousins would help us, would teach us. But the high-ons, they don't like it if anyone else has strength. So they sent an army and killed my kin. Things were better before the Cousins came."

"The Order says that the Cousins are good; they bring gifts."

"We *pay* for those gifts," I say. "With craken dye and ore and land. And with our own ways. Anywhere the Cousins come, things get bad."

It gets darker. Chalcey wraps herself in my cloak, and I hunch over the tiller. It isn't that the boat needs much sailing; there's a light wind and the sea is blessedly calm (Someone seems to favor us, despite our attack on the green-robed boy to get this boat), but the boat is too small for me to go anywhere else, so I sit at the tiller.

The spray keeps the back of my left shoulder damp, and the breeze seems to leach the warmth out of me. My teeth start chattering.

"Chalcey?"

"What?" she murmurs sleepily from the prow.

"I am feeling a bit under, littleheart. Do you think you could sit with me and we could share the cloak?"

I can feel her hesitation in the dark. She's afraid of me, and that pains me. It's funny, too, considering. "I don't want anything other than warmth,' I say gently.

She feels her way slowly from the prow. "It's *your* cloak," she says, "you can have it if you want."

"I think we can share it." I say. "Sit next to me, the tiller will be between us, and you can lean against me and sleep."

Gingerly, she sits down next to me, the boat rocking gently with her movements, and throws the cloak around our shoulders. She touches my arm on the tiller and jerks back. "You're hot," she says. Then she surprises me by touching my forehead. "You have a fever!"

"Don't worry about it," I say, oddly embarrassed. "Just sit here." She curls against me, and, after a few minutes, she leans her head on my shoulder. Her hair smells sweet. It's soothing to have her there. I try to keep the constellation southerners call the Crown to my right.

"How old are you?" she asks.

"Thirty-one," I say.

"That's not so old."

I laugh.

"Well," she is defensive, "you have white hair, but your face isn't old."
Sometimes I feel very old, and never more than now.

I jerk awake from scattered dreams of being back on Barok's boat. It's
dawn. Chalcey stirs against my shoulder and settles again. I think about the
sea, about our journey. Celestial navigation is not my strong point; I hope
we haven't drifted too much. I hope that Chalcey's chart is good, and I wonder
how much Barok will get paid for a boat with a chart carved on it, even if the
chart isn't very good, but blue flames lick the chart, and I'm on Barok's boat
again. . . .

I jerk awake. My fever feels low; because it's morning, I'm certain. I try to
open my pack without disturbing Chalcey, but she's asleep against my right
shoulder, and I'm awkward with my left hand and my side is stiff, so after a
moment she straightens up. We have five boxfruit left, so we split one. I'm
too thirsty for red peanuts, but Chalcey eats a few.

As the sun climbs, so does my fever, and I start dreaming even when my
eyes are open. At one point, Trevin is in the boat with us, sitting there in his
blue jerkin with the gray fur low on the shoulders, and I must be talking to
him, because Chalcey says, "Who is Trevin?"

I blink and lean over the side and splash cold water on my sunburned face.
When I sit up, I'm dizzy from the blood rushing to my head, but I know where
I am. "Trevin was a friend," I say. "He's dead now."

"Oh," she says, and adds, with the callousness of youth, "How did he die?"

How did Trevin die? I have to think. "The flux," I say. "We were marching
to Bashtoy, we were retreating, Trevin and I had decided to fight against
Scalthalos High-on since he'd burned out Sckarline. It was winter, and we
didn't have much to eat, and the people who got sick, many of them died." I
add, "I joined the fight because of Trevin." I don't add, "I was in love."

When it gets hot, Chalcey soaks her veil in water and covers my head with
it. I clutch the tiller. It seems that I am not sailing the boat so much as it is
sailing me. She doles out the boxfruit, too, peeling them and splitting the
purple segments.

"I think," she says, "that maybe I should look at your side."

"No," I say.

"Don't worry," she says, moving toward me in the boat.

"No," I snap.

"I could put some cool seawater on it," she says. "Saltwater is good for an
injury."

"I don't take off my shirt," I say. I'm irrational and I know it, but I'm not
going to take off my shirt. Not when someone is around. We were finally in
Bashtoy and almost everyone I knew was dead, and the MilitiaMaster said,
"Boy, what's your name?" and I didn't know that he was talking to me. "Boy!"
he shouted, "what's your name!" and I stuttered "Jahn, sir." "We'll call you
Jahn-the-clever," he said, "you're in my group now," and the others laughed,
and after that I was Jahn-the-clever until they discovered that I was really

clever, but I still wasn't going to take off my shirt.

My thoughts run like squirrels in a cage, and sometimes I talk out loud. Trevin comes back. He asks, "Would you rather have grown up anywhere but Sckarline?"

Chalcey soaks her veil in water and tries to keep my face cool.

"Wanji taught us about the cities," I say, "and she was right. I've been there, Trevin." My voice is high. "Wherever the Cousins come, they use us, they live like Scalthalos High-on, and we clean their houses and are grateful for light and glz stick on Sixth-day night. People don't care about kin anymore, they don't care about anything. Wanji told us about culture clash, that the weaker culture dissolves."

"Wanji and Aneal, Ayuedesh and Kumar, they dedicated their lives to helping us," Trevin says.

"Aneal *apologized* to me, Trevin!" I say. "She apologized for the terrible wrong they had done! She said it would be better if they never came!"

"I know," he said.

"Jahn," Chalcey says. "Jahn, there's nobody here but *me!* Talk to me! Don't die!" She is crying. Her veil is wet, and so cold it takes my breath away.

Trevin didn't know. I never told him about Aneal apologizing, I never told anyone. I blink and he wavers, and I blink and blink and he goes away. "You're not Trevin," I say, "I'm arguing with myself."

It's bright and hot.

I have my head on my arm.

The sky is lavender and red, and there is a dark stripe across the water that I can't make go away, no matter how hard I blink. I think that the fever is making my vision go, or that the sun has made me blind, until Chalcey, crying, says that it is Lesian.

There is no place to land, so we head up the coast northeast until we come to a river. "Go up here!" Chalcey says. "I know this place! I know that marker!" She is pointing to a pile of stone. "My grandmother lives up here!"

The night comes down around us before we see a light, like a cooking fire. I call instructions to shift the sail in a cracked voice; Chalcey has quick hands, thank Heth.

I run the boat aground, and Chalcey leaps out, calling and pulling at the boat, but I can't move. People come down and stand looking at us, and Chalcey says that her grandmother is Llasey. In the village they know her grandmother, although her grandmother lives a long walk away. I have a confused sense of being helped out of the boat, and I tell them, "We have silver, we can pay." Blur of people in the dark, and then into a place where there is too much light.

Then they are forcing hot seawater between my teeth, I can't drink it, then I think, "it's broth." The fire flickers off a whitewashed wall, and a bareheaded woman says, "Let me help you."

I don't want them to take off my shirt. "Not my shirt!" I say, raising my hands. They are talking and I can't follow what they are saying, but with gentle persistent hands they deftly hold my wrists and peel off the torn jacket and the shirt. The gentle voice says, "What's *this?*" and cuts the bindings on my chest.

Chalcey says, startled, "What's *wrong* with him!" I turn my face away.

A woman smiles at me and says, "You'll be all right, dear." Chalcey stares at me, betrayed, and the woman says to her (and to me), "She's a woman, dear. She'll be all right, there's nothing wrong with her except a bit of fever and too much sun."

And, so, stripped, I slide defenseless into sleep, thinking of the surprise on Chalcey's face.

I sleep a great deal during the next two days, wake up and drink soup, and sleep again. Chalcey isn't there when I wake up, although there is a pallet of blankets on the floor. And perhaps if I wake up and hear her, I pretend to be asleep and soon sleep again. But eventually I can't sleep anymore. Tuwle, the woman with the gentle hands who has given me a bed, asks me if I want a shirt or a dress, and, running my hand over my cropped hair, I say a shirt. But I tell her to call me Jahnna.

They bring me my shirt, neatly mended. And they won't take my silver.

Finally, Chalcey comes to see me. I am sitting on the bed where I have slept so long, shucking beans. It embarrasses me to be caught in shirt and breeches, shucking beans, although I've shucked beans, mended clothes, done all manner of woman's work in men's clothes. But it has been a long time since I've felt so self-conscious.

She comes in, tentative as a bird, and says, "Jahn?"

So I say, "Sit down," and immediately regret it, since there is no place to sit but next to me on the bed.

We go through the old routine of "how are you feeling?" and "what have you been doing?" She holds her veil tightly, although the women here don't go veiled for everyday.

Finally she says, in a hurt little voice, "You could have *told* me."

"I haven't told anyone in years." In a way, I almost didn't think I *was* a woman anymore.

"But I'm not just *any*one!" She is vexed. And how could she know that in a fight you become close comrades, yes, but that we know nothing about each other?

The snap of beans seems very loud. I think of trying to explain, about cutting my hair off to fight with Trevin, and learning long before Trevin died that fighting makes people strangers to themselves. Heth says life hinges on little things, like the fact that I am tall for a woman and flat chested, and when the MilitiaMaster at Bashtoy saw me, half-starved and shorthaired, he thought that I was a boy, and so after that I *was*. Snap. And I run my thumb down the pod and the beans spill into the bowl.

To break the silence, she says, "Your sunburn is almost gone," and, amazingly, she blushes scarlet.

I realize then how it is with her. She had fancied herself in love. "I'm sorry, littleheart," I say, "I didn't intend to hurt or embarrass you. I'm embarrassed, too."

She looks at me sideways. "What do you have to be embarrassed about?"

"It's a little like having no clothes on, everybody knowing, and now that my kin are gone, I am always a stranger, wherever I go —" but she is looking at me without comprehension, so I falter and say lamely, "it's hard to explain."

"What arc you going to do now?" she asks.

I sigh. That is a question that has been on my mind a great deal. Here there is no chance of saving passage money to get back to the mainland. "I don't know."

I told my grandmother about you," Chalcey says. "She said you could come and stay with us, if you would work hard. I said you were very strong." Again she blushes scarlet, and hurries on, "It's a little farm, it used to be better, but there's only my grandmother, but we could help, and I think we could be friends."

As I learned during the long walk to Bashtoy, you may be tokked, but if you just look to the immediate future, sometimes eventually, you find the way.

"I'd like that, littleheart," I say, meaning every word. "I'd like to be friends."

The future, it seems, does, indeed hinge on little things.

A Long
Way Home

SHELIA FINCH

ABOUT SHELIA FINCH
AND
A LONG WAY HOME

A Long Way Home *was first published:*
Isaac Asimov's, *December 1982*

Shelia Finch is one of the basing lights of the 80s and 90s. Each story is distinguished by quality, depth and craftsmanship. Not surprisingly, her first sales were to literary magazines, beginning in the early 1970s. "A Long Way Home" was her first science fiction sale. It began a long relationship with Isaac Asimov's *magazine which has continued under several changes of editorship.*

All her work seems to turn on problems in communication, including novels like The Web of Infinity *and the* Shaper Exile Trilogy. *The following story is no exception. Mistrust on one side and failure to understand a differing perspective on the other hand, cause a "failure to communicate" that threatens to bring a mission of mercy on a distant world to a tragic end.*

A Long Way Home

by SHEILA FINCH

THE SUN STRUCK like a giant fist flattening an insect as Mayva emerged again onto the marketplace. She moved slowly, seeking the bars of brown shadow that alternated with the burning amber stripes of sun-blackened mud. Ahead of her, an old woman scuttled crablike, one hand clutching the shawl to her head against the heat, the other cradling the folded palm leaf containing a gray powder Mayva had just given her.

"You! Come here! My boy needs help."

The man who stood scowling in the doorway of the small, flat-roofed hut was Ruk, spokesman of the village by virtue of the fact that his vocal cords did not yet show signs of developing the nodes that robbed so many of their voice in adult life. He was a thickset man with heavily muscled arms on which the hairs grew long and dark, but he reached only to Mayva's shoulders, for his legs had ceased to grow while he was still a child. He held back the hide curtain through which he wanted Mayva to pass.

She drew her gray skirt up and stepped through the narrow opening. She said nothing, for there was nothing to say, and loose talk angered Ruk.

The interior of the hut was dark but almost as hot as the marketplace; what breeze there was outside was barred from the room by heavy cloths at the door and the one window. Mayva felt the sweat start out on her brow as she approached the bed, her eyes adjusting to the gloom. Ruk's oldest son, Gelor, lay motionless on the grimy pallet, his eyes sunken and closed, his mouth parted. For a moment she feared he was already dead and that Ruk would blame her for not coming sooner.

An old woman sat by the bed, stroking with one hand the boy's lank hair; six thin fingers crawled like centipedes through the tangles. She looked up as Mayva came near and opened her mouth soundlessly; her tongue was gray and bloated. Mayva knew the woman would not outlive her son by very long. The boy stirred feebly, and she turned her attention to him.

The ulcers that covered much of his body were suppurating, and the stench that rose from the bed sickened her. She forced herself to take his thin wrist in her hand and test his pulse. It was weak but constant.

"Goodwife Ruk, bring water and clean cloths that I may wash the sores on your son," she said.

She had tried so many times to explain to them that it was important to keep their bodies clean, but they seemed incapable of remembering her words once she was gone. Sometimes she wanted to scream at them for their stupidity, at the way they let the dogs crawl on the beds where sick children lay, the flies that they seemed not to notice laying eggs on the uncovered meat till it glowed with the green-blue phosphorescence of decay. Yet she held her tongue, knowing that although they needed her help, they feared her skills, and it would not take much to cause them to rise up and stone her to death.

The mother returned with a cracked pottery bowl in which tepid water sloshed, and Mayva could not be sure as she took it from her that the gray cast to the water was only a reflection from the clay. The cloth she knew was not clean, for the goodwife tore it from her own soiled robe. Mayva shut her lips firmly to hold back the protest that rose to them, feeling the burning anger of Ruk's gaze on her.

"Gelor," she said softly, "if you can hear me, I'm going to wash the sores and put a little salve in each. It will take away some of the pain."

But it would not prevent the boy from dying. There was nothing she could do to halt his death. And perhaps it was better that he die, for he had been slowly sinking into idiocy, unable to feed himself or know when he needed to eliminate, so that the mother had to maintain a constant watch on the bed, batting away the hordes of flies that signalled each new lapse.

Mayva worked methodically, rinsing off the filth that surrounded each ulcer and replacing it with a layer of sweet salve. The bowl had to be emptied and refilled with fresher water three times before she was done. Then she straightened up and replaced the jar of salve in her leather satchel.

"I can do no more for him," she said in answer to Ruk's unspoken question.

"Witch woman!" He spat, his face contorting in his hate, one eye pulled upward by a sudden spasm that threatened to tear the left half of his face from the right. "Monster! Where do you get such powers?"

She pushed back the tiredness that dragged at her. "Do you wish me to do anything else for you?"

Ruk shook his head and pointed to the opening. He would not feel comfortable until his hut was purged of the abomination of her presence. Mayva lowered her eyes and turned to the doorway.

"Do you find them in the desert, Witch? I've seen you go into that place of evil!"

She went out without replying, and the filthy curtain fell behind her. The sun hit her full on the brow again, but the air moved a little now and then, and for this much she was grateful. She continued on through the village.

It was a good question Ruk had asked. She did not know the answer. One day, a very long time ago, at sunset, she had stumbled into the village from the desert. Her robe had been dusty but not torn, and her arms and legs bore only minor scratches, so she could not have been long in the desert's furnace. In her mind she had found knowledge: which herbs and roots were helpful against sickness and where to find them. And her hands were skillful at setting bones and soothing pain. But that was all she knew. She could not remember where she had been before she was in the desert, or anything other than her name.

Nor did she know why hers was the only body in the village that had grown straight and tall; whose arms were the same length, both hands displaying five fingers of matching shape (unlike Goodwife Ruk, who had six on one hand and three on the other); whose two legs bore her weight without limping; whose two eyes were set evenly in her brow, the ears likewise on either side of her head, neither one larger than the other; whose nose was a slight protuberance on her face, not a beak the size of a fist or a gaping hole; whose thick, dark hair grew only on her head.

The people of the village called her witch and monster. The little children loped on hands and feet after her in the street to throw stones, because they found her ugly. And the only thing she knew was she must help them. It was as if she had a debt to repay, though she had never seen the people of the village before that day at sunset, nor had they seen her.

And one more thing she knew, a thing she kept like a precious stone, wrapped and hidden from the eyes of thieves, to be taken out and turned over in her mind when she was alone. She knew that though she was the one who was different, hers was the body that was right.

"Woman!" a voice accosted her from a doorway. "Come tend to my goodman, who cannot take food."

There was little she could do for the goodman, whose tongue had swollen to fill up his mouth. But she persuaded the goodwife to brew him a little herb tea and trickle it slowly between the parched lips. At least it might ease the pain. He would not last long.

After him there was a baby born with two heads, and another with a head as large as its body. And then there was a girl with her face pulled in a perpetual snarl more suited to a dog, an old man who vomited continuously, and one whose abdomen had swollen like a seed pod about to burst.

So it went all day, every day, till it seemed to her that there was nothing in this village but decay, deformity, and flies. Yet on some days she could find a tiny shard of time to slip away from the village to the edge of the scorched emptiness that surrounded it. There in the desert she searched for the sparse, elusive plants to replenish her store. In one patch of soil beside an outcropping of rusty boulders, she had coaxed a few stunted vegetables to grow, carrying water from the village well and thatching palm strips across the dead scrub bush to give them a little shade. The villagers paid her for her services with food, but she was careful to eat as little as possible, both because they had so little to give and because what they had was often contaminated and spoiled. And some, like Ruk, were more likely to give her blows than payment, when the help she gave them did not match their hopes.

At sunset, the desert rim was streaked with mauve and rose, and a cloudwrack settled golden and glowing on the distant peaks. A trick of the light at this hour made the cloud-covered mountains behind which the sun set take on the shapes of towers and fantastic spires, so that she could imagine a city rested there. She did not allow herself such dreams for long. They aroused a wild longing in her to be free of the villagers and their torment. But she had nowhere to go, and they needed her; and such visions as arose in her mind at sunset only increased her pain.

The sky turned aquamarine as the sun vanished, but the heat still rose off the desert floor as she faced the west. As she did so a small shadow detached itself from the last wall of the village and came near.

"Mayva?" the small voice said.

"What are you doing here, Bryn?" she said, dropping her satchel and kneeling in the dust.

The child came confidently into her arms and kissed her. "I was waiting for you. I knew you would be coming by. I've seen you working at your plants."

Ruk's youngest son was not like the rest of the children born in the village. His body was symmetrically formed, and he ran easily on two legs. The only sign he bore that guaranteed him kinship with his people was a dark red stain that spread like a mask over half his face and down his neck. But it was not enough to shield him from the anger of his father.

"You must go home, Bryn." Her heart cried out against the advice, for she had seen the bruises on his legs and arms, the cuts that blossomed suddenly on the child's lips. But she was an outcast too and could do nothing for him.

"Let me go with you, Mayva," he pleaded. "I can pour the water on the roots carefully and not waste a drop."

"I'm not going to the garden tonight. I have to seek the herbs I use in my medicine."

"I'll help," the boy said. "I see well by moonlight. I'll find whatever you tell me to look for. Don't send me away. I wish I lived with you, Mayva," he finished wistfully. "I love you."

The weariness of the day's work flooded over her. She embraced the boy briefly, then set him at arm's length and rose from her knees.

"Someday, perhaps, but not now. Come, I'll walk back with you. I'll tell your father you were with me so he won't beat you."

She took the small hand in hers and turned her back to the desert. The child sighed but accepted her words without argument, as if he had not expected better luck. His difference stirred her deeply, speaking to something buried and out of reach in her closed memory. But she was too worn out by her labor to take on the boy's problems. They walked silently, hand in hand, and a sliver of new moon climbed up the sky behind them.

Lamplight spilled from Ruk's house, and a high wail greeted them. Bryn shivered and drew close to Mayva's side. As they stepped up to the door, the curtain was suddenly ripped aside and Ruk appeared, his twisted face wild with grief, his older son hanging limply in his arms. Gelor was dead.

Mayva's first reaction was relief for Gelor. Her second was fear for Bryn. She pulled the child close to her skirt, as if to hide him from the wrath of his father that would come pouring down on the unmarked and still living child.

But it was she that Ruk was staring at, for her the cry of rage that escaped his thickened lips.

"Witch! What did you do to my son? You've killed my son!"

The corpse in his arms shook, its fingers brushed the floor at the father's feet, scattering dust.

"Goodman Ruk," she began, "you know I did not kill Gelor. I tried to help him."

Fear rose within her as Ruk's hatred flowed like an almost visible wave against her. If he believed she had bewitched his son, he might kill her.

The goodwife appeared in the doorway behind her man, the six-fingered hand clawing the empty air. She saw her younger son hiding in the folds of Mayva's skirt, and shrieking, she reached for him and dragged him free. He stumbled against the doorpost, but she ignored his cries.

Ruk took a step toward Mayva, but the corpse made his movements clumsy. He roared at her but seemed unable to decide to put the dead boy down and pursue the one he accused as murderer. He swayed on the threshold, his face suffused with blood so that he looked as if he were about to burst into flame.

"Run, Mayva!" Bryn cried from around his mother's arm. "Run!"

Mayva ran.

She did not stop running until she reached the spot where she had left her satchel and the shouts of the goodman faded behind her. Then she sank onto the warm dust and buried her face in her arms and wept for all the ignorance and bestiality in the village, for the unending toil and hardship that was her life among these people, for her own cowardice in not staying to protect Bryn from his father.

After a while the tears stopped and she stood up. She would not go back to the village. Her fear shamed her, and the tears welled again as she thought of the child she would be abandoning, but she fought the memory down. She did not belong to the village. They had never accepted her, nor had they ever been thankful for her help. Whoever or whatever she was, she was not one of them.

She could not cross the desert from which she had once come, for there were no roads across it. The villagers feared the desert and never set foot in it. The older ones still told of the days when the devil fires had flickered at night, the fires that killed at a distance. Nothing lived in the deep desert,

Mayva knew. There were no trees to give shelter at midday, no water to stop death that would surely come from dehydration.

The road from the village did not enter the desert, but wound toward a distant line of low hills. Whatever lay beyond those hills could not be any worse that what she had just left. She set off along the road.

The crescent moon rose weakly up the sky a little as she walked, then flopped back behind the hills. The stars flamed in the darkness and wheeled overhead like torches carried in some faraway procession. Hour after hour she walked, thinking of the sky, until her legs would no longer hold her. Then she wrapped herself in her cloak and lay down in a ditch beside the road and slept.

Day was streaking the eastern sky with opal swirls of pink and lemon when Mayva came over a slight rise and saw the looming shadows of another village ahead of her. A light wind was rising, ruffling her hair and drying the sweat that glazed her skin. She stared at the village.

Apart from the child, Bryn, she had never seen another like herself. By what right could she expect the next village to contain people who would welcome her? She did not know if all the world was filled with people like Ruk and his goodwife, or whether there were others like herself. Again and again in the early days of her coming out of the desert, she had pushed her mind back to what must have happened to her. And again and again she had come to the point where the wall had been erected in her mind, separating before and after. She had found no way of scaling that wall. There was simply no way she could know. She would have to take a chance.

Then she saw a figure coming toward her on the road. She pulled her hood forward, shadowing her face. She did not wish to be too quickly marked as different. The figure grew in stature, and she could see from its gait that it did not suffer from deformed legs. It too was muffled in a cloak. In a moment it had drawn level with her as she stood waiting on the dusty road.

The figure walked purposefully down the middle of the path, and Mayva stepped off to one side. Awkwardly, her ankle struck against a boulder, and she cried out at the blow, her hood slipping back a little. Hastily she stifled her cry and tugged the hood back in place.

The figure hesitated and peered at her.

"Are you all right?"

"Yes."

The figure nodded and began to move on.

"Wait!" she said. "I mean, please wait a moment more. I am a healer. Tell me if I can find work and lodging up ahead."

Again the figure peered at her. She was aware of dark eyes burning in the shadows of the hood. It was a little taller than she and carried itself straighter than over half the people in the village she had left.

"Who are you?"

"Mayva," she said. "I've been living in the village at the desert's edge, though I share no kinship with those people."

"Mayva," the voice repeated.

Then the figure suddenly reached up and threw back its hood, revealing a dark, angular face with dark eyes under a sweep of black hair. The surprise of realizing there was no deformity in the face was swept away by the shock of recognition that raced through her. She knew the face!

"Shen," she said.

Immediately, a flood of images tumbled in her mind. Shen's face beside a shining wall, Shen's long-fingered hand reaching for hers, lights twinkling in a pattern like stars captured on a board. And nothing else. No more came. Though she strained to catch the images, it was as if she tried to grasp a swirl of mist.

"So you also remember?" he asked.

Bitterly she shook her head. "Only your name."

"More will come," he said. "That's the beginning."

"How can you know?"

"Do you think you're the only one they did it to? Look!" He thrust his hands out, allowing the cloak to fall back, exposing bare arms. The dark fingers splayed for her inspection. Five on each hand.

"Mayva, you and I don't belong here with these pitiful creatures."

Again the images rushed through her mind. The city flaming at sunset on the mountain top, Shen kissing her cheek beneath a tree whose leaves were carved from jewels, someone speaking in a high arched room. Her eyes filled with tears and she clung to Shen's outstretched hands.

"Why is it so difficult to remember?"

"Perhaps if we had remembered, we would not have stayed."

She stared at Shen as the sun came up behind her and sat like a fur cape on her shoulders. The little wind of dawn had subsided, and in the distance the desert had begun to shimmer as if it were underwater. He led her aside from the road to a place where boulders crouched beside a dry stream bed like a group of mutants gathered to beg. He spoke to her in a voice that trembled on the edge of great pain.

"We were mindwiped, Mayva, you and I and the others scattered in villages and settlements across this doomed land. They took away our memory of who we were and where we came from, and left us each only one skill. Yours was a knowledge of healing, mine of building."

Once again he displayed the five-fingered hands, and she saw the calluses on them this time. She recognized the truth in his words, though she could not have said them herself

"There was someone who had an idea," she said slowly, creasing her brow in the effort to remember. "How long have we been here?"

"A very long time!" he said.

This too was true. How many times had the little moon grown full and wasted away again since the time she had walked out of the desert? How

many times had the insufficient rains blown out of the west in their season?
A very long time.

"I feel as if I have been wandering in a nightmare for too long." Shen
laughed, splintering the morning quietness. "Spoken like one of us!"

"But who are we?"

His laughter stopped. "I don't know. There are things I still can't
remember. Damn them! They did a magnificent job on our minds." He
looked intently at her. "But the fact that we remember anything despite
their mindwiping proves we must be very strong. We can recapture the
rest, Mayva, if we try."

She let the thoughts flow easily into her mind this time, not grasping
any, letting them settle into their own constellations. It was as if she had
been unchained and given the sky to fly in. The image startled her. She
stared at Shen.

"Where were you going when I met you?"

"Home," he said simply.

The word roared in her ears like the noise of a great waterfall. A river of
memory came rushing toward her, knocking away the wall that separated
her from the knowledge of herself, lighting up her mind with a thousand
simultaneous pictures. She saw the ship-city perched in the clouds on the
high mountaintop, golden at sunset; she heard the hum of its life support
system, endlessly renewing itself and the life within the metal walls. She
saw the vaulted rooms, the silver floors, the artificial trees with a whole
world's treasure for fruit; she heard the lilt of harp and flute, caught the
glimmer of thousands of tiny lights floating in a ballroom where the citizens
took their ease, saw the flash and sparkle of luminous gowns and opalescent
cloaks passing on a wide glass stair.

Home.

She stood up. "Let's go home."

"Do you know where to find it?"

She smiled. "It's in the sunset."

Together, hand in hand, they walked away from the villages, leaving the
path behind and striking out across the open desert. Now that they had
remembered who they were, it seemed that the ferocious heat could not
touch them. The twisted landscape swam in browns and ambers, but they
walked as if through a cool forest.

Once she stopped and gazed into Shen's dark eyes.

"Do you remember yet why?"

He shook his head. "A jest? A trial? Perhaps a punishment?"

She looked startled at that. "No, though for a moment —"

They walked on.

"Someone was speaking," she said as they crossed a dry lake and the
heat rose up in waves from the sand. "Someone had an idea. It's no use. I
don't remember."

"Don't try," he advised.

Shortly before midday, they heard a cry and, turning, saw a cloud of dust rising behind them.

"We're being pursued," Shen said.

Now in the dust she could see figures carrying staves and axes, hobbling and loping after them like creatures in a bad dream. The heavy air shattered with their raucous cries, and the echoes of their hate reverberated among the misshapen rocks.

"Monsters!" Shen cried.

He extended his hand toward them suddenly, then dropped it slowly, his face puzzled, as though he had forgotten the rest of it. His eyes searched Mayva's for the answer. But if she had remembered it, she knew it would not have been the right way.

"Run," she said, tugging her skirt above her knees. "They won't dare follow us far. They fear the desert."

Shen threw back his cloak, and they ran on strong, straight legs. Her mind balked at the easy assignment of words to objects, but still she felt that truth lay behind a closed door. They ran, and the sounds of pursuit fell away in the distance, until at last, breathless, they knew they were safe.

At sunset they came in view of the foothills that marked the beginning of the rise toward the high range of mountains on the western horizon. From this point, the land sloped relentlessly upward like a cracked and broken table tipped on its side. It was harder now to make progress, for the heat pressed down like a shield, holding them back. The sun began to slide faster down the sky, and the cloudwrack on the peaks flamed scarlet and gold. And as they looked, the outline of the starship emerged from the clouds, its domes and spires wreathed in mist so that it was difficult to tell where the clouds ended and the ship began.

"I remember our coming," he said in a low, tense voice. "I remember the darkness of space between, the emptiness of time on the voyage."

She shivered despite the late afternoon's lingering heat. The sunlight reflected on the clouds darkened briefly, and the ship grew indistinct.

"There was another ship," Mayva said. "There was a battle."

Shen answered her fiercely. "The planet was ours! We found it. We'd searched for so long."

"So had they. And their need was as great as ours."

"Don't think of that now," he advised. "Save your strength till we get home."

They climbed in silence as the vision ahead grew clearer. But she could not rid herself of the thoughts that crowded one upon the other. Every step opened another door and let them in. Time had passed too slowly by the shining wall. The beautiful faces had been bored. There had been an idea. A voice. It was so long ago.

Darkness came creeping across the desert, and still they climbed. Stars leaped in fire above their heads, and the tiny moon crept shyly out from behind a drift of cloud. Their own had been so much bigger and more bold, she remembered.

Toward midnight, when the liquid fire of the home galaxy tilted directly overhead, they came to a narrow ledge before a vertical rock wall, into which was set a metal door. Shen set his palm flat against an engraved circle in the middle of the door. It swung silently open, admitting them to a room carved in the rock, filled with pale yellow light that cast no shadows. The door slid shut behind them, and a faint hum of distant machinery began. The air shimmered, and a slight sparkle rose before them as if someone had sprinkled a handful of luminous dust. The column of bright motes coalesced into a pillar of light, which took shape. A woman stepped out, tossing back her brilliant cloak to reveal a clinging, diaphanous gown that seemed spun out of particles of light. She held out jeweled arms, and her bright laughter chimed like a bell in the rock chamber.

"Welcome home! You stayed longer than all the others."

Shen was already in the woman's embrace, but in Mayva's mind the door swung wide, allowing memories to crowd upon her.

"Will they concede defeat, Dema?" Shen asked, laughing.

"Teleren has already ordered the feast!" she replied.

She held out her hand to include Mayva in the welcoming, but Mayva held back.

"It was an accident," Mayva said. "We did not mean to harm this planet's people. We did not intend them to suffer as they did." How lightly they had always taken such things!

"Let it go now, Mayva," Shen said. "We're home."

Home. Inside the ship-city, their home, there was no pain, no deformity, no sorrow or loss, only music and feasting and endless pleasure. Inside the city there had been an idea, a game. But there had been a voice too that spoke of guilt. And she remembered whose voice it had been.

"I'm not going with you."

"Are you mad?" Shen asked. "I remember it all now. We wagered on it, to pass the time. The mindwipe was a kindness, so we could bear the unspeakable horror. But we don't have to stay once we remember. Those were the rules!"

"It was no game for me, Shen," she said. "It was our fault it happened to them. They were innocent victims, caught like animals in the crossfire of our battle. They had been human once like us, and we made monsters of them."

"You've done your share of helping them," Dema said. In Dema's eyes she saw neither love nor hate, only the cool dispassion of those who have lived a very long time, journeyed a very long way. "You were always too emotional, Mayva."

"They don't concern us," Shen said. "They're ignorant and brutish, and they aren't going to change. Perhaps it would have been kinder to finish them when we destroyed the other ship."

She thought of Bryn, only the bloodmarked face linking him to his people.

"But they can change. We can lead them back to being men."

"We're bound by the Code not to interfere," Dema said. "You know that, Mayva. No world may deliberately use its knowledge to change the course of evolution of another. That's why you were only allowed to take such rudimentary skills with you in the game."

"We changed their world the day we came to it!" she argued. "Our war changed their history. We would be justified in changing it back."

"An interesting point," Dema conceded. "The Elders will be glad to debate it with you."

Mayva thought of the endless discussions, the brilliant concepts threaded like shining beads on a string to pass the years. They too were a game. It was not enough.

"We deserve to come home," Shen said.

Where is home, she thought, but the place where the work is, and the love?

"Goodbye, Shen-Who-Once-Loved-Me," she said. 'I'm going back."

She turned and touched her hand to the door. As it opened, revealing the deformed and barren land lying at the foot of the mountain, bathed in pale radiance from the planet's tiny satellite, she heard Dema's bright laughter. The perfection of music from the ship drifted down to her. This time, she would remember that, and a lot more.

She could not go back to Ruk's village; she had done all she could for them. But there were other villages, other men in whose hearts she could plant seeds that would blossom into remembrance of their lost humanity. There was so much to do, and so little time to do it in. She would need an apprentice, one who loved her and followed her ways. And she knew where to find him.

It was a long way home.

The Lake
Was Full Of
Artificial Things

KAREN JOY FOWLER

ABOUT KAREN JOY FOWLER
AND
THE LAKE WAS FULL OF ARTIFICIAL THINGS

The Lake Was Full of Artificial Things *was first published:*
Isaac Asimov's, *October 1985*

Karen Joy Fowler has been writing for less than a decade as of publication of this anthology, yet she has already earned an enviable reputation in the field. Like a number of new authors, of both genders, her work has a high literary polish and focuses on such fundamental concerns that it has often been accused of not being science fiction. This is especially true of her first novel, Sarah Canary — much to Ms. Fowler's surprise. However, its receipt of the prestigious mainstream Commonwealth Award seems to have put her beyond the need for consolation.

Like many of the newer women writers represented here, she is a multiple Hugo and Nebula award nominee. Her work has appeared in Isaac Asimov's, Omni, F&SF *and numerous anthologies. In "The Lake Was Full of Artificial Things," a therapist uses a new breakthrough in psychotherapy to help the central figure exorcise the ghost of her dead lover; just as the author uses this breakthrough story to help the reader exorcise the ghosts of the Viet Nam War (now called "conflict" in most media accounts to shield the U.S. psyche from having lost a "war"). Ms. Fowler remarks that having attended the University of California at Berkeley, the hotbed of antiwar activism, may have had something to do with the genesis of this story and her particular New Eve.*

The Lake Was Full Of Artificial Things

by KAREN JOY FOWLER

ANIEL WAS OLDER than Miranda had expected. In 1970, when they had said good-bye, he had been twenty-two. Two years later he was dead, but now, approaching her with the bouncing walk which had suited his personality so well, he appeared as a middle-aged man and quite gray, though solid and muscular. She noted with relief that he was smiling. "Randy!" he said. He laughed delightedly. "You look wonderful."

Miranda glanced down at herself, wondering what, in fact, she did look like or if she had any form at all. She saw the flesh of her arms firm again and the skin smooth and tight. So *she* was the twenty-year old. Isn't that odd, she thought, turning her hands palms up to examine them. Then Daniel reached her. The sun was bright in the sky behind him, obscuring his face, giving him a halo. He put his arms around her. I feel him, she thought in astonishment. I smell him. She breathed in slowly. "Hello, Daniel," she said.

He squeezed her slightly, then dropped his arms and looked around. Miranda looked outward, too. They were on the college campus. Surely this was not the setting she would have chosen. It unsettled her, as if she had been sent backward in time and gifted with prescience, but remained powerless to make any changes, was doomed to see it all again, moving to its inevitable conclusion. Daniel, however, seemed pleased.

He pointed off to the right. "There's the creek," he said, and suddenly she could hear it. "Memories there, right?" and she remembered lying beneath him on the grass by the water. She put her hands on his shoulders now, his clothes were rough against her palms and military — like his hair. He gestured to the round brick building behind her. "Tollman Hall," he said. "Am I right? God, this is great, Randy. I remember *everything*. Total recall. I had Physics 10 there with Dr. Fielding. Physics for non-majors. I couldn't manage my vectors and I got a B." He laughed again, throwing an arm around Miranda. "It's great to be back."

They began to walk together toward the center of campus, slow walking with no destination, designed for conversation. They were all alone, Miranda noticed. The campus was deserted, then suddenly it wasn't. Students appeared on the pathways. Long-hairs with headbands and straights with slide rules. Just what she remembered. "Tell me what everyone's been doing," Daniel said. "It's been what? Thirty years? Don't leave out a thing."

Miranda stooped and picked a small daisy out of the grass. She twirled it absentmindedly in her fingers. It left a green stain on her thumb. Daniel stopped walking and waited beside her. "Well," Miranda said. "I've lost touch with most of them. Gail got a job on *Le Monde*. She went to Germany for the re-unification. I heard she was living there. The anti-nuclear movement was her permanent beat. She could still be there, I suppose."

"So she's still a radical," said Daniel. "What stamina."

"Margaret bought a bakery in San Francisco. Sixties cuisine. Whole grains. Tofu brownies. Heaviest cookies west of the Rockies. We're in the same cable chapter so I keep up with her better. I saw her last marriage on T.V. She's been married three times now, every one a loser."

"What about Allen?" Daniel asked

"Allen," repeated Miranda. "Well; Allen had a promising career in jogging shoes. He was making great strides." She glanced at Daniel's face. "Sorry," she said. "Allen always brought out the worst in me. He lost his father in an air collision over Kennedy. Sued the airline and discovered he never had to work again. In short, Allen is rich. Last I heard, and this was maybe twenty years ago, he was headed to the Philippines to buy himself a submissive bride." She saw Daniel smile, the lines in his face deepening with his expression. "Oh, you'd like to blame me for Allen, wouldn't you?" she said. "But it wouldn't be fair. I dated him maybe three times, tops." Miranda shook her head. "Such an enthusiastic participant in the sexual revolution. And then it all turned to women's liberation on him. Poor Allen. We can only hope his tiny wife divorced him and won a large settlement when you could still get alimony."

Daniel moved closer to her and they began to walk again, passing under the shade of a redwood grove. The grass changed to needles under their feet. "You needn't be so hard on Allen," he said. "I never minded about him. I always knew you loved me."

"Did you?" asked Miranda anxiously. She looked at her feet, afraid to examine Daniel's face. My god, she was wearing moccasins. Had she ever worn moccasins? "I did get married, Daniel," she said. "I married a mathematician. His name was Michael." Miranda dropped her daisy, petals intact.

Daniel continued to walk, swinging his arms easily. "Well, you were always hot for mathematics. I didn't expect you to mourn me forever."

"So it's all right?"

Daniel stopped, turning to face her. He was still smiling, though it was not quite the smile she expected, not quite the easy, happy smile she remembered. "It's all right that you got married, Randy," he said softly.

Something passed over his face and left it. "Hey!" he laughed again. "I remember something else from Physics 10. Zeno's paradox. You know what that is?"

"No," said Miranda.

"It's an argument. Zeno argued that motion was impossible because it required an object to pass through an infinite number of points in a finite amount of time." Daniel swung his arms energetically. "Think about it for a minute, Randy. Can you fault it? Then think about how far I came to be here with you."

"Miranda. Miranda." It was her mother's voice, rousing her for school. Only then it wasn't. It was Dr. Matsui who merely sounded maternal, despite the fact that she had no children of her own and was not yet thirty. Miranda felt her chair returning slowly to its upright position. "Are you back?" Dr. Matsui asked. "How did it go?"

"It was short," Miranda told her. She pulled the taped wires gently from her lids and opened her eyes. Dr. Matsui was seated beside her, reaching into Miranda's hair to detach the clips which touched her scalp.

"Perhaps we recalled you too early," she conceded. "Matthew spotted an apex so we pulled the plug. We just wanted a happy ending. It was happy, wasn't it?"

"Yes." Dr. Matsui's hair, parted on one side and curving smoothly under her chin, bobbed before Miranda's face. Miranda touched it briefly, then her own hair, her cheeks, and her nose. They felt solid under her hand, real, but no more so than Daniel had been. "Yes, it was," she repeated. "He was so happy to see me. So glad to be back. But, Anna, he was so real. I thought you said it would be like a dream."

"No," Dr. Matsui told her. "I said it *wouldn't* be. I said it was a memory of something that never happened and in that respect was like a dream. I wasn't speaking to the quality of the experience." She rolled her chair to the monitor and stripped the long feed-out sheet from it, tracing the curves quickly with one finger. Matthew, her technician, came to stand behind her. He leaned over her left shoulder, pointing. "There," he said. "That's Daniel. That's what I put in."

Dr. Matsui returned her chair to Miranda's side. "Here's the map," she said. "Maybe I can explain better."

Miranda tried to sit forward. One remaining clip pulled her hair and made her inhale sharply. She reached up to detach herself. "Sorry," said Dr. Matsui sheepishly. She held out the paper for Miranda to see. "The dark wave is the Daniel we recorded off your memories earlier. Happy memories, right? You can see the fainter echo here as you responded to it with the original memories. Think of it as memory squared. Naturally, it's going to be intense. Then, everything else here is the record of the additional activity you brought to this particular session. Look at these sharp peaks at the beginning. They indicate stress. You'll see that nowhere else do they recur.

On paper it looks to have been an entirely successful session. Of course, only you know the content of the experience." Her dark eyes were searching and sympathetic. "Well," she said. "Do you feel better about him?"

"Yes," said Miranda. "I feel better."

"Wonderful." Dr. Matsui handed the feedback to Matthew. "Store it," she told him.

Miranda spoke hesitatingly. "I had other things I wanted to say to him," she said. "It doesn't feel resolved."

"I don't think the sessions ever resolve things," Dr. Matsui said. "The best they can do is open the mind to resolution. The resolution still has to be found in the real world."

"Can I see him again?" Miranda asked.

Dr. Matsui interlaced her fingers and pressed them to her chest. "A repeat would be less expensive, of course," she said. "Since we've already got Daniel. We could just run him through again. Still, I'm reluctant to advise it. I wonder what else we could possibly gain."

"Please, Anna," said Miranda. She was looking down at her arms remembering how firmly fleshed they had seemed.

"Let's wait and see how you're feeling after our next couple regular visits. If the old regrets persist and, more importantly, if they're still interfering with your ability to get on with things, then ask me again."

She was standing. Miranda swung her legs over the side of the chair and stood, too. Matthew walked with her to the door of the office. "We've got a goalie coming in next," he confided. "She stepped into the goal while holding the ball; she wants to remember it the way it didn't happen. Self-indulgent if you ask me. But then, athletes make the money, right?" He held the door open, his arm stretched in front of Miranda. "You feel better, don't you?" he asked.

"Yes," she reassured him.

She met Daniel for lunch at Frank Fats Cafe. They ordered fried clams and scallops, but the food never came. Daniel was twenty again and luminescent with youth. His hair was blond and his face was smooth. Had he really been so beautiful? Miranda wondered.

"I'd love a coke," he said. "I haven't had one in thirty years."

"You're kidding," said Miranda. "They don't have the real thing in heaven?" Daniel looked puzzled.

"Skip it," she told him. "I was just wondering what it was like being dead. You could tell me."

"It's classified," said Daniel. "On a need to know basis."

Miranda picked up her fork which was heavy and cold. "This time it's you who looks wonderful. Positively beatific. Last time you looked so — " she started to say *old*, but amended it. After all, he had looked no older than she did these days. Such things were relative. "Tired," she finished.

"No, I wasn't tired," Daniel told her. "It was the war."

"The war's over now," Miranda said and this time his smile was decidedly unpleasant.

"Is it?" he asked. "Just because you don't read about it in the paper now? Just because you watch the evening news and there's no body count in the corner of the screen?"

"Television's not like that now," Miranda began, but Daniel hadn't stopped talking.

"What's really going on in Southeast Asia? Do you even know?" Daniel shook his head. "Wars never end," he said. He leaned threateningly over the table. "Do you imagine for one minute that it's over for me?"

Miranda slammed her fork down. "Don't do that," she said. "Don't try to make me guilty of that, too. You didn't have to go. I begged you not to. Jesus, you knew what the war was. If you'd gone off to save the world from communist aggression, I would have disagreed, but I could have understood. But you knew better than that. I never forgave you for going."

"It was so easy for you to see what was right," Daniel responded angrily. "You were completely safe. You women could graduate without losing your deferment. Your goddamn birthday wasn't drawn twelfth in the draft lottery and if it had been you wouldn't have cared. When was your birthday drawn? You don't even know." Daniel leaned back and looked out the window. People appeared on the street. A woman in a red miniskirt got into a blue car. Then Daniel faced her again, large before Miranda. She couldn't shut him out. " 'Go to Canada,' you said. 'That's what I'd do.' I wonder. Could you have married your mathematician in Canada? I can just picture you saying good-bye to your mother forever."

"My mother's dead now," said Miranda. A knot of tears tightened about her throat.

"And so the hell am I." Daniel reached for her wrists, holding them too hard, hurting her deliberately. "But you're not, are you? You're just fine."

There was a voice behind Daniel. "Miranda. Miranda," it called.

"Mother," cried Miranda. But, of course it wasn't, it was Anna Matsui, gripping her wrists, bringing her back. Miranda gasped for breath and Dr. Matsui let go of her. "It was awful," said Miranda. She began to cry. "He accused me . . ." She pulled the wires from her eyes recklessly. Tears spilled out of them. Miranda ached all over.

"He accused you of nothing." Dr. Matsui's voice was sharp and disappointed. "You accused yourself. The same old accusations. We made Daniel out of you, remember?" She rolled her chair backward, moved to the monitor for the feedback. Matthew handed it to her and she read it, shaking her head. Her short black hair flew against her cheeks. "It shouldn't have happened," she said. "We used only the memories that made you happy. And with your gift for lucid dreaming — well, I didn't think there was a risk." Her face was apologetic as she handed Miranda a tissue and waited for the crying to stop. "Matthew wanted to recall you earlier," she confessed, "but I didn't want it to end this way."

"No!" said Miranda. "We can't stop now. I never answered him."

"You only need to answer yourself. It's your memory and imagination confronting you. He speaks only with your voice, he behaves only as you expect him to." Dr. Matsui examined the feedback map again. "I should never have agreed to a repeat. I certainly won't send you back." She looked at Miranda and softened her voice. "Lie still. Lie still until you feel better."

"Like in another thirty years?" asked Miranda. She closed her eyes her head hurt from the crying and the wires. She reached up to detach one close to her ear. "Everything he said to me was true," she added tonelessly.

"Many things he didn't say are bound to be true as well," Dr. Matsui pointed out. "Therapy is not really concerned with truth which is almost always merely a matter of perspective. Therapy is concerned with adjustment — adjustment to an unchangeable situation or to a changing truth." She lifted a pen from her collar, clicking the point in and out absentmindedly. "In any given case," she continued, "we face a number of elements within our control and a far greater number beyond it. In a case such as yours, where the patient has felt profoundly and morbidly guilty over an extended period of time, it is because she is focusing almost exclusively on her own behavior. 'If only I hadn't done x,' she thinks, 'then y would never have happened.' Do you understand what I'm saying Miranda?"

"No."

"In these sessions we try to show you what might have happened if the elements you couldn't control were changed. In your case we let you experience a continued relationship with Daniel. You see that you bore him no malice. You wished him nothing ill. If he had come back the bitterness of your last meeting would have been unimportant."

"He asked me to marry him," said Miranda. "He asked me to wait for him. I told you that. And I said that I was already seeing Allen. Allen! I said as far as I was concerned he was already gone."

"You wish you could change that, of course. But what you really want to change is his death and that was beyond your control." Dr. Matsui's face was sweet and intense.

Miranda shook her head. "You're not listening to me, Anna. I told you what happened, but I lied about why it happened. I pretended we had political differences. I thought my behavior would be palatable if it looked like a matter of conscience. But really I dated Allen for the first time before Daniel had even been drafted. Because I knew what was coming. I saw that his life was about to get complicated and messy. And I saw a way out of it. For me, of course. Not for him." Miranda began to pick unhappily at the loose skin around her nails. "What do you think of that?" she asked. "What do you think of me now?"

"What do *you* think?" Dr. Matsui said and Miranda responded in disgust.

"I know what *I* think. I think I'm sick of talking to myself. Is that the best you therapists can manage? I think I'll stay home and talk to the mirrors."

She pulled off the remaining connections to her scalp and sat up. "Matthew," she said. "Matthew!"

Matthew came to the side of her chair. He looked thin, concerned, and awkward. What a baby he was, really, she thought. He couldn't be more than twenty-five. "How old are you, Matthew?" she asked.

"Twenty-seven."

"Be a hell of a time to die, wouldn't it?" She watched Matthew put a nervous hand on his short brown hair and run it backward. "I want your opinion about something, Matthew. A hypothetical case. I'm trusting you to answer honestly."

Matthew glanced at Dr. Matsui who gestured with her pen for him to go ahead. He turned back to Miranda. "What would you think of a woman who deserted her lover, a man she really claimed to love, because he got sick and she didn't want to face the unpleasantness of it?"

Matthew spoke carefully. "I would imagine that it was motivated by cowardice rather than cruelty," he said. "I think we should always forgive sins of cowardice. Even our own." He stood looking at Miranda with his earnest, innocent face.

"All right, Matthew." she said. "Thank you." She lay back down in the chair and listened to the hum of the idle machines. "Anna." she said, "He didn't behave as I expected. I mean sometimes he did and sometimes he didn't. Even the first time."

"Tell me about it," said Dr. Matsui.

"The first session he was older than I expected. Like he hadn't died, but had continued to age along with me."

"Wish fulfillment."

"Yes, but I was *surprised* by it. And I was surprised by the setting. And he said something very odd right at the end. He quoted me Zeno's paradox and it really exists, but I never heard it before. It didn't sound like something Daniel would say, either. It sounded more like my husband, Michael. Where did it come from?"

"Probably from just where you said," Dr. Matsui told her. "Michael. You don't think you remember it, but obviously you did. And husbands and lovers are bound to resemble each other, don't you think? We often get bits of overlap. Our parents show up one way or another in almost all, our memories." Dr. Matsui stood. "Come in Tuesday," she said. "We'll talk some more."

"I'd like to see him one more time," said Miranda.

"Absolutely not," Dr. Matsui answered, returning Miranda's chair to its upright position.

"Where are we, Daniel?" Miranda asked. She couldn't see anything.

"Camp Pendleton," he answered. "On the beach. I used to run here mornings. Guys would bring their girlfriends. Not me, of course."

Miranda watched the landscape fill in as he spoke. Fog remained. It was early and overcast. She heard the ocean and felt the wet, heavy air begin to curl her hair. She was barefoot on the sand and a little cold. I'm so sorry, Daniel," she said. "That's all I ever really wanted to tell you. I loved you."

"I know you did." He put his arm around her. She leaned against him. I must look like his mother, she thought; in fact, her own son was older than Daniel now. She looked up at him carefully. He must have just arrived at camp. The hair had been all but shaved from his head.

"Maybe you were right, anyway," Daniel told her. "Maybe I just shouldn't have gone. I was so angry at you by then I didn't care anymore. I even thought about dying with some sense of anticipation. Petulant, you know, like a little kid. I'll go and get killed and *then* she'll be sorry."

"And she was," said Miranda. "God, was she." She turned to face him, pressed her lined cheek against his chest, smelled his clothes. He must have started smoking again. Daniel put both arms around her. She heard a gull cry out ecstatically.

"But when the time came I really didn't want to die." Daniel's voice took on an unfamiliar edge, frightened, slightly hoarse. "When the time came I was willing to do *anything* rather than die." He hid his face in her neck. "Do you have kids?" he asked. "Did you and Michael ever?"

"A son," she said.

"How old? About six?"

Miranda wasn't sure how old Jeremy was now. It changed every year. But she told him, wonderingly, "Of course not, Daniel. He's all grown up. He owns a pizza franchise, can you believe it? He thinks I'm a bore."

"Because I killed a kid during the war. A kid about six years old. I figured it was him or me. I shot him." Miranda pushed back from Daniel, trying to get a good look at his face. "They used kids, you know," he said. "They counted on us not being able to kill them. I saw this little boy coming for me with his hands behind his back. I told him to stop. I shouted at him to stop. I pointed my rifle and said I was going to kill him. But he kept coming."

"Oh, Daniel," said Miranda. "Maybe he didn't speak English."

"A pointed rifle is universal. He walked into the bullet."

"What was he carrying?"

"Nothing," said Daniel. "How could I know?"

"Daniel," Miranda said. "I don't believe you. You wouldn't do that." Her words unsettled her even more. "Not the way I remember you," she said. "This is not the way I remember you."

"It's so easy for you to see what's right," said Daniel.

I'm going back, thought Miranda. Where am I really? I must be with Anna, but then she remembered that she was not. She was in her own study. She worked to feel the study chair beneath her, the ache in her back as she curved over her desk. Her feet dangled by the wheels; she concentrated until she could feel them. She saw her own hand, still holding her pencil, and she put it down. Things seemed very clear to her. She walked to the bedroom and summoned Dr. Matsui over the console. She waited perhaps fifteen minutes before Anna appeared.

"Daniel's the one with the problem," Miranda said. "It's not me, after all."

"There is no Daniel." Dr. Matsui's voice betrayed a startled concern. "Except in your mind and on my tapes. Apart from you, no Daniel."

"No. He came for me again. Just like in our sessions. Just as intense. Do you understand? Not a dream," she cut off Dr. Matsui's protest. "It was not a dream, because I wasn't asleep. I was working and then I was with him. I could feel him. I could smell him. He told me an absolutely horrible story about killing a child during the war. Where would I have gotten that? Not the sort of thing they send home in their letters to the bereaved."

"There were a thousand ugly stories out of Vietnam," said Dr. Matsui. "I know some and I wasn't even born yet. Or just barely born. Remember My Lai?" Miranda watched her image clasp its hands. "You heard this story somewhere. It became part of your concept of the war. So you put it together now with Daniel." Dr. Matsui's voice took on its professional patina. "I'd like you to come in, Miranda. Immediately. I'd like to take a complete read-out and keep you monitored a while. Maybe overnight. I don't like the turn this is taking."

"All right," said Miranda. "I don't want to be alone anyway. Because he's going to come again."

"No," said Dr. Matsui firmly. "He's not."

Miranda took the elevator to the garage and unlocked her bicycle. She was not frightened and wondered why not. She felt unhappy and uncertain, but in complete control of herself. She pushed out into the bike lane. When the helicopter appeared overhead, Miranda knew immediately where she was. A banana tree sketched itself in on her right. There was a smell in the air which was strange to her. Old diesel engines, which she recognized, but also something organic. A lushness almost turned to rot. In the distance the breathtaking green of rice growing. But the dirt at her feet was bare.

Miranda had never imagined a war could be so quiet. Then she heard the chopper. And she heard Daniel. He was screaming. He stood right next to her, beside a pile of sandbags, his rifle stretched out before him. A small, delicately featured child was just walking into Miranda's view, his arms held behind him. All Miranda had to do was lift her hand.

"No, Daniel," she said. "His hands are empty."

Daniel didn't move. The war stopped. "I killed him, Randy," said Daniel. "You can't change that."

Miranda looked at the boy. His eyes were dark, a streak of dust ran all the way up one shoulder and onto his face. He was barefoot. "I know," she said. "I can't help him." The child faded and disappeared. "I'm trying to help you." The boy reappeared again, back further, at the very edge of her vision. He was beautiful, unbearably young. He began to walk to them once more.

"*Can* you help me?" Daniel asked.

Miranda pressed her palm into his back. He wore no shirt and was slick and sweaty. "I don't know," she said. "Was it a crime of cowardice or of cruelty? I'm told you can be forgiven the one, but not the other."

Daniel dropped his rifle into the dirt. The landscape turned slowly about them, became mountainous. The air smelled cleaner and was cold.

A bird flew over them in a beautiful arc, and then it became a baseball and began to fall in slow motion, and then it became death and she could plot its trajectory. It was aimed at Daniel whose rifle had reappeared in his hands. Now, Miranda thought. She could stay and die with Daniel the way she'd always believed she should. Death moved so slowly in the sky. She could see it, moment to moment, descending like a series of scarcely differentiated still frames. "Look, Daniel," she said. "It's Zeno's paradox in reverse. Finite points. Infinite time." How long did she have to make this decision? A lifetime. Her lifetime.

Daniel would not look up. He reached out his hand to touch her hair. Gray, she knew. Her gray under his young hand. He was twenty-four. "Don't stay," he said. "Do you think I would have wanted you to? I would never have wanted that."

So Miranda moved from his hand and found she was glad to do so. "I always loved you," she said as if it mattered. "Good-bye, Daniel," but he had already looked away. Other soldiers materialized beside him and death grew to accommodate them. But they wouldn't all die. Some would survive in pieces, she thought. And some would survive whole. Wouldn't they?

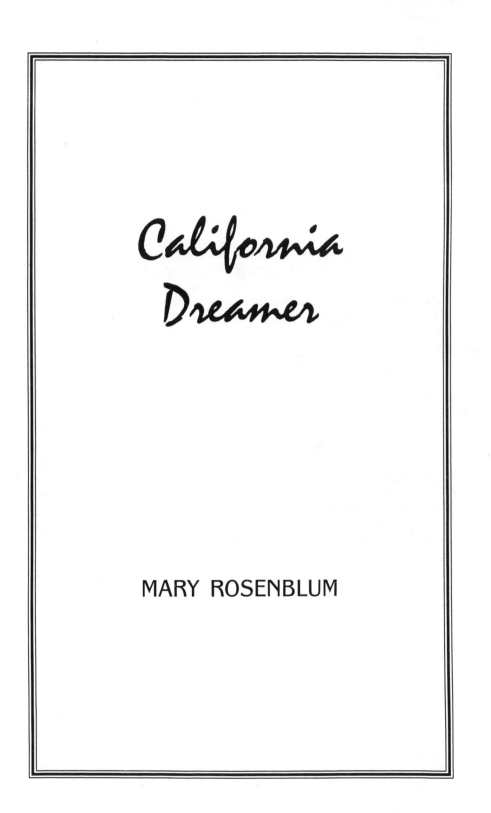

California
Dreamer

MARY ROSENBLUM

ABOUT MARY ROSENBLUM
AND
CALIFORNIA DREAMER

California Dreamer *was first published:*
The Magazine of Fantasy and Science Fiction, *October 1993*

Mary Rosenblum is one of the important new women writers (her first story appeared in Isaac Asimov's *in 1990) whose work blurs genderlines. Gay men and lesbians are prominently featured in her short stories and novels* (Chimera, The Stone Garden). *Although her growing body of work is still small, each story and novel has been critically acclaimed for its ingenuity, deft characterization and burnished prose.*

"California Dreamer" concerns two women and a young girl struggling to survive in the aftermath of a major West Coast earthquake and offers telling comments on the nature of survivorship and accommodation. Of it Mr. Rosenblum has written: "I visited the Marina district where the worst of the earthquake damage occurred. All the debris and burned-out buildings had been cleared away. The streets were lean and empty. Most of the buildings were still unsafe, so it was a small ghost town within the rush of downtown San Francisco. I found it very eerie to walk down those empty streets and see the glyphs the rescue teams had scrawled on the doors and walls. Those quiet streets disturbed me more than the media scenes of fire and death had done. Perhaps it was because evidence of such tragedy lurked beneath a skin or normalcy. "California Dreamer" grew from it. I began to wonder just how deep and far reaching the effects of human cataclysm might be."

California Dreamer

by MARY ROSENBAUM

THE RELIEF BOAT came once a week. This morning it had been a sturdy salmon fisher, hired down from Oregon. The crew had unloaded the usual relief supplies, canned milk and shrink-wrapped cheese, cans of peanut butter and stuff like that. It had unloaded mail.

Mail. Letters. Junk mail, for God's sake. No power yet, no telephones, but the US Postal Service had come through. Neither rain nor snow nor earthquake . . . Ellen struggled to swallow the hurting lump in her throat as she walked slowly homeward. Back on the beach — the new, Wave-scoured beach — people were sorting through envelopes and catalogues and cards. Crying and laughing. Britty Harris had gone into hysterics over a postcard from her vacationing brother. *Wish you were here*, he had scrawled on the back of a glossy picture of Fisherman's Wharf.

Wish you were here. Neither Fisherman's Wharf nor her brother were there anymore.

There had been no ghost mail from Rebecca. The lump swelled, threatening to turn into more tears. Ellen ducked her head and walked faster. Her shadow stretched seaward, a tall, thin caricature of herself. Perhaps she was *becoming* a caricature, turned hollow and surreal by the force of the Quake. Changed.

Beanpole, Rebecca had called her, and said, *Why can't I be thin like you?* at least once a week. Then Ellen would tell her to quit eating so much junk food and Rebecca would call her a Jewish mother and they would both laugh, because Scandinavian-blonde Ellen had grown up Catholic, and Rebecca was Jewish. It had been a ritual between them — a lightly spoken touchstone of love. As she turned up the walkway to the house, the unshed tears settled into Ellen's stomach, hard as beach pebbles.

It was a cottage, more than a house. Weathered gray shingles, weathered gray roof. Rebecca's house, because she'd always wanted to live near the sea, even though she had called it *ours*. Scraggly geraniums bloomed in a pot on the tiny front porch. The pot — generic red earthenware — was cracked. Ellen had watched it crack, clinging to this very railing as the earth shuddered and the house groaned in a choir of terrifying voices.

Earthquake, Ellen had thought in surprise. *That's not supposed to happen here.*

They'd heard it was the Big One on Jack's generator-run radio. But it was only after the relief boats started coming that they got to see the news photos of San Francisco and L.A. Ellen stomped sand from her shoes on the three wooden steps, went inside. A long worktable filled half of the single main room. Boxes of beads, feathers, and assorted junk cluttered the floor, and unfinished collages leaned against the wall. Rebecca's workspace. Rebecca's *life.* The room looked . . . unfamiliar. The Quake had changed everything, had charged the air with something like electricity. Angles and familiar lines looked sharp and strange and new, as if the unleashed force had transformed flowerpots and people and houses on some subtle, molecular scale.

Ellen set the bundled mail down on the stained formica of the kitchen counter and worked one of the rubber bands loose. Bank statements. Mail order catalogues, bright with spring dresses and shoes. A sale flyer from an art supply dealer. The second rubber band snapped as Ellen slid her fingers beneath it. The unexpected sting filled her eyes with tears. They spilled over and ran down her cheeks. She sobbed once, clutching the stupid, useless envelopes, fighting the tide that would rise up if she let it, and sweep her away.

Mail. It meant that Rebecca was dead. Ellen's tears made round, wrinkled spots on a glossy sportswear catalogue. All these endless weeks, she had told herself that Rebecca had survived, had cowered in the safety of some doorway or park while San Francisco dissolved in rubble and flame. She had told herself that Rebecca was in some schoolhouse shelter, frantic with worry because she couldn't call. As long as Ellen believed this — as long as she really — *believed* — then, Rebecca was alive.

How could you believe in a miracle, with a sportswear catalogue in your hands?

I have never lived without Rebecca, Ellen thought in terror.

That wasn't quite true. She had passed through childhood without Rebecca, had only met her in college. Rebecca had been struggling through art-majors' bio, as it was called. Ellen had helped her, because she was a bio major and Rebecca's outraged frustration made her laugh. *You need someone to take care of you,* Ellen had said lightly . They had moved in together a month later. Fifteen years ago. Ellen looked up at the cupboard above the sink.

The bottle of pills was up there, on the top shelf behind the glasses, with the aspirin and antacids. Sleeping pills, prescribed for Rebecca years ago, after she hurt her knee skiing. Would Ellen die if she took them all? She had a hard time swallowing capsules. They would stick to the back of her throat, hard, gelatinous lumps of oblivion. She would have to drink glasses of water to get them down.

Someone knocked on the door.

Rebecca? The traitorous rush of hope made her dizzy. "Coming!" Ellen flung the door open.

"Mom's sick." A girl stared up at her, dirty-faced, tousle-headed, a stranger. "Please come."

Not Rebecca "Who are you?" Ellen said numbly. "Where did you come from?"

"I'm Beth. Our car ran out of gas and we got lost. Please hurry."

Ellen blinked at the girl. Eleven? Twelve? Gawky and blonde, but you noticed her eyes first. They were a strange color, depthless blue, like the sky after sunset.

"All right." Ellen sighed and stepped out onto the porch. "Take me to your mom."

The girl turned unhesitatingly inland, trotting up through the scraggly spring grass toward the forested ridge above the cottage. "Wait a minute," Ellen called, but the girl didn't slow down, didn't even look back. Ellen hesitated, then ducked her head and broke into a run, was panting after only a dozen uphill yards, because Rebecca had run every morning and Ellen hadn't.

The girl crouched in the tree shadows, cradling a woman in her arms. The woman's face was flushed and she breathed in short, raspy breaths. Her hair stuck to her face, dark and stringy, as if she had been sweating, but when Ellen touched her cheek, her skin felt hot and dry.

"How long has your mother been sick?" Ellen asked the girl.

"A couple of days. It rained on us and it was cold. Mom let me wear her jacket, but then she started shivering."

"We've got to get her down to the house somehow." This was a crisis and Ellen could handle crises. She'd had fifteen years of practice, because Rebecca *didn't* handle them. She squatted beside the sick woman, shook her gently. "Can you wake up?"

Miraculously, the woman's eyelids fluttered.

"Come on, honey. Got to get you on your feet." Ellen slid her arm beneath the woman's shoulders.

Another miracle. The woman mumbled something incoherent and struggled to her feet. Ellen kept her arm around her, frightened by her fierce heat, supporting her. Step by step, she coaxed the woman down the slope, staggering like a drunk beneath her slack weight.

It took forever to reach the house, but they finally made it. Ellen put the woman into Rebecca's empty (forever, Oh God) bed. The rasp of her breathing scared Ellen. Pneumonia? In the old days, before antibiotics, people had died from flu and pneumonia. The Quake had smashed the comfortable present as it smashed through the California hills. It had warped time back on itself, had brought back the old days of candles and no roads and death from measles or cholera. Seal Cove had no doctor. Big chunks of the California coast had fallen into the sea and you couldn't get there from here.

"I'll walk down to the store." Ellen poured water into a bowl from the kitchen jug, got a clean washcloth down from the shelf. "Jack can call Eureka on the radio. They'll send a helicopter to take your mom to the hospital. I'm going to give her some aspirin and I want you to wipe her all over while I'm gone." She handed the washcloth to Beth. "We need to get her fever down."

"Okay." The girl looked up at Ellen, her eyes dark and fierce. "She'll be all right. I love her."

She'll be all right. I love her. That incantation hadn't saved Rebecca. Ellen swallowed. "What's your mom's name, honey?"

"Laura Sorenson." The girl dipped the folded washcloth into the water. "She'll get well. She *has* to."

Her hands were trembling as she wiped her mother's face. Ellen groped for reassuring words and found only emptiness. "I'll be back in a little while," she said.

Clouds were boiling up over the horizon again by the time Ellen returned to the house. The wind gusted on shore, whipping the waves, snatching wisps of spume from the gray curl of the breakers. There had been a lot of storms lately, as if the Quake's terrible power had been absorbed into the atmosphere, was being discharged in raging wind and waves.

"Jack called the relief people up in Eureka." Ellen flinched as the wind slammed the screen door behind her. "They'll send the helicopter for your mom, just as soon as it gets back in." If the weather didn't stop it. She closed the wooden door against the building storm. "How is she?"

"Asleep." Beth hovered protectively in the bedroom doorway. "Better, I think."

Ellen edged past her and bent over the bed. She was worse, struggling to breathe, burning with fever. The woman's eyelids fluttered and Ellen shivered. There was a disinterested glaze to her eyes, as if the woman was on a boat, watching a shoreline recede into the distance. She is dying, Ellen thought and shivered again. "Beth?" Distract her. "Come have something to eat, okay? I don't want you getting sick, too."

"If you want." Beth sat reluctantly at the kitchen table. "What a pretty woman." She nodded at the watercolor on the wall "Did you paint it?" she asked with a child's transparent effort to be polite.

"No." Some art student had painted it, years ago. Rebecca was smiling, head tilted, one hand in her dark, thick, semitic hair that had just been starting to go gray. The student had caught the impatience, the *intensity* that kept her up all night working, sent her weeping into Ellen's bed in the dawn, full of exhaustion and triumph and doubts. *Tell me it's not awful,* she would whisper. *God, EL, I need you.* "It's a picture of my friend." Ellen busied herself peeling back shrink-wrap and slicing the yellow block of salmon-boat cheese. "Is a cheese sandwich all right?"

"Fine."

Silence. The rasp of the dying woman's breathing filled the kitchen. "She was an artist," Ellen said too loudly. "She did collages. When they started selling, I quit my job and we moved out here." *You supported me*, Rebecca had said, grinning. *While I was a starving artist. Now you get to be my kept woman.* "I took care of her. She needed a full-time keeper when she was working."

Beth nodded politely, eyes on the bedroom door. "Where is she now?"

"She's dead." The words caught Ellen by surprise. "She was in . . . San Francisco. When the Quake happened." She set the plate of sandwiches down in front of Beth with a small thump, aware of the pill bottle up on the top shelf. "I'll get you some water."

"I'm really sorry." Beth touched her hand. "That your friend died."

"Me, too," Ellen whispered.

Storm wind whined around the corners of the house, banging a loose piece of gutter against the eaves. Shadows were creeping into the corners. She switched on the fluorescent lantern, hung it on its hook above the table. The shadows cast by its gentle swinging made the watercolor Rebecca smile, but her eyes looked sad. "In a hundred years, we'll have forgotten how California looked before the Quake," Ellen murmured. "Everything will seem so *normal.*"

"We lived in Berkeley. " Beth lifted a corner of bread, stared at the yellow slab of cheese beneath. "We had an apartment near the doctor's office where Mom was a nurse. I was across the street telling Cara about Mr. Walther's giving me a referral at school and all of a sudden we fell down. I saw our building *sway*, like it was made out of rubber. Pieces cracked out of it and started falling. Cars were crashing into things and Cara was screaming. Her voice sounded so *small*. All you could hear was this giant roar. I thought . . . Mom was dead."

"She wasn't dead." Beth had won that terrible lottery and Ellen had lost. Outside, the wind rattled the screen door against its hook. Beth was trembling and Ellen's twinge of anger metamorphosed suddenly into sympathy. "C'mon, eat." She put her arm around Beth's shoulders. *Eat*, she had said a hundred times a week to Rebecca. *You can't live on corn chips and pop, you idiot.* "Take your time. I'll check on your mom," she said.

The lantern streaked Rebecca's bedroom with dim light and shadow. Beth's mother — Laura — lay still beneath the light sheet. She didn't react as Ellen wiped her hot face with a washcloth. Her breathing was shallow and uneven. Outside, wind fluttered the shingles with the sound of cards riffling in a giant hand. No helicopter would land to save her.

"Ellen?" Beth's butterfly touch made Ellen jump, raised gooseflesh on her arms. "What's wrong?"

"Nothing."

"Don't lie to me." Beth's face was pale. "You think she's dying."

Ellen opened her mouth, but the lie wouldn't come.

"She can't die," Beth whispered. "She *can't*. I need her."

Need couldn't save the one you loved. "Your mom's sleeping and you need some sleep, too." Ellen steered Beth firmly out of the room. "You can sleep in my bed tonight. I'll sit up with your mom."

"She'll be better when she wakes up." Beth's shoulders stiffened. "She *has* to be."

"I'm sure she will be," Ellen said, but Beth's eyes told her she knew the lie for what it was.

Ellen found an extra nightshirt and tucked Beth into her own bed. Such bitter, bitter irony, to survive the Quake just to die from the busy breeding of invisible bacteria. "Go to sleep," Ellen whispered. "Your mom will be fine."

"She was making fudge." Beth looked up at Ellen, golden hair spread across the pillow. "She always made fudge on Wednesday, because Wednesday's her day off and fudge is our favorite thing in the whole world. The corner where our apartment is cracked and just fell down. This big chunk of concrete landed on a man and you couldn't even see what happened to him. Just dust, lots of dust. It hid everything and then there was smoke and fire and Cara was screaming that everyone was dead, that Mom was dead. She ran away, but I waited for the firetrucks. They didn't come and then the whole building fell in and Cara's building was on fire and I had to run away after all."

Teams filled those depthless eyes. "It's all right, honey." Ellen stroked her face. "Your mom got out, remember?"

"Cara was lying," Beth said shrilly. "She always lied. I knew Mom wasn't dead, but I couldn't find her. I saw a body lying in a pile of bricks. It was a man with black hair. He didn't have any pants on and one of his legs was gone. Some firemen in yellow coats told me they'd help me, but they didn't. They took me to this park and it wasn't even in Berkeley. There were tents and lots of people. I told them I couldn't stay, that I had to look for my mother, but they wouldn't listen to me. There was a fence around the park. And soldiers. They wouldn't let me out. They said that Mom would come look for me there, but how could she *know?*"

"She found you. She's right here, Beth." And dying. Ellen put her arms around the shaking girl, held her close, rocking her gently.

"I found *her*," Beth whispered. "We're going to Grandpa's house, up in Oregon. We'll be safe there. You think she's dying." Beth pushed Ellen away. "She's *not* dying. I won't let her die."

"There, there," Ellen soothed, but tears stung her eyes. "You sleep now." She kissed Beth gently on the forehead. "I'll take good care of your mom."

"She won't die." Beth turned onto her side and closed her eyes.

But she *was* dying. Ellen sat beside her bed, wiping her fever-hot body with the wet cloth. Had Rebecca's last moments been full of terror and pain? Had she bled to death, trapped under fallen ceilings and walls, or had she burned, screaming? Outside, the wind hurled itself inland, slamming against the house with the Quake's absorbed power, shaking it to its foundations. Ellen rinsed the cloth. It was warm with the woman's heat. She didn't look like Beth. She had dark hair and an olive tint to her skin. The lantern cast long shadows across the floor and something creaked in the main room. Rebecca's ghost?

Need shapes our lives, Ellen thought dully. Need for food, for attention, for power. The need for love. That's the foundation, the rock on which we build everything. "How can I live without Rebecca?" she whispered.

The woman's eyelids twitched. "Joseph?" she whispered. "Have to get back . . . Love . . . don't worry . . ." The feeble words fluttered to silence.

Joseph? Ellen wiped the woman's, forehead. Beth's father? Beth hadn't mentioned a Joseph or a father.

Ellen woke to gray dawn light and the morning sounds of surf. Her head was pillowed on the sick woman's thigh and the washcloth made a damp spot on the quilt. Afraid, Ellen jerked upright.

"Hello," Laura Sorenson whispered.

Still alive! "Good morning." Guilty and relieved, Ellen stifled a yawn. "I didn't mean to fall asleep. How are you feeling?"

"Tired. What . . . happened?"

"You're in my house. You've been sick." Ellen touched the woman's forehead. No fever. "Beth's here, too, and she's fine. Your daughter's a brave girl."

"Beth? I . . . don't have a daughter." She clutched weakly at the sheet. "Why did you call me Laura? That's not . . . my name,"

"Just take it easy." Ellen patted Laura's shoulder, hiding dismay. "You had a high fever."

"Oh." Fear flickered in the woman's dark eyes. "Did I hit my head? What day is this? I feel as if . . . I've been dreaming for a long time."

"You were just sick," Ellen murmured. "It's March 25. Don't worry about it now. I'll get you some water, or would you rather have some orange juice?"

"March?" the woman whispered brokenly. "It *can't* be. Why can't I remember?"

In the kitchen, Ellen spooned orange crystals into glass from a white can, trying to recall the effects of a prolonged high fever. Seizures, she remembered, but Laura hadn't gone into convulsions. Amnesia? Ellen shook her head, stirred the fake juice to orange froth. She carried the glass back to the bedroom and found Beth already there, her arms around her mother.

"Mom, it's *me*," Beth was saying in a broken voice.

"It's . . . coming back." Laura stroked her daughter's back. Beth. Honey, it'll be all right."

There was a tentative quality to the gesture and a frightened expression in her eyes. "Here's your juice," Ellen said, holding out the glass. "How are you doing?"

Beth almost snatched the glass from Ellen's hand. "I told you she'd get well," she said.

Voyeur, outsider, Ellen watched Beth help her mother drink. Side by side, they looked even less alike. There was a protective possessiveness to Beth's posture; a confidence that was lacking in Laura. Beth might be the mother; Laura the fragile child.

"Thank you." The woman sank back on the pillows, trying for a smile. "Thank you for taking us in. We must be a horrible burden."

"Not at all." Ellen collected the empty glass. "I'm just glad you're better."

Laura stroked her daughter's hair. "Beth said I was in our apartment when it happened. I'm . . . starting to remember." She spoke hesitantly, like an actor groping for half-learned lines. "What about . . . Joseph? Oh . . . God, Joseph!"

"What's wrong? Who's Joseph, Mom?" Beth stroked a strand of hair back from her mother's face. "Someone at the office?"

"No. I . . . don't know. I don't know a Joseph, do I? It was a . . . dream, I guess. From the fever." She squeezed Beth's hand, her fingers trembling.

"You'll sort it out." Ellen touched Laura's shoulder, moved by the anguish in her face. "I've got to run into town." She had almost forgotten the helicopter. "I'll be back in an hour. There's more water in the jugs beside the kitchen counter."

Laura nodded weakly, but her eyes never left her daughter's face. She is afraid, Ellen thought.

Of what?

At the store, Jack eyed her over the fake tortoiseshell rim of his glasses as he called Eureka and canceled the helicopter. "They were busy anyway," he drawled. "Guess the storm hit real bad up there. Your visitor wasn't so sick, huh?"

Dumb woman, his expression said. *Don't know sick from dying.*

"She was *dying*." Ellen snapped, but she hadn't died, had she? "I guess I was wrong." she said lamely. "Thanks for calling Eureka." She turned away from Jack's cool, judgmental face. She had no real friends in this Godforsaken town. Ellen-and-Rebecca had been a complete and seamless universe. She could feel the shattered bits of that universe crunching beneath her feet. "I'd better get back," she said.

"Oh yeah." Jack crossed his arms on the top of the old-fashioned wood-and-glass counter. "Aaron McDevitt was in yesterday, to pick up his share of the food. He said he found a car up on the old logging road across Bear Ridge." He cleared his throat. "Aaron brought this in." He fished around behind the counter, laid a brown handbag on the scarred wood, put a woman's wallet down beside it. "Wasn't no money in it," he said.

Aaron would have made sure of that. Ellen picked up the leather wallet. The bag was leather, too. It looked expensive. She opened the wallet. Credit cards from stores and oil companies. A check guarantee card. All in the name of Julia DeMarco. Ellen started to say that it didn't belong to Laura, but she closed her mouth without speaking. Laura's dark oval face smiled at her from a California driver's license.

Julia DeMarco!

"This is her bag." Ellen folded up the wallet, stuffed it back into the bag. "I'll take it to her. Thanks," she said too quickly. "Thank Aaron, too, when you see him."

She left the store, feeling guilty, as if she was partner to some crime. There were hundreds of reasons to lie about your name — some good, lots of them bad. Ellen stopped at the bottom of her driveway and opened the bag again. It held the usual stuff, checkbook, wallet, makeup items and a leatherbound datebook. Ellen found a leather card case full of business cards, printed on creamy stock.

Julia DeMarco

Attorney at Law

The address was San Francisco. Beth had told Ellen that her mother was a nurse in Berkeley. The datebook listed court dates, appointments, and reminders to pick up dry cleaning or visit the dentist. Ellen paged through it. *Joseph's Birthday* was written neatly at the top of the page for next Wednesday. Joseph. A dream, Laura had said with her face full of anguish. Ellen stuffed everything back into the bag and hurried up the lane to the house.

Inside, the watercolor Rebecca glowed on the wall. Ellen tossed the bag onto the cluttered worktable and went into the bedroom.

"Hi." Laura smiled wanly at Ellen. "Beth went to get more water. She said she saw a pool up above the house."

"The spring." Ellen nodded. "That was nice of her."

"Beth's a good kid. She had to grow up a little too early. There was a divorce — a custody battle. I think . . . it was ugly. I think it . . . hurt Beth."

Again, the sense of lines being recited. "You're remembering?" Ellen asked.

"I don't know." Laura's eyes flickered. "I remember scenes or faces — and I don't know them, but I do. I'm not making any sense, am I?" Her laugh was fragile, edged with hysteria. "Did our building burn down? I remember it burning and . . . I remember picking up pieces of a broken vase and thinking how *lucky* I was. I keep wanting to remember that it was a house, but it was an apartment, wasn't it?"

Ellen took a quick breath. "Who's Julia DeMarco?"

"I . . . don't know. Do I?" Laura whispered. "Joseph . . .? Oh, God." She buried her face in her hands. "Why do I want to cry? What's *wrong* with me? I don't even know where we are or why we're *here*."

"Take it easy." Ellen stroked Laura's back. "You'll straighten everything out eventually." Would she? Who *are* you? she wondered, but she didn't say it out loud.

"Hi, Mom." Beth stuck her head through the doorway, a wet jug in each hand. "What's wrong?" She dropped the jugs, ran to the bedside. "Mom, what's *wrong*?"

"Nothing . . . nothing." Laura straightened, struggling to smile for her daughter. "I'm still feeling . . . shaky."

"Oh, Mom." Beth clutched her mother. "You'll remember again. You have to."

"Of course I will, sweetheart." Laura buried her face in her daughter's hair. "It's all right, Beth. Really."

Was it? Ellen tiptoed out of the room. Perhaps it would be all right. Perhaps Laura Sorenson would wake up tomorrow and remember the burning apartment. And what about Julia DeMarco? What about Joseph? Not my business, Ellen told herself fiercely. Not at all. She got a pot down from the kitchen cupboard, filled it with water from the dripping jug.

"What are you doing?" Beth asked from the doorway.

"Fixing brunch."

"I'll help you." Beth perched herself on the table. "What can I do?"

"Nothing just yet." Ellen measured dusty flakes of oatmeal into the water. "Why were you going to your grandfather's house? Half the roads in the state are closed. Why didn't you and your mom stay in San Francisco?"

"We . . . couldn't."

Aha. "Why not?"

No answer.

Ellen lit the little white-gas camping stove, set the pot of oatmeal on to boil.

"They wouldn't let me go," Beth spoke suddenly. She sat rigidly straight, hands tucked beneath her thighs, eyes fixed on her knees. "I saw her one afternoon, but she was outside the fence and she didn't see me. When I told them, they said she was dead, that she'd died in our building. They said I'd have to wait for my father to come. He'd never let me go back to Mom. Never. The firemen told me they'd help me find Mom, but they lied. They just took me to that place." She looked at Ellen at last. "The man at the gate hit me, when I tried to run after her."

Such terrible eyes, dark as the Quake-storm yesterday. They were full of desperate need. Full of power. Power to tear apart the landscape of reality, to reshape it like the Quake had reshaped the hills? A hissing startled Ellen and she snatched her gaze away from those depthless eyes, grabbing a potholder. Sticky oatmeal foamed over the lip of the pot and bubbled down the side.

Oh, yes, she understood the power of need. Ellen stirred the boiling cereal, Rebecca's absence a gaping wound in her heart.

"Grandpa won't let Dad take me," Beth went on in a flat monotone. "He won't let them take Mom. We'll be safe there. We'll be happy. They want to take her away." Beth's voice cracked suddenly, became the cry of a frightened child. "They *can't!*"

"Honey, it's all right." Ellen's arms went around her. She knew the terror, had felt it every dark, post-Quake night, as she waited to hear from Rebecca. It had seeped into the marrow of her bones and would never go away. "It's all right," she murmured. Beth was sobbing, her thin body shaking as Ellen held her close.

Nothing was all right. The Quake had shattered the earth. It had shattered buildings and freeways, it had buckled lives, smashed them into ruin. So much power, but it was an innocent power; destruction without choice or anger. The sky had absorbed some of that power, had transformed it into the wild, unseasonable storms that were battering the coast. Children were such *sponges*. They absorbed experiences so easily . . .

Beth's sobs were diminishing. Ellen stroked her hair back from her damp and swollen face. "Why don't you ask your mom if she wants honey or canned milk on her cereal," she said.

"She puts milk on it." Beth hiccoughed. "And brown sugar."

"I think I have a little brown sugar left." How did Julia DeMarco like her oatmeal? Ellen fished in the cupboard, found a plastic bag with a few brown lumps left in it. It didn't matter, she thought as she crumbled rock hard lumps onto the steaming cereal. Beth's mother had liked brown sugar on her oatmeal and Beth needed her mother. Desperately. With all the power of the Quake.

She had found her, on the other side of a barbed-wire fence. She had reshaped Julia DeMarco into Laura Sorenson, as innocent and destructive as the Quake that had reshaped California.

"I'll fill yours," Beth said gravely. "Do you want honey and milk on it?"

"Thank you," Ellen said. She picked up the tray, carried it into the bedroom.

"I could eat at the table with you." Laura sat up straighter as Ellen put the tray down on her lap. "I'm feeling much better."

She wore a gold wedding ring on her left hand. "You can get up anytime." Was Joseph searching frantically for Julia DeMarco, praying that she was still alive?

"I'll come eat with you." Beth came in with her bowl, her eyes bright with love.

How many days had Beth huddled behind the barbed wire of a refugee camp, filling the black hole of her loss with the Quake's power, waiting for a mother who would never come? Ellen tiptoed into the kitchen. In the bedroom, Beth laughed and Laura joined in tentatively. Maybe Julia had been a volunteer at the refugee center, or had been hired to untangle the miles of legal red tape. Ellen wondered why Beth had chosen her. Perhaps the choice had been as random as the Quake's violence.

She's not dying, Beth had said and those words had been an incantation. This woman couldn't die any more than she could remain Julia DeMarco. Beth needed her mother. Julia DeMarco had had no choice at all.

A bowl of oatmeal cooled on the table, flanked neatly by spoon and napkin. With honey and milk. Sunlight streamed through the window into the cluttered room, and the watercolor Rebecca smiled gently from the wall. "I will always love you," Ellen whispered to her. Standing on her toes, she took the bottle of pills down from the cabinet shelf.

The helicopter from Eureka landed at dusk. The blades flattened the grass in the front yard and whipped a small sandstorm into the air. "In here," Ellen told the tired-looking paramedic who climbed out of the hatch. "She's unconscious." She had put three of the sleeping capsules into Laura's hot chocolate, had been terrified that it might be too much.

The paramedics took Laura's blood pressure, shone a light into her eyes, frowned, and asked Ellen questions. "She seemed to be getting better," Ellen told them. "And then, all of a sudden, she just collapsed I had Jack call you right away."

"Does she have any ID?" the taller of the two men asked her. He had black hair and dark circles beneath his eyes.

"She had this." Ellen handed them Julia DeMarco's handbag. "Off and on, she'd forget who she was. She was confused. I don't know how she ended up out here."

"Lady, we've seen stranger things." The dark-haired paramedic shrugged. "She's pretty unresponsive. We'll take her in."

They lifted her onto a stretcher with remarkable gentleness and loaded her into the belly of the waiting helicopter; Laura Sorenson, Julia DeMarco. Tomorrow, she would wake up in the Eureka hospital and for a while, she would wonder where she was and who she was. But she would remember. Someone would contact Joseph. He would hurry out to Eureka in an ecstasy of fear and relief, and he would help her to remember. Happy birthday, Joseph.

Outside, the helicopter thundered into the sky. Ellen left the lantern on — a flagrant waste of precious batteries, but she couldn't face the darkness. The room looked strange in the feeble glow of yellow light — streaked with shadows and memories. Each item, each tool in Rebecca's cluttered workspace, carried echoes of laughter and tears and *life*. Memories. Ellen picked up a leather-gouge, envisioning Rebecca bent over her work table. How can you be sure that what you remember really happened? She tucked the gouge into a box and reached for a basket of feathers.

She spent the night sorting through shells, beads, and tools; through the moments of their life together. On the wall, Rebecca's watercolor eyes were full of life and love, full of death. Ellen packed everything into the cartons left over from hauling home the relief supplies. In the gray pre-dawn light, she stacked the last of the filled cartons in a corner of the shed out behind the house.

The first beams of sunlight streaked the sparse grass in the front yard and stretched shadows westward toward the beach. In a few weeks, they would have power again, and running water. Slowly, the scars would be covered by new buildings, new grass, new roads, new lives. Scars on the soul were harder to heal. Ellen closed the shed door, snapped the padlock shut.

Beth waited in the neat, uncluttered house, a little unsteady on her feet. "What are you doing? Where's Mom?" She rubbed at her eyes, words slurring a little.

A whole capsule had been just right. "I couldn't sleep." Ellen's heart began to pound, but she kept her tone casual. "I thought I'd clean up Grandpa's house."

Beth's eyes widened.

"I was going to take a walk on the beach," Ellen said quickly. "Do you want to come along?"

Beth nodded slowly, silent and wary.

The rising sun burned on the rim of the hills as they walked across the smooth white sand. The Wave had washed out the road in some places, left it hanging like an asphalt cliff in others. Beth remained silent, her twilight eyes full of shadows and unconscious power. I should be afraid, Ellen thought, but she wasn't afraid. She had lost her capacity for fear when she had contemplated the pills, with her hands full of mail.

The watercolor crackled as she pulled it from her pocket and unfolded it. Rebecca smiled at her, eyes sparkling in the morning light. "Rebecca, I love you," Ellen whispered. "I will always love you, but you were the strong one. Not me. I am not strong enough to use the pills and I am not strong enough to live without you. Forgive me." She wrapped the stiff paper around a beach stone and fastened it with one of the thick rubber-bands that had come on the mail. The rising sun stretched her shadow seaward as she drew her arm back and hurled the painting-wrapped stone far out into the offshore swell.

The Quake had released so much power. It charged the air like electricity, it shimmered in Beth's twilight eyes. Innocent power. The power to reshape reality, like the Quake had reshaped the land. Rebecca had needed her, but Rebecca was dead. Beth needed her mother. Ellen could feel that need seeping into the hole Rebecca had left in her life, filling her up like the tide. Behind her, waves curled and broke, dissolving the painting. She didn't want to look at Rebecca's face one day, and see a stranger.

What will I remember tomorrow? Ellen reached for Beth's hand, shivering a little at the cool touch of the girl's fingers. She could feel the change shuddering through her, an invisible Quake across the landscape of the soul. "There's chocolate in the cupboard. We've got margarine from the last relief boat and canned milk," Ellen smiled. "We could try to make fudge. It's Wednesday, after all."

Beth's slow smile was like the sun rising, bringing color to the gray world. "It *is* Wednesday." She put her arm around Ellen's waist, face turned up to hers, eyes full of twilight and love. "I'm so *glad* we're here," she said.

"Me, too," Ellen whispered. She could almost remember it — the apartment and the doctor's office where she had worked. Tomorrow, or the next day, she *would* remember it. Beth needed here. She would take care of her daughter and they would be happy together.

Beth had said so.

Down Behind
Cuba Lake

NANCY KRESS

ABOUT NANCY KRESS
AND
DOWN BEHIND CUBA LAKE

Down Behind Cuba Lake *was first published:*
Isaac Asimov's, *September 1986*

Nancy Kress has become one of the most important science fiction writers of the late 1980s and early 1990s. The quality of her work has already earned her an prominent place in the history of the field, but only the staying power necessary to produce a large body of work can secure it. Meanwhile a fine line-up of distinguished novels like The Golden Grove, The White Pipes, An Alien Light *and* Beggars in Spain *keep her multitude of fans satisfied, although eagerly begging for more.*

In the meantime her multiple awards and award nominations ensure her current popularity and high prestige. In "Down Behind Cuba Lake" Ms. Kress's heroine finds herself trying to resolve a problem multitudes of women have faced: how to break off with a captivating married lover who won't break off with his wife. When the protagonist drives off the edge of reality into an alternate world (perhaps), she resolves her own dilemma by discovering a profound secret of the universe, and an even more profound one about relationships.

Down Behind Cuba Lake

by NANCY KRESS

hen Jane finished reading the letter for the third time, she picked up the phone. Anger bubbled up through her like bad champagne, heady and perversely sweet. One hundred twenty miles away, Nick answered on the second ring.

"Hello?"

"This is Jane. I got your letter."

"Jane . . ."

"Yeah, Jane. You remember me. It was a lovely letter, Nick. Chatty and friendly and sweet."

Silence .

"It was really lovely to hear such great detail about the remodeling of your garage."

He said, very quietly, "Don't, Jane."

"Don't what?" she said automatically, before his quietness hit her. Then it did. This was Wednesday.

'Your wife is home."

"Yes."

Non-commital, neutral. Was the woman in the same *room?* "You can't talk."

"No."

" 'Yes,' 'No' — What are you pretending, that I'm a fucking *construction client?"*

In his silence, Jane heard that he was doing just that. Tears bit her eyes. She moved to slam down the phone, stopping herself at the last possible moment before the receiver smashed into the erect double buttons.

"I'm coming down there, Nick. Tonight, after my evening class. I'll be there by 11:30. Meet me at the bar, and you damn well better be there this time, I swear it. I have to talk to you. If you're not there, I'll come to your house and ring the bell and talk to you there."

She didn't wait for Nick's answer but she heard part of it anyway, while the receiver was on its way down: "Wait, tonight isn't —" The words already sounded tinny with distance, ghostly with loss.

She knew she was a better teacher when she was angry, was perhaps even at her best then. Even Freshman Composition sat up straight in its chairs, stopped doodling in its collective margins. During Romantic and Victorian Poetry, Jane sparkled with irony, grew passionate with the sort of literary scorn that impresses graduate students. Her notes strode across the board in a forceful hand she scarcely recognized as her own. The better students' eyes took on that thoughtful look that was at once public reward and a kind of private, sly seduction.

Not tonight, chickies. Sorry. Teacher has a headache.

Jane let them go at 8:45, fifteen minutes early, knowing she would need the time to peel them both off Wordsworth and off her, and escape to the car. By 9:02 she was pulling away from the campus, the lights of the high-rise dorms shining in her rear-view mirror in erratic patterns like some indecipherable message from the sky itself. The October night was cold, desolately beautiful. She could feel her anger begin to slide away; she whipped it up again, afraid to feel what might take its place.

Dear Nick,

Don't write me, not even about the fascinating progress in remodeling your garage. I'll just have to live without finding out how much the in-sulation exceeds federal energy specifications. Don't write me, don't call me, don't try to drive up and walk into one of my classes —

Fat chance.

She was crying again. *Fuck it.* She swiped at her eyes with a Kleenex, hunkered down over the wheel like a bad parody of a race car driver, and concentrated on the road. One hundred twenty miles south through the Allegheny foothills and over the border into Pennsylvania, the last section expressway but the rest New York State Route 19 south through decaying small towns and comatose cabbage farms. Two and a half hours, if it didn't rain. In two and a half hours she would slide into a booth in a roadside bar across from Nick and say . . . what?

Don't call me, don't write me . . .

Fat chance.

Not tonight, chickies. Teacher has a heartache.

She lost Route 19 at Pike, without at first realizing it. Clouds had rolled in from the west, and there were no street lights except for the sole traffic light at the sole major crossroads of Pike itself. On campus, life went on twenty-four hours; this empty blackness, mile after mile of it broken only by an isolated farmhouse and her own headlights, was at first unsettling and then calming. Beyond the spectral sweep of her high beams lay sullen hills, sensed rather than seen even when the road rose and fell between them.

Jane rolled down the window. The air smelled of late autumn bitterness, wet leaves and wetter earth, violated out of season for the planting of winter wheat. Plows behind yellow tractors biting the ground. There would be thick raw furrows, naked without snow.

Twenty minutes past Pike, Jane knew she was lost. No more farmhouses, no more winter wheat, just dense woods crowding close to the road, which seemed to have shrunk. Jane scowled into blackness. *Let there be a roadsign. And lo, there were roadsigns! It's a miracle she's cured she can . . . . she can read again!*

There was no roadsign.

A hundred feet, a quarter mile, a half mile more of nothing but sullen void. Even the trees had retreated back from the shoulder of the road. When she pulled over to consult a map, the quality of the silence startled her with its velvet indifference, its country blackness.

My dear Nicholas,

Am writing this from the depths of nature, where I have gone to experience the fullness of the land and my own inner self, a Wordsworthian sentiment your pretty and illiterate little wife is Incapable of feeling. Please forgive the turds smeared on the back of this birchbark. They are not a personal message but rather a social statement as writing paper has come to seem a desecration of living timber which might provoke the ancient sleeping forces to retaliate —

The map was only limited help. The last landmark she remembered was Pike, where she must have missed the way Route 19 abruptly twisted southeast and instead had taken some branching local road. But the map, a gift from Mobil Oil, showed only main routes, and Jane had no idea in which direction she had branched, or if she had done so more than once. It was so damn dark . . .

She could either retrace her route north back to Pike, or forge on ahead. She had come maybe ten miles off 19—retracing would lose her another fifteen or twenty minutes. Since she had not twisted east when 19 did, she was probably still heading south, and if that were so she ought to be able to keep going until she rejoined 19, or else came directly to the Expressway at some point or other. The Expressway ran east and west; if she drove south long enough, she would *have* to come to it.

On impulse, Jane twisted the door handle. Outside the car, the darkness seemed even more furry, soft in the way heaps of banked ashes are soft, with the underlying sense of something alive, mute but not extinguished. She could not remember the last time she had stood alone this deep in wooded countryside. Maybe she never had. There was no sound, not even insects. Was it too late in the year for insects, were they all dead? When in the fall did insects die? What if the car broke down out here?

Inside, she rolled up the window as tight as it would go. Three miles down the twisting road, just when she was beginning to eye panic warily, as if it were a potentially dangerous student, she saw the glow of curious green lights through the trees. Green, surrounding a red and glowing blob.

She had met Nick a year ago. As part of a Faculty Exchange Program that had started mostly because there was State Arts Council money to start it, the community college in Pennsylvania had requested a guest lecture on World War I poet Siegfried Sassoon, and Jane had lost the political tussle not to go deliver it. Why Siegfried Sassoon? She never found out.

Nick had sat in the second row, a big glum man with gray in his dark beard and the serious tan of a man who worked outdoors. Throughout the lecture he scribbled dutifully in a notebook, asking no questions and showing no real interest in Sassoon's sing-song and bitter pacifism. Nonetheless, Jane found herself aware of him throughout, and when he came up to her in the coffee hour afterward, she put on her best can-I-help-you-understand-some-point bullshit smile, slightly curious to hear what this aging undergraduate would ask. But she hadn't been prepared for what he did say.

"It's gone, you know. All that Georgian anguish over war, and then all that sixties pacifism. The men I know who didn't go to Nam wish they had."

Jane froze. Stupidly — later she would see it had been stupidly, had given him some early indefinable advantage she never regained — she said, "No, they don't."

He smiled. "Afraid so. Me, too. We missed something."

"Missed?"

He looked at her more closely, and his expression shifted.

"Missed?" She heard her own voice, scaling slightly upward, the acceptable contempt not quite enough to cover the unacceptable panic. "I lost a brother in Vietnam. The men you know must be fools, or bastards, or both!"

His glumness seemed to deepen, settle over him like a mist, out of which his eyes watched her with the first hint she had of his astonishing ability to turn an attack into an occasion for reassurance. "Oh yes, they are that. All of us. Both."

Jane had found herself grinning: coldly, reluctantly, her anger not completely gone. It was a strange sensation; the skin around her mouth tingled with it. She had raised her eyes to his, all glum compassion, and the dreary room had suddenly seemed too bright, full of glare and sunshine, hot with possibility.

The greenish light turned out to be Christmas tree lights, half of them broken into jagged ovals, circling a window with a red COCA-COLA sign. Even in the dark, Jane could see the wooden store was unpainted. Gutters sagged below the roof line. She parked her Chevette next to the biggest pick-up truck she had ever seen, a monstrousity painted screaming yellow, and took the keys out of her ignition. To grasp the doorknob she had to reach through the soft worn ribbons of a screen door.

Inside, there were high half-empty shelves, one littered with the dusty yellow fallout from a bag of corn chips. Three people stood under a dim bulb, arguing fiercely. None of them looked at Jane.

"— paid last week, the full damn amount —"

"Like hell you did!"

"Like hell I didn't, Emma —"

"Excuse me," Jane said. The three looked up, annoyed. Uneasiness nibbled at Jane.

The woman — Emma — was huge, middle-aged muscle gone to fat stuffed into jeans and sweatshirt balanced over surprisingly small—even dainty—feet in Western boots. The boy, a gum-chewing ten or eleven, she would have passed a dozen times without noticing. But no one could not notice the man, if only because he matched the store too perfectly. In another setting Jane would have found him fascinating; in this one he seemed to her the creation of one of her second-rate students, a stale literary contrivance. Scrabbly-haired, wild-eyed, bearded, his knobby frame dressed in torn overalls and a dirty sheepskin-lined jacket.

"I'm lost," Jane said. "I'm trying to get back on Route 19, and I think I turned off it at Pike. What's the fastest way to pick it up south of here?"

The three stared blankly.

"Route 19," Jane repeated, more loudly. Were they all feeble? Rural inbreeding, exhausted chromosomes.

They went on staring. Then the woman stepped forward, a half-step in her delicate leather boots.

"Can't get there from here."

Exasperation flooded Jane, washing out her momentary uneasiness. "Of course you can get there from here I just *was* there. I left Route 19 at Pike and now I could just drive back the way I came, but I thought there might be a faster way to rejoin 19 farther south. I'm heading for Pennsylvania."

"Can't get there from here." the woman said. Her voice had changed, gone curiously gentle.

The wild man said, "She can go by down behind Cuba Lake."

The boy stopped chewing gum. The woman whipped around her huge body to turn on the man. "Down behind Cuba Lake! I'd like to see her try to go down behind Cuba Lake, you big fool! She'd get lost on them back roads before she knew it!"

"Huh," the man said, and there the discussion stopped. Man and woman glared at each other, Jane apparently forgotten. Their fury was inexplicable to her, but obviously unconnected to getting back to Route 19. She scanned the Mobil map. There were numerous tiny splotches of blue, most of them unlabeled.

"Which one is Cuba Lake?"

Everyone ignored her.

"Look," Jane said, "I'll just retrace the route I came. Thanks anyway." She turned to the door.

"Wait," the man said. He stepped closer; she smelled fetid whiskey on his breath. "There's a faster way. You just follow me half a mile. Then the road splits in three, I'll pull over and get out and show you which way to go. It goes on a ways, put you back on a main road that hooks into 19 south of Oramel."

Jane looked at him. At the edge of his flannel collar, a roll of gray flesh worked up and down.

"No, thanks. It'll probably be simpler to just drive back to Pike."

He shrugged. "Suit yourself."

"Hold still a minute," the woman said sharply. She took the map, not asking first, from Jane's hand and studied it. "Lose you half an hour. Maybe more. Yeah — more."

More. And she had already lost time she wouldn't get to Nick before 1:00 a.m. The bar would be deserted if it were open at all, the lights long since out behind Nick's Austrian pines.

"She can't even get down behind Cuba Lake," the woman said, still studying Jane's map. Her voice held a curious mixture of triumph and pique. Pique — that was reassuring, wasn't it? Pique wasn't an emotion that went with condoning a set-up for crime. "Not on that split."

"Huh," the man repeated. He raised one scrawny leg and stood balanced on the other like some extinct waterfowl, yellowed teeth chewing on his bottom lip and eyes gone inward. He looked so bizarre that Jane was suddenly sick of both of them, suddenly longed for the slick normality of a Safe-way. Clean plastic, college kids buying chips and beer, housewives with whining kids. An hour and a half.

"Look," she said with sudden decision, "when the road splits in three, which one do I take? Left, right, or middle?" She watched not the man but the woman, searching for some sign of complicity, some shifting of eyes or muscles that would map the woman as knowing him capable of . . . whatever. She didn't find it.

"Left," the man said. "But you could miss it, the middle curves a trick left too. I'll stop, get out, show you."

"Just honk," Jane said. "Honk at the split and I'll find it." She was still watching the woman, who showed only annoyance at having her opinion ignored. At the edge of her vision the man, still on one foot, nodded.

"Okay. I honk, you bear far left. Come on, boy."

Outside, the boy climbed into the cab of the huge yellow pick-up. Jane felt further reassured. It didn't seem likely a man bent on rape or robbery would bring along a child, did it? She locked her car doors and started the engine.

The road seemed even darker, more desolate than before. Jane's high beams glared off the rear of the pick-up. Despite herself, she peered at the window: no gun rack.

Dear Nick,

Literary models, like Newtonian physics, cause equal and opposite reactions. Put it in your course notes. I start to love you because you say something so outrageous that you can't possibly mean it. I follow a hillbilly derelict because he looks so much like a crazed killer that he can't possibly be one. The world is not that anthropomorphic, except in bad novels, which I've been reading a lot of lately in a stupid effort to not think about you —

The pick-up honked, slowed, and veered right. Jane caught her breath, unexpectedly panicked that it had after all been some sort of trap, that the man would shoot out her tires or follow her down what would turn out to be a deserted dead end. "Dead end" . . . who the hell coined these metaphors?

The yellow truck honked a second time and picked up speed, disappearing around a bend. Jane pushed her foot to the floor. Pebbles clattered against the underside of the Chevette. She slowed down, angry at herself: even if there were some sort of cut-off and the yellow truck suddenly bore down on her, it wouldn't help to be piled up against the dark woods.

Crouched over the wheel, she strained to see the twists and turns of the dirt road. Her high beams were unaccountably focused too high; they showed clearly the undersides of leaves clawing at each other from opposite sides of the road.

A few miles after the fork, the road ended.

First it climbed an abrupt rise, which descended even more abruptly. Jane's headlights, now pointed down, shimmered over a flat blackness. She slammed on the brakes and skidded, stopping inches from the water's edge.

Panic gripped her. Mud — the bank could be soft mud, cars sank in mud and then the pressure kept the doors from being opened from the inside — flinging open the door, Jane hurled herself out of the car and clambered back up the rise. Her heart slammed in her chest as she stood looking down on the smooth top of the Chevette, still shining its lights out over the lake.

Minutes passed. The top did not move. When Jane finally crept back down the slope, she tested the ground with each step. It held firm. Cautiously she reached into the car for her purse and pulled out a penlight. Hard ground, covered with tough weeds, extended clear to the water's edge. Beyond, the lake sighed softly. A breeze sprang up; the surface rippled like black muscle.

Cuba Lake?

In her haste at the triple fork, she must not have veered far enough left, and so had ended up on the middle road. The man had said . . . the man . . .

Jane scrambled back into the car, slammed the door, and switched off both headlights and flashlight. But after a moment anger began to burn away fear. She yanked the key to the right and began to back up the rise. Her beams again pointed down onto the lake, and for a moment it seemed something moved over the surface, far from shore. Jane turned her head back over her shoulder and tried to stay out of the underbrush.

At the top of the rise she did a three-point turn in seven points, then barreled back under the leaves that were like dark hands.

Nick —

I do not believe in ancient terrors stirring to life in the menacing country-side, shaping the lives of men as in some modern horror novel, any more than I believe in ancient benevolence stirring to life in the pastoral countryside as in the sentimental Romantic poets you unaccountably love so much —

Poets. What was she doing in possibly mortal danger, thinking about poets? *Nick, Nick, you corrupted me, my dissertation was on Zola — stay on the road, Jane you idiot, it turns here —*

Beyond the turn, the yellow pick-up blocked the road.

It was positioned with hood touching the dense trees on one side of the road, rear bumper on the other. There was no way around. Jane peered at the truck, one hand frozen halfway in the act of hitting the lights. The yellow cab seemed empty.

Then where was he, where were they . . . the boy, too —

Nick —

Carefully, fingers trembling on the wheel, she backed the car through the overhanging trees. A hundred yards before the turn, there had been a gap in the woods, something that might have been the remnant of another dirt track. If it angled upward, it might bypass the occupants of the pick-up, wherever they were.

She found the track, choked with weeds at its beginning but becoming surprisingly clear as she pushed along it. At one point Jane had the eerie sensation that she was driving on fresh asphalt, not dirt. The road seemed to neither curve back towards the lake nor to angle upwards — until it precipitately descended and Jane was again staring at the dark water of the lake.

She hit the brakes, stopped just short of the bank, and laid her forehead against the cold plastic of the steering wheel.

In her headlights, something dark moved over the water.

She tried to pull herself together, to think rationally. Of course all the dirt tracks would lead back to the lake; the lake was probably where everyone — or such "everyone" as there was around here — wanted to go. Kids fishing. Hunters out after deer. Lovers looking for a lane.

She resisted the impulse to open the car door and let the penlight search for used condoms.

This time there was room to turn the Chevette around by the water's edge, a wide shelf of weedy ground that nonetheless left her shaking each time the wheels approached the bank. The shaking made her inch up the rise, and so she was going slow enough to notice the nearly-hidden fork at the top. On the right, the clear road she had come down; on the left, a weed choked path.

She turned left. The path, wherever else it took her, headed away from the yellow truck. And after a hundred yards, it was even easier to drive on than the previous road. Caught between curiosity and dread, Jane stopped the car, opened the door just wide enough to take the width of the penlight, and shined it straight down.

Asphalt.

As she again drove forward, a sudden giddiness seized her. She even laughed out loud, a sound so high and abrupt that it made her shake her head ruefully. The car shimmied lightly.

Dear Nicky,

You my love are a fool to prefer your domestic little wife to a woman who can — single-handedly! yes! — defeat a mad hillbilly rapist AND a child-midget murderer AND — not to mention! — the dark forces rising from the gaseous swamps to ooze around the souls of the sinful, a group for which you and I definitely qualify. A pioneer of femininity, hacking her way through this slightly banal underbrush while your —

Ahead, the pick-up blocked the road.

Jane cried out. This time she nearly smashed into the passenger side of the cab before she was able to make her foot hit the brake. The tires squealed, laying rubber. Scabs of scrofulous yellow paint loomed at her.

There was no sound. After unbearable moments of dark silence, Jane leaned into the horn. Thin blatting leaked out into the thick air, was absorbed by it as by soggy wool. No one came.

The truck could not be there. There hadn't been time, the road beyond angled even farther to the left, even farther away from where the pickup had been parked before. It could not be there. It could not.

Shaking, Jane studied the truck. The front bumper was jammed against an outcropping of New England granite. But between the rear bumper and the trunk of a pulpy-looking tree Jane couldn't identify, was a gap that might be just large enough to ease the Chevette through. Or might not.

And if there *was* someone hunkered down in the yellow cab — someone small, a child — who reached up to turn on the ignition, to pull the clutch into reverse, to lean with both hands on the accelerator as the Chevy was easing through the gap, the pick-up would easily crush the passenger door. Would that make it easier or harder for someone to get inside? If the pick-up kept on crushing, would it twist the steering wheel into her chest?

She could back up again, look for yet another side road. But this time she had been watching; there were no more side roads. Behind her was only the lake.

For a long moment Jane squeezed shut her eyes, opening them only when the images inside the lids became worse than the one outside. Carefully she edged the Chevy toward the rear of the pick-up.

The right door handle caught the bottom edge of the bumper, scraping a bright gash in the dirty chrome. On the driver's side, bark smeared across-the window. Once off the asphalt, the Chevette sank a few inches into loam and rotten leaves, and there was a moment where Jane thought it would not continue to move forward. But it did.

Clear of the truck, Jane accelerated wildly. Four hundred yards down the road the trees suddenly withdrew and she was flying past flat fields, empty as deserts. The rear-view mirror revealed the pick-up still motionless, still solitary.

A drink — what she would give for a Jack Daniels, how late did Pennsylvania bars serve . . .

Her watch said 10:03.

Shocked, Jane slowed the car. That wasn't possible. She had left Pike perhaps an hour ago, at roughly 10:00. There was no way it could be that early —

Directly ahead, her high beams skimmed out over water.

She stopped at the water's edge, the road behind her both flat and straight, stretching like a plumb line to where she had left Cuba Lake receding in the other direction.

Another lake . . .

But she knew it was not. Even as she watched numbly through the windshield still spattered with leaves and pulpy bark, something spectral moved over the distant surface.

Wearily, with muscles that no longer seemed her own, Jane opened the door and walked towards the water. She sat at its very edge, knees clasped to her chest, tough weeds rustling under her weight and pressing their shapes through the wool of her slacks. It no longer seemed to matter whether she protected herself by staying in the car; whether she tried another road; whether she tried at all. There was no other road. There was only the yellow pick-up and the derelict with gray in his dark beard and the black thing over the water, and all roads led to Cuba Lake.

"You can't get there from here."

Dispassionately, with the curious clarity that comes from having worn out all emotion, Jane studied the darkness moving over the water. A kind of mist, without form, neither rising from the lake nor descending from the sky. *"And darkness was upon the face of the deep, and the Spirit of God moved upon the face of the waters."* Breshith, en arkhei, Beginning, Jane thought and, despite herself, smiled jeeringly. A professor to the last. The quotation created the reality.

Dear Nick,
  Ask for me tomorrow and you shall find me a grave man —

Nick . . .

Her purse was in her hand, although she didn't remember carrying it from the car. On impulse, eyes still hopeless on the dark lake, she fumbled among the make-up and wallet and glasses case for his letter. When she held it again, lukewarm colorless tasteless hemlock on sixteen-pound bond, anguish pierced her so sharply that she bent her head over her raised knees and rested it there. She thought it would be helpful to cry, thought it in just those detached pop-theory bullshit words: "It would be helpful, Jane, to cry." But she knew she wouldn't. The thought of the echoes of sobs returning to her from across that lake — that alone would have been enough to stop her.

A long time later she released the straining clasp around her knees and lay, exhausted, on her back. The sky above was featureless. Jane stared at it, equally empty. She stared until the gray blank might have been either miles or inches above her eyes. Until the boundary between the flat void of the sky and her skull disappeared. Until her clothing was soaked with dew and her fingers so chilled they would not open around Nick's letter.

It took that long.

Her watch said 10:03.

Eventually, Jane rose, staggering on numb legs. She got into the car and started back along the flat, perfectly straight road. Glancing in the rear view-mirror she saw, as she knew she would, the surface of the water empty behind her. After a few miles, the road roughened, swerved and joined New York State Route 19. A little farther along, road signs re-appeared; farther still, she came to a caution light, blinking like a single yellow eye.

Dear Nick,
  Not Wordsworth, not Byron, not even Stephen King. They all had it backwards. We shape it.

Just before Pike, halted at a barren intersection, Jane rolled down the car window. The crumpled paper arced over the dirt shoulder and into an unseen ditch. There was the faint splash of water. Driving only slightly faster than the speed limit, she was able to glimpse the last light in Lehman Science Hall before whoever was still up there working winked it off.

Dear Nick,
  But not each other.

Her watch said 11:30.